BROTHERS3

SCOTT REINERS

PAGE PUBLISHING, INC.
New York, NY

First originally published by Page Publishing, Inc. 2017

ISBN 978-1-64082-186-6 (Paperback)
ISBN 978-1-64082-187-3 (Digital)

Printed in the United States of America

Power is the ability to control the mind of a man through the fear of pain or death. Real power is the ability to manipulate and perverse facts to persuade and control all men and women, giving them the disillusion of freedom.

Freedom comes from the power within one's self. True freedom can only be achieved through a combination of autonomy, self-respect, and humility.

Liberty cannot be achieved through negotiation but only by the uprising of the masses of people. Liberty won through blood, guts, and war. Only when the oppressor, his allies, and his ideals are gone can one revel in liberty.

Those who look to their government for food and security will soon be living with rations and enslavement.

To my wife and son, I love you both dearly
To my whole family and friends

In memory of my father and to all the special
family that I have lost along the way

Special thank you to Debbie for your editorial assistance

CHAPTER ONE

....

IN A CHICAGO HOTEL, SEVERAL men met for the first time at the Red Room. The whole hotel was recently commandeered by the mayor. His reasoning for this confiscation was that the hotel could be used as a political awareness center for minorities and economically challenged. The people in attendance included the mayor, senatorial candidate John Barrack, Congressmen Dodd and Jacklow, leaders of OCORC, and several leaders of semimilitant groups. All of them were there to discuss the political direction of who they hoped will soon be the leader of the world, John Barrack. They discussed how to fund the most elaborate campaign to bring their group into control of the United States government, thereby a position of power to control the world. Their goal is wealth and power.

At the same time, a group of forty-five men drove into a small town in Virginia. They rode into town aboard two buses. When the buses stopped, the men ran through the town like a riot of drunken thugs. Most of the men were drunken violent criminals recently paroled. They were hired by OCORC (Operative Community for Organizing a Reformed Country) to bring about the OCORC directives. Because OCORC needed to look like an upstanding group in the eyes of America, they needed a group to do their dirty work. This group is known as the YUPPIs (Youths Unified for Political Policy Initiatives).

The YUPPIs were to incite fear in people across the nation and raise money through extortion, theft, and drug sales. Today's goal is to find a methamphetamine lab base that is out of the scrutiny of the local population and a center of operations. The town visit today is to incite fear into the people in the surrounding community. The YUPPIs are showing the townspeople, the law does not apply to them.

A guy with orange spiked hair named Poot walked into the police station followed by two men; one is carrying a baseball bat and the other is carrying a large canvas bag. Poot is the leader of this small group of YUPPIs. He is a well-educated man with a master of science degree in chemistry from Illinois State University. His real name is Paul Olive Olivia Thurston, but he got tired of kids calling him Olive Oyl, so he changed it. He got into a lot of fights growing up in Chicago. He was moved in and out of several different foster homes. If anyone would call him by any name other than Poot, he would beat them mercilessly. Poot had always been an angry young man but learned to control it. After Poot got out of college, he started working in a fertilizer plant in Iowa until one day someone called him Olive Oyl. He didn't really like working there anyway and he found it extremely boring. He quit the fertilizer plant and returned to Chicago. Poot used his chemistry degree producing a more lucrative product, a very potent top-notch methamphetamine. He was one of the biggest producers of meth in the state of Illinois. His reputation was the reason the YUPPI group picked him. The YUPPI's promise of fortune without rules made it very attractive to Poot. Now he is walking into the sheriff's office to buy off the local sheriff and his son for the YUPPIs.

Sheriff Bill Tamms and his son, Deputy Sheriff Cecil Tamms, were contacted earlier by Congressman Dodd. Dodd had told them that the YUPPI group was going to be coming into the area. Both Tammses were happy with that as long as the money was right. Sheriff Bill Tamms is a sixty-year-old man that has been the Sheriff of this town for thirty-nine years. People would describe him as a rude and crude asshole that would not be fit for dining with buzzards. Over the years, he has funded his drinking, smoking and hunting trips with donations from people who needed "a little less law" around the community. Sheriff Tamms's son is thirty-something, not that anyone cares and is the extreme version of his father.

Poot walks straight into the sheriff's office like he owns the place. They ignore the man at the front desk and the sheriff's secretary, both who tried to stop the three of them from entering. The two men following Poot dropped the bag in the office and then left to go join in the fun of tearing the town apart.

"There ya are, just as that old bastard promised," Poot says to old man Sheriff Bill Tamms.

Bill is sitting in his chair with his feet up on his desk. He just glances over at Poot, pours a shot of tequila, and drinks it down. "Boy, isn't you a funny looking bastard? Now who the hell are you?"

The sheriff's comment pissed Poot off. Poot's face flushed red with anger, but he held his temper. "They call me Poot," Poot says very sarcastically and loudly, "and I'm the new sheriff in town."

"Is that right?" Sheriff Tamms says with a stern raspy voice. "I hope that's my gift in that fucking bag." He gets up out of his chair and walks over to the bag. He unzips the bag and opens the top flap, which reveals five hundred thousand dollars in cash.

"I hope that will keep your dumb ass out of our way," Poot says in a very authoritative voice.

"That should about do it. Now get the fuck out of my office and don't get into any trouble, ya hear?" Sheriff Tamms laughs. He grabs his bag of money and pulls it over to the other side of his desk. He takes a bundle of one-hundred-dollar bills and stuffs it into his inside vest pocket.

Poot just turns and walks out. He walks down to the local restaurant, which is only two blocks away. Most of the YUPPI crew are in there eating already and have chased the locals out into the street. Only two waitresses and a cook are left in the place. A couple of the men are eyeing the one young waitress. She is a twenty-year-old blonde who lives on a farm with her grandfather, Tommy Schultz.

Tommy is a retired old farmer. The years of farming have taken a toll on Tommy's body, and he can no longer get around like he needs to. He sold his stock cattle and part of his farm but still tinkers around with fixing farm machinery for neighboring farmers.

The waitress walks hesitantly over to where Poot sat himself down. The young waitress asks Poot in the nicest voice she can conjure up, "Hello, welcome to Art's Bar and Grill. My name is Carly. What can I get you today?" She is tired from working double shifts for months on end. Her voice has gotten hoarse over the last few months from trying to talk over the loud music that is played at nights.

Poot looks up at the waitress and stares. He is instantly attracted to the waitress and knows he is going to have her as soon as he eats. "I'm going to have two cheeseburgers, fries, and pie. I also want a Coke," Poot says in a sickeningly polite voice much like a child molester talking to a child.

Behind the waitress stand two men. One keeps picking up Carly's skirt. The other sticks his tongue out and flicks it around like a snake. Both men laugh as Carly brushes away the hand that is lifting up on her skirt. One of the men sticks his hand up between Carly's thighs and grabs her panties. She quickly slaps his hand away and readjusts her skirt. Carly is furious, but she has to keep on working. Carly turns and walks toward the kitchen. Poot stares at Carly's butt as she weaves through the crowd of people and chairs. When he notices other men in his group doing the same, he slaps the table and gives a piercing stare at all those who look over at him. They all know that it means for them to back off.

Carly returns to Poot's table with a glass of Coke. Poot holds out his hand, and one of the YUPPIs places a bottle of Jack Daniels in his hand. Poot pours some Jack into the glass and then takes a big guzzle of Jack right out of the bottle. Carly watches.

"Sorry, but we cannot allow outside drinks in this place. Please put that away. If you want a drink, I can get you one," Carly says in a polite but stern voice.

Poot picks up the bottle, looks Carly straight in the eye, and then guzzles down the rest of the bottle of Jack Daniels. When he is finishes, he slams the bottle down on the table and the YUPPIs roar and cheer for him. Poot lets out a loud long burp and the YUPPIs roar again. Carly stands there and looks at Poot in disgust. Poot sees that the waitress is repulsed by his behavior, so in anger he throws the bottle across the room. The bottle bounces off the top of the cash register and hits the older waitress in the face. Blood erupts from her broken nose and runs down her chin. She stands there, stunned for a moment, and then quickly covers her nose with her hands. Blood flows between her fingers like someone trying to stop the flow of water from a water hydrant with their hands. Blood runs down over her name badge with the printed name "Gale" on it and then soaks her uniform. Gale looks around the room like she is looking for someone to rescue her, and then her eyes go blank and she faints. Carly runs over to assist Gale as the room erupts with laughter. Carly applies a towel over Gale's nose. Minutes go by and Gale comes to. Carly helps Gale to her feet and places another clean towel on her nose. Gale rushes to the restroom followed by two of the YUPPIs, Vic and Kroop. Gale closes and locks the door just before the YUPPIs reach it. Vic and Kroop just leaned up against the wall. They wait outside the door, not saying a word, but both know what they are going to do.

Carly picks up Poot's order, then walks to the table and sets it down on his table. Three men surround her so that she can't leave. Poot immediately starts to devour the food. Carly just stands there with her hands on her waist. "Can I get you anything else?" Carly asks sarcastically. She is very tired of the constant harassment from the YUPPIs.

Carly thinks, "These guys think they are tough, but they are just assholes. One on one they'd all would cower if confronted."

Poot has his mouth full of food, so he just holds up his index finger until he is done eating. "You forgot my pie." Carly turns to get the pie and squeezes between two of the men. She returns with the pie, but the three men are still standing there. "Please, get out of the way," Carly says.

The men let her pass and one of them grabs her butt. She sets the pie on the table and turns. She slaps the one that grabbed her. The other two men grab her by the arms just as the one that just got slapped is getting ready to punch her. Poot holds up his hand and they all stop. The two men let Carly go and she goes about her business.

Vern is the cook at Art's. He is a young man just out of high school. He decides that things are getting out of hand and knows he has to find help. Vern is not a fighting man, so he went out the back door when Gale got hit in the face with the bottle. Vern runs down to the police station to get the sheriff. He runs into the sheriff department, and he barely gets out his words because he is out of breath. "I need to talk to the sheriff immediately."

The man at the front desk turns and looks at the sheriff's door. When the sheriff's door is open, it meant it was OK for people to go in and talk to him. The man at the front desk nods and points toward the sheriff's door.

Vern hurries back to the sheriff's office. "Sheriff Bill, you need to get down to Art's right away. There are a bunch of men tearing the place apart and throwing bottles at Gale. They hurt her. You need to come right away!" Vern is in a panic.

"Don't tell me my job, boy!" Sheriff Bill Tamms yells in a scolding way. "I'll get down there in a bit and check this incident out. Just try to get everyone's name and address so if they leave, we can find them." Sheriff Bill just sits in his chair with his feet on the desk drinking tequila.

"How the hell do you think I'm going to do that?" Vern yells inquisitively. He is panicking and unsure.

"Well, hell! That is what you want me to do. I thought since you are trying to tell me my job, you knew how to do that," Sheriff Bill says and then leans forward. "Now get the fuck out of my office."

Vern flips off the sheriff and runs out of the sheriff's department. He runs down the street to Art's to see if he can do anything.

Vic and Kroop get tired of waiting outside of the restroom door. Vic knocks on the door and Gale yells, "Just a minute." Gale is still in the restroom trying to gather her wits to come back out and put up with more harassment.

Kroop says, "Fuck it! I'm tired of waiting." Kroop kicks the door open and they both rush in and shut the door behind them. Gale screams as Kroop grabs her with one arm around her neck. Vic starts laughing in a sick, slimy way. Vic grabs Gale's breast and starts laughing almost uncontrollably. He continues to squeeze her breast with one hand and then works his way down to her crotch. He grabs her panties and tears them off her. Gale screams, "Noooo!"

Vic responds to the scream with a punch to her abdomen. Gale lets out a grunt and the air just leaves her lungs. She is unable to bend over or fall to the ground because Kroop is still holding onto her neck. She almost faints and is barely able to stand. Now Kroop starts laughing and cheering Vic on. "Go ahead, Vic! I gots her. I thinks she's liken' it."

Vic's eyes got a wild look to them. Then he punches Gale in the chest and knees her in the crotch. He says with a sinister laugh, "How ya liken' the foreplay, bitch?" Gale can say or do nothing. Vic grabs the collar area of Gale's dress with both hands, and with one big yank, the dress is ripped down the front. He pushes up her bra so that her breasts are exposed. Kroop grabs the bra and holds on to it like a choke collar around a dog's neck. Vic stops laughing for a short moment as he stares at Gale's body. He runs his hands over her body like an artist with a sculpture, almost like he is thinking about what to do next.

Vic puts his right hand to his chin and says, "Look, Kroop, a clean canvas." He pulls his knife out of it sheath that is hanging on the right side of his belt. Then he starts poking at Gale's breast with the tip of the knife, not really sinking the blade in but just a giving her little prick. He continues until Gale's grunts out a scream. "Stop!" Kroop starts laughing again, "YEAH! YEAH! You go, Vic."

Vic moves his knife over to the left nipple. He grabs the nipple with his left thumb and index finger. He twists and squeezes the nipple before he slowly cuts it off. He cuts it off slowly with a sawing motion, savoring the moment, like someone cutting into a new block of cheese. Drool trickled down the corner of his mouth and mixed with some of Gale's blood that sprayed from her nipple. Vic brought the severed nipple up to his mouth and slowly licked it, then held it out in front of him, examining it. He looked at Kroop and he broke out into a sickening sinister laugh. Vic says, "I think we's havin' fun now. Throw that bitch on the floor!" Tears rolled down Gale's cheeks. She could barely breathe, let alone scream or cry.

like a kid getting a new toy. Kroop pulls down his pants and lies on top of Gale's body. He humps her abdomen until he finishes with a yell—"YEAH!"

Vic hands Kroop Gale's dress to wipe the blood off. Vic starts to laugh and Kroop instantly joins in with the laugher. Vic walks over to Gale's body and drops his pants to the floor. He kneels down and pushes Gale's legs up to her shoulders. Vic looks over at Kroop and says, "Here, hold these legs. I'm not letting good pussy go to waste." Vic rapes Gale's dead body again.

Once they both were finished, they just leave Gale's body on the floor. Vic opens the bathroom door and yells, "Free fuckin'. Help yourself boys." Six more men head into the bathroom and they rape Gale's body in every way possible. Before the last one finishes, he starts laughing and says, "This is the best kind of woman! You can get yer rocks off and she don't bitch before or after." They all laugh.

The word gets around the restaurant that the older waitress is dead. Carly overhears and slowly makes her escape through the kitchen.

Vern is halfway down the street when he sees that Carly is running for her car. He stops on the sidewalk and watches as Poot and a few of the other YUPPIs come out of the restaurant. They stop a man in a truck that is driving down the street. Poot waves the truck down. When the man stops the truck, one of the YUPPIs runs over and pulls the man from the truck. Another YUPPI, carrying a baseball bat, beats the man in the head. The YUPPI swings his bat like he is trying to hit a home run. The right side of the man skull caves in on the first swing and the second and third swing completely open the skull. Blood, crushed bone, and bits of brain tissue run from the opening in the man's head. They leave the pulverized body in the street. All three of them jump into the truck in pursuit of Carly.

Carly speeds down the highway toward her grandpa's place. Poot catches up to Carly but keeps his distance. He is waiting to find out where she goes, just in case he wants to come a calling on her someday. They follow her from afar until she turns down a long driveway. On one side of the driveway is a large hay field next to a very tall hill of trees. The other side is all trees. The farm is about a half mile in from the road. The farm place consists of a large barn with an apartment above it and a large two-story white house.

Carly speeds up the driveway till she reaches the farm place. She stops the car and runs inside the house. She quickly locks the door and leans her back up against it for just a moment. Her grandpa Tommy is sitting at the kitchen table feeding Carly's two-year-old boy. Carly's slamming the door startles both Tommy and the young boy, Lucas. Tommy jumps up from his chair. Lucas starts screaming.

"What in tar nation is going on?" Tommy Schultz asks. He is really worried. He has never seen his granddaughter so upset—well not since the day she caught her husband having sex with her best friend.

"Papa, they killed and raped Gale down at Art's. I think they're coming after me." She grabs Lucas and hugs him tight. Lucas stops screaming and gives his mom a kiss.

Tommy goes over to the door and looks outside. "I don't see anyone out there, but let me get my gun. You go upstairs till I tell you that the coast is clear." Carly carries her son upstairs to her bedroom and locks the door behind her.

Tommy walks over to the broom cabinet and grabs his sawed-off 12-gauge shotgun. He loads the gun with his shells he loads himself. He loads his shells with steel ribbons and bits and pieces of steel that come from the metal lathe in his shop. He goes over to the door to stands watch.

Poot with the two other YUPPIs, Germ and Dirk, come speeding up the driveway to Tommy's farm in the truck they jacked. Poot licked his lips in expectation, "I ain't waitin' any longer fer a taste of that bitch." They stop the truck behind Carly's car. They get out of the truck and Poot folds down the back of the bench seat to see what he can find behind the seat. He finds a tire iron and puts it into the back of his belt. Germ holds the baseball bat behind his back. All three men slowly walk up to the front door like they are walking up to the front door of their grandparents. Tommy opens the door and points a shotgun at the men before they could even reach the top of the steps to the front door.

"I believe you all will be turning around and going back to wherever you came from," Tommy says with a shaky voice. His adrenaline is on high and it is affecting his voice.

"Hold on," Poot says and holds up an open hand. Poot's other hand slowly reaches behind his back for the tire iron he has tucked in his belt. "We're here to pick up your daughter. We are new in town and she was going to show us around." Poot is just stalling long enough to get Tommy lower his guard just slightly.

"Don't believe that is it at all. Now leave before I let you have it," Tommy says. Tommy's voice is relaxing a little.

Poot senses that Tommy has relaxed a little, so he grabs for the barrel of the shotgun, at the same time; he swings his tire iron at Tommy's body. Tommy is quick enough to see Poot grab for the gun and he pulls the trigger. The bits of metal and the metal ribbons tear through Poot's left ear, almost completely removing it. The rest of the metal hits Germ, who was standing behind the left side of Poot. The force of the shot completely removes the right side of Germ's head. Germ's body stands rigid as blood sprays over onto Poot and Tommy. The whole right side of Germ's head is reduced to pieces of bone, ribbons of tissue, and blood lying on the ground behind Germ. Germ is dead, but his body just doesn't know it yet. His arms start flapping like a bird and his body starts shaking until Germ falls backward to the ground. When the remainder of his head hits the ground, part of his brain pops out onto the ground. Dirk dives for cover over the side of the stair steps and lands in some bushes. Poot stands stunned with the loss of his ear along with his hearing. He can feel a burning sensation on the left side of his face and something running down his neck, but he stays focused on Tommy.

Poot manages to hit Tommy in the head with the tire iron. Tommy drops his shotgun as he falls to the porch floor. Tommy lies there unconscious. With Tommy knocked out, Poot relaxes a little and then the pain rushes over his whole head like of bucket of hot coals. Poot screams in pain and looks behind him. He is looking to see why no one has come to his assistance. He quickly sees a headless torso lying half on the stairs and half on the ground. Dirk is trying to crawl to the truck they had jacked. Poot sees Dirk crawling, so he rushes down the stairs to kick him in the butt.

"Get up you chicken-shit bastard and help me!" Poot screams at Dirk. Poot is in a lot of pain but is more pissed off at Tommy. Dirk gets up off the ground. He sees that his buddy's head has been shot off. Blood is scattered everywhere on the ground. Germ's head looks like it had been removed with a meat grinder, and blood is still running from the torso's neck. "What the fuck, man. He lost his fuckin' head." Dirk starts laughing, not because it was funny but out of nervousness.

"Fuck him," Poot yells. "He's dead and my ear is fucking killing me. Now give me your goddamn head band." Dirk removes his handkerchief from his head and hands it to Poot. Poot wraps it around his ear and head.

"Let's get this fucking asshole farmer into the house. We are going to fuck him up just like he did me," Poot says. Both men drag Tommy up into the kitchen. They throw Tommy onto the table, and Poot punches him the face.

"You fucking stay here while I find that bitch!" Poot screeches at Dirk. Poot is both angry and in pain. Poot rushes through the house and finds no one on the lower level but sees that there is a stairway to the upstairs. Poot rushes back to Dirk and Tommy in the kitchen. When Poot gets to the kitchen, Dirk rushes out to the porch and grabs Tommy's shotgun. He walks back inside, grabs a chair, and then sits next to Tommy, who is still lying motionless on the table. Poot looks around the room and opens cabinet doors, trying to find some sort of alcohol. He only finds beer in the refrigerator. Poot takes a beer and throws one to Dirk. Poot opens two of them and drinks them both like a man who just came out of the desert. He goes over to one of the drawers that he has opened and takes out a roll of duct tape. He tapes Tommy's arms and legs to the legs on the table. "There! Now we don't have to worry about him getting away. Help me find the bitch," Poot says to Dirk.

Dirk sets the shotgun down on the kitchen cupboard. Both men go through the house kicking in doors. Poot finds the bathroom. He walks in and opens the cabinet doors and drawers. He finds a bottle of expired Darvocet. He pours out six of them into his hand, throws them into his mouth, and washes them down with beer. He finds a washcloth and wets it. Carefully, he wipes away the blood from his face. He finds tweezers and plucks out some of the small pieces of metal that have embedded into the left side of his head. Once he is satisfied with his minor surgery, he wraps gauze around his head to cover his left ear and then places the headband back over the gauze.

Once they are satisfied that no one is on the bottom floor, they go upstairs. One by one, they kick open doors until they reach the last room at the end of the hallway. They rush into the room and find Carly and Lucas hiding under the bed. Poot grabs Carly by the hair and drags hers out from under the bed. Dirk grabs Lucas by his arms and pulls him from under the bed. Carly gets to her feet, Poot keeps ahold of her hair and rushes her down the stairs. Carly is half-crawling and half-dragged. He pulls her into the kitchen, pulls a chair away from the kitchen table, and shoves her into it. Dirk carries Lucas down to the kitchen and sets him on the countertop. Then he stands there and holds him. Lucas starts squirming and crying trying to get out of the arms of Dirk. The more Lucas struggles, the harder Dirk squeezes. Soon Lucas is squeezed so hard, he has difficult time breathing. He lets out a cry, but it only comes out as a little squeak. Tears flow from his eyes.

"Stop it, you bastard! You are killing him!" Carly screams at Dirk. Dirk stops squeezing Lucas and Lucas just sits there crying. Poot slaps Carly across the face and almost knocks her off the chair. "Shut the fuck up, bitch! I'll tell ya when ya can talk!" Poot yells at Carly.

Tommy regains consciousness. He is still confused and looks around the room to try to get his bearings on what is happening. Nothing looks familiar to Tommy. He has never lain on the kitchen table and looked around the room before now. Tommy does realize that he is bound to the table and his head feels like a baseball bat just hit him. He looks over and sees his granddaughter sitting alongside of the table with a man who has orange hair and a bandana tied around his head. He looks over to the kitchen counter and sees Lucas sitting there crying with Dirk holding onto him. Tommy looks over at his granddaughter. "I'm so sorry. I am so sorry. I love you." Tommy figures that the men are going kill him.

"Shut the fuck up, old man! You fucking shot me in the fucking ear and now we are going to make you pay!" Poot screams. Then Poot looks over at Carly, "You and me are going to have us a good time. Your old man and kid are going to watch me screwin' ya. Now get them fucking clothes off or I'll have him do it for you." Poot raised up his chin in the direction of Dirk, in order to point to him.

Carly quickly gets up off the chair and rushes to try to reach the shotgun on the kitchen counter. Poot catches her by the hair and yanks her back. Carly's head flies back, but her body keeps going forward. She flies backward and her feet come up off the ground. While she is in midair, Poot punches her so hard in the side of the face that she falls sideway on top of Tommy. She lies there for a brief second and then falls to the floor. Then Poot kicks her in the side of the right calf muscle. He jumps on her to hold her down, but she is not really struggling. Carly is just barely conscious at this time. Dirk grabs a knife from the drawer and hands it Poot. Poot cuts Carly clothes off with the precision of a surgeon. After he cuts up Carly's clothes, he grabs her by the hair until she stands up.

"Hey, old man, have you ever seen a snatch like that." Poot grabs Carly's crotch.

Poot starts to get excited and dances around a little. He looks Carly over like a sculptor would look over his creation, to decide what he is going to do next. Poot grabs Carly by the hair and pushes her over the back of the kitchen chair. "Stay there, bitch, or I'll have him carve up your little boy. That's just what he likes, little boys!" Poot says sternly to Carly.

Carly couldn't struggle anyway. Her leg is hurting and she is barely holding onto consciousness. Carly screams with a cry in her voice, "Please let us go. We won't tell anyone."

Poot pulls her head back up to his face so he can yell into her ear, "Well, bitch, there is no one to tell!"

Poot kicks the chair out of the way and shoves Carly on top of Tommy, who is still lying on the table. He lets go of Carly's hair and slaps her on the back of the head. "Don't fucking move." Poot says to

and stick it up yer loose asshole and blow your fucking insides out." Dirk starts laughing at the thought of what Poot just said.

Carly continues to stay bent over onto Tommy. She has basically given up. Dirk pulls down his pants and inserts his penis into Carly's vagina. She doesn't even move or make a sound. Dirk starts thrusting forcefully as Carly keeps her eyes shut tightly trying to make her mind go somewhere else.

Poot says, "But I like ya and ye'r pretty, so maybe we just keep ya here and the boys can use ya for a while. Hmmmm? Nope, I don't like to share." Poot sits there for a short minute and then looks at Dirk using "his woman." Poot gets pissed off at Dirk. "Get the fuck off her right now," Poot says to Dirk. Dirk looks over at Poot in puzzlement but just keeps thrusting. "I said get the fuck off her before I cut your dick off." Dirk immediately stops and then pushes Carly to the floor. Carly curls up in to a ball and lies on the floor without saying a word.

Dirk pulls his pants back on, "What the fuck, man?" He is pissed off that Poot didn't let him finish.

"Let her go. I need a hit and we need to go back to town to get the boys. We just found a new home," Poot says to Dirk. Poot didn't give Dirk the pleasure in acknowledging that he is mad.

Poot looks over at Carly lying on the floor, "Get up and get the hell out of here before I change my mind. I may want another round or maybe a little boy."

Carly struggles to her feet and grabs a coat off the coat rack in the corner of the kitchen. She puts on the coat and looks over at Tommy and Lucas.

"Go! Go now! Get some help," Tommy yells.

"Go! Go get help." Poot laughs at Tommy. "Shit, mister, you ain't going to need any help."

"I love you, Grandpa." Carly says as she grabs Lucas off the kitchen counter and then rushes out the door. She gets to her car and puts Lucas in the car seat in the back. She gets into the driver's seat and starts down the driveway. Anger, fear, and pain shoot across her body, and she begins to cry uncontrollably while driving into town. She is also disappointed. She should have never gone home and endangered her son and grandfather like she did. She thinks home is a safe place. She thinks she should have fought more and better. She blames herself. She will never trust anyone again.

"OK, old man. My fucking head hurts and I want to get to town, so what should we do to you?" Poot was sitting in a chair, looking at Dirk. "Do whatever. Just get it done quickly. I need a hit of meth something bad."

Dirk grabs the kitchen knife off the kitchen counter and goes over to the table where Tommy is bound. Dirk walks around to Tommy's legs and cuts the tape binding Tommy's legs to the table. Tommy starts kicking at Dirk, but Dirk gets out of the way. Dirk rushes up to Tommy's head and punches him in the face until he stops kicking. He takes the knife and puts the point on to Tommy's shoulder. Then he slowly leans on the knife as it slides into Tommy's shoulder. Tommy screams in pain. "Oh God!"

Poot just sits there watching and then gets up. Poot goes over to the refrigerator and gets two beers. He sits down on the kitchen counter, drinking the beer and enjoying the show. Dirk walks over to the kitchen counter, grabs another knife, and cuts the cords off the microwave and blender. He ties Tommy's left leg to one table leg where the left arm is bound and then ties the right leg to the other side where the right arm is bound. Dirk then scoots Tommy's butt around to the side of the table. He grabs the kitchen knife and cuts Tommy's pants off.

"Well, ya old fuck, since I didn't get to fuck yer girl, I gonna do you," Dirk says to Tommy. Tommy didn't say anything. His mouth and eyes are swollen from the beating. Most of Tommy's teeth were broken. Tommy tried to spit out the broken teeth and blood so he doesn't choke on it but it doesn't work, so he swallows it. Tommy is having a hard time breathing all folded up. He knew there was nothing he could do but take it.

Dirk pulls down his pants and starts anally raping Tommy. Dirk has a big smile on his face. Poot just sits there and enjoys the show. Once Dirk is done, he walks over to the stove and grabs a towel that is hanging on the stove handle. He wipes himself off and then pulls up his pants. Dirk then grabs the kitchen knife off the table and looks Tommy in his swollen eyes. "I think that my buddy would want me to castrate your ass for shootin' his head off." Before Tommy can beg for mercy, Dirk cuts Tommy's testicles off slowly like cutting a log with a hacksaw. Tommy screams with every knife stroke, but his screams are muffled from the blood in his mouth and the swollen lips. Blood sprays everywhere from Tommy's testicular area, and the more blood that sprays, the more excited Dirk gets. He is having a hard time cutting slowly because he is so excited. Dirk finishes removing the testicles and scrotum and throws them up on to Tommy's chest. "Well, that is fun. What should I do next?" Dirk says, all excited.

Poot finishes his last beer and is tired of waiting. Poot wants to leave. "Shut him the fuck up. My head is killing me. I want to get the fuck to town."

Dirk sets down the knife and grabs Tommy's shotgun. He walks over to Tommy's anus and shoves the barrel up his rectum. Dirk pulls the trigger. Blood, flesh, and ingesta explode from Tommy's abdomen. The explosion of flesh covers Poot. Tommy is still screaming as the air and life finally leaves his body.

Poot is furious. "You asshole!" Poot grabs the shotgun from Dirk. "Ya could've killed me, ya fuck!"

Dirk is just amazed. He is so excited and amazed. "Did ya see that shit? Did ya see that?" He is stopped in midsentence when Poot shoves the barrel into Dirk's open mouth. Poot pulls the trigger and the gun goes *click*. It didn't fire because it was empty. Poot drops the shotgun and walks out to the truck. Dirk comes running out and jumps into the truck. They both take off to town.

That night after gathering up all of the YUPPIs, they all head back out to Tommy's farm and move in.

CHAPTER TWO

TWO YEARS LATER.

Sam wakes up to the sound of his cellphone. Sam quickly shakes the sleep out of his head and grabs the phone. Sam holds the phone up his ear, and with a low grumbly voice, he says, "Hello, this is Dr. Kelley, how can I help you?"

"Hey, Sam, this is Artie. I hope I didn't wake you up but my mare is limping and it looks bad. She's breathing hard and her left front leg is all swollen up. I gave her some bute and it didn't make a difference. Do you think you can come out?" Artie says to Sam in an excited voice.

Sam wipes the sleep out of his eyes, "I'll be out there as soon as I can. I have to stop by the hospital and get my x-ray machine and ultrasound. Just keep her quiet and I'll see you in a little bit."

Artie says in a panic, "OK, hurry."

Sam is barely awake, but he never liked to let his clients know that they caught him sleeping. He can never understand why he thinks it is wrong for him to be asleep when one of his clients calls. Sam thinks that they have to know that he slept. Sam slides out of bed and into the clothes he wore the day before since he didn't want to wake up his wife with digging through the closet. Sam says to himself, "I've got to at least put on clean underwear and socks. I hope it doesn't look too obvious that these are the same clothes I wore yesterday. If anybody notices, they'll probably think that I got them dirty from the last horse I was looking at." After getting his clothes on, he walks downstairs to his bathroom. Every step he makes, his knees and ankles crack and creek. He looks in the mirror and says to himself, "Damn, you're looking older every day. I know I'm getting fatter every day." He brushes his teeth, reaches under his shirt, and puts on some underarm deodorant. Sam pets the cats and feeds them some treats. Sam loves his cats as if they were his kids. All three cats look at him like, "Where the heck are you going all the time? Spend some time with us." Sam puts on another layer of socks because he knows its cold out, since he could feel it on the cold bathroom floor. He puts on a fleece sweater and then a wind shirt over top. Then grabs his vest and keys on the way out the door.

It is a cold morning, of course it is only 5:00 a.m. and the sun is not up yet. Sam never likes this time of the morning. This time of the morning is when he is most tired and it's the coldest part of the day. Sam always feels tired. He has been working too many late nights. He is the main income for the hospital that he and his wife own. He has to work when there is work to be done because the hospital is a monster that needs to be fed constantly. Now he is up and outside and he needs to score some coffee and Copenhagen. He figured it's going to keep him going for the rest of the day.

"Hope this vehicle starts." Sam says to himself. The vehicle can never hold a charge when the cooler has been plugged in all night. He thinks it has been cold all night and the cooler may not have run his battery down. He gets in and starts the vehicle. He turns on the radio to the news. At this time of the day, the news is just rehashing what he heard last night when he was coming home at midnight. The news is all about the big presidential election. Sam already knows how he is going to vote. The decision isn't too hard. You either vote for an old businessman that has no personality but knows that there are hardworking Americans out there that do not want government in their business or a younger socialist. The socialist has never had a real job his whole life and just wants to be elected so that he can fulfill all his and his crooked buddies' worldly needs. Sam thinks that the younger man just doesn't care about anyone but himself. Sam says to himself, "The asshole is going to get elected because most of the people that are going to vote just can't see through this guy's bull-shit." Sam knew a bullshitter when he saw one. Sam always says that

"You can't bullshit a bullshitter" and Sam could really pile it on when the time calls for it. He thinks he acquired the art from his dad, but for the most part, Sam prides himself on his honesty and integrity.

Sam goes to the hospital and through the back door where the hospital horses are kept. He looks over all the horses really quick. Then Sam's brother Dakota comes out from the pharmacy. Kota puts some syringes in a drawer of the crash cart. "Whatcha doin?" Sam walks into the hallway where all the lights are turned out except for a few stall lights. At night, everything is quite enough that you can hear the sounds of a horse chewing on hay or the cats walking across the rubberized floor. Sam always thought his hospital is the best place to rest at night.

"Oh, the Sikes called. He says that one of their horses is lame and not doing well. I hope it's just a foot abscess because they just can't afford to have any major problems," Sam says to Kota. Kota's real name is Dakota, but since he was a kid, he has been called Kota.

Sam looks over at the horses in the hospital. "You may want to get a stall ready for another horse. I'll call you if this horse is coming in."

Sam starts loading the radiograph equipment and Dakota grabs the ultrasound equipment. Then Sam runs back into the hospital and looks through the assortment of splints. Before he can grab a splint Elvis, Driz and Harold show up. Elvis starts telling him that they are hungry, so Sam feeds them some cat food and gives them each a treat.

Kota walks into the storage room and says, "What ya lookin' for? Hey, I already fed those cats tonight!"

Sam pets each cat like each one is his only cat. "Yep, but Elvis says he's hungry and I hate to see any animal go hungry."

Kota stands in the doorway, looking at Sam petting the cats. "Do you need me to get you anything else?"

Sam puts Elvis back down on the floor and Elvis runs over to the cat food. Then Sam starts rummaging through the storage cabinet that is full of splints. "Oh, I better take the front leg Kimzey splint just in case it turns out to be a facture and they decide they want to fix it."

Sam hates not having everything he needs when he goes out on calls. He always tries to think of every scenario that could be going on before he goes out on a call. Sam had developed long ago an instinct about what is going to happen, but it is never foolproof. Anyway, if he doesn't have something, he can usually "jimmy rig" something together that would work. Sam grabs the splint that he thinks he might need and heads for the door in a quick pace.

"See ya later, and remember, there are some doughnuts up in the front office," Sam says to Kota.

Kota is holding the door open for Sam. "I know. I found them when I was getting coffee. See ya later. I'm going to get a stall ready for you no matter what."

Sam gets into his vehicle and takes off down the road. In his mind, he is trying to come up with every possible thing that could be wrong with this horse. He likes to do that and it comes to him naturally. It might have been developed when his dad would always need something and then send him running to get it. Now he just did it with everything he is doing. He hates to be wrong, but he hates even more to not be able to find out what is wrong. Sam never lets anything go from his mind. He still reevaluates everything he did in his past, especially things that ended up going wrong.

Sam stops at the nearest truck stop and runs inside. He pours himself a big cup of black coffee. Then he goes up to the counter and pays. He usually doesn't talk much to anyone that works in the truck stop, especially when he is in a hurry, so he just puts two dollars on the counter. It's not that Sam doesn't like the people that worked there; everyone is always busy. When Sam gets his change back, he bids the gal a good day.

Sam is forty-plus years old and grew up in South Dakota on a farm with two younger brothers and an older sister. Bud, one of Sam's brothers, was a year younger then Sam. Dakota, Sam's other brother, was nine years younger. Sam's sister, Gina, was a few years older than Sam. They grew up like other farm kids at that time. They went to school and came home to work the rest of the night. Taking care of animals and getting the farm work done were always the most import thing. They never had much money even though they worked hard.

Sam's mom, Elaine, is a registered nurse and worked hard all her life trying to take care of the family. Sam considers her the nicest person in the world, but sometimes she is too nice. She will never turn anyone away from a meal. This part is what always bothered Sam about his mom and dad. People would often take advantage of her kindness. On the weekends, Sam's mom cooks for several uninvited guests.

Sam's dad, Darrell, was a hardworking farmer. He worked day in and day out just to keep the farm going. Sam's dad never really spent much time teaching or giving praise. Sam usually learned by doing on his own. Sam knew that his dad meant well, but it just wasn't in him to show it.

Sam's whole family is a little what they call "western." The family is simple and down to earth. They have what they need and want what they have. They value hard work, fertile land, and good horses.

Sam loves competition but never really pushes himself. His father never pushed him at competition and often discouraged it. He is good at almost anything he does but never is excellent at anything. Sam's one drive is to make himself better. Many times in the process of trying to be the best caused him to "overdo" most things. Sam's wife, Carol, is much like Sam except she excels at everything she does. Sam often wonders why such an intelligent woman would marry someone like him.

Sam drives off and gets on the interstate setting the cruise control at seventy-three mile per hour. The morning news has just started. Sam's thoughts run wild as he listens to the news. "Don't really care about this local news garbage. It's kind of hard to give a crap about most of the people on the news. Most of the people just want to get on television and get their few minutes of fame. Shit, this is the first place where we hardly know the neighbors and the neighbors don't care to know us. Not like back home. Nothing stays a secret for very long in the valley. People just don't have much to talk about or they're just plain nosy. Oh well."

Sam never cared for politics before he and Carol built the hospital. Now Sam takes politics very seriously because it always affects his business. Sam takes a drink of coffee and slips back into his thoughts, almost a driving trance. "I'll never understand how people that work day in and day out can fall for a politician's bullshit. Every politician in the federal government is a millionaire and most of them have never worked a real job. Politicians always talk about how they understand the American people. Politicians tell everyone how much they are going to help everyone, but they really don't care. People still believe the politicians. If those dumb-ass politicians would just stay out of everyone's business and life, things would work out all by themselves. The poor would get food and money from people and businesses that have more to give. Businesses would all have more money to give if they didn't have to give half of it to the government. People would have jobs if they wanted jobs. Those that don't want to work could just starve for all I care. People need to work to make fun worth having. People need to work so that life has value. If you value yourself, you would develop pride. A nation of proud people would be a very strong nation that could produce quality products and wealth. Another good thing about proud and assured people is that pride usually becomes contagious and spreads to those around them. People always say, 'I worked hard for that stuff, and by gosh, I'm going to keep it and take care of it.' But you don't hear people say, 'I got that for free and I'm going to do everything I can to keep it.' People don't take care of things they get for free, and that includes life. Too bad those stupid politicians don't understand."

Sam arrives at Artie's place in about an hour. Artie is waiting in the barn, which is unusual because he usually waits in the house. Sam thinks to himself, "It must really be bad if he standing in there holding the horse."

Sam walks in to the barn and immediately sees the horse's problem. Sam says, "Morning, Artie."

Artie says, "Good morning, Doc. I hate to call you out so early but her leg just didn't look good. I felt it for heat but she really doesn't want me to touch it. I put the hoof testers on it and got nothing. What do you think it is?"

"Now Artie, I just walked in here. How am I supposed to tell what's going on?" Sam says. "From here it looks like she fractured a bone somewhere in that pastern region, but we need to do a radiograph before I can say for sure."

Sam turns and starts walking out of the barn to go get his radiograph equipment when Artie starts to tell him why he is up so early in the morning. Sam just acknowledges to him that he is listening, but Sam is still headed out the door. When Sam returns to the horse, Artie is still talking about his long night and how he just got back from some training thing, and since he was up, he thought he would just go to the barn and check things out. "It must be a sixth sense that I have about these horses," Artie says. "That is why I came over to the barn to check on things. I knew there was something wrong."

Sam takes a few images. "Well, looks like we got a comminuted P1 fracture. I can count about four fragments. It's a poor prognosis for return to soundness. She may be pasture sound if we fix it, but the fracture is into the fetlock joint and the pastern joint. There's not one big fragment to attach the other fragments to but there appears to be enough left of the bone that we can put the two joints back together. Then put two five-hole plates on P1 and put her into a transfixation pin cast. She'll need about two to three cast changes before she leaves the hospital." Sam gives Artie a lot of information all at once so Artie will stop talking and start thinking. Artie just stands there and stares.

"Well, I am going to have to call my dad and see what he wants to do. He'll have to come down here." Artie snaps out of his standing coma. Artie called his dad. Sam puts his equipment back into the vehicle. He wraps the horse's leg and then applies Kimzey splint.

Artie is still talking to his dad on the phone when his dad and brother come in the door. Artie, without missing a beat, hangs up the phone in midsentence and starts talking directly to his dad. As Sam listens to Artie and his dad's conversation, he realizes that they are not even talking about the problem at hand but about Artie's adventure to Kentucky. Sam interrupts the conversation. "So what have you guys decided about Queeny?"

"Well, what is wrong with her?" Bob asked.

"She has fractured a bone in the lower limb." Sam points out on the other front leg. "It is going to be difficult to fix, but I can fix it. I don't think she will be a riding horse again, but maybe I can get her to be comfortable enough to be a broodmare. It is going to be expensive and she is going to have to stay at the hospital for at least two months."

Tears start to well under in Bob's eyes. "How could this happen? Is it something that we did?"

Sam can never handle the crying part. He empathizes with owners, but more so he feels like he has failed the horse or God in some way if he has to euthanatize a horse. The hardest horses to euthanatize are the ones he knows he could fix but the owners are unable because of money. When he and his wife, Carol, started the hospital, they would just do the surgeries. They would have the owners pay what they could or would give. Many times people would just give them the horse. Now they can't do that because their pastures are full and it just about bankrupted the hospital. Sam guesses that no good deed goes unpunished.

"Well, we got to fix her. I can't see her suffer and I don't just want to kill her," Bob said. "How much do you think it will cost? Just a ballpark figure, I'm not going to hold you to it."

"Well, by the time she comes home, you may spend around fifteen to twenty thousand dollars, depending on if there are any complications." Sam knows better when he hears the words "I'm not going to hold you to it," the only thing they remember is the lowest number. Then they come back with the phrases, "Well, I guess I own part of your hospital now," "It costs that much?" "I don't mind helping you pay for all those new toys, but I don't what to pay for the whole hospital," and on and on. It pisses Sam off that people will go to their own doctors for a simple knee surgery, and it costs twenty to thirty thousand dollars. Then they brag about how much it costs them. Sam does the same surgeries, and he charges less than two thousand and they complain about how much it costs. Hell, he paid just as much for school as any MD, and all his costs for doing business are more than theirs. He has to keep costs down so that people will do the surgeries instead of letting the horse suffer.

"I'll see you at the hospital in a little bit," Sam tells Artie. "I'm going to go ahead of you and get things ready." Sam gets in his vehicle before Artie can say anything and takes off. In the rearview mirror, he can see everyone loading up into the truck. Sam knows it is going to be a long day again. As he starts down the road, he gets his cell phone out and calls into the hospital. He checks the time as the phone is ringing; its eight thirty in the morning, but no one is answering the phone. "Damn it! Why the hell are they not answering the phone?" Sam says to himself. "They'd better all be there today. Mondays are always hard to get everyone there on time." Sam hangs up and calls his wife's cell phone. There is no answer, which is not unusual; she seldom answers her phone. She always says that she didn't hear it, but most of the time she just doesn't answer, which always upsets him. Sam hangs up and calls his brother Bud, who is the farm manager. Once again, there is no answer but Bud always calls back. So Sam hangs up and turns on the radio.

Fox News is on the radio. Sam thinks as he is driving, "News anymore is more for entertainment than it is for facts. They think that they need to make the news entertaining in order for people to watch it. It's pretty bad when they have to hire a model to read the news and give commentary."

"Who gives a damn what her opinion is?" Sam says out loud to himself. "Just read the news. I just want the facts."

"Congressman John Barrack is now in the lead in all the polls. He is very popular and has had fifty thousand people or more at every campaign rally. He is running on a fresh start," the news lady says with almost erotic excitement.

"Oh, he is very well-spoken and good-looking, but do we really know what he stands for? He really talks to the people." Then she babbles on some more and switches to some other non-newsworthy story.

The phone rings and it is Bud on the other end, "Hey, you called, I was on the tractor and didn't hear the phone."

"Hey, how are you this morning?" Sam says.

"Fine, but it's a bit cool out this morning." Bud says.

"Do you know where everyone is?" Sam asked. "No one is answering the phone."

"Nope, but I will go check it out," Bud says as he drives tractor up to the hospital.

"Well, will you go in there and tell them that we have a fracture on its way and that they need to call me ASAP?" Sam says. "And can you get the sling ready for this horse?"

"Yep, I'll go do that right now," Bud says. Bud can always tell when Sam gets pissed off. It is when people are not doing their job and when people don't answer their phones.

Sam hangs up and starts to go over in his head how this fracture is going to be fixed. He can see the fracture in his mind and go over the repair step by step before he even gets to surgery. This always seemed to make things easier and faster during surgery. Sam always took the old saying that "Slow and smooth is fast and efficient" to heart.

Sam's phone rings and he quickly grabs it up. "Hello, this is Sam." It was the receptionist at the hospital. Marsha was always on the ball. They really couldn't function without her.

"How are you getting along this morning?" Marsha says.

"Artie is hauling Queeny in to the hospital, she has a broken leg, and we need to get things ready for surgery. She needs to be in dorsal recumbence and we need to get all the fracture equipment. Can you get everyone going on this ASAP? We need to see if we can change some of the appointments around." Sam says.

"I'll see what I can do," Marsha says. "When will they get here?"

"I'm about thirty minutes from the hospital," Sam says. "They left after me, so about forty-five minutes."

"OK, see you when you get here. Do you want your messages or just get them when you get here?" Marsha asks, knowing full well what the answer is going to be.

"I'll get them later, see ya later." Sam hangs up and turns the radio back on. On the radio is more news about the presidential candidates. John Barrack wants to make the rich pay more money to the government because they are not paying enough and all the poor are poor because these privileged people are holding them back. Sam shuts the radio off because the news is just pissing him off.

Sam gets to the hospital and goes up to the reception area. "Marsha, did you get my appointments changed?"

"No, I got this morning's appointments changed to Saturday, but your afternoon appointment with the lameness can't change days because they need this horse sound by next week. They are going to a show," Marsha says as she types away at the computer. "You have a lot of messages so check them. Some of them need to be called back as soon as you can."

"Where is everyone?" Sam pages through his messages.

"They should be in the surgery room getting things ready," Marsha says.

Sam walks back to the surgery room and checks to make sure everything is ready. It appears that everything is in order. He goes out and grabs the radiograph equipment and brings it inside and sets it up to be ready for the surgery.

Sam goes up front and grabs a cup of coffee and scrounges around like a rat to come up with some old cookies that have been setting around for a while. "I should have stopped and gotten something to eat but I thought they would beat me here," Sam says to himself. "Where the hell are they?" Just then Artie and Bob Sikes' truck and trailer enter the gate at the end of the driveway. Sam leaves the reception area when the Sikes head into the reception area. Artie, his brother, Bob, and his wife enter in the front door of the reception area. Artie can see that Sam is not there waiting, so he leaves to find him.

Artie shows up to the trailer and starts giving orders on how this horse is going to be unloaded to the technician that is out shutting the door. Sam sees Artie out there jabbering to the technician and goes out to save the tech from the lingual massacre that is about to take place. Sam interrupts Artie. "Did you get everything finished up with Marsha?"

Artie starts opening the door. "My dad is finishing up everything. Should we get this horse off? Here is how we should unload—"

Sam interrupts Artie again. "Artie, we already got her off the trailer and we are prepping her right now."

Artie just shuts the door again and walks into the hospital and watches as the technicians are getting the horse ready. The Sikes family came back to the prep area and started hugging and talking baby talk to the horse. They're getting in the way and crying again. Sam is getting pissed because they need to get this horse into induction, and they are swarming around the horse getting in the way. Sam tells the techs, "Time to go. Let's get the sling fitted and drop this horse." The technician leads the startled horse into the induction room. Sam locks the door and gives a sigh of relief that now he can start doing what he needs to get done without interruption.

After four hours in surgery, Queeny goes into the recovery room. Sam is relieved that everything went without a hitch. After writing a surgery report, Sam heads up to the reception area to talk to the Sikes family.

"Well, surgery went well. Everything went back together well. I removed some small fragments from both joints, and everything should heal well. The next biggest part is getting her up without any incidences, like breaking her leg or the implants. After she is up, the next hurdle is going to be keeping her comfortable and keeping her from getting laminitis or destroying her pin cast. Hopefully she can wear that cast for four to five weeks, and then we will remove it and maybe put on a regular cast. We will just have to see." Sam looks around the room; he sees that all the Sikes family members are chopping at the bit to say something. Sam thinks, "If I let them start talking, I will never get out of here and I've got to get this horse up."

"You all think about what questions you what to ask. When Queeny gets up, I'll be back," Sam says as he backs out of the room and closes the door.

Sam goes back and changes clothes. The horse gets up without a problem. After thirty minutes of the horse standing in the recovery room, they remove the sling and walk the horse back to a stall. She is walking well on the cast and the technicians tend to the horse. Sam goes back up front to meet with the Sikes family. When he gets there, the Sikeses are gone.

"Where did they go?" Sam asks Marsha.

"They got tired of waiting and they went to get something to eat. They wrote out two pages of questions for you before they left. They said that you might want to look over them so when they get back here, you can be ready to answer them," Marsha says with a laugh.

Sam hates when people write papers of questions. It was more like a test than a question-and-answer period. He also hates when people leave and expect him to just sit around and wait. "Well, I can't wait for them. I've got to get to my two o'clock," Sam says. "I'll call them on the way to my appointment. Just call me when they come in."

Sam is on his way to his appointment. All the while Sam is thinking about the surgery he just finished. He always tries to think about how things could've gone better. Sam can't think of anything, so he just decided to concentrate on the next job. Sam turns on the radio to the old-time rock station and relaxes.

Sam gets back to the hospital at 8:00 p.m. after he was done with his last appointment. Sam thinks, "I wonder why Marsha hadn't called when the Sikeses came back. They probably just went home." Just then, the phone rings. "Hey, Sam, this is Artie. How is Queeny doing?" Artie asks.

"Well, she's eating and everything is OK right now," Sam says.

"Everyone is here and we want to go over the questions we wrote out. Can you just read the question and then give us the answer," Artie says.

"I just got back from appointments and I don't have the papers in front of me," Sam says with a lot of irritation.

"That's OK. We took a nap earlier so we'll wait until you go get them," Artie says.

"Just ask me what you want. I'm not going to go get the papers." Sam says.

"We don't remember the questions and there were things we really need to know," Artie says.

Sam sends the technician up to the reception area to get the question sheets. She runs up and grabs them and runs back, rolls her eyes, then hands them to Sam. Sam reads the first question, "When can we start riding her?" Sam is irritated. "I told you we have to wait and see. She may not ever be sound enough to ride. Besides, when did you start riding her anyway?"

"Oh, we never ride her but we thought we should ask just in case we want to start," Artie says.

Sam reads through the rest of the questions, and all the questions are completely ridiculous. "You guys, we really need to just wait four to five weeks to see how she is doing. I can't answer any of these questions to any accuracy until after the first cast change," Sam says sternly. "And no, your other horses can catch this problem, and there really isn't anything you can do to prevent it in the future."

"Well, OK, Sam. We're just worried but we'll just wait. I think we'll let you go. We had a long day and we'll see you tomorrow," Artie says.

"OK, then, have a good night," Sam says.

"One other thing, my dad wants to know if he can call you tonight if he gets worried about her," Artie asks.

"That's fine but I'm not going to know any more than what I know now," Sam says. "Have a good night." Artie hangs up.

Sam sends the technician home and stays to watch the hospital horses until Dakota comes in at midnight.

Chapter Three

"SATURDAY, YAHOO!" SAM THINKS TO himself. "I haven't had a weekend off for at least six weeks. There are no horse shows, and the appointment I had to day changed to next week." Sam takes a shower, gets dressed, and heads into the hospital. He walks out to the parking lot of the hospital and stops, looks around, then takes a deep breath. Sam looks up at the clouds in the sky just like his grandpa used to do. Sam says to himself, "It's a perfect day outside, sixty-five degrees, sun is shining, and a slight breeze from the south. It's going to get cold later on today and maybe rain tonight."

Sam walks on in to the hospital to check all the horses and their charts. Dr. Whim is there with the technician doing treatments. "So what are you doing today?" Dr. Whim asks. "You probably don't even know what to do with a weekend off, do you?"

"Bud, Kota and I are going to a shooting range. There's one over by West Virginia that we can shoot long-range targets and they have a pistol range. So I think we will go over there for a while," Sam says with a little smile. "I'll call you when we get over there to ensure that you can get ahold of me." Sam hates to be out of touch when something is needed, so a while back, he went out and bought a satellite phone. The only thing that interferes with it is some of the buildings.

Sam hasn't had a chance to shoot for a long time. He and his brothers love to go out and see how far they can shoot. It's almost a competition between them and they are about even. Each one has his favorite rifle. Sam shoots a .300 Super Mag and the .338 Lapua. Kota likes the .338 Lapua and the .22-250. He also has a .50-caliber

Barrett, but it is too expensive to shoot, so if he brings it out, it has to be a special day. Bud likes to shoot a .308 and a .45-70. He also has a .45-70 pistol that can shoot the same rounds as the rifle.

Bud walks in the door as Sam finishes his checks. "Me and Kota got everything loaded and we're ready to go. Are you?"

"Yep, just got to put these files away." Sam carries the files to the pharmacy and puts them back to the file holder. "OK, I've just got to grab my vest and I'm ready."

"We already got your vest. We got everything, rifles, pistols, water, power bars in case you get hungry, and about three thousand rounds of ammunition." Bud opens the hospital's exit door and bows jestingly. "After you, madam." Bud gives a big laugh. They go out of the hospital to the truck where Dakota and two kids are waiting. Luke and Montana are Bud's and Kota's kids. The kids go everywhere with their dads. They are becoming the outdoor, do everything kids just like their dads. The kids are not yet old enough to shoot with the big weapons, but they are learning about living outside, camouflage, judging distances and wind. Next year they can start shooting a .22 rifle, but for now, they will have to stick with their pellet guns.

Bud jumps into the driver's seat and Sam gets up into the passenger seat. Bud and Dakota always like to drive, but Bud always drove when they were all together. Sam was a great driver, but he didn't like to drive when he didn't have too. He would rather sit and think about things, not really paying attention to what was going on around him. Some of Sam's best ideas came while he was on the road or riding a horse. Bud starts the truck and Sam shuts the door.

Dr. Whim comes running out of the hospital, yelling, "Stop! Stop! We have a colic coming in about an hour from now." Dr. Whim opens the truck door. "Do you want me to just call you, or are you going to wait to see if it needs to go to surgery or not?"

"Damn it, we haven't had a colic in four weeks. Now when I want to go do something this happens." Sam gets out of the truck. "Do you know where they are coming from and if they will go to surgery? I know that sounds terrible of me, but today I'm being a little selfish."

Dr. Whim leans up against the truck bed. "The owners are from Bonatti Farms, and no one has treated this horse yet. They just found it rolling around the field, gave it some Banamine before calling me."

Sam reaches in the back window of the truck and starts tickling Luke and Montana. "Well, I'll stay here and see what this horse looks like and if it looks OK, we will go. If not, I'll stay." Sam gives the kids a shove and they start wrestling.

"I'll call you when the horse gets here." Dr. Whim is looking at the kids fighting while talking to Sam. "Go have fun for a while and I'll call you as soon as I check this horse."

Sam pulls his arm out of the window just in time before the two kids close in on his arm. "OK, we will be around." Sam looks over at Bud. "Well, I have to stay here for a little while. If you guys want to go without me, that's fine, or we can take these two hellions down to the targets and have them shoot the pellet guns till I know if I have to do surgery or not."

"Yep, let's just go have the kids shoot." Kota starts wrestling with Montana and Luke. "You got them all wound up and they need to get out and blow off some steam."

Bud says, "Get in and let's go before you can't go." Sam jumps into the truck and they drive to the bottom of the field where there's a mini target range. They get the kids out and have them run around for a while until the kids start stick fighting. Kota went over and broke up the stick fight.

"Luke! Montana! Get your rifles ready so we can start shooting!" Bud yells. Both kids run over to the truck and climb up in the bed. Immediately they go from messing around to getting very serious. They both have been taught that when you are dealing with weapons, you have to be serious and stay focused.

The kids kept saying, "Move smooth and confident, smooth is fast." They carefully hand their rifles to each other and climb out of the truck in a rhythmic manner, almost like they know what each one is thinking. Both of them go over and sit in front of their targets. They wait for their dads to tell them what to do next. Kota points to Luke and Montana, then points to the targets he wants them to shoot. Luke runs over and sits behind a rock, sets his rifle on the rock. Bud goes over and loads Luke's pellet gun. Montana runs over into some tall grass and lies in prone position. Kota goes over and puts one pellet in to Montana's rifle. Both kids take careful aim, knowing that they may only ever get one shot. Both dads watch over their kids shoulders and instruct them through their every move. Both kids fire and hit their targets dead-on. Their dads reload and the kids change position. They go on like this until Luke misses and then the switch targets.

Sam sits on the tailgate of the truck and watching the kids shoot. Sam wishes he could drink beer, but guns and alcohol don't mix. Some rules are just set in stone and this is one of them. Besides he may have to go to surgery, so it wouldn't be good to drink anyway. After about an hour of shooting, neither kid has missed more than one of their targets. They start running low on ammunition. Another rule is that you always leave yourself some ammunition; don't shoot it all up target practicing.

Bud says, "We only have a small amount of ammunition left, so what do we do?" Both kids yell, "Never use all your ammunition on practice. Time to load up!"

The kids check their rifles to make sure nothing is in the chambers. The kids put their rifles back to its proper area of the truck. Both kids jump out of the truck and start running around like wild animals, chasing each other, and wrestling around on the ground. Suddenly, the kids turn their attention on to Sam and both of them are trying to wrestle him to the ground. Sam's phone rings. "Hello," Sam says, all out of breath. "Yep, I'll come on up."

It was Dr. Whim on the other end. Sam tells his brothers, "Well, I got to go up to the hospital, you guys gonna stay here?"

Bud is trying to wrestle Luke out from a tree. "No, we'll go up and help so you can get done." Kota comes up to the truck carrying Montana over his shoulder like a sack of feed and Montana is laughing while holding on to the back of Kota's belt. Kota sets Montana down on the ground, and then both kids climb in the truck into their car seats. Bud drives the truck up to the hospital. Sam gets out and goes into the hospital. Dr. Whim is in the process of performing a belly tap. Sam asks Dr. Whim, "So what do you think is going on with this horse?"

Dr. Whim finishes what she is doing and stands. "Hey, Sam, I think this horse is going to be OK and won't need surgery." She lists his vital signs and diagnostic findings. Sam is relieved and goes out to give the boys the good news.

"Well, let me know if things change!" Sam states as he walks out the door.

"Let's go, she won't need me after all!" Sam says enthusiastically to Kota and Bud.

Sam gets into the vehicle and turns the radio on while riding to the shooting range. He turns it to the election news coverage. The election coverage was about the only thing on the radio except for the news about the racism of the white American male. The news these days just turns Sam's stomach because he has a feeling that John Barrack is going to win the election. Sam knows that Barrack is a lying crook that is running this country into debt and socialism. "I hope that bastard Barrack doesn't win again," Sam says to Bud. "He'll ruin this country even worse than he has already. He keeps saying he is going to clean up congress even though he is one of the do-nothings. He hides behind the senate majority leader and attorney general. He's so crooked, he can see his butt by just looking up."

Bud looks at Sam and shuts the radio off. "We're not going to talk about politics today. We are going to do some shooting. Get your head together."

"Here, drink this Dr. Pepper," Kota says as he hands Sam the pop, "and quit your whining around about some stupid election that never even happened yet. Nothing you do is going to matter."

"OK, OK, when the heck are we going to get there?" Sam pops open the can and it sprays all over the truck. The kids in the back roar in laugher.

"Do it again! Do it again!" both kids scream.

They arrive at the shooting range and there are several groups of people already shooting. Sam and Bud grab the cooler out of the back of the truck and go find a spot on the range. They leave the cooler at the spot. They go back to get the guns. Kota gets the kids out and put on their ear protection. Sam and Bud load themselves down with a .50, .300 Super Mag, .22-250, .30-06, and .338. They grab ammunition bag and they all head for the spot. The kids are always very cautious and conscientious when they are around people shooting. They don't run off nor tear around.

The kids get to the spot first, and they recognize the cooler that they always take along. The cooler didn't just hold drinks and snacks but held the two spotting scopes that they use. The kids open the lid and take out the spotting scopes. One scope is for them and the other is for the spotter. Kota stands behind the kids and watches them get things ready. The kids try to stack sandbags just how their dads like them but could not quite lift them high enough. While Bud and Kota stay with the kids and get the rifles ready, Sam checks his pockets to make sure he had his wallet with him. Sam goes back to the shooting shack where the range boss rents out space. Sam likes this range because the targets drop when hit and they automatically stand back up. At about 1,500 yards, there is a moving target that moves at about thirty miles an hour. It cost a little more, but it is always worth trying to hit the target.

"We have three people shooting today and we have five rifles. We would like all targets including the moving target," Sam says to the man in the shack.

"Well, that will be two hundred dollars. Read the rules and sign this paper. Let me know when you want the target to move by pushing the call button, and then I will turn it on for you. Just go and pick your spot. Shoot at your own pace. Range closes at 10:00 p.m., and no shooting the wild animals that may come into the range. Be careful and have fun." The range boss takes the paper from Sam without even looking at him. Sam notices the range boss was different from the last time he was here. This guy never looked at Sam the whole time he was talking to him. Sam gets a little suspicious when someone does that kind of stuff. He starts thinking something may be up.

"Oh well, we'll be at the farthest spot on the line," Sam says to himself. Sam walks out of the shack and looks back at the man. The man just stares out at a group of shooters with AK-47s and Uzi's.

Sam looks over at them and notices they are just burning up ammo. Sam says to himself, "They have hit everything except the target that they we're shooting at. They look like they're members of a street gang or something, just yelling and drinking. In the rules, it says that there is no drinking. It was also an unwritten rule that no one drinks while there is people shooting unless you were behind the spectator line, which these guys clearly were not." Sam sensed trouble if those guys didn't leave but kept on walking. Out of the corner of his eye, Sam notices that two of the guys were staring over at him.

Sam gets back to the spot just as Bud and Kota got the .22-250 and the .338 set up and ready to shoot. "Hurry up." Bud is looking at Sam from his sitting position. "Why does it always take you so long to do something so simple? It's shooting time. Now get on the scope and spot us."

Sam looks over at the kids, who are sitting on the cooler drinking a pop. He kneels down behind the spotting scope. "Just keep an eye out for anybody coming over here," Sam says to the kids.

Sam sits behind the scope and tells Bud which target is live. "First target one hundred yards, wind five miles from right to left, fire when ready." Bud fires three times.

"Hit, hit, hit," Sam says, "Second target two hundred yards, winds the same, fire when ready." Bud fires three times. "Dead center, hit, hit. Third target four hundred yards, no winds at the target, fire when ready." Bud fires three times. "Three inches off center, center, center," Sam says. "Fourth target seven hundred and fifty yards, five-mile-an-hour winds swirling, target ready, fire when ready." Bud fires three times. "Dead center, hit, hit, same target, target ready, fire when ready." Bud fires three times. "Dead center, hit, hit. Reload, it's Kota's turn." Sam gives Bud a "great job" sock in the shoulder.

Each brother takes their turn shooting. It is almost like a shooting competition between the three of them but Sam always conceded that Kota and Bud are better shooters. None of the brothers really cared who was better; they just like to shoot. This shooting rhythm goes on for about three hours, switching from Bud to Kota to Sam. They each shoot several rounds through all the rifles that they brought along. Finally, Kota sets up his .50-caliber for the long-range shots. Kota gets to shoot first because it's his weapon of choice. Bud and Sam put the other rifles in the rifle stand. Kota shouts, "I'm ready." He is sitting behind the .50 with it already loaded and ready. The kids are napping on top of a pile of sandbags. Bud sits down next to Kota and looks through the spotting scope. Sam hits the button for the target to start moving. He put his ear protection over his ears. He glances over at the shack to make sure that the range boss was paying attention. Sam notices that the little "gang boys" are looking in his direction, but the range boss is keeping an eye on them.

Bud gives Kota the "Fire when ready" touch on the back. Kota fires and the target falls over. "Damn," Sam says, "that's good shootin'!" Just then, Sam senses something behind him. Sam quickly rolls forward and comes up on to his feet where he comes face to face with an AK-47.

"Hey, puta, you sons bitch, why you think you's better than me," one of the "gang boys" screams at Sam and points the AK-47 at him.

"Shoot him, Dirk!" the small gang that came with Dirk yelled.

"Put that damn gun away before someone gets hurt, you stupid bastard." Sam stares directly into the guy's eyes. Sam sees a little bit of shutter and uneasiness in the guy's movement. Sam knows that the guy did not expect him to just jump up and start yelling at him, especially when he's holding a gun.

"You's a stupid man, and I am going to kill you," Dirk says with a little bit of confusion on what to say or do. Dirk looks away from Sam to mess with the weapon.

That's all Sam needed. Sam grabs the barrel of the AK-47 and pushes it to Dirk's right shoulder. This small movement of the weapon put the barrel out of sight of Sam's face and exposed Dirk's right arm. Sam pulls out his tactical knife from his front pocket. With the quickness of a cat, Sam slices the forearm of the Dirk's right arm before Dirk could pull the trigger. He then follows through with slashes across the left bicep muscle, then across Dirk's abdomen. Then he buries the knife deep into Dirk's thigh. He leaves the knife in Dirk's thigh and grabs the butt end of the AK-47 and jerks the rifle from Dirk. Dirk still has his right index finger in the trigger guard when Sam jerks the rifle away from him. The finger went with the rifle. It came off at the first knuckle. Dirk stands there stunned. Sam swings the rifle butt and hits Dirk between the nose and the upper lip. Dirk falls backward toward the ground, but before he falls flat, Sam jerks his knife out of Dirk's thigh. He puts it back in his pocket just as fast as he pulled it out. The slash across Dirk's forearm cut through all the flexor tendons and muscles. Blood sprays from the severed arteries of Dirk's arm. Dirk's fingers are made useless. He could not grip anything or pull the trigger. Sam makes a second cut across Dirk's abdomen, causing only a small hole for some of the small intestines to start herniating. Cutting the left bicep muscle rendered Dirk unable to throw a punch with that arm.

Dirk is lying on the ground unconscious with blood and small intestine oozing into his shirt. Blood streams from his severed finger and cut bicep. When Dirk hits the ground, one of Dirk's men runs toward Sam, trying to tackle him. Sam hits the guy in the forehead with the butt of the AK-47. The man is stopped cold in his tracks. He stands there for a couple of seconds and then drops to the ground. His body goes rigid with his arms reaching for anything but nowhere.

"Now listen up, you dumb bastard"—Sam points his finger at Dirk—"I told you that someone was going to get hurt." Dirk is curled up in to a fetal position with his arms crossed across his belly holding his arms. Sam crouches down in front of the Dirk's face. "There are kids out here and you will stop acting stupid with these weapons. If you hurt one of these kids or any of my brothers, I will kill you. If I ever see you out here or ever see you again, I will take it that you have come to challenge me. I will strike first without hesitation and with no remorse. Now get yourself to a doctor and get those tendons put back together before they retract so far that they will never get them back together."

Sam sees a bunch more of Dirk's men running in his direction. Sam glances over at the two kids, and they had buried themselves in the pile of sandbags. He could just see their eyes peeking through the bags. Sam then quickly glances over at his brothers. Bud has his .45-70 pistol out and ready. Kota has the semiautomatic .300 Super Mag in position and ready to fire. Sam stands with his hands on his hips as the gang of Dirk's men coming running over to him. The little gang stops a few yards from Sam. All of them point their weapons at Sam but ignore Bud and Kota. Sam has faced a gang before, but there were no guns involved. Sam figures the way to handle this situation will be the same. Sam stands there and looks the gang over while they yell some incomprehensible cussing and gang crap language. One man of the gang is kneeling down by Dirk on the ground trying to help him out. Dirk did not want any help and is very vocally resisting. Sam picks out the one who is probably the leader of the gang; they called him Poot. Sam notices that some of the weapons don't have clips in them. Some have the chambers open, which meant that they were out of ammunition. Poot is the only one with a loaded and ready weapon.

Sam stares at Poot, which made him come in closer to get into Sam's face. Sam thinks, "This guy is so stupid. He is trying to intimidate me by jumping in my space. Next he'll stick his weapon into my face."

Just then, Poot jumps up close to Sam and starts yelling at him, "You's going to die foockin' piece of shit. That's ma bro and no one mess with ma bros."

Poot slowly lifts up his weapon and points it in to Sam's face. Sam pulls his tactical knife and slashes in an upward stroke through Poot's crotch, all the way up to his chest. At the same time, Sam grabs the weapon and flips the weapon's safety switch to safe. Poot is stunned and instantly lets the weapon go. As Poot grabs his crotch, Sam grabs the weapon and swings the butt end of the stock. Sam sees that the gang member kneeling next to Dirk grabbing for a pistol. Sam hits him square on the bridge of his nose with butt of the weapon. In one quick motion, Sam points the weapon at the others and throws the safety. The others in the bunch are still standing there like they don't have a clue of what to do. Sam figures that the cluelessness is caused from a combination of stupidity, drugs, and alcohol that have got them in such a stupor.

Sam looks the gang over. "All of you, who want to go home in one piece, drop your weapons and lay down on the ground. Anyone that doesn't drop their weapons in one second will be shot instantly. Are you ready? Go!" All of them just stood there and dropped their weapons before Sam could finish his sentence. One of them pisses his pants.

Without speaking a word, Sam motions to Kota to get the gangs weapons. He fully understands what Sam wanted. Sam and his brothers always thought alike, and many times, it was like telepathy. Kota scoops up the weapons and brings them back to their shooting spot. Sam looks over at the bunch. "Now on the ground and make it quick." Just like in a football team training drill, they all hit the ground. "If any of you guys move, I am sure that you will get shot by one or both of my brothers."

Sam goes over to Poot, who is now lying flat on his back with his hands over his crotch. Sam crouches down next to him. "If you guys would have left us alone, you could be still having fun, but this is what happens to tough guys like you. Now, let's have a look at that wound and see if you are going to live or not." Sam pulls the clothing away from the wounds to reveal an open scrotal laceration with one testicle opened up and oozing, a small superficial laceration just below the belt. He had a deep laceration cutting through muscle tissue from just above the belly button up to the rib cage. None of the wounds are life-threatening and can easily be repaired. Sam flips the shirt back over the laceration. "You'll live but don't move till the ambulance gets here. Otherwise, you'll lose a testicle." Sam walks over to the other three wounded guys and they are all still on the ground. The last guy's nose is definitely broken. Sam leans over and grabs his nose and gives it a squeeze, "You shouldn't point guns at people. It can be dangerous."

By now, the other shooters at the range gather around the fight scene. One of the shooters says to Sam, "I seen the whole thing and I'll stick up for you, mister. I know these guys and they are never up to no good. I seen that guy come over here and come after ya. I never seen a guy bring a knife to a gunfight before."

Then another guy from the back of the crowd steps up, "Mister, do you know who this bunch is? They's a gang from over by Covington that sells them drugs and they's own the law around here.

They's not good people, I heards they's killed old Tommy Schultz because he'd not sell them his farm place. That's where they stay now and there's a bunch of them there. This ain't even a half of thems. I hope they don't come after you, but if they do, you let me know I'lls give you a hand."

There was a low roar through the crowd.

"Yeah, I'll give you a hand."

"Yeah, me too."

Through the crowd, County Sheriff Bill Tamms pushes his way up front. "What in the Sam Hill is going on here! Can anyone of you brainless hicks explain why these men are on the ground? Why are these three men bleeding over here?"

One of the gang members stands. "That sons-bitch just—" He is cut off in midsentence by a stare from Poot, who is still holding his crotch and sitting up. "Nothing is going on around here except your stupid loud mouth is moving when it should be calling me an ambulance. Now, you stupid bastard, get your sorry ass out of here and go eat some fucking doughnuts. I got everything under control, can't ya see? I just got my newbies out here learnin' how to shoot."

Sheriff Bill Tamms takes his hat off and slicks back his hair, then puts his hat back on. "Well, well then, I guess I'll be gettin' along. The ambulance will be along in a minute or two. I suggest the rest of y'all be gitn' along home for supper. I think you have had enough excitement for the day. I'll be back later to make sure everything is back in order, say about in an hour."

The ambulance arrives blipping it's siren as the crowd parts around it. The ambulance crew jump out with a gurney. They lift Poot and Dirk on the gurneys. The other injured gang member walks to the ambulance with the help of the ambulance crew. The other gang members gather around the leader like they were going to a wake. They all surround their leader, awaiting instructions. "Y'all get back to the farm and wait there till I get there. Do not talk to anyone and do not go into town." Poot points to one of them and motions him closer. "You get them boys back to the farm and find out who this son of a bitch is that did this to us. I want to know by morning. Got it?" The guy nods rapidly.

Sam watches the gang disperse. Bud and Kota gather up their rifles and the gang members' rifles. The kids dig themselves out of the pile of sandbags to do their job of putting the scopes back into the cooler.

Sam turns to the kids. "Are you guys all right?"

Both kids nod, "Yes, we hide really good. Nobody finds us when we hide."

Sam gives them both a hug. "Yes, you both did really well. I could hardly tell where you were hiding. Should we go and get some ice cream?"

Both of the kids yell, "Yeah, me likes strawberry."

Sam lets the kids go and they both run to their dads. Sam helps to pick up the area along with two arms full of rifles. They all start walking toward their truck when Sam stops. "Wait, you guys, I'll bet one of those guys will be watching which vehicle we get into and try to find us. We need to be careful that they're not watching."

Just then the ambulance gives them a blip of the siren. They step to the side with the kids. Sam watches as the ambulance disappears down the road. Kota sets down his rifles next to Sam and Bud, "Montana, stay here with Sam and Bud. I'll be right back." Kota darts off as quickly as a cat and disappears among the vehicles in the parking lot. After he surveys the area to his satisfaction, he appears just as fast as he disappeared. "Coast is clear. There are no gang members out there that I can see, only a few of the shooters loading up. I'll bet that sheriff got everyone's plate numbers while he was here. He's in with those guys big time."

Sam hands Kota and arm full of rifles. "I suspect so."

The brothers and kids walk back to the truck and quickly load up everything. They store the confiscated weapons into sidewall panel of the truck bed. They all climb into the truck. Bud starts the truck. They start pulling out of the parking lot, when Sheriff Bill Tamms turns his lights on to pull them over. Bud pulls over and the sheriff pulls in behind them. Sheriff Bill Tamms gets out and walks up to Sam's window. Sam rolls down the window, "Yes, Officer, what can we do for you?"

Sheriff Bill Tamms tilts back his hat. "I thought I told everyone to leave."

Sam looks at him. "Yes, you did and that is exactly what we are doing. It took us a while to pack up, but we are on our way home."

Sheriff Bill Tamms rubs his head like he is got a headache or something. "Well, y'all are just not moving fast enough for my liking. Maybe I should run ya in. I'm going to have to check your truck for drugs and weapons. I want you"—the Sheriff points his finger at Sam—"and just you to get the hell out of this truck and do it quick."

Sam knows this sheriff is up to something, but he is just going to go along with it for a little while till it gets a little dangerous. Sam gets out of the truck. The sheriff walks around to the back of the truck and looks in the bed of the truck. Sam walks behind the truck to where the sheriff is standing and leans on the back of the tailgate. Sheriff Bill Tamms fusses with his hat again. "Ya know that you could be in a heap of trouble if those boys press charges. I should just run you downtown and book you for attempted murder among other things. Or maybe I should just whip your ass now for coming over to my county and stirring up trouble. Which one would you chose?"

"Well, maybe an ass whipping, but then again maybe I would just like to go to jail. Oh, Sheriff, I just can't make up my mind. They both sound so good, but I guess you better start whipping ass." Sam turns to the sheriff and gives him a stare that pierces the heart and soul of the sheriff. "I guess I'll just have to press charges on those guys. My actions are all self-defense and I have witnesses to such. It was not attempted murder because I could have killed every single one of those lowlife good-for-nothings before they could have even pulled a trigger. You can't arrest a man for self-restraint. So I guess you had better start whipping my ass, but you had better get some more help so that it is a fair fight."

Sheriff Bill Tamms faces turns beet red with anger. He puts his hand on this pistol and stands there looking at Sam. "Smart guy, huh?"

Sam takes a glance at the sheriff's hand and notices that the holster is still snapped, then stares directly at the sheriff. "Well, Sheriff, I like to think so. I know I'm smarter than most but dumber than some." Sam could tell he was irritating the sheriff because the sheriff started getting fidgety and would not look Sam in the eye anymore.

Sheriff Bill Tamms fixes his hat again. "Well, then maybe you just tell me what you do for a living and you just get on your way."

Sam fixes his cap and doesn't look at the sheriff. "I'm a veterinarian and I believe we will be getting going now."

Sheriff Bill Tamms is so mad, it is giving him a headache. He rubs the back of his neck, which cracks as he turns his head. "I'll be seeing you around. Soon! Now you try to stay out of trouble, ya hear?"

Sam walks back to the passenger side of the truck all the while he keeps one eye on the sheriff as he climbs into the truck backward and gets the door shut. Sheriff Bill Tamms quickly walks up to the door and puts his hands on the window. "Did you boys see any illegal weapons when you were at the range?" The sheriff sticks his head through the window in order to search around.

Sam just starts rolling up the window. "Nope." Sheriff Tamms gets his head out of the window just before it closes. He then takes one step back. Bud puts the truck in gear and takes off. Sam looks back in the rearview mirror. He sees the sheriff take out his phone and put it up to his ear.

Sheriff Tamms calls Poot, "I got the plate number, and I'll run it for you. He's a veterinarian, so it will be easy to find him. Did they get you patched back up?"

Poot is still lying on the gurney in the ambulance. "No, you stupid bastard. We just left the range about fifteen minutes ago. You tell me where that bastard lives. I want to know everything about him. Did you get my guns back, you stupid shit?"

Sheriff Bill Tamms twisted his pinky in his ear and pulls out some earwax. "No, I didn't see them in their pickup. They might have left them at the range. You should send someone over to look because I'm not going back in to the range. If I go back there, then there will be no doubt that you and I are together."

Poot gives a big groan when the ambulance hits a bump. "I'll send Shack right over."

Bud heads for home with everyone all buckled in. "What the hell was that? That was some really bad stuff. What did you do to that guy to make him come over there in the first place?"

Sam turns in his seat to face sideways so that he could talk to Bud and Kota. His adrenaline was still flowing pretty high. "I didn't do anything to that dumb bastard. I saw them guys over by the spot closest to the range shack when I went to pay the range fee. Those guys were drinking and just shooting everything but the target. Hell, they're too dumb to have fully autos anyway, so I'm glad they came over and we got them away from them. Anyway, when I was leaving the shack, I looked over at the bunch and some of them took notice of me. I guess we looked like easy prey."

Kota grabs the back of Bud's seat and pulls himself up from the back of the seat. "We're going to have to clean those rifles and Glock 18s up but they looked fairly new. What I want to know is, where did that shit Sam did come from? Where did you learn to do that stuff? I was about to piss my pants when that first guy came up."

Sam sits fidgeting in his seat. "Ah, that's just a little something I picked up in China." The brothers all start laughing. Sam always says that when he just winged it. He's never been to China. "Let's go get some ice cream before we go home."

The kids start chanting, "Ice cream, ice cream."

Bud continues on toward home. They stop at the Dairy Mart before finishing the trip to home. When Bud pulls in the parking lot, Kota notices that one of the guys that were at the range had followed them. Kota taps Sam and Bud on their shoulders and points to the car that is just pulling into the parking lot. The car's driver pulls around to the back of the building. Kota tells them that the guy in the car was one of the guys with the gang. He remembers because of the bright red hair that the guy had been sporting. The brothers and kids go inside and walk up to the counter. As they stand in line, Kota glances outside to see that more cars are pulling in and driving toward the back of the building. Kota swallows hard, "Hey, guys, I think they're here."

Sam turns toward Kota, "Who's they?"

Kota points toward the window. "Looks like a gang, probably those guys from the range."

Sam tells them, "Just hurry and get the ice cream. I'll meet you back at the truck. If I'm not back by the time, you guys get ready to leave, just leave without me. Just come back in about thirty minutes and pick me up along the road."

Sam goes out the front door and grabs the binoculars out of the glove compartment in the truck. He runs up and into the tree line that lies on the side of the parking lot. He sneaks along the tree line till he can get a clear view of the gang. All the gang members are out of their cars. The red-haired gang member goes up to two men who just got out of one of the cars. They slap and bump hands. Two other men are digging in the trunk of their car like they were disassembling it. They take the spare tire and the carpet out of the trunk. They take out two duffel bags that look fairly heavy from the trunk. They carry the bags and drop them on to the hood of the car that the other two came in. Then they step back. The two other guys and the red-haired guy walk up to the bags and open them up.

Sam gets a good look into the bags. "Meth or something like that," Sam says to himself, "This is just a drug sale. They're not following us." Sam looks on as one of the two buyers goes back into their trunk and brings out a duffel bag. He opens it up on the hood. "Holy cow," Sam can barely keep himself from saying anything out loud. "That is the most money I've ever seen."

Sam sneaks back to the truck just in time as Bud was driving out of the parking lot. Sam jumps in, "You guys would not believe how much money I just seen. They're selling meth and a lot of it. They had stacks and stacks of one-hundred-dollar bills in a large duffel bag."

Kota hands Sam an ice cream cone. "I knew you would make it back."

Bud stops eating his ice cream. "We should go get that money from them guys. Not like they are going to report us for robbing them."

Sam tries to catch up to the dripping ice cream. "If the kids weren't along, then I would say yes. Then we could just follow them out of town. We'll get to have another chance. We'll just watch the place for a while. Those idiots probably meet here all the time to sell the shit. We can sit up in the tree line and watch. When they go to sell the stuff, we'll just take both the drugs and the money. That way, we can get some drugs off the street and get paid at the same time."

Kota kicks back in his seat. "Home, James, home."

CHAPTER FOUR

SAM'S ALARM GOES OFF ON his cell phone. Sam and Carol don't have a clock or a calendar in their house. Their days consist of getting out of bed, go to work, and then come home and go to bed. They usually work six to seven days a week and about ten to twenty-four hours a day. Ever since they open their own hospital, they have worked non-stop. They built a beautiful hospital with the help of their family, but they owed a lot of money to the bank. They had hoped that someone would have partnered up or they would have had investors by now, but they never could find anyone. So they just try to make it the best way they knew how. It is hard work providing the best medicine and surgical treatment for horses anywhere. But now, since the economic recession, people are not coming in, nor are they paying their bills. People either just don't have any money, or they just wouldn't give it up. Sam and Carol hate to turn any horse away when it needs help, but working on horses for free just causes them to go deeper in debt. Now for the first time, they have to turn horses away if the owners can't afford the services. The hospital could no longer afford to give away services. They didn't like it, but it was either that or bankruptcy. Carol had to stop getting paid from the hospital. She started working a second job since her work at the hospital was very seasonal. Sam's job was all the time; otherwise, he would have gotten another job also. They had to let some of the employees go and others got their wages lowered. It didn't sit well with the employees, but it was that or lock the doors. Sam and Carol started arguing a lot since the business was in trouble. Sometimes they were like cornered feral cats; they just hunch up and fought the world every day. They tried to think of other ways to make and collect money, but each amounted only to a little more income. They would have been better off if they didn't owe money on everything they had, including their education.

Sam tried to go back to sleep, but his good friend Boogie, one of his cats, is head-butting him and pulling up his eyelid. He's probably the only reason Sam gets out of bed because Sam seldom hears his alarm anymore. Sam opens his eyes, and Jack Royal and Phoenix were sitting on his chest, staring him in the face. "I guess it's time for breakfast, aye, guys?" Sam says to the cats as he scoots out from under the covers. Sam throws on his sweatpants and goes downstairs with all three cats running in front of him. He holds up a few different kinds of canned cat food. Boogie is there to pick out what flavor they wanted that morning. "So its seafood this morning for you guys." Sam holds the can and shows it to the others. "Is everyone in agreement?" Jack gives a big meow and Phoenix heads for the dish. Sam feeds the cats, then heads for the shower. "If I go back to bed, I'll never get up," Sam thinks to himself. Sam takes a shower and gets dressed. He goes back up to the bedroom to get a second pair of socks. He looks outside. "I hate waking up to a crappy rainy morning. It's going to be a cold and miserable day and I've got lame horses to look at today."

Sam reaches over and turns the TV on. He sits on the corner of the bed. The news is on and they are talking about tomorrow's election. John Barrack and Herman Bashert are on the Democratic ticket, and Merlin and Poole on the Republican ticket. Sam watches the news and says to himself, "What the hell are people thinking? Anyone that votes for Barrack doesn't know what he stands for or they think he's going to give them something for nothing. The guy stands for anti-American and prosocialism. He hung around known criminals, and you know that jerk doesn't have an original idea in his head. If you run with outlaws, you die with outlaws. People are suckered into his 'change' speeches. They think he is such an elegant speaker, but he just reads it off a teleprompter just like a news reporter." The news goes on about all the polls and several experts that say who is going to win and by how much. Barrack has it in the bag. Sam pulls on his second layer of socks. "I know that jerk is going to win and taxes are going to kill the hospital and us. Hell, he hates small business and loves the celebrities. Somebody will probably kill him off, but then that would leave Bashert, that stupid loudmouth and drunk bastard, in charge. That's probably why Barrack picked that idiot for a running mate so that nobody will kill him off in fear of having Bashert for a president. Both of them are an embarrassment to the United States."

Sam gets off the bed and goes around a gives Carol a kiss. Sam goes downstairs and puts his shoes, sweatshirt, and cap on. He goes out and drives to the hospital.

Sam arrives at the hospital and checks on the horses. All of them look like they are doing well, bandages still in place. The colic horse he cut last night is standing there at the stall door, looking for more food. So he goes out to the feed shed and checks the chart to see when the horse had gotten feed last. He grabs a pound of senior feed and goes in to the hospital to feed the colic horse. Sam goes up to the reception room to grab a cup of coffee. "Maybe that will wake me up and get me out of this foul mood," Sam thinks to himself. But then, Sam opens the door the reception office and finds that the technicians and Marsha are all standing around, just shooting the bull. Sam immediately gets irate. "Is this all you guys have to do? Is everything ready to go so we can get these lame horses looked at quickly, so you guys don't get so much overtime? Hell, I can barely keep the lights on and you guys are screwing around up here. Let's get things done so I can go home and wallow in self-pity. Then you guys can do whatever you want." Then he gives a little chuckle and everyone else smiled and rolled their eyes. Everyone scatters. Sam gets mad quick and then changes just as quick. He always thought that he got his grandpa's quick temper that blew up like a volcano and cool down just as fast.

Carol comes in the front door of the hospital. "Are you done with your day already?" It really wasn't a question more than a snide remark. Carol is grumpier than Sam in the morning. Sam just ignores her comment. One thing Sam never can understand was how Carol could get ready so fast in the morning. Sam could get up at 6:00 a.m. and still not get to work till 8:00 or 8:30 a.m. Sam goes back to the office where Carol is sitting at the desk piled with magazines and bills. Sam could see that she was about ready to have a nervous breakdown. Carol just stares at the desk and puts her hands over her face and starts crying. "There are so many bills and we don't have enough money to pay even half of them, and we've got to pay the mortgage, payroll, insurance, and oh hell, they are all overdue. The bank is not going to give us a working loan this winter. I went in and talked to them last week and they just said no. We're just supposed to tighten our belts and manage our business better. Business sucks, and if we don't get any money in soon, we are going to have to shut the doors."

Sam goes over to her and gets on his knees. He gives her a hug. "Things will work out. We'll get by somehow this winter. We've just got to think of new ways to make money. We can talk about that later tonight. So just pay as many as you can. Call the others and tell them we will get them paid as soon as we can. The bank can just wait or just take everything back. They've got just as much invested in this place as we do. They'll wait." Sam gets up and opens the door. He takes one look back and sees her digging through the bills and sorting them into piles. Sam always stresses but he never shows it much. He was always good at getting through situations somehow, someway. This time he really didn't have a clue how he was going to work this out. Clients are just not paying their bills, and there was nothing Sam could do about it.

Sam goes to the back of the hospital to see the horses that were here. He goes up and shakes hands with the owners and gets busy with his day.

"Can I help you?" Marsha pushes her chair from the desk and stands up to greet the four men that just came in the front door. One of the guys had bright red hair and dressed in a punker look. He is wearing a leather jacket that is too big. He has chains on his clothes that lead to a wallet. He has pants that are falling down below the top of his underwear. He has a neck tattoo of some Japanese symbols on one side and "Shack" on the other. Shack has tattooed knuckles that spelled "LOVE" on one hand and "PEACE" on the other. He has multiple piercings including two sharp pointed studs in his lower lip and one below his eye that looked like a safety pin. The others are dressed fairly similar. They all have the same symbols on their neck and wearing the same kind of motocross type boots.

The red-haired punk, Shack, walks over to the counter, "I wants to sees a Sam Kelley."

"May I have your name and what this is concerning?" Marsha shies away a little with the aggressive approach of Shack.

"My names Shack, and none of your fucking bizz about concerning." Shack leans in over the counter and sneers at Marsha.

"Well, if this does not have to do with the care of an animal, then I suggest that you make an appointment to see him." Marsha face turns red with anger but controls it very well for as much crap as she has to put up with on a daily basis.

Shack's face turns red and distorted from anger. He thinks to himself, "No one has ever not done what I tell them to do. This bitch, how dare she not jump when I tell her to." He grits his teeth and looks back at the other three guys. The other three are just standing around, looking through horse magazines and not giving one bit of attention to him. "You's dumb asses gets rid of the mags and pays attention." Then he looks over at Marsha and stares. "Listens up, you dumb bitch. When I tells ya I wans to sees someone, yous will git'em for me, NOW!"

Marsha stares back at him, "When I tell you you need an appointment, I mean YOU need an appointment. Now get out before I call the police."

Shack draws back his right arm like he is ready to give Marsha a punch, when Kota and Bud walk in the front door. Kota quickly notices the guy and grabs his arm just as he is about to hit Marsha. Marsha had slid her chair away from the desk in a defense reaction and is now sitting in the corner. Bud and Kota have a good hold of the guy and appear to be waiting instructions from Marsha.

"Throw him out and don't let him back in ever again." Marsha moves around the counter and opens the door. Bud has a hold of the guy by the hair and by the back of his pants. Kota has the guy's arm twisted around to his back and another hand on his coat collar. Together, as if running a battering ram to break a castle door, they pick Shack up and throw him onto the parking lot concrete. Shack's right cheekbone hit first and a burst of pain shot through his brain as he leaves a skid mark of blood and bits of flesh on the parking lot. He just lays there as if he is dead.

The three others that are with Shack drop their magazines and move on out the door. The first one walks in between Kota and Bud as if parting the sea. He gives Kota a push as he moves by. Kota immediately punches the guy in his right ear, and the guy drops to the ground instantly. The other two step around Bud and Kota as if dancing around a rattlesnake, keeping an eye on them yet making steady movement to their two buddies on the ground.

By this time, Shack is slowly trying to get up off the ground. Blood combined with dirt and small stones are stuck to the right side of his face and jacket. Trickles of blood are dripping from Shack's chin and mouth. He takes his hand and wipes the blood off his mouth and flicks it to the ground. "You's shouldn't done that," he said, looking up at Bud and Kota. Shack's buddy grabs him by the left shoulder and tries to pull him up to his feet. Shack pulls his shoulder away, says "Fuck off," then gives his buddy a shove. Shack gets to his feet, walks to the car, and gets in the passenger side.

The jerk that Kota dropped is being helped up from the ground. He is staggering a little while holding his right hand to his ear as if to feel if it was still there. They both head to the car and the staggering jerk turns just as he is ready to get in and yells, "You fuckers, I get ya back, you fucking asshole motherfuckers."

Kota and Bud are just standing there on the sidewalk, smoking cigarettes. Kota flips off the jerk who is yelling over to them. The jerk slams the door and the car backs up. As they are pulling forward, the two on the passenger side roll their windows down and start throwing garbage out the window. Then they just drive off. Kota and Bud look at each other and start laughing. They both flick their cigarettes and put a toe of their boot on them and twist. They walk over to pick up the garbage that the punks had thrown out the window. Most of it was fast food bags and cups, but two of them were brown paper bags.

Bud picks up one of the paper bags and looks inside. "Meth!" he says as he pulls a plastic bag of crystals out of the paper bag.

Kota grabs the other bag and looks inside, "Holy shit, it's money!" Kota reaches in the bag and pulls out rolls of one-hundred-dollar bills—eight rolls altogether. Kota shoves the money back in the bag. "Those dumb asses just threw their shit out by mistake. Their loss, we're keeping the money and getting rid of the meth." They both gathered up the garbage and headed for the shop. They throw the garbage into an old feed sack that they are using for a garbage bag.

Bud clears a spot on the workbench, which is covered with horse supplements, jars of nails and screws, and a feed scale.

Bud puts the bag of meth on the scale. "About two and a quarter pounds. I wonder how much this is worth." Then he gets his cell phone out of its holster and starts dialing. "I'm going to call Carol's brother's friend who is a cop and ask him how much meth is worth."

Kota dumps the money on the bench and starts undoing the rolls of bills. "Well, don't tell him we have any, you dork. He'll come over and arrest us and probably go home and smoke the stuff or whatever they do with it."

Bud holds the phone up with his right hand and holds left index finger over his mouth as to shush Kota. Bud gets the cop on the phone and bullshits with him for a while, and then he leads the conversation over to drugs and meth. Then Bud hangs up the phone. "It's worth from eighty to a hundred and thirty dollars a gram. How much money you got there?"

Kota holds up his index finger as to shut Bud up and he finishes counting the bills. "There is eighty thousand dollars here, and here is your half."

Kota hands Bud a stack of bills. "Should we share it with Sam?"

Bud just looks at the money. "Well, I don't know."

Kota starts tapping his stack of money on the bench to get them all in line. "I don't think he would take it, but at least we can let him in on what is going on. Besides by the time I pay him back what I owe him. He'll have most of my cut. Let's go get him." Kota grabs an empty Cosequin container from the shelf and shoves his money in. Bud does the same and then closes the lid. Kota takes a Sharpie and draws a line from the bottom of the lid to the container. "This way

I will know if anyone has opened this besides you or me." Bud puts the bag of meth into another container.

Bud and Kota both walk over to Sam, who is just finishing his lameness exam. The clients were loading their horses. They both walk up to Sam and stand on both sides of him. Sam watches the horses load as he finishes writing a report. "What's up, guys?"

Bud pulls up his sunglasses. "When you're done and before you go up to the office, we need to show you something."

"I'm done right now." Sam hands his report to the technician. "So let's go see what's going on."

As Sam, Bud and Kota walk back to the shed. Bud and Kota give Sam a play by play of the incident that had happen. "I know that was the same guy that was at the range and at the ice cream place," Kota said as he was opening the shop door, "and this time they left presents."

Bud gets out the two containers and shows Sam. "There's eighty thousand dollars in here."

"Well, good, there is your tip for showing them to their car." Sam takes a handful of money out from one of the containers. "Now don't you guys waste it all on stupid stuff. Kota, you can pay your bills off and put a down payment on a bigger house. Bud, you can pay all your bills off and you'll probably have a bunch left over so that BOTH of you can have some well-deserved fun with this money."

"Yeah, but don't you want a cut?" Bud gets the money back from Sam and he stuffs it back into the container.

"I do but ya know that wouldn't be right. You guys found it, so it's yours." Sam gives Bud and Kota a "that a boy" punch in the arm, "But don't waste it on stupid stuff and don't pay your bills off in one lump sum. Spread it out a little so that no one takes notice."

"Well, they gave us one more present." Kota reaches up high on the shelf and brings down the other container, opens it up, and shows it to Sam. "And this would probably be meth."

"Hmmm, what the hell are we going to do with that?" Sam reaches in the container and takes out the bag. "We can't just throw it in the Dumpster, and we don't know anything about selling this stuff. Let's just hide it where no one will find it and then figure out what to do with it."

"It's supposed to be worth a hundred and some thousand dollars." Kota holds the lid to the container open and Sam puts the bag back. "Where we going to hide it?"

"How about putting it in another container and we'll put it with those weapons we took from those punks? Maybe we can just take the backhoe loader and open one of those old empty coyote holes down by the shooting range. We'll put in a large septic tank vault. That will store this stuff. I guess we'll have to use some of you guy's money to get one because I'm broke." Sam starts looking for another container. "I just hate to get rid of it because we may need it for a bargaining chip someday. But we better not let Carol find out about all this stuff that we seem to be accumulating, she'll blow a gasket."

"That's fine, we can use this money." Bud starts pulling a handful of money from one of the money containers. "I can take the trailer tomorrow and go get a tank to put in. We should have it done by tomorrow night, if it doesn't rain."

They all leave the shed. Bud heads for the house and Kota gets in his vehicle to drive home. Sam heads for the hospital to finish up more paperwork and check on tomorrow's calendar.

Chapter Five

THE NEXT MORNING SAM GETS up a little late and takes his time getting ready for work. There are no appointments this morning and maybe none for this afternoon if things don't go right. After dressing, he goes down to the local community center to vote. At the community center, there are signs everywhere for John Barrack and his lackey but not a single sign for the less-than-fabulous Republican candidate. Barrack's OCORC group, which is paid by the federal government, is all around handing out campaign paraphernalia. People are coming out of the center in droves with Barrack stickers on their shirts. Inside the center are people wearing Barrack stickers and holding up the voting lines. Sam is about tenth in line. As Sam observes the people in the room, he thinks to himself, "Many of these people are too stupid to be voting. They take several minutes asking stupid questions like "Now when I get up there to the voting booth, which buttons do I have to,push and what if I make a mistake can I erase it and start over?" If you can't read and push a couple of buttons on a screen, then you should not bother to vote. For that matter, if you don't pay taxes or never have paid taxes, then you should not get to vote.

While standing in line, five people had to have the attendant come back and restart a booth because they had messed up on their voting. Sam thought to himself, "I thought that there was only one thing to vote on and that was for the president. There are no other issues to vote on. Maybe I am wrong and there are more bills to vote on."

After three minutes of waiting in line, it is Sam's turn to vote. He goes into the booth, touches the screen three times, then he is done. Sam voted in less than thirty seconds. As he walks out of the room, he says out loud, "If you are stupid, please don't vote. It's not good for me or you, but especially for me."

The door attendant quickly shut the door after Sam stepped outside. Sam was outraged as he walks out the door as he sees the OCORC people outside. All the OCORC people are swarming around everyone walking up the sidewalk to vote. As Sam walks to his vehicle, several of OCORC people surround him with cameras. "Sir, you just voted. Can we ask who you voted for and why you voted for him?"

"Well no, that is really none of your business now, is it?" Sam turns his back to them.

"I guess we can just assume that you voted Republican. We can also assume that you are a racist because you don't like change and you wouldn't vote for a black candidate." One of the OCORC assholes snidely told Sam. Sam hated people like this one, especially when they do the little quotation mark thing with their fingers. Sam immediately wanted to rip this person nose off and stick it on those quoting fingers.

"Well, if you're going to be like that, then yes, I voted Republican because I love America and my ancestors did the same. They fought in the Revolutionary War. You young pukes probably know nothing about the history of this country, nor do you like this country the way it is. You want everyone to vote for a crook. Barrack is not only a racist but is one of the biggest do-nothing in the senate today. He is one of the most bloviating narcissistic, American hating, stupid assholes that has ever run for the president of this United States of American. Barrack's mother was a liberal whore and his daddy was a nomadic do-nothing from Kenya. I do not believe Barrack was even born in the USA, which does not entitle him to run for the presidency. His wife is some loudmouthed bitch who also hates Americans. She can only look ahead and see dollar signs, not how much 'good' she can do as a First Lady. They are both socialites that only want to know you if you can do something for them. If you have to grab people from their homes and give them stuff, those types of people don't need to vote. People living off the government payouts should not get to vote. The 'get out to vote' crap is just that, a bunch of uninformed dumb asses voting for people they don't know anything about. Now for you all, all of you are also criminals by involving yourselves with a company that has committed several acts of voter fraud. You people are too stupid to vote and to be talking to me. I also believe if you have never paid taxes or are too stupid to run a voting machine, then you should not vote. You are not Americans, you are anti-Americans. I guess OCORC stands for Organized Citizens of Racist Criminals organizing dumb asses for indoctrination in to liberal never-never land?" Sam stands and stares right into the camera.

"You are stupid, you don't even know what OCORC stands for," some fat old lady got into Sam's face and starts yelling. Sam just turns and grabs the Yukon's door handle. A fat bald guy comes running up to the vehicle to speak his mind about what Sam has just said. Sam opens the door just as the guy comes running up to tackle Sam. The fat bald guy runs into to the Yukon door head first, then hits the ground like a lead brick. Sam shut the door to inspect it for dents. The door has a big dent. Sam looks down at the guy on the ground, who is rolling around like a turtle trying to get off its back.

Sam points a finger at the guy. "I hope you got insurance because you are going to pay for this dent in my door."

"He is not going to pay anything!" Some blond chick with pseudo dread locks pointed a finger in Sam's face. "I seen everything and you hit him with that door. That is assault and battery. I am calling the police. You are a bastard, how dare you hit this poor innocent man."

"Lady, I have had it with you people. Since you are on his side, then I can only assume that you are willing to pay for this dent in my door." Sam grabs the camera from a guy who has had it in his face the whole time. "Now someone get their money out since I have the real eyewitness right here." Sam pops the DVD out of the camera and puts it in his pocket. Then he hands camera back to the guy. "Now who is going to pay or do I have to call the cops?" Soon as Sam said that, people started to shy away from him like a group of people who were out bid at an auction.

The fat bald man is still trying to get to his feet, so Sam reached down and extended his hand out to him so that he could help the man off the grounded. The guy instantly curled up in a fetal position and start screaming, "Don't hit me. Don't hit me." The crowd that had dispersed turned and moved in on Sam. Several of them have their cell phones out either taking pictures or making calls. The fat man continued to lie on the ground and continued screaming.

Sam just stepped back and looked at the guy. "This guy is the biggest wimp I have ever seen." Some people from the crowd walk over and help the wimp off the ground. They walk the wimp back into the crowd to console him. Sam just rolls his eyes and turns to his Yukon when from behind, someone hits him in the back of the head with a Barrack sign. Sam turns to face his assailant. When he turns, more people start hitting him with signs. Sam instantly goes into an offensive mode and grabs the sign from the nearest assailant. He started using his martial art skills to throw his assailants to the ground. He has to throw seven people to the ground before they would stop their attack. This scrimmage all took place within a matter of seconds without too much physical damage to anyone. Sam gets into his Yukon. He starts the vehicle and slowly creeps forward to head out of the driveway. People start jumping on his vehicle and standing at protest in front of his vehicle.

The county sheriff shows up with five cars. Sam stops his vehicle and sits there until the crowd has been controlled by the cops. Cops come up to his vehicle and pull their guns. "Get your hands on the steering wheel." Sam puts his hands on the steering wheel and thinks, "Nothing more dangerous than an itchy cop with a gun."

Three of the cops keep their weapons pointed at Sam, and two come up to the door. "Open your door."

Sam doesn't comply, and he just yells to the cop, "How do you think I am going to open the door if my hands have to stay on the steering wheel?"

The cop closest to the door is slightly embarrassed but yells, "Ah, take one hand off the steering wheel, but keep it where we can see it."

Sam is thinking, "These guys are the biggest dumb asses, they must be rookies, or they are videoing this for some reality show." Sam just opens the door anyway and slowly turns to get out, when the other cop with the shaved head runs up to the door. The cop slams Sam's leg in between the door and the vehicle. Sam quickly glances at the cop's name tag and it reads, "Sheriff Cecil Tamms." Sam yells, "You asshole, what the hell did you do that for?"

"You're moving a little too quickly," the tough guy cop holsters his weapon and opens the door. "Now step out of the vehicle and get down on the ground." Sam gets out of the vehicle and slowly kneels on the ground. His knees ache from years of working and riding horses. Sheriff Tamms kicks Sam in the back just between his shoulder blades and Sam goes crashing to the ground. Sheriff Tamms sticks a knee in Sam's back, pulls his arms around, and handcuffs him. The crowd cheers. Two of the cops pick Sam up and set him next to the Yukon.

Sam was always good at facial recognition. He takes a good look at Sheriff Tamms and says, "You must be the son of that old bastard sheriff in Highland County. You both have that same face that looks like a dried-up bull scrotum." Sheriff Tamms face turns beet red and then punches Sam in the stomach.

Sheriff Tamms tells Sam, "It's not my beautiful face people love, it's the power I have. Not that it is any of your business, but he is my father, so fuck you." Sheriff Tamms turns and looks the crowd over. He sees the excitement in their faces as everyone watches like there is going to be a major car wreck. He then walks over and turns to look at Sam. He scratches his head and then grabs Sam's chin. "Listen up, you. You are under arrest for assault and battery, disturbing the peace, and inciting a riot." Then he grabs Sam by the collar and waves his nervous finger in his face.

Sam could see that this guy was wired on something. Sam could see that this cop's pupils were dilated and his veins are about to pop from his forehead. Then the camera crew came out from the back of

Sheriff Tamms's car. "Now I know why this guy is acting so tough, it's his fifteen minutes of fame," Sam is thinking to himself while the tough guy takes his pose for the camera. "Dumb shit, they got it all on tape and this is police brutality. I will get this dumb ass fired."

After posing for the camera, Sheriff Tamms turns to Sam. "Got anything to say for yourself? Maybe you can try to convince America that you are innocent before we haul you in."

"Well yes, I do have something to say," Sam stares directly into the eyes of the cop. Sam sees that Sheriff Tamms's eyes moved away and started fidgeting a little. All the while, the other cops have helped themselves to Sam's vehicle. They were going through his vet box and taking stuff out and throwing it on the ground. They have stuff spread everywhere. Sam looks at the camera, "First of all, this is an intrusion on my rights. Secondly, I am the one who got attacked by these people because I didn't vote for the fascist bastard Barrack. Third, this is a clear case of police brutality, which all you will be summoned to court for along with that tape. Lastly, you just invaded my privacy and impinged on my freedom to vote without retaliation. You people in the crowd, along with you shithead cops, have just violated something that we as Americans hold true too—voting without repression. So I have eyewitnesses and a camera that has seen all of this. Do you still want to arrest me?" Sam looks directly at Sheriff Tamms, who at some time in this whole fiasco has wet his tight pants.

"Well, we have a call here from several people that you assaulted a short fat man." Sheriff Tamms looks down at his little notebook. "You hit him with the door of your vehicle and then started to batter him while he was on the ground. There is a dent in your door. Can you explain this?"

"Yes, I can show you if you take these fucking cuffs off me." Sam moves his arms to the side closest to the cop. "I got a computer in my vehicle that should show you everything."

The cop fumbles for his keys and unlocks Sam's handcuffs. Sam moves around to the other side of the Yukon and finds his computer on the ground out of its case. Sam grabs the computer and puts it on to the hood of the car. "I hope you bastards plan to pay for anything that gets lost, broken, or stolen. The drugs are covered under rules of the DEA and any of them missing will result in you guys getting busted." Sam starts the computer and the camera crew moves in to video the screen. Sam pops the DVD into the computer. He fast-forwards to him walking into the voting area and walking out, then the confrontation with the group of OCORC pukes and then, "Ohhh! Looky there, out of nowhere some dumb shit bald fat cretin comes running out of the blue and runs into my door. Now explain to me how any of this is my fault. I ask you, who is going to pay for my door?"

Sheriff Tamms turns into the camera, "Even as great of a job that we do day in and day out we sometimes make a mistake." He puts his hand on Sam's shoulder, "Sir you may go free."

Sam again asks, "Who the hell is going to pay for my door and why are you not arresting all of those that were mobbing me? I want to press charges. I want justice and I want it now." Immediately people scattered. Sam walks up to one of the quiet cops, "Why are you not arresting anyone? You come out here and treated me like a criminal and now you won't haul any of those that assaulted me in to jail. And who the hell is going to pay for the door and for you assholes breaking my equipment?"

"Sir, take one step back." The cop grabs for his gun. "We will review the camera footage and determine who needs to be arrested. You need to make a list of all equipment damaged and turn it into the county treasure office. They can determine its worth and write you a check. But for now get your crap back into your vehicle and depart from these premises."

Sam walks over to Sheriff Tamms and leans up to his ear then whispers, "You and I know that if I turn you in for police brutality that nothing will ever happen to you, right? So either you owe me and I will call on you for a favor sometime or I will break you into so many pieces that you will wish you were dead. What do you think?" Sam takes a step back and waits for an answer.

Sheriff Tamms throws out his chest and adjusts his belt. In a semiquiet voice, "Are you trying to threaten me? Are you just that stupid? I am an officer of the law. I will pretend that I did not hear that. Now leave or I will run you in."

"I guess you had the choice and you just gave me the answer. Let me know if you change your mind." Sam walks over and throws all his stuff in the Yukon. He gets in and takes off down the driveway. On his way out, he runs over every sign that is out there, including the one in the ditch. Sam drives to the clinic and hands the keys to the technician, "Please go through the vehicle and make a list of anything broken or missing. Then make sure that all the equipment still works. The cops broke into the vehicle and threw all my stuff out." Sam walks in the hospital and tells Carol what had happened. She told him that there was only a few of those OCORC people out there when she went and voted. Sam goes in to his office and starts his daily paperwork. He can hardly concentrate because he is so mad.

Later that night, Sam and Carol sit in front of the television and watch the election results. Sam looks at Carol. "I can't believe so many people fell for that phony communist crook Barrack. He won by a lot. I think that will be the end of America as we know it. That crooked bastard will run this country right into a hole. He really doesn't have clue on how to run anything, let alone a country. Hell, he has never even had a real job in his life."

Carol just gets up and shuts the television off. "We will just have to make do. We can't stress ourselves over things that we can't change. I just hope those that voted for him will soon learn that he is not on their side. He's just like every other politician, only there to fill their pockets with what we work for day in and day out. Let's go to bed."

The next morning Sam and Carol get up just like every other morning, they are both grumpy in the morning. Sam drives to the gas station and fills up the Yukon with gas. "I'm sure the gas prices will go up pretty fast now that the crooked bastard is in office." Sam thinks to himself. Then gets into the Yukon and drives to work. Carol is already at work and has started doing paperwork in her office. Sam goes back to the office, "How did you get here before me?" Sam asks Carol.

She looks up from her paperwork, "I don't dillydally." Sam laughs and turns, then goes out and starts talking to his brothers. They told him that they got the biggest septic tank that they could find and that it was safely in the ground.

"We buried that tank about eight feet into the hill," Bud said. "No one can find that unless they walk right up to it and notice that the sod and rocks are different.

"We did a great job." Kota tells Sam.

"Well, great, I'll have to go out and see it this afternoon." Sam gives Kota a punch in the arm.

Sam gives them the lowdown on what happened yesterday. Kota tells Sam that he went to fill up the ambulatory vehicles last night and that there was a sheriff's car sitting at the end of the road when he left and when he came back. Sam told him that he didn't see anyone when he came in. Carol comes back and breaks into the conversation, "Sam, since you don't have any out calls today, can I take the Yukon to go the bank? My vehicle is almost out of gas."

Sam laughs, "Well, Miss No Dillydally, I filled it up this morning, so you should be good to go. I'll go get your vehicle filled up as soon as I get done with my first appointment." Sam hands her the keys.

Kota says, "I'll just go now and fill it up before I go home and get some sleep." Carol hands her keys over to Kota. Kota takes off and drives down to the gas station. On his way, he notices that the cop car is sitting at the corner again. Kota calls Sam. "That cop car is sitting down here again. Better tell Carol to watch herself."

Sam hangs up and runs out to the Yukon, but Carol had already taken off. Sam calls Carol, "Hey, there is a cop car down at the corner."

Carol cuts him off short. "I know he just pulled me over and he's coming up to the door with his gun out. Got to go."

Sheriff Cecil Tamms, the very same one that roughed up Sam yesterday, decided that Sam had ruined his television day view and he was going to make Sam pay. He walks up to the car with his Glock in hand and taps on the window with his weapon. "OK, roll down the window and then hands on the wheel."

Carol rolls down the window and hands her drives license to him, "Why did you pull me over?"

Sheriff Tamms slaps Carol across the face. "I told you to put your fuckin' hands on the wheel and don't question my authority." Carol looks away and grabs her face and starts crying.

Sheriff Tamms opens the door and grabs Carol by the hair. "Now get the fuck out of the car, bitch."

Carol slaps the cop in order for him to let go. "Let go, you ass-hole. I didn't do anything."

Sheriff Tamms unbuckles Carol seat belt and grabs her again, then drags her out of the Yukon by her hair. He throws her to the ground and pulls her arms behind her back then handcuffs her. "You, bitch, are under arrest."

Kota drives by after going to the gas station. He sees that Carol is on the ground. Kota races past the cops and up to the hospital but calls Sam on his way. "Sam, they got Carol on the ground with hand-cuffs on." Sam runs out to one of the vehicles and takes off down the road. At that time, two more cop cars pull up to the scene. The cops get out and run up to the Yukon where Sheriff Tamms is yelling at Carol. "So what do we got going here?" the first cop, Officer Rose, says.

Sheriff Tamms says, "Well, I pulled her over for a broken tail-light, broken window, and no rearview mirrors. But then she was talking on the cell phone and didn't have her seat belt on. I went up to the door to get her driver's license, and she started yelling obscen-ities at me and failed to produce a driver's licenses. So I asked her to step out of the car, and when she did, she slapped me. I'm arresting her for all those traffic violations, resisting arrest, and assaulting a police officer."

Just then Sam pulls up to the scene and jumps out of his vehicle and runs up to Carol, who is still lying on the ground. "What the hell is going on here?"

Both Rose and the second cop, Trevor, pull their weapons. "Halt, step away from the prisoner."

Sam stops. "She's not a fucking prisoner, and why the hell is she lying on the ground? I'm her husband and I want some answers,

NOW!" Sam looks over at Sheriff Tamms and gives him the eye. "YOU, I warned you."

Sheriff Tamms walks over to the Yukon and takes out his night-stick and starts smashing the windows, taillights, and mirrors. Then he kicks dents on the side of the vehicle. "Looks like you need a little bodywork. You should get this fixed before you drive this vehicle. I think I'll just have it towed. As for your bitch wife, you can see her down at the county jail. Now get the fuck out of here before you are arrested for obstruction of justice." Both Rose and Trevor have picked up Carol and are putting her into one of the cop cars.

Sam yells to Carol, "Hang in there, Carol. I'll meet you down at the jail." Sam looks over at Sheriff Tamms. "Now for you, I warned you. You just wrote your own death warrant."

"Are you threatening me?" Sheriff Tamms walks over to Sam. "I'm an officer of the law and you can't talk to me like that." He points a finger at Sam but is shaking like a leaf.

Sam looks over at the other two cops, and they have already started driving off with Carol. After seeing that they are alone, Sam grabs Sheriff Tamms's finger and bends it until the cop drops to his knee. "I am promising you that you have just declared war. I will make you pay and pay dearly," Sam says in a soft raspy voice. Then Sam gives the finger a little twist and dislocates it. Sam lets the finger go and walks away. Sheriff Tamms just sits there on one knee and grabs his finger.

Sheriff Tamms yells to Sam, "I am going to fuck up your wife and your family for this. I'll ruin you for this."

Sam turns and does a running front kick to the sheriff's head. It looked much like someone kicking a field goal. The sheriff's head whips back from the force of the kick just under the chin. The sheriff's teeth and lower jaw cracked, and he fell to the ground uncon-scious. Sam stands over him for a brief moment make sure the sheriff was still alive. Once the sheriff took a breath, Sam spits on the sher-iff's forehead. He turns and walks to the vehicle he drove down. He gets in his vehicle and drives off toward the jail. He calls Marsha. "I won't be in today, so can you cancel all my appointments. I have a really big emergency to handle."

"I'll call every one. You just go do what you need to do," Marsha says in panic. "Is everything going to be all right? Do you need help?"

"No, just tell Bud and Kota that I'll be calling and to get ready. I'll tell you about everything when we get back." Sam hangs up and dials the phone for Bud.

Bud answers, "Hey, what's up?"

"Is Kota with you or did he go home?" Sam asks.

Bud motions Kota to come over to him. "He's here and he's standing next to me." Bud pushes the button for the speakerphone.

"Here's the deal. That asshole cop that was harassing me yesterday just hit Carol and beat the crap out of my Yukon. I pissed him off quite a bit. The cops took Carol to jail, and I'm on my way there right now. I suggest you guys get ready for a war with this asshole, a quiet war. We need to do some surveillance on this guy and find out what he does after work and where he lives. Then I'm going to make him pay." Sam turns his vehicle into the police station.

Bud asks, "Do you know his name or where he is right now?"

"On his shirt tag it said Sheriff C. Tamms." Sam parks the vehicle. "You may want to drive down to the corner and see if the Yukon has been towed or if it is still sitting there. If it is still sitting there, then bring it home. If it has been towed, I'll find out where it was towed to right after I get Carol out of jail. So I'll talk to you later." Sam hangs up the phone and walks into the police station.

Sam walks up to the front desk, "I'm here to see Carol Kelley."

At the front desk was a lady cop named Officer Oscar. "She is still in booking and will not be released until she goes before the judge, which will be tomorrow."

"I am her husband and I will see her today." Sam gets a little angry at the snide way Officer Oscar spoke to him like he was a child.

"Well, sir, I don't care who you are. The only person that is going to see her today is a lawyer and she has not been able to call one yet," Officer Oscar snidely says to Sam. She doesn't even look up from her computer.

"Can you tell me where the vehicle she was driving is towed?" Sam asks.

"I am not sure it was towed. After I am done with this, I will try to find it on the computer," Officer Oscar says.

Sam walks outside and calls Bud. "Hey, did you guys go down and see if the Yukon is still there."

"Yeah, it's still here but we had to call the tow truck because they shot all the tires and there is a hole in the computer and the radiator," Bud tells Sam while he is still scoping out the vehicle.

"Well, just have it moved to Cash's place and tell him to take pictures and get an estimate." Sam tells Bud what was going on at the police station, then tells him that he has to call a lawyer. Sam hangs up with Bud. He calls Carol's dad, Mark, who knows about everyone around and asks him for a lawyer for Carol.

Mark tells him, "Call Terri Logan, she is the best lawyer around. She will get Carol out of jail today and handle everything."

"OK, I'll call her right now if you can text me the phone number." Sam hangs up with Mark and looks at the text message and gets the number and calls the lawyer. "Hello, this is Sam Kelley. I would like to talk to Terri Logan about an urgent matter."

"Is this Dr. Kelley?" Caroline the receptionist asked.

"Yes, this is," Sam says questioningly. Whenever Sam gets asked that question, it puts a little chill up Sam's spine. They either really like him or they are mad because their horse died or they thought they spent too much.

"This is Caroline Gimbal. You saved Buck, my pony from that riverbed last year."

"I remember Bucky very well. It was a long night but lucky everything worked out," Sam says in a happy tone. "Is Bucky doing well? Have you been trail riding lately?"

"He is doing great and my daughter has been riding him since the accident. They are almost inseparable," Caroline tells Sam while she brings up Terri's appointments on the computer. "Sam, Terri is booked all day, but for you, I am moving all her appointments and I will get her on the phone immediately. I hope she can get everything straightened out for you."

"Well, thank you very much, Caroline." Sam starts getting a little anxious. "I wish you a good day."

Caroline puts him on hold, and about fifteen seconds later, Terri is on the phone, "Sam this is Terri, Caroline says this is an emergency. How can I help you?"

Sam fills Terri in on what happened the day before and on today's events in as much detail as he could give her. "She is still in booking and they will not let me see her," Sam finishes.

"Sam, I am coming down there right now. There has been a lot of trouble with the county sheriff's department since this Officer Tamms has started working there. I'll get her out today and you can go about your day but just wait there until I get down there," Terri says in a calm voice. "Oh, and, Sam? Try not to stir the hornets' nest before I get there."

"OK, I'll just wait for you," Sam says with a little laugh.

Terri grabs her brief case and heads out of the door to the reception desk. "Caroline, please reschedule my appointments. I think this may take all day."

"I will handle everything," Caroline tells Terri, knowing that she had already changed all the appointments while Terri was on the phone. Terri gets in her yellow H3 with license plates that reads "LAW DOC." As she is driving, she thinks about the weekend coming up. She is supposed to go to the beach and relax with her family. She is hoping this does not take long because she wants to get everything finished before she leaves this weekend. As she gets about six miles out of town, she is pulled over by a county deputy sheriff. She reaches into the glove compartment a grabs the registration and insurance card. Then she sits and watches while the deputy gets out of the car and puts his hat on and adjusts his belt. He then unsnaps his holster and draws his weapon. Terri just watches and thinks, "What in the hell did he pull me over for, and why does he have his weapon drawn." She quickly gets her video camera out and turns it on and sets it on the dash.

Deputy Trevor walks up to the H3 and stands next to the back door and looks in to inspect the vehicle, all the while he has his weapon drawn. "Get out of the vehicle, now." Terri opens the door and puts her feet out but does not get all the way out. She wants him to come up to the front door so that she can get everything on video in case there is a problem.

"I am not getting out until I see some form of identification," Terri tells Deputy Trevor. This instantly enrages him, and he rushes the door and grabs her by the shirt collar, then yanks her out of the door. Terri screams, "You bastard, how dare you treat me like this?"

Deputy Trevor then grabs her by the hair and then swings her around the door and slams her up against the front of the vehicle. "When I tell you to do something, bitch, I don't want to hear anything except 'Yes, sir!' You got that law bitch?" Deputy Trevor holsters his weapon and pushes himself up to backside of Terri. "Now, you spread those pretty little legs of yours and we will see if you are carrying any weapons. He kicks her ankles until she spreads her legs. Then he reaches under her suit jacket and starts cupping her breast. "Oh these firm tits could make me do things that only a whore like you could love." Then he slowly moves his right hand down underneath her skirt and sticks two fingers into her panties. He runs his fingers into her vagina and pulls up like he is trying to open a drawer. He then pushes himself up against her and licks her ear. "I bet a whore like you would enjoy a good fucking, wouldn't you?"

Terri just cringes and hopes that all of this is gotten by the video camera. His breath was nauseating with the smell of alcohol, onion, and a hint of meth. "You son of a bitch, I will have you jailed for the rest of your life for this," Terri screams at Deputy Trevor.

"Oh, no, you won't! You are under arrest for grand theft auto and resisting arrest." Deputy Trevor pulls his hand out from underneath Terri's skirt, then grabs her shoulder and pulls her around. He then sticks his two fingers in his mouth and pulls them out and licks his lips. "You little bitch, I think before I bring you down to the station, I will bring you out to the farm and just have some fun. Then when I'm done, I bet the boys would love to have a turn or two. Yeah, I bet you would just love that, and maybe you wouldn't be such a bitch after that." Deputy Trevor then reaches around his back to grab for his handcuffs but fumbles a little. Terri seizes the moment and kicks him right in the nuts. She kicked him so hard that she thought that she heard something pop. Deputy Trevor drops to the ground and tries to scream, but he can barely catch his breath.

Terri quickly jumps into her vehicle and throws the vehicle in gear then speeds off to the station. She looks into her rearview mirror and sees that the deputy still has not moved from the ground. "I'm so glad that I took karate from Master Clemons. That kick was perfect. I'm glad that Master Clemons made me practice those kicks over and over and keeping my cool while under pressure," Terri thought to herself. "That bastard has been waiting for a chance to get me since I got him suspended for two months for sexual harassment about six months ago. If this video turns out, I have him locked up for the rest of his life." Terri is still trying to compose herself so that she was not so fired up when she had to deal with the morons at the station.

Terri drives in to the parking lot and sees Sam sitting on the sidewalk. She parks her vehicle, grabs her brief case and walks up to Sam. She throws her arms around Sam and gives him a hug. "I hope you are Sam. If you are not, please forgive me."

Sam hugs her and then holds her out at arm's length. "I am Sam and I have never have been greeted by a lawyer like this before."

Terri whisks her fingers through her hair and composes herself. "Well, I needed that and thank you. I have had a real bad time getting here." She then tells Sam about what had happened. "I am sorry to be telling you all this. I know you already have a lot to deal with, but I just needed to tell someone. Thank you for listening. Now let's see what we can do for Carol."

"That deputy is one of them that had been out at the community center, and he is one of them that were out there when Carol was picked up." Sam starts to look a little worried. "I hope to God that Carol was actually brought here." Both Terri and Sam run into the station.

They rush through the front door and Terri walks up to front desk. "I am here to see Carol Kelley, I am her lawyer."

Officer Oscar just looks at her. "There is no one here by that name."

Sam hears this and moves up to front desk. "You just said about an hour and a half ago that she was in booking. Now, where the fuck is she? Your shithead Sheriff Tamms brought her here about two hours ago."

Officer Oscar jumps back when Sam flew up to the desk. "Back off, before I have you arrested. I told you she is not here."

Terri slaps the desk. "You will go and check the cells and booking room and make sure that she is not back there. If she is not, I want to know where she is and where Sheriff Tamms is at this time."

Officer Oscar walks into the back room and returns in five minutes. "She is not back there, and as a matter of fact, no one is back there." Officer Oscar starts typing on the computer. "Sheriff Tamms is not even scheduled to work today, and so you must be mistaken about who picked her up. If she cannot be found in twenty-four hours, then we can fill out a missing person report. If she did leave you, I can see by your abusive behavior why she left."

"You fucking bitch, we have your number and we will be back." Sam was fuming and the same time very worried. "If I don't find her in twenty-four hours, then in twenty-four hours you will be in jail." Sam looks at Terri, who is on the phone to a private detective friend of hers, and they walk out the door.

Sam phones Bud. "Have you found out anything about that fucking Tamms or anything?"

"Yeah, Henry Bahr, the PI, I was talking to, knows that Tamms is the son of that jerk cop out at the shooting range, and he says that they hang out over near the town we were at. How is Carol?" Bud says.

"Where is Kota?" Sam starts down the steps to his vehicle.

"He is here." Bud looks over at Kota, who is sleeping in the hay.

"Well, Carol and that cop never showed up here at the station. That fucking bitch at the front desk lied to me and we will deal with her later. You and Kota get the guns in the truck. Go to the house and get my knife belt and the night vision goggles. Then go over to the gun shop and pick up plenty of ammo and get each one of you some goggles. We are now going to find Carol, and if there is one hair out of place, then I am going to war. I'll be there in an hour." Sam looks over at Terri then hangs up.

Bud gave Kota a shove and gives him the lowdown on what was happening. They grab the container with the money. They jump in the truck and take off.

Sam looks over at Terri who has just hung up the phone. "So what did you find out?"

"Well, that was Chad, who is a PI, and he has had to look into these cops matters before for another disappearance of a farmer. He says that Sheriff Tamms's dad is a sheriff over near a town by West Virginia. They appear to be on the take from a gang of drug-dealing thugs. The gang members are paid thugs of the OCORC group. They are used by OCORC to stir up trouble around the polling sights, bankers' homes, and other odds and ends to help change people's minds. That is why the sheriff took the side of the OCORC people at the community center. They are all dirty as dirty can be." Terri unlocks her vehicle door and opens it. "I am going to go back to the office and see if I can get some of this worked out. If Carol turns up, call me. Otherwise, I am going to get the state or federal people on this right away."

"OK, I'm going to look for her and you may want to have your law books in hand if and when I do find the sheriff."

Sam shuts Terri door for her and she rolls down the window. "Sam, do not get into any trouble that can get you thrown into jail. We will handle this legally."

"I'm only going to do what needs to be done and nothing more. I will call you later." Sam goes over to his vehicle and gets in. He starts it up. Just as he is leaving, a sheriff car pulls in to the parking lot. Sam sees it is Deputy Trevor. Trevor gets out of his vehicle. He is as pale as a ghost. Sam thinks to himself, "I'll wait to see if he leaves and then start with interrogating him first."

Sam calls Bud. "You and Kota are going to have to meet me. I'm going to stay here until this fucking Deputy Trevor leaves and then I'm going to follow him. I'll call when I know where to meet up at." Sam waited in the parking lot for about a half an hour when deputy Trevor came limping out of the station carrying a bag of ice. He got into his Chevy Blazer. Sam started his vehicle and followed him out of the parking lot and on to the highway headed west. Sam called Bud again. "Are you guys on your way?"

"We are loading everything right now." Bud shuts the door to Sam's house. "We just got your stuff at the house loaded. Do you need anything else?"

"While you are there, can you grab my camouflage gear and hunting clothes from the downstairs closet?" Sam does not ask a question but gives an order. Sam watches as Trevor turns up a dirt road. "When you are done, I will meet you guys at that place that we got ice cream. Trevor just turn up a dirt road, and I'm going to follow until he stops. Then I will go and find you guys. Make sure you get something to eat and bring plenty of water. It may be a long night," Sam tells Bud.

Sam follows Deputy Trevor up the dirt road to a house in the woods. Sam stops short to the entrance to the driveway and then backs up. The place is surrounded by trees and weeds. It looks like Trevor never did any grounds keeping or even picked up any of his junk. Sam stops and jumps out of the vehicle and walks into the trees. Deputy Trevor is still hurting and moving very slowly with the bag of ice between his legs. Sam sees Deputy Trevor shut the front door. He waits for about ten minutes. Sam thinks to himself, "Ten minutes is enough time for him to get relaxed. It will catch him more off guard." Sam walks up to the front door and knocks.

"This better be important or it going to cost you," Deputy Trevor yells and then takes a long deep draw from his meth pipe. He crushes a small crystal of meth and snorts it in. Instantly he gets a rush and shakes, almost convulsing. Trevor jumps up, not feeling much pain at this time. He stomps over to open the door. Sam doesn't say a word. He just keeps knocking.

"You assholes better have a good reason or you bastards are in for a world of hurt," Deputy Trevor says and grabs the door handle.

Sam could hear the door handle moving. A rush of adrenaline fills Sam's body. He is still unclear what he is going to do when the door opens. Maybe it was a little fear or maybe excitement, but soon as the door began to open, Sam gives the door a kick that would kill a buffalo. The force of the door knocks the deputy on to the floor. Sam rushes in and holds Deputy Trevor on the ground. Trevor starts cussing, kicking, and punching. Sam gives Trevor a punch just below the ear, dislocating the left jaw, sending a wave of pain through Trevor's head that would last months. Trevor instantly quit struggling.

Sam screamed at Trevor, "Where did you guys take my wife?" Trevor mumbled something that sounded like "Fuck you," so Sam hit the side of Trevor's nose with one knuckle. It makes you feel like someone just broke your nose without breaking it. "Last time, and then the hurting is really going to start. Where did you take my wife?" Sam was high on adrenaline; he knew he had to calm down.

Trevor screams like he has a mouth full of cotton. "FUCK YOU!"

Sam glances around the room and sees a fork lying on the floor within arm's reach. He grabs it and shows it to Trevor. Sam says in a threatening way, "Last time!" Trevor shakes his head without saying a word. Sam places his knee over Trevor's neck so he can't move. Then Sam stabs the fork into thigh. Sam can feel the fork break through the skin and then hit bone. Once the fork hit bone, Sam moved the fork around scraping the periosteum. Scraping on the periosteum made it very painful. Sam repeats the procedure in a rapid repeating fashion. There is very little blood and the puncture wounds are a good cause of infection. Sam is hoping to start an infection. He is feeling very hateful right now. He stabs Trevor with the dirty fork about five times until Trevor starts mumbling. Sam looks at Trevor and just says, "Well?"

Trevor mumbled, "The farm, the farm on Highway 250. You fuck. I am going to—" That is the last thing that Trevor said before Sam stood up and kicked him in the kidney area. Trevor sent a stream of vomit across the floor. Then Sam kicks him in the ribs just under the armpit. Sam knew that is going to make it difficult for Trevor to breathe without a lot of pain.

Sam leaves Trevor lying on the floor and then looks through the house. Sam finds several guns, which he puts in his pockets. He then goes through all the dresser and kitchen cabinet drawers. He finds knives, handguns, jewelry, and other stuff that looks like Trevor probably took from other people. As Sam works his way through the house, he notices that there is only one picture on a wall in the whole house. Sam walks over and moves the picture. He finds a load of cash stacked in the wall. "What an idiot, if there was a fire, it would have burned the money. Besides, any moron could have found it," Sam says to himself. Sam finds a garbage bag and fills it with the guns, jewelry, knives, and money but leaves the drugs and other paraphernalia, then heads for the door.

Trevor is drooling and groaning on the floor. He tries to crawl after Sam but then gives up and heads to the phone. Trevor's arms are stretched out, pulling himself over to where the phone is on the end table. Sam decides that he needs to keep Trevor from alerting any one. Sam goes over and cuts the phone line, then gives one last kick to Trevor's right shoulder. Sam hears a loud pop, which meant the ligaments in Trevor shoulder just gave way as his shoulder dislocates. He grabs Trevor by the legs and drags him over to the corner of the room. He helps Trevor sit up and gives him the drugs he found. Trevor quickly loads his crack pipe with one hand and takes a hit. He immediately starts screaming at Sam. He tries to get to his feet and move toward Sam. Sam kicks Trevor in the chest, and Trevor falls back into a chair. Sam is growing tired of Trevor and his constant insistence of trying to come after him. Sam goes into the kitchen and opens a "junk" drawer. He pulls out a hammer that he had seen earlier. He takes the hammer and walks over to a coat hook rack that is nailed to the wall. He uses the claws on the hammer to pull it down. He hammers out two of the nails from the wood. He walks over to Trevor, who is basically all but passed out in the chair. He takes one nail and positions it over Trevor's right hand that is sitting on the arm of the chair. Sam hits the nail three times with the hammer. He nails Trevor's right hand to the wood in the chairs arm. Pounding the nail through Trevor's hand made him come to. Sam just continues on and nails the left foot to the floor. Trevor lets out a scream. Sam looks at Trevor and says, "I should just kill you, but I never killed a man before. Not that I can't, just that I don't want to start. You should count your blessings. You are a man that needs to die." Sam pauses a moment. "Maybe if I see you again, I may kill you." Sam bends the nail heads over so Trevor can't just pull the nail though his hand. Then he sets the hammer on the floor and turns on the television. He grabs his newfound bounty and opens the front door. Sam takes a look back at Trevor and thinks, "I may regret this later. He is a scumbag and he will be out of service for months." Sam turns and shuts the door. He throws the bounty in the vehicle and takes off to meet Bud and Kota.

Sam arrives at the Dairy Mart. Kota and Bud is waiting in the truck, eating cheeseburgers and fries. Sam parks alongside of the truck and jumps out of the vehicle he's been driving. Bud and Kota put down the burgers and open up the truck doors. "Here are your clothes. You go change and we'll get you something to eat," Bud says to Sam. "How about a cheeseburger and fries?"

"Sounds good," Sam says to Bud and Kota. "I'll run into the restroom and change. We have to find this farm, wherever the hell that is, on Highway 250." Sam grabs the duffel bag. "Hey, look in the vehicle. I have a surprise for you all." Sam heads to the Dairy Mart door when someone pulls up to the front door parking space.

"Hey, y'all, whatup?" Bill from the rifle range leans out his pickup window and reaches a hand out to Sam. "Ya remember me from the range a while back, don't you?"

Sam shakes the guy's hand. "Yes, I remember you there but I don't remember your name."

Kota and Bud find the guns and all the money in Sam's vehicle. They take it and put it into the gun box in the back of the truck. They notice that Sam is talking to someone at the front door.

"Name's Bill Schaefer, and this gal I got here with me is my wife, Joy." Bill and Joy get out of the truck and shut the doors. Joy goes on in to the Dairy Mart and Bill is then surrounded by Bud, Kota, and Sam.

"I'm Sam, and these are my two brothers, Dakota and Bud. We are the 'Brothers3,' if you please." Sam points each brother out as he introduces them. Kota and Bud each give Bill a handshake. "I've got to run inside to change clothes right now. I'll leave you with these guys and be back in about ten minutes." Sam heads into the Dairy Mart.

"Do you remember when you were talking about the farm that the gang had taken from some farmer?" Bud asks Bill and then leans against Bill's truck.

"The Brothers3, hey." Bill gives a little sigh. "What's ya looking for that place for? You don't want anything to do with that place," Bill spits on the ground, then turns his head slightly and then stares at Bud.

"Well, you did say we could call on you when we needed some help with those guys in the gang. Can we trust you?" Bud leans back and puts a hand on his knife that is hooked to the back of his belt.

"Hell yeah, you can trust me. I hate those guys. They beat up my dad and grandpa when they went to vote the other day. Then when I went to vote they had blocked the roads so no one could get through except for some folks." Bill spits again.

"Well, this Sheriff Tamms from over in our county pulled Sam's wife over, and they never showed up at the jail. Sam thinks that they are tied in with the gang and the sheriff in your county." Bud takes his hand off his knife.

"Well, we gots the Sheriff Bill Tamms over in our county. That's the guy that shown up over at the range," Bill explains.

"We're going over to look around and see if we can find his wife. The cops aren't looking, so we have to do it ourselves. I'm afraid the shit just hit the fan for those guys. They pissed us off at the range, and now if they have Sam's wife, he is going to come unglued," Bud says with excitement.

"He don't look very worried or pissed off," Bill questioned Bud.

"Oh, he's mad, but he just never shows it. He says that you have to have a cool head in order to think and react. I guess he learned all that stuff when he was in those karate classes or whatever it was that he was doing. He used to get really mad and almost loose his mind until he settled down. So he must have learned something some place," Bud says.

"I can't tell you where that farm is. I'll have to show yas. It's not to fer from here. There is only one way into the farm and there's pasture ground to the east of the farm place, and the other side is all covered with trees, so I don't think that you will be able to drive up there. Ya're probably going to have to walk about a mile or so," Bill says.

"That's what we wanted anyway. We are going in stealth mode and running in with the chariots," Kota says. "Let me runs in here a minute and thens I'll show you guys hows to gets there and anything else about the farm you wants to know." Bill spit all his chew out on the parking lot and then went in to the Dairy Mart.

Bud and Kota went in to the Dairy Mart and gets Sam some food to go. Sam is inside putting on his scent-proof Gore-Tex under-clothes and his high-tech hunting clothes. They had cost a fortune, but it has lasted him about six years now. Sam can stay in the freezing cold weather for days no matter if it is raining or snowing with these clothes. Sam thought the clothes were so good he bought his brothers the same. Sam puts all his other clothes back into duffel bag and goes out to the dining room.

"Are you guys ready to go?" Sam heads for the door.

"Yeah, as soon as Bill gets his food. He is going to show us where the farm is." Kota hands Sam the bag of food. Sam and his two brothers leave the building. They get into the truck so they are ready to leave. Bill and Joy come out. Joy gets into their truck. Joy takes off and waves as she is leaving.

Bill walks over to Bud. "If you guys are going out there and giving those bastards a whopping, then I think I'm going too. Joy is going to gets some of the other boys together. If you need them, they'll be ready. If you don't, they'll still be ready," Bill says.

Bud opens up the back door. "Well then, let's go."

Bill gets in the backseat of the truck and everyone shuts their doors. Bill gives some direction to Bud. "Go out here and take a left, then goes for about twenty minutes, and we are going to take a left after the ol' gas station. We needs to go into the hayfield and park ups along them there trees." Bill sits back and starts eating his food. Sam does the same.

On the way to the farm, Bill fills everyone in on the details of the farm. The barn had a closed hayloft, there was a cellar under the barn, the house had a basement that could only be accessed from the outside, and the house had four rooms upstairs and five downstairs. "That's about it, but I haven't been in the house for six years."

"That's OK, I'll scout it out before anyone else has to come in," Sam says.

Sam finishes his food and drinks a bottle of Dr. Pepper. He takes out his can of Copenhagen and takes a chew before he puts it back into his pocket. Bill finishes his food and takes a chew of his Skoal. Bud and Kota are both smoking, and no one is saying anything. After driving for twenty minutes, Bud pulls into a field and drives up along a bunch of trees finds a good place. He backs the truck up as far into the trees as the truck would go. They all get out and Bud and Kota grab the machetes and cut some brush to cover the front of the truck. Sam jumps up into the bed of the truck. He puts on his utility harness and hiking pack, which has three liters of water, a slingshot, first aid supplies, extendable nightstick, a machete, and power bars. Sam holsters a semiauto 9-mm., and a Ka-Bar knife. He grabs the .300 Super Mag and several ammunition clips. Bud and Kota climbs up into the back of the truck after they are done covering the front of the truck. Kota grabs his old buck knife and holsters it. Kota grabs the semiautomatic .357 Magnum and the .50-caliber Barrett. He puts on his hiking pack and grabs his ghillie suit. Bud grabs his gear and chooses the .30-06. They both grab their extra rounds of ammunition and the two night vision scopes. Sam reaches for his most reliable weapon, which is his homemade tomahawk, and stuffs it into the back of his utility harness. Bill just stands there with his mouth open and staring at the three brothers.

"What the hell do you guys expect to do, fights a war?" Bill spits and wipes his mouth.

"Well, we hate to be caught unprepared. Do you want a weapon or do you want to just stay here?" Kota asks.

"Well, I'll stay here out of sight but maybe you can lend me a rifle," Bill hesitantly says. "I don't want to be unprepared."

"Here's a .243. It's a good rifle, shoots dead on at 150 yards so adjust the scope with this elevation dial; One click to the right for each fifty yards. Here is the safety. Here are 150 rounds. Now if you see someone coming, then click twice on the walkie-talkie.

Remember *twice*. Now stay low or in the truck and don't call anyone." Kota hands Bill the weapon and a walkie-talkie.

"I got it. What do you guys plan on doing?" Bill nosily asks.

"Nothing, if they give us no trouble, then they get no trouble," Kota tells Bill as he turns away. Kota grabs his gear and they head up the hill through the trees. It's still light out and they may have about twenty minutes of light left. The air is getting cool, so it will be a good night. The three of them reach the hill next to the farm place. They sit down and scope out the farm place.

"I'm going to go down too check out the buildings. You two get into a good area where you can see everything. If you see anything funny, you shoot at it. If it has a gun, you wound them. If it shoots at you or me, then you kill it. I'm totally relying on you guys." Sam slings his rifle.

"We got your back, no worries." Kota and Bud move into action and start finding an area where they could see the whole farm.

Sam heads down to the farm. He slowly moves in near the house and sees only one light on upstairs. There are no cars or motorcycles anywhere around. He pulls out his tomahawk. He turns the doorknob, and to his amazement, it is not locked. "Guess they thought no one would be dumb enough to come out here," he thinks to himself. Sam slips into the house and looks around the room. "What a fucking pig sty!" Sam thinks to himself as he looks around the kitchen. Sam moves on in and looks around the other rooms, and no one was around. Sam thinks to himself, "Looks like they had a party." There are beer cans and Crown Royal bottles everywhere. On one of the coffee tables is a big mirror that still has a half-done line of cocaine on it. He sees four meth pipes lying around the house. Sam finds the stairway and slowly moves up, being careful to only step on the outside corners of the steps. Sam remembers sneaking up the stairs of his parents' house when he was in high school, "Steps creek and if you step closer to their supported area, there is a less chance of creaking." Sam reaches the top of the steps. He slowly walks to the first door and turns the doorknob. It's dark so he quickly puts on his night vision and looks in. No one is in the room so he moves on down the hall. The next room didn't have a door so he peers into the room. On the dresser, there is a badge and a Sheriff's uniform along with the gun belt with a Glock 40 in it. Sam unloads the Glock, then takes the clips and throws them down under the dresser. He grabs the handcuffs and keys. He stuffs it all into his pack. He looks at the uniform. The nameplate is still there. "Tamms, the son of a bitch was here," Sam thinks to himself. Sam looks through the drawers and finds some AA batteries along with a bundle of cash. He grabs the cash puts it into his pack. He takes an AA battery and grabs the Glock. He sticks the battery into the end of the barrel. It doesn't really fit, but he pushes the end of the barrel to the floor and the battery wedges into the barrel. "I hope this jerk tries to fire this," Sam thinks to himself. He slowly looks through the other two rooms, and there was nothing but bunk beds. There were garbage and cans lying everywhere. He has to watch his step to avoid stepping on anything and making a noise. Sam takes off his night vision and slowly moves over to the last room that has the lights on. He lies down on the floor and looks under the door. He can see no feet on the floor, so he stands to one side of the door and slowly turns the doorknob. It is locked and that meant that there is something important behind the door. Sam stepped back, pulls his 9-mm. with his right hand and holds his tomahawk with his left hand. He kicks the door just below the doorknob. The door flies open and Sam dives into the room, does a somersault and ends up standing next to the bed. Sam holsters his two weapons and sits down on the bed when he sees Carol there.

On the bed is Carol handcuffed to the bed frame. She has her mouth taped and is completely naked. Sam quickly unlocks the handcuffs and removes the tape. Carol screams and cries. She then grabs Sam so tight that he could not believe the strength she has. "It's going to be OK now." Sam kisses Carol on the cheek and on the forehead. He tries to wipe the tears, but they flow like a river. Sam is so happy and mad at the same time, he can hardly control his emotions. Carol cannot let go. She is shaking and crying. Sam knows they need to get out before anyone gets back. Sam gently pushes Carol away so he can find some clothes for her. "Carol, I need you to be strong for me and you. We need to get you out of here to some place safe." Sam searches the room for some clothes and finds her shirt and pants in

94

the closet. They had been just thrown on to the floor along with her shoes. "I'm going to help you get dressed right now so that we can get going." Carol is still crying uncontrollably, but she manages to nod. Carol steps into her pants and holds up her arms as Sam puts the shirt on to her. Carol is now starting to take control of herself. She puts her shoes on and turns to Sam and hugs him.

"Why did they take me, why?" Carol starts crying again.

"Because they are evil bastards. They will pay dearly for what they done to you. I love you very much. I want to get you to some place safe." Sam takes both of her hands and holds them. "Carol we've got to go now!" She nods and they start down the steps. Sam could hear the clicks coming over the radios. "Shit they are coming," Sam said. Sam grabs Carol by the arm and goes out the back door. They run into the woods. He slips his night vision on and they move up toward the area he had left Bud and Kota. Carol starts slowing down so he picks her up. Sam carries her to the top of the hill. "It's all downhill from here. Are you doing OK? Can you make it the rest of the way?" Sam says. He is breathing hard. He is out of condition.

"I'm fine now and I can make it if it's downhill." Just then Bud and Kota appeared in the darkness, which made both Carol and Sam jump.

"Guess we should have said something." Bud and Kota came up and gave Carol a hug. "Are you OK?" Kota asks.

"I'll be OK when I see that fucking sheriff dead," Carol says.

"Let's get Carol to the truck and then I'm going back to take everything worth taking from that place. Then if they all come back it will be the biggest slaughter since the civil war." Sam takes Carol by the hand. He gives her the night vision glasses. Kota and Bud lead the way down the hill. After walking for about ten minutes, they all stop instantly. Kota motions to them to get down. Sam crawls up next to Bud and Kota. Carol sits quietly as the brothers talk.

"I don't see Bill and there is a lot of activity down there. I don't know if those are his buddies or if they are the gang," Bud says.

"Do you want me to move on down there and check it out?" Kota says.

"Have you heard anything from Bill on the radio?" Sam says.

"Earlier, we couldn't get him to shut up, but then we haven't listened since we put radios back into the pack," Kota says.

"I heard clicking on the radio before we left the house," Sam says. "Did you guys hear it?"

"Yes, but that dumb shit was clicking since we started. We finally asked him and he said he was just practicing. So I'm not sure what's up but we didn't see anyone coming down the driveway." Kota takes out his radio. "Bill, come in. Bill, come in."

"Well, maybe we should get a closer look at what is going on down there. If that is that gang down there, I don't know how they would have found Bill unless he was turning the truck lights on or told them where he was. Its pitch dark out here and no one could find you out here." Sam sets his rifle down and starts taking off his pack.

"I'll go, I can move faster than you two old farts, I'll be back in five minutes," Kota drops his pack and rifle, checked his .357 Magnum Desert Eagle, put on his night vision, and takes off into the darkness. Bud monitors his movements. After five minutes, Kota runs back to Bud.

"They're the gang all right and they got Bill pretty well beat up. He is lying down by the hay. I don't think that they know where the truck is because the footprints around the truck are ours and Bill's." Kota takes a deep breath and concentrates on his breathing. He is a good runner but his years of smoking have slowed him down.

"Sam, give me a chew." Kota needs a nicotine fix, but he knew that smoking is off-limits while trying to stay camouflaged. Sam hands him the Copenhagen and Kota takes a chew. Then hands Sam back the can.

Carol wrinkles her nose. "I wish you guys would stop that shit. It's going to kill you." The three brothers look at each other and smile. Carol is starting to come back to her old self now. She realizes what they are going to do. She doesn't like it but she hates those bastards, and they deserve anything that is coming their way. It will be pure hell.

"Here's the plan. I want to go and get a closer look at that farm place. That fucking Tamms has been staying there, or at least I found his uniform. I'll go down to the farm and you guys stay here with Carol. When I'm done, I'll start a diversion and one of you go down and grab Bill. One of you, stay up here and be an angel. No warning shots. Take out the vehicles and anyone who sticks his head up. Carol, just stay here and I'll be back. Then we can get you home and talk," Sam says. Then Sam takes out a rescue blanket and turns it inside out. It is black on the inside and foil on the outside. Carol is getting cold and Sam didn't bring a jacket along. He then grabs the ghillie suit and wraps her up in it. "That should keep you warm." Then Sam gives Carol a kiss. "I'll see you in an hour or so."

"OK, please be careful," Carol tells Sam. Bud grabs his pack and hands it to Carol. Carol drinks some water and eats a power bar.

Sam hands his rifle to Kota and put on his night vision, then disappears into the hills. Bud and Kota set up the .50-caliber rifle as Carol sits on the ground, shivering and eating. Carol never was much for the cold weather. Bud turns the rifle's night vision on so that he can watch what is going on with the gang of idiots down below. Kota is planning his route to grab Bill. He plans on moving up to the round bales of hay. Then sneak between the bales and pulling Bill back through. Kota moves over to Bud, and they go over the plan of attack. They both agree and also come up with another plan just in case the first one did not work.

Sam moves quickly through the woods and makes it up to the house. He is still careful just in case someone has come back to the house while he was gone. The lights are still not on in the house, so Sam is pretty sure no one is home. Sam had searched the house fairly well but did not look in the basement. He quickly finds the outside door to the basement. It looks well used. There is a path up to the doorway. The walkway and doorway is free from weeds. Sam opens one of the doors, and it makes a loud squeaking noise. "If anyone is around, it will bring them out," Sam says to himself. Sam moves down the stairs and tries to open the bottom door. It is locked. He backs up and kicks the door just below the doorknob, but the door doesn't budge. "Damn, I'm must be getting old," Sam thought to himself. He pulls out his tomahawk and starts making cuts around the doorknob. He steps back and gives the door a kick. This time the door flies open. Sam looks around and whistles. The basement is an arsenal with more weapons than Sam has ever seen. "I wish I had help, we could take every one of these and supply a small army," Sam says to himself. Sam moves on through looking at crates of weapons, mostly automatics, handguns, and some weapons he has never seen before except on the military channel. At the end of the room is another door. Sam tries the door, but it is locked. Sam takes his tomahawk and cuts around the doorknob. The door opens without a kick. "This door is falling apart," Sam says quietly. Sam looks in the back room. Sam jaw drops. The room is full of cash all wrapped up in plastic wrap. "There has to be millions of dollars here," Sam starts thinking. "I need to make a new plan to get this stuff out of here. I thought I would just burn the place to the ground, but I am not doing that now. If we take this, it will hurt them more than just killing them," Sam thinks to himself. Then he grabs the radio. "Hey, guys."

"Yep," Bud says.

"Listen, I found millions of dollars and a whole arsenal of weapons ranging from rifles to stuff I have never seen before. What do you think we should do?" Sam asks.

"Ah, give us a minute and we'll come up with something," Bud says and then turns to Kota.

The radio goes silent and Sam moves on out to look into the barn. Sam opens the cellar to the barn. "Looks like someone has been remodeling," Sam says to himself. The whole basement is encased in concrete. Even the ceiling is concrete. In the center is a huge lab with barrels of chemicals with tubing attached. It is a massive methamphetamine production lab. "They must be able to turn out thousands of pounds of meth in this lab, not that you know anything about cooking meth," Sam says to himself. Sam shuts the door and quickly moves to the ground level of the barn. Sam looks at a stairs leading to the loft of the barn. He runs up the steps and looks into the window. All he can see is beds everywhere and a big screen TV. Sam decides he has had enough and goes down to look into the ground level of the barn. He walks into the barn. "This is my lucky day," Sam thinks to himself. Inside the barn is an old 1960 something stock truck. "The truck looks in runnable condition. Tires are fairly new. The windows are still clean," Sam says to himself. He opens the truck door and the keys are in the ignition. He gets in and turns the key halfway. The truck is half-full of gas. Sam turns the key and the truck starts immediately. He jumps down and opens the doors. He runs back to the truck and jumps in. He shifts it into gear and the truck creeps out of the barn. Sam takes the truck and parks it behind the house but keeps it running. He runs over and shuts the doors to the barn, then runs down to the house basement and starts carrying everything that he could carry.

"Hey," Sam calls over the radio.

"Hey, we think we got a plan but there are a lot of headlights coming down the road," Bud says over the radio.

"Never mind that, I found a truck and I just about got everything loaded. When I radio you, I need you to create a diversion so I can drive this thing out of here." Sam says.

"Will do," Bud says.

"When I drive out, they may be on my tail and I'll need some backup. This truck is like the old truck we had on the farm and it is not going to go very fast. Be ready to pack up and get the hell out of there," Sam tells Bud.

"Sam there's vehicles are coming into the field right now," Bud says with a little excitement in his voice. Sam runs and a grabs another crate and drags it up the stairs. He had loaded the money first. After thirty minutes, he finishes loading the rest of the crates. He has taken everything of value from the place.

"Hey, all those cars I think are those friends of Bill, and I think there is going to be a big rumble out here. About forty to sixty people that just got out of their vehicles, and they are not looking happy." Bud radios Sam.

"Good, let them fight maybe just help it along a little bit. Do you think you can shut down the gang's vehicles?" Sam asks Bud.

"Got just the ticket, does that mean you are coming through?" Bud asks.

"Right now, so let it rip," Sam says with excitement.

Bud sights in on his first target, which is a nice new three-quarter-ton lifted truck. "You guys get ready to pack it up and get the hell out of here. We'll pick up Bill if he is still there when we drive by," Bud tells Carol and Kota. "Carol, are you ready to go?"

"Yes, anytime you say," Carol whispers. She unbundles herself and then rolls up everything. She slings the rifle and pack over her shoulders.

Bud fires the first shot and the truck's hood blows off. Then he targets the next car. He blows the car's hood off and it starts on fire. After firing seven shots and killing seven vehicles, Bud slings the rifle. Bud, Carol, and Kota run down the hill to the truck. Kota jumps in the back of the truck and secures the weapons while Bud starts the truck. Carol jumps into the passenger seat. Bud throws the truck in gear and drives out wearing the night vision goggles. He drives right past the burning vehicle. Sam has already made it to the highway before Bud even got done shooting. Bud drives by the hay bales and Bill is still there. Bud slams on his brakes. Kota jumps out and picks Bill up. He puts Bill into the bed of the truck. Bud throws the truck in gear and drives off down the highway. He takes his goggles off and turns on the lights.

"Hey, are you guys doing OK?" Sam radios Bud.

Bud hands the radio to Carol. "We're right behind you, are you OK?"

"I'm OK, did you get Bill?" Sam has the truck floored and is doing about fifty-four miles per hour.

"Yes, he seems to be OK but I don't know how bad he is hurt. We are coming up behind you right now. Drive faster." Carol is fidgeting in her seat. Her adrenaline is flowing high.

"I am going as fast as this truck will go. You guys just follow me and let me know if anyone is coming up behind us. Tell Kota to sit in the back and have the 50 cal ready." Sam looks in his rearview mirrors and notices both of them are broken.

"He's already in the back with Bill. He's got Bill all wrapped up in a blanket and it looks like he is loading the rifle," Carol says to Sam. "Where are we going to put this truck?"

Sam says, "I don't know yet but we will have that figured out when we get home."

"Sam . . ." Carol pauses for a few seconds. "Thank you for coming to get me. I knew you would find me and get me home. Oh, and, Sam, I love you."

"I love you too. I would do anything for you. Now let's concentrate on driving and we will talk later when everything is settled down." Sam sets the radio down and then adjusts his utility harness that was digging into his back.

"OK, be careful," Carol sets the radio on the seat and turns around, then unbuckles her seat belt and climbs into the backseat. She opens the sliding back window and tells Kota what Sam said. Kota gives her a thumbs-up.

"How is Bill doing?" Carol yells back to Kota.

"He's still alive but really beat up." Kota offers Bill some water. Bill drinks it down and then coughs.

"Got a chew, I swallowed mine," Bill asks Kota. "Hey, is there any Copenhagen up there?" Kota yells up to Carol. Carol turns around and Bud digs around the center console. He pulls out a can of Copenhagen and it hands to Carol. Carol climbs half through the window and gives it to Bill. Bill gives her a nod. The ride home seemed to take forever. When they pull into the hospital lane, they all breathe a sigh of relief. Sam drives up past the hospital and on out to the field. Bud follows him out there. Sam stops next to the compost pile and shuts the truck off. He goes over to Bud, Carol, Bill, and Kota.

"Hey, come and see what I got in the truck. We need to unload it so I can get rid of the truck," Sam says to Bud.

Sam goes over to Bill. "How are you doing? We'll get you to the hospital as soon as we unload our weapons from our truck."

Bill lets out a short groan and puts a hand out to Kota to help him up, "Oh hell, I'll be fine. I never go to them doctors. Shit! My wife can lay down a better whoopin' than those shitheads. Just get me up and give me a shot of shine. I'll be up and going like new."

Kota reaches into the side compartment of the custom build truck box and brings out a bottle of Crown Royal. He hands it to

Bill. Bill looks at him like the tooth fairy just showed up. "It's a 'just in case' bottle. You just never know." Kota shrugs.

Kota, Bud, and Sam go over to the truck. Kota jumps in to the box. Carol walks over to the truck with Bill trailing behind. Carol asks, "Can I see?"

"Well, of course, my dear. This is your bounty." Sam helps Carol into the truck box.

"Shit, do you know what is in here?" Kota says to everyone. "There are two M32s, a .50-caliber McMillian, four M110s, a crate of Glock 9-millimeters, a crate of shock grenades, a crate of AA12, several M16s, and two new tank killers the AT4-CS, a crate of .338s with Lapua rounds, and I don't know how much ammo."

"What the hell are you talking about? What is an M-something, something and a McDonald-whatever?" Bud asks.

"Some of this stuff is probably not even available to the military yet. This stuff is new and top-notch. You could fight a small war with this stuff." Kota just kept digging though the truck.

"Sam do you know how much money is here?" Carol peels open the plastic of one of the bundles of money.

"Well no, I really didn't have time to count it. I just grab everything." Sam leans against the truck box.

"These are hundred-dollar bills and there is hundreds if not thousands of bundles. There are at least fifty of those bundles in here." Kota kept going through the bundles of money.

"Well, then give everyone a bundle and we will hide the rest," Sam says.

Carol hands everyone a bundle of bills and leans over to Sam and gives him a kiss. "Sam, I love you. You do know that don't you?"

Bud, Kota, and Bill, what little he could do, start to unload the truck. Sam lifts Carol off the truck and sets her on the ground after he gives her another kiss. "Yes, I do and I love you." Sam looks at her a little questioning.

"You found me naked and handcuffed, but they didn't do anything to me. They were going to use me for the entertainment tonight after the damn sheriff got done with me. The whole gang was going to rape me. Sam and you saved me," Carol starts crying.

"I'm glad I found you. You know I would do anything for you." Sam reaches over and wipes a tear away with his thumb. Sam hugs her and holds her for what seems to be an eternity. They have gone through so much in the last few years that they just forgot about what really mattered. Now they knew—each other.

For the next hour, they unload the truck. After they are done, Sam drives the truck to the next county. He drives into the self-car wash bay. Sam is not sure if the gang he stole it from would try to find it. He decides he is going to wash away all the evidence of him being in the truck. Kota, Bud, and Sam power wash the truck inside and out. Afterward, Sam drives the truck to a Wal-Mart parking lot and leaves it there. He makes sure that there are no cameras in the parking lot where he parks it. Everyone comes along to pick up Sam. Bill is getting pretty drunk by now and is talking more and more. Sam climbs in to the passenger seat of the pickup. He buckles up and Bud takes off.

"Wait till Joy finds out about this," Bill says loudly.

Sam turns in his seat and grabs Bill by the shirt. "She will never know, you will never tell anyone, you will keep your mouth shut about everything that happened tonight. As far as Joy knows, you were out drinking with us and we got into a fight. You got your ass kicked. OK!" Sam yells at Bill.

"OK, OK, we were out drinking. What's the big deal?" Bill sank in his seat.

"The big deal is a lot of bad people in that gang, if you hadn't noticed. No one here will tell anyone and you are new. If word gets around, then you are the one that talked. If I find out you were shooting your mouth off, I will castrated you and then remove your mouth. Got it Bill? Now, I'm not trying to be mean, but this is very important and I want to make sure you understand the extreme importance of no one saying anything. So just forget about everything. There is plenty of money for everyone. If you need some, we will get you some, but don't get stupid with spending money," Sam says to Bill in a soft, threatening tone.

"No, I'm not like that. I'm not like that at all." Bill sits back in his seat and takes a drink, then hands it to Sam, who also takes a drink. They all go back to the hospital.

CHAPTER SIX

BACK AT THE HAY FIELD after Sam, Carol, Kota, Bud, and Bill had left, some of the cars and trucks that are shot start on fire. The fires spark a huge fight to break out between Bill's friends and the gang. Most people are using bats and ax handles for weapons, but some are using machetes. People on both sides of the fight start to drop like flies being sprayed with bug spray. The fire from the cars causes a grass fire, which causes a gas tank on another car to heat up. The gas expands and the car explodes, causing the hay bales to burn. The embers start drifting into the brush and the undercover in the trees. A small forest fire starts, and with all the dry weather along with the fifteen-mile-per-hour wind, the fire blows on up the hill fairly quickly. Somewhere between the car explosion and the trees starting on fire, the fight stops. There are injured people laying everywhere. Those people that are still standing dragged and carried the injured to the driveway. Some of Bill's friends brought the wounded people to the hospital. A car driving by the field notices the fire and calls it in to the fire department. Soon Sheriff Cecil Tamms and the old Sheriff Bill Tamms show up along with the fire department. The fire in the trees is moving very quickly toward the farmhouse and barn.

"What in the Sam Hill is going on here," Bill Tamms yells over the loud speaker. Soon everyone stops yelling and screaming. The fire trucks move on down the driveway to start to put out the forest fire. "God damn it! I want everyone to get there asses over here in the next minute before I start shooting," Sheriff Bill Tamms says over the loud speaker. The crowd slowly gathers around the sheriff's car. Everyone is standing into two separate groups. No one intermingled with in the other group. It was Bill's friends on one side of the sheriff and the gang on the other side.

"Now that I got your attention, someone tell me what is going on." Sheriff Bill Tamms puts down the microphone. Sheriff Cecil Tamms just stands there with his legs spread and his arms crossed.

A blond woman pushed her way through the gang until she made it up to the sheriff, "I seen everything, Sheriff, those people came driving in here and started our cars on fire and then they attacked us with sticks and stuff." This woman is the same one that was at the community center that gave Sam all the trouble when he was voting. Many people standing on the gang side had been at the community center.

A young farmer points his finger at the blond woman. "That bitch is lying. We came over here because they had one of our friends. They started their own cars on fire."

"Hold on, you two!" Sheriff Bill Tamms holds up both hands and then points over Bill's friends' group. "What in the hell are you people here for?"

"I told you, we came over to . . .," the young farmer told the Sheriff before he is stopped short by the Sheriff Cecil Tamms walking over and punching him in the mouth.

"You stupid shit, we ain't askin'a question. Y'all are tres-pas-sin', so yur goin' ta jail," Sheriff Cecil Tamms stands over the young farmer, leaning and pointing a finger in his face. "And for you boy, yur goin' for assaltin' an officer of the law." The young farmer crab-crawled backward a little, then kicks up and hits Cecil Tamms in the nuts. The kick causes Sheriff Cecil Tamms to fall to his side as he grabs his crotch.

"You ain't takin' anyone anywhere. We are tired of you and your dad and your crooked friends. We ain't goin' to take it anymore," the young farmer yells. Sheriff Bill Tamms walks over and pistol-whips the young farmer. The farmer grabs the back of his head and screams, "God damn you!" and he meant it.

While the Sheriff Bill Tamms is abusing the farmer, the father of the young farmer runs up with an ax handle and hits the sheriff in the face. Blood explodes from Sheriff Bill Tamms's face. The sheriff just stands there in a daze. As he stands there in a daze, an old lady walks up and stabs him with a five-tine pitch fork. The sheriff slowly works up a scream and stands bent over with blood pouring from his mouth. His jaw is broken along with several teeth and his nose. The sheriff draws his secondary handgun from his boot. With him still bent over, he shooting in all directions. Bullets fly hitting several people on both sides and shooting a large hole in his car. Sheriff Cecil Tamms finally makes it to his feet. He decides to abandon the scene. The gang side immediately starts attacking Bill's friends and the fight starts all over again. Sheriff Bill Tamms finally runs out of ammunition in his weapon. He tries to replace the clip, but several people start beating him down with clubs.

While the fight is raging, Sheriff Cecil Tamms jumps in the car. He calls for reinforcements as he speeds down to the farm. He is pissed off. He screams, "How dare they disrespect the law. I am the law. Those bastards will pay." As he drove past the fire trucks, he realized that the fire was getting close to the farm. He says to himself, "Oh shit, I still got that bitch cuffed to the bed. I'll just roll that bitch over and stick it to her, then go back there as those bastards are hauled in. When I get them all in the station, I'll work those people over but good." He stops at the house at the front of the door and ran inside straight up the stairs. He notices the broken door of the room at the end of the hallway. "How did that cunt get away? Fuck it, I'll get another," he said out loud. Then he runs into his room and puts on his gun belt. He goes over to the dresser drawer to grab some money, but it is gone. He screams, "Who the fuck took my money? I know I wasn't that high and left it someplace else. Oh! I bet that bitch took it when she left." He grabs his gun and checks the clip. Empty. This confuses him. He thinks to himself, "I was pretty high earlier and I may have shot at something." He goes down to the car and is about to get in when he notices the roof to the house is starting to glow. He stands there watching until it bursts into flames. He thinks to himself, "Fuck, I got to get the money from the basement." He runs down to the basement doors and notices they are broken. He stands there in the doorway surveying the empty room. He thinks,

"Fuck! The back room door is busted." He runs to the back room door and stands there stunned. He yells, "All of it gone. Damn it! Who the fuck would take it?" He runs up the stairs and into the kitchen. He opens the refrigerator door and grabs a large bag. He shakes it a little and then holds it up to inspect it. He goes over to the table and pulls out a meth crystal. He puts the crystal on the table and smashes it with the butt of his gun. He bends over and snorts the powder off the table. The meth sends him into an instant high and a rush of power. He says, with the voice of someone that just quenched a thirst, "Now I will get those fuckin' farmers." He grabs the bag and runs outside to his car.

As he drives off, he looks in the rearview mirror to see the house's roof totally engulfed in flames. He races down the lane swerving around several fire trucks that are moving up to the farm. He gets up to the crowd of fighting people just as the other deputies were coming into the field. Just before jumping out of the car, he takes another hit of meth which shoots him into a fury. He gets out of the car and looks around. He runs up to the first person and punches them in the side of the face. The person he punches is a fifty-year-old housewife that is tending to an injured gang member. She falls to the ground unconscious and with a broken jaw. Then Sheriff Cecil Tamms grabs a man by the neck that is fighting with a gang member. The sheriff snaps the neck with a quick twist of the man's head. Then Sheriff Cecil Tamms grabs another man and twists him down to the ground. He bounces the man's head on to the ground like a basketball. He motions for one of the gang members to give him a club. Sheriff Cecil Tamms puts his foot on the man's neck that he has just thrown to the ground and begins to hit him in the head with the club until the man's head caves in on one side. Blood and bone lay next to the man's head with part of the brain herniating from the wound. The man starts convulsing. Sheriff Tamms just wipes his boot off on the man's shirt and goes to the next victim.

A forty-year-old man is fending off three gang members when the sheriff walks up behind him and hits the man in the back of the neck with a club. The man drops to the ground. Immediately, the three gang members go to work on the man beating him until the man's body is just a hide filled with blood and pieces of bone. The sheriff grabs a machete from one of the gang member and starts walking through the rumble of people. He walks through the crowd chopping on arms and legs like he is test driving the blade. "Ah, this feels great!" he thought to himself. The blood that is everywhere increases the sheriff's frenzy for more blood and gore. He walks up to the car and grabs another hit of meth before returning to the crowd. The sheriff walks up to the first man he meets who is fighting with a gang member and strikes him in the head. A quarter of the man's skull is sliced off. The piece that is removed only hangs by the twisted hair and blood. The man just holds up his hand to the side of his head as if to see if there is anything on the side of his head. He starts walking in circles just staring into space. The gang member that he has been fighting stands there, watching him for a moment. Then the gang member hits the man in the face with a pipe, caving in the man's face and taking whatever consciousness the man had. The sheriff screams with enjoyment as he once again walks through the crowd slicing and chopping.

More of Bill's friends and friends of friends show up. Bill's friends outnumber the gang members four to one now. They quickly overtake the gang and surround them until the gang surrendered. The sheriff is still running ramped until a sand shovel to the face brings him down. The deputies that are standing on the sidelines watching quickly move in when Bill's friends subdue and disarm the gang. When the deputies move in, they start arresting gang members and putting them in handcuffs. The ambulances showed up to pick up several people with severe lacerations to the head, arms, and torso. Eight people die from severe lacerations, head trauma, decapitations, and severe beatings. There are thirty-eight severely wounded and several others that are wounded but not badly.

Sheriff Cecil Tamms is picked up from the ground and placed in handcuffs. He regains consciousness and starts screaming, "Hey! Hey! What the fuck are you guys doing? I'm the Sheriff here, now damn it! Let me go! I got a job to do!" The deputies take Sheriff Cecil Tamms's gun belt off and throw him into the cop car.

The firemen, who are all volunteers, get the house fire out, but the trees continue to burn strong with flames shooting a hundred feet into the air. The firemen move over to the barn. They begin to soak the barn roof to try to prevent a fire. Some of the firemen go inside and make sure there is nothing smoldering on the inside. When they make it into the basement, they immediately vacate the barn. "Hey, everybody out of here, now!" one of the fire captains yells. "Everyone concentrate the water to the barn, it's filled with explosives." The firemen work diligently for about two hours until the wind picks up, pushing the flames down from the hills. The fire captain notices that the flames are moving in toward the barn quickly. "Pack it up quick, boys, and move out. We've got to get the hell out of here." Soon the farm place is engulfed in flames. To the fire captain's disbelief, the barn's contents didn't explode. Overnight the fire moves into to field, and they are able to put it out. The next morning, the Drug Enforcement Administration is out in full force to look at the meth lab.

Sheriff Bill Tamms is taken to the hospital with severe head wounds and one severe laceration to the spine just below the ribs, severing the spinal cord and lacerating a kidney. He also has several puncture wounds to the abdomen, which starts a severe peritonitis. The deputies haul Sheriff Cecil Tamms and the other gang members along with some of Bill's friends to the county sheriff department. Everyone is booked and jailed.

The deputies start fingerprinting Sheriff Cecil Tamms, and he goes into one of his rages. He starts screaming, "You can't put me in jail! I'll have all you bastards fired! Just wait till my dad gets in here!"

He starts punching and kicking, knocking one deputy to the floor. The other deputy gets a broken nose, which sent him to the floor on his butt. The deputy with the broken nose draws his Taser as soon as he hits the floor and shoots Sheriff Cecil Tamms in the chest. Sheriff Cecil Tamms is stunned and falls, bouncing his face on the tiled floor. Blood and teeth ooze from his mouth creating a crimson pool as the deputy continues to Tase him. The other deputy gets up, wipes off his bloody mouth, and walks over to Sheriff Cecil Tamms.

Sheriff Cecil Tamms is just lying on the floor, slowly moving around as if trying to swim through mud.

The deputy looks down at the sheriff. "You asshole! Your father won't be coming back any time soon! You practically chopped him in half." The deputy then kicks the sheriff in the lower jaw, splitting the skin at the point of the chin and shattering the jaw into several pieces.

Sheriff Cecil Tamms recovers handcuffed to a hospital bed. The doctor comes into the emergency room where Cecil is lying in the bed groaning. The doctor explains, "We are going to have to operate to put that jaw back together. You will have to have your jaw wired shut for about six weeks. We are going to bring in a specialist to work on those teeth. We'll have you all fixed up in a jiffy. The nurse will be in any minute and get you prepped. So you won't see me until tomorrow."

Sheriff Cecil Tamms could barely say a word, but he mumbles, "Where is my father, Tamms?" The doctor bent over to listen closer. Sheriff Tamms mumbles it again. "Where is my father?"

The doctor looks a little closer at the medical record, "You are Sheriff Tamms's son. He is in stable condition now but is going to be flown to AMC for surgery. He has puncture wounds to the abdomen but the main problem is someone slashed his spine and kidney. Someone must have had a sword or a machete and really did a lot of damage."

Sheriff Cecil Tamms just stares at the ceiling like "What have I done?" or more like "How the hell am I going to get out of this?" Soon the prep nurse comes in and starts prepping him for surgery. Then a police officer comes in and uncuffs him after the anesthetist sedates him. He is wheeled into surgery.

Back at the jail, the gang members had been processed. They are all screaming like a pack of wild dogs in their cells. Poot is one of them in the jail cell. Poot starts screaming, "I want to make a phone call to my lawyer!" One of the deputies comes back and opens the jail cell. The deputy handcuffs Poot and then brings the phone. Poot dials in a number.

A woman on the other end answers, "Hello, this is Jacelyn with Youths Unified for Political Policy Initiation. How can I help you?"

Poot speaks in his gang voice, "Shuts up, bitch, this here's Poot! I needs yus to come to the Appalachian Jail."

"I'm sorry but you cannot speak to me this way. I work for YUPPI and I do not think we get people out of jail," Jacelyn says angrily.

"Listen, yus dumb bitch, gets Links on the fuckin' phone!" Poot is screaming in the phone.

"There is no one here by that name," Jacelyn says.

"Links, the damn congressman, you know him. He gave me dis number ta call when I's needs things." Poot is a little confused but more irritated.

"You mean Congressman Dodd, do you not?" Jocelyn says in a condescending voice.

"Yeah, I's do." Poot is getting worried now because this is the number he always calls. No one besides Links ever answers the phone. "That asshole better not have stood me up this time after all the fucking work we did to get those bastards elected," Poot thought to himself.

"Let me check and see if I can transfer you to him, hold one moment," Jocelyn says. Then she puts him on hold.

The deputy in charge is getting antsy and starts motioning Poot to hurry up. The deputy gives Poot the five-finger signal meaning Poot has five more minutes. Poot gives the deputy "the bird" and mouths "Fuck you." The deputy slaps Poot in the ear hard enough to make Poot's ear go numb. Poot just rubs his ear and stays on the phone.

"I am transferring you to Congressman Dodd now, thank you for holding," Jocelyn says and then switches the lines.

"Now what the fuck did you guys get into?" the congressman screams into the phone.

"Well, we did like you said and got your ass elected and we just had a little party. Then Sheriff Tamms got us all in trouble by killing a few people and he probably killed his dad too. The townspeople, they just jumped us." Poot spoke very clearly when talking to the congressman. Poot was actually an educated man but he gave that all up when he was hired by OCORC to start the YUPPI division up. He never did like working very much and this was great money and freedom. He had a free rein on anything he wanted to do and no one could touch him. These freedoms lead him to revert into a gangster like mentality. All he had to do was to raise hell when hell was needed to be raised.

"That son of a bitch, I knew I couldn't trust that Tamms to stay out of trouble. I thought I could trust the old man to keep his fucking son on a short leash. What the fuck do they think I pay them for? They are constantly going off on their own tangents and not sticking to my plan," the congressman says. "Now where are you?"

"I am in the Appalachian County Jail. We are all in jail. The old man Tamms's deputies were pretty pissed when they saw that he had been beaten to a pulp. So they hauled us all in and took young Tamms somewhere. We haven't seen him since—" Poot is cut short when the deputy grabs the phone from him.

"You fuck, let me get done talking," Poot says to the deputy. The congressman can be heard screaming through the phone.

"Why should I?" the deputy asks Poot.

"Because I can do a lot for your piece-of-shit career, that's why," Poot says arrogantly.

"How the fuck can a piece of shit like you do anything for me?" the deputy asks.

"Give me the phone! And I will show you!" Poot tells the deputy and then gives him a look of hate.

The deputy gives the phone back to Poot. "Hey. What the fuck just happened?" the congressman asks.

"The deputy took the phone away," Poot says, glaring up at the deputy.

"Let me talk to him," the congressman says.

"He wants to talk to you," Poot tells the deputy and then hands him the phone.

"Yeah, this is Deputy Allen," the deputy says with detestation.

"I am Congressman Dodd and you are now the sheriff in charge until there can be a new election. I will get all the paperwork over to you today. Now the first thing you are going to do is let my boys go. Kick them in the ass hard before they do go, but they must go nonetheless," Congressman Dodd says.

"How do I know you are going to do what you say you are going to do? I don't have any authority to let these criminals out," Deputy Allen asks.

"Listen, you little piss ant. I will get the paperwork done and sent over now, so get your ducks in line and shit in a ball so that this can happen as smoothly as possible," Congressman Dodd says with anger in his voice.

"When I see the paperwork, I will think about letting these guys go, but don't count on it." Deputy Allen is trying to show some authority.

"OK, son. What kind of price are we talking?" the congressman asks.

"Price? No one said anything about a price," Deputy Allen says.

"How does forty thousand sound? Cash in your pocket." The congressman knows money talks.

"How ya going to do that?" the deputy asks.

"Do you know who OCORC is? If you do, then we have a special division for people like you. There are millions in the account so that we can get things done. All you have to do is do your job and your job is to do what we want. Shit boy, you could be rich before too long." Congressman Dodd is now in his campaigning mode.

"Well, OK, but I got to see some paperwork first," the deputy says with interest.

"It will be coming over the fax in about five minutes. Now this is hush-hush. We don't want the others there getting the idea they can take advantage of this jackpot now, do we?" Congressman Dodd says.

"Ahh, no, sir," Deputy Allen says.

"That a boy. Now go do your job." Congressman Dodd hangs up.

The new sheriff, Allen, hangs up the phone and helps Poot to his feet. "OK, back to the cell."

Poot turns around and the sheriff kicks him right in the tailbone. This made Poot stumble a little and then he quickly turns
around. "What the fuck did you do that for?" Poot says.

"I was told to kick you all in the ass before I let you guys out,
so I'm practicing. You should expect another in about a half hour,"
Sheriff Allen says with happiness in his voice.

"You dumb shit. He didn't mean to literally kick us," Poot says.

"I don't care, it feels good," Sheriff Allen says. He gives Poot a
shove down the hall and puts him back into the cell. He walks up to
check the fax machine. "Boy, I hope this is the real deal. I can use that
money. Shit, the judge will just let them go anyway, so this will just
save the taxpayers a few dollars," Sheriff Allen thought.

The papers come over the fax, it read, "By the order of
the Department of Interior under the Division of the Political
Development for Youth and Policy Initiation, I, Congressman Dodd,
command that under the dire circumstances with the grave development of Sheriff Tamms of the County of Appalachian, that Deputy
Allen is now acting sheriff of this county and all the benefits and
responsibility that is afforded to the sheriff position. If there are any
questions, please address them to the Youths Unified for Political
Policy Initiation." Sheriff Allen grabs the paper and calls a meeting
with all the deputies and staff at the station.

Most of the deputies are still at the station because of tonight's
activities. Everyone gathers into the conference room. Sheriff Allen
goes to the front of the room and sits on the table. "I don't have to tell
you who I am, everyone here knows me. The situation that happened
tonight was nothing less than tragic but very preventable. I am not
going to point fingers or dwell on the event. The past is the past." He
is trying to be very authoritative but everyone just looks at him like
the idiot that he is. "I am now the sheriff in charge as of a few minutes ago. This is under the direction of Congressman Dodd. If you
have any questions, I will be in my new office. Thank you." Sheriff
Allen turns and almost runs out of the room.

Everyone just stares at the person next to him like "What the
hell?" They all know Deputy Allen as the person that screwed up
everything. They can't even trust him to drive a car let alone be

Sheriff. "Who the hell is Congressman Dodd? He don't make rules around here." Everyone is thinking. Everyone gets back to work and finish their paperwork.

Sheriff Allen comes out of his new office. "All paperwork for tonight's incidence needs to come to me and I want it now." Everyone looks up and shrugs. Whether they are done or not, they hand the papers over to the sheriff. This way is not the protocol that they are to follow, but what the hell do they care? It isn't their ass that will be in a sling when court came around. Sheriff Allen takes the paperwork and runs it through the shredder in his office. He doesn't even hide the fact that he is doing this. He walks back the deputy on cell duty. "OK, we don't have anything to hold these guys on, so we are letting them go."

"What are you talking about? They and Sheriff Tamms butchered a lot of people tonight. This should be an open and shut case. We saw it ourselves," the deputy says with puzzlement.

"Well, I'm in charge now, and I say there is no evidence and we are letting them all go," Sheriff Allen says.

The deputy shrugs. "It's your ass. I'll put this in the logbooks."

"Do what you want but turn in your logs for the night immediately in the morning. I want them on my desk by six," Sheriff Allen says.

The deputy just looks at the sheriff like he just got done talking to the high school principal. Then he goes back and opens the cell doors. All forty-eight of the gang members and twelve of Bill's friends gather their belonging at the front desk. Once again, they all become loud and obnoxious, screaming obscenities and threatening to sue. Then Poot walks over to the loudest ones in his group and punches them in the side of the face. Immediately, the whole gang shuts up. Sheriff Allen takes Poot and five others out to the car and gives them a ride to get what vehicles are left. Only one truck remained intact. The others are burned and disabled. When the sun comes up, the gang is gone from the station.

CHAPTER SEVEN

THE NEXT MORNING SAM AND Carol wake up late. Sam gets ready for work, but Carol stays in bed. Sam thought it would be a good idea for her to take a few days off from doing any work. She needed to get her thoughts together. Sam knows she is a strong woman, but the emotional trauma of yesterday will hit sometime. Sam knows that she will have to work out the "if only I would have done this" type of stuff in her head and then she will be all right.

"Maybe today when you get moving around, we can go see that lawyer, Terri Logan. We can see what can be done about the whole situation. Besides, if they find out what we did, we may need a lawyer. I don't know. It's just a thought," Sam says and then gives Carol a kiss.

"I'll think about it," Carol says and then rolls over to fall asleep.

Sam tells her, "You should call your dad and tell him that you are OK." He just wants her to keep engaged with people so she doesn't sit around thinking too much.

"OK, I'll call you later." Then Carol dives back under the covers like she is freezing.

Sam leaves and goes to the hospital. He goes into his office and thinks about the day before. "Everything is going to be OK now. Carol is safe. Everyone made it through the night safely. We have plenty of money and we are set. I just hope those bastards don't show up here." Sam goes out and asks the technicians about the day's schedule. Then Sam goes outside to look for Bud and Kota. Bud and Kota are in the shed talking.

"Hey, what you guys up to?" Sam asks.

"Oh, nothing. Just talking about yesterday," Bud says.

"Where is Bill? Did he go home?" Sam asks.

"Hell no, that guy is still on the couch, sleeping," Bud says.

"Well, we better wake him up and have him call his wife before someone starts looking for him. See if he has a job and if not, have him start working here," Sam says.

"We don't need him to work here. What do you want him to do?" Kota says in a protesting manner.

"I don't care what the hell he does. Have him cut some brush, pick up rocks, anything. I just want to be able to keep an eye on him for a while," Sam says. "I really don't trust him yet and I want to see how big of mouth he has when he sobers up."

"OK! We'll go wake him up and see what we can do," Kota says with a little ease in his voice now that he knows the plan.

Then Sam starts the day of work. Most of his day is on the road. He has to make up all the appointments he missed yesterday. When he gets back to the hospital, he finds Bud and Bill hauling limbs and brush. Sam walks out to where the men are working to talk.

"So you're going to start here?" Sam asks Bill.

"Yeah, my other job sucked, so I'll just stay here and work," Bill says and then spits a stream of chew to the ground.

"Did you call your wife and let her know how you are?" Sam asks.

"Yeah, she came over here and brought me some clothes," Bill says.

"Well, take it easy today. You had a tough night last night," Sam says but not really caring if Bill hurt or not; he is just being nice. Sam thinks, "He is one lazy ass. He will be trouble but I'll let the boys work him until he becomes a real problem."

"I'm OK, got a little hangover but the rest of me's good," Bill says.

"Well, we'll get together tomorrow and work out anything you need." Sam says and then heads on in to the hospital. He finishes the daily paperwork and then calls Carol. "How are you doing?" Sam asks with concern.

"Oh, I'm fine," Carol says but with a little tension or concern in her voice.

"What have you been up to all day?" Sam shuffles through some papers.

"I went over and saw Dad. I told him everything that had happened. He told me to go see Terri Logan, so we both went over there," Carol says. Sam could sense she is about to tell him something that he didn't want to hear.

"You didn't tell him about the money and the guns and the shooting, did you?" Sam stops shuffling papers and gets really concern. A knot starts to form in his stomach.

"Well, it kind of slipped out, but don't worry, he won't tell anyone," Carol says, knowing she messed up.

"I hope you didn't tell that lawyer about that stuff. Between your dad and her, it will be all over town and then we are screwed," Sam is past worry and almost mad.

"I only told her about part of it, but she won't tell anyone. She does not like those guys at all," Carol says.

"I knew you were going to tell everyone, who else did you tell?" Sam says to himself. Now Sam is mad. He thought that Carol was going to tell her mother and father but not the lawyer. Sam asks, "Who else did you tell?"

"My mom was there but they are the only ones. Terri told us that she had had a private detective working on one of the deputies and on Sheriff Tamms for about a year now. She also told me she was about raped yesterday by the detective and that she told you about that before you found me. Why didn't you tell me?" Carol asks like it is some big secret she just found out him.

"Well, I really didn't have time to tell you all that had happened, nor could I fill you in on all the details of the day. That deputy is the reason I found you, but he won't be up and around anytime soon. What are you doing now?" Sam is trying to change the subject in order to cool down.

"I'm at Mom and Dad's still. Do you want to come over?" Carol asks while eating something while she talks.

"Yeah, I'll be over there in a little bit. See you later," Sam says and then Carol hangs up. Sam gathers his paperwork and puts it on the front desk for Marsha to deal with tomorrow.

Sam drives over to see Carol at her parents' house. Mark opens the door. "I thought you could take better care of my daughter than this. She's not accustomed to your 'Wild West' ways. I think she needs to stay here for a while until all this is straightened out."

"First of all, I ain't the one who pulled her over and took her off to some farm to rape her. Secondly, if I had waited for your fucking lawyer to find her, she may have been dead or raped or both. So what the fuck do you want from me? You didn't do anything to help." Sam stares at Mark straight in the eyes and then walks on past him to Carol, who is in the kitchen. Carol comes up and gives him a hug. Mark comes into the room right behind Sam, storming in like someone just pissed in his cereal.

Mark went on the other side of the kitchen's center island and then looks at Sam. "So now what are you going to do to fix this mess?"

"Dad! It's not Sam's fault. Not everything that happens to me is Sam's fault. If it wasn't for him, I would probably still be there hand-cuffed to the bed," Carol snaps at her dad.

"What about the money and guns?" Mark yells back.

"Shit, if that is all you are worried about, I got that covered as long as everybody"—Sam points to Mark, Carol, and Carol's mom, Marilyn—"keeps their mouths shut. Now you guys already blabbed to the lawyer. How many other people did you guys tell today?"

"I never told anyone, except for Kirk, Allen's friend. He works for the state police," Mark said. "He is going to look into the matter right away."

"You are a dumb ass. Now we are going to have police and shit all over the place. That money was a reward for Carol having to endure the crap she went through and we need that money to save the hospital. Shit! This economy is killing our business," Sam tells everyone. "Besides, this problem is mine and Carol's. It is obvious that you guys can't handle anything! So stay the fuck out of my business. You all can help Carol along, but I don't need any help with this whole thing. If they come for a fight, there is going to be a lot of food for the buzzards."

"Oh, Sam, he's just trying to help," Carol says and touches Sam on the hand.

"I know but now we've got to keep everything in hiding until the coast is clear. Anyway, I will work it out. Now what did the lawyer say?" Sam asks.

"Henry Bahr, the PI who works for Terri, said that Sheriff Tamms and his dad have been working for Youths Unified for Political Policy Initiation and they call their group YUPPIs. The YUPPIs work under OCORC. Their job is to make people do what OCORC wants and when they want it. Like for instance, if they want a bank to loan money to someone who can't afford it, the YUPPIs go to the banker's place and make him give the loan. During the election, they are the ones who kept some people from voting by standing outside of voting centers and making sure only Democrats voted. Both of the sheriffs were getting paid a lot of money from OCORC. They could do whatever they wanted and get by with it. The gang works with the sheriffs but is paid by OCORC. OCORC has someone in congress calling the shots, but he was unsure exactly who it was. He is still looking into it," Mark says with a pouty voice.

"I need to get home and make sure things are all in place," Sam says. "I think Carol should stay here until we know everything is OK. She should be safe here. Never know if there is going to be retaliation from those guys if they find out who took all their stuff."

"I can handle this myself. I am going home and going to work tomorrow," Carol says in a sassy voice.

"I really think you should stay here for at least a couple of days," Sam says sternly.

"I have to get back and pay bills and get the order done," Carol says like she is bargaining for a position.

"No, you don't have to go to the clinic for that. Please, just stay at least for one night so I know the coast is clear. Please! Everything else can wait for a few days," Sam pleads with Carol. He knows she really doesn't want to go back to work, but she always wants someone to talk her into it.

"OK, I'll stay, but call me in the morning." Carol leans over and gives Sam a kiss on the lips and a hug. "Good night, Sam, I love you."

"I'll see you tomorrow. Good night." Sam walks out of the kitchen and then goes out to his vehicle. Sam starts thinking about what needs to be done about the guns and money. "Nothing will be the same anymore. Somehow things went from bad to worse in just a short period of time, everything is moving too fast. How the hell can I get the money hidden before the cops get it all? First, we need to make another investment company and buy some land. A lot of the money can be run through the clinic without any question. I could make fake clients, and no one will suspect anything to do with services. We can split the money up and hide the majority of it. I'll be damned if I give that drug money to the government. We can do a lot of good with this money. Maybe set up a fund for treating animals where there is no owner or the owner can't afford treatment. But I'll talk it over with everyone later."

Sam drives home and feeds the dogs and cats. Then goes to bed but he cannot sleep very well. At 4:00 a.m., Sam gets out of bed and goes to the hospital. Kota is there doing chores. Bud comes out about 5:00 a.m. The three of them go to the local restaurant for breakfast after they hurry and finish chores. When they get to the restaurant, they sit in the back of the room next to an exit door just like they do every time they go somewhere. They're not paranoid but just cautious. The three brothers and their sister were raised on a farm out west. They always worked and almost never went to town except for school or church. Being around people was never comfortable for any of them. They're always very cautious when they are in a crowd or public places.

"Here's the deal," Sam says, "Carol is at her mom and dad's place right now for safekeeping. She told them all about what happened and about the money and guns."

"What the hell did she shoot her damn mouth off for?" Kota says and becomes really uneasy. He starts shifting in his chair like he is getting ready to jump and run. Then quickly settles down a little and starts chugging cups of coffee.

"I don't know. It probably just came out, but it is probably good. I never did trust that any of this would stay quiet, but I was hoping for more time. I didn't think that Bill would ever keep his mouth shut, and if someone ever did catch up to him, he would probably just squeal on us anyway," Sam says in a calm voice and then drinks his cup of coffee.

"Bill has been very good so far. He's not much of a worker. He's about as lazy as they come," Bud says as he stirs more sugar into his coffee.

"I figured he would be like that but we have to have some way to keep a handle on him. If he works with us, maybe he will build a bond with us. But we can't trust him or anyone else," Sam says and then picks up a menu and pages through it even though he never reads a menu. He just orders what he wants. "We should probably move everything then. They will probably find where we hide the guns and money if any one searches the place. Besides, Bill knows where everything is hidden." Bud flips open a menu and starts looking through it. "What do you guys think we should do? I think we need to take the money and store it in different places. Spend some of it and pay everyone's bills and then buy some land out west. The guns we need to store in a different location, but do you have any ideas?" Sam looks around for the waitress.

"I think we should." Kota stops as the waitress comes over.

"What will you guys have to eat?" the waitress asks.

"I'll have the hungry man's breakfast and a glass of milk," Kota says with a stern voice.

"I'll have the three pancakes and the bacon and egg combo and I'll take some milk," Bud says.

"I want three eggs, bacon, and toast. If you have that in a combo, that's great. I also would like a large glass of milk. Thank you," Sam says and gathers all the menus. He gives the menus to the waitress, trying to rush her away so they can finish talking. When the waitress leaves, Sam asks, "So, Kota, what was your idea?"

"Well, shit, here she comes again." Kota motions with his eyes to let the others know the waitress is coming.

"Here is your milk. Can I get anything else right now?" the waitress asks and looks around the table like she is trying to find something.

"Yes, we'll take some more coffee. Thank you," Sam says. The waitress picks up the coffee carafe and leaves.

"I need to get a different house, probably a modular home. We can get it put up really fast. What we can do before putting in the electricity and plumbing, we can build a huge vault room in the ground, and no one will suspect that we are up to something. The kids and my wife are going to go to her mom's for Thanksgiving. The kids get four days off for Thanksgiving, and that will give us enough time to dig, but when they get back, we will have to live somewhere till the house gets put up." Kota explains.

"You guys can stay with us for a while. We don't have a lot of room but we can make it work. My house is a crappy house but you are welcome to stay," Sam tells Kota.

"OK, that will be it then. I will order the house today and we will get the ball rolling. Bud, we need to get the backhoe greased and ready to roll," Kota says.

The waitress comes back with the breakfast and coffee. The three of them start eating immediately without a word. They then get up and Sam pays the bill along with a huge tip. When they get back to the hospital, Bill is there waiting.

"Hey! What y'all doing?" Bill asked.

"Oh, we just went to breakfast and discussing what we need to get done before winter," Bud says as they all get out of the truck.

"Ya guys want to hear something about the other night?" Bill says with a shit-eating grin on his face. "Well, you guys knows about that there two sheriffs and that gang? The old man sheriff is in the hospital, may not make it. His son chopped him in the back with a machete among other people. The young sheriff went mad. Killed a lot of people and chopped a lot of peoples. Then the deputies hauled him in and beat him up really good and put him in the hospital, but he is out now but not working yet. One of his deputies also got beat up that night in his house, and he is still in the hospital but mostly for detox. The gang was arrested but they just let them go along with everyone else that night."

"How do you know all of that?" Kota asked with extreme curiosity.

"Well, my cousin is a cop and he knows all about what has been going on. But I never said anything about what we did," Bill says in a nervous voice. "I will never tell anyone about that."

"Bill, here's the deal. We are going to split up some of the money so that everyone can pay off their bills and then put the money away where no one can find it. Don't put it in a bank. Bury it in the barn or somewhere else that is safe, and no one will suspect anything," Sam says. "What do you think of that?"

"Well, I think that would be great. I'll hide the money in the basement. No one ever goes down there and I can put a safe down under the floor while the wife is gone, if you guys can help me," Bill says.

"We can do that," Bud says, "We better get this done in the next few days. If those guys are out of jail, they may just find out who procured their treasure."

"Bill and I will go get a safe," Kota says to Bud. "If you want, you can get a dolly and the climbing ropes and pulleys. We'll meet at Bill's place."

"OK, let's get going. We got a lot of work to do before the end of the week. Bill, I need directions to your place," Bud says and then rips a piece of paper off a feed bag. Bud gets directions. Bill and Kota take off in Bill's truck and head to town. Bud goes into the shed over to the toolbox and digs around for everything he will need. Sam goes to work in the hospital.

Bud, Kota, and Bill meet later that day at Bill's house. Bill's truck is weighted down with a large safe. The safe weighed so much that the tires are rubbing on the fender wells of the truck bed. When Bill and Kota arrive, smoke is rolling out from under the bed of the truck. They pull up to the house as Bud stands there laughing. "Bill, you dumb shit. Didn't you see that the tires are getting torn apart?" Bud walks up to the truck and looks at the rear tire on the driver's side.

"Yeah, we's jack up the truck on the ways over here and put somes them two-ba four blocks in the springs but they's broke about four miles back," Bill says as he gets out and walks back to the rear tire, "Jus says fuck it ans kept goin'. Didn' have nos more wood."

All three of them looks over the tire situation and then go into the house. Bill leads the way with Bud and Kota following with a tape measure to measure every doorway and hallway. When they get into the kitchen, Kota felt a soft spot in the floor. Kota jumps up and down and says, "Shit, this floor is about had it."

Bud moves over to the area where Kota is standing. "Yeah, Bill, this floor will never hold that safe to run it across to the basement. I guess if we do get it this far, it won't take long to get it into the basement." Everyone laughed.

"Yeah, then you can just throw a new rug over the hole and your wife will never know. Hell, she may even be happy because you got her a new rug," Kota says jokingly.

So the three of them walk outside and Kota sees the tack shed out back. Kota says, "I think that we should just slide this shed to one side and then dig a hole and throw the safe in. We can move the shed back, and you can cut a hole in the floor after we get the safe in the ground."

"Sounds good fer me," Bill says.

They all get to work on the project. They get done just in time, just before Joy got home. Kota and Bud go on home as they load the backhoe loader on the trailer.

The next day Sam, Bud, and Kota go down to their hiding place and sit inside the tank. They open one of the ten bundles of money and count out the stacks of hundred-dollar bills. "There's at least a couple of million dollars or more here in this bundle. Shit, there's millions and millions of dollars in here. That means a whole bunch of trouble if those assholes ever find out who took it," Sam says as he flips through the stacks of money.

"Maybe we bit off more than we can chew this time," Kota says with a little smirk on his face. "So I think we should just give them the money back and tell them we are sorry." They all bust out laughing for a minute or two.

"We are going to have to be very alert from now on if any-one comes snooping around. We can't just go hog wild on spending money because it may send up a red flag. Kota, we can get you a new house, and all of us should pay off all our bills. If you want to buy any land, do it through a corporation and only buy through the corpora-tion. We are going to have to build that underground room that we always talked about. We can put a barn or an indoor arena over the top of it and that will hide it even more. If it goes well, we are going to put up another one which can be a shelter for storms and such. So let's spend this bundle and the rest we are not going to touch until we have too. We need to get some training to use those weapons we found. Kota, I'm going to leave it up to you to see if you can get us training at a place like Black Swamp." Sam sort of had a plan.

"Well, I'm just going to take enough money to pay off my bills and a little extra to buy the wife and kids a little treat. I'll leave the rest here for now."

Bud starts counting out some bundles of bills. "I'll call a couple of people tomorrow and maybe they can find out who we need to go through to get some training. When do we want to do this?" Kota says.

"Anytime, I'm not going to be too busy this winter, so I'll just take a vacation and we can do this. We'll all just say we are going home at the same time or maybe a boy's vacation that we never had." Sam says.

"We should pay off Mom and Dad's bills and maybe Gina's bills. We'll call up Rick and he can just go to work and fix up the farm place," Bud says with excitement.

"Just tell him that we need to hire him full time for the next two to three years. Give him about three hundred thousand and that ought to be a start. If he doesn't want to do it, have him find someone else. Tell him that we'll hire any help he needs. Then call Gina and have her open a building account for him and a shopping account for Mom and Dad. She will be in charge of it. We have to do this a little under the table so Gina can hide this a little with some fuzzy accounting," Sam says.

"Well, I'm going to have to take enough for a payment on a new house and we got to get everyone in line for electric and plumbing. I think we will have to get DH's track trencher for the room. We can use the backhoe to dig my vault room, but the trencher will be faster. Bud and I can run it and may need his trucks to haul dirt. I'll have to get a building permit for a basement and a house, so I'm going to do that today," Kota says.

"OK, well, Bud, give Bill his share and read him the riot act on not telling anyone or spending too quick. Tell him to take the rest of the day off. I've got to go to work and look at a couple of lame horses. We'll meet in the morning. Bill is not to know about the basement." Sam put his money back on the pile and then crawls out with Bud with a bag of money in hand right behind him. Then Kota comes out with two pockets full of money. He closes the lid and locks it up. They all put the camouflage back in place.

Sam goes off to work. Bud and Kota go to meet up with Bill. Bud gives Bill the bag of money. Bill opens the bag and turns bright red with fury. "What the hell is this shit?" Bill starts yelling at Bud. "There is a hell of a lot more money than that down there and I want the rest of my share. You cheatin' me?"

"You ungrateful fuck." Bud stands in front of Bill. "That is your share for now. We don't really have to give you anything. As a matter of fact, it is really all Sam's, but he just shares everything and he said this is the only amount we are splitting now and keeping the rest until needed."

"I want my share or else I'll just take it." Bill throws the bag on the ground and gets up into Bud's face. "Where is that asshole at now, on vacation with all our money? I'll kick that fucker's ass."

Bud just stands there and starts to laugh in Bill's face. Kota stands off to the side and watches just in case he has to jump in and help. Bill starts to get more irate. His face starts to twitch and tensing up like he is going to throw a punch. Bud has been in enough fights that he senses it is time to put Bill in his place. Bud gives Bill a shove. Bill flies back off-balance and then recovers. Bill lunges forward with a punch at Bud. Bill's plan of attack may have worked, but his nose runs into Bud's right fist. Bill only hears a crunch from broken cartilage in his nose. Then instant heat and darkness comes over Bill as he drops to the ground stiff as a board. Blood rushes from his nose and his face swells under his eyes. Bud and Kota look over Bill to make sure he is still breathing. Bill comes to in about a minute. He looks up and stares at Kota and Bud. Kota bends over and tells Bill, "If you like that, Sam will probably do a lot more of that, if you want to keep shooting your fucking mouth off."

"Yeah, I've seen him castrate a guy while the guy was holding a gun on him," Bud adds in with a smile on his face. "Now, you still want more or did this satisfy you for now? When I tell Sam what just happened, he is not going to be happy and we may have to bury you somewhere. Do you have any place in mind?" Bill is regaining his senses. Bud and Kota give him some help up off the ground. Bud looks at Bill's nose. "Yep, looks a little broke. Stand there and I'll fix it for you." Bud places a hand on both sides of Bill's nose and squeezes everything in line. Kota hands Bud some duct tape and Bud puts a stripe of it over Bill's nose. "There, just like uptown," Bud says.

"I guess y'all is right. I should be grateful for all ya done for me. Sometimes I just gits a little bent out of shape. Sorry, guys. Please don't tells Sam I's so ungrateful," Bill says and messes around with his broken nose. He wipes his nose on an old shop rag that Kota hands him. Bud takes Bill up to the hospital. A technician gives him some Advil and a cold pack. Then she makes him sit in the break room and watch TV. Kota takes off and goes over to DH's place. Bud goes into the house and calls Gina to tell her what is going to happen.

When Kota arrives at DH's place, DH and his dad, Harold, are working on a dump truck. They have the hydraulics all torn apart. Harold is cussing at DH. DH is cussing at the hydraulic pump system. "Hey, guys, what ya up to?" Kota asks, knowing exactly what they are doing.

"The damn hydraulic pump hose just broke and we are trying to get the end out of the pump." DH says in a disgruntled tone. "The dumb ass tightened it up with a pipe wrench and broke that new hose, busted the threads off inside the pump," Harold says, staring at DH.

"Ahh! Shit! I've put more of these damn things together than you have," DH says just as he gets the treads moving out. DH continues to remove the damaged part. When he is done, he holds it up like a bounty of reward. "There, I told ya I would get it if you would just leave it alone." DH sets the parts down and wipes his hands. Then goes over and shakes Kota's hand. "How ya doing?"

"Good, and y'all?" Kota shakes DH and Harold's hands. "You guys busy?"

"No, not right now. We may have a big job coming up in few weeks, so we are getting everything ready," Harold says.

"Sam wants to know if we can rent your trucks and loader for about a week. We got a couple of deep holes to dig," Kota says.

"Well, it's not that I don't trust that you can't run the equipment, but I'd really don't like to rent it out. There are a few little things that the loader does that makes it, so only I can really run it. Hell, Dad can't even run it," DH says. "Besides, I owe Sam a favor or two, so I'll just do it for him if you guys want to haul."

"Let me have you talk to Sam." Kota dials his cell phone and gets Sam on the line. "Hey, DH doesn't really want to let us rent the machine because it has its quirks to it. Here let me have you talk to DH, he's standing right here." Kota hands the phone to DH.

"Hey, Sam! How ya doing?" DH says.

"Good, and you?" Sam says.

"Hey, it's not that I don't want to let you rent my loader, but the thing is really a bitch sometimes. I would prefer to run it myself. If you can't afford to pay me, I'll do it for nothing and you just work on my horses sometime." DH starts to fidget.

"That's fine. I need you to start today. Can you do that?" Sam asks. "And I can pay you, but if you want to trade, that is fine with me."

"Soon as I get this hydraulic pump on, me and Dad will haul everything over. Are we digging at the hospital?" DH asks.

Sam tries to make up a good lie but one that fits with what he wants done. "Not at first, we need you to go over to Kota's place and dig a deep basement. We are going to put a house on it. Then we need to dig a deep, deep hole in the barn that we don't have up yet.

We are going to put in a cistern for a swimming pool. I want a giant water reserve so we never have to pump water to the pool."

"Well, let me get this done and we'll be over in two hours." DH hands the phone back to Kota.

"Kota, just call me when you leave," Sam says.

"OK." Kota hangs up and puts his phone away. "Well, I'll see you guys later I got to get going."

"OK, good to see you again," DH and Harold say. "We'll be over in a couple of hours," DH says and waves goodbye. Then he goes back to work.

Kota gets back into his Bronco and drives toward the modular home place in Harrisonburg. He calls Sam, "Hey."

"Hey, DH is going to come over and dig. We will have him dig at the hospital first and then over at your place. So change of plans. Look for an in ground storm shelter for your place. They make really nice ones and that will be better. When I think about it, you really don't want all those munitions under your house. We'll just dig this hole in the barn first until you get a building permit and find a shelter up in Harrisonburg. We'll say that we are putting a cistern in for the swimming pool and I'll just draw a little plan tonight. Call Bud and give him the lowdown. Then call DH and have him come over here first," Sam says.

"OK, I'm headed up to Harrisonburg right now and I'll see you in the morning," Kota says and then hangs up with Sam so he can make his other calls.

Sam arrives back at the hospital about three hours later after finishing his farm calls. DH and Harland are waiting there with their equipment unloaded. They are standing outside talking to Bud, Carol, and Marsha. They are all waiting for Sam like he is in some kind of big trouble. Sam pulls around to the other side of the hospital and the technician start unloading the vehicle while Sam walks over to talk to everyone.

"So what's going on?" Carol asks before Sam even made it all the way over to them. She is standing with her hands on hips and lips are tight. "Can you explain what you think you are doing?"

Sam walks up and shakes DH and Harold's hands. "Why yes, I can, and if everyone will follow along, I will show everyone." Sam thinks to himself, "Obviously Kota didn't tell Bud what was going on, or he was just waiting for me to tell the lie so we are on the same page."

They all walk over to the barn area. "This is going to be a new swimming pool barn. We just got a huge grant to build this and there is a time limit on it. I need to have this done in two weeks or so. We need two areas to put in under water reserve tanks. One is here and one is in the hill over there. We are going to increase reserve even further by putting in a six-foot pipe between them. I need the holes as deep as you can put them, down to bedrock if we can get that far in both of them." Sam stands there and points out the location.

"What do you need all the water for? One tank will be enough," DH says.

"Well, the problem here is that we have very little water. If we use too much, it takes a long time for the well to recharge. I want enough water so if I leave the water on all day I still have enough water to refill the pool," Sam explains.

"OK, how big of tank?" DH inquires.

"I don't know. We can make it twenty feet by twenty feet by ten feet both of them, if we can get that deep."

"Now what are we doing?" Carol jumps in. "This is the first I heard of this and who the hell gave you a grant?"

"Carol, if you showed up to work once in a while, you may know about some of this stuff. I will show you later." Sam cuts her down in front of everyone so she will shut the hell up.

"Do you know anything about this?" Carol turns to Marsha.

"Don't look at me. This is the first I have heard of this," Marsha says.

"Don't you start digging!" Carol looks at DH. "We are not putting a swimming pool in. We can't afford it and there sure the hell is no grant."

Sam grabs Carol's hand and escorts her away from the crowd. Everyone starts babbling among themselves and looks questioningly over at Sam. "Carol," Sam says in a stern voice. He is mad as hell.

Carol always throws a fit at any time, and it didn't matter if they were in a crowd or wherever. "Thanks for being a bitch again in front of everyone. You really show your true stars. Now here is what we are doing. We are building a swimming pool and we are building panic shelters also so that we can hide all the stuff we just confiscated. We have millions of dollars and I can't tell them what we are doing. We are trying to keep it a secret. Do you remember?"

"Don't you think you should run this by me first?" Carol screams at Sam. "This is my place, too. Maybe I don't want to spend the money that way. Besides the police want to see the money and guns we got. They may have the FBI come in and investigate this whole thing. They are coming tomorrow."

"You and your dad just can't keep your mouth shut." Sam is pissed. "That money is nobody's except ours, and the weapons are now mine and ours. Now, what the hell are you guys going to tell them when all of it is not here tomorrow and the cops come rolling in?"

"Well, I want the sheriff arrested." Carol starts crying. "All you care about is the money."

"That's not true and you know it. As for the sheriff, he is in the hospital. They arrested him and the gang, but they let them out right away. So that just tells me that this runs higher up more than just that fucking cop. You know that the guy is getting paid from high up, so what makes you think that the cop you talked to isn't on the take?" Sam tries to explain.

"Well, I don't," Carol says while pouting.

"So they take the stuff back and say fuck you. They do nothing to the sheriff." Sam wipes away Carol's tears. "I will make the sheriff pay dearly. This is not over yet, not by a long shot."

"OK, so now that I messed everything up, what are we going to do?" Carol says and sniffles.

"I'll handle it. Just trust me, OK?" Sam says with a reassuring voice.

"I do, and from now on I'll follow your lead," Carol says.

"OK, let's go get some stuff done." Sam walks over to the crowd. "OK, so I was trying to save you all from a lot of trouble in your life, but if you want to really know, then you are in neck-deep and sworn to secrecy."

"Well, just tell me what is going on and then I'll decide if I want to continue or not," Marsha says.

"No, I'm sorry but this is really serious stuff and you are all in or all out. What you know can hurt you and may get you killed. If you don't want to know more than I suggest you just not hear this and never ask about it. If you all are in, we are bound by secrecy and you can't even tell your spouses. Got it?" Sam says sternly and points to Marsha, DH, and Harold.

They all stay and say at one time, "I'm in."

Sam gives them the whole summary of what happened the last few days only, leaving out the stuff about the amount of money. He tells them about Bill and the sheriffs. "So what we are now building is a bunker to store the weapons and a place to hide if need be. We can pack up and leave, but I kind of like working here and all. So what do you think?"

They all just stand there staring at Sam, and then DH says, "So then you do have enough money to build this. Now that we know a little more about what we need, we can build something a lot better. I helped build some of the army bunkers that are hidden out west. We need to get a drill and a crane. If you got enough money, we can get it done right, but it will take about a month or more. We will need to hire a few people."

"Well, how much are we talking?" Sam asks.

"We are talking about a million or a little more. And for the weapons, just leave them where they are for now. If they look like they are getting hot on the trail, then we will get them out of here," DH says.

"We've got enough money, so I am putting you and Bud in charge of this project, but I still want to put in a pool and cistern. That will divert people's attention. Bud you know where the money is, so you are the finance director," Sam says.

Sam signals Bud to move away from the crowd. They always had secret signals even when they were kids. Bud walks away with Sam, leaving the others to babble among themselves. "Don't let anyone see the money. No one else! You know how money makes people stupid. They don't need to know how much money we have. Marsha will get a big raise and that will shut her up and the other two will get paid well, so we should be safe. What about Bill? Do I need to deal with him?" Sam asks Bud.

"No, I think he just needed to be shut down and rebooted and I did just that. But we need to keep an eye on him," Bud says with a grin.

"Don't let Bill know what is going on. I don't want him to know anything about the bunker. I just don't trust him," Sam says.

They go back to the group and everyone is on the same page of what to do. DH, Harold, and Bud go off together to discuss things. Carol and Marsha go back into the office. Sam goes back into the hospital to finish up with the hospital horses. Later that night, Sam and Carol draw up a floor plan for the equine rehab center. They already had plans from long ago when they were going to add it but didn't have enough money. They changed a few things around in the plans and add some more luxuries for the horses.

"I think we need to hire some more construction crews," Carol says. "It will never get done with just DH. I want to have this done in a month."

Sam rolls his eyes. Carol always thinks things can get built overnight. "They may be lucky to get this up in six months. There is a lot of building and several different construction crews that need to do their job in a coordinated manner."

Carol says, "Well, I want it done as fast as possible so we are not working on this during our busy season."

"That means every one of the construction crews have to be moving fast. If they have too much time, they will poke around and start snooping around," Sam says. "We can add some bonuses for the first crew done. That will give them all an incentive to hurry."

Carol looks at Sam like he just farted. She says, "Really!"

"I just want this thing to go up quick," Sam says. "I want to have this done before February."

"Yeah, I'll have Dad get the blueprints drawn up as soon as possible, and he will have to give one to the pool people so they can get started with their plans. So tomorrow I will coordinate everyone on the construction plans." Carol packs away the drawings they just made.

"OK, I'm also going to call the guy on the coverall build, and he can put the one up we had been planning. We will just attach it to the rehab center," Sam says. They both get in the Sam's vehicle and drive home.

Chapter Eight

Two weeks later, DH has already started to pour concrete. He had gone out and hired twenty people to help build the bunker. It wasn't hard to find twenty people to work because of the housing market going bust. Construction workers are a dime a dozen right now. The downfall of the housing market is purely the government's fault and OCORC for making banks and lending institutions loan money to people who couldn't afford a new house.

Bud calls Sam late one afternoon. "Hey, you've got to get back here as soon as possible."

Sam is out on a farm call but is on his way back. "Now what happened?"

"DH was finishing the digging and hit a cave or something. We dropped a rope and it's about a hundred and fifty feet deep," Bud says. He is so excited, he could barely speak.

"Well, I'm on my way back. Don't let anyone get around the opening. All we need is to have one of those workers fall into that hole," Sam says sarcastically.

"I put up a barrier and the workers are pouring concrete at the other end of this trench. Kota went to get the climbing gear and some lights," Bud says.

Sam tells Bud, "Call him and see if he can find someone with a methane or gas reader. I'd like to see if there is good air down there before we go in and look."

Bud says, "I'll tell him. When are you going to be back?"

"Thirty minutes, see you then." Sam hangs up the phone and keeps driving. Bud sets up barriers and gets ready for some cave exploration. DH stops digging and checks the concrete work that the workers are doing.

Sam shows up and Bud is standing on the hill of dirt along with DH. Sam gets out of his vehicle and goes up to Bud and DH.

"What the hell, DH? You broke my ground," Sam says sarcastically.

"Ahh, it was broken before. I just cracked the lid," DH says with a smile.

"Well, who wants to climb down and see where the hell it goes? I hate climbing in caves, but I will if I have too," Sam says and looks around for someone to volunteer. "Kota will be here in a few minutes. We can tie off everything to the loader. That pulley system we have can lower one of us down, and that way you don't have to climb or repel," Bud says, looking at Sam.

Sam's eyes got big and he takes a deep breath, then lets it out. "Right. Let's do it. I'll get mentally prepared."

Kota shows up with two big duffel bags of climbing gear. "I got a methane gas reader, but it is just a methane alarm, so it doesn't measure levels but just if there is any methane."

"Well, that will have to do for right now. Let's lower that down first." Sam says.

"Shit, there is no methane in that hole. As much as we sparked the area when we were digging, it would have blown up or something," DH says. "And besides, there is a draft coming out of the hole."

"I think you are right, there is a draft." Sam walks over and grabs some grass. He climbs down to the hole and throws the grass into the hole. The grass blows out of the hole. "Well, there is definitely a draft, so it has good air. Let's throw in a ChemLight." Bud hands Sam a ChemLight. Sam snaps the light and throws it in. "Wow!" Sam says.

The other three get closer to the hole and look down. In the hole is a huge cavern about the size of a big indoor arena. The ChemLight makes the whole area light up by illuminating the crystals in the walls.

"Well, who wants to go first?" Sam asks. Sam really hated crawling in to closed spaces ever since he was a little kid. When he was very young, he got stuck in a culvert.

"I'm already to go, so I'll go first," Kota says with excitement.

Sam goes over to Kota and double-checks his gear. Then he gets ready lower him into the cavern. "Now if you don't stay talking, I'm going to take it that there is some bad air down there and I'm pulling you up immediately," Sam tells Kota.

Kota smiles and says, "I'll stay talking. I'm never at a loss for words."

Kota backs up to the hole and leans back. DH and Bud slowly lower him into the cavern. Sam keeps a close eye on him and continues to talk to him on his descent. Kota makes it to the bottom. He yells, "OK, I'm at the bottom. The ground down here is very smooth, almost like a concrete floor. The air appears to be good, but I'm going to stay hooked up until I look everything over. There is a lot of air movement coming from the tunnel over here to the left. Send down some rope, more light, and some Chem sticks."

Sam turns and motions to Bud to hand him one of the duffel bags. Sam ties a rope to the bag then cracks a ChemLight and tapes it to the handle of the bag. He lies down next to the hole and lowers the bag to the bottom of the cavern.

"Kota, here is the bag," Sam yells but there is no answer, so he yells again, "Dakota, where are you?"

No answer. Sam gives a tug on the rope. Then there are three returned tugs on the rope from the other end, which always meant everything is all right. In about five minutes Kota appears at the bottom of the cavern below the hole. He yells up, "Hey, you need to get down here and check this out."

Sam gets up and puts on his climbing gear. DH and Bud lower him to the bottom of the cavern. Sam pounds a stake into the floor and attaches two carabiners. Kota leads the way into the tunnel and Sam drops ChemLights as they go along. At about five hundred feet in the tunnel, there are old digging tools, an old sword of some type, an ax that is made from what looked like some type of old metal, a pile of decayed furs, a decayed bag of gold trinkets, and brass armor. "Shit, that's pretty neat," Sam says.

"Someone stayed in this cave, so there has to be entrance somewhere. Let's go find it," Kota says with excitement.

Sam tugs on the rope three times to let Bud know everything is OK. Then they both unhook the ropes and go on without any lines. After another three hundred feet, the tunnel opens into another cavern that looked like at one time it housed a lot of people. There are ruins of shelters made from rock and wood. The wood has long since rotted away and some of the rock walls have caved in. All around the cavern is several artifacts that show people stayed here but no skeletons. Kota and Sam continue and finally see light coming through one of the tunnels in the sidewalls. A remnant of a ladder remains. Sam free climbs the wall to the tunnel opening and Kota follows. They continue to the end of the short tunnel and come out in the trees on the west side of a hill on the property that the farm leases.

"Well, it looks like we need to buy some more land," Sam says to Kota. Sam and Kota are happy that they decided to go on exploring the cavern. It would go down as one of their best adventures.

Sam calls Bud through his cell phone. "Hey, come and get us with the Mule. We'll meet you at the top of the hill."

"You assholes unhooked. We are just getting ready to go down in after you. You jackasses know that you never do that, ever," Bud says with concern and anger.

"I know and it won't happen again. Wait till you see what Kota found down there. Bring the extension ladder when you come." Sam tells Bud.

Bud tells DH to pull up the rope and untie from the equipment. Bud puts everything in the duffel bag and then puts the barriers around the hole. "We need to cover this for today and figure out what we are going to do with it. Come on lets go get those guys and kick them in the ass for making us worry," Bud says jokingly to DH.

Bud and DH jump into the Mule and drive up to the top of the hill clear across the pasture. There Sam and Kota wait. Sam and Kota grab the ladder and a bunch of ChemLights and head down the hill.

"Come on you guys, you won't believe this," Kota says like a giddy little kid. Bud and DH follow and soon they stand at the cavern entrance. Sam pops a ChemLight and lays it on the edge of the tunnel then lowers the ladder. Sam pops another ChemLight and throws it down at the bottom of the ladder. They all climbed down one at a time. Sam leads the way as they search the whole bigger cavern.

Bud exclaims, "Shit this is a small town down here. We should call this the city cavern."

Kota agrees, "That's a good name for it."

Sam says, "It is too bad we don't have any champagne to Christen this place."

Kota says, waving a stick in the air, "I pronounce this place to be, from now forward, City Cavern."

Everyone chuckled and then they follow the other tunnel back to the other smaller cavern.

"This is great. We can put in a cable elevator in the bunker down to the cavern. Shit we can rebuild a city in to this place." DH thinks out loud as he looks around the cavern walls.

"Yeah, but we need to get this capped off and then figure out who lived here. Maybe we can get an archaeologist at the university to look at some of this stuff. If it's important, then maybe we will let them down here." Sam says but with some hesitation.

"We can take this sword and armor. They can look at that along with a few things from these huts," Dakota says. "But I want the stuff back. I found them."

"Yep, we'll do that," Sam says, "Let's get out of here for right now until we find out more. DH and Bud, maybe we can get that back entrance so we can drive in and out." Sam says.

DH says, "I think we can open that entrance up and maybe put concrete walls in. That will stabilize the entranceway and we can put some thick doors in to seal it off if we have to."

Bud jumps in, "Yeah, we need blast doors, but we need to camouflage the entrance also. I will look into that tonight. We can work it out tomorrow."

They all make their way out of the cavern picking up all that they dropped on their way out. They put all the stuff into the Mule and drive on back to the hospital. Everyone goes back to work.

Bud and Kota move the storm shelter in for Kota the next day. They spend the whole day filling in and preparing the area for the crew to put in electricity and plumbing before they pour a concrete slab. Kota has a huge modular home arriving in three days. Everything is moving right along and without any problems.

At the equine hospital, there's not a lot to do. The horse cases are down, so Sam has a lot of free time. The hospital is always slow this time of the year. Sam decides that it would be a good idea if all the families of his brothers and wife's families get together for Thanksgiving. He calls up one of his clients that owned and operated a charter service to pick up all the families. Carol called the Stonewall Jackson Hotel in Staunton to set up enough rooms for all the families. Bill on the other hand was becoming a pain in the ass to Sam.

"Bill, can I talk to you?" Sam calls him on the walkie-talkie. Bill is over with DH inside the cab of the crane.

Bill jumps down and swaggers over to Sam. "What can I do for ya?"

"Well, Bill, you can start by leaving DH to do his work. He doesn't need you over there bugging the shit out of him." Sam looks at Bill straight in the eye. He did this when he confronted people. He is always ready for someone to take a swing at him.

Bill shuffles around a little bit with his feet and then kicks at some rocks. "Well, I was just making sure that he knew that cistern didn't need that much damn concrete in it and he put floor drains and pumps in it. I don't think he knows exactly what he is doing."

"Bill, he knows exactly what he is doing. He's doing exactly what I told him to do," Sam says sternly.

"Why the hell do you have pipe out to the back there? It don't make sense," Bill inquires.

"We are building a water storage facility. We can pump water from anywhere in the storage system. Now, for the last time, I am telling you to leave it alone, he knows exactly what he is doing," Sam warns Bill.

"Well, do you have a job for me?" Bill asks.

"Yes, you go help Kota. He is getting his place ready for the house he is having moved in," Sam says.

"OK, I'll go over there until you need me to come back." Bill walks to his new truck and leaves. Sam has warned him not to show boat any money. So Bill financed the truck and put a small down payment on it. It is good timing because he just started a new job. Sam has a feeling that Bill is probably spending more than he let on. Sam really can't trust Bill, and later it will probably bite him in the butt for even involving Bill in any of this.

CHAPTER NINE

OVER THE NEXT THREE WEEKS, Kota gets his house put up. DH has dumped a foot of epoxy to the entire length of the bunker and covered it. Gravel, sand, and sod had been laid over the dugout areas. The project is going very quickly even the steel building crew started pouring footers for the new rehabilitation center about a week ago. The swimming pool company is finishing the final touches on the rehabilitation pool and underwater treadmill. Sam and Carol had set a deadline for the project to be done in February, but with the incentive money, all the crews worked night and day to finish quickly. They paid all the crews the incentive money because they all finished quickly.

DH and Bud were able to put a rope elevator from the bunker down to the cavern in the area that DH had opened up. The other entranceway to the cavern was widened and a large thick steel door was put in so that a small sized vehicle can drive down into it. DH has an out of state company work on the door so that they would not be around after the job was done.

Thanksgiving had been good but none of the families really got along with each other. Many of them thought that the others are getting something for nothing. Sam just sent them all home after Thanksgiving Day except for Gina (Sam's sister) and Darrell and Elaine (their mom and dad). Sending the families home made some of them mad because they didn't get to go shopping on that Friday morning. Sam really didn't care he just wanted them to leave.

Early Monday morning before the sun came up, Bud calls Sam. "Hey, get in here right away," Bud says in a panic. "There are about fifty people that I think are cops here and half of them could be ATF. I can't read what's on the uniforms those guys are wearing. They are tearing shit up in the hospital and in the barns."

"I'll be right in there," Sam says "What time is it anyway?"

"It's 5:30 a.m.," Bud says. "Just park down at the road and sneak up here along the tree line. There's no moon, so it's dark and they won't see you."

Sam throws on his clothes in a hurry. He jumps into his vehicle and drives to the hospital. He shuts his lights off before he gets to the hospital entranceway. He parks in the field across the road. Sam carefully runs up through the trees and then up to the back of Bud's house. Bud was waiting for him at the bottom of the stairs.

"So who is in charge of this crap out here?" Sam asks Bud.

"I don't know," Bud says. "No one has come up to the front door. They are just going to the buildings. I don't think they are cops. Cops would have come to the house."

"Where is Dakota?" Sam asks with concern.

"I haven't found him yet. I called you as soon as I came out of the house." Bud has a look of panic on his face. He had completely forgotten about Kota being on the grounds somewhere. Bud knows that Kota would have greeted someone when they drove up in the middle of the night. Sometimes clients arrive really early or an emergency shows up before Sam or Carol gets there.

"Well, as soon as I find out who is in charge, then we'll go find Dakota," Sam says to Bud. They start walking over to someone wearing a police uniform at the front door of the hospital. Sam whispers to Bud, "I'll just grab this fucker and find out what they are doing."

Sam walks silently up behind the cop at the front door. Sam taps the guy on the shoulder, "Excuse me, but what the hell do you think you are doing here?"

The man in the police uniform spins and draws his revolver. When he draws, Sam blocks the barrel from pointing at him. The guy has his finger on the trigger. When Sam blocks the revolver the weapon fires and a round goes into the ground.

Sam thinks, "This guy is a real rookie or isn't really a cop. When did cops carry a .357 revolver? No one that is trained in shooting puts their finger on the trigger when drawing their pistols. You will shoot yourself in the foot."

Sam traps the weapon's hammer after the round is fired with one hand and spins it around with his other hand. This motion traps the finger in the trigger guard and snaps the finger in two. Sam yanks the weapon from the man's hand, removing part of the trigger finger with it. Bud jumps in and punches the guy in the side of his face before he can start screaming. The guy drops to the ground and his body gets stiff. The guy lies unconscious on the ground with blood pouring out of the end of the finger that has been ripped off. The gunshot causes several other men in police uniforms inside the reception area to take notice. They all stop what they are doing and look toward Sam and Bud but just for a moment. Then they go back to what they had been doing. Sam figures, "The light inside and the darkness outside the glass windows make the windows like mirrors. The men inside cannot see outside without opening the door or turning the lights off."

"You asshole muthafucker! Give me my fucking gun back!" The guy in the uniform yells at Sam when he regains consciousness. Sam is crouched down along side of the man. The guy reaches for his knife. Sam's and Bud's attention was on the people inside. The guy draws the knife and swings it wildly at Sam. Sam and Bud roll backward out of the way. Sam rolls up to a standing position with the revolver pointing at the guy.

"You need to just settle down," Sam says. "I took it away from you before you killed someone. Now who the fuck are you?"

"I'm a cop, you dumb ass, and we's comes here fer the money." The guy takes another wild swing at Sam. Blood flies from the removed figure and rains over Sam's and Bud's faces. While the man slashes at Sam and Bud, Sam slaps the guy's knife hand. The knife is redirected enough during the slash that it slices over the guy's thigh. The cut enraged him more and he stands up. He starts slashing more wildly than before at Sam. Sam glances over at Bud. Bud knows exactly what Sam wanted and lunges forward with a kick. The kick lands to the guy's testicles. The kick landed so well that Bud could feel the testicle crunch. The guy stands like a statue completely stunned until Bud finishes him with a roundhouse to the side of the head. The guy falls to the ground without even a grunt. Sam grabs the knife and gives Bud the .357. Sam tucks the knife into his coat sleeve.

"This is no cop," Bud says as he looks the guy over. "I think this is the guy Kota knocked out a long time ago, here at the hospital. You know the dumb asses that threw the money and drugs out of their car."

"Well, let's put his handcuffs on him and cuff him to the tree until we find out more." Sam grabs one arm and Bud the other. They drag the guy over to the tree in the small garden at the front of the hospital and cuffed his hands around the tree. Sam rips off part of his own shirt and ties it around the bleeding finger to stop the bleeding. They check the guy for more weapons. Bud takes the ammunition and the cuff keys from the guy's belt. He puts it into his coat pocket.

"Let's find Kota, this is not a good situation," Sam says.

Sam and Bud sneak around the hospital up to one of the horse trailers. They see lights on and men in the hayshed. They crawl under the trailer to scope out the hayshed. They see nine guys dressed in some other type of black outfits that look like police uniforms. The men are all wearing bulletproof vests. Kota is sitting on the ground with his handcuffed behind his back and around the shed post. Several of the men are gathered around Kota.

Bud whispers to Sam, "He looks really beat up and isn't moving, but I think I still see him breathing."

Sam can see Kota's breath in the cold morning air. Sam looks at Bud and whispers, "You got the men on the outside of the shed. I'll take the rest. You got enough ammo. Reload fast and watch your back because those guys scattered about will be coming when this all starts. But first, I'm going up to talk to them and see if they are real cops or not. Just wait for my signal."

"Got it, be careful. I got your back," Bud says checking the .357 to making sure it's loaded and ready.

Sam backs out from under the trailer. He figures that the best approach is to just walk up and ask them what the hell is going on. Sam runs around to the corner of the hayshed and then just walks in.

"Will someone here tell me just what the fuck you are all doing here?" Sam yells, startling all the men. Just as he moves into the building, he recognizes three of the people standing there. One is Sheriff Cecil Tamms, one is Deputy Trevor, and the other is the orange-haired punk (Poot). Sam takes one look at Kota just sitting there on the ground bleeding. Sam flies into a rage. He knows these men cannot be dealt with diplomatically. He knows that he has to get these guys off his family's back once and for all. With them hurting his wife and Dakota and one being a rapist, that just sent him over the edge of his restraint. Sam gives Bud the quick five-finger signal and then drops the knife from his sleeve. The men are still startled and are trying to grab for their guns. Some of the weapons are still holstered and some have their weapons sitting on the hay bales away from them. Sam throws the knife and buries it deep into the leg of the guy with red hair (Shack) that moved for his weapon next to the hay bales. Shack falls to the ground, grabbing at the knife and screaming in pain. The knife is buried deep into the Shack's femur. Then Sam grabs for the sixteen-penny nails that lay on the bench as he jumps across the bench. When his feet touch the ground, he punches two nails into the lower jaw of Deputy Trevor. Deputy Trevor has his pistol partially drawn. Trevor drops his pistol and grabs at his face with both hands. He tries screaming but is unable to open his mouth because the nails go through the chin and up through upper hard palate exiting out both sides of his nose. Sam spins around and grabs a broken ax handle that is lying on the ground at Kota's feet. In the same spin, he comes around with the ax handle and hits Poot in the teeth. Poot's lower jaw explodes with blood and teeth. Poot hits the ground like a lead brick.

Bud at the same time shoots five of the guys dead center into breastplate of the vest. The force of the .357 Magnum round sends them tumbling backward and knocking the wind out of them. Those men just lay on the ground, not moving. Sam continues his next swing and hits Sheriff Cecil Tamms in the right hand, making him unable to grab his weapon quickly. Sam lounges over to Shack and hits him in both elbows shattering the ulna in both arms. All Shack could do is lie on the ground screaming.

Sam then spun to the Deputy Trevor, who has given up trying to pull the nails from his face, and now reaching for his weapon. Sam does a spin hook kick to Deputy Trevor's face knocking him to the ground but not before he is able to reach his 9-mm. pistol. Deputy Trevor hit the ground on his back but fires his weapon and catching Sam in the left shoulder with a slug. The 9-mm. round shattered Sam's left collarbone. Sam spun to the left from the force of the bullet hitting him. Deputy Trevor gets off another shot but misses Sam and hits a post in the barn. Sam is dazed and drops to the ground on his knees like a man out of breath. He drops the ax handle and crouches there for a second. As Deputy Trevor is getting to his knees, Sam finds a steel pry bar that is lying on the ground. Sam, still writhing in pain, throws the bar like a javelin and hits Trevor in the forehead. Deputy Trevor's skin splits and his skull cracks like a sledgehammer on a car window. Trevor drops to the ground and fires two more shots. One of the two shots hit one of the guys that had been shot by Bud. This shot hits the man in the neck. Blood, cartilage, and flesh fly from his neck, ripping a large hole in the side of the exit wound. The other shot hits the horse trailer that Bud is still under.

Sheriff Cecil Tamms started running away when Deputy Trevor started firing. He has his weapon drawn in his left hand; his right hand is tucked into his belt. Sam sees Sheriff Tamms on the run. He grabs the ax handle and throws it. He throws it in a spinning motion so the handle flies just above the ground at leg level. The handle hits Tamms in the legs, tripping him up and sending him falling face first into the gravel. He slides on his face and lies there, not making a move. Sam rushes over to grab Tamms before he is able to recover from the fall. When Sam is about fifteen feet from him, Tamms turns and fires his weapon. The weapon explodes, sending pieces of the weapon flying. The shrapnel takes off two of Tamms's fingers and tears some of the flesh from his face.

Sam would have laughed if he hadn't been in pain. He says to himself, "The dumb bastard was too stupid to clean his weapon. I could have been dead if he had cleaned his gun."

Bud in the meantime is busy holding off the others that are running to the rescue of the fellow gang members. He reloads and continues to shoot the gang members in the breastplate. Each one drops like someone just hit them with a sledgehammer. Many of the others see what is going on and run back in to the hospital for cover. Sam confident that he is not in immediate danger runs over to check on Kota. Sam looks Kota over and covers him with his coat. He rushes over to the toolbox and gets bolt cutters. On his way back to Kota, he steps over Shack and Poot. Shack kicks at Sam. Sam in turn greets him with the swing of the bolt cutters to his teeth. Blood and teeth shoot out of Shack's mouth, and he turns his head to spit. Shack didn't move for fear of another beating. Sam continues to walk toward Kota when Poot starts to come to. Sam turns and examines him for a second. He decides it is better to keep the man down when you get him down. Sam kicks Poot in the side of the head, sending Poot back into unconsciousness. Sam goes over and cuts the chain to the handcuffs on Kota.

"Bud! Get over here right now!" Sam yelled. Bud crawls from under the horse trailer and walks toward Kota but always on the lookout for any one moving. As he walks past Sheriff Tamms on the ground, he gives him a kick in the ribs and one in the nuts. The sheriff just groans and curls up in to a ball. Bud notices no one is moving around, so he walks over to Kota.

"See if that key you got will unlock these cuffs." Sam tells Bud and then winces in pain. Sam's left arm is almost useless and the pain is getting more intense. Breathing is painful to him. Bud gets the keys out of his pocket and quickly unlocks the handcuffs.

"He's pretty beat up. He's got some broken ribs, maybe a broken nose and jaw, and probably got a concussion. I don't know if his legs are broken but they are really swollen. We need to call the ambulance right away and get him to the hospital," Sam says to Bud. The pain makes Sam want to vomit.

"You need to get to the hospital too. Let's see that wound." Bud whips out a tech knife and cuts Sam's shirt open. The wound goes all the way through the top of Sam's shoulder. "I can see a bone, I'm pretty sure this is not good."

"I'll be OK. What time is it?" Sam asks and then grits his teeth.

"It's 7:45 a.m., about time for everyone to show up," Bud says.

"Well, just call the ambulance and—" Sam stops when he hears a truck coming down the road outside the hospital gate. Bud calls the ambulance and gives them the lowdown on everyone's condition.

Sam recognizes the sound of the truck. He calls DH. "Hey, DH, just stop where you are right now and don't say anything just listen." DH slams on his brakes immediately.

Sam says in an urgent voice, "There are about forty or so people dressed in police uniforms and in black uniforms. They busted up Dakota and have been tearing shit apart. I think they may be looking for the money or weapons. Do you have your .40 with you?"

"Yes, I'll park at the bottom and block the driveway," DH says.

Sam says, "Great, we'll take them from up here."

Sam notices the guys that Bud had knocked down are moving again. Some are peeling off their vests and the ones in the hayshed are just crawling but not really moving anywhere.

"Looks like they are trying to burn the hospital down." Bud points out the smoke coming out of the hospital to Sam.

Sam says, "I don't think it will burn. The sprinkler system should kick on in the barn area. The horses will be fine but wet." Sam thinks, "I'm glad we put a smoke detection system on to the sprinkler system."

"Maybe they will leave, so we don't have to shoot the whole lot of them," Bud says with a little sigh of relief.

Down by the gate, DH has the driveway blocked and he is ready for anyone coming down the driveway. DH sees the smoke coming from the hospital and the people running out like rats from a sinking ship. The people run out to the parking lot and stand there like they are on a smoke break. DH decides to focus their attention on him to keep them away from Bud, Sam, and Kota. He knows it will be a long shot to hit one of them from this distance, but he fires one round anyway. He hits one of the guys smoking in the parking lot. All of them hit the ground and start firing down toward DH but didn't hit anything. Not even his truck. They all quit shooting at about at the same time.

DH says to himself, "Jerks probably ran out of bullets."

A car comes up to the road and turns the corner into the hospital entranceway. Cars keep turning the corner and start driving up to the entranceway. Everyone is showing up for work at the same time.

DH runs over to each car and tells the two technicians and Marsha. "You guys need to back up and get out of the way. Then get out of your cars and hide in the ditch or go home." They all back up and Marsha jumps out of her car. She grabs her 9-mm. and joins DH. The two technicians get out of their cars, grab their cell phones, and jump in to the ditch across the road. They lie down and start texting people.

The guys in the parking lot start shooting again. Bullets hit all around and in front of the truck. On bullet hits the back tire and it goes flat.

DH yells, "God damn it! That was almost a new tire." DH is pissed off, so he shoots two rounds up toward the guys in the parking lot and hit one of them in the foot. Another burst of bullets fly down to DH and Marsha; they both stand behind the front wheel.

"I hear a siren," Marsha says to DH.

DH gets a little panicked and tells Marsha, "Well, shit, we are going to get busted now, go toss your weapon in the weeds over there near the mailbox and I will cover you. Then go take cover over with the girls. I'll take the heat for this. Now go!"

Marsha runs over and tosses her weapon in the weeds and then looks down the road. She yells to DH, "It's an ambulance!"

DH breathes a sigh of relief. He looks up to the parking lot and sees a bunch of people are running toward their vehicles. As the ambulance turns into the driveway, DH throws his weapon into his truck. DH waves down the ambulance. The ambulance driver stops next to DH and rolls down the window.

DH tells the ambulance driver, "You might want to just sit here a minute. Those guys in those cars have been shooting down here.

They just shoot out my new tire. But I think they thought you are the cops and are on the run."

The ambulance driver tells DH, "The state police are on their way. Someone called in a shooting. Was it you?"

"No, I hadn't had time," DH says.

Marsha and the two technicians come running over to the ambulance. One of the technicians asks DH, "Is it safe to drive up there yet? We got appointments coming in early and Sam should be here fairly soon."

DH informs everyone around him, "Sam is already here. He called me when he heard me coming up the drive. And we should wait a little bit so that we know them guys are on the run. I don't really know how they are going to get out unless they find their way to the old road in the trees."

"Sam is going to be mad if we are late for work," the tech says.

"I don't think you are going to be doing anything but cleaning today. They tried to burn the hospital. See the smoke?" DH says.

"Well, I called the police," the other technician says.

"Hey, let's call Sam and see what is going on," Marsha says. Marsha phones Sam. Sam answers his phone and Marsha asks him, "Sam, this is Marsha, is everything all right?"

Sam tells Marsha, "Well, I think all of those that could leave have left, so if you are down with DH, you can come on up. We need to get into the hospital and see what is going on in there. They tried to burn it and I need to get those horses out. Bud is going to make sure no one else is in there but he can wait for DH." Sam is breathing hard like he is out of breath. He is in a lot of pain but still trying to take care of Kota and instructing people.

Marsha informs DH, "DH, Sam wants you to go up and help Bud check out the hospital before we go up."

"Tell him I'm just going to back the truck up and then I'll be right up," DH says.

"Sam, he is just backing up his truck now, and he will be right up. Are you all right?" Marsha asks.

Sam tells Marsha, "I'll be OK, but Dakota needs to get to the hospital. I think you had better call the clients and put them off for a few days. We need to get this mess cleared up first."

"I'll do that as soon as I can get in." Marsha hangs up the phone. Marsha tells the ambulance driver, "You guys need to get up there right now."

"I'm not going up there and getting shot," the ambulance drive says.

DH walks over after moving his truck and tells the ambulance driver, "I'll ride up with you."

"OK, but do you have a weapon?" the driver asks DH.

"Right here." DH pulls his .40 from the back of his belt.

The ambulance driver and DH drive up to the side of the hospital. Bud waves them over to the hayshed.

"Holy shit, there are bodies everywhere!" The driver yells back to the two EMTs in the back. The ambulance comes to a stop at the hayshed. Everyone jumps out. DH and Bud run over to the hospital to see if the coast is clear. The driver and the EMTs unload their gear and rush over to Dakota.

"He is the worst. You need to get him going right now," Sam tells the EMT.

"We will make that assessment as soon as we examine all the people," one of the EMTs arrogantly says to Sam.

"Listen, you asshole! I'm telling you get a catheter in him and start him on fluids and get him to the hospital. These other buzzard baits are the ones that tried to kill him. So leave them for someone else and take him now," Sam starts yelling at the EMT.

"I'm not going to listen to you. You are not in charge here. I am a trained EMT. What are you?" the arrogant EMT says.

"I'm a fucking veterinarian and that means I'm a doctor, so do it now!" Sam yells.

"No," the EMTs says.

"Well, fuck you, I'll do it myself." Sam gets up and walks over to his vehicle, but it has been shot up and the interior has been set on fire. Sam looks at the other vehicles and they all have been shot up or set on fire. Sam calls Marsha, "I need you to get up here right now and bring Dakota to the hospital."

"I'll be there in one minute." Marsha runs to her vehicle and races up to the side of the ambulance. Sam meets her there. They walk over to Kota.

Sam says to Marsha, "Let's lay him down in the backseat. I don't think I can lift anything."

"I'll get him," Marsha tells Sam. Marsha being a farm girl is pretty strong and picks Kota up. Kota groans but stands as best as he can. Sam slips under Kota's left arm to support him and Marsha takes the other side. They get Kota into the backseat and Sam sits in the back with him. Marsha speeds off to the hospital while Sam holds Kota all the way to the hospital.

The ambulance crew continues to examine everyone on the ground. The ambulance driver calls in for two more ambulances. Two Augusta County deputy sheriffs arrive about twenty minutes after Sam has left. Bud and DH had already checked out the hospital and found no one left inside. DH takes his weapon and the one Bud had been using. DH hides the weapons in one of the trees where no one will find them. Bud stays and talks to the police. He tells them the whole story about what went on, except for him shooting the guys in the chest. He figures he was using one of the guy's guns and he didn't kill anyone. He basically just hit them with a super-sonic sledgehammer. Both deputy sheriffs go into the hospital and check out the damage. The reception and office area is burned along with the lab and the ICU stall area. Nothing in the stall area burned because of the sprinkler system. The lab equipment is all smashed. The drugs that were on the shelves are broken on the floor. The MRI machine has been dented. They probably tried to destroy the MRI machine, but the magnet grabbed the sledgehammers and they are still sticking to the machine. The MRI computers and all the electronic hardware is all smashed. Just about anything that could be broken is broken and anything that could be burned is burned. The hospital is not usable at this time, and it will take weeks before it is operating again.

One of the deputy sheriffs named Cal Benz tells Bud, "I suggest you call the insurance company and get them over here and assess the damage. Go around and make sure you list everything that is broken or missing." Then he asks, "What is in the safe?"

"Just controlled drugs and some files," Bud says with hesitation, "and stuff."

From the hospital, Marsha had called Carol and told her the story. Carol walks into the front door and says with despair, "Oh my God! What happened?"

Bud tells Carol, "It's a long story, but to put it short, a gang of people that were dressed in police uniforms broke in here. They beat up Dakota and shot Sam. Sam and I fought off a bunch of guys and the rest of them broke in here and destroyed the place."

"Well, did they catch the people?" Carol asks Bud. She ignores Deputy Cal Benz standing in room.

Bud tells her, "They got the few guys that Sam had fought with and they took them to the hospital. The rest of them took off through the field and must have gone out the old driveway through the trees."

"Madam, do you own this place?" Deputy Benz asks Carol.

"Yes, I do!" Carol answers.

Deputy Benz says in a slightly hesitant manner, "We want permission to search to whole property. We want to look through all the buildings and search the grounds."

Bud is standing behind the police and shook his head no toward Carol. Carol is flustered and not thinking well, but she did remember that lecture Sam gave her. "You can look through the buildings, but we are building everywhere and I would prefer you not drive around on the property and into the fields. I don't want anyone to get in the way of the workers and get hurt. Why do you need to look over the property?" Carol asks Deputy Benz.

Deputy Benz says, "We need to look for anyone that may be around or more evidence into what happened here. I called in more men to help with this situation because of the arson, gunfire, and the possibility that some men have died. My men will be very discreet and they will be very careful."

"Well, they must stay with Bud. He will take three men on the Mule around the property and show you everything." Carol gives Bud a little wink.

Deputy Benz says, "That would be very helpful and may get things done faster. We will file all this in the report, and we will need to talk to the two men that were hurt. So I will be heading for the hospital and I will get back in touch with you. In the meantime, please write down as much as you can of why these men would come up here and do something like this."

Deputy Benz leaves the office with Bud. Outside two other officers join the deputy sheriff and Bud. They all walk over to the Mule and climb in to the front and the bed. Bud takes them on a tour of the property. When he gets back to the hospital, they get into their vehicles and leave. Carol and the two technicians go through everything and write down everything that is broken. Bill shows up later, strolling in at his leisure.

Bill says to Bud with a groan, like someone just woke him up. "Mornin'."

Bud is not in a good mood and he hated Bill. Bud says in an angry voice, "Where the fuck have you been, Bill? You're fucking late again." It was not a question. Bud knows Bill was probably sleeping off another hangover. Bill knows Bud hates him and the feeling is mutual.

Bill snaps back at Bud, "I ain't late. I can come in when I want."

Bud is fuming in anger. He walks over and cups his hands over Bill's ears. He picks him up slightly off the ground and then slams him to the ground. "Now, you piece of shit." Bud holds Bill to the ground with a knee in the chest. Bud shakes a finger in Bill's face. "I make the rules when it comes to you. When I say you are late, you are late."

Bill knows that Bud is about to kick the shit out of him. He is already hurting with a hangover and decides not to push it with Bud. He tells Bud with a shaky voice, "OK! OK! What ya want me to do?"

Bud instantly becomes calm. He tells Bill, "We need to start cleaning this place up. Grab a wheelbarrow and we will start in the hospital."

Bill and Bud start cleaning up the hospital. Later that day, the insurance man shows up.

Meanwhile, Kota's wife and Montana join him at the hospital. The doctors have started him on IV fluids and pain medication. He has three broken ribs, a concussion, compartmental syndrome in his legs, and multiple bruises and lacerations. The doctors told him that he is going to be OK in a few weeks.

Sam is in surgery getting his wound debrided and his clavicle repaired. He is going to be all right, but it will take a couple of months for his wounds to heal. Since Sam's mom and dad were still around, they go and sit with Kota while Sam is in surgery. Their mom and dad are not strangers to waiting in the hospitals. When the brothers were young, Kota raced cars, Sam did rodeos, and Bud was just wild. They all had been in the hospital several times. Sam comes out of surgery after about three hours. He is still groggy but conscience of his surroundings.

Deputy Sheriff Cal Benz comes to see Kota. Deputy Benz says to Kota in a soft but demanding voice, "We need to know what happened this morning."

"Well," Kota says and then swallows hard. He reaches over to the bedside stand and grabs a glass of water. He takes a long drink of water thinking about what to say next. "I was in the hayshed getting the feed ready to do morning chores when a bunch of cars drove up. I recognized a couple of the guys that got out of the cars. They were all dressed in police uniforms and bulletproof vests. They were packing automatic weapons and started running into all the buildings. I asked them what they wanted, and then one guy hit me with a nightstick. They handcuffed me to the post and kept asking me where the stuff was and where the money was. I kept telling them I didn't have any idea what they were talking about. They just kept hitting and kicking me. Then that asshole that attacked us at the gun range one day came up and kicked me in the head. That is the last thing I remember until I came to when Sam and Marsha put me in the car."

"So you have seen some of these men, which ones?" Deputy Benz inquires. He keeps writing things in his little table.

"The orange-haired guy and the red-haired guy that we threw out of the hospital one day," Kota says and takes another drink of water.

Deputy Benz is getting more curious. He asks Kota, "Why would they show up at the hospital and do this to you all?"

"I don't know. Maybe that red-haired guy is mad about getting thrown out of the hospital. Maybe the orange-haired guy is mad for Sam kicking his ass at the gun range," Kota says sarcastically. "Hell, I really don't know who was even there. If you tell me some of the names, maybe I can give you more information."

Deputy Benz sees that Kota is getting frustrated, so he obliges Kota's request. He tells Kota, "One is a Sheriff Cecil Tamms. The two that you mentioned go by the name Shack and Poot. One is Deputy Sheriff Trevor. No one else was recovered from the scene."

Kota repositions himself in the bed. His blinking slightly increases in frequency and a bit of anxiety is lifted. Kota tells Deputy Benz, "Well, I know there were a lot more than four men there. That sheriff, I think, is the one that kidnapped Carol."

"What do you mean they kidnapped Carol? When did this happen?" Deputy Benz is puzzled and concerned at the same time. He had not heard about any kidnapping. He knows that there would have been an alert. His anxiety level rises.

"A while back," Kota says. He thinks a second and wonders if he should even say anything, but he continues on with caution. "He pulled Carol over and then busted up the vehicle and took her. She turned him into the police, but I don't think anything came of it. That's all I know about that."

"Well, we will have to look into that. Sheriff Tamms was treated and released because he is the sheriff of Rock County. Deputy Trevor, Poot, and Shack are all going into surgery," Deputy Benz tells Kota.

"Well, that's all I know, so I really got to sleep now," Kota says. He is getting tired of the questions and concerned that he has said too much already. He knows nothing will be done about the situation anyway.

"Right, we will go talk to Sam. Thank you for your information," Deputy Benz says. Then leaves the room and goes to see Sam.

Sam comes out of recovery fairly quickly. He is moved up to an ICU room for further monitoring. After Sam has been up in the room for an hour or so, Deputy Benz shows up.

Deputy Benz walks into the room like he owned the place. He walks slowly but steadily, like someone sneaking in to a meeting when they come in late, up to the foot of Sam's bed. He says almost in a whisper, "Mr. Kelley, my name is Cal Benz. I am with the deputy sheriff from Augusta County. I have spoken with your wife and brother. I need to ask you a few questions. Do you feel up to this right now?"

Sam is half-asleep. He is tired not from the anesthesia but from late nights of working and worrying. He says in a raspy, dry voice, "Yes, I am fine. I'm still a little groggy but I'll answer anything I can."

"When did you get to the hospital?" Deputy Benz asks.

"I have no idea. Sometime this morning," Sam says.

"Why did you come in at that time in the morning?" Deputy Benz asks. "Do you normally come in at that time?"

Sam is a little puzzled by the question, and then it comes to him that Benz is asking about the equine hospital. Sam says, "Sorry, I didn't know you were talking about my hospital."

Benz smirks a little and then asks again, "When did you get to *your* hospital and is that a normal time you show up?"

"About five thirty in the morning," Sam says, "and no, not unless I have an emergency. This morning Bud, my other brother, called me and said there was a lot of people running around outside. Dakota was not answering his phone. So since I am one of the owners of the hospital, I came in to find out what was going on."

"When you got there, did you try to find out who was in charge?" Deputy Benz asks in a more interrogating voice. "How did you determine that something was going wrong? They were dressed in police uniforms and that should not alarm you, should it?"

Sam started not to like Benz's tone. He figures Benz is trying to trip him up and confess to something. That is why Benz is asking a lot of questions at once. He knows that later Benz will ask the questions again one at a time, and if the answers don't match, then they will think it's a lie. Sam knew about police interrogation techniques. This interview is not his first rodeo.

"Why the hell would people in police uniforms be running around my hospital at five thirty in the morning not alarm me?" Sam really is not asking but more sarcasm. He asks in a stern tone, "If they were running around your place at that time, wouldn't you be alarmed?" Sam is starting to get a little upset.

Deputy Benz says snidely, "Well, I don't think that would happen to me. No one has any reason to come and raid my place."

"So what the hell are you really getting to? Are you accusing me of something?" Sam asks with a little anger in his voice.

"Well, right now I am just trying to find out what happened to set this all in motion. A gang of people don't normally raid a vet clinic and try to destroy the place and the people that are there," Deputy Benz says in a defensive tone.

"When I got there, the first person I saw coming outside from the reception area, I went up to ask him who was in charge. He immediately drew his weapon, a .357, and fired a shot." Sam is almost yelling. "In self-defense I took his weapon away from him before he killed someone. Then he got pissed off and pulled a knife on me, so we had to knock him out. Now you tell me what cops carry a .357 pistol and a Ka-Bar military knife?"

"It is not normal equipment for any one of the state police, but the county makes their own rules." Deputy Benz looks down at his table and keeps writing. "What happened after that?"

"Bud and I went to look for Dakota. We found him beat up in the hayshed. There were nine guys in the shed. I recognized three of them right away. One was Sheriff Tamms who kidnapped my wife and tried to rape her, the orange-haired guy that we saw at the gun range. He and his gang tried to kill us there. Then there was the rapist Deputy Trevor. Soon as I asked them what they were doing, they all started drawing weapons," Sam says.

"Well, two of those are in the hospital now. Can you explain why you didn't call the police as soon as you noticed something was wrong?" The officer asks but he already knows the answer.

"I really didn't have time. I had to defend myself or to be killed. We had someone call soon as we knew it was safe," Sam says.

"Well, it seems you overdefended yourself. Don't you think you were a little excessive? You could be arrested for assaulting an officer. But for right now, we are going to gather all the facts and we may be seeing you soon. Now why do you think they were there?" the officer asks calmly.

"I don't know why they were there at that time. Why don't you arrest the bastard Trevor that shot me and those guys for destroying my hospital and for beating up my brother! As a matter of fact, I think I will call the TV station and see if they want a good story." Sam is mad again. He had calmed down, but when someone talks about arresting him, he just doesn't take kindly to that kind of threat.

"I would advise you to keep this out of the media. If you choose to do that, we may have to take legal action against you," Deputy Benz says in a snide and threatening manner. "Now I suggest you seek legal counsel and get healed up. We will be seeing you soon."

"Is that a threat?" Sam asks. He didn't like the snide attitude Deputy Benz has taken. Sam thinks, "They always try to make you think you did something wrong. I really don't have much use for police of any kind. They have never done anything to help him out when he was younger and needed help. I know they are needed, but I really don't need them. I will handle everything myself. Shit, do any police ever pull you over to tell you how good you were driving or come around and tell you how much they appreciate you being a good citizen? Never! They are there to fine you or throw you in jail. Fuck this, as soon as I'm out of this bed, those assholes that came up to my place will surely regret that their Mom and Dad ever had sex."

"No, that is not a threat," Deputy Benz says as he is a little taken aback by Sam's response. "We, ah, may just have a few more questions so we may be back that is all."

"Well then, have a good day," Sam says abruptly like he is dismissing Deputy Benz.

"Yes, good day," Deputy Benz says as he turns and leaves the room.

Sam shifts around in his bed to get comfortable. He takes a drink of water and falls asleep. He sleeps for a few hours until a nurse comes in and wakes him up. He gets out of his bed, and she offers him a wheelchair. Sam declines the wheelchair and says to the nurse, "I need to walk and stretch my legs. I am not used to lying around this long."

The nurse says, "It is hospital policy that we use a wheelchair to transport patients. I will walk with you with the wheelchair so if you get tired or dizzy, you can sit down."

Sam stands up and he is a little unstable at first but as he moves, he is fine. The nurse brings him up to Kota's room. "Dakota, are you doing OK?" Sam asks. Sam is excited and worried at the same time.

"I'll be all right," Kota says.

"Sorry I wasn't there earlier. I am the one that should have gotten hurt, not you," Sam says almost apologizing.

"I'll be all right! Damn, Sam! You didn't know that they would come. I should have been paying more attention to the cars that came up. They just came up so fast that I didn't even see them until they had jumped out of the car and were on top of me immediately. Someone came up behind me when I was arguing with the sheriff. I didn't have a chance after that." Kota is more upset with himself than anything else.

"You did great. You're still alive and I am very happy about that. I can't even explain to you what I felt when I saw you lying there. I just hope you forgive me." Sam is almost crying.

"Nothing to forgive. We'll both heal up and start everything again," Kota says.

"Cool," Sam says. After that, Sam greets his parents and sister. They all talk for a while. Later that night Carol, Bud, and Luke come up to visit. They all talk about the day. It is almost like a family reunion.

CHAPTER TEN

THE BROTHERS FLY THEIR FAMILIES to South Dakota for Christmas and New Year's. They have a huge party that hundreds of people, old friends, acquaintances, and family attendants. Dakota heals up well and Sam has healed well but still has his arm in a sling. Everyone has fun. After what the three brothers and Carol had gone through, this was a well-needed vacation. This vacation was the first time all three brothers and the extended families had been together. For the first time, Carol's mother and father go to South Dakota.

"I have never been anywhere that it has been this cold out. It has to be ten below outside," Mark says as he looks out the window at the convention hall at the Holiday Inn.

"Oh, you get used to it. If you live her long enough you just learn to live with it." Darrell (the brother's father) says with a little chuckle. Darrell thinks, "Everyone says that. Toughen up a bit."

"I really don't want to live with it. It is just uncomfortable to live here. Does the wind ever quit here?" Mark asks.

"Oh, at night it usually stops and on a clear night you can see all the stars in the sky. It's beautiful and at the same time shows you just how small we all really are," Darrell says. He stands there drinking a beer and looking out the window.

"Yes, but you can see stars in places where it is warm all the time," Mark says.

"Yeah, but this is home and you live here long enough it will make you tough. There is not much you can't endure. There aren't many places that get as hot and humid or as cold," Darrell says assertively.

"Well, I can see your point, but don't you think it would be good to live where it's a little warmer in your later years? I know I do," Mark says in a salesman-like manner.

"Well, I can't leave HERE!" Darrell exclaims. "I've lived here all my life."

"Why don't you just move out with Sam and come back here in the summer?" Mark asks.

"I can't afford to do that. We are lucky that we can get to see the boys once a year. We don't have that kind of money for two places, and I know the boys don't have that kind of money," Darrell explains.

"Oh, I think they just came into some money lately. I bet they could probably set you up if you asked them," Mark says.

"Where did they get that at?" Darrell asks, puzzled by Mark's remarks. "Is Sam's business doing that well?"

"He does well, but I know they just ran into some extra money. You should probably ask them," Mark says as he is taking the last swallow of his drink. He lifts his glass like he is examining it to make sure no more drink is in the glass. He tells Darrell, "Going to get another, can I get you one?"

"Oh, sure, I'll have a beer," Darrell says and then swirls the beer around in the bottle. He walks over to some other people to see if he can strike up a conversation.

Sam is making his way through the crowd with Carol in hand. He has talked to just about everyone there, but he had to drag Carol along to meet people. Carol is never much for small talk or holding conversations with people she doesn't know. Sam can talk to anyone about nothing for hours. He got the gift of gab from his dad.

"Hello, folks, are you having a good time?" Sam asks some people that he vaguely remembers seeing a long time ago.

"Well, we are having a great time. I think that your mom and dad really enjoy having everyone home for Christmas. Last Christmas we all went out to your folks' house. And they just couldn't keep from talking about all you kids," one of the ladies in the group says to Sam.

"That's my mom!" Sam says with some sarcasm. "She loves to have company over and loves to bake. If more people were like her, America wouldn't be in such rough shape."

"Yeah, but Mr. Barrack will get us out of this mess in a big hurry and we won't even have to pay our own rent by the time he gets done," the lady says in a sweet but naive older lady voice.

"Sorry, but that guy is a big crook," Sam says in slightly harsh tone. "He's a radical, a socialist that has never done anything."

"I can't believe you would say something like that about our president. Bush is the liar. All he wanted was to start a war and make a lot of money. He has been ruining the economy by all the wars and giving those corporations money. He made it easy for the rich people and we older poor folks just stay poor," the lady says in an angry voice.

"Mamma, you are grossly misinformed," Sam says sternly. "The war is more about control in the Middle East in order to keep track of Iran. They say there are weapons of mass destruction. They probably just have not told anyone about what they found because you people wouldn't believe it anyways. All the world's intelligent agents say it is there and they can't all be wrong. Bush did not start the war himself. Congress voted on it. He is not a king. As for the economy, it is people that bought homes and other things that they could not afford. The banks were pushed to loan money to those people by OCORC and the Democrats control the house and senate. Now John Barrack will drive this nation in to socialism. He is an extreme radical, whose friends are extreme radical socialists. You will see in about a year or so. Then come see me so I can say I told you so." Sam didn't give a shit if he makes this woman mad. He remembers her now—"She and her family are freeloaders that hang out at mom and dad's house. They are the ones that lived in grandma and grandpa's old place. They go over to his mom and dad's place two to three times a week to eat. Sometimes they show up at breakfast and stay through supper."

"You're just one of those rich people. We don't have the money and easy life like you, Mr. Big Shot Doctor," the lady says in a sassy, angry voice.

"I came from here, just like you all did. I have to and still do work my butt off on a daily basis. I just don't wait around for scraps that are thrown away by others," Sam says in a stern voice.

"I don't wish to speak to you anymore. Your mother spoke so highly of you, but you have forgotten where you come from," the lady says.

"Say what you will, but my freedom and livelihood comes from what my family and I do. Not from what someone or a government is willing to let me have. I take what is mine. I protect my family and friends, no matter what. Will you ever be able to say the same?" Sam asks. The woman just turns and walks away. Her face is beet red and she is mad as hell. Sam just shrugs. "I wish the rest of you a fun night," Sam says to the others around him. Sam and Carol walk away from the little group. Carol is a little embarrassed by Sam's comments, but she knows how he feels. She knows he would never back down unless he knew he is wrong. She has tried to shut him up before, but it never works. Now she just stands behind him.

Carol ventures off on her own to talk to some of Sam's old high school mates. Bud and Kota are making their rounds around the room talking to everyone like they have known them all their lives. There is an open bar, so around midnight many of the people are getting fairly snockered. The band, whose bass player was a guy that worked with Sam in the construction business, is playing until 2:00 a.m. Most people are dancing, drinking, or talking. Sam goes over to talk to his dad. They never really ever talked much. But in the last few years, his dad started calling him just to talk.

"So did ya get enough to drink and eat?" Sam asks his dad and hands him a beer.

"Oh yeah, plenty to eat," Darrell says and set his other beer down so he can take the one Sam just gave to him.

"It's pretty cold out tonight. Good thing we had the party inside," Sam says with a little laugh.

"Well, we wouldn't have had it outside anyway, would you?" Darrell always did that when Sam is trying to joke with him.

"No, Dad, I'm joking," Sam says and looks at his dad like he is nuts.

"Yeah, but I bet the bar bill would have been cheaper if it was outside," Darrell says jokingly.

"Ha, yeah, it would." Sam gives a chuckle. He looks at his beer bottle and swirls the beer around. He says, "And I don't think everyone would have fit in the house."

"No, no, they wouldn't. Do you guys still live in the same house? How big is that house anyway?" Darrell asks Sam.

"Yeah, we still live in the same crappy house. It's cold in the winter and hot in the summer. It needs a lot of remodeling, but I don't have time. Maybe this spring we will be able to put up a house or remodel this one. I just hate to put a lot of money into it. It's not worth anything because it's small and it only has one bathroom. It's smaller than the house we lived in across the road from you," Sam explains.

"Mark said that you've run into some money. Why don't you use that to fix up the house?" Darrell starts swirling his beer bottle. He is uncomfortable even trying to ask his son where the money came from. He doesn't think that Sam is doing anything illegal, but he wants to know without asking.

"Got too many bills. If things go good this spring, I can probably build," Sam explains.

"Where did you run into some money? Maybe I can run into some?" Darrell asks Sam but doesn't look at him. Darrell puts his bottle down on the table sticks his hands into his pockets.

"Dad, you have money. We sent up a fund for you and mom and Gina. You know about that, don't you? You can do whatever you want with the money," Sam explains.

"I didn't know that came from you," Darrell says with a surprise, and then he tries to downplay his excitement by saying, "I don't need any money. I don't have anything that I need."

"Dad! You and Mom are supposed to use that money so you can pay bills and go on vacation whenever you want. You can visit us when you want. You can move some place warm for the winter. Hire some more help with the farm and not work so hard." Sam looks up from his beer bottle, knowing his dad is being curious about where the money come from, but he isn't ready to tell any more people.

Sam thought, "Dad really doesn't give a shit about where the money comes from, nor does he care about the money. He probably doesn't even remember about the money. Gina probably told him but he wasn't really listening, kind of like he always does when you tell him something important. I'm glad we only rationed it out because he would just buy a bunch of junk but never spend it fixing up the place. Glad we hire the people to go out and work for the place."

"I didn't know we had that much money," Darrell says in a thankful way but not coming out really saying it. "We got enough people working out there right now. Those guys are hard workers," Darrell says.

"It's not my money, it's everyone's money. Bud, Dakota, and I are just in charge of it," Sam says.

"Oh, well, that's good. Who's running the clinic while you are gone?" Darrell asks but not really caring to know the answer.

"I hired another guy to clean stalls and take care of some of the stuff Bud and Dakota are doing. I also hired another surgeon because I hurt my shoulder, and I wanted to spend some time on other things," Sam explains as if in passing. He then looks his beer over as if looking for an exit from a conversation that will go nowhere, he asks, "You want another beer?"

"Yeah, I'll take another one," Darrell says unenthusiastically.

Sam looks over to the bar and waits for the bartender to look over at him. Then he raises his arm and two fingers. The bartender nods and immediately brings over two beers. Sam thanks him and the bartender goes back to wait on people at the bar.

"You should come back and see what we done at the farm," Sam tells his dad, then takes a swallow of beer. He leans up against the wall.

"I knew you were working on something, but you guys got it done now, huh?" Darrell asks, then takes a drink of his beer.

"We got DH, you remember him, to do the project. He and Bud set up everything and got it done in no time. We put a pool for horses and an indoor lameness and rehab area. It should be completely done by the time we get back home. We also put in a huge cistern that will hold enough water to fill ten Olympic-size swimming pools. And I put in a bunker," Sam excitedly tells his dad.

"I can't leave now. I got to do chores and I got to sell some horses next week." Darrell gives an excuse. Darrell is always worried about doing chores even though there are plenty of people to do them if he left.

"Dad, you got two guys who work for you to do anything you want them to do. You got Rick building stuff along with a bunch of guys. You got nothing that you need to do except what you want to do, and you can do it when you want to do it. If you don't have enough land to run horses on, we will buy some more before we go," Sam explains in a pleading way.

"Well, we will have to ask your mother first, she might have to work." Darrell always has an excuse not to leave. Just then Bud, Kota, and Elaine (the brother's mom) comes up.

A moderately drunk Kota says, "Let's all go out to dance. You guys need to grab your girls and go dance."

Sam seizes the opportunity to get a final answer from his mother and father. He asks Elaine, "Mom, will you and Dad come back with us. Dad thinks you guys are too busy to come out and see what we done to the place."

"I might have to work next week and I have to cook for the guys that are working on the farm. We are really too busy," Elaine says.

"Mom, you do not have to cook for anyone and you can just quit your job. You don't need to do that stuff, but if you don't want to come out, you don't have to. You can come out later," Sam says. He is a little upset, but he will get over it like he always does.

"I think that would be better, but for now we are going to have fun," Elaine says and grabs his hand and they goes out to dance.

After the holidays, things at the hospital start getting back to normal. The whole office area and lab is remodeled, and all the equipment has to be replaced. One ambulatory vehicle and Bud's vehicle was covered by insurance, but they only covered part of it. The hospital ended up paying for most of both vehicles. Bud got a new truck and the hospital got a new Yukon. Business begins to pick up early this year compared to last few years. Sam and Carol decide the reason is due to all the news coverage or they are just getting popular because of the new rehab and lameness center. The breeding season for horses is in shambles because of the poor horse prices. Sam is working every day, and the new doctor is picking up the slack, such as a lot of the emergencies. Sam in his off hours starts to work on his little projects such as his new line of horse products. Deputy Benz has been back several times to question Sam and his brothers. He usually asks the same questions. They all think that he comes out just to drink coffee and talk to the women technicians.

"I want to know what happened to the weapon that shot those men in the chest," Deputy Benz asks. "None of them died, but they were wearing bulletproof vest. It could be considered attempted murder, but we are not going to press charges at this time. Now where did the weapons go and where did it come from?"

"Wait right there," Sam says as he is getting into his interrogation mode. "Did you actually find more bodies or men that attacked us up here or are you asking because someone told you that is what happened?"

"No!" Deputy Benz says. He is a little taken aback by the reverse interrogation. "No, we didn't find any more men or bodies. We are just going by what Sheriff Cecil Tamms told us."

Sam snort laughs and asks, "You actually believe that piece of shit? Did you ask him about the kidnapping and how he about trying to kill his own father?"

Deputy Benz feels like a cornered chicken; he either gets caught or makes a run for it. He says, "Well, I am just trying to get to the bottom of things. I feel no one is telling the whole truth. I'll just leave and you can think about it and the contact me when something comes to you." He gets up from the chair he is sitting and picks up his cup of coffee.

Sam starts feeling a little sorry for the guy but only a little. Maybe if he just tells the whole story, then they will quit hanging around. Sam motions Deputy Benz to sit back down and says, "Just sit down," he says in a calm voice. "If you really want to listen, I can tell you all that I know but you cannot record it."

Deputy Benz sits back down and takes a gulp of coffee. He tells Sam, "I'm not going to record anything, so tell away."

Sam explains, "I don't know where the .357 went to. I was shot, remember? The weapon came from the son of a bitch that tried to shoot me out front here. I took it away from him along with his knife. He fired a round or two at me and my brother before we got the weapon away from him. We also knew that they all were wearing vests, and by hitting them in the breastplate, they were in no way in danger of getting killed, so you can take your attempted murder and stick it up your ass."

"OK, then," Deputy Benz says. "We should have the weapon to finish up this investigation."

"I don't know why you need the weapon," Sam says in a calm voice. "Maybe they took it with them when they all left. If there are no bodies and no one to report a shooting, then there was no gun."

"Well, the sheriff and his men that were in the hospital told us that you guys took the first shots. They do admit that they were rough on Dakota, but that is all." Deputy Benz defends the questioning.

"I don't care what they admit to or say, they are the ones that attacked us first," Sam says. "We just got the hospital back together again, and they say that they were the only ones here." Sam knows what is going to happen; he always has a sixth sense when people are about to tell him something he doesn't want to hear. He would get this tightness in his stomach and in the middle of his head. Most of the time he ignored it, but he is always dead on when the news came.

"So we have been given orders to not investigate the sheriff and his men. They have promised not to come around and harass anyone here. Right now we don't have any evidence against them that it was not self-defense on their part." Deputy Benz looks down at his feet, knowing he is lying and ashamed of it.

"You are letting them go. Shit, they just about killed my brother, what about that? Who the hell is giving you orders?" Sam asks.

"Well, Dakota will be compensated through your workers' compensation and the courts also ordered that the Deputy Trevor pay a fine. Dakota will also be compensated by Rock County a sum of ten thousand dollars if he signs papers to not sue the county." Deputy

Benz looks up at Sam's eyes. Sam could see that Deputy Benz knows this is all crap, but there is nothing he could do about it.

"What a load of shit. Tell me, what are you going to do when these guys come back here and try to finish what they started?" Sam asks sternly. "Did you ever find out what they were doing here in the first place?"

"They are on a restraining order not to come within two hundred yards of here. They cannot even pull you or anyone that is associated with this place, over for a speeding ticket," Deputy Benz informs Sam. "Now, they said that they had dropped a package out of their car a while back and they were just trying to retrieve it."

"Do you really believe that the restraining order is going to do anything?" Sam asks. "And do you really believe them about any of that?" Sam is so irritated that the answer didn't matter.

"Between you and me, no, but I am taking orders from higher up, so that is that," Deputy Benz says in an apologetic manner. He then gets up and starts out the door.

"I guess I will be seeing you in a little while when these guys come back," Sam says as Deputy Benz is walking out.

"I hope I don't have to come back for something like this again," Deputy Benz says with concern as he is walking out the door.

Sam calls his brothers, Carol, Marsha, Bill, and DH in for a little meeting for that night. Everyone meets in their new hideaway. The new hideaway is well lit and can hold several people comfortably. It is well stocked with food, water, alcohol, tools, computers, and monitors from cameras at various places on the farm. There is a filtered airflow system, small treatment area, and much, much more. The place would make any CEO of a Fortune 500 company to be envious.

Everyone comes in and sits on the couches. Sam comes in and gets a beer from the refrigerator. He then passes them out to those that want one.

"The reason I want to have this meeting with you all is one: we are the only ones that know that this place is a new little hide out or a get away from it all. You all know about the cave and the stuff we found down there. We need to keep this place a secret and I mean a *secret*. Secondly, the artifacts we took to the archaeologist were found to be those from some Spanish warrior dated somewhere around the late fourteen hundreds or earlier. Some of other stuff is from the Native American tribes that were nomadic in this area. The archaeologist wants to come in and mark the area, then look for more artifacts," Sam informs everyone. "So I need to give her an answer on that stuff. Last but not least, the shitheads that attacked Kota may be back, but I will let Kota tell us about what has come about with that. Deputy Benz visited Kota and I today. They still want a .357, but it really doesn't matter now." Sam cracks open a beer and chugs it down then opens another.

Kota takes a drink of his beer then clears his throat. "They let the assholes go. They have to give me some money and pay a fine, but that is it. Somehow, they got let go and the cop told me that they are not pressing charges against me, but they are still looking in to Sam case. They never mentioned Bud at all."

Sam jumps and interrupts. "Benz came in again today and told me that there were no real charges for anyone. He also told me that it is coming from a higher up and that he has to drop the case on them. He wouldn't tell me who, but maybe he really didn't know." Sam takes another big drink and then sits back in the couch.

"So do you think that they will come back or do you think they are done?" DH asks Sam.

"Oh, I am pretty sure that they will be back, so I think that we need to be ready for them this time. I want to hire another person to be here with Kota at night. I don't think that anyone should be alone until the jerks stop coming around. I don't know when that will be, but there will be an end sometime," Sam says.

"Well, what about during the day? Do we dare let anyone go out by themselves on farm calls?" Marsha asks with concern.

"I am not too worried about the day, but we should always have two go out and not just one. We have enough people now so that shouldn't be a problem," Sam says with authority. "Carol, that goes for you also! You should have a tech or an assistant go with you.

Mostly, I think they will be trying to sneak at night or try to get us at home."

DH jumps in on the conversation and starts laughing. "I'll be ready for the sons of bitches. I got some lead that will stop them just short of the door." He has already had a couple of rum and Cokes.

"That's great, but you got to know they are coming first and you need to get the jump on them. I think we should all get alarm systems put in our houses, and I don't mean those cheap-ass alarms," Sam says. "Here, I think we need to put up perimeter sensors and outer perimeter cameras. DH and Bud, I want you guys to get after that and make sure everyone's house gets fitted up also. Maybe call Closed Circuit and Thomas can get it all fixed up." Sam chugs his beer down. He gets up and takes another one out of the refrigerator.

"We'll get after that tomorrow, if that is all right with you, DH?" Bud says.

Sam comes back and sits down on the couch. Carol gives him the evil eye, which means that she thinks that he has enough to drink. Sam just wrinkles his nose and opens the beer can. Sam inquires, "What do you think we should do about the archeologist?"

"I think we should let them come in and look the cave over," Carol says.

"I think they can just stay the hell out of the cave. Do we even own that place yet?" Bud asked.

"We will close on the property, I think next week. Carol, do you know when that is going to take place?" Sam asks.

"Yes, we got to go in next week and sign the papers. We bought it through a new company name and all of us will own it. If you leave the group, you leave the property and you get nothing. I brought the papers for everyone to sign, so before you leave, make sure you sign the papers. Otherwise, you are left out," Carol informs everyone and then she starts pulling papers out of her computer case.

"Anyone else got a comment on whether we let them into the cave or not?" Sam asks.

"If they come in and find all this stuff, then they will get the cave involved into some stupid program. We will never get to use it," Kota states. "There will be people snooping around here all the time.

I think they can just stay the hell out. We can just encase the area so we don't disturb it if we find something."

"I would like to see if there are any dead or buried people here. If there is, then I'm not going to use the place. There will be ghosts," Sam says and everyone laughs except for Sam. Sam believes in ghosts and had a couple of times felt the presence of a ghost. He isn't joking. "How about we let one or two of them in with the agreement they can document everything, but they will be under direct supervision at all times. They cannot go up into the entrance that connects to this place. That way, they can get the crap out of the cave and tell us if anyone is buried down there. What do you think of that?"

"I think that is a great idea. Let's vote. All in favor of Sam's idea raise your hand," Carol says. Everyone raises their hands.

"OK, I'll call her tomorrow. Kota, I'm going to have you supervise, so you won't be working at night when they start their stuff. Carol will have to get a night person for that time. Anyone have anything else?" Sam asks.

"Yeah, we need to turn that TV on and get some more drinks," DH says. "I think I'll just stay here for the night." DH gets up and makes another drink. Then he flips on the TV. Marsha and Carol get up and go back into the hospital. The brothers stay awhile and then go home.

The next morning, Carol and Sam go to see Terri Logan about Carol's kidnapping. Terri has been working on the case. She is supposed to have information of when the court case is going to take place. Carol and Sam first stop at their accountant's office to drop off the last quarters accounts. Then they go on to Terri's office.

"Oh, hello, doctors. You are right on time," Caroline Gimble says in a kindly manner. "Terri is waiting for you. You can go right on in."

"Thank you, Caroline. Did you have a good Christmas?" Sam asks.

"Yes, the whole family was there. We had so much fun. How was your Christmas?" Caroline gets out of her chair and knocks on Terri's office door.

"The best I have had in years, thanks," Sam says.

"I enjoyed Christmas this year. This is the biggest Christmas I have ever had," Carol says.

"Carol and Sam, please, come on in." Terri walks up to the door and shakes hands with both of them. Terri greets both of them. "Please have a seat."

"How are you doing?" Carol asks. Sam doesn't say much; he can feel it in his gut that Terri doesn't have anything that they want to hear. Sam thinks, "This is like going to the principal's office, nothing is going to be good."

"I am doing well, and how have you been doing? I know you went through such a traumatic event. You must be a very strong woman," Terri says to Carol with a fake sense of concern in her voice and on her face. "Well, here is what I have for you."

"I just need to know when the court date is so I can get things scheduled," Carol says reading through Terri's fake "I give a shit" attitude.

"We don't have a court date," Terri informs Carol with exasperation. "There will never be a court date. Neither Sheriff Tamms nor Deputy Trevor will be arrested or even appear in court. They are untouchable." This time Terri has a real frustrated look on her face.

"Why the hell is that?" Carol screams at Terri. "That bastard kidnapped me and was going to rape me. The only reason I'm here is because Sam came and got me."

Terri explains with some anxiety. "I brought the case in front of the district attorney and he started pushing the case through but it suddenly stopped. I called him and I was told that the case would not go to trial and there would not be any charges filed. I asked him why and he said he was under strict orders directly from Governor Kane not to interfere in the sheriff's business." Terri leans into her desk and then runs her fingers through her hair. She grabs her hair in frustration. "I sent my private detective out to find out what is happening, so as soon as I get any information, I will call you. Do you have anything else that I can do for you?"

"No, I just don't understand how these jerks keep getting away with everything," Carol says with a lot of anger but is not screaming anymore. "The deputy sheriff had to let everyone go that destroyed our hospital and just about killed Sam's brother. Someone high up is running this and we need to find out. Maybe we should look up the line more."

"I think we will just deal with it. My brothers and I will take care of it," Sam says calmly. "Terri, you can continue to do your thing and we can meet somewhere in the middle. Thank you." Sam gets up and then holds out his hand for Carol. Sam helps her to her feet. They both say goodbye and then go on home. On the way home, Sam just listens and doesn't say a word while a very upset Carol rants about everything. He knows saying anything would not help. She just has to get it all out. When they get back to the hospital, Sam tells Carol, "We will fix this problem and get to the bottom of all this crap. That sheriff will pay dearly one way or another. I thought I had him that night when he trashed the place, but next time, he will not get away with anything."

"I know you will fix everything." Carol gives Sam a kiss and they both go back to work.

Chapter Eleven

BARRACK TAKES OFFICE OF THE president in January; he spends three hundred million dollars on his inaugural party and all the doings. He has celebrities of all kinds singing and giving long heartfelt supporting speeches. About two million people show up at the inauguration; most of them are drones that are bused in by OCORC with taxpayer money. Barrack's most spectacular part is that he cannot be officially sworn in because he refuses to repeat the proper order of the pledge. In his speech, he swears that he is going to change government and make it very transparent, fix the budget, and make corruption and waste disappear. He is going to "change America." All the drones stand and cheer. Many of the people that are interviewed after the inaugural dress tell reporters, "I'll never have to worry about my mortgage, and I will not have to worry about paying bills." Many people soak up Barrack's rhetoric and believe he is the new chosen one to save America and its people. Barrack believes he isn't he great and powerful messiah.

Sam watches the inauguration as if it is the end of America as he knows it. Sam is stuck working at a horse show. He is sitting down in the break room of the coliseum, drinking coffee and talking with Ike, the emergency medical technician, and Smitty, the farrier.

Sam says to himself out loud, "That Barrack is too big of a crook to be the leader of America. He is going to try to make this the socialist republic of America. Just you mark my words. This economy is going to hit an all-time low with massive bankruptcies and small businesses and big businesses closing. There is going to be massive unemployment and taxes going through the roof—not only that but the government will want to take the roof."

"You got to at least give him a chance," Ike refutes the statement. "I think that he was dealt a bad hand. He's got quite a job to clean up after Bush."

"What the hell are you talking about?" Sam exclaims. "President Bush did a wonderful job. Everyone that wanted a job had a job. We could feel safe and business was good."

"That son of a bitch lied to everyone," Ike says brazenly, "and he started a war that we have no business being in."

"What did he lie about exactly?" Sam asks.

"He said there were weapons of mass destruction in Iraq and there is none," Ike tells Sam like he is a kid in an argument that he can't win. He is also to get Sam riled up.

"When are you darn liberals going to quit spreading the same damn rhetoric around? Bush is only one man, congress voted on the war, and all the world's intelligent agencies all said that there were biological weapons there." Sam is riled up but not mad. "Saddam Hussein used the weapons against his own people." He knows that liberals like Ike couldn't help themselves for being ignorant.

"He lied and it cost us a lot of money. He caused this recession," Ike says but really just wanted someone to blame. "This last year, the banks went bankrupt because of him. If he wouldn't have caused the war, banks would have had more money. I can't sell my house because of him."

"Once again it is the Democrat Barry Frank, who was supposed to overlook the banks and their policies. OCORC and their cronies made banks loan money to people that didn't even have jobs so that everyone could have a house, a big-screen TV, and a new car. Ah, the American dream," Sam informs Ike. Sam is growing tired of talking politics especially with someone that has no knowledge of any facts.

"It's all Bush's fault and Barrack is going to fix it all. He promised that there is not going to be government waste, and no one will have to worry about jobs and paying for health care," Ike says in an almost whining fashion. "That is the way it should be and it will be.

This country should pay for health care it can afford it." Ike loves the fact the government is going to try to pay for health care.

"Who do you think will pay for it? The government doesn't make money. Everyone that makes money will have to pay for it," Sam tries to explain. "Besides, you may just lose your job to make room for a younger more productive model, especially if you get sick."

"The government has lots of money. They should pay for it like they do in Canada and Europe. We won't have to pay for a thing," Ike says and then leans back in his seat.

"How the hell did you become an EMT? Did they brainwash you in EMT school or were you this stupid all on your own?" Sam asks sarcastically.

"You're such an arrogant asshole, not everyone is as rich as you. We all can't afford the luxuries of life like you." Ike gives his ranting sermon much like the lady at the Christmas party. "Most people cannot afford doctors, a house, a car, and food. They have to make choices to what they want most. You doctors are way overpaid."

"That's me! Living high on the hog. I pay twenty-five hundred dollars a month for student loans. I live in an old house that is a piece of crap. I work about a hundred hours a week and barely have enough money to pay for the rest of my bills. I don't go to the doctor unless I am on the verge of death or a broken leg. I give my employees all that the hospital can afford, and I live on almost nothing. I give my family all that I can afford and ask nothing in return. Where do you get off calling me arrogant and rich? I work for a living. I started with nothing, and no one gives me anything except a hard time. That's more than I can say for you." Sam is now getting upset. "Don't you live in a three-thousand-square-foot house in the suburbs? You don't even pay for your health insurance and I'm sure you have a paid pension, don't you?"

"Well, that is beside the point. It's people like you that make the government make businesses have to pay for things. You wouldn't give your employees anything if they didn't make you," Ike says.

"Bullshit, my employees get as much as I can give them. The government doesn't give anything, they just take. They will take more and more, then they waste it on bureaucratic waste projects and administration fees." Sam takes out his can of Copenhagen and takes a chew. It usually calms him down.

"Barrack is going to fix all of that. He is the hope that we have all been waiting for to come to the government. He knows how to fix this crappy economy. You just wait and see." Ike sees Sam take a chew and curls up his nose. "That stuff is not good for you. It will probably kill you."

"We'll see, but mark my words, in one year when we are both sitting here, I will be saying I told you so. I got to go and look at some horses, you have a great day." Sam leaves and goes to the stall barn to look at a couple of horses with coughs. Sam thinks, "Me being an 'arrogant asshole.' I am a surgeon. If I was arrogant, then this would be far beneath me."

After the show was over at eleven o'clock at night, Sam goes back to the hospital and checks on the other horses before he goes home to bed. He has to be back at the show grounds by seven in the morning to help measure ponies.

Several weeks go by and President Barrack goes right to work after a week of partying at the White House. He and his wife host parties every Wednesday at the White House for celebrities and others who gave him a lot of money for his campaign. His cabinet, he makes up is full of left-wing radicals and some are convicted felons. Many of his newly announced cabinet members have years of outstanding unpaid taxes. Some of his cabinet members are fired just because they have brought on some much criticism. With all this, Barrack's cronies (the undying supporters) still tote him as the new messiah.

Barrack and his armament of a liberal-filled congress and senate go right to work changing America. Their first order of business is to make sure that those groups that help get them all elected get paid. Unions, OCORC, and businessmen that gave thousands of dollars all get money or a new government jobs. Barrack gets his so-called stimulus package passed without a single opposition from the Democrats but total opposition from the Republicans. The stimulus package is filled with more than nine thousand earmarks for pet projects and payoffs. Five billion goes to OCORC, twenty billion goes to saving some rat in Nancy Pelosi's district, and on and on. It only costs the taxpaying public about a trillion dollars and then comes the government takeover of General Motors. They take the car company away from the shareholders and tell them that their stock is no longer worth anything. Then the car company is given to the auto union. All the stockholders lose every dime they have invested into the company. Some have millions of dollars of their retirement invested and lose it all. All of this is Barrack's idea to "save or create jobs and spur the economy."

Barrack is on television every day to tell America how great of a job he is doing. "I inherited a mess from failed policies over the last eight years. I won't fix this mess overnight, but it just didn't happen overnight. My plans and policies will save and create three million jobs. Unemployment under my plan will not go above eight percent. We will help new businesses and entrepreneurs create new jobs. The world will respect the United States again. We will do this by reforming health care that is plaguing small businesses and the middle class. Green energy with carbon dioxide controls in place in the form of cap-and-trade is needed to bring new jobs to help thousands of Americans. There will be more job creation in this year's budget. This budget is going to be a little expensive, but it is an investment into America. We are going to spend more so that we can save money and give middle-income families a long-earned tax breaks. In the long run, this will create jobs and new opportunities and this will bring back the economy." Blah, blah, blah.

Week after week, it is the same speech on how he is going to make America better and people's lives better through free health care, controlling banks and big businesses, and controlling energy. After congress passes the biggest budget ever and drives the country's debt up to fifteen trillion dollars with a budget deficit of almost two trillion dollars, they went to work on passing a twenty-seven-hundred-page health care plan with thirty thousand new regulations.

Chapter Twelve

Sam gets a call from his friend from grade school, Darwin Arin. "Hello, Darwin, how ya getting along?"

Darwin very sorrowfully says, "Well, not good. My Gladys, she just passed away. Can you come back home and give me a hand? I need some help. Danny has been over here but I need some of your old-time advice."

Sam used to give Darwin all kinds of advice when they were young. Most of it was not worth anything, but Sam always had plenty of it. Darwin always needed someone, but his mother had died a few years ago of congestive heart failure. It hit him fairly hard, but he had his wife, Gladys, to cling to. They had been married for twenty-some years but had no kids.

"Oh my word, I feel so bad for you. I'll try to get a plane ticket out there tomorrow, and if I can't, I will drive out there. You guys were so good for each other," Sam tells Darwin in a sincere way. Sam learned a long time ago never to say, "I'm sorry for your loss." That, to him, meant that he was responsible somehow for whatever happen. If he was responsible and he was sorry for the outcome, then he would say he was sorry. It would be demeaning to the word "sorry" if he just used it all the time.

"I hope you do come. I'll pick you up from the airport if you fly. Call me tomorrow and let me know." Darwin says.

"I'll call you tomorrow either way. In the meantime, go see my mom. I'll call her and let you know that you are coming. She will want to know," Sam instructed.

"Well, I don't want to bother her, she might be busy," Darwin says.

"She is never too busy to see you, and you know you are just like one of her kids. Just go see her. I mean it, Darwin! If you don't go see her, I'm not coming," Sam says as he types on the computer to bring up his schedule for work.

"OK! OK, I'll go over there right away." Darwin is still in a daze.

"She can help you get things started. Now as soon as we get off the phone, I will start making plans, so I'm going to let you go now and call my mom. I'll talk to you later," Sam says in a slow, calm voice like he is talking to a kid.

"OK, talk to you later," Darwin says and then hangs up the phone.

Sam hangs up and calls his mom. She is at home baking bread. Sam tells her about Darwin. Sam says, "I am going to come home and help Darwin out for a few days till he gets himself straightened out. I have to make arrangements first, so I don't know if I am driving or flying. I also told Darwin to come over and see you. You are like a second mom to him, and it sounds like he needs a motherly talk right now."

Darwin is alone now for the first time in his life. His wife just died of complications from an accident. He and his wife had been out riding motorcycles when a drugged, crazed lunatic driving a Cadillac Eldorado hit her from the side at eighty miles an hour. She never made it to the hospital. It took the rescue people four hours to remove her and her motorcycle from the car. They found out the driver of the car was left without a scratch, and he also was a congressman named Bud Jacklow. Darwin saw the whole thing. He was about a one hundred feet behind her on his motorcycle. Congressman Jacklow was not charged with anything except for not stopping at a stop sign. The congressman had over hundred and eighty traffic violations, ranging from speeding, driving while intoxicated, to drug trafficking, but he never served time or even paid a fine. All his crimes had been swept under the rug. When this news came out, it had enraged many people. The news was the trigger that caused Darwin to sink into a deep depression, and that is when he called Sam.

Darwin always keeps up with everyone from grade school and high school. Sam never keeps in touch with anyone. Sam likes Darwin, he is kind of like family, but he just didn't take the time to keep up with anyone from his past. Sam never really had any friends. He is mostly a loner except when it comes to his family, but even more he really doesn't care about most people. Darwin is and never was a popular person in grade school or high school, but then neither was Sam. They were both the quiet and the shy type in school. Both of them are from the farm. Darwin was from a small farm and Sam from a moderate-size farm. Darwin was always a little on the wimpy side, but Sam always got along with him. Sam could actually have an intelligent conversation with Darwin, unlike most of the high schoolers. To both of them, material possessions mean nothing. Both men were raised with very little extras in their lives.

Darwin started to play with computers while they were seniors in high school. Sam recalls that there was one computer in the whole high school at that time. He always regarded it as useless expensive piece of equipment that he would probably never use. Darwin would sit down at that computer and print out pictures in dot matrix. He would do letterhead and other things that no one else in the school could do at that time. After high school, he went on to write software that most of the financial institutions built their software over. He helped develop software for most of the imaging companies that most cities use for their video surveillance. He is still writing software for many large corporations, such as Citibank, AIG, Bank of America, and others. Darwin is like a Mozart of the computer. Darwin finally got married and went to a community college to get a degree in computers, which is very funny since the software that they were studying is based upon Darwin's early designs. Sam always thought that they should just give Darwin an honorary computer doctorate degree and save everyone some time and money.

Money was one thing that Darwin never had all his life. With all his accomplishments, he never got paid what he was worth. One time, Sam and Darwin had to go to Darwin's first employer's house to pick up part of his pay. The guy handed Darwin a bag of change, which amounted to about one hundred dollars. It pissed Sam off so much that he went back that night to the guy's house and tossed him around a bit until the guy came up with another one thousand dollars in cash. By the time Sam was done, the guy was happy to give it up. Sam went over to Darwin's house and gave him the money. Darwin was embarrassed and angry at the same time. He didn't do his job for the money; he did it because he loved it. He was afraid that he would lose his job, but Sam assured him that would never happen. The next day Darwin was made manager of the company.

Darwin's mother had been having heart problems for two or three years. Darwin had been taking care of her for most of those years. He and Gladys had moved in with her because she wouldn't stay in town with them. He paid all her medical expenses and cooked for her. He always said that "It's the least I can do for raising me." Then Darwin's mother died one night. She just went to bed and never woke up. Darwin found her the next morning when he brought her breakfast into her. He was devastated, but Sam gave him some good old advice and he was back on his feet.

Sam just told him, "Dying is as natural as being born. As soon as they slap your behind and you start crying, you start living until you die. Your mother lived her life to the fullest. She was rich in love and never had an ounce of hatred in her heart. You should remember her in greatness and not dwell on death. I'm pretty sure she would want you to live on and reach for everything that you can in life." Darwin took a day to come around but then he was back to normal.

Darwin had a brother, but Sam never had met him. Darwin's brother never was around the farm and he didn't go to the same school as Sam and Darwin. To the best of Sam's knowledge, Darwin's brother wasn't even at the funeral.

Darwin's father was a World War II veteran and fought against the Japanese. His dad was a sharp shooter in the military. After the war, he was a farmer and an inventor. Darwin's dad could make anything that was mechanical. He used to sit around his shop most of the time working on many different things at one time. Sam used to go over and test out some of the inventions. Darwin was sometimes embarrassed that his dad spent so much time working in the shop, but Sam always thought it was a treasure chest of great stuff. Darwin's dad didn't farm a lot of ground, but he raised enough to feed his family and always had some unusual animals at the farm. The farm was sometimes like a zoo, and it was a great change of pace for Sam to go visit.

Sam gets off the plane at the Sioux Falls, South Dakota, airport and it is unseasonably hot. September is usually cooler, but today it just seems hot. Sam is met by his mom and dad at the airport. His mom is all smiles and hugs him like always, but this time, his Dad gives him a hug. This hug is the first time in Sam's life that his dad has ever given him one. Sam's dad had never shown any affection toward any of his kids, but he was always good to them and provided for them. Sam's dad just wasn't raised to show any affection; his father and mother never did, even as grandparents. It bothered Sam some, but he didn't dwell on it.

"How was your flight?" Sam's mom asks with a smile.

"It was fine, it went by fast, and I only had one layover," Sam says.

"We are going to go eat before we go home. Are you hungry?" Sam's mom asks.

"Yeah, that's great. Let's go," Sam says and then grabs his bag of clothes. Then they head out to the parking lot.

Darrell and Elaine always park in the long-term parking lot because it saves them two dollars an hour. They've probably only been there for an hour and it's not like they don't have a lot of money now. They have access to as much money as they would ever need, but they just live like they have all their lives. Darrell is still driving the old broken-down truck that barely starts. There are holes in the seats, covered with a nice blanket that Dad bought at a sale somewhere. The radio is only an AM radio with one central dash speaker. The heater lever is broken, so the heat stays on. The window knob on the passenger side is broken, so a small vise grip was attached to it to roll the window down. The inside door latch is broken off on the driver's side, so you have to roll down the window in order to open the door. All this and they refuse to buy a new pickup.

"Hey, after we eat, I want to go look at some trucks if you guys feel up to it," Sam says with a little apprehension.

"Why, don't they have any trucks out there? I thought you guys have a truck. What do you need another one for?" Sam's Dad asks.

"Oh, we use it for the farm and Bud has been hauling a lot of horses, so when Carol takes the truck to horse shows, Bud can't haul horses. I think it's time we get another one and we can probably get a better deal here then out there." Sam lies a little.

"Well, what kind of truck you want to get?" Elaine asks in a contemptuous tone but not in a hateful way. "One with all those fancy-dancy electronic gadgets and pretty seats in it?"

"Probably get everything I can get in it because Carol will probably be taking it to shows. I don't like to drive much, so the more comfortable, the better. What would you get in a truck if you could get anything you wanted?" Sam tries to question his mother without her knowing.

"I don't understand why anyone would want all that stuff in a truck. It's just more to break. I don't think I would get any of that fancy stuff if I got anything new, but I'll never be able to afford a new vehicle in my lifetime," Elaine says like she is almost bragging about being poor.

"We'll see if you can, you're not dead yet, Mom," Sam says.

Sam's dad pulls into the truck stop after running two stoplights.

"Dad, you just ran two stoplights and you were only going about fifteen miles per hour all the way here. Didn't you see them?" Sam asks but knows his dad just doesn't give a shit if he stops for stoplights. Sam's dad is always like that and has gotten worse now that he is older.

"I'll stop for them twice the next time. They just put them in there to piss me off," Darrell says in his only little joking way.

"Dad, I swear, you are becoming the driver that you always hated to meet on the road," Sam says.

"Let's go eat," Elaine says not because she is hungry but just to change the subject before it turned into an argument. Elaine never likes an argument. It takes a lot to ever get her to discuss anything in depth, let alone a fight.

Sam's Mom and Dad has always thought that the truck stop is the best place to eat, especially this one, because the truck lot is always full. Darrell always says, "Truck drivers can eat anywhere in the country. If they take the time to stop, then that is the best place to eat. Truck drivers always know the best places to eat."

Sam always thought sarcastically, "Surely, truck drivers were all great food connoisseurs. They would only eat healthy and well-made food and drive out of their way to get a wonderful meal."

Anyway, the food is OK and it didn't cost an arm and leg. After they eat breakfast and drink what seems to be at least a gallon of coffee, they drive back across town to the Ford dealer. Darrell drives into the Ford dealership and drives around the lot for about a half an hour. He then stops his truck in the middle of the main driveway into the lot. They all got out and start to walking and looking at the new trucks. They open doors and sit in a bunch of trucks, looking under the hoods and under the boxes. After about another half an hour, some salesman in a suit comes out to them.

"I am going to have to ask you all to move your truck. It is blocking the way for real customers to get in here," the salesman says in a very arrogant tone.

It instantly infuriates Sam. Sam's thoughts instantly turn to hateful thoughts, "That son of bitch didn't even greet us in an appropriate manner. How dare he speak to us like that? I should just knock this asshole out and then leave him bleeding in these new trucks."

"Darrell," Elaine says timidly, "give me the keys and I'll go move the truck so you guys can keep looking."

The salesman just stands there with his hands on his hip looking like he is something of great authority.

Sam looks over at Elaine, "Mom, don't do that, it is fine right where it is." Then he points to the salesman. "You sir, come over here and speak to me like I am a person and a customer."

The salesman just looks at Sam with contempt and walks over to him. "You and the other two need to move your pile of junk before I have it—" The salesman starts coughing and gagging. The salesman goes down to his knees, holding his hands to his throat like he is going to open it up for more air.

Sam has had enough disrespect from salesman. Sam suddenly remembers this man from when he was a freshman in high school. "Dale Bickert." When the salesman got close enough, Sam slaps him in the throat with a knife hand. Not hard enough to crush his larynx but enough to make breathing difficult.

"Now you will shut up and be more respectful to your customers. I remember your stupid ass in high school when you pushed me down the stairs and always peed in my locker. You are Dale Bickert, and I have hated you for all these years," Sam says in a stern yet soft-toned hateful manner, "The truck is not in the way, there is not a lot of traffic coming in here, and as a matter of fact, we are the only ones out here barring the other salesman that are running out to save your ass right now. Now we came here to buy two trucks, but I may just go elsewhere since we have been treated like a bag of shit." Sam reaches over and helps the man up off his knees. "You'll be just fine in about an hour. Maybe you will be more respectful next time."

"I am calling the cops, you fucking asshole," Dales squeaks out in a very harsh voice. He can barely breathe let alone get the words out. Dale brushes himself off and heads toward the building. The other salesmen come running up to Sam and surrounded him.

A man about Sam's age, wearing a suit and an ugly tie, walks toward Sam with a swagger. He has his arms held out like one of those body builders. He pushes through the circle of salespeople then immediately walks up to Sam and put his face only a few inches in front of Sam's face.

"Nobody—and I mean nobody!—strikes one of my men. You should be glad that I am in a good mood today. Yesterday I would have given you a beat down. Now what is your fucking problem, mister?" the man yells at Sam in a really cocky and big-shot tone, something that reminded Sam of some TV gangster. All the salesmen standing around start flexing and acting like they are going to see a big fight. They look like people who, if the fight didn't go the right way, then are going to jump in and take over.

Sam glances around and then says to the man in front of him, "Do you really think you can scare me. Anyone that would wear that ugly of a tie and is short as a leprechaun can probably only fight like a fish." Sam and the man start laughing.

"You old son of bitch, I thought you fell off the face of the earth." The man reaches and gives Sam a hug. "How the hell you been Sam?"

All the salesmen that are standing around just drop their jaws and look like someone just took away their coffee and doughnuts. Dale has made his way into the building. Sam can see him through the big windows in the front. The guy is pointing toward Sam and yelling at a lady sitting at a desk.

"I've been doing good, Jay. I thought you were fighting fires and not babysitting a bunch of pussy salesmen," Sam says sarcastically. Then he looks around with contempt at all the salesmen surrounding him. Sam can see the sigh of relief in some and the disappointment in others.

"Well, Dad retired and I took over the place. I retired after twenty years as a firefighter. I thought it was time to take it easy," Jay informs Sam. "What have you been up to? I haven't seen you since the class reunion about seven years ago."

"My wife and I still have the veterinary hospital in Virginia, so it keeps me busy working all the time. How's your family all doing?" Sam asks.

"My boy is in college right now, and Sarah, you never met her, she's is still in high school," Jay says with a proud voice, "My wife is working at the hospital as a nurse. So what are you doing here?"

"Darwin Jenson's wife just died. I'm here to help him out. But today I'm going to buy two trucks from you." Sam looks around and sees that Dale Bickert is on the phone. He is throwing his hands and arms around like he is in a fight. "I think the first thing I need you to do is to go in there and talk to that salesman. Maybe explain the more simple things in life, such as if you mess with the bull, you may end up with the horn." Sam is pointing out Dale to Jay.

Jay shrugs and says, "Don't worry, he needs this job and I'll talk to him right now. He's a real asshole anyway." Jay gets on his phone and Sam can see Dale in the window set the other phone down and answer his cell phone. Then Jay gives Dale a talking too. Sam watches

Dale stomp his feet and throw a temper tantrum, then picks up the other phone for a brief minute and hangs it up. "There, that fixed that. Now what trucks were you looking at?" Jay asks with a smile.

"I need the biggest dually with everything in it and something my mom and dad want, but make sure it is loaded full of everything," Sam says.

"Do we need to make sure you can get the financing first or should we wait till you find what you want?" Jay asks with a little concern.

"No, I'll just pay you in cash or give you a check. So let's go look," Sam says with confidence.

"Holy shit, you got that much. I guess the vet business is good," Jay says.

"I do pretty well. Let me go get my mom and dad out of their truck and then they can look. If you can get some guys lined up and find those trucks, we can just take each one for a ride," Sam requested.

"Great," Jay says. Jay gets on his phone for about a minute and then hangs up.

Sam goes over and gets his Mom and Dad out of their truck. "Mom, you and Dad need to come and look at trucks. I'm going to buy you one today," Sam says.

"Oh no, we are fine with this one. We don't want to look too highfalutin, and besides, you can't afford it. You need to save your money for a rainy day," Elaine says. Sam can see she is almost a little embarrassed at the thought of even driving a new vehicle. She is a very modest person, the kindest person Sam has ever known. Even though Sam's mom and dad never had any money, they would feed anyone that came their way.

"Mom, Dad, I have saved my money, and now it is time that I give you something back. I really want to give you something you need and something you can enjoy every day," Sam says almost pleading.

"Oh well, we can look, but I just don't think we can really find just anything here," Elaine states but not really believing what she just said. "We don't know what we want." Elaine gets out of the pickup walks around to the driver's side of the truck. Darrell reaches out the window and grabs the outside door handle. He bumps the door with his shoulder and the door opens. Darrell gets out and sticks his hands in his pockets. Darrell walks round like a man that was shopping with his wife in the mall.

The salesmen all drive up in some of the best trucks on the lot. Elaine and Darrell both get in and out of each truck. All the trucks are fully loaded with everything that there is to put in one. Finally after about an hour, Elaine and Darrell don't get out of a truck. That is the one.

"Do you like it?" Sam asks.

"Oh, it's so comfortable. Your dad can sit in here and his back doesn't hurt," Elaine says. "Dad, what do you think?"

"It will work," Darrell says in a nonchalant way but in reality, he is overjoyed.

"So that's it then. One of you can drive this home and the other one drive your other truck home," Sam says.

Jay drives up in the best truck that is around and Sam gets into the driver's seat. He knows right away that this is the one he is going to take.

"I'll take it. Let's go do the paperwork and get a drink and some food. I'm buying," Sam says to Jay, Elaine, and Darrell. They all went in and did the paperwork. Sam writes a check. Jay gets on the phone and calls Sam's bank to make sure the check is covered. Then they all drive to a steak house to eat.

That night, all of Elaine and Darrell's friends and Gina's friends, and Jay's family come over and crowd into Elaine and Darrell's house. Some sit in the house and some sit around a campfire outside. The conversation of the night is all directed at the new trucks, old times, Sam's life now and the way he was, and politics. Sam has always lived a fairly exciting life. He was never one to sit on the sidelines and watch. If he wasn't into what was going on, he wasn't there at all. He's never the best at anything, but he is very persistent at making himself the best he could be at anything he set his mind to doing. This usually leads him in several different directions and in several different situations. Sam's life always seems like a topic of conversation whenever he goes home. It always starts with "Do you remember when . . . ?" Then Sam ends up telling stories for the rest of the night. It is not exciting to Sam but people seem to like to listen to his stories. If someone else has a story, Sam happily lets them tell it. The story telling goes on until Elaine serves up an early morning feast. Everyone eats. Then they fall asleep in a chair or go home. Sam's parents often have overnight visitors.

Sam's family was never much into politics. In their farm life, they just didn't have time to worry about things like that. They were sort of isolated into one side of political opinion. There was only local newspaper and two TV stations when Sam was growing up. Political opinion was based on whatever his grandpa had to say about the way things ran. But when Sam moved to Virginia, he became more enthralled with the way the country was run. He started reading and understanding the Constitution and reading bills brought into congress, and now he is involved in local political group.

Jay is the first to bring up politics. "If this president and congress have it their way, no one will be buying trucks. I've had to lay off half of my salesmen and servicemen, and with the way the banks are, we can hardly get anyone a loan. Everyone needs such a big down payment to even qualify that vehicle sales are ten percent of what they were."

"Business has been way down for me. People just don't have the money and those that do are holding on to it in case they lose their jobs," Sam says sincerely. "Those people that are up near the DC area are still doing well because most of their clients are government workers. The government workers are not hurting. As a matter of fact, they just got a raise and don't have to worry about getting laid off. I think that the government should start getting pay cuts."

"Yeah, but those government workers get a raise and benefits every year that are more than we can ever get. Even when I was in the fire station, we didn't get that good of benefits because we were paid by the city here. I think some fire stations in other states are paid by the state. Our retirement plan at that place was a 401K. We did have a pension until last year, when the city said that the pension money was gone because of the stock market crash. My 401K is pretty much worthless so that's why I have to keep the truck lot going," Jay says. Then he takes a big swig of beer and opens another. He is all fired up now and his face is turning red.

"Well, something has to change and for the better. Otherwise, everyone is going to be in the bread line. Especially people that have worked all their lives and now what they did invest is gone. The government just doesn't even care. I have a client that had two million in stocks in GMC, but when the government took it over, they just got a letter telling them that their stocks are no longer any good. So instantly their retirement is gone. They are completely broke and now they are looking for jobs and are going to lose their house. President Barrack just took their life's investment away and told them to fuck off. That son of a bitch then gave it all to the auto union. Something needs to be done," Sam says with a little anger in his voice.

"Nothing can be done until those bastards are up for elections, but they will probably just get voted back in again," Jay says and pounds a fist on the table, which sends a fork flying to the floor.

"I know the biggest problem is that they let stupid, lazy people vote. Those stupid college students run out and vote because they think that the government needs to help all the poor people. And the lazy just vote for those that they will get them stuff and they will never have to work. Most of them don't pay taxes and some never will pay taxes, so why the hell do they get to vote on how taxes are spent? It all just needs to change. We are starting a group back home to lobby and maybe protest against politicians' piss-poor performance, and if they pass all the crap like the health care bill and cap-and-trade, then America as we know it is done for," Sam rants.

"Well, let me know when you get that going. I'll be there with you," almost everyone in the room said.

"Well, right now we are having trouble with OCORC. Mostly their offshoot, a group called YUPPI. So far we have found out that they are funded by OCORC and methamphetamine sales. They own a bunch of cops, and the gang is pretty ruthless. My brothers and I have tangled with them a couple of times. One of the sheriffs that they own kidnapped my wife, but we went and got her back, then took everything that fucking group had. I found a huge meth lab that looked like it could cook a lot of stuff. It was automated like a factory. Are there any of them out here?" Sam asked.

"No, not that I have heard of, but is that lab still there?" A friend of Gina's whose name was Snoop asked in a very drunk voice. Sam didn't know him; this is the first time that he ever seen him.

"As far as I know, I didn't destroy it. I guess I can sneak back in a look, but this time it might be booby-trapped," Sam says.

"Boy, it would be fun to go see if it's still there," Snoop says.

"Why you want to go along?" Sam asks.

"Yeah, I do. If you go back in then I will come along," both Snoop and Jay say in unison. They were both a little drunk.

"OK, when I leave, pack your clothes and grab your wife or whoever you want. You guys can come back with me and we will go look," Sam says.

"Ah, I don't know if I can leave that long from work," Jay says. Snoop just sat there and nods and kept saying "Yeah coooool. A little Rambo action."

"Don't you own your own business? Hell, just sell the business and move on out there," Sam says as he is starting to get drunk along with everyone else.

"Oh hell, I can't sell my business. Just let me have a couple of days to think about it," Jay says.

"Yeah, it's getting late," Sam says.

"So you are telling us that you went in and took all of this gang stuff. What did you take? Even for you this is a little bit out there." Harold, one of Gina's friends, says with skepticism. He usually is a big fan of Sam's story's, but this time he has to call bullshit.

"I'm not going to tell you what I took, besides my wife, but if you are bored, then you can also pack your bags and come along," Sam says.

"I'm just calling bullshit on this one. It's not that I would put it past you, but bullshit!" He finishes a cigarette and mashes it out then sucks down a beer like it is a shot.

"I'm just saying, if you wouldn't pussy out, you can come on an adventure that you may or may not come back from. More than likely, we won't even run into anything bad, but we did have two big battles and we put a bunch of them in the hospital. I got shot and Dakota got beat up pretty good. So make sure your ducks are in line before you go," Sam says.

"I can't afford to go and do that stuff. If I leave work I will get fired," Harland says.

"Let him fire you." Sam takes out his billfold and pulls out a blank check. "How much do you make in a year?"

"I make thirty thousand and you are not going to pay my way out there. This would be for me and not anyone else," Harland says. He is an honest and hardworking person. He didn't like to take anything that he couldn't pay for.

Sam wrote a check out for forty thousand dollars and pushed it over to Harold. "I'm not paying your way out there. You are working for me if you take this check. You will start as soon as you take the check."

"I can't just quit now, but maybe tomorrow." Harold grabbed the check and looks at it. He then grabs his phone. He did a little nervous laugh and starts dialing. "I guess he won't mind if I call him this late since I am quitting. We didn't have much construction business anyway." Harold gets up from the table and walks outside. He is gone for about five minutes then comes back in with a sigh of relief on his face. "I guess I work for you."

"Good, we will start tomorrow and not early," Sam says. Everyone is shocked that at the drop of a hat Sam just hired him and paid a full year salary. Then everyone starts talking and making plans to come out to see Sam. The conversations begin to taper down to a dull roar and people begin to feel the early morning heaviness. Yawns and tired eyes start to travel through the crowd and people make plans to meet at nine in the morning.

Everyone tires out and slowly start to go home. Within about an hour, everyone has left and Sam and his parents and his sister are the only ones left. They all go to bed. Sam goes into his old room that he had growing up. It is exactly the same as it was then except instead of the posters on the wall, there were pictures of him and his brothers and sister. All the kids' rooms are like a memorial to the kids' lives. Sam's family is very much family orientated. Family is the most important part of their lives, and nothing comes before it. Sam always knew that it was family, God, friends, and country, and it came in that order, always. People that become friends are always treated like family, but if they ever did something to harm that relationship, they are shunned for life. Even worse if they harm anyone in the circle or steal from any of them, the consequences could be worse.

After a great night sleep of about three hours, Sam's parents are up and going. Sam could hear them stirring about the house at about seven in the morning. He could smell the coffee brewing on the stove and smell the biscuits in the oven. His mom loves to bake and Sam always gains several pounds whenever he came home. Sam gets up and takes a shower, trying to wake himself up. He always had a hard time waking up. He gets dressed and breakfast is waiting for him on the table.

"Are you tired? I hope I didn't wake you up," Elaine says with an overly cheerful attitude.

"Well, it's hard to sleep when you can smell a breakfast like this on the table." Sam sits down at the table and the coffee is poured and milk is in a glass.

"What else can I get you?" Elaine asks.

"Not a thing, thank you," Sam says to his mother. Elaine would make anything he wants, but Sam never really wants anything and with a meal like this. Who could ask for more? "I think that after breakfast I will go over and see Darwin. I'm sure he was expecting me to come over yesterday. Did he come over here and visit with you?"

"He came over once. The day that you called me, I called him and he came over. He was really broken up and confused. We got it all worked out and I got the funeral organized for him. Everything went well. He'll be happy to see you," Elaine says.

Sam finishes eating breakfast. He jumps into his new truck and drives over to Darwin's place that is his mom and dad's place. When Sam drives into the yard, he didn't recognize the place. The place is overgrown with trees and weeds. The barn is leaning to the right and appears to be about ready to fall down. The shop that Darwin's dad always worked is missing a door. The roof is caving in on one side. The screens on the house are hanging off the windows. The house has numerous areas where the siding is ripped off. Shingles are missing and a large tree branch has fallen on the house and caved in an area of the roof. Sam wades through the weeds and carefully walks up the front door steps. One of the steps is broken and Sam pulls himself up by the handrail. The handrail gives way, but with Sam's great balance, he kept himself from falling down the stairs. He makes it to the top of the stairs and opened the screen door, but when he does, the whole screen door comes off the door jam, hinges and all. Sam starts to think that no one even lives in the house and that maybe Darwin had moved back to his old place in town. He knocks on the door anyway and then listens for any movement in the house. After knocking a couple of times, he hears footsteps on the inside. The curtain in the window next to the door moves and Darwin's face appears in the window. Sam's first thought is, "Darwin looks like shit." Darwin smiles when he recognizes Sam. Darwin unlocks the door and opens it up. Darwin leaps at Sam and gives him a big hug. Sam is caught off guard and just stands there for a minute. He gives Darwin a pat on the back and then gently pushes him away.

"I'm so happy you are here," Darwin says in a voice of relief. He let Sam go and took a step back. Darwin is wearing clothes that have not seen a wash machine in quite some time. He is dirty and stinky.

Sam thinks, "How the hell did you let yourself go? You stink like you haven't showered in weeks."

"I'm happy to see you, my friend. I am so sad that you lost Gladys. She was a good person and she was good for you. Now, I think you need some help," Sam says with sincerity. He walks into the house. The house is a mess. Boxes and garbage were everywhere. The floor barely has a path to walk through. Sam follows Darwin into a room in the back of the house. This room has not been violated with garbage. It has four computer screens and a huge computer set up that is bigger than any Sam has ever seen. Darwin has three flat panel televisions that are playing CNN, C-SPAN, and Fox News. The only other furniture is a huge comfortable chair in the center of the room. "Darwin what have you been up to?" Sam asks in a calm voice.

"I've sort of been working on a project that I got started on and I can't quit till I get some answers," Darwin says in a very tired voice.

"Well, this place and you don't look like the last time I was here. What have you been up to since I last saw you?" Sam asks with concern.

"This place has been going downhill since my mom died and left it to us. The taxes had not been paid since my Dad died. Mom didn't have enough money to pay them since she was just living off Dad's pension and social security. Gladys and I tried to keep the place up and help pay taxes, but we just couldn't keep up. I'm not much of a handy man, so I couldn't keep the buildings in good shape. We did hire a carpenter a year ago and we paid him a deposit, then he never showed up to do anything," Darwin explains.

"So who is this carpenter you hired?" Sam asks.

"You remember Brian Macky? We went to school with him. He came out and gave me an estimate. We had to give him ten thousand dollars to start. He said the whole thing would cost about thirty thousand to fix everything. He never came back out here," Darwin explains.

"Did you go and ask him why he didn't start?" Sam asks. He knew Brian Macky. The guy was an asshole since he was born. Sam met him when they both were five years old and had been fighting with him since. Brian has been in and out of prison so many times that they just keep the cell free for him.

"Yeah, I waited a couple of months, and then I went to talk to him. I found him at the bar in Hartford. I went up and asked him when he was going to start and he said, "Start what?" I told him about the deposit and working on the farm. He said, "What fucking deposit? You didn't pay me to do anything." So I asked for my ten thousand back and he knocked me out. When I came to, I was lying in the bar booth with ice on my head and everyone standing over me laughing at me. He just kept sitting at the bar drinking. So I left and told the cop in town, but they never did anything. I took him to small claims court, but the judge said that since I didn't have a contract or receipts, I didn't have a case against him. Sam, I could have used that money to pay some of the taxes on this place," Darwin summarizes with some reluctance.

"Well! We will just have to go get that money back. I can call some people and get this place looking tip-top. What about the tax problem? Did you get them paid up or are they still after you for the money?" Sam asks.

"They are going to take the place away at the end of the week and auction it off," Darwin says, "Sam, I can't lose this place because of taxes. My dad would never have let this happen. I have failed my dad." Darwin just plops down into the chair and starts crying.

Sam realizes now how much stress Darwin is under. He is probably on the verge of breaking. "Darwin, I will get everything fixed. Now you need to pull yourself together and go take a shower right now. Then I'm going to take you to town and get you something to eat," Sam says in soft voice. Sam gives Darwin a pat on the back. Darwin gets up and hugs Sam again. He then heads off into the other room to clean himself up.

Sam sits down in Darwin's only chair in the computer room. He starts playing around with the computer, not that he is any computer expert, but just to pass the time. The screen saver disappears and Darwin's project appears on all the screens. The project that Darwin has tapped into is Bud Jacklow's financial accounts, all his transaction that were done while he was in office, and all his people that he had ever talked to. On two other screens are the FBI and police computer system and files. Sam always knew that Darwin was a computer whiz, but he never knew he could do this. Sam just left the computer alone before he messed something up. He just sits there contemplating his next move. He thinks that Darwin will make a good partner back at his place. He needs someone that could fix his shabby computer system and run everything.

Sam calls Rick, the carpenter at Sam's mom and dad's farm. "Hey, Rick, hope you had fun last night."

"Yes, I did, but I had to leave because I had to work today. Maybe I'll see you later at the farm," Rick says.

"Yeah, I will be back there later today and we can drink a few more beers," Sam says with mild appetence. "Hey, I got a friend who is in great need of your services. Can you bring your crew over and fix up another farm?" Sam knows that Rick will do it since Rick is working for him, but it is always better to ask then to demand. It lets Rick feel more in control, which is what Sam wants Rick to be.

"Sure we can, if it is all right with you. You're the boss," Rick says, "Where is it? We will be there in a half hour."

Sam gives him directions, and within twenty minutes, there are ten men at the farm. Sam goes out to greet them in the driveway. He can tell that the men are not looking excited about tackling this job, but no one voices any opposition. Sam shows Rick around the farm. Sam tells Rick about the overall expectations of the new project, which is to make the farm almost new without tearing the whole place down. He tells them to fix anything that can be fixed and take down anything not worth fixing. Rick and his crew go right to work, walking around the farm assessing buildings and making a list of supplies they need.

"I'll get the supplies and we will start tomorrow on the repairs. Today the guys will start cleaning up. I have a loader and a dump truck coming," Rick tells Sam.

"Great. Have fun and turn all the bills over to the same farm account. You have to make sure to save the house and the workshop, but anything else is free game," Sam says in a propitious manner, "Oh! If you know any house-cleaning people, get them over here. Please."

"I know just the people." Rick goes to work. Sam goes back into the house and sits down in Darwin's big chair.

Darwin comes back in and sees that Sam has been looking at the computer. "Ah, just a little project I've been working on. Um, do you think it's bad that I'm, ah, hacking?"

Sam stops him in midsentence. "Au contraire, mon frère, I think this is great what you can do with computers. I need you to come work for me. I need someone like you. I never knew you could do this stuff," Sam says to Darwin. "How the hell did you figure this stuff out?"

"You know I've been writing software since I got out of high school. Well, all the banks and government systems are all built on my basic software that I made for the first job. The company sold the software to other software companies. Those companies just built on my software. Since then, they have been just adding securities crap over top of it without changing any of the basic stuff. I made a back-door into my software that is so basic, no one has ever changed it or found it. They can add all the secure stuff they want to and I can get into it in a split second and never be detected, a sort of a hidden tunnel that a mountain got piled on to. So I can get information from wherever I want, whenever I want, without a trace," Darwin explains.

"Great, I always knew you were far ahead of your time," Sam says. "I got some guys outside fixing the place up and they will probably be here for a few weeks."

"Sam, I don't have any money," Darwin says. He is embarrassed.

"It is part of your benefit package, or you can consider it a signing bonus," Sam tells him.

"That is mighty nice of you, Sam," Darwin says with sincerity.

Darwin now has a giant grin on his face. What Sam did is just what he needed to put a smile on his face.

"Let's go eat." Sam grabs Darwin and they go outside.

Darwin looks around at all the men working. Darwin thinks out loud, "This place will never be the same."

Sam reassures him, "They are just going to clean up the place today and tear apart some of the rotten buildings and stuff like that. It will all look new and clean when they are done. Look what they did with my mom and dad's place."

"All right, Sam," Darwin says, "I trust you."

Darwin and Sam jump in the truck and head to town. They go to eat at Kenny's, the local restaurant. The whole time that they are eating, Darwin talks about Gladys. Sam just listens and gives a few words of encouragement every now and then. After eating, they jump into the truck. Sam heads downtown.

"Now where are we going?" Darwin asks.

"We are going to have a little talk with Brian Macky. He is still hanging around the bar downtown, isn't he?" Sam always had a problem with bullies. He grew up with kids in school picking on him because he was different. He wasn't a sports hero, nor was he the most intelligent person. He was just a farm kid that could do everything. Sam always stood up for the little guy even though he was one of the little guys. He never backed away from his principles even if it meant a big fight or even worse. Sam can't stand the thought of evil people getting by with anything, but what he hates worse is good people standing by and watching with indifference, never stepping up and helping when help is needed.

"Well yeah, but I don't know if he is going to be down there now. You have to watch him. He has hurt a lot of people that cross him," Darwin says timidly. Darwin is nervous at just the mention of Macky's name.

"Let's just go have a little drink then and we'll talk some more," Sam says in a calm voice. Sam can see that Darwin is really nervous.

Sam pulls into a parking spot on main street about two blocks away from the bar. They both get out and walk to the front door of the bar. Sam learned a long time ago never to park right in front of the bar. You could get your vehicle wrecked if trouble breaks out. Also people may see what you are driving and then try to find out where you live. Sam observes all the vehicles along the street. The town is pretty much quiet except for a few trucks pulling into the co-op and the people just passing through town.

Sam and Darwin walk in to the bar and sit down on the corner barstools closest to the door. At the other end of the bar Brian Macky is sitting on a barstool and is surrounded by a couple of women and several men. Darwin points Macky out and Sam recognizes him immediately. Sam stared down the bar at Macky. Sam's mind takes off in a place of long ago; he remembers just how much and why he hated Macky.

Sam and Darwin order some drinks. Darwin never drank alcohol ever in his life until today. Darwin orders a Tom Collins and drinks it down like it is Kool-Aid, then orders another. He is extremely nervous, but the alcohol is just starting to take a little of it away. He starts staring at Macky like he is stalking a kill. The more he drinks, the less he talks and the more he stares. Macky sees that Darwin is staring at him. It is starting to bother Macky that someone keep staring at him. Macky turns to his entourage and points over at them. He then turns and looks at Sam and Darwin and laughs. Macky turns and stands up. He says something to his entourage and they all laugh. He put his drink down on the bar and shrugs back, then walks over to Sam and Darwin. Macky put his hands on both Sam's and Darwin's shoulders. Sam just sits there facing straight forward, evaluating Macky's entourage. Darwin turns toward Macky.

"I want my money back," Darwin yells. He is drunk and his words are slurring.

"Is that what you came down here for? Didn't I explain myself well enough the last time you were down here? Why don't you and your friend just sit here and finish your drinks? Then get the hell out of here before you both get hurt," Macky says and then laughs. He squeezes Darwin's and Sam's shoulders.

"Don't you know who is with me, you dumb son of a bitch?" Darwin asks Macky.

Sam turns around and looks Macky in the eyes. Macky takes a step back. "You? What are you doing here?" Macky asks in a shaky voice. He signals to some of his friend. "Hey, boys, look who's back. It's Sam. He's Darwin's bodyguard or something like that. You all remember him. We used to beat the shit out of him in school." Macky pats Sam's face. "What, Sam, you come back so you can get an old-time beating?"

Without saying a word, Sam punches Macky in the throat. Macky drops to the floor trying to catch his breath. Sam gets up slowly from the barstool. He picks up Macky's hand that had patted him on the cheek then wrenches back each finger one by one. The finger's joints snap loudly as the ligaments and tendons tear and the joints dislocate. Macky would scream, but he really is having a hard time breathing. Sam kicks Macky in the lower rib cage, causing the last ribs to snap. The sound of cracking ribs echoed through the bar. Sam would have been satisfied with that, but he looks over at Macky's entourage, and they are quickly making their way toward him. One of the women in the entourage that is sitting at the bar stands quickly and throws a beer bottle at Sam. Sam turns his body slightly and catches the bottle in his left hand. It amazed Sam that he caught it. As soon as he catches the bottle, he immediately throws it back at the woman. The bottle hits her in the nose and breaks on her forehead. Blood erupts for the nose and shards of glass impale into her forehead. She falls backward to the ground and grabs for her nose. She starts screaming and kicking like she just became possessed. Blood flew everywhere around her. The other woman sitting with her quickly kneels besides her trying to console her but to no avail.

The men in the group rush Sam, thinking that he is distracted by the beer bottle incident. Sam is ready for them. The first man to throw a punch at Sam is an overweight tough guy. The man ran at Sam at the same time he is throwing the punch. Sam grabs the guy's wrist at the same time circles to the guy's back. It is an aikido move Sam had learned. The momentum of the twist sends the guy's head crashing into the bar and knocking him unconscious. A second man throws two punches. Sam dodges one of the punches but is caught with the second. Sam falls back a little. As he is stumbling back, he gives the guy a front kick right to the chin. The guy drops to the floor on to his knees. He spits blood and a couple of teeth on to the floor. The guy wipes his mouth then looks at Sam in a bewildered rage. Sam kicks him in the face again. This time, the guy falls backward on to the floor unconscious with his legs bent under him. Three more guys rush Sam. Sam reaches into his pocket and pulls out a weighted chain about six feet long. The chain is a calf-pulling chain. It is lightweight with weights Sam had put on it to make it a useful weapon. The guys stop then circle around Sam. Sam had been trained in weapons in karate class and became very proficient in the use of traditional weapons. The chain is one that Sam can always carry around. Sam starts to work the chain around and around. All the guys just stand there, ready to attack. One of the guys works up enough nerve to lunge toward Sam. Sam snaps the chain like a whip and hits the guy in the forehead. The guy's forehead cracks, leaving a slight dent, and instantly a hematoma forms. The guy drops to the floor and sits there shaking his head like a dog with a tick in its ear. The other two seeing how brave their comrade was, didn't want to be out done. They both lunge forward at the same time. Sam swings the chain, and it wraps around one of the guy's necks. Sam jerks on the chain, sending the guy flying forward and into other attacker. They both fall to the ground and Sam jumps over to them. Sam stomps on the face of the attacker that is lying on his back. The guy goes out like a broken lightbulb. Sam grabs the other one around the neck and chokes him out. When the guy quits moving, Sam unwraps the chain and puts it back into his pocket.

The other people in the bar never say a word. To Sam, they all appear to be both surprised and happy that Sam has just beat the shit out of the whole lot of them. Sam walks over to Macky, who is just sitting up and coughing now. Sam bent over and put his face about one inch from Macky's face. "I hear you owe my friend ten thousand dollars! I also hear that you haven't changed a bit. I'm here now to show you that when you think you are the big tough fish in the pond, there are even bigger and meaner ones that will tear you apart." Macky just sits there and looks at Sam. Not that Macky can really say anything, but he can barely breath.

"I'll tell you what. In two days, I'm going to leave town. You will have Darwin's money by tomorrow. Otherwise, I will be taking your body parts with me and I'm going to start with your nuts. Got it?" Sam says in a calm voice. "And you dumb bastard, this is how the fights used to end up." Sam reaches over and grabs Macky's billfold. He takes out the money Macky has along with his driver's license and credit cards. The billfold contains about a thousand dollars. Sam gives the cash to the bartender. "This here is for anything that may have been broken and a tip." The bartender grabs the money and puts it in his pocket.

"Doesn't appear anything was broken and the drinks are on the house," the bartender says with a smile on his face.

Darwin was still sitting on his stool with his mouth wide open. All the fighting took place over a couple of minutes and there are people on the floor everywhere.

"Let's go, Darwin. These guys will be all right. We've got to go visit a few people." Sam grabs Darwin's hand and gives him help off the barstool. Darwin stares at Macky sitting on the floor. Sam starts through the door when he turns around to see Darwin kicking Macky in the nuts.

"You heard him. Those come off first," Darwin yells to Macky.

Macky makes a funny harsh noise and grabs his crotch with his good hand.

Sam and Darwin hurry down the street and jumped in to the truck. Sam starts the truck and drives off. Darwin just sits there not saying a word.

"Are you doing all right? You look a little pale," Sam says to Darwin.

"Ah, I never thought . . . like sumptum happen. I never drunkin' before. He gunna look fer me," Darwin says, slurring his words. He is drunk and sick.

"Nah, by the time we get done with him, he isn't going to bother anyone again," Sam says with confidence.

"Why, what you gunna do? Shit gunna be illegal or sumptum?" Darwin asks.

"No more than what we already did. I think by the time we get done, he won't have any friends left," Sam says.

"Where going?" Darwin asks but didn't care. He is just trying to keep from vomiting.

"We are going to go to the gunsmith shop right now and then we are going to go see Danny," Sam explains.

"Why a gun for?" Darwin asks. He starts to hiccup and saliva starts filling his mouth.

"Look, when we go get your money tomorrow, those guys are going to have guns and they are going to be ready. We need some firepower just in case. It is not going to go well tomorrow but we will make him pay one way or another," Sam lectures Darwin. Sam sees that Darwin is getting sicker. Sam stops the truck. Darwin opens the door and vomit erupts. Sam grabs Darwin by the belt just as he is about to fall out the door. Once Darwin is done vomiting, Sam hands him a Dr. Pepper. Darwin washes his mouth out and spits. Once Darwin is ready and the door is shut, Sam takes off again.

CHAPTER THIRTEEN

THEY DRIVE TO THE GUNSMITH shop that has been around since they were kids. The guy who owns the shop is called Gunny. He is a genius with weapon making. Sam never really knows what his whole name is, but he always loved going into the shop and looking around. Gunny was an old man when Sam was a kid. Gunny was the only black man that Sam had ever seen when he was young. Sam remembered that Gunny's hands looked like he was wearing gloves. He had big strong hands that looked like leather, probably came from the years of working with hot steel. The weapons he made were very precisely made and well balanced. Sam never could afford any of his weapons, but now he can get what he wants.

The place is in the middle of nowhere. It looks like an old barn. Nothing has changed. The barrel that was almost cut in half with bullet holes is still sitting out front. The windows have never been washed and the dirt on the windows made it impossible to see inside. The porch on the front is in great need of repair. Trees and weeds had grown up around the building, but there is still a place to park and it was never busy. Sam and Darwin pull up to the front door and walk in. Sam's eyes just open wide like a kid walking into a toy store for the first time. Any knife, gun, camouflage, old-type weapon, or antique weapon that anyone could want or need is in the gunsmith shop.

"Howdy, boys. What can I do for you all today?" Gunny says with a smile. "If you are just here to look, then feel free, but watch out—these are real weapons, not toys." Gunny meets them at the door carrying an old tin cup filled with coffee. "Ya boys want coffee? I just made some. If ya do, it's warmin' on the stove."

"Hello, Mr. Gunny, you are still looking well," Sam says. "I would love a cup of coffee and my friend here really needs some coffee." Sam reaches out to shake Gunny's hand. Gunny's hand is a catcher's mitt compared to Sam's. Sam had seen Gunny squeeze pliers together and breaks the center bolt with his bare hands.

"Sam, I don't drink coffee." Darwin looks over to Sam. Darwin is still a little peaked.

"*You don't* drink alcohol either until a few hours ago and you need coffee." Sam walks over to the stove and found two fairly clean tin cups. Sam looks the cups over. He could tell that the cups were definitely handmade and well done. No seams or sharp edges. Sam pours two coffees and then hands one to Darwin. Darwin smells it and shakes his head. Sam looks over at him gives him a stare like "you drink it or else." Darwin starts to sip his coffee.

Sam looks around the shop for hours. There is so much to see. Sam finds two perfectly made tomahawks that are sharp as razors, a short sword that would make a ninja envious, and two crossbows with scopes that had a two hundred fifty pound draw to them. Sam goes and looks at the handguns and find two .45 Colts, three 9-mm. fully automatic machine pistols that have thirty-round clips, and a .50-caliber desert eagle—all of which had been modified so that they are totally illegal to own. The rifles that are there were limitless. Everything you need to either shoot a far distance or for home defense. Sam looks for Gunny and finds him at his workbench making a weapon that looks like a small double-sided hook knife at the end of a ten foot chain.

Without looking up, Gunny said, "Ya know you look like that young man that used to hang around starin' at all the stuff on my walls years ago. Where have ya been?" Gunny puts down his work and turns. He looks over at Sam. "I should have recognized you as soon as you walked in, but it wasn't until you started to handle the tomahawks that I knew it were you. You always took great interest in my work. I should have taken more interest in you."

"You are right, I am Sam. I used to come here and stare at your stuff. I think it is incredible the way you can make anything. I am a veterinarian now in Virginia, so I didn't just waste my life, if that is what you think," Sam says and then sits down on an old bench stool.

"No, boy, I didn't mean it that way. Let me ask you something. Did you go off and get some training in the arts of fightin'?" Gunny asks with intent.

"Yes, how did you know?" Sam asks inquisitively.

"I just know. I could tell when you were a kid that you had some warrior in you. That's what I was meaning, that I should have trained you then," Gunny explains.

"You know about the use of all these weapons?" Sam knew he had just asked a stupid question.

"Ya think I just make this stuff. You can't make them if you can't use them," Gunny says with pride. He is proud of his weapons knowledge.

"I had no idea, but how did you learn this stuff?" Sam asks.

"My dad was in World War II. When japan surrendered in 1945, my father was stationed there. My father a few years later married a Japanese girl who was the daughter of a swordsmith. The sword-smith was a samurai as was his father and his father before. I was born in Japan and was taught at an early age to work with metal and use weapons. When I was seventeen, we moved back to Madison, South Dakota, and then when I turned eighteen, I was drafted into the army to be sent over to Vietnam. They put me into some special forces division and I spent six years sneaking around the bush all through Cambodia, Laos, and Vietnam. There were only eight of us and we were called Whisper. No one knew we even existed. We traveled from village to village, killing VC. We then would send back for troop support but most of the time we got nothing. We had to live off what we killed or obtained from villages. We lived like Vietnamese for six years. We never went into any of the army outpost except if we needed more ammunition, and then it was only at the cover of night where we would sneak in and out. We didn't even know about the fall of Saigon until we went to an outpost and found it empty. We found a paper that said that everyone was pulling out. We had to make our own way back to the States. The army had forgotten about us. When we got back they just gave us are discharge papers with a handful of medals. They told us that we 'made America proud.' They gave us our six years of paychecks and then I came here and set up shop with the money I had."

"That is amazing. Do you ever see any of your buddies?" Sam asks.

"Haven't seen any of them for years. When we got back, we really didn't fit in with anyone or anywhere. I know that Rice—we just called him Rice because if he ate rice, he would fart for two days straight—went and got killed flyin' choppers for the oil company. He crashed in Alaska somewhere. Slug and Crow became trackers in the Rocky Mountains—they may even still be up there. I did see Lee. Lee never did have a nickname. He was on his way to California to become a policeman out there. He said he wanted to round up the dirt in the big city. He stayed for a couple of weeks and I never saw him again. The others I have not seen," Gunny recalled. Gunny tried to remember the rest of his group but he figure that they were just gone.

"You are an amazing man. Would you tell me some more stories? I really am very interested," Sam asks.

Gunny got up from the bench stool and handed Sam the weapon he just made. It is a bladed whip chain. "This is for you. This is your weapon. This is the weapon you should be using. It will fit you like another hand. Practice it and it will be your favorite weapon," Gunny says with authority. "Now let's go into the sittin' spot and I'll tell you a story. You go get us some beer out of the icebox."

Sam accepts the weapon and twirls it around. It felt right in his hands. He goes and grabs some beers out of the refrigerator. He sits down in an old rocking chair. Darwin is still messing around rummaging through drawers and through the rooms upstairs. Gunny tells Sam several stories about how he grew up and about Vietnam. After about four or five hours, Gunny's stomach starts to rumble.

"Gunny, I want to take you out to eat. Anywhere you want?" Sam says. "It is the least I can do to thank you for the stories and for making this special weapon.

"Oh, I don't know. I don't like to go to town. I haven't been to one of them eatin' places since I don't know when." Gunny is shy about accepting the invitation.

"We're going for steaks and beers. Darwin, are you getting hungry?" Sam yells to Darwin.

"Yes, I am. But before we go, are we going to buy anything?" Darwin asks.

"Yes, we are if Gunny will sell us anything," Sam says. "Gunny, do you want to sell any of your things?" Sam knows it is polite to ask if craftsmen like Gunny will sell their work.

"Well, boy, everything is for sale. That is what I am here for. What do you guys want? If you don't see, it I'll make it," Gunny says with enthusiasm.

"How much for everything?" Sam asks with a straight face.

Gunny's jaw drops and he starts to mumble a bit. "What are you going to do with it all? Some of this stuff you'll need special training to use. How the heck are you going to haul this stuff?"

Sam looks at Gunny. "What I was thinking is that I could maybe hire you to train my brothers and me and maybe their kids," Sam explains. "You could set up shop in Virginia for a while and still keep this place. You can come and go as you please, but I will pay you whatever you want. So think about a price tag for all of it and a good wage for you. I will call and get a truck over here tomorrow and load up everything if you want."

"Well, I, ah . . ." Then a big smile comes across his face. "I always wanted to be a millionaire, so one million dollars." He laughs and shakes his head like he just told a joke.

"OK, I'll get my brother to bring out your money tomorrow," Sam says.

Gunny just keeps laughing and shaking his head. Then he mumbles something under his breath and he kept saying, "I'm rich, I'm rich, ha, ha, I told you I'd strike it rich."

Sam just looks at him and smiles. He calls Bud on the phone. Sam tells Bud to grab a million and a half and have him, Kota and DH bring a truck and trailer out to pick up everything. Sam then calls Carol and tells her about what has been happening except for

214

the bar incident. Sam knows he'd better tell her before she found out about spending all that money from Bud.

Sam explains to Carol about everything he has been doing. He tells her about the new trucks he bought and the gunsmith shop he just bought. She is OK with most of it until Sam tells her about the three people that he hired.

Carol says in a snarly manner, "Why the hell do we need more people on the payroll? With you spending all this money and all the building we just did, we may be broke before you get home. So get home and be prepared to get back to work. I don't want to lose this place."

Sam tells her, "We ain't going to lose anything. We got plenty of money and I'm sure if I find them guys again, I can get more money."

"Sam. I don't want you to find those guys again. I don't want more of their money. We are a veterinary hospital. We work on horses. That is what I want us to do," Carol says with sincerity.

"I know, I know," Sam answers like he just got scolded. "I'll be home soon and we will get back to normal. OK."

"OK, Sam. I got to go get things arranged since the boys are going to be gone," Carol says in a calm manner. "I love you."

"I love you too," Sam says. Then they both hang up the phone.

"Well, Gunny, you got a deal. I'm going to take a few things now and then tomorrow the money and my brothers will be here," Sam says.

"Take what you want, it's all yours now. Just remember that these weapons are not legal anywhere, so don't get caught with them," Gunny says.

Sam takes his new weapon, two machine gun pistols, two tomahawks, several boxes of ammunition and clips, and a shoulder harness. Darwin takes a little 9-mm. handgun and a knife. They all headed for the truck and Gunny locks the door to the shop.

"This is the first time I am leaving this place at night in years." He shakes his head and laughs. Then, he keeps saying under his breath, "I'm rich, I'm rich."

They go out to eat and they all talk for hours. After eating, Sam stops at the store and buys more beer and coffee to resupply Gunny's store of goods they used up. Sam and Darwin bring Gunny back to shop.

"You boys just stay here tonight. It's a long way back to your place and I'll cook some breakfast in the morning." Gunny carries out a handful of blankets and sets them on the bench.

Both Darwin and Sam agree. They are tired both from fighting and drinking. They sack out on some army cots that are in the store. They both fall asleep instantly.

Sam feels a hand on his mouth and he quickly opens his eyes. Instantly, before opening his eyes, his hand comes up with a tomahawk in his hand ready for action. Another hand grabs his tomahawk hand.

"It's me, Gunny. Be quiet, there are some people outside by your truck. I've never seen them before," Gunny says in a calm whisper.

Sam slides out of the cot on to the floor. Gunny then wakes up Darwin. Darwin just mumbles and Gunny yanks him out of the cot. Darwin wakes up when he hits the floor.

Gunny falls into combat mode and gives Sam commands. Gunny tells Darwin to hide upstairs and Darwin does just that. Gunny takes an AR-15 automatic with laser site and night vision on it, then tells Sam to go around back and sneak up on them. Gunny goes to the upstairs window and sights in on the intruders. Sam grabs his tomahawk, night vision goggles, and his new chain weapon. He works his way down through the overgrowth of trees and weeds.

"Son of a bitch, I can't believe I let myself get followed," Sam says to himself. Then he remembers someone in the restaurant looking over at him. "That fucking Macky is here. He just doesn't know when to quit. I guess it is better here than mom and dad's place."

Sam counts eight men and two trucks. Four of the guys have handguns out, one has an ax, and the other three have what looks like pipes. "I can't believe I didn't hear the damn trucks," Sam says to himself. He is mad at himself but he will have to think about that later. Sam figures the best thing to do is to trust that Gunny will get those with guns before they shoot him. He can get a few before they catch him and have to do some close hand-to-hand combat. "It shouldn't be too hard. Half these guys are still wounded from the bar fight. Macky's arm is in a sling. What a dumb ass," Sam says to himself. Sam picks up four fair sized rocks and moves in a little closer still in the cover of some weeds to one of the trucks. Sam positions himself perpendicular to their trucks in case they turn their lights on. He takes the first rock and throws it at Macky. He hits him square in the forehead. Macky falls back and his gun goes off, then falls to his back and just lies there. The others start turning wildly pointing their guns and other weapons in all directions. One guy runs to their truck and turns the lights on. Sam takes his night vision goggles off.

"Those dumb shits, now I can see them and they can't see me." Sam says to himself.

Sam takes another rock and throws it at another guy that has a gun. It hits him in the mouth and the guy falls to his knees. He throws his gun to the ground and starts spitting blood and teeth, all the while screaming. The other six become confused. One starts shooting, but it is in the wrong direction. The guy empties his gun and Sam takes another rock and hit him in the back of the head. The guy drops like a lead brick. The last guy with the gun goes into crotch position like someone from a TV show looks like when they are ready to shoot. The other four stand there twirling there pipes and axes around like Conan the Barbarian. Sam threw another rock and hits last guy with a gun right in the nose. Blood shoots out of his nose like a sledgehammer hitting a watermelon. The guy drops his weapon and drops to both knees with his hands over his nose like he is trying to stop the blood flow. Sam quickly moves in and hits the guy with the ax in the side of the head with the side of the tomahawk. Sam then takes the chain weapon and whips one of the guys with a pipe with the blunt end of the chain. He then jumps up and grabs the pipe away from him and hits both of the others in the shins. They drop to the ground and throw away their pipes.

"OK, OK, we're good, we're good," the one guy says. Sam quickly rounds up the weapons and removes any bullets from the guns. Then he throws the weapons up by the door.

Gunny comes up and pats Sam on the back, "Just like I would have done."

Gunny stands with his weapon pointed at the men on the ground. Sam goes over and checks out the damage done on the guys. "Nothing serious, they'll heal up in a couple of weeks," Sam says out loud.

Darwin comes out with his knife in his hand like he is ready to fight. "Darwin, skin that knife before you cut yourself." Sam tells him. Darwin takes the sheath out of his back pocket and put it onto the knife instead of the knife into the sheath.

Sam walks over to Brian Macky, who is now able to sit up. Sam grabs Macky's hair and drags him over to the porch. Sam kicks him in the abdomen and lets him fall. Then Darwin turns the porch lights on.

"Now, since you are here, I am sure you brought Darwin's money. Otherwise, I can only assume that you are here to hurt me. If the latter is true, then I will remove your nuts first and then I will cut each and every one of you fucking dirtbag's head off. I'll assume that they are here to try to kill me since you brought along guns. So do you have the money?" Sam asks Macky. Sam is not being nice; he has his new chain kama out. Sam set the point of the kama blade on Macky's collarbone, as Sam talks to Macky; he burrows the point of the blade into the bone. Macky is wincing in pain.

"Aaaah! You son of a bitch! I should have killed you when we were kids." Macky looks up at Sam and flips him off.

Sam kicks him in the ribs. Sam reaches over and grabs the finger that flipped him off and dislocated it.

"Aaaah, fucking asshole." Macky grabs his finger with his other injured hand.

"Are you going to sit there and cuss me or are you going to start talking? Otherwise, you are in a world of hurt. I'm sure Gunny here can keep you a hurting for weeks before you die," Sam yells at Macky.

"I don't have any money yet. You asshole you broke my finger." Macky is furious.

Sam grabs Macky's dislocated finger and cuts it off with the kama blade. Sam throws the finger over to Darwin. "That's yours till he gets you your money."

Darwin catches the finger and holds it up to look at it like he is inspecting a glass of wine. "Let's take the nuts next," Darwin says in a sinister way. Darwin is caught up in Sam's fury and adrenaline rush. He is turning half-nuts.

"There now, quit whining. You don't have to worry about breaking that finger ever again," Sam says in a calm manner. Sam rips off the bottom of his shirt so he can bandage Macky's bleeding stump. "Let me tie this on. I don't want you bleeding all over the porch." Sam says with a stern voice. Sam ties the cloth on to the severed stump and it quits bleeding. "Now! What do you have to trade? I should say, how much are you worth?" Sam asks Macky. Sam knelt down in front of Macky. He takes his blade on the chain and places it under his chin. "As a matter of fact, all you need to think of what you've got to trade for your life. What the hell are any of you worth?" Sam says in a loud but calm voice. Sam looks and points out to the rest of the guys.

"I got something to trade," Macky says. Sam picks up a little hard on the blade. A trickle of blood starts to run from Macky's chin. "I got some meth that's worth some money. We just got a pound from the lab. We can get you more if you just let me go."

Sam's ears sort of twitched. Sam asks with interest, "How big is this lab? And what the hell are you doing with meth?"

"We sell it. We sell it for the YUPPIs. I'd have the money if we hadn't just paid for more products," Macky tries to explain.

"I don't think I can let you guys go. You might just try to do something stupid again or try to hurt someone I know," Sam says and removes the blade. He goes over and gets the others on the porch. Gunny stands there with his weapon pointed on to the eight guys. Sam looks over at Gunny, "Should we kill them or let them be, Gunny? Maybe just hang them out back and then feed them to the pigs," Sam says with sarcasm and winks at Gunny.

"I think we will skin this one with the broken nose. This one thinks he has had military training, so I think I will show him what happened to those the Vietcong we caught back in the day," Gunny says and points to the broken nose guy.

The guy holds up a hand and shakes his head. He screams, "No, no!" Gunny takes out his knife and the guy wet his pants.

"We ain't heathens. We ain't going to kill anyone. But this is the last chance you guys get, and then we will skin you all alive and throw you out in the middle of the badlands. The buzzards and ants will eat you alive over a few days." Sam says will some seriousness." All the guys are shaking and scared. "Now I'm the new boss in town, and you will do what I tell you when I tell you. Does everyone have that?" Sam says nice and loud.

Everyone nods.

"Now, first things first. Where is this lab?" Sam asks.

Darwin finds some paper inside of the shop and brings it out to the guys on the porch. One of the guys with a sore shin starts drawing a map, but it didn't really make sense. He couldn't remember a single road or the direction he was going.

Sam knows that Macky will surely try something stupid as soon as he gets the chance. Sam could never trust Macky and he can't just kill him. He is going to have to either get him thrown into jail or throw him to the wolves.

The sun is coming up. Sam goes over to their trucks to see if there is anything that needs to be taken. Sam finds some money under the seat, which amounts to about a thousand dollars. He takes the money and puts it in his pocket. He finds two 9-mm. handguns, which are junk, but he takes them anyway. He finds a sawed-off shotgun, a box of shells, and two bottles of Crown Royal. Then he looks in the back of the trucks and finds two cases of beer. He looks around for any secret compartments that may be hiding drugs or money. He finally finds a box under the truck. He calls one of the guys over to open the box. They all hesitate and look at Macky. Sam grabs up his findings along with the beer and walks over to the porch. Sam hands the weapons to Darwin and the beer to the guys on the porch. They all quickly grab a beer and drink it down like they are dying of thirst. Sam grabs a beer and drinks part of it then walks over and grabs Macky by the throat. "Open the fucking box now or we will finish this now," Sam threatens Macky.

Macky shakes his head. "I ain't opening that fucking box for no one. If I do, they will kill me for sure. So fuck you."

"I'll do more than kill you. In ten seconds, Darwin is going to cut your nuts off and he has never done it before. It's going to hurt and it is going to take a while. Then we will start at your toes and start removing parts. Take your pick," Sam says sternly.

"I ain't going to do it," Macky says.

Sam motioned Darwin for the knife. Sam grabs the knife and cut open Macky's jeans. Then he hands the knife back to Darwin. Say warns Macky, "Last chance."

"Fuck you, I won't do it anyway, you motherfucker," Macky says very nervously. Macky is sacred. He stands up and prepares for a getaway or death.

Sam kicks Macky's legs out from underneath him and Macky falls to the ground. Sam puts one knee on Macky's neck and the other on his chest. Darwin walks over and gets down on one knee ready to cut Macky. Darwin's hands start shaking like a leaf.

"OK, OK, Slim, go over and open the box!" Macky yells. Sam isn't sure if it is a bluff, but so far things have not gone well.

"Darwin, give me that shotgun I gave you and make sure it is loaded," Sam says to Darwin. Darwin grabs the shotgun and injects a shell into the chamber. Then he hands it to Sam.

Slim is one of the guys that Sam had hit in the back of the head. Slim grabs another beer. He goes over and opens the box while Sam watches from a far. "If there is a gun in there and you touch it, I will kill you before you can turn around," Sam warns Slim.

Slim opens the box and then gets up off his knees and steps back. Sam looks at Slim. Sam can tell there is something fishy going on. Sam looks at the box and it is empty. On closer inspection, there is a thin wire inside the empty box. Sam gets up and walks over to Slim. He points the shotgun at Slim and then kicks him in the nuts. Slim bends over in pain and tries to catch his breath. Sam says to him, "Get down there and open that fucking door. That thing is booby-trapped." Slim nervously undoes the wire and opens the door. "Now take the contents out of the box and put it down on the ground." Slim reaches in and pulls out the .45 Colt that is in the box. Sam sticks the shotgun up to Slim's head and Slim slowly set the .45 on the ground. Sam walks over and picks up the handgun. Slim pulls out two large plastic wrapped bundles and sets them on the ground. Sam walks over and opens them up. The two bundles are money, a lot of money. Sam tucks the .45 into his belt and then grabs the money. He carries the money over to the porch. Macky is standing there, holding his pants up. Sam drops the money into Darwin's hands. "Here count this," Sam says to Darwin.

"I thought you didn't have the money?" Sam looks over at Macky.

"That's not my money. They will kill us if we don't bring that back," Macky screams.

"WHO is they?" Sam asks with intense curiosity.

"The YUPPIs, they run all the meth around here and they will kill us and you," Macky yells out in nervousness. Macky is mad and scared at the same time.

"No, they won't. I have run into them many of times. Now you will tell me where the lab is and I'll get them first before they get me or you. If not, I'm going to turn you loose and you can go tell them where I'm at if you can still talk." Sam gives them an ultimatum.

"Hey! There has to be at least two hundred thousand dollars in here," Darwin says with excitement. Sam goes over and takes out twenty thousand dollars and gives it to Darwin and then hands the rest to Gunny.

"There, Darwin, this is your money back with interest, and, Gunny, there is a down payment," Sam says.

Sam walks over and looks around under the other truck, but there is no box. Sam grabs Slim and asks, "You got anything else hidden that I might want? Is that all you guys are worth is a few thousand dollars?"

"That is it, one truck is the hauler, the other is the blocker," Slim explains. "We were going to bring this money back and pick up another meth delivery today. But Macky wanted to come after you first so he had something to brag about. We didn't want to do this, but he is the boss."

"OK, you and the boys will just sit here till my brothers get here and then you can all go. When do they expect you to show up?" Sam asks.

"Not until tonight," Slim says.

"Gunny, you got any handcuffs so these guys will stay awhile?" Sam asks.

Gunny goes into the shop and comes out with handcuffs, and all eight guys are handcuffed to the porch rail. Sam gives them all beer and Gunny cooks them all breakfast. Gunny brings out a half-gallon jug of Lord Calvert whiskey, and the boys passed it around along with the two bottles of Crown Royal. Within an hour, all eight of them are too drunk to even stand up, which made it easy to guard them. Darwin delighted in the duty of sitting in a rocking chair holding the sawed-off shotgun on them. It gave him the feeling of real power he needed.

Sam calls his Mom and tells her that he will probably not make it home today but that later Bud, Dakota, and DH will be coming. She is excited and kind of questioned why they are coming. But Mom and Dad are always happy when they come home. His Mom starts to act worried, so Sam just tells her that he is with Darwin and they are visiting friends. Darwin never got into trouble, so Sam's Mom is much relieved.

Sam then calls his sister, Gina, to get Harland's number. Sam is going to ask for Scubby's number, but he really didn't trust him.

Sam calls Harland. "Harland! Are you working for me yet?"

"Yes, I am, what do you want me to do?" Harland asks.

"I want you to come over to the gunsmith shop and do not tell a soul where you are going," Sam orders.

"OK, do you want me to bring anything?" Harland asks.

"Yeah, stop and get me some Copenhagen and about ten cases of beer. Not that cheap shit either, good beer. Then get two big bottles of Jack Daniels. Then go pickup about ten pizzas and two boxes of power bars and a case of bottled water. Then go and get a lot of bandage material, Betadine solution and Neosporin, and a bunch of Band-Aids of the large size and some of those nasal strips," Sam says.

Harland is completely baffled. "What the hell do you want all that for?"

"Just bring the stuff here and make it snappy," Sam says snippily. Sam thought, "I just fucking hired him and now he was questioning the first order of business. What the fuck?"

"OK, it will probably take me a couple of hours but I will get there," Harland says. He can tell by the tone in Sam's voice that he is not happy.

"OK!" Sam says.

Harland jumps into his truck to leave Sam's parents' place. Harland had been talking to Darrell when Sam called.

"Where you going in such a hurry?" Darrell asks.

"Sam called and told me to get to work. *Sooo* I got to get going now. I'll probably talk to you later," Harland says as he looks for his keys for the truck.

"Well, mind if I ride along?" Darrell asks as he makes his way to the passenger door. He has already made up his mind that he is going even without an answer.

"Well, Sam told me not to tell anyone but I suppose he won't mind if you just ride along," Harland says.

"Hey, Mother! Mom!" Darrell yells toward the house to Elaine, "I'm going with Harland and he's going over to where Sam is."

"OK, Sam just called and said he's not going to be back tonight, so maybe you should take some of his clothes along." Elaine says, She quickly gathers up some clothes for Sam.

"He's probably fine, but . . ."

Elaine just shoves Sam's clothes into Darrell's hands. She knows that Darrell will just hem and haw about it. "Just wait and I'll make some sandwiches for you guys to take along in case you get hungry."

Darrell just accepts the clothes. "We'll be all right. We will just grab something on the way. Harland is in a hurry."

Elaine just goes into the house and starts making sandwiches. She never likes to hear the words "No, thank you, I'm not hungry." She quickly makes sandwiches and puts them in a bag. She goes outside and hands them to Darrell. "Now you guys don't get into any trouble." Then she chuckles.

Darrell throws the stuff in to Harland truck. He gets in and shuts the door. Harland quickly drives out of the driveway and races into town.

"What is the hurry?" Darrell asks.

"Sam told me to hurry," Harland says with anxiousness.

"Well, where are we going?" Darrell asks. He doesn't really care where he is going. He is just making small talk. The important thing to him is that he is going somewhere.

"I can't tell you but we have to stop in town to get some things for Sam. He gave me a list of things to bring." Harland tells Darrell with a little annoyance. Harland is not easily annoyed, but now Darrell is getting on his nerves. He knows that Darrell doesn't care where they are going.

They drive into town and stop at the liquor store first. Scubby and Digger are at the liquor store. Digger is one of Snoop's friends and is also one of Gina's friends. Sam doesn't really like Digger. Sam always thought that Digger is a useless arrogant asshole. Sam had known Digger for a long time. Digger sometimes would go along with Sam to rodeos. He seldom would participate in the rodeo, but it didn't keep him from bragging about how he rode bulls. Then one weekend while Sam was gone rodeoing, Sam went to a rodeo dance and Digger was with Sam's girlfriend. Sam never could tolerate being around either one of them ever again.

"What'cha doing? Having a party without us, boy?" Digger says and slaps Harland on the back like they are friends. "We're going to come out tonight and see Sam anyway. We'll just get some more beer and meet you out there. Do you got enough ice? Oh hell, we'll get ice."

"Yeah, we want to talk some more about going out east with Sam," Snoop says with excitement. Snoop is already a little drunk.

"We're not going back to the farm yet, we're just getting this for Sam and he ain't going to be back tonight anyway. But you can help us carry this stuff," Harland says in kind, irritated voice. He grabs an arm full of beer, whiskey, and a roll of Copenhagen as did Darrell.

Snoop and Digger grab the rest and carry it to the truck. Snoop and Digger then run in to the store and buy a bunch of beer, ice, and cigarettes. They run out to Snoop's truck and follow Harland. Harland has driven across the highway to the grocery store to pick up the food and other things. Harland and Snoop do the same and then go into the store to find Darrell and Harland. Harland is racing around the store with a shopping cart, only slowing down long enough to throw stuff in the cart. Then he runs up to the checkout counter, and that is where Darrell, Snoop, and Digger catch up to him. Harland pays for all the stuff with a credit card and then pushes the cart out to his truck. Snoop helps Harland load everything into the truck while Darrell and Digger stand around and talk. Harland jumps into his truck and starts it.

"Ahh, Darrell. We, ah, need to get going like right now," Harland says with urgency.

Darrell finishes his conversation with Digger. Then he slowly climbs into the truck. Darrell turns and looks at Harland some annoyance and says, "I still don't know what all the hurry is for. Sam can wait if he wants this stuff. Just don't know why we are in a hurry."

Harland just looks at Darrell. He really just wanted to hurry and get out of the parking lot to see if he could keep Snoop from following him. Harland races down some back roads, but Snoop is right on his tail. The dirt plume flew high and thick behind the two trucks as they raced down the back dirt roads.

Sam and Gunny are talking and drinking coffee. Gunny starts to show Sam some of the tricks of using his new chain weapon. Gunny demonstrates the weapon to Sam by whipping the chain around and hitting a small tree. Gunny cuts the tree down and then recoils it faster than a snake strike. Sam just stands there watching in awe. Gunny hands Sam the weapon. Sam twirls it around like a rope then lets the kama end go. It flies through the air and around a small tree. He jerks on the chain and blade slices through the small tree. The kama and chain flies back, but Sam misses the catch, narrowly missing his ear. Sam whips the chain again and this time he catches it.

Gunny smiles and says, "Very good recovery, Sam."

Sam, relieved that he missed his face, smiles and says, "Just like the whip I had when I was a kid. Definitely need a lot more practice."

Gunny slaps Sam on the back. Sam hears a truck coming down the road and looks to see who is coming. Sam sees Harland's truck pull in along with one behind it. Snoop and Digger get out of their truck, whopping and hollering like they are at a party. Darrell gets out and walks up to the shop with his hands in his pockets. Harland slunk up to the shop. Sam and Gunny just stand there waiting for everyone to walk up to the shop.

Sam is upset. Sam motions for Harland to come over a long side of the shop. Harland nervously walks up to the side of the shop where Sam and Gunny are standing. Sam looks at Harland and says in a soft stern voice, "What the hell did I tell you?"

"You told me to get the stuff, hurry up, and don't tell anyone where I was going. I didn't tell them, they all just followed along," Harland says in his defense. Harland looks down and puts his hands up with his palms out. "Sorry. I couldn't tell your dad he couldn't come and the other two were at the liquor store."

"Well, I guess, now there is going to be a bunch of people getting involved. Get all the stuff out and we are going to have a little meeting," Sam says almost in an apologetic voice.

Harland grabs Snoop and Digger, who are both drinking again, to help him with the stuff. They take it and set it all inside the shop.

"Sam, you doing all right?" Digger asks as he walks up to Sam with his hand held out for a handshake.

"I'm doing just fine, but you guys just got yourselves in a whole bunch of shit," Sam says while shaking Digger's hand.

Digger with draws his hand and steps back like he has been slapped. He then notices the eight beat-up drunken guys handcuffed to the rail and Darwin sitting shotgun.

"OOOOOKKKKAAAYYY, I give up. What up?" Digger asks with anxiousness.

"These assholes came out here to put a killing on us and we kicked their ass. Now we are going to go to the big boys and whip their ass. Any questions?" Darwin says in a cocky way. He jumps up like he is now the man in charge. Sam thought it is great that Darwin for the first time in his life is feeling like he is "the man."

"OK, but are we going to party man?" Snoop asks while he jumps over to his truck and grabs the rest of the beer. Both he and Harland are dumping ice on the beer. They had found an old steel and porcelain bathtub in the weeds. Once they are done dumping ice, Snoop starts passing beers all around. Darwin even has one.

"Mom sent along your clothes if you what them," Darrell tells Sam. "So what are you doing over here?"

"We just came over to look at the shop and see Gunny. You remember Gunny, don't you? Gunny, this is my dad," Sam introduces them.

"Hello, Mr. Jackson," Darrell says as he shakes Gunny's hand.

"Hello, I think you and I are a little old for this stuff. Let's go in and sit a spell," Gunny says and then walks in to the shop with Darrell. They both sit down in the shop and start talking. They talk and drink for hours.

Everyone digs into the food, even the chained-up bunch. The gang of eight have already drank two cases of beer and most of the whiskey. Now that there is more alcohol, the eight of them keep on drinking. When Sam thinks that the gang of eight is incapacitated enough, he unhandcuffs them so they can move around on the porch. Darwin has been watching them very closely and Sam is sure that Darwin will keep them under control. Some of the gang of eight helped themselves to the bandage supplies. One of the gang rebandaged all of Macky's wounds. Sam was going too, but he hated Macky so much, he didn't bother. The guy with the broken nose put a couple of nasal strips on his nose and the rest iced some wounds. Macky is still holding on to his pants, so Sam goes into the shop and finds a pair of camouflage pants for him to put on. One of the gang helps Macky put his pants on.

Sam thinks, "Things are going well so far. This little gang is drunk and happy except for Harland, Darwin, and me. Those others should be here sometime tonight."

Sam decides to call Bud, "Hey, how's it going."

"Good, we'll be there in a few hours. We are going to fill up in Sioux Falls and then you can meet us," Bud says.

"No, just fill up and get some food. Then hurry up and come out to the gunsmith shop. Do you remember where that is?" Sam asks.

"Yeah, I've been there a bunch of times. I can find it with my eyes closed," Bud says.

"Good, because we've got another big night. Those damn YUPPI groups are out here too. Do you remember that fucking Macky?" Sam asks Bud. "He's selling for them and tonight we are going on a little raid." Sam gets a little glint of excitement.

"OK, do you have any weapons or anything?" Sam asks Bud jokingly.

"We didn't bring anything except DH's .40," Bud says with a little confusion.

"I'm just joking about the weapons," Sam says with a little smirk.

"I was a little confused. Don't they have some weapons at the shop?" Bud says sarcastically.

"I just bought us the whole gunsmith shop and he has everything. Wait till you see it all," Sam says with excitement.

"Holy shit, how did you get that old guy to sell you all that?" Bud asks.

"I had HIM make me an offer that HE couldn't refuse," Sam says.

"Well, we'll call after we fill up," Bud says and then hangs up.

Sam puts his phone away. He notices that Macky and Snoop are talking a little too much. Sam knows that they know each other, but he doesn't know how much. Sam can sense that there is going to be trouble with Snoop. His senses are usually right. Sam decides to keep an eye on Snoop. He walks over to Darwin.

"Hey, my brothers are on their way and will be here in a few hours. I think it would be best if no one but us and Harland go into the shop, could you watch the door for me?" Sam says to Darwin. "Like put your chair in the doorway so no one gets in. I'm going to send Harland down the road a ways and let him be a lookout. Then I'm going to make sure no one can get in the back way."

"Yeah, I noticed that Snoop guy is a little chummy with Macky. He's been talking on his phone too. I think the shit may hit the fan before we even turn it on," Darwin says in an authoritative voice. He slides chair over to the doorway.

Sam motions to Harland to come into the shop. "How well do you know this Snoop?" Sam asks Harland.

"He just started to hang around Gina's place a lot. He seems to be always around at your dad's place or in town when I go there. I just don't know him that well. I don't even know if he has a job," Harland explains.

"Well, I think him and Macky are buddies or something. There may be trouble on the way and I want to be ready for it if it comes. My brothers won't be here for a few hours. I'll feel more comfortable when they get here," Sam says with a little concern.

"I'm sorry I let him follow us out here. I didn't know all of this was going to be such a big to do," Harland says.

"No worries. You go hunting, don't you?" Sam asks.

"Yeah, all the time," Harland says almost in a questioning way. Harland looks at Sam a little puzzled.

"Do you think you can sneak out through the trees and up the road, say about a mile and be a lookout? Maybe if you see trouble coming you can make a few tires go flat." Sam says.

"Hell yeah, just get me a rifle." Harland says with enthusiasm.

"Hey, Gunny, I hate to interrupt," Sam butts in on Gunny and Darrell conversation.

"Yes, Sam, what can I do for ya?" Gunny turns and looks over at Sam while still sitting in his chair.

"Ah, Harland here needs a rifle with a sound suppresser and night vision." Sam says almost as a question, but Sam figured that Gunny could come up with something.

"Just happened to have one." Gunny and Darrell get up and walk over and into the back room. Then they both come back with Gunny carrying an M110 semiautomatic with night vision mounted behind a scope and a sound suppresser. "You think this will work?" Gunny says with a smile on his face.

"I think that will be great. Maybe about two hundred rounds of ammunition in magazines to go, and we will need a radio, and some camouflage," Harland says with a smile on his face. He takes the weapon from Gunny like he is a kid that just got a present.

Gunny walks Harland over to camouflage clothing shelf. He takes out some camouflage fatigues and a ghillie suit. Harland hands the weapon back to Gunny and takes the clothes. He goes into a more secluded part of the shop and changes clothes.

Harland returns up to the front of the shops interior, where Sam, Gunny, and Darrell are standing loading ammunition clips. Harland says, "What do you think?" Harland has a smile on his face like a man that just put on a tux for the first time.

"I think that will do. Now when you get there, you radio me. Do not let anyone see you moving out there, and I mean no one. Don't call anyone, don't make a noise. I want you to be invisible even if you have to shoot. I want you to be invisible and silent. Can you do this? If you can't I need to know now." Sam is still a little untrusting of Harland for bring that asshole Snoop out here.

"I can do it. I did this in the marines. I was a marine sniper. I never saw any action but I can shoot and stay invisible. Don't worry, this is right up my alley," Harland says with confidence. He is excited; this is the first time that he may be able to use some of his skills.

"I am sorry. I did not know that you had training. I thank you for your service to the country. I am ashamed that I under estimated your skills. I will not ever do that again," Sam says with sincerity. He is embarrassed about telling Harland how to do a job that he had been so highly trained for.

"I'll be going know," Harland says and then he disappeared. Sam watches him go out the back of the shop.

Sam goes out on the porch to see if anyone is watching the trees. Sam does not see or hear any movement in the trees. Sam says softly to himself, "Damn, he does know what he is doing."

Sam watches Snoop and Macky. Sam thinks, "They are definitely buddies." Sam notices that Snoop is on the phone and then he hands the phone to Macky. While Macky is on the phone, he looks worried and almost pleading to whomever he is talking to. Sam walks over to Snoop and Macky. Snoop walks away like dog that just got caught peeing on the carpet.

Macky looks at Sam and hands him the phone. "It's for you," he says.

Snoop starts to bounce around the place smoking cigarettes and drinking. He goes over and grabs a bottle of Crown Royal and brings it back to where Sam and Macky are standing. He leans up to the porch post and stands there like he is king shit. He takes a hit off his smoke. Then he tilts his head back and blows smoke. After each puff, he laughs and shakes his head. Sam stares in disgust at Snoop. He hates like him, big fish in a puddle, but when thrown in the lake, they swim for the shore.

"Hello!" Sam says to whoever is on the phone.

"My, you are a busy man today. Taking out some of my employees and then you had the nerve to take my money too," the guy on the phone says.

"Well, you have very bad employees. They should have been fired for incompetence. Obviously, they can never stick to the job that is given to them. Otherwise, I would not even be involved. Macky here, cannot pay his bills so basically you just gave him a loan. He'll pay you back like he paid my friend back." Sam is calm and cool. Sam treated this call like one of his clients' calls.

"You are probably right, and as soon as he comes back to work, he will probably, let say, ah, be terminated. But that is just between him and me. We, on the other hand, need to figure out how that money that I so-called loaned him is going to make it back to me. You see it is not my money neither, its federal property, or sort of," the guy on the phone says.

"You loaned your money to the wrong person, the federal government should know all about that. Unfortunately for you, I at this point, hate the federal government and its agencies. Basically, I will not give the money back. You can have Macky work it off," Sam says.

"It is not possible that you keep the money. So I guess if you don't give it back to Macky, then I will come and get it. As you know, the government imposes huge penalties for those that don't pay on time," the guy on the phone says with some sarcasm but more of a slighted threat.

"Might I ask, not that I don't already know but I want to confirm, what agency are you a part of?" Sam asks.

"Youth Unified for Political Party Initiatives, we are OCORC. That money is charity money for the community of sorts. Now give Macky the money back and this will be over." The guy on the phone is getting upset with Sam.

Sam looks at Snoop and Macky. Both guys are smiling from ear to ear like sixteen-year-olds at a striper club. Sam's eyes just narrow and he grow a big scowl on his face.

"Well, I am not going to give the money back. I just gave it to part of the community, and by the looks of it, they are not going to give any donations. Just say it went to a veterans of foreign wars fund and your higher-ups should be happy," Sam says.

"Well, that is unacceptable, and we will be on are way to claim what is government property," the guy on the phone says.

"Let's just say this is the start of a new revolution. I am going to take my country back and give it to the people," Sam says and then he snaps the phone in half. He hands it back to Snoop and says to him, "I reckon this is yours."

"You fucking prick, you broke my new phone!" Snoop yells at Sam. Snoop holds the phone in his hands like it is a dead baby.

Sam slaps Snoop. He hits in the left ear and Snoop falls to the ground. Snoop starts rolling around, screaming and kicking. He held his hand over his ear rubbing and grabbing at it.

Sam put his foot on Snoop's chest. He put half his weight down on to Snoop's xiphoid process just enough to make it painful and difficult for him to breathe. Snoop grunted as Sam applied weight. Sam leaned over and looked Snoop in the eye. "You disrespectful bastard. You are part of this whole fucking YUPPI thing," Sam says in a calm hateful voice. "Now I am going to have to kill you."

Snoop has fear in his eyes and is truly afraid Sam is going to kill him. Sam stands up and takes his foot off Snoop's chest and kicks him as hard as he could under Snoop's armpit. Snoop lets out a yell.

"Aaahhh!" Then Sam leaves him there with a cracked rib and a numb arm.

Sam walks over to Macky who is standing there smirking. Macky thinks he will be saved in an hour or so by his boss. Sam says to Macky, "You fuck! You think they are coming to save you?" Sam gives a sarcastic laugh. "They just want their money and they are going to kill you. You are too much trouble."

Macky starts laughing and says, "When they get here, I am going to have them drag you back to the barracks. If you are still alive, I'm going to gut you."

Without flinching, Sam punches Macky in the side of his face. Macky falls back against the wall of the shop and then slides down on to the porch. The trajectory of the punch knocks Macky's left mandible out of place. Instantly Macky's left side of his face goes numb. Macky had nothing else to say.

Darwin sees what is going on and he goes in to a wild dance type move. He starts waving the shotgun around at everyone. "Nobody move, nobody move. Stay calm or I'll let ya have it. Ya know I will."

"Darwin, Darwin! Easy up or you are going to shoot someone!" Sam yells over to him. Sam walks over to Snoop, who is sitting in the parking lot. Sam grabs him by the hair and drags him over to the rail. Then he grabs Macky by his bad arm and drags him closer to the rail. Gunny sees that things are happening and brings out the handcuffs. He quickly cuffs the two to the rail.

Digger is way too drunk to react to anything. He drank most of the Jack Daniels by himself but he did manage to say, "What the fuck did ya hit him for? He's ma friend."

Darwin walks over to Digger and sticks the shotgun under his chin, "Any friend of his is not any longer a friend of mine. You may want to think that out a bit."

"Easy, easy, he is an asshole. I really hate that son of a bitch," Digger says and then walks over and looks down at Snoop. Snoop looks up with the face of shame. Digger smiles and then gives him a kick in the ribs. "That's what you get for messing up a good party," Digger says to Snoop.

Darwin looks at Digger and says, "You're a hell of a loyal friend you are."

Sam looks at the others, who are pretty drunk, and then Sam gives them an ultimatum. "Here is the deal. You all get in your trucks and get on home. If I see you here or anywhere for that matter, I will make you wish you were dead. If you want trouble, stay here and we can redo last night. You got thirty seconds to decide and make your move."

The seven of them look at each other and then they look at Macky cuffed up to the rail. They all turn and head for their trucks. Slim turns around and looks at Sam. "We'll be going now. Thank you for the food and drinks. None of us wanted to come out here anyway, this was all Macky's idea. He's the boss, but I reckon he's not going to be much of anything anymore. Good day." Sam throws them their keys. Then they start their trucks and leave.

Sam and Darwin go inside. Gunny is sitting at his workbench, and Darrell is just standing there with his hands in his pockets looking out the door.

"What's going on?" Darrell asks Sam.

"Well, Dad, do you remember when we would go hunting and you always made some great shots? Well you'd better have Gunny set you up with whatever weapon you want because you may have to make several of those shots. I think we are now fighting the US government," Sam says.

"Oh shit, well, let me get over to Gunny," Darrell says.

Gunny is over at his bench, already setting up rifles. He is mounting scopes and adjusting this and that. Darrell jumps in and helps out with whatever Gunny is telling him to do. They worked well together and seem to understand each other.

Sam leaves Gunny and his Dad to what they are doing and goes outside to get some information from Snoop and Macky.

"Well, Macky, this is your last chance. Where are those guys coming from?" Sam asks.

"I ain't telling you anything. You guys are all fucked," Macky argumentatively mumbles to Sam. Macky remains siting there like he is going to be made king.

Sam grabs Macky by the hair and pulls his head back. Sam tells him, "Oh, you will tell me whatever I want and in a very short time." Sam lets go of his hair. Macky just starts laughing while keeping his jaw shut. Sam goes in to the shop and grabs a garbage bag from under the sink in Gunny's kitchenette. He grabs some para cord on his way back out the door. He goes out to Snoop and Macky who are just drinking and have a good old time tell each other what is going to happen to everyone as soon as the big boss gets there. Macky's jaw is working better. Somehow Snoop put it back in place by having Macky bite down on a shoe and hitting him the face.

Sam is calm but he is pissed off. When he asks a question, he wants an answer. Sam takes the para cord and cuts two four-foot lengths of rope. He stands in front of Macky and Snoop and ties a modified Roeder knot in each piece of rope.

Sam says, "These knots are great. They are like zip strips. Once they are tightened down, they cannot come off unless you cut them off."

Macky and Snoop just sat there and looked at Sam. Sam opens the garbage bags. He quickly puts one of the garbage bags over Macky's head along with the para cord.

"What the fuck are you doing, you stupid asshole?" Macky yells. He tries to grab at the bag with his good hand. Sam grabs Macky's hand and stands on it while he slightly tightens the knot. Macky screams, "Ooouchh! Get the fuck off my hand, God damn you!"

Once Sam got the bag and para cord on his neck, he slightly tightens the knot a little more just a little, not enough to choke him but enough to seal the bag. Sam tells Macky, "Now you listen, I think you may have about one minute before the CO_2 builds up in that bag. You have a couple of minutes after, and then you will die. So if you start talking and tell me exactly what I want to know, I will take the bag off your head. Now where are they coming from?"

"Fuck you!" Macky says and starts to struggle to remove the bag. Sam just pulled the knot down a little tighter.

"Well then, you are going to die. Snoop, you are next, do you want to answer the question?" Sam says. Snoop just sat there staring at Sam.

"Aaah! Yeah!" Snoop's jaw drops when Macky quit struggling and goes limp. Sam removes the bag and cuts the para cord. Sam checks for a pulse. Sam shakes his head as to say, "No pulse." Snoop understood it to mean that Sam has killed Macky. Then he moves over to Snoop, who is trying to get his handcuffs off and move away from Sam. Sam lifts up the bag. Snoop quickly blurts out, "Their coming from the other side of Chamberlin. They'll be here in about five hours or so." Snoop wets his pants. At that time, Macky comes to and struggles to sit up. Snoop look at Macky in amazement and says to Sam, "He ain't fucking dead. I thought you killed him. Otherwise, I'd never told you shit."

Macky shakes the cobwebs out of his head then looks at Snoop. "You fucking dumb ass, what the hell did you tell him? Man, the boss is going to fucking kill you when he gets here," Macky says and then punches Snoop.

"Didn't matter if you talked now or not," Sam says, "I would have skinned you both alive if you wouldn't have told me." Sam knows that Snoop is lying about the time or the place. Chamberlin is only about two and half hours from where they are. He figures that part of it is true and knows he doesn't have much time before the YUPPIs get there.

"Aaahh, hey, boss, aaahh, there's a semi coming up the road," Harland calls over the radio.

"That's probably my brother is there anyone following the truck?" Sam radios back.

"Yeah, there are five cars and four trucks filled with people. The one truck is your dad's new truck," Harland says.

"Can you see who is in it?" Sam asks

"It is your sister and your mom," Harland says.

"Well, let them through, but keep a watch on things," Sam says.

The semi rolls in as well as a bunch of other vehicles. Sam can see DH is driving and Bud in the passenger seat. DH turns the truck around so that it is heading on its way out. The truck stops and the doors open. DH, Bud, and Kota get out and walk up to Sam.

"Hey," Bud says.

"Hey," Sam says.

"Well, we got the stuff in the truck minus some traveling expensive. What do you want the truck for again?"

"Well, we need to start loading everything this shop into the truck in a hell of a hurry. I reckon that there is probably going to be big trouble from YUPPIs again," Sam informs Bud. "You remember Macky and Darwin, don't you? Old Macky here is part of that shit group. We just took about a quarter million off them. I gave some to Darwin and the rest to Gunny for a down payment on our new place. We need to get loaded and get the hell out of here with in the next hour or so." Sam reaches over and shakes DH's hand and slaps Kota on the back. Sam tells Bud, Kota, and DH, "Well, go get what you want and put it in the pickup over there and then let's load up." He points over to the new truck in the parking lot.

The three men walk into the shop. They all glance at the two handcuffed to the rail while they are walking. The two brothers and DH walk in the shop with big smiles on their faces. They run around the shop, picking things up and setting them down like kids who are turned loose into a toy store and have been told they can have anything he want.

Elaine, Gina, and a bunch of other people get out of their vehicles. "How come you all came out here?" Sam asks.

"Dad called us a long time ago and told me to get some people together to help Gunny move all this stuff and that Bud is coming by with a truck to load it on," Elaine explains to Sam. "I called Gina and she got a bunch of her friends to help you move." Elaine gives Sam a hug.

Gina walks over to Snoop and asks, "What the hell did you do?"

"I didn't do a damn thing. Your fucking brother just went nuts. Now he's got all of you in big trouble, so I suggest you get the hell home," Snoop screams a warning to Gina and the group standing around as he looks up from the porch floor.

"I told you about him, I told you not ever to cross him," Gina says to Snoop.

"Yeah, and you said all those stories that he tells were true too. I still think he is full of shit, and as soon as my boss gets here, I will show you that he just someone who is full of shit. Hell, I just about kicked his ass until he jumped me," Snoop says in cocky manner.

"I bet you did," Gina says with sarcasm. "Is that why you pissed your pants?"

"I didn't piss my pants, I just spilled something," Snoop says with embarrassment.

"You shouldn't saddle up if you can't ride like the big boys. I told you he was one to bring a knife to a gunfight and now you are on his bad side," Gina says "I told you so without actually saying 'I told you so.'"

"I didn't do anything. Tell him to just let me go and I'll leave and that will be that. If he doesn't, then as soon as I get out of these cuffs, I'll kick his ass." Snoop tries to bargain with Gina.

"You'll be lucky if he don't bury and let the buzzards eat you alive. I'll tell him that you want to kick his ass and maybe he will let you go." Gina turns and walks over to Sam. Sam is talking to his Mom. Gina interrupts, "So what did they do to get cuffed to the rail?"

"Well, you know Macky? He comes out here with a bunch of his buddies and is going to kill us. I sent his buddies on their way a while ago. Snoop follows Harland and Dad out here and then call someone they call the Boss. The Boss is part of the YUPPI group that I told you all about the other night. Now they are on their way here and it won't be good if we are here when they arrive," Sam explains to Gina.

"OK, well, Snoop told me to tell you that if you let him go, there won't be any trouble. Oh yeah, he says he could kick your ass," Gina says to Sam.

Sam walks over without saying a word and motions for Darwin to unlock Snoop's handcuffs. Darwin unlocks the handcuffs and puts them in his pocket. Snoop looks up and then rubs his wrist. He stands up and walks off the porch to the center of the parking area. He looks at everyone watching him, then warns everyone, "You all are in deep shit, and if you hang around that crazy bastard, you'll probably all get arrested or killed." Snoop points toward Sam standing next to the porch.

"Now, Snoop, if I see you again, I will not let you off so easy," Sam warns Snoop with a calm voice.

"WHAT DID YOU SAY TO ME?" Snoop yells with almost a laugh or sarcasm in his voice. "Let me off. I can kick your ass at any time. I may not let you off so easy next time." Snoop throws his head back and shakes it. He grabs a smoke and lights it. "Matter of fact, I am going to show everyone. Right fucking now! How full of shit you are. I'll prove that you are nothing but a lying sack of shit." Snoop takes another puff of his smoke and then throws it on the ground. Then takes out a small container and opens it. He reaches into the small container with two fingers and brings them back out. He holds his two figures up to his nose and snorts some of the white contents. This sends him in to frenzy. He screams and runs at Sam. Sam watches him coming toward him. Snoop lunges at Sam and swing his fist in circles like one of them wind lawn ornaments. Sam jumps to the left as Snoop lunges by him. Sam punch Snoop with a right hand to the Snoop's left ear. Sam grabs Snoop's hair and jerks him back. At the same time Snoop stumbles back, Sam hits him with a knee into the kidney area and then again to the back of his head. Snoop drops to the ground. Sam punches him in the mouth, xiphoid, and testicles, all in one quick consecutive motion. The fight is over in fifteen seconds. Snoop grabs his crotch and tries to scream but all he could do is let out a squeak. He starts breathing rapid shallow breathes writhing in pain everywhere. Sam grabs him by the left leg and pulls him up close to rail. Darwin pulls the handcuffs out of his pocket and cuffs Snoop's leg to the rail.

"You had a chance to leave, and I guess you choose to stay. Your stupidity or pride has probably just got you killed. Not by me but I am sure your boss will finish the job. You know the rules of my family," Sam lectures Snoop. Then he turns to everyone else. They are all watching. They all thought that they were going to see a long drawn-out fight. "I know you all wanted to see a big fight, and I'm sorry to disappoint you but this is how most fights go. So if you all are here to help, then we need to get this place loaded and get out of here in the next hour. We really need to hurry and get out of here so let's get busy. The faster we get done, the faster the party can start over at Mom and Dad's place," Sam says.

The crowd says, "Yeah!" and they all rush into the shop. DH, Bud, and Dakota have Sam's truckload to the brim. DH already has the semitruck started and is ready to back up to the door as soon as the crowd moves. By the time DH has the truck backed up, the crowd is already bringing stuff out to the porch. DH, Dakota, and three others jump in the trailer and stack things up as people lift it up into the trailer. Gunny, Darrell, Elaine, Gina, and Sam pack crates and take stuff down. With all the help, the shop is loaded into the trailer in about seventy minutes. They even take the kitchen sink with them. DH starts the truck and the others all gathered outside.

"OK, the last one to Mom and Dad's place is buying the beer for the night!" Sam yells. The crowd rans to their vehicles and in a cloud of dust they are gone. Sam sends Gina, Gunny, Darrell, and Elaine back to the farm. Gunny keeps ahold of the first half of this money while he sat in Darrell and Elaine's new truck. He is still smiling from ear to ear. Darwin and Bud helped him up into the truck. Sam leaves Macky cuffed to the rail. He throws the keys on the floor next to the shop door. Digger had sobered up enough, found the keys to his truck, and then took off with the others.

"You are going to stay here and maybe your boss will help you out or not." Sam lays the disassembled handgun on the porch just in reach of Macky. "Now he may be pissed that you lost his money, so I'm going to leave this gun with you and you can defend yourself or shoot the cuffs off. Whatever you prefer," Sam says to Macky in a calm manner. He sets the clip onto the porch. "If I see you again, ever again, I will bury you." Sam, Bud, and Darwin get into Sam's truck and take off.

"Get out to the road as fast as you can and call me on the radio when you get there," Sam says over the radio to Harland.

"I'm already there, so pick me up at the corner," Harland radios back.

Sam drives down the road and stops to pick up Harland. Harland throws his gear in the back of the truck then jumps in the passenger side. "Boy, Snoop, you look like shit. What happened to you?" Harland asks Snoop with a little laughter in his voice. Snoop just grunts.

"The dumb shit tried to tangle with Sam. He got the bad end of the stick," Darwin says and starts laughing.

"Well, why is he in here?" Harland asks.

"He is going to tell us where the lab is, and while they are coming for us, we will be checking out their place. So what we need to do is go pickup Dakota and DH. Then we are going to head out to find this place. We may find something and we may not, but we need to look. If anyone doesn't want to go, then they need to speak now," Sam says as he drives toward his parents' farm.

"I don't want to go. Why don't you just let me out somewhere and I'll just forget all about this little misunderstanding," Snoop says with a little trouble. His chest still hurt him, but nothing is permanently damaged. There is no immediate danger of dying.

"You can leave when you show us this place. You owe me, you lied, and you were trying to call the enemy in on me. This is going to be your payment, but if you don't what to do it, you and I are going to the badlands and feed the coyotes. Take your fucking pick. You get until we get to the farm to decide," Sam says sternly to Snoop.

"OK, I'll show you but these are really bad people. You may not want to mess with them. You are already in deep shit, and they won't let up until they find you," Snoop warns Sam.

"We'll worry about that later. Harland! Bud! Darwin! Are you all in?" Sam asks.

"You bet," they all say.

CHAPTER FOURTEEN

SAM DRIVES TO THE FARM. DH and Dakota have already parked the semitruck in the trees next to the barn. The rest of the people are already drinking and cooking on the grill. Darrell and Gunny are still talking and drinking beer.

Sam walks over to the semitruck to talk to DH and Kota. He tells them the full lowdown on the last few days. DH and Kota both agree that they should leave immediately and find the lab. They all walk over to Sam's truck and start unloading and loading gear and weapons. Gunny and Darrell come over to find out what is going on.

"Don't you think all this stuff can stay in here for now?" Darrell says and hands everyone a beer. "You can park the truck in the shed and it should be all right. Come and join the party."

"Well, Dad, we are not quite done yet today. We are going to take a little trip to a lab and check things out. If you can get Snoop some Advil and maybe get him a shot of whiskey, he may feel a little better and quit whining," Sam tells his dad and then drinks down the beer.

"What do you need to go stir up trouble for? Just leave those people alone and they won't bother you. Remember, you can't get the bees to make honey if you keep kicking the hive," Darrell says.

"What the hell does that mean?" Sam says not with a question but more questioning the stupidity of the statement. "Dad, these people are bad people. Remember what happened to Dakota and me in Virginia? These are the same group of people and they cannot be dealt with in any other way. They will come here if we don't stop them there," Sam explains.

"Well, do what you have to do but don't get hurt. I'll go get those aspirin." Darrell leaves and heads into the house.

"I'll get these weapons set up in a jiffy. You guys start loading magazines and get your gear on," Gunny says and gets to work. He quickly puts night scopes on and checks trigger pulls and actions of the rifles and handguns.

Sam goes in the house and finds his old slingshot that he used when he was a kid. Then he grabs some food from the cupboard and goes out to the truck again. Everything is quickly put together. DH and Kota got some fatigues and bulletproof vests for everyone from the trailer. Everyone changes clothes and jump into the truck. They start to drive out of the driveway when a truck pulls in. Sam pulls his truck up alongside the truck and rolls down the window.

"How ya doing, you old two-bit?" the man in the truck asks in an excited voice.

"Well, shit, what have you been up to?" Sam asks. Sam hadn't seen Kim, his old friend, in several years. They had run around together getting into trouble and getting rid of trouble long ago. Kim had been the toughest and meanest fighter Sam had known when they were running around. Kim then joined the marines, and they just sort of went in different directions from then on. Now Kim is married and has two kids.

"Where are you going? I heard you were in town and thought we'd stop over and kick your butt. Are you leaving already?" Kim asks with curiosity.

"Well, I am not leaving for good. I got a little job we have to finish before morning. You want to come along, it will be like old times, and I mean just like old times. If you know what I'm saying," Sam says.

"I'm with my wife and kids, but if we are just going and coming back . . ." Kim stops talking and looks questioningly at his wife. Then he asks her if it is all right that he goes with them. She tells him it would be all right since he hadn't seen Sam in a long time. But he is not supposed to get into any trouble. Kim turns back to Sam. "I'm in. You got any room?"

"We've got room for one more. Jump in!" Sam says. Bud opens up the back door. It is getting pretty crowded in the truck with eight people, but they would manage. Sam drives and tells the whole story about what is going on and where they are going. Kim's face lights up like old times, like they were headed for the bar where they knew they would be in a fight.

Snoop still hasn't told them exactly where the lab is located. Sam yells back, "Well, Snoop, where is the lab?"

"I ain't tellin' you all nothing. You can't make me tell you shit." Snoop flips Sam off. "As soon as I get the hell out of here, you and your brothers will be going to jail."

"Pull over for a minute," Kim tells Sam. Sam knew exactly what Kim is going to do.

Sam pulls over to the side of the road. Kim opens the back door. He grabs Snoop by the side of his mouth and drags him out. Snoop sort of crawls with resistance across Bud. Bud pushes Snoop and he lands on the side of the road, knees and arms first. Snoop screams in pain. His knees feel like a hammer just hit them. Kim takes his foot and pushes Snoop over onto his back. Then he places a boot on his chest. Kim leans over and yells, "You need to tell Sam exactly what he wants or"—Kim takes out his tactical knife and opens it up—"I'll show up what pain really is."

"You ain't shit. If you're with them, you and your family are just as good as dead," Snoop screams and spits in to Kim's face.

"Oh, you're going to talk." Kim grabs Snoop's earlobe with the diamond stud and cuts the earlobe off. Snoop grabs for his ear and starts screaming.

"You son of a bitch, I'm going to kill you!" He starts kicking and screaming, trying to get off the ground. Kim steps down harder on his chest then lets him go. Snoop backs away by scooting on his rump, then gets up on his feet. Snoop screams at Kim, "You think you are a tough guy with that knife, don't you? Well, fuck you! Now I'm going to fuck you up."

Kim folds his knife and puts it back into his pocket. Snoop starts to move from side to side like some Brazilian martial artist. He moves in closer to Kim and then throws a kick. Kim grabs the leg and at the same time slaps Snoop in the face so hard it knock him down. Kim lets him go. Snoop gets back up to his feet and starts throwing wild punches. Kim just leans back and all the punches miss him. Snoop seems to run out of strength and sits down on to his knees. Kim just stands there.

"Are you done or do I have to start kicking your ass now?" Kim looks down at Snoop and takes out his knife again. "Start talking or I'll ankle you to the truck hitch and drag you until you vanish. Your choice."

"We need to go to Platte. The lab is around there at an old army ammunition bunker. I'll show you, but it's your guys' asses that will be getting shot off." Snoop has had enough. With all the drinking and getting beaten, he is worn-out.

Kim helps Snoop off the ground and pushes him into the truck. Kim tells Sam, "Well, Sam, Snoop has a better attitude now. Head toward Platte. Do you remember that old ammo dump that we rode through a long time ago? That is where we are going."

"I'm glad that you got that all worked out," Sam says with a smile. Then he drives off.

"You said it was going to be like old times," Kim says with a smile.

Two Bradley troop carriers, three large trucks, four armored Hummers, and a helicopter arrived at Gunny's gunsmith shop an hour after everyone had left. The place was empty except for Macky, who had shot off his handcuff and is sitting on the porch finishing the bottle of Crown Royal that Sam had left for him.

A man in a blue camouflage pattern uniform with a star on both collars steps out of the helicopter. About a hundred men climb out of the trucks and carriers. All of them are well-armed and move like infantry but the uniforms all have some red lettering. The letters read "YUPPI." The men surround the building in matter of minutes but never look at the outbuilding, nor did they secure the area. Macky just sits there drinking and watching. The guy with the stars swaggers up to Macky, "So where are they?"

"Well, General! It fucking appears that they have fucking left. They packed the fuck up everything and fucking left," Macky says. He is very drunk.

"Where are your troops, and most of all, where is the money?" the Boss asks.

"Gone, you stupid shit. If you would have come when I told you to, you could have gotten everyone and everything," Macky says.

"Where did they go?" the Boss leans over and grabs Macky's chin.

"They took off, maybe to find you and your fucking lab," Macky says. Macky knows that he is probably going to get killed. He has lost a lot of money and that's never tolerated. He figured it's no use helping the toy general with anything.

"Well then, pull yourself together and get into the chopper. We will talk on the way back to base." The general turns and starts to walk to the helicopter. Macky drinks down the last of the Crown Royal, then gets up and quickly pulls the .45 semiautomatic pistol up from the porch. He starts shooting in rapid fire. He manages to shoot the general in the left shoulder and hit the helicopter with several rounds. Oil and smoke spray out of the helicopter. The pilot jumps from the pilot seat. Flames start coming from the helicopter. Within less than a half a minute, the helicopter is engulfed in flames, and soon after, the fuel tank explodes. When the helicopter explodes, fragments of composite steel, fuel, and burning oil fly everywhere acting like a giant firebomb. Several of the YUPPIs' clothes catch fire from the flying flaming oil and fuel. When the flaming oil and fuel hit the men, the skin on their faces melted in to an oozing black gel. Flaming hot smoke from their burning clothes filled their lungs, and they slowly and painfully suffocated on their own exudates. Many of the YUPPIs were hit with shrapnel from the helicopter. Fragments of metal and composite material rip through bodies severing limbs and tearing large gapping wounds. Blood, bone, and flash erupted from the bodies as fragments tore through them.

Macky drops to the ground to save himself from the blast. The shop caught fire, and since it is old, it burned quickly. Macky gets up and starts to run to a truck but is quickly brought down by a gunshot from the pilot. Macky tries to get up but a pain goes through his chest makes it impossible to do so. He rolls over and starts coughing up foaming froth of blood. Blood runs down the back and front of his shirt. His shirt soaks up the blood and it flows from his chest. Macky struggles to breathe as he continues to try to get to his feet. He coughs one last time spewing foamy froth over the ground in front of him. Then he dies.

YUPPI men are running around like a bunch of chickens being chased with firecrackers. No one knows what they are doing. The pilot runs over to the Boss to see if he is still alive. The Boss is alive but badly burned on his back and blood is flowing from a baseball-sized exit wound in his chest. The .45 hollow point bullet had hit the shoulder blade before going through the rest of the chest. When the bullet hit the shoulder blade, it expanded and made it start tumbling. Clothing material, bone, and flesh involute as the bullet traveled through the chest cavity slowing down the bleeding. The pilot knows it is unlikely that the general will make it. He stuffs a piece of shirt in the hole and ties the rest of the shirt around the chest. Two of the other men come over and help carry the Boss to one of the Hummers. The men that have not been wounded pick up those men that are wounded and still alive. They load them into the Hummers and trucks. They leave the dead and those that look dead. When they think they are ready, everyone leaves as quickly as they arrived and head for the hospital in Sioux Falls.

None of the YUPPI men are associated with the armed forces. They are just a bunch a men hired by the YUPPI group. They are trained but very poorly and informally trained. They are taught how to shoot and act tough. Most of them are addicted to meth or some other substance. Some of the men are on anabolic steroids. With the steroids along with methamphetamines make them very unpredictable. The pilot did have training in the army. He flew helicopters until he was released from the army because of a positive drug test after one of his weekends in Mexico. He has been pissed off at the

Army since then and found comfort in the YUPPI group. With the YUPPIs, he is free to do what he wanted and drugs are free. The YUPPIs are more like a bad gang than anything else.

The YUPPIs arrive at the hospital and pull up to emergency entrance. They pull the wounded from the trucks and carry them in to the emergency door. The pilot carries the Boss into the hospital and drops him onto one of the couch in the waiting room. He is pretty sure that the Boss is dead, so he just left without saying a word. The pilot thinks, "Fuck it, it's not like they were friends. It's just a job." He goes back out to the Hummer and gets out his cellphone. He calls Congressman Bud Jacklow. "This is Captain Nate Lavean with the South Dakota YUPPI division. I want to report that the Boss is dead along with about ten to twenty men. He's at Sioux Valley hospital right now along with all the wounded."

"Now what in the hell did you all get into out there?" the congressman screams. He knew that if the pilot was calling, nothing that could be good.

"We had to apprehend a lost shipment and something went wrong. One of the charity shipments is lost along with a dispenser and collector," Captain Nate explains in sort of coded message.

"Where the hell did the charity shipment go?" Congressman Jacklow quizzes. "Who the hell took it?" The congressman is both scared and mad.

"We're not sure yet, but we will find out and I will contact you after that. Right now we need a plan for County Sheriff in Minnehaha. What do we need to do with that?" Captain Nate asks.

"You don't do a damn thing. You and your bunch go lie low for a few days until I handle this mess you all created. The good thing is that we own the sheriff and a couple of judges there. I'll make some calls. Do nothing until I call you on this phone." The congressman hangs up.

Nate hangs up and yells to the men, "OK, men, I'm now in charge and we are instructed to go out and drink for a couple of days. Let's load up and head out. We will come back and check on them in a couple of days."

The YUPPI group didn't need any more convincing. They all jump in to vehicles and leave. They all head for a stripper bar just outside of the city limits. The bar never closes and there is plenty of entertainment.

Congressman Jacklow calls Congressman Dodd to let him know of the incident in South Dakota. Both of them agree that the sheriff should get this cleaned up and shut up as quickly as possible. Getting the money back is not that important at this moment. Congressman Jacklow agrees and then calls the sheriff. He tells him what is going on and then lets it go at that.

Sam and the boys pull into a field close to the old bunkers. Kim grabs Snoop and asks him, "Where is the security in this place? Is there anyone on the road or are there cameras? Start talking, you little bastard." Kim starts shaking Snoop.

"Iiiieeeeee dooonn't knooooow," Snoop says as he is being shaken. Kim stops shaking him. "I just drive in and drive out. They never gave me a grand tour of the fucking place."

Kim kind of thought that Snoop wouldn't know anything, but he doesn't like Snoop, so shaking him just makes him feel good.

Everyone gets out and puts on their gear. Sam tells everyone, "Kota and Harland are on sniper duty in two different locations. Bud and DH are spotters and backup for me and Kim. We will move into the bunkers and look around. If the area is clear, then Bud and DH will move in and help look around. Darwin, you are in charge of Snoop."

Darwin handcuffs Snoop to the truck bed and puts duct tape on his mouth. Darwin is still clutching a sawed off shotgun. Harland helps Kota pick out a perfect spotting area where they could see the bunker entrance and the road in and out. Sam grabs his new chained knife, a tomahawk, his old slingshot, and a Glock 18. Kim grabs a rifle and a .45. Sam and Kim carefully move in close to the bunkers. They look around for security beams and cameras. They find four cameras mounted on each of the bunkers and two cameras on each of the housing areas that were just old FEMA trailers set up on blocks. They did not find anyone guarding the area.

Sam radios to Harland and Kota, "Do you see anyone around here?"

"Not a soul in site," Harland radios back.

"No one here," Kota radios back.

The doors have alarm systems on them, but Kim disables them easily. He had worked for an alarm company when he came back from the marines. Kim tells Sam, "This type of alarm system goes off in house first then will dial the alarm company after two minutes if a code is not put in. Or you can just take the cover off the numbers pad and cut the incoming wire and nothing will sound, not even in house. They are the economic household version that they quit selling in his first year working."

Sam and Kim scout each trailer. The trailers are pigsty, but no one is home. They move into the first bunker. There are two bunkers placed about a hundred yards apart from each other. Kim disables the alarm quickly. Sam and he move through the darkness looking for any signs of people. They look through every room and then move through bunker number two and find the same.

Sam radios Harland and Kota, "If you guys are all right, send over DH and Bud. We marked the trail, so just tell them to keep on it and they should be OK."

"You know we have radios too, you dumb ass. We can hear you just fine," Bud radios.

"Oh yeah, I forgot. Well then, get your ass down here and let's check this place out," Sam radios.

"Be right there," Both Bud and DH chime in.

Kim finds the lights in the second bunker and turns them on. The bunker is filled with armored vehicles, a weapons room and a machine shop, a couple of offices, a locker room, a half-court basketball floor, and a weights room. Bud and DH come through the door. Sam radios up to Harland and Kota to tell them what is going on. "Keep one eye on the open door. Make sure that it only is a quarter of the way open. If it is any more than that, you need to give a yell, immediately."

"Holy shit, what a jackpot this is," DH says and runs over to the vehicles, "These two here are Stryker infantry carriers. They carry about eleven people and go about sixty miles an hour. They used these over in the war, but they put blast cages on them. They do have three layers to them and you can drive them night or day. Hell, even if you can't see it can with thermal image. Shit, we need one of these. What for, I don't know, but I want one. These three are the armored Hummers like those used in the middle of the Iraq war. Now they have better ones but they still use these things. This helicopter is an AH6 or an MH6 Little Bird, I can't remember which one. I think the AH is the armed one or something like that. They are fast and can carry about six men or so. I worked on all this shit when I was in the army. The helicopter, though, I don't know a lot about, but I know who can work on it if we needed to." DH is so excited, he just keeps rambling on and on.

"None of us know how to fly. How the hell would we move this chopper? Can you load it on a trailer or truck? Maybe take the propellers off or something?" Sam asks. He is wondering if he should even bother with this stuff.

"Hell yeah! In the marines, we had to move these things all the time on and off the ships. We could make a trailer really quick with all these spare parts. Shit with two of us welding, we could have this thing trailered within an hour," Kim says with great enthusiasm.

"Well, if you and DH want to get after that, we will have ourselves a helicopter to take home. Hell, it doesn't really belong to anyone. These assholes got it from the government, so technically we are just appropriating this stuff. Either that or it came from drug sales, but we haven't found the lab yet. Bud lets go look at the weapons room," Sam says.

Sam and Bud go into the back room. The room is full of weapons of all kinds.

"Enough to fit an army," Bud says.

Sam and Bud leave the room and go back out to the shop. DH and Kim have already got the helicopter's blades off and on jacks. Bud informs them that they are going to look through the other bunker. Sam radios Harland and Kota, "We are coming out to go to the other bunker. Is the coast clear?"

They both radio back, "All is clear. It's a go."

Sam and Bud search around in the dark for the lights. They find the switch and turn the lights on. The bunker is filled with several rooms on both sides of the main area. The main area appears to be a dining area. There is a huge room in the back that is separated from the main area by a solid concrete wall. Sam opens the door and looks in.

"Bingo! Here's the lab," Sam says.

Bud comes over and looks in. "Crimony, this is something."

"This is ten times bigger than the lab I found in Virginia," Sam says. "Well, screw this. If they've got a lab, they've got money stashed somewhere. Let's go find it."

"Right behind you," Bud says.

Bud and Sam look in every room for a safe or any place that might hold some money or anything. Bud finds a small safe in one of the offices and a hard drive. Sam finds a pallet lift in a food storage room and wheels it over to the safe, and they tip the safe onto the jack. Sam grabs the hard drive and puts it on top of the safe. They wheeled it out to the front door. Then they go back in for one more look around. Sam goes back into the food storage area and decides to take a look in the walk in freezer. He had seen on a movie where there was a fake wall in the freezer and a security room behind it.

"There's no way any one is dumb enough to really do that," Sam thinks. He kicks and knocks on some of the walls. Then noticed on the floor a worn area like a shelf had been slid away from the wall many times. Sam slides the shelf away from the sidewall. On the wall behind where the shelf was, there is a handle. Sam yells to Bud. Bud comes in to the freezer. Sam pulls the handle and opens a panel to the wall. He looks in and sees a ramp that goes down into a dark area.

"You stay here and I'll go look. Don't let these doors close," Sam tells Bud and then slips on his night vision goggles.

"I'll be right here," Bud says. He wedges the freezer door with box of frozen steaks and then wedges the panel open with a box of frozen pork chops. Bud thinks, "These guys eat pretty damn good! There are no leftovers in here."

Sam slowly walks down the ramp. Sam says to himself, "Ah, that's where all the security personnel are." At the bottom of the ramp are two men sitting in recliners sound asleep or passed out. Beside each chair is a pile of beer cans. Between the chairs is an end table that has an empty bottle of Cuervo and a .45 Colt handgun sitting on it. Sam slips down off the ramp and moves up behind the chairs. He spots the light switch and quietly radios Bud. "Hey, there are two men sleeping in chairs down here. I'm going to take their guns and if they move I'll crack their heads with the tomahawk. Give me fifteen seconds when I say go and come on down quickly but quietly." Sam reaches over and grabs an AP90 off the side of one chair and the .45 Colt lying on the end table. Sam says, "Go."

Bud waits fifteen seconds and comes down the stairs. It is dark, but when Sam sees Bud at the bottom of the ramp, he switches the lights on. Neither one of the men in the chairs wake up, but one man snorts and moves his head. The other one farts and rolls onto his side. Bud goes back up the ramp and into the food storage room. He finds a small amount of rope and some pallet wrap. He brings it down to Sam. Bud and Sam wrap both of the men up, chairs and all, leaving only their noses and mouth unwrapped. In the process, one of them wakes up but quickly goes back to sleep.

Bud keeps a watch on the two men while Sam figures out how to open the locked door. It has a metal roll up door that has three locks on it. Sam looks it over and thinks, "I can shoot the locks but it could ricochet. Even if I do shoot the locks, they still may not open up. I can't hammer them open, but these dumb shits may have just hammer-drilled the latches to the floor." Sam takes his tomahawk out and chips away at one of the locks on the floor. The concrete quickly broke around the latch. Sam continues on to the other two then rolls the door open.

"Oh my God, would you look at that?" Sam says to Bud.

"Damn, I've never seen and I will never see it again." Bud says as his jaw drops and then he walks into the doorway.

In the room are four pallets of money all bound with the pallet wrap. Silver and gold bars are sitting on the floor next to the pallets. Sam looks at Bud and gives him a high-five.

"Score!" they both yell.

"You or I have to go and get some help. Get two of those troop carrier things and we can hall this stuff in there. Now I know why there was that pallet jack sitting in the food room. That is what the carriers are for. Not for people but for transporting money," Sam says to Bud.

"I'll go get Kim and DH and a couple of vehicles," Bud says. He runs up the ramp and over to the other bunker. Bud radios Harland and Kota before opening the door. He tells them that they are going to be loading things up. They give him the all clear. Bud doesn't want to tell them about their find until later so that they will concentrate on the job at hand. Bud goes into the second bunker. Kim and DH have the helicopter already trailered and hitched to one of the Hummers.

"I told you we would get this done. Hell, we even loaded the Hummers full of the weapons and gassed everything up," Kim says. "So what have you guys been doing all this time? Find anything worth loading up?"

"Well, yes. We need those troop carriers backed over to the other bunker. I think we should hurry, Sam is getting anxious," Bud says. He is a little out of breath.

"OK, I'll get one of the carriers. They drive like a skid loader so they are easy to drive," DH says.

Kim opens the door to the bunker. DH and Bud drive out two of the carriers and back up to the big door in the first bunker. Kim runs over and opens the big door to the bunker. The whole backend of the carriers opens down to a ramp. Kim and DH follow Bud. They drag the pallet jack with the safe on it into the carrier.

"Is that it?" Kim asks and then laughs. "That took you guys all this time?"

"Hell no, we just need the jack for the next bunch of stuff," Bud says with excitement.

Kim and DH follow Bud down into the money room. They notice the two men all cocooned in their chairs as they walk into the money room.

Both of them just stand there and stare. "Is it real?" Kim asks.

"Yes, you dork. Let's get this money loaded and we can stare at it later. I can't imagine anyone would leave this stuff without more security than what we have run into," Sam says.

They all push and pull the pallets up into the carriers. Then they go back and load the stacks of gold and silver that is left. Sam then runs back and leaves two bottles of water on the end table. "If these two dumb shits are smart, they can get out by midafternoon or so," Sam says to himself and then shut all the doors and turns the lights off.

DH and Bud jump in the driver's seats of the carriers. Sam radios Harland and Kota, "Come down to get a vehicle."

Within a few minutes, they are both down and picking out a vehicle. Kim drives the Hummer with the helicopter. Harland and Dakota both jump into the last two Hummers. Sam closes all the doors, turns the lights out, then jumps in with Harland, who is in the last Hummer out.

"OK, Darwin, are you out there?" Sam calls over the radio.

"Yeah, I'm still here watching this maggot. Can I shoot him yet?" Darwin asks playfully. He had turned into Barney Fife.

"No, you can't shoot him. Listen, I need you to drive my truck and follow us. We will be in three Hummers and two troop carriers. We will be in a formation of a Hummer, carrier, Hummer, carrier, Hummer. The middle Hummer has a helicopter on a trailer. I need you to pick me up at the road and we will throw Snoop into one of the Hummers. Everyone hear that?" Sam instructs everyone.

"Yeah," everyone radios back.

"Does anyone have a plan on how we are going to get this stuff to the farm without anyone, like the cops, seeing us?" Kota asks over the radio.

"Hell, we'll just drive right down the highway. The cops won't pull us over because they will think we are military. Just don't speed. And if they do try to pull us over, shoot them!" Kim says over the radio.

"No, we are not going to shoot them. We need to hide this stuff and find some way to haul it, like in a truck. Do any of you guys know where we can hide out for a few hours and find some trucks?" Bud asks over the radio.

"My cousin has a farm about fifteen miles from here. He has a machine shop and a barn we can hide these vehicles in," Harland says over the radio.

"Yeah, and we can drive up to the truck stop or up to Mitchell and get some trucks and trailers. We don't want new ones so maybe we can get some used trucks from those at the truck stop," Bud says over the radio.

"Well, DH, you know the most about trucks and trailers. You, Bud, Dakota, Harland, and Kim go find some truck drivers who want new trucks in the morning. How much do you think it would take to buy somebody's truck and trailer?" Sam asks over the radio.

"I suppose we could get one for about a hundred to a hundred and fifty thousand," DH says over the radio.

"Well, give them double and make sure the trucks are full of diesel. Harland and Kim, do you have class A licenses?" Sam asks over the radio.

"I do," Harland says over the radio

"I don't have a CDL, so I can't drive," Kim says over the radio.

"Well, when we get to Harland's cousin's place and get this stuff hidden, Darwin and I will watch Snoop and stand guard. You guys take my truck and go. Kim you can drive my truck back," Sam says over the radio.

They get to Harland cousin's place and hid the vehicles. The boys get out a bunch of money and load it into Sam's truck.

"Hey, take Snoop and dump him off at a truck stop or whatever. I'm tired of dragging his dumb ass around. Just give him some money and don't let him go until you get the trucks. Don't let him see what you are up to either because you know he'll rat us out as soon as he gets the chance. I don't want an army following us," Sam says and then goes back to the truck and takes the handcuffs and duct tape off Snoop. "We are going to let you go. Now you made good on your part, so I'm going to make good on my part." Sam looks around and finds a bag in the barn. Sam goes back to the carrier and takes a hundred grand and put in the bag. Sam goes back over to Snoop. He hands him the bag and warns him. "I put a hundred thousand in this bag. That's a damn good payday for a piece of shit like you. Now it is yours if you just disappear. If you rat us out, I am going to find you and skin you, and then I am going to feed you to the pigs. Do you understand me or do you think I am still full of shit?"

"No, that sounds good to me. I'll take the money." Snoop says and then gets into the truck cab. "You can drop me off in Sioux Falls."

"Well, these guys are going somewhere near there so Harland can give you a ride," Sam says. "Darwin lets go, we'll stay here until they come back, unless you have to go home or got somewhere else to go."

"No, I'm good. This is the most fun I've had in a long time," Darwin says and jumps out of the back of the truck.

The boys take off. Sam and Darwin go and look around at all the bounty they just captured. Sam is really interested in the helicopter. He had always wanted to fly helicopters. Now he has one and he can't fly it. He makes a mental note: "Soon as I get home, learn to fly a helicopter." Darwin sits on the pallets of cash and just rolls over top of it like a horse in new shavings.

"You know, Darwin, part of this is yours. You can take some and take off or you can move on back to Virginia. We can finish your project you started and more," Sam says.

"Oh, I think I'll hang around with you guys for a while and see where we go. I'm tired of being scared and since I've been with you. I've had the shit scared out of me, but it wasn't me being scared. Do you know what I mean?" Darwin says in some philosophical manner.

"Yep, happens to me all the time," Sam says. "Weeellllll, good! I think we all work good together and this is a good team. Now if we can just make it back home in one piece, I will quit being nervous."

"You really can't tell that you are nervous, tired maybe, but not nervous," Darwin says.

"I am tired but I'm used to that. Well I think we need to find a place to watch for incoming traffic. So you can find a place around here to hind or fight if you have too. I'm going to take these two rifles and go up and hide in the bushes close to the road. This one will stop anything that I can hit," Sam says and he picks up a .50-caliber Barrett sniper rifle. "And this one will slow everyone else down." Sam grabs a 5.56-mm. SAW (squad automatic weapon) and thinks, "God damn, these things are heavy." Then he puts on his bulletproof vest and heads down the driveway.

Harland's cousins are just going to stay in the house and stay in bed till the sun comes up. Harland had convinced his cousins to leave because they just stolen part of the drug dealers' stuff. Harland's cousins have had a run in with the drug dealers, and they were very happy to accommodate them.

Sam sets up his weapon's nest in the field about a hundred yards off the road. He has camouflaged himself in the bush. He can see down both sides of the road, the barn and shed entrance from where he is sitting. He watches Darwin pick through the weapons and feeling them out. Darwin picks one up and pretends to shoot then sets it down and picks up another. The only thing is that most of the rifles are loaded. Sam hopes Darwin doesn't accidently shoot himself. As time goes on, Darwin quits playing around with the weapons. He climbs up on top of one of the carriers and to lies down.

The DH, Bud, and the others make it to the truck stop up by Interstate 90. They found four owner operators that are happy to sell their rigs and buy all new rigs. After the group gets done purchasing the rigs, DH, Harland, Bud, and Kota took off with the rigs, leaving Kim to deal with Snoop. Kim drove Snoop about ten miles out of town.

Kim stops Sam's truck alongside of a highway and tells him, "If it was just me, I would just fucking kill you and throw you in the river, but Sam wants to let you go."

Snoop puffs out his chest and tells Kim in a cocky tone, "Oh yeah, next time I see you will be the last time you see anyone."

Kim gives a little laugh and tells Snoop in a stern voice, "Get the fuck out or we will see who pushes daisies."

Snoop grabs his bag of money then opens his door and gets out of the truck. He slams the door shut just after he yells to Kim, "Fuck you, you asshole motherfucker!"

Kim ignores Snoop and puts the truck in gear. He starts to take off when all of a sudden a rock comes through the back window. Snoop had picked up the biggest rock and throws it through the back window. Kim stops and puts the truck in reverse. He speeds backward toward Snoop. He hits Snoop, who is running down the center of the highway, just enough to make him trip and fall on his face. Kim stops the truck and looks out his review mirror to watch Snoop skid on his face and chest along the highway. The moneybag falls open and cash starts to fly everywhere. Kim laughs and then takes off leaving Snoop out in the country. Snoop doesn't even think about his injuries; he just starts chasing his money.

No YUPPIs show up at Harland's cousins' place while everyone is gone. When Sam sees the trucks coming down the road, Sam calls them and tells them to load up while he stays and watches the road. The loading of all the equipment goes smoothly but slowly. Kim and DH had loaded and unloaded this type of equipment several times while in the military.

Sam tells everyone, "Let's get going. We may run into trouble along the way if we just happen to pass by those fucking YUPPIs."

Kim says, "We got enough weaponry to hold off an army."

Sam nods and says, "Yes, we do, and the bunker size can hold an army so that might be what we will run into out on the run. Just be on the lookout and be ready."

Everyone went to their trucks they are going to drive. Harland tells Sam, "I am going to leave a note for my cousins and tell them that we are gone and appreciate them let us stay here."

Sam says, "I think your cousins could use a little money for repairs. Let's leave them a hundred grand to help them out. That is if it is all right with you."

Harland smiles and says, "I think they would be very appreciative."

Sam says, "Well, we'll wait."

Harland wrote a quick note on a piece of old feed bag with an old carpenter's pencil he found lying in the barn. He wrapped the money in the rest of the feed bag. He ran up to the front door of the house and put it all on the inside of the porch doorway. Harland ran back and jumped into one of the semitrucks, and they all headed for the brother's grandparents' old farm place. The place is well hidden by a grove of trees that wrap around the place on three sides. The open area of the trees opens up to a large pasture that has a deep creek running through it. Hills wrap around the farm on two sides on the outside of the trees. From the top of the hill, it is possible to see in all directions for miles. The nearest neighbor is three miles away. The place has been empty for several years and has not been kept up with much needed maintenance. The house, hog barns, milk barn, and shop are all falling down. The roofs have been leaking for years, and the place is really unlivable. The good thing is that there is plenty of space to park all the trucks and one lookout can watch the whole area.

They park the trucks in the main yard that is overgrown with weeds. Once parked, Kota and Harland look through all the treasure that they just confiscated under the authority of part of the people of the USA. Bud, DH, Kim, and Sam all call their wives to let them know that everything is fine and not to worry. Then Sam and Darwin dig out the hard drive out of the carrier, but Darwin gets interested in the safe. Darwin looks over the safe and decides he is going to try to crack it. Darwin sits down in front of the safe turning the combination dial. For several hours, Darwin works to try to open the safe while the rest of them look the farm over. They are trying to decide whether or not to leave the trucks here or move on to a different location.

After a couple of hours, Kota walks over to Darwin and asks sarcastically, "Ain't got that thing open yet, ay?"

Darwin glares at Kota and says, "I just about had it open a few times but it's not that simple. If you can do a better job, you try."

Kota looks at the safe and says, "Hmmm!"

Kota walks away without saying anything else. He goes back to the garage, where he has seen some tools. He comes back with a drill and two old drill bits. Kim finds an extension cord in the barn. The troop carrier has a power inverter build in to the vehicle so Kim plugs the extension cord in to a socket. Kota plugs the drill into the extension cord stands over Darwin.

"I'll get this thing open." Kota gives Darwin a little push with his knee and sits down in front of the safe with the drill. "I've had to open a few of these damn things when Sam has forgotten the combination."

"You have to be very precise with these things. If you mess it up, we may never get it open." Darwin cautions Kota. He stands over Kota's shoulder watching. "You don't want to drill into far, just through the outer plate."

"Just go find me a hammer and a screwdriver or something," Kota tells Darwin. Kota is getting a little annoyed at Darwin's constant yakking. Darwin climbs over the heaping palates of cash and other stuff. He runs over to the garage and digs around until he finds an old broken screwdriver and a hammer with a broken handle. He runs back to the carrier but by the time he gets back, Kota has the door to the safe open.

"Shit is this all there is, a bunch of papers and notebooks," Kota says with disappointment as he digs through the safe. "Ahh, a gold bar. Shit that is hardly worth opening the safe. Here, Darwin, you can have the bar and all this other shit."

Darwin takes the bar and puts it in his pocket. He starts looking through the papers and notebooks. He gets through most of the papers and then yells for Sam, "Sam! Sam, come here quickly! I need to show you something very important."

Sam comes running over to the carrier and yells from the door, "What's wrong, what's going on?"

"Nothing is wrong. I just wanted to show you this right away." Darwin throws the notebook to Sam as Sam makes his way back to the safe.

Sam looks though to notebook real quick. "Damn, that lab made a hell of a lot of money. I see they may be making about two billion a year. Shit, I wonder how much we have of that money?"

"Yeah, and in this other book is banks that they own and accounts that they put money into. I bet they are payoffs or something," Darwin says.

"I wonder what is on the hard drive. The dumb asses probably are keeping names and other shit on that hard drive. Let's take this stuff to your place and hook up the hard drive. Can we do that and see what is on this thing?" Sam asks.

"No sweat. I'll have that damn thing hacked and downloaded in no time," Darwin brags.

Sam grabs the hard drive and Darwin grabs the papers. They go out and load it all in Sam's truck.

Sam says to everyone really loudly, "We're going to Darwin's house and look over this stuff. Does anyone got to leave? Kim?"

"No, I called my wife and she said it was OK that I am out with you, but I will have to get home later today. I got to work tomorrow," Kim says.

"What the fuck do you think you got to go to work for?" Sam says with a laugh. "We got enough money here that none of us will ever have to work."

"I didn't think that it is any part mine. I was just along for the fun of it," Kim says with surprise.

"OK, guys, let's gather around. We now have a lot of money and weapons and other stuff. I for one think that we all are going into business for ourselves as in taking everything we possibly can from these government crooks. We will watch the money and dish it out as needed, and if anyone needs something, we will take care of it immediately. Otherwise, we leave the money and stuff in one location and work from there. What do you think?" Sam gives one of his little lectures.

"Well, someone needs to watch how much we spend so we need a treasurer," Bud says. "Maybe we can get Gina as the treasurer and I vote Sam as president."

"That sounds good to me. I'll take care of the mechanic parts and such," DH says.

"I'll do what I can and do whatever else needs to be done," Kota says.

"I'm working for Sam, so I'll do what I'm told," Harland says.

"I'll be the computer geek, but am I in on this? I was just along for the ride," Darwin says and then looks around to see if anyone had anything to say.

"We are all in on this. So if I'm president, then I put it up for a vote that Darwin, Kim, and Harland are in with us, if they swear to secrecy. They have to swear loyalty and allegiance to us and family and no one else. So, you guys, if this is OK, then let's all vote on it first," Sam says. Bud, Dakota, DH, and Sam all hold up a hand to vote yes. "OK, now let's all swear all of us in." Everyone held up their right hand, Sam says, "We pledge allegiance and loyalty to each other and to family. We will not live in extravagance or lavish style. We will do as a group and as friends. If anyone of us has a problem, it will be said in our group openly and never complain outside this group. Secrecy is ours and no one else will hear of anything that we do under penalty of death or whatever we decide is worse. So help us GOD." Sam just made something up. It was kind of like a pinky swear.

They all say, "I do."

"OK, let's rebuild this place. DH, can you build another bunker?" Sam asks. "Bud or Dakota, can you go get Dad's workers and have them get a crew in here to rebuild this place. I know that Rick can get this place in shape. Harland, I hate to tell you but we need a lookout and need to get this place secured. You guys work it out. Darwin and I are going to look at this hard drive. Someone might want to go get some food and some tents and whatever else might be needed. We're going to be here for a few days or weeks. But first Bud, Kota, Harland, and I will go set some traps all around just in case we have visitors that we don't know about," Sam says.

They go out and set traps through the grove of trees just in case someone tries to sneak in. Bud and Sam use to build traps when they were kids. Kota is very good at mechanical things and can build just about anything, so once Kota got the hang of building traps, he goes very fast. Harland never learned how to trap, but he is a good hand. They set up forty nonlethal but very effective traps in about two hours. They mark all the traps and then go back to the farm place. Bud and Kota call their Dad to come over to pick them up. Harland goes out on the hill and finds a great location for a lookout.

Sam and Darwin drive over to Darwin's place. The place is looking great. The workers from Sam's parents place had already started repairing and cleaning up the place. Sam and Darwin go inside and

Darwin hooks up the hard drive. Darwin hacks through the hard drives passwords with a software program that he had written for the IRS. Within minutes he is opening all the files. One file opens up and a bunch of places and names come up with dollars amounts.

"That must be more labs all across the country. I think we just discovered our new business venture. We are going to bust every one of these and take everything that they have," Sam says with excitement.

"Oh, there's more. This business of selling meth is bring in about thirty billion a year, and it's all going to this bank in New York City. It looks like they have been doing this for years. They are making billions of dollars," Darwin says.

"Well, keep looking and maybe we can find out who controls this group," Sam says.

"Well, this is all a group called YUPPI. Annnnndddddd . . . that son of a bitch," Darwin says.

"Who, who?" Sam asks.

"Jacklow! He is one of the assholes who's making a fortune from this group. There's Congressman Dodd and Franks in here. Shit, they are all on the take. Hold it, Senator Barrack. Holy shit, the president is all in this. This is how he got enough money to buy his presidency," Darwin says with excitement.

"You know if we shut this group down, they will be hurting for money in the next election. Maybe we can get some real people in office," Sam contemplates.

"Well, if you can get that done, then great, but I want Jacklow to pay deeply. Sam, can we get to him somehow?" Darwin asks.

"You've got his account numbers in front of you. Can you do anything about taking his money and transfer it to an account we can use?" Sam asks.

"If I do it from here, they can trace that to me," Darwin says.

"I thought you could go anywhere without anyone knowing?" Sam asks.

"I can look, but if I start changing, that is a whole different thing. They can trace transactions back to this computer no matter how many subs I go through," Darwin says.

"I have a place in Virginia that is in a bunker. You can set whatever you need to do from there, and we will get him where it hurts. Right in the pocketbook! All of them," Sam says.

"OK, I'll pack some stuff," Darwin says.

"Pack what? What the hell do you need? It will all be here. Just call in the maid service and clean this dump up. Change your clothes and we'll grab the hard drive and we'll send you on a plane back to my place in Virginia. You can set stuff up and we'll stay in touch. I'll have to drive back anyway as soon as I get everything in place here," Sam says.

"OK, let's see when I can get a ticket." Darwin starts typing. "Where am I going?"

"Roanoke, Virginia?" Sam says.

"OK, I can get on the plane in two hours, but it is going to cost me fourteen hundred dollars and only one layover. I can be there by 10:00 p.m. I'm going to use the money you gave me at the gun shop. Can you pick up my car from the airport later?" Darwin says.

"When you get to the airport, just give your car to someone and give them your title? You can buy a car when you get to Virginia. Carol will give you some money and you can buy clothes and computer equipment. Just get what you need or want. I'll call Carol to have her pick you up when you get there," Sam says to Darwin.

Darwin says with objection, "But I like that car. It's a classic."

Sam says, "Well then, keep it in long term parking. Or we'll pick it up sometime."

Darwin thinks for a minute and says, "Well, I'll let you know if I leave it or not."

Sam calls Carol and tells her everything. Meanwhile, Darwin changes clothes. He grabs a suitcase and packs the hard drive.

Sam tells Carol, "I won't be back for a week or so."

Carol jokingly says to him, "Everything is going fine with the three new doctors we hired. So we can still keep the hospital open while you are out having fun."

Sam says, "Well, good. I'll talk to you later. Love you."

Carol says, "Love you."

Darwin drives into Sioux Falls to the airport. He finds a woman who is trying to get a taxicab ride to the downtown area. He walks up and hands the woman the keys to his car along with the title. The woman just stands there in disbelief until Darwin says, "Really, the Chevy is yours if you want it. If not, just take it and sell it. I'm not going to be back." Then Darwin walks away.

Sam goes to the Army Surplus Store and buys large tents and other supplies. After loading his stuff into the truck, Sam drives to a large sporting goods store. He calls Kota to see what they needed. He gets a whole list of stuff and then goes in a buys everything he can and more. He calls Kim and Kim gives him a list of alarm systems and surveillance equipment that they needed and where to get it. Sam drives across town. He buys everything that they have in the way of video and motion detection devices. The store manager starts to get suspicious.

The store manager apprehensively says to Sam, "You know if I knew what you are doing, I could advise you better on what to buy."

Sam just looks at him and says, "Oh, you wouldn't really understand if I told you."

The store manager says to Sam, "You would be surprised at what I have heard over the years." He tries to act like he has heard everything. "I don't think you could tell me anything that I haven't heard before."

Sam likes a challenge and the truth is more surprising than a lie to most people. So Sam says, "I will bet you that I can tell you something you haven't heard before."

The store manager is fairly convinced that he has heard everything. He knows that he could just lie and say he heard about it. He says, "I will give you a fifty percent discount if you tell me something that I haven't heard before but if I have then full price plus ten percent for me."

"OK," Sam says, "here is the story. Some friends and I have just busted a secret major government drug lab. They have a small army running the place. We took everything they had and now found out that the drug lab involves several politicians including the president of the United States. They haven't found us yet, but we are pretty sure they are hunting us. We are hiding out and we need some surveillance equipment to help us. We need the surveillance equipment to surround a wooded area of about three-mile range. My friend used to work in home security after being in the marines recon. He says he can make just about anything work."

The store manager just stood there like he just saw a pink elephant. He looks at Sam and laughs. He says, "Yeah, right."

Sam says, "No, sir. That is the God-honest truth."

"Well, why would you tell me?" the store manager asks. "I could be a government nark and turn you in."

"Really, a paid nark for the government working in downtown Sioux Falls?" Sam says with sarcasm. "Besides, if I thought you were going to rat me out, I would just cut your head off and take what I wanted."

The store manager gets a little nervous and says, "Ahh, you got a point."

Sam says, "Besides, the truth is usually more exciting than a lie, so why not tell the truth?"

"Well, you win," the store manager says. "You can go ahead and clean the place out at fifty percent off."

Sam says, "If you help me find a place to get a big-ass generator and help me load this up, I will make it worth your while. I really don't want fifty percent off."

"Great!" the store manager says with a sigh of relief. "I would have been so busted if I would have given you that discount."

Sam says with a smirk on his face, "I know."

They load the backseat area of the truck with all the equipment leaving no room whatsoever for anything else. The store manager then tells Sam directions to a place he can purchase a commercial grade generator. They shake hands and Sam takes off across town again. He purchases a Generac MMG205 with a John Deere engine and it sat on a trailer. He hooks up to the trailer and heads to the farm since he has no more room for anything.

Bud and Kota quickly say hi to their mom and then have their dad drive them back to their grandparents' farm place. Sam gets back with a truckload of stuff. Everyone helps unload the truck. Kim,

Dakota, DH, Bud, and Sam start setting up tents and a full camping area. They start cutting out trees in the grove in order to hide the trucks out of sight from the air or the road. They camouflaged the trucks so well, it is even hard to see the trucks when you are looking at them and you knew what they are. After a full day of work, it is beer time and meeting time. Sam calls Harland in for a break and when Harland gets down to the camping area, Sam starts his meeting. Sam tells everyone about what is on the hard drive and what he wants to do. Everyone is in agreement that it is their job to take this organization down. As night falls, Sam's parents and Kim's family come over for a cookout. Elaine is a little upset that she didn't get to cook anything. After the cookout everyone picks a time, two at a time, to be on a lookout until the electronic surveillance equipment is put up.

CHAPTER FIFTEEN

SNOOP MAKES IT BACK TO the truck stop and immediately buys a cellphone. He calls the Boss but there is no answer. He waits for several hours and Captain Nate calls back.

"You called this phone, what do you want?" Nate asks with annoyance.

"This is Snoop, one of your distributors," Snoop says with authority. He can hear the music in the background and a bunch of men that sound like there is a party.

"Yeah, OK, what the do you want? I'm fucking busy," Nate asks. He is in the middle of a lap dance and he is drunk off his ass.

"Just want to let you know that you have been cleaned out. That's it," Snoop says nonchalantly.

"Cleaned out, what the fuck are you talking about? Who the hell are you?" Nate screams in surprise. Nate sobers a little, but his concentration is still elsewhere.

"Never mind then. I just fucking thought you'd want to know. If you don't believe me, go back to the bunker and look yourself," Snoop says. He hangs up and calls Digger for a ride home. Digger comes to pick him up.

Nate sits there, trying to think for about ten minutes, and all of a sudden, it just hits him. Nate grabs the stripper by the butt and throws her to the floor. "Get off me, bitch." He gets up and pulls up his pants, then rushes out to the main area. "Come on, you bunch of assholes. We have to go," Nate yells to the YUPPIs. All of them are drunk; some of them are passed out in booths and on the floor. The men that can walk carry out the others who can't walk.

"No one left behind," one of the YUPPIs yells like a war cry.

They all load up in the trucks and carriers. They head down the interstate. They are swerving all over the road. One of the Hummers hit a car and then swerves and hits a sign before rolling over into the ditch. The convoy just leaves them there and continues on toward the bunker.

When they arrive at the bunker, they find that their vehicles and weapons are gone. Nate runs over to the freezer. He finds that the two guards are still wrapped in their chairs. One of guards had vomited all over himself. Nate runs into the money vault and finds it completely empty. He feels a sickening feeling well up in his stomach. "Who the hell would have ever found this?" he said to himself. "That fucker that called me—aahhh, Snoop. But how would he know where this place is?"

Nate walks out of the vault mad as hell not because of the money being gone but now he has to call the fucking congressman again. Nate looks at the two in their chairs and unwraps their heads. Two of the other men come down to help Nate out.

"Aaahh, sir, the lab is still intact and does not appear to have been touched," one of the men tells Nate.

"Well, thank God for that," Nate says. "What were you two doing while all this shit was happening?"

"We were watching the place real good when about twenty men come haulin' ass down here. It was like an army. They's on us and we couldn't do nothin' but give up. We didn't give up the keys though." The man in the chair looked worried and very shaken. The other never spoke; he was too sick to speak. He had drunk the most and is dehydrated from being wrapped in plastic.

"What did this army look like? Did they wear any uniforms? We're they black, white, or Mexicans? Come on, boy, speak up," Nate says with a stern, angry voice. He turns to the one that hadn't spoken anything.

"I, aaahhhh, don't recall off hand it was dark and they jumped us so quick," the guy says.

"Didn't the alarm go off?" Nate asks.

"No, we didn't hear any alarm. They were like ninja," the first man says.

"Hmmm." Nate just turns and walks upstairs where he can get cellphone reception. Nate calls the congressman. "This is Captain Nate. I am calling because our distribution center has been attacked while we were on a mission."

"Jesus H. Christ, can't you people do anything right? I hope for your sake that the charitable donations are still there," Congressman Jacklow screams.

"Well, no, no they are not. The charitable donations, transportation, and protective devices are all gone," Nate says in a shaky voice.

"You find that charity and you find it now. You go get help from the Iowa division or from who the fuck ever, I don't care, just find the shit. That is close to a billion. I want that back now!" Congressman Jacklow screams. He is infuriated and worried all at the same time. How the hell would someone have the gall to steal from them? "You stupid shit, don't you mess this up! Got it?" Congressman Jacklow finishes screaming.

"Listen, I'm just a pilot. I don't know about any of these divisions you are talking about. According to my security guards, an army of well-trained men moved in here and took everything," Nate tries to explain.

"An army, hey? Well then, look for an army that is running around the fucking countryside, you stupid fuck. Shouldn't be too fucking hard to find a damn army. Hell, there are only about a couple of hundred people in the whole fucking state. Now go into the office and in the computer should be contacts for the others. In the safe is the information for the banks that this charity should go to as soon as you find it!" Congressman Jacklow explains. He is still screaming but is calming down a little.

Nate walks over to the office and looks around. Nate tells the congressman, "Aahh, there is no safe and the computer thing is gone."

"Jesus, you need to get that shit back. That shit has highly classified information in it that if it falls in the wrong hands, you don't know what could happen. An empire may fall and it all rests on you to keep it up!" Congressman Jacklow starts screaming again. He is extremely worried.

"Well, where the fuck is the division and I will go get help? Then we can find all this shit," Nate asks.

"I'll send you the GPS coordinates as soon as we hang up," Congressman Jacklow says without screaming.

"What do you want to do about what happened yesterday?" Nate asks.

"Don't fucking worry about the small shit, we have a pile to clean up now," Congressman Jacklow says.

The congressman hangs up and sends the coordinates. Nate goes out and gets the four most sober men and has them load up into the Hummer. Nate leaves one of the security guards in charge of the place.

"Get the lab going again! Get this place in order and send out half of the men to find out who the hell had attacked this place!" Nate yells to everyone.

"It will be done, sir," one of the YUPPIs says.

"No more fucking drinking, and go pick up the men at the hospital," Nate yells.

"Yes, sir!" several drunken men yell.

Nate takes off to find the Iowa division. He calls them and tells them exactly what had happened. They are going to meet him in Larchwood, Iowa, to discuss plans.

Everyone gets a good rest even though they all were on guard duty. When morning comes, Elaine has a huge breakfast waiting. During breakfast, they discuss what is needed and what their goal is going to be. With the information that Darwin got from the computer, they know exactly where all the labs are and where all the money is hiding.

Sam knows he will have to return to Virginia soon but there is too much to do here. DH and Kim elect to stay and finish the bunker. Sam has already got a crew going on the farm. Bud and Kota need to get back to their families. Sam needs to get Gunny to

Virginia to set up his new shop and get his money in a safe place. They also need to get their stuff from the gun shop back to Virginia.

Sam comes up with a plan of buying new horse trailers and trucks. They will unload the semitruck into the trailers. They can pack hay all around and lessen the chance of getting caught with all the illegal weapons and other stuff. Bud, Dakota, DH, and Sam headed into town to buy trucks and trailers. Sam figures that the biggest problem is protecting the money and other stuff they just acquired.

Harland and Kim stay behind to set up motion detectors and other surveillance around the farm so that no one can enter the farm without detection.

Once Sam and the others reach the city, their first stop is to see Jay at his truck sale lot. They all get out and walk inside. The salesman Sam tangled with the last time walks up in his snide swagger and halfheartedly greets the four of them.

"Can I help you gentlemen or are you here to, as you say, 'look around,'" the salesman says in a snide tone. Then he looks Sam in the eye and knows he is in deep shit again. He barely kept his job the last time.

Sam just smiled at him and says, "No, I'm here to see the boss."

"Aaahh yes, I will tell him that you are here, immediately. Please make yourself comfortable," the salesman says and then he quickly goes off to find Jay.

Bud, Dakota and DH all check out the vehicles in the building. They open hoods and sit in seats. All the salespeople stand and just watch. No other salesmen come up to see if they can help them out except for a young saleslady. She comes up to Kota immediately and starts giving him all the specs on the new truck he is sitting in. Sam opens a tailgate and sits down.

Jay comes out on to the floor. Jay jokingly says, "Sam, come to trade in that old truck already." Jay smiles and shakes Sam's hand. Bud, DH, and Kota come up and shake hands with Jay. Then the three of them go back and start talking to the saleslady.

"No, not today. But my brothers and DH over there, need to get one ton dually four-wheel drive trucks and they need them now," Sam says.

"Well, I think we can fit you all with a truck. What are you looking for?" Jay asks.

"I want one with everything in it and it has to be at least a ton and half truck," Bud says loudly from across the room where the three are flirting with the saleslady.

"And I'll take the same but I want a blue or red," Kota says loudly.

"I have just the trucks for you all. I'll have them bring them up front right away so you can test-drive them," Jay says.

"I don't want to test-drive anything! Just bring me one that has everything and is full of diesel. I know how they drive," Kota says loudly.

"Hey, you guys. Do you think I can get this one? She kind of convinced me to buy this truck," DH yells over to Sam and Jay.

"I'm sure it will be OK," Bud says. Then DH goes on chatting up the saleslady.

"So, Sam, is this going to be a cash or credit this time?" Jay asks and laughs. "I'll get the credit guys on it right away. You shouldn't have any problems financing this."

"Well, Jay my credit is shit so I think we will just pay you in cash." Sam says. "How much is it going to be so I can go get it?"

"Oh, bullshit!" Jay starts laughing because he thinks Sam is pulling his leg. He takes out his calculator and starts punching numbers. "Shit, Sam, that is two hundred and twenty thousand dollars and that includes the discounts for a cash buy."

"OK!" Sam goes out to the truck and comes back in with an arm full of money. He drops it on the tailgate he was sitting on and says, "Here you go. Now make sure they all are trailer equipped."

"Yes, they will all be ready in an hour or so," Jay says as he stares at all the money.

"Well, Jay, are you going to come on back with us to see Virginia," Sam asks.

"Oh, I can't leave. I thought a lot about it but right now is not a good time. Sorry," Jay says. Sam knew that Jay would never leave his business.

"That's OK, it's an open invitation. You will be welcomed anytime," Sam says.

"Let's go, Sam, we got a lot of places to stop before we are done today." Kota says. "Jay, can you drop those trucks off over at the Tomson's trailer place?"

"Not a problem. You guys, thank you," Jay says. "Sam, great to see you again." Jay waves.

Bud pries DH away from the saleslady and then they leave to go buy trailers. They buy four of the biggest trailers that the place has on the lot. Then they all go to Dakota Western Wear and shop for some new shirts and jeans. They had been wearing the same clothes for a couple of days. No one had bought new clothes in several years. They are due for some new clothes.

"These shirts all look like a bunch of girls' clothes. Whatever happened to real western clothes?" Bud asks the salesman who just happens to be wearing a pink shirt.

"These are the new styles. Everyone is wearing them now. Colors are not just for women," the salesman tells Bud.

"Bullshit, where are the real western clothes like the Brushpopper shirts and the Wrangler jeans that are supposed to be made in America." Bud asks as he looks through the rack of clothes.

"Wrangler is now made in Mexico with American fabric. They are the same jeans. The Brushpopper shirts have not been around for several years. They are too hot and unflattering," the salesman explains.

"Well, shit," Sam says to Kota. Sam and Kota are looking at clothes and boots but didn't see anything that they liked. All the brothers like plain clothes, nothing to flashy.

"What we need to do is start making real clothes. I bet we can get them made at home. There are plenty of sewing people around there." Sam says.

"Yes, that would be a good company to make. When we get back, we can look into it. But for now, we can just all get a change of clothes and be on our way," Kota says. Kota notices that DH has an arm full of clothes. "DH, did ya find anything you like?"

"I love these new clothes," DH says. He notices that no one else is buying anything but a change of clothes, but it didn't stop him from buying an armful.

They all leave to pick up the trucks and trailers. After picking up the trucks, they head over to Darrell and Elaine's farm to unload the semitruck into the trailers. They load some hay to cover the weapons not because it hasn't been done several times, but as a matter of fact, you see it all the time on television. The hay just gives someone looking at the trailer something else to look at instead of a trailer of weapons, which would turn police into a feeding frenzy. Bud, DH, and Kota immediately go to work putting in false floors and boxes under the trailers. Sam sorts through the weapons putting those that need to be hidden and those that are not so bad. He rearranges the semitrailer to keep the machines, shelves, and clothes in the trailer. The automatic weapons and explosives are put into false floors. The least illegal weapons are placed inside the trailers in the hay bales. The knives and other hand weapons are put in the tack rooms. They are able to load everything into four trailers. Everyone is happy about the concealment. The loading takes all day and most of the night. They all stay at Darrell and Elaine's place that night. In the morning, they go back over to the grandparents' farm. Harland and Kim got all the security put in place. Harland already got an excavating crew over, waiting to start digging the deep trenches for the bunker.

"Looks like everything is going well," Sam says to DH. "Now remember what we talked about. The water for this place is only about thirty-five to forty feet deep. The gravel pit area is probably the best place to put a bunker. I think you can dig at least a hundred feet there."

"Got it under control." DH socked Sam in the arm. "We will start digging there and go until we find water. By next week, we will be pouring footings. I want to get at least five different crews to come into work. No one will know exactly what it is they are going to be building. We'll get the electricians started next week. We will have solar, wind, natural gas generator, and power grid electricity. So everything is going to work out. It is just a matter of time. I hope to have this place done in about a month or so." DH shows everyone the plans he had drawing up during the night.

"So then we are going to go back and get everything going back home. Where is Kim?" Sam asks Harland.

"He had to go back home for a day because his wife was yelling at him. He hasn't been home for a while, and she was pretty pissed off. He'll be back tonight with a couple more men to help with guard duty," Harland says.

"What! This is supposed to be on the hush-hush. Does he know these guys or what?" Sam says. He is a little upset and worried at the same time.

"He said they are some of the guys he worked with in the marines. They are out of work, so he is going to give them a job they are good at," Harland says.

"OK, but keep an eye on them. You have about a billion dollars to look after. My sister will be over to take some of the money to start setting up some bank accounts, but other than that, no one goes near those vehicles," Sam says sternly.

"I'll make sure nothing happens to anything, but I think maybe Kota or Bud should stay." DH jumped in the conversation.

Bud and Dakota look at each other and discuss who is going to stay. Both of them decide that they cannot stay any longer, but they can go and then come back. Harland volunteers to stay, but the whole idea is to have one of the three brothers there. Sam decides he will stay and his dad is going to have to go out with the truck and trailer.

"I'll stay until we get this place secured," Sam says. "Then I have to get back to work."

"Shit, you don't need to go to work anymore. Just hire some more doctors," Kota says.

At that moment, he almost felt free for the first time in over twenty some years. Somehow the weight of stress is lifted off his back by the few words Kota said to him. "I already did that, but I still have to show up once in a while. It can wait though. When you get home, you and Bud need to get a construction crew over to the farm and get Gunny's building started. Put up any building that he wants but make sure it looks good. Maybe put him in the back by the trees or hell, I don't care. You guys can handle it," Sam says.

Bud, Kota, and Harland take off. They go pickup Gunny and Darrell. Then they immediately leave for Virginia. It was a little difficult the brothers to convince Darrell that he could go. His excuse was that he was too busy to leave. Gunny convinced him that he needed someone to talk too. Dad was more than willing to go after that. They make it back to Virginia without a problem. It took them thirty-six hours to their normal twenty-four because Darrell had to stop about ten times.

Sam calls Carol and tells her what is going on. She decides to fly out to see Sam for a few days. Sam tells her, "We are camping out here at my grandparents' old farm."

Carol says, "Sam, I used to love camping. That will be fun."

She flies out to South Dakota. She isn't too happy about the accommodations, but she doesn't complain. Sam knows that Carol does not like the fact of living in a tent. They talk and go out for dinner. They visit the falls and the palisades while she is there. She fills Sam in on what has been happening at the hospital and with the rehab center. She tells him, "That damn archaeologist tried to bring in a group of people. I told her she could bring only one person at a time. She got pissy with me, so I had to kick her out."

"Good," Sam says, "she probably would want to declare the cave as some preserve or something."

"That's what she was starting to get too before I kicked her and her stupid group out," Carol says. "She says the place needs to be preserved and everything needs to be documented. I hope she doesn't come back."

Sam says, "Yeah, I wish I hadn't let here in in the first place."

Carol stays for two days. She really didn't like camping all that much.

Chapter Sixteen

Snoop is on his tenth hour of drinking in the Frontier Club in downtown Sioux Falls. This bar has always been a place of acceptance for him and his type of business—that is, methamphetamine sales. It is also the place where if you were in need of any product, you can get it there. Snoop was the primary supplier of crystal methamphetamines for the place and most of Sioux Falls until a new distributor bought out his business. Snoop decided that with the money Sam gave him and the sale of his business that it was time to retire. Snoop's new hobby is just drinking all day.

Snoop has several of his so-called friends and women surrounding him in a back booth. They all are very drunk, and the only thing keeping them going is the meth they are snorting and smoking all night. They all are laughing it up until Captain Nate Lavean walks up with twenty uniformed armed men.

Nate sticks a .45 Colt up Snoop's nose. "You'll be fucking coming with me," Nate demands. Nate has been trying to find Snoop since the day he got the call. He finally tracks him to the Frontier Club, not that Snoop was in hiding. Nate could have found him earlier, but he had been in such a drunken state when he had received the phone call that he barely remember Snoop's name.

"OK, dude, just take the piece out of my face," Snoop says without any panic. Snoop's friends just slunk out of the booth and leave quickly. Snoop slithers out of the booth and staggers out with Nate.

Once outside, Nate turns to Snoop. "Who busted into my place? Now before you answer, I will tell you this—I want that money back and all those weapons. I want to know where it is. I will only ask once and I will kill to get it back. Now speak."

"His name is Sam Kelley and he lives in Virginia some place. I don't know where your fucking money is, but I'm sure they are having fun spending it. I suppose they took everything to Virginia since they loaded it all on trucks the night that I fucking called you," Snoop yells in a sarcastic tone.

"Why did they go to the bunker?" Nate asks in a calm voice.

"Macky tried to kill him over at the gun shop. You should ask that dumb shit," Snoop says. He quit yelling because he is about to puke out all the alcohol in his stomach.

"I can't ask him, he's dead," Nate says with a little laughter in his voice.

"Then Macky shouldn't have pissed off Sam. You better not piss off Sam," Snoop warns Nate. Snoop turns quickly away from Nate and vomit erupts from his mouth and on to the sidewalk.

"Christ's sakes, boy! Get your shit together here!" Nate says and cringes at the sight of Snoop vomiting.

Snoop stands up straight and splits. He wipes his mouth with the bottom of his shirt. Snoop gives a little smile and says, "Aahh, I needed that."

Nate shakes his head and tries to get back to the interrogation. He says, "Now! What the fuck are you talking about? I have an army. We have thousands of men. Well-paid men. I will do as I want." Nate is now a little arrogant.

"He'll kill you and take everything you have and everything that the company has. Beware," Snoop warns Nate. Snoop gets real serious. He now believes all the stories Sam told him.

"I am going to find him. I'm going to kill him and all those around him." Nate is furious. "Men, let's go! This shit knows nothing." Nate and his men, along with several others from the Iowa division, load up into trucks. They head out of town back to the bunker. Their next job is to make contact with the Virginia division to find out if they know anything about Sam Kelley.

Snoop feels kind of guilty for giving up Sam even though Sam did kick the shit out of him. Snoop is smart enough to know that it really was his own fault. Gina and her parents had always been good to Snoop. He had never ridden a horse until Darrell took him on a ride. Snoop really didn't want to see them get hurt because of his doings. He also knew that if Sam found out about him narking, Sam would kill him. Snoop grabs his cell phone and calls Gina, "Hey, Gina! Snoop."

"What do you want? You get into trouble again?" Gina asks. "This time you may have to just work it out yourself, after turning on Sam," Gina says in nice calm voice.

"Aaahh, yeah. I am sorry about that, ya know. I was pretty high and drunk, and I do stupid stuff. I never wanted to piss off Sam. He is kind of my ideal. But now there are a bunch of guys looking for him," Snoop says with sincerity.

"Who is looking for him? Is it that group you've been selling for?" Gina was now upset and worried at the same time.

"Yeah, listen, I don't want Mom and Dad to get hurt or anything. Just tell Sam that a bunch of guys in blue-and-white camouflage are looking for him and the money. He'll know what I mean. And look, I'm sorry. I'd like to stay friends if we could. I'm not going to sell anymore," Snoop says. Elaine and Darrell had always made him feel like one of the family. All of Gina's friend refer to Elaine and Darrell as Mom and Dad.

"Right, well, we will see. You keep your word and maybe we can get around this mess. I got to go," Gina says and hangs up the phone and immediately calls Sam.

"Sam, I just talked to Snoop."

Sam cuts her off. He is irritated that she would talk to that asshole after he helped out Macky. Sam asks in an irritated tone. "What did you talk to that asshole for?"

"Oh, simmer down!" Gina says to Sam. "He just wanted me to let you know that some guys in blue-and-white camouflage are looking for you and the money. He also said he was sorry."

"Well, thanks for the warning. I guess I'd better find them before they find me or you or Mom and Dad," Sam says nonchalantly.

"Sam, what money is he talking about?" Gina asks.

"Well, come out to Grandma and Pa's old place tomorrow and I will explain everything. Bring your books and a calculator also," Sam says. "I was going to call you tonight or tomorrow to come out and see what we found."

"Oookkkay, I'll see you about seven then." Gina always got up early. She would always start milking cows in the morning before anyone else would get out to the barn.

"All right then, I think in the meantime, you should stay at Mom and Dad's tonight. Just so you are close and also keep an eye on the farm," Sam suggests.

"I'm going out there now and I'll call if there is any problem." Gina hangs up and leaves her house for the farm.

Sam hangs up and gets Kota on the phone. "Hey, how is it going?" Sam asks.

"Good, we already got Fort construction out here and they already got the building laid out. They'll be digging tomorrow for footings. So what's up with you?" Kota asks.

"Nothing, just getting the place going out here. How is Montana doing?" Sam asks. He loved his nephews just as if they were his kids.

"Good, he wants to go see Grandma next time I come out. He's pretty wound up about all the stuff we brought back. We put it all in the cave. We made a new bridge down into the back of the cave. Now you can drive a truck in and out the back entrance. We're trying to figure out how to put a better door on the entrance," Kota says with excitement.

"Well, just put the door on the inside of the cave. You can concrete some walls to hold doors. Drill deep all around the entrance into the rock and pour a wall with a hole in it. Then put a heavy blast door on the thing. Carol's dad can figure up the engineering stuff on that," Sam says.

"Yeah, we already thought of that but we have to just work on it for a while," Kota says.

"I know you guys have, but I'm just thinking out loud. Well, the other reason I called is that Snoop must have ratted us out to the people we took all the money from. They may try to track me down out there so everyone be on alert. If the alarm system goes off, get into the bunker or better yet, just have everyone stay in the bunker. There is plenty of room for everyone and it's comfortable so just stay there till we get everything under control. How is Darwin doing?" Sam asks.

"We hardly ever see him," Kota says.

"What does he do then if you never see him?" Sam asks.

"He is buying shit left and right. He has changed the computer room in the bunker into a giant room of screens and computers. I have no idea what he is doing but he is doing it big," Kota says with a little laughter.

"That's great. Maybe when he gets done with that, he can work on the hospital computer system and make that work," Sam says with a little sarcasm.

"I'll ask him to work on it and I'll get everyone rounded up and get them into the bunker. You know Carol ain't going to like it," Kota says.

"I'll call her and maybe she can go over to her mom and dad's place," Sam says. He knows Carol will put up a big fuss. She always did what she wanted, but maybe she will listen this time.

"OK, well I'll call you later," Kota says.

"OK, bye," Sam says.

Sam hangs up the phone and then calls Carol to let her know what is going on. She decides to pack up all the cats and dogs and bring them and herself over to her parents' house. Sam then calls Kim to get his guys over as soon as possible and gather any men or women that may want some work.

Sam finds DH looking over some of the plans that he had drawn up for the bunker. DH has made it so that the bunker would hold several trucks and vehicles. It is going to be a three-story underground shop and garage in the hill. The way to the housing bunker is through a tunnel. The bunker will branch several times to different parts of the farm. DH said that it is much like the bunkers that are built in Montana that held the people and vehicles for the missile silos.

"Looks good to me," Sam says. "How long do you think it will take to get it done?" He goes over to the cooler and grabs two beers. He hands one to DH and they both pop them open.

DH drank down half the beer and tells Sam, "Probably take about five months to get the concrete poured, but we could use precast and get most of the tunnel done quickly. We can just pour footers for the precast, but the garage bunker needs to be poured. We are going to have to almost move a hill to do that, but it can be done if we can get enough of a crew."

"Well, let's go find about five or six construction crews and see if we can't entice them to get here early by giving them some bonus money. Then give each one a section and have a race on who gets it done first. First one done gets a million dollar bonus," Sam says. He really didn't want to wait five months. They had plenty of money to throw around, so why not buy speed and quality if you can afford it? He knows construction crews work faster with more money sitting in front of them. "Tell the contractors that not only do they get a bonus, but every one of their men will get a bonus," Sam says.

"We can probably get it done in a month or two that way. I will get it all set up and find the crews tomorrow. We don't have blueprints, so I'll just have to watch everyone really close. I will need some help though. Kim can probably watch the electrical, plumbing, and heating. I'll do the rest." DH is excited.

"Why don't we just find some old plans they used for building those government bunkers. I'll get Darwin to find some plans and we can build off that," Sam says.

"That would be the best if we had some blueprints. See what he can find," DH says.

"Sounds like a plan. Kim should be here in a little while. He should be bringing some help. We may have to get rid of a little problem before long," Sam says. "Snoop, that guy you all dumped off, he ratted us out or at least me. I am going to have to find the guys he told and get rid of them before they find us."

DH starts looking serious and asks Sam, "What do you think is going to happen? Do you think they can even find this place?"

"I don't know if they can find this place and you don't have to get in the middle of it if you don't want," Sam says. "It may get bloody from here on out." Sam is a little worried but figured it would all work out in the end. He wasn't a military man, but he would never back down from a fight.

"Oh, I'm in with you all right. I'll help you get them. Remember we are all in this together. Ya know the 'all for one and one for all' shit?" DH says in a tough tone. Then he drinks down the last of his beer and grabs another.

"OK. Tonight I'm going to go and find Snoop so I can find this group or we can wait for them to find us here. What do you think?" Sam contemplates out loud.

"I think we let them come find us and we can make it really easy. We will have a perimeter set up and they can come get us," DH suggests.

"Yeah, they are kind of dumb from what I've seen so far. We don't want them to come here though," Sam says as he is trying to think of a good place around the area that he is familiar with. Then he says, "Maybe we can use this place behind the racetrack about five miles from here. The place is surrounded by hills and trees. There is an open field that we used to farm when I was a kid. We could stage an ambush there, if they would fall for it. I can go talk to the people that own the place. It may have changed hands, but if it did, maybe it is for sale or rent for a few weeks."

"Tomorrow we can go check it out and come up with a plan," DH says.

Sam calls Bud on the phone. "Hey, tell Darwin to look for some government bunker blueprints."

Bud says, "Hey. I'll tell him if I can track him down."

Sam says, "Well, sit in front of his computer room door for a little bit and I'm sure you will be able to catch him there."

Bud says, "I'll find him. I'll have him tracked down by tomorrow."

Sam says, "Just have him call me as soon as he can."

Bud says, "Will do. Bye." Then he hangs up the phone.

Sam hangs up the phone and says to DH, "Darwin is running wild in Virginia."

DH says, "Yep."

DH and Sam sit around the rest of night drinking beer and talking about horses and other bullshit. Kim shows up later on with ten people.

"I got some good men—well, some are women, but they're all are good," Kim says and then goes over to the cooler and grabs a beer. He leaves the cooler open and motions to the new people to help themselves. "Sam, DH, this is . . ." Kim introduces everyone as he goes around from person to person to point them out. "Mike, we were in the marines together. He can find and obtain anything you want or need. He's so good he found us a camper in Kuwait. Dan is one of the best drivers around here. He has been in several rally races overseas until he ended up in the hospital for about five months and lost his sponsors. Whiskers works with me down at the shop. He's a hard worker and can get into anything you point at, lock or no lock. Sarah flies for the hospital and is tired of working for them, so she can fly for us. Skids is a very good aircraft mechanic. Bozzel and Poppers, they can shoot and fight and they both are good carpenters. Mickey, he used to rodeo but he works as a truck driver. He needs a different job. Lisa and Beth are both from the farm. They can hunt and fish. Right now, they both work down at the hospital with my mom. They are both RNs. And last but not least, do you remember my two brothers, Bobby and Tom. They grew up and they are ready to do anything we tell them to do. So that's all of them. We can probably find some more help, but these guys are all I could find on a short notice."

"Well, everyone, I'm Sam and this scruff is DH. Welcome to your new office, for now anyway," Sam says as he points out the tents. "We are in the process of fixing up the farm and building us all a nice new building," Sam announces and then goes around and shakes everyone's hand.

"Hey, y'all," DH says and shakes everyone's hand.

"Now does anyone know what they are doing here or what we do?" Sam asks with a serious tone.

Tom raises his hand and Sam points at him to give him the go ahead to answer, "We are here to be lookouts so that no one steals any of this machinery and stuff. Or work on fixing the farm."

"Well, yes and no." Sam turns to Kim and motions his head for Kim to go outside the tent to have a talk. "You all help yourself to the food and drinks, we'll be right back."

Sam, DH, and Kim all walk outside the tent and about a hundred feet away. "Well, Kim, we have a dilemma. That Snoop ratted me out. I am going to go after this group before they come after us," Sam says in a serious tone. DH stands there with his arms crossed and nodding.

"So what are you saying?" Kim asks with excitement, "We're going to war?"

"Exactly!" Sam says and then asks Kim, "Are these guys ready for a fight, or do we need to leave them here to tend to the farm?"

Kim takes off his cowboy hat and rubs his head. He takes a deep breath and says, "I think some of them are good to go. Maybe we should ask them."

"Well, that is a problem," Sam takes off his old black cowboy hat and adjusts the hat brow band that has been falling out for years. Then he puts is hat back on and says, "If we ask them to fight with us, then we are going to have to let them in on everything. Now I don't think these guys really need to know how much money we got because people get a little different when a lot of money is involved. How much can we trust to tell them about our plans of going around and busting these places or do we just not involve them?"

"They all can be trusted. I will stake my life on it," Kim says with sincerity.

"Well, they will have to take and say the oath, but they are going on a payroll or salary. Ya think?" DH says. Not that he cared— he just wanted to make a command decision.

"OK with me, but no talk about the money and no one sees it except for us. DH, we need to get a concrete tank buried in the barn tomorrow. It needs to be big enough to hold all the money and make sure it is waterproof. I'll get some waterproof bags. Tomorrow we can bag and store the money for a while after my sister gets here and counts it," Sam says.

"Good," Kim and DH say in agreement.

"Give each one a job and we'll tell them tomorrow exactly what is going on. Tonight we can split up guard duty. They can settle into the tent. I guess we should tell them how much they are going to get paid, so if it ain't enough, they can leave now," Sam says to Kim and DH. "You think a hundred fifty grand and we pay off their bills will be good enough to start. Or what you all think?"

"Yeah, we got plenty of money and we'll get more." DH nods in approval and goes on to say, "I think that would be fair and if their family needs a little help we can do that."

Kim puts his hat back on and says, "Sounds good. Let's do it."

All three walk back into the tent. Everyone is eating and drinking. They are having a good time.

"OK, everyone, here's the deal," Sam says with authority, "Kim is going to give you each jobs for today and tomorrow. But first, I just want to tell you exactly what you are going to get paid in case it is not enough, you can leave now. There will be no negotiations on salary and every one of you will get paid the same. Your salary for the year is one hundred and fifty thousand. Your house and all your bills will be paid off as of the first day you work here so you will not owe anything. You keep ownership of the property. You will not have expenses from work. You can stay here or go home every day, but you have to be available twenty-four hours a day, seven days a week. No exceptions unless it happens to be a family emergency. We work almost every day, and when we get done this year, you may get a bonus. You can never tell anyone about anything we do here or anything do anywhere. Your lips are sealed. If not, we will seal them surgically. Any questions, concerns, or hate mail?" Sam looks around at their faces. No one looks angry but no one looks happy except for Bobby and Tom.

"So if we work for you, we get all this stuff?" Sarah asks. "Why the hell would you pay us this much? Is the job dangerous?"

"Sometimes it is but most of the time not. There is a chance you can get killed, and we expect loyalty. We expect you all to be dedicated to what we are setting out to do as much as we are. Some of the stuff we may do may be considered illegal, but I will be responsible for that. If you are scared or reluctant, then leave now. If not, you are with us forever," Sam says. Everyone is nodding like they understood, so Sam knows that none of them understands. "Let me put this simple: you are going to get paid well upfront, you get your years pay in cash tomorrow. We also pay all your debt. For this, we expect divine loyalty, and you can get your ass killed or other bad stuff. We will have fun but also work hard. If you seek adventure, this will be the place to find it, if not please leave now. Kim will take you home and there will be no hard feelings. We will give you a ten-thousand-dollar stipend for your time here if you go home now," Sam explains it as well as he could.

"Sam, sir, I'm in and I'm staying," Sarah says.

There is a round of "Me too" that went around the tent. Everyone is in and no one leaves. Kim goes around and gives everyone a job for the night.

Everyone stays the night and no one goes home. Everyone does guard duty without whining.

Chapter Seventeen

The next morning, Sam goes back to the infantry carrier with an old feed sack and fills it full of money. He knows he will either have to buy the farm they are going to set up the ambush on or rent it. Plus they had a little shopping to do. Then Sam finds Kim and DH.

"I'm going to go find a place to try to set up an ambush for these pukes that are looking for me." Sam tells Kim and DH, "Then I'm going to find a caterer to hire. They can bring out three square meals a day while everyone is working out here. I'll buy some snacks and get some waterproof bags."

"OK, sounds good to me," DH says, "Where you going to find a Caterer?"

"I don't know yet," Sam says.

"Well, while you're out," DH says, "get me some Marlboro lights and a new Zippo lighter."

"Got it," Sam says.

"I'm going with you," Kim says. "These guys all got jobs to do and we need to check some shit out."

"Sounds good," Sam says. "First thing, we are going to find Snoop to get the ball a rolling. We can use him to get those guys that are after me to find me. Why hide?"

"Great," Kim says, "let's bring Whiskers along."

"OK!" Sam says. "Let's get going. DH, we'll leave you to holding down the fort."

"Got it under control," DH says. "See you in a bit."

Kim rounds up Whiskers and they all jump into Sam's truck. First stop is to pay Snoop a visit to get the plan in place. They arrive at Snoop's house. Sam had found out where the house is from Gina. Whiskers unlocks the front door within seconds. They quickly and quietly move around the house and looking at everything.

"This place is a shit hole," Whiskers whispers. "Does anyone even live here?"

Kim slaps Whiskers on the back of the head and whispers, "Quiet!"

The house is a large open house with a loft. Sam goes up the stairs. He sees Snoop still in bed with two naked women lying next to him. Sam had brought along his new chained weapon so he takes the chain and puts a loop around Snoop's feet. Snoop starts to move a little but doesn't wake up. Sam looks over the rail and motions for Kim to come up and for Whiskers to watch the door. When Kim gets to the top of the stairs, Sam pulls on the chain, ripping Snoop out of bed. Snoop has a rude awakening when he hits the floor. Sam instantly puts his knee on Snoop's chest and wraps one end of the chain around Snoop's neck. The two women wake up and look around but go right back to sleep. Snoop finally comes to his consciousness and realizes what is going on.

"Snoop! Snoop! You there! You stupid bastard!" Sam says in a quiet soft voice. He tightens the chain a little and slaps Snoop.

Snoop nods but doesn't move his arms or legs. Sam loosens the chain.

"You ratted me out and now I'm going to remove your liver." Sam moves the knife's point up to Snoop's lower abdomen.

Snoop starts screaming and crying, "Oh my God, oh my God, NOOOOO!"

Sam pushes the knife in a little harder and tells him in a stern but quiet voice, "Well, if you want to save your liver, then you will do exactly as I tell you. Otherwise, I will be back for body parts. Now, here is what you are going to tell those guys you ratted me out too. We are moving into a farm over by the racetrack. We are going to hide all the stuff in a field behind the farm in about two days from now. Right now, we are just hiding in several different locations and we are never in one place for very long. We just bought this farm and are going to hide the stuff because we are tired of running. You will not tell them for two days. GOT IT?"

Snoop nods. Sam removes the chain. Then Kim, Whiskers, and Sam leave as fast as they came in.

The three of them jump into Sam's truck and head to the store. They buy a bunch of beer, pop, water, ten cartons of cigarettes, a Zippo lighter, and snacks. They head on over to the Outdoor Store and get giant vacuum packing bags for storing the money and several other things that they need, like sleeping bags, backpacks, more tents, rope, cots, and several other things that would make camping more luxurious. After loading everything into the pickup, they drive back to Hartford to find a caterer.

They stop at the only restaurant in town. Sam, Kim, and Whiskers order cheeseburgers and Pepsi. When the waitress brings the order out Sam asks her, "I got a big caterer job that will last for several weeks or months, do you all do catering?"

"Well, I never have known Kenney to do any catering but don't really know if he has been asked." The waitress says in a kind and friendly voice.

"Please excuse my manners," Sam says. "My name is Sam Kelley. This is Kim and Whiskers." Kim and Whiskers keep eating but give a wave.

"I'm Adeana," the waitress says. "I'll go back and ask Kenney. He owns this place."

"That would be great," Sam says.

Five minutes later Kenney comes out from the back of the restaurant with Adeana. Adeana introduces them. "Kenney this is Sam, Kim and Mr. Whiskers."

Sam stops eating and stands up. He shakes hands with Kenney and says, "Sir, I used to eat here a long time ago before I moved away. This was the place to come to, especially in the summer. I am in need of a caterer for several weeks and for several men. Would you be interested in something like that or do you know of anyone?"

"It is good to meet you, Sam," Kenney says in a tired voice. "I would be interested but I just don't have the equipment to haul food anywhere. Business is not like it used to be and I could use the work, but I am underequipped."

"If money for the equipment was not an issue, could you get the equipment to do something?" Sam asks and then looks at Sam to make sure he is OK with what he is thinking. Kim nods and smiles.

"I could get the equipment to day and start catering tomorrow if I had the money to do so, but how many meals and how often?" Kenney say with seriousness.

"How much money do you think it would take?" Sam asks.

"Probably about five to ten thousand dollars. I could probably borrow my brother's van to haul the food or rent a truck. The main thing is to get heating cabinets and coolers and pans and other stuff," Kenney thought out loud.

"OK, we got that covered," Sam says and then gets up to leave. "I will be right back." Sam goes out to the truck and takes out fifty thousand dollars out of the bag of money. He goes back in and sets the money on the table. "This should get you started."

Kenney and Adeana's eyes open wide and they each pick up a stack of money. Kenney says in a slight stutter, "Ah, ah, that is a lot of money. How many men, did you say?"

Sam shrugs and looks at Kim before saying, "What? Maybe, a hundred to hundred twenty men, three times a day."

"Oh," Kenney says as he is thinking. "Do you want menus or how do you want to do this?"

"I'll make this easy for you," Sam says. "I have a large generator out there and a tent. You can set whatever you want out there. All your equipment will be safe. You can bring the whole breakfast menu out in the morning, a light dinner of multiple choices at noon, and a big meal at suppertime, say around seven o'clock. There will be less people at breakfast and supper. I will get you more money tomorrow at breakfast if you decide to do this job. If you don't, then keep this money and just bring us a good breakfast in the morning. No strings attached."

"No, Sam. I will do this job," Kenney says. "I like to cook and this is a chance to get back on my feet again."

"Good," Sam says and looks over at Kim and Whiskers just sitting there, waiting to go. "We've got to go so we will expect you tomorrow. One other thing, we need to keep this quiet. I really don't want a bunch of people to be coming out and getting in the way of the construction crews. Can you do that?"

"Our lips are sealed," Kenney says. "But where do I bring the food to?" Adeana is standing there, nodding in approval.

"Do you know where the old Pipgras farm is?" Sam asks.

"Ah, oh, the farm down the road with Voe's Salvage Yard about five miles from here," Kenney says as he looks down at the floor, trying to remember.

"Exactly," Sam says. "See you tomorrow." He looks at Kim and Whiskers and says, "Let's go."

Sam, Kim, and Whiskers get up and leave. Kenney and Adeana lock the doors on their way out to go shopping.

After eating dinner, the three of them drive out to visit the land-owners of the old farm where they are going to have the show down. When they get there, a man is working on an old M. Farmall tractor. The tires are bald and the motor is covered in oil. The tractor is in desperate need of repair. The house and the barn are falling apart. There a couple of cows in a pen behind the barn. The pen's fence had been repaired with baling wire and twine string. Some of the fence is old woven wire, and some is barbed wire. In the backyard is a bunch of pigs just wallowing in the dirt. The pigs look like they are supposed to be in a pen at the corner of the farmyard, but several of the fence posts are lying on the ground. The pigs can just walk out of the pen. Just on the other side of yard is a garbage pile next to a burning barrel that is sitting by a grove of trees. In the front of the house, there is an old couch on the pouch. On the couch are two dogs that look like they hadn't moved in quite some time. In the yard, up by the road, is an old toilet that is full of dirt and dead flowers. The windows on the house are either broken or missing.

Sam drives up to the man working on the tractor. He gets out of the truck and walks up to guy. He says, "Hello, sir, my name is Sam Kelley. Do you own this farm?"

"I'm not buying anything and I don't want to hear anything about how great God is, so you can just leave now and save both of us a lot of time," the farmer says without looking up from the work he is doing with the tractor.

"Sir, I'm not selling anything and you can deal with God at your own choosing. What I have for you may make us both happy and content," Sam says convincingly.

"Is that right? What would make me happy is a sack of twenties. If you got, that I got all the time in the world for you." The farmer says.

Sam goes back to the truck and dumps out the contents of one of the grocery bags into the cab of the truck. He fills the bag full with bundles of hundred-dollar bills. Then he goes back to the farmer who has gone back to working on his tractor.

"I thought you left," the farmer says, not looking up from the tractor.

"I thought you wanted a sack of twenties," Sam says. The farmer turns around and looks at Sam. Sam hands him the grocery bag.

The farmer opens the bag and looks inside then drops the wrench he is holding. "Well, son, just what can I do for you?" he says with a big smile.

"I need to borrow your farm for about a week. Do you own that land out back there?" Sam asks.

"Yes, I do," the farm says with a questioning tone.

"Well, sir, some real bad men are going to be coming here in about two days or so. It would be a great time for you and your family to go on vacation. When you get back here, we will be gone," Sam informs the farmer.

"So you what to buy my farm. Well, I'm not really selling. I'd have nowhere else to go," The farmer says.

"No, I'm giving you the money to fix this shit hole up. I just want you to leave this place for me. I want you to take your animals some place for a week or so. Then come back. Make sure you take anything that means something to you or your family. Your place may get destroyed while you are gone. You should have enough in there to rebuild anything that could get destroyed. Now, I suggest you take the money and get your ducks in a row and your shit in a ball," Sam explains as calmly as he can.

"Well, we could go to see the in-laws. We haven't been there for a while. Let me talk it over with my wife and see what she has to say. You can come on in and have some sun tea," the farmer says. He wipes his oily hands on his pants and rolls the top of the grocery bag to close it. He turns to take Sam up to the house.

"Thank you, but no, thank you. I don't have time. I need you to decide in the next five minutes or give me the money back. I'll just go somewhere else," Sam says a little bluntly. He is getting pushy because he really didn't want to go into the house. "Ya know? I find it hard to believe that you would just throw away a quarter of a million dollars just because you have to ask your wife if it is OK to go on a vacation and see her family."

"I reckon you're right. We'll be leaving tonight. I'll get the truck and haul all my critters over to the neighbors," the farmer says without any expression of gratitude or remorse.

"Wise decision. Thank you for your time," Sam says.

Sam jumps into the truck and leaves with Kim and Whiskers. They go back to Sam's grandparents' farm. When they arrive at the farm, Gina is there with DH. DH has given her the grand tour of the farm place but did not take her into the trees. There are too many traps in the perimeter and in the trees. The traps are nonlethal but can maim a large man fairly easily. Everyone else is working at the jobs assigned to them. Sam, Kim, and Whiskers unload the truck.

"Did the tank get put in today, DH?" Sam asks.

"We got the tank but we didn't get the hole in the barn dug yet. They are still digging and it has to be mostly dug by hand. The last time I was over there it was about half-done," DH says.

"Well, let's run over there and see if it can be buried yet. I would like to get it in and buried by tonight, but by morning is OK. I want those guys working until they get done. So I don't want them to leave until it is done," Sam says with authority.

"I don't know if they will stay, but let's see how close they are," DH says.

Sam and DH walk over to the barn where the hole is being dug. When they get there, DH looks in the hole and takes out his tape measure. "This hole needs to be another five feet deeper and another two feet wider and three feet longer." DH looks up at Sam.

Sam looks over at the foreman and asks, "Are you going to get it done today?" Sam really isn't asking, he is telling the foreman. The foreman knows it too.

"Nah, we're probably looking to getting it done in the next couple of days. We have to dig most of this and that just takes time," the foreman explains.

"Well, I want it done today or by morning, so you either work faster or get more help in here," Sam tells the foreman point blank since he didn't take the order in a less blunt way. Sam is a little upset on how long it taking for eight men to dig a hole.

"We're just not going to get it done today and that is just the way it is." The foreman is trying to exert some type of power trip and hoping Sam will back down.

Sam is getting annoyed; he knows that the foreman probably did this power trip thing before and people would just back down. Sam is not backing down and tells the foreman in a stern tone, "Here is what is going to happen, so listen—this hole is going to be done before anyone goes home, and by morning, that concrete tank will concreted in to this hole. The only thing I want to see is a metal door sticking out of the ground."

"Like I said, we ain't workin' overtime to get this done. It's an extra and we'll get this done in due time," the foreman says in a stern, definitive voice as steps up close to Sam. He then pokes Sam in the chest with a finger.

"Take one step back or else," Sam tells him.

The foreman doesn't move and just gives Sam a little push. Sam just steps back two steps to keep his balance. The foreman steps forward into Sam and reaches out to give Sam another shove. Sam in the blink of the eye grabs the foreman's hand and spins him around with a hapkido move and then throws him to the floor. The foreman's wrist is bent in a direction that is very painful. Sam makes it hurt without dislocating it. The foreman doesn't move.

Sam bends down on one knee and informs the foreman, "I don't like men touching me, so when I say to you step back, I pretty much mean it. Now you obviously don't know who you are talking to. I am Sam, and if you don't get this done, you will not be working here tomorrow or ever. Do you understand?"

"I do, I understand," the foreman grunts.

Sam lets the foreman up. The foreman brushes himself off, then goes over to his workers and tells them they wouldn't be going anywhere until they are done. The foreman gets on the phone and calls in another crew. Within the hour there are fourteen men working in the barn.

Sam, DH, Kim, and Gina go into the trees, back to the hidden troop carriers. Sam opens up one of the carriers on one of the trailers. Sam climbs over top of the carrier and opens the drop down gate. Gina climbs in.

"My God, where the hell did you get all this money?" Gina asked all excited.

"You don't want to know. We have four of these piles. I need you to count it and then take part of it and start some bank accounts. We also need to get the ten new people paid and pay off all their bills. I will send each one to you when you are ready, and you can go over all that. Give each one a hundred and fifty thousand in cash. The big thing is that no one sees this money or hears how much there is. As soon as you are done counting, we are going to move most of it over to the barn and bury it," Sam informs Gina.

"It's going to take a while to count it, but I'll get it counted today, so leave me alone to my job," Gina says and then pushes Sam out of the carrier.

"OK, but I'm going to leave Kim here to help you and as a guard," Sam says and then calls Kim over. "Can you help her? If you go through the trees, remember how we walked through, or better yet just call me so I can help you through. I'm going to bring you guys some drinks over. Do you guys need anything else?"

"No, not right now," they both say.

Sam and DH go over to the weapons that are in the Hummers. "I think we need to get these two trucks out and look over the weapons. We need to do an inventory on the ammunition," Sam says to DH, "Let's take and bring out the helicopter and get Skids and Sarah to look at it. We may need to get a fuel tank or something to get that thing flying."

"Yeah, we can to that right now, but can we get out without triggering the traps?" DH asks.

"I'll have to disarm three of the traps and then we can move them," Sam says. "You go start those trucks up and I'll get that done."

Sam goes and disarms the traps while DH starts the trucks. DH gets into one of the trucks and slowly backs it out the narrow path out to the main yard. Sam helps guide him out. Once out, they leave the truck running. They both go back into the trees and move the other truck out. They park it close to the main tent. Sam calls over the ten new people. He has Bozzel and Poppers make a tent around the back of the truck with the two Hummers. Whiskers, Mickey, Dan, and DH build a huge tent around the back of the truck and over the truck containing the helicopter. They use all the tarps and scrap wood that they can find.

"I guess we need a circus tent. Does anyone know where we can find one?" Sam asks.

Mike's ears perk up and he says, "That is right up my alley. I'll be back before morning with one big enough to park both trucks in." Then Mike grabs Kim's truck and takes off.

"Well!" Sam says to everyone. "Aaahh, OK, we are going to unload those two trucks and try not to kill yourself or anyone else."

They open the two trucks and set up the ramps. There are a few "oohs" and "aahs" but they get everything unloaded. Sarah and Skids immediately inspected the helicopter. The others start rummaging through the Hummers and unloading them. Lisa and Beth write down everything that they had in the Hummers. The job goes quickly and they get it all done before the caterers deliver supper.

Sam goes back into the woods and sets the traps back up. Then he goes over to the trucks with Kim and Gina. They had finished counting the first pile of money and Kim had bagged it as they went along.

"Each one of these blocks is a million dollars, and on this pallet, there are two hundred and ninety of them. This is a lot of money here, more than any bank would ever have in it. I know you wouldn't rob a bank, so where did you get it?" Gina says.

"You have to keep it secret, all of this, no one can know about it. So if you promise, then I will tell you," Sam tells to Gina.

"I promise. Besides, I already saw the money so that is beside the point," Gina says sarcastically.

"This money and all the money I have in Virginia, we took from meth labs run by the government. Remember what I was telling you about the first night I was here. It's OCORC's way of funding some of the government funny business. We have a bunch of files and a hard drive. Darwin is working on the files right now in Virginia. We are going to rob every government run meth lab in the US and shut down all those who have been getting money and power from this over the years. What do you think of that?" Sam says and then he looks at Gina for a blessing on his brilliant idea. He knows it is a long shot, but he is fed up with the drug dealers and the government getting rich. He has worked hard all his life and is always broke. This time, he is going to be the superhero with the help of his friends.

"I think you are going to be in big trouble, so you better get it done before they catch you," Gina says with concern.

"We are working on it. That is why we are building this bunker here like the one in Virginia. So you'd better get counting because soon I hope, we will be getting a lot more money," Sam says.

"I'll have it done in an hour or so. We are just going to count bundles and that should be pretty close to right. I'll take two bundles and put into ten different banks, and that way we have it spread out. Then we can just add to the accounts as needed. I can set them all up under a nonprofit corporation. Then we should turn a lot of this money into gold or other investments. It will be easier to control. We can set up a corporation that buys gold and silver from everyday people and that way no one will know how much is coming or going. Good idea, huh?" Gina tells Sam like it is a new idea. People have been laundering money through the gold-buying scams for years.

"Great, I'll leave it all up to you and Kim. I'm going back to the yard and I'll be back here in an hour. We'll take the trucks over to the barn. You, Kim, DH, and I will have to unload the trucks," Sam tells her. Then he treks through the trees. He walks in to the shelter area to check on how DH is coming along with the inventory.

"So how is everything going?" Sam asks DH.

"Well, Skids got the copter back together and Sarah is going to take it for a test drive. She wants to know if you want to go along. We got an inventory on the weapons and ammunition and there is a lot there. We have enough weapons to equip a platoon. We even have explosives and timers, but I have no idea about using that shit so if you are going to use it some place, then we need to find someone else," DH informs Sam.

"Well, did they get that damn hole dug yet?" Sam asks.

"I was just over there and they are about done with the hole. Then they are going to mix concrete in a mixer they brought over to pour the base for the concrete tank. That thing is huge and if they don't put some base down it may just tip. They can set the tank in the morning and a truck will be here at seven in the morning to pour around the tank. We can load the tank at about nine or ten. That is the best they can do." DH informs Sam.

"OK, that will have to work. We will have to hurry to set things up over at the ambush area but I think we can get everything ready. We need to get a truck in here to fill these vehicles up and to fill the helicopter. Maybe put Mike and Dan on that job. Where the hell is Mike anyway?" Sam asks.

"He called about fifteen minutes ago and he said he's on his way back. He'll be here in about an hour or so." DH says.

Sam goes over to the other shelter to see when the helicopter of going to be ready. Everything is ready so they take the make shift shelter and move it so the helicopter is no longer covered.

"So have you flown one of these MH6s before?" Sam asks Sarah.

"Not exactly but I have flown a helicopter before. I trained on one in the army but it was a Blackhawk. The principle is the same but I will have to get the feel of it," Sarah says with confidence.

"You can fly it though, right?" Sam asks with a little concern.

"Yeah, yeah, no problem," Sarah says with a little hesitation.

"Well then, let's go." Sam says.

Sarah climbs into the helicopter and starts it up. Sam jumps into the copilot seat and DH climbs into the back. Sarah handles the helicopter nice and smooth. Sarah flies around the farm for about ten minutes. When she is comfortable with flying it, she flies over to Sam's parents' place. Sam wants to show Sarah where they are going tomorrow so they fly over to the farm.

Sarah says to Sam, "This helicopter is fast and responsive." She wiggles the helicopter like Sam needed a demonstration. Sam never liked flying unless he was going to skydive. He felt safer with a parachute rig on his back. Sarah drops the helicopter down to tree top level in the blink of an eye. Sam almost vomits but quickly recovers. DH didn't buckle himself in and he is getting thrown around. He struggles to find his way back to the little fold up seat and buckle himself in. After flying over the ambush area, they head back to base. Sarah lands the helicopter down as smooth as she took off.

"Shit, that was so much fun!" Sarah says with excitement "I hope we can do that again." Sarah throws off her headphones and climbs out.

Sam climbs out and looks around. Everyone is looking at them. DH is still hooting and hollering inside that back of the helicopter. "I'd say, Sarah, you really know how to fly," Sam says with a sigh of relief that he is on the ground. "So, yes, you will definitely be flying this thing with one catch, you have to show me how to fly it."

Sarah holds out her hand, and Sam extends his. She shakes it, "That's a deal."

"OK," Sam says and then goes to check on Gina and Kim when a rental truck rolls into the yard. It is Mike. Mike turns the truck and backs up to the two semitrucks and then gets out.

"What's in the truck, Mike?" Sam asks.

Mike says with a smile on his face, "You wanted a circus tent? I got you a circus tent."

"Good job, Mike, where did you get it?" Sam asks.

"I got it from a circus," Mike says while looking at Sam strangely like, where else would you get a circus tent?

Sam asks, "Did you steal it or buy it?"

"Neither, I traded," Mike says and is still smiling like the Cheshire cat.

"Well, either way, good job. Let's put it up," Sam says and calls over the crew, "Let's get this tent up before it gets dark." Once he is sure that they are all OK with setting the tent up, Sam let DH take over. Sam says to himself, "What the hell do they need me for? I don't have a clue on how to set up a circus tent." Sam walks into the trees to check on Gina and Kim.

"Hey, you all, are ya about done?" Sam asks.

Kim says, "Guess how much you have here."

"Aaahh, eight hundred million dollars," Sam says. He has no idea.

"Close, but it is nine hundred ten million and some odd change." Kim says.

"Shit, the government is going to want this back," Sam says in a little sinister way. "I don't think we will give it back. We can do so much good with this money unlike the way it was gotten. Another thing is that there is probably more out there. We are going to get that too." Sam gives a little laugh. He felt like it is his time to get a little greedy. This money is really no one's and he doesn't feel guilty for taking it.

Gina warns Sam again. "You are really going to get into trouble this time, Sam."

"No, no," Kim jumps in. "They can't say a thing, they aren't even supposed to have this money. It really doesn't exist in the eyes of the law or anyone, besides those directly involved. Thus, we can keep it and any other money we get. We just may have to kill a few people though, but all is fair in love and war. This will be a war so we need more help."

"I guess you're right," Sam says reluctantly, "but where the hell we going to find more people?" Sam wasn't reluctant about tell Kim he is right but reluctant that he has to find more people.

"We'll find them. It will just take a little while," Kim assured Sam.

"Let's lock up and go get something to drink. We can't put the money away tonight anyway," Sam says in a melancholy tone.

"OK, we're ready," Kim and Gina say.

Chapter Eighteen

Darwin finally gets his computer system set up just exactly the way he wants it. He has basically worked night and day setting everything up. During the day, he would shop for materials, and during the night, he would assemble everything. With his new computer system, he would be ready for anything. It makes NASA's computer system look like a video game. Darwin doesn't come out of the bunker much; no one ever sees him except at night when they all stay down there. Darwin basically moved into the bunker full time. He really doesn't have much need for the real world except if it comes across the computer.

First thing Darwin does is look for the plans for a government bunker. After a day of looking through government archived documents in some library files, he finds them. He calls Sam, "Hey, I found some plans for a government bunker. It looks like complete blueprints that were made in the nineteen sixties."

Sam says, "Good job. Can you print them and send them or how are you going to get them to me?"

Darwin says with a snort, "Go get a computer, pad, or something and I will e-mail it to you."

Sam says, "I don't have time for that shit, maybe someone here has one."

Gunny and Darrell have become best friends. They spent most of their time talking about old times. Dad about growing up farming and Gunny talks about the war and his life in Japan. Gunny keeps saying he is the last black samurai and Darrell says he is last of the old farmers. Both men are proud of their past and what they had accomplished even though they never got rich doing it. Both knew they could be proud of hard work and a job well done.

Gunny's building is not done as of yet, but it doesn't stop him from making things. Bud and Kota set up an anvil and a temporary coal forge in a tent. The local farriers come over at night and work with Gunny on the finer intricacies of metalworking. Darrell sits around and talks horses with everyone. The hospital became the place to hang out and it seemed to bring in more clients.

Carol has the hospital running like a clock. The new veterinarians that she hired made everything run smoothly. They are very busy especially with the new rehabilitation wing added. Carol also started making plans for a twenty-four-hour full-service small-animal emergency and rehabilitation center. The local area needs a good emergency clinic. The hospital now has the money, so building the clinic is going to happen. Carol has already started advertising for small-animal doctors.

Sam always let Carol go with anything that she wanted to do with the business. He just puts in his two cents' worth and usually things go well. Some things didn't go well, such as their horse-breeding business. It wasn't the worst business idea, but they never made any money with it. Both Carol and Sam worked every day just to keep their heads above water. Until now, Sam has never been gone this long from his business. This is the first time that he has let other doctors do his work and take over. Sam was finally able to relax and have fun again.

The next morning Sam wakes up early. The caterers are not due to come for another hour or so. DH and Kim are already up and drinking coffee when Sam walks out the dining tent.

"Is the vault ready for us to put the money in?" Sam asks.

"I haven't been over there yet, but we can walk over and look," DH says. Sam, DH, and Kim walk over to the barn after grabbing some flashlights. The vault has been set on the concrete footers, but the concrete around the vault was not poured.

"What do you think?" Sam asks them. "Can we load it or do we wait?"

"I'd say we can load it and lock it." DH says as he shines the flashlight all around. "They can still pour around it and we can get everything loaded before anyone shows up."

"I think we should load it before the concrete trucks get here. Otherwise, we will have to wait all day. We still have to go set up at the other place," Kim says as he opens the steel lid to the vault. Kim shines the light into the vault and then jumps down inside of it. He looks around and then looks back up through the opening and says, "Damn, this is the size of my kitchen at home."

"Good, I think we are going to need several more of these before we are done," Sam says and looks down into the vault. "Let's go and get those two troop carriers and unload."

Kim climbs out of the vault with some help from DH and Sam. They all go over to the tent camp to make sure no one is hanging around. Then they make their way through the trees. Sam disarms the traps while DH and Kim open up the two trucks. The good thing about these trucks is that they are able to be ground loaded without ramps. DH unchains the carriers. Both Kim and DH start the troop carriers up and back on down. Sam guides them and then jumps up on one of them for a ride up to the barn. They back right up to the door of the vault, which made it easy to unload the four pallets of money. DH and Kim stack the money in the vault as Sam drops the blocks of money down the hole. It only takes about a half an hour and they are done. DH and Kim climb out of the vault and Sam ran over to get the lock that he had bought when he was in town. They lock it up and drive the troop carriers to the tent. The ten others are waiting for them when they drive up.

"Wow, where the hell did you get those?" Bobby, Kim's brother, asks.

"We found them. Now you and Tom get over to the barn right after you eat breakfast and take two handguns each. You two need to guard that concrete tank and don't let anyone open it up. I mean no one. If they do, I will shoot you myself," Kim instructs his brother.

"Can we take any gun?" Tom jumps in to the troop carrier.

"Yes, that's what I told you! Now get your breakfast and get over there right now. Remember—no one, including you guys or anyone, except Sam, me, or DH, gets in there. Do you get it?" Kim starts yelling at his brother.

"Yeah, I heard you the first time," Tom yells back. Then he sulks to eat breakfast.

Everyone eats and then Sam gathers everyone around for a meeting except for Tom and Bobby, who go over to the barn.

"Today we are going to go and set up for an ambush. We don't want to get anyone hurt, nor are we going to shoot anyone unless we need too. So we are going to setup and kind of rehearse some things. We may be met by ten people or a hundred people. We need to be sharp and precise and there can be no screw-ups. Last and foremost, do not shoot me or anyone else on this team. Lisa and Beth, I need you all to stay here and be prepared for any emergencies, such as gunshot wounds, and you need to guard these troop carriers. Dan, Mickey, and Whiskers, you guys will be in charge of driving the Hummers. We will leave two Hummers in the valley as bait and the other is a get-away car. You guys will also act as snipers can any of you shoot?" Sam says.

"We can all shoot but we never shot anyone," Mickey says with a little hesitation.

"Well, you don't have to shoot them unless they are shooting us. Just scare them," Sam assures them. "Mike, have you ever shot at anyone?"

"Hell yeah, I killed a few in Kuwait. I'm not afraid of shooting a couple more," Mike says with enthusiasm.

"Good, you are going to be mine and Kim's guardian angel. We will be down on the line somewhere near the Hummers," Sam says. "We will also be bait if need be, if that is all right with you, Kim?"

"Just like old times," Kim says with a smile.

"Great! Sarah, you will fly surveillance? We need a count on vehicle numbers, type, and whatever else you can get. Bozzel and Popper, I'd like you to stay here and keep things going also be the reserve in case we need backup. I'll have Sarah fly back and get you if we need you. Skids, you and DH are also going to be rovers. You guys are going to moving around where needed. So with that said, we will go set up. Bozzel and Mike will help everyone with a good weapon selection," Sam says, and then he goes over to the barn. Kim follows him out of the tent. They need to go check up on the two brothers because they can get a little off track sometimes.

As they walk into the barn, Sam yells, "What the hell are you guys doing?" He sees the two brothers with a crowbar and a sledge-hammer trying to break into the vault. They had hammered and cracked the concrete around the lid to the vault. The lock is smashed but it did not break. Sam is furious as well as Kim. Kim rushes in and grabs the sledge and bar. The two brothers are startled and a bit scared at the same time. Kim slaps both of them and they go flying.

"I trusted both of you and you disgraced me and Sam by doing this." Kim is so mad, he grabs the sledgehammer and is going to hit one of his brothers. Sam jumps in and grabs Kim before he does something stupid.

"Kim! Kim! Settle the fuck down," Sam yells.

Kim drops the hammer and just stands there. He looks at his brothers and screams, "Damn it, you guys. You can never listen. Now what the fuck are we going to do with you? I can't kill ya and I can't trust you to stay here or leave here. Shit. Sam, what do you want to do?"

"I think we should shoot them in the stomach. That way, we never actually killed them but they will just die from the infection and blood loss. May take a day or two, but oh well," Sam says. Then he goes over and grabs one of the brother's handguns off the vault. Kim looks at Sam a little suspiciously. Sam gives him a little eye flutter but not quite a wink. Kim knows that Sam is just trying to scare the two brothers and he's going to play along with it. Sam walks over to Bobby and tells him, "Take your shirt off so that you don't get blood all over it. After I shoot you in the belly, you can cover up with the shirt so it won't look so bad."

Bobby takes off his shirt and then Tom takes off his shirt. "I'm ready now, so do your thing." Bobby says. "Is it going to hurt a lot? Because if it is, I may just puke."

"Oh, it's going to hurt a lot. Now, turn around and bend over," Kim says to the both of them. Sam takes the clip out and ejects the round, which sounds just like loading a round. Bobby whimpers a little and Tom wets his pants. Kim looks around and finds a board. He picks it up and runs over behind the two brothers. He swats them both on the butt as hard as he could swing. They both drop to the ground and scream.

"Now, next time you two fuck up, I'm going to let Sam 'gut shoot' the both of you. Got it? Kim yells.

Both of the brothers get up, rubbing their butts and cussing under their breath. They both say loudly, "YEAH." Then they put on their shirts.

"Now get back to work and don't open the fucking vault," Sam says as they leave.

Snoop wakes up from a drunken stupor with no idea on how much time has passed since Sam had been there. He thought it was time to call but wasn't really sure where he is supposed to tell them to go. He thought about calling Sam but knows Sam will probably be mad. "Oh, well, he'll just have to be mad," Snoop says to himself. He grabs his phone and calls Sam.

"Sam, this is Snoop," Snoop says.

"Hello," Sam says.

Snoop says with hesitation, "Aaahhh, I forgot where I'm supposed to send those guys to. Just remind me so I can call them now and tell them."

"Well, you are not supposed call them until tomorrow but I suppose you can call them now," Sam says in a calm voice. "The place is at the old farm behind the racetrack. Do you know where that is?"

"Yeah, I know where it is. It's by Scott's Slew," Snoop says with confidence. "Should I call them now or later?"

"Just call them now before you get high and forget again," Sam says with sarcasm.

"Got it," Snoop says and hangs up the phone. He calls out to the bunker. Some guy answers the phone but Snoop doesn't know who it was.

"Yeah?" The guy says in a grumpy voice like it is a big inconvenience to answer a phone. He is a man that is extremely overweight and underbathed. He stank of sweat, garlic, and decaying food that is caught in his scruffy beard. Everyone on called him Skunk.

Snoop says, "Hey, I need to talk to the guy in charge."

"Aaahhh, nobody here that fits that d'scriptin," Skunk says.

"Let me talk to that Nate," Snoop demands.

"Nate who?" Skunk is not really playing dumb, because he is extremely stupid. He is also very lazy and doesn't want to go get Nate.

"Well, tell any fuck in charge, I know where your fucking money is, you stupid asshole. Does that ring a FUCKING BELL?" Snoop yells.

"Aaahh, hold on, I'll get someone on the phone," Skunk says with a tone of urgency. He runs back and gets Nate out of the bunkhouse. He breathes heavy and rapidly because he is out of breath but manages to say to Nate, "There's some guy on the phone that says that he knows where the money is."

"Who the fuck is it?" Nate asks in a grumpy tone. Nate was fast asleep but is more appalled at the stench Skunk exuded. Just the sight of Skunk appalled Nate.

"I dun know. I didn't ask," Skunk says.

Nate gets up out of his bed. He put his pants and shirt on, then walks over to the office. Skunk walks in front of him like he is leading the way to the phone. Nate wrinkles his nose and says to Skunk, "You will shower and shave and be done by the time I get off this phone. If you can't do that, we will help you out a little."

Skunk says with some hesitation, "Ahh, sure thing, right away." He is a little embarrassed and offended that Nate would say something to him.

Nate gets on the phone. "Yeah what up?" Skunk stands there to listen to the conversation.

Snoop says in a stern, perturbed voice, "This is Snoop. I got some information for you but I want to get paid."

"What is it?" Nate inquires.

Snoop tells Nate, "I know where your fucking money is, and for a hundred Gs, I'll tell you."

Nate says in an irritated manner, "Why you fucking piss ant? I should just wring your fuckin' neck till you tell me?" He knows that he would have done the same thing, but he is upset because it is Snoop and not him.

Snoop tells him point blank, "A hundred grand and you can meet me at the fucking truck stop in Mitchell. I'll be there in one hour and I'll have a map for you."

"OK, but what makes you think I need you to find that guy who took my money?" Nate asks. "Hell, I got an army after him. I already know where he is, we are probably going to go get the money back today." Nate tries to bluff Snoop.

"I know if you knew where he was, you would already be there but you're not. You stupid lazy bastards will never find him but I did. I know where your trucks are and everything. Bring the fucking money or I disappear." Snoop gives his ultimatum and calls Nate's bluff. He hangs up the phone. Snoop is dumb but he has been around the block a few times. He knows Sam took all the YUPPI money, but the YUPPIs are probably still cooking and selling, so there is still money. Snoop figures that the truck stop is the best place to be when they meet. Snoop needs people around when the trade is made. He knows he can still be killed with a lot of people around, but at least he has some form a safety. He grabs a piece of paper and starts drawing a map from the interstate to the farm. He stuffs it into his pocket and jumps into his car. He drives to the truck stop.

Nate is not happy when he gets off the phone and he could still smell Skunk behind him. Nate says out loud, "I thought I told you to get cleaned up?"

Skunk had sort of stood the whole time in kind of a daze. He shakes his head when Nate yells. "Yep, yeah, I guess you did."

Nate thinks, "I fucking give a command and these assholes just don't listen. I can't stand it." Nate is still furious over Snoop and how all this place is so unorganized. Nate can still smell Skunk in the room. He draws his .45 Colt from his shoulder holster as he spins in his chair. Skunk is still standing there, fiddling with his scruffy beard, when Nate turns his chair. Nate raises the .45 and shoots Skunk in the face and in the chest. Skunk's body just stands there with the first shot and the slug enters just above the bottom of the nose and exits out the back of his head. The slug rips most of the back of his head apart sending shards of bone, bloods, and brain on the wall behind him. The second slug to the chest sends Skunk's body flying backward to the wall, and then it hits the ground.

Two guys come running into the office and see Nate in the chair and Skunk on the ground. The two never ever asked what happened. They just look at Nate. Nate motions them with the .45 Colt to remove the body. They each grab a leg and tuck the foot under their arms. They drag Skunk outside and with the help of several other men; they throw the body into the incinerator. One of the men starts the incinerator up and burn the body along with the garbage. One of the men gets a mop and bucket. He goes and cleans up the office. Not one of the men says anything.

CHAPTER NINETEEN

SAM CALLS EVERYONE TOGETHER AFTER the phone call. "We have to get moving now. Things are going to move today and not tomorrow. If you don't remember what your job is, then speak up now." Sam looks around but no one looks confused. "OK, then let's grab some water and supplies for the day and lets go. We need to be set up in a couple of hours."

Everyone climbs into their vehicles and take off. Sam and Kim climb into the helicopter. Sarah flies over to the farm to make sure the farmer has removed his livestock. Then Sam directs her to fly over to the meth lab bunker so that she knows the area to keep surveillance on for any movement out of there. When they fly over the bunker, Kim sees a seven-vehicle convoy leaving the bunker. It is moving north up the road that goes to Mitchell.

Kim says to Sam and Sarah, "It's not really heading toward the farm, maybe to Mitchell's or something."

Sam has Sarah fly a circle around the bunker. It looks vacant. Sam says to himself, "They wouldn't be dumb enough to leave this place empty again, would they? I bet they are still selling and they probably have more stuff to take." Sam has Sarah land behind the trees where they had driven into the last time. Kim and Sam get out.

Sam says to Kim, "Let's just go look and see what they have been up to since we were last here." Kim agrees.

They follow the same path that they had made the last time. They search the sleeping quarters and no one was around. They search the vehicle bunker and find several more weapons. They just leave them for now and go to the bunker with the lab. Looking into the lab, they notice that the lab is very much still producing meth. Then they move over into the cooler. Sam looks at Kim and says, "They wouldn't be stupid enough to store money down here again, would they?" It wasn't a question but more a statement. They open the secret door and look down the walkway. No one is watching the place. They both go down to the vault area. They had broken the door before and no one fixed it. Sam opens the door and on a pallet on the floor is another pile of money. Kim runs up to the lab where he had seen a pile of knapsacks, which were probably used for carrying out the meth. He grabs an armful and brings them back down to the money room.

Kim throws the knapsacks on the floor and says to Sam, "Here, we can carry this money out in these."

Sam says, "Good idea. I wondered where you'd gone off to."

They fill four of the knapsacks with about forty pounds of money. They each sling up two knapsacks each and then head up to the main area of the building. Sam sees a door start moving and stops Kim, who has already knelt down. Someone is coming out of the restroom in the cafeteria part of the building. Sam instantly drops his knapsacks and grabs his chained weapon. He readies his weapon, and when the guy steps out around the door, Sam whips the bladed end of the weapon. The blade flies like a fly on a fly-fishing line. The knife end flies around both legs of the guy. The chain wraps around the legs. The blade cuts through the left calf muscle and all the tendons and ligaments in that area. The blade ends sunk deep into the tibia (shinbone) of the right leg. Sam pulls tension on the chain and chain buries deeper into the severed calf muscle. Blood sprays from the calf muscle and form a deluge on the floor around the guy's feet. Cutting the muscles, tendons, and ligaments makes it impossible for the man to use that leg. The guy screams in pain, then instantly drops to the floor. He grabs at the blade stuck in his tibia but cannot remove it. Sam keeps tension on the weapon as Kim runs up to the man to hold him down. Kim takes the guy's pistol away and tosses it to Sam. The man did not move. Sam walks over removes the chained weapon by wiggling the blade out of the bone. The removal of the blade is so painful the man screams until he passes out. The wound continues to bleed profusely. Sam gets up and looks around the bunker. He finds a well-stocked first aid kit. He flushes the wounds with Betadine solution and pours in Celox to stop the bleeding. He wraps the legs with a pressure bandages. Sam goes over to the lab and gets the guy some meth and leaves it next to him. The bleeding had stopped but the man will need surgery to get the legs repaired. About the time Sam gets done bandaging the legs, the man regains consciousness. He looks around and starts to struggle. Kim holds him down to the floor.

Sam kneels down and says to the man, "Now if you get up, you will probably break this leg or bleed to death. If you move before we leave, I will remove your leg with the blade. I suggest you just lie here and then call for an ambulance as soon as we leave. You need to go to the hospital. Do you understand?"

"Yes! You fucking asshole. Just leave me alone!" the guy says and then takes out his meth pipe and lighter and then takes a big hit of meth.

"OK, let's go," Sam says to Kim. Sam gets up and grabs the knapsacks full of money. They both take off to the other bunker to grab as many weapons as they can carry. Then they head out to the trees and get on to the helicopter that is all ready to go. As soon as they get in, Sarah takes off.

Sarah flies up along the road until they spot the convoy. Then she turns and flies to the farm to drop Kim and Sam off. Sam and Kim get out of the helicopter. They just leave all the new bounty in the helicopter. Then Sarah takes off to track the convoy. The others are already there waiting for instructions. Sam and Kim give everyone their last instructions and they all make sure that the radios and weapons work. Each one also takes three test fires of their weapons to sight them in. Everything was all set except there is no plan. Sam is hoping that once they show up and they find nothing may be they will just go. The other option is to grab the leader and coerce him to just leaving them well enough alone. Sam never really had any other idea except the ambush. He just knows everything will fall into place once things start. Now all there is to do is to wait.

Nate and five others walk into the truck stop restaurant. They look around until they see Snoop sitting at the counter with one empty seat next to him. Nate walks up with a brown paper bag and drops it on the counter in front of Snoop then sits down next to him. He asks Snoop, "Ya got something for me?"

Snoop hands him the map and looks into the bag. He sees what looks like a hundred grand in cash.

Nate stands up and slaps Snoop on the back of the head, then leaves with the five others. Snoop just laughs and he says to himself, "That was easy. I thought it would be more trouble than that."

Snoop grabs his bag and pulls a hundred-dollar bill out. He lays it on the counter then gets up. As he walks across the floor toward the door, the bag explodes. Snoop is blown to pieces. Bits and pieces of his body are blown throughout the restaurant. The windows to the restaurant explode outward. Pieces of booths and other debris fly everywhere. Several people are being ripped apart from Snoop's body parts acting as shrapnel along with the other debris rifling through the air. Thirty-one people die.

The YUPPI convoy is long gone down the road, heading toward the location on the map. Nate is finally happy that he got rid of Snoop. Now, he is going to go get all the money and weapons back. He got rid of one problem with a bag of Semtex wrapped in about ten thousand dollars. As soon as he gets rid of his other problem, then he can go back and live like a king.

Sarah radios to Sam, "Sam, the convoy is moving. They just fucking blew up the truck stop. The fuckers actually blew up the truck stop. I can't believe they blew up the truck stop."

"Say what? Shit. You watch yourself. If they see you, they may fire at you. We'll get them when they get here. You just watch for them. I need at least fifteen minutes notice," Sam says with anxiousness. "Did you all hear what Sarah said?"

All of them radio back, "Copy."

Sam radios back, "Don't hesitate to shoot if you have too. They are bad people. They will kill you if they see you. Everyone got it?"

"Got it," everyone radios back. Then they are all silent. Mickey has friends that work at the truck stop and the news disturbed him a lot.

Captain Nate gets on the phone to the Iowa YUPPI captain. "I got the location of those bastards that took the money and we are now heading there."

The YUPPI captain asks, "Will you need assistance?"

"I don't need any fucking help. I'm just telling you because the Boss told me I had too. But if you want to come and get the money and keep it there until pick up, I don't have to rely on these dumb asses that I work with to watch it," Nate says almost with excitement.

The YUPPI captain says, "Just send the location and we will be there."

Nate turns to the guy in the back of the Stryker and asks, "Can you fucking send this map somehow?"

The communication man says, "Right away, just get the number." Nate gets the number of the YUPPI captains fax and gives it to the guy. The guy grabs the map and runs it through the portable fax machine, then sends it. The communication man says, "It should be coming through any second now."

Nate says to the YUPPI captain, "It should be coming through right now."

"The map is here," the YUPPI captain says. "We can be there in an hour."

Nate hangs up.

Sarah radios Sam, "They'll be there in fifteen minutes or less. I don't know how many people there are, but get ready."

"Copy," Sam says with excitement. "Everyone, awake. Get your ducks in a row."

Everyone radios back, "We're ready."

When the convoy drives into the yard, the Stryker goes through the barn and knocks it over. Two of the Hummers go the fence and across the lawn. The convoy is tearing up as much stuff as they can.

They all drive up and surround the two Hummers that Sam had parked in the bottom of the field. This area was surrounded by a hill on three sides. The hill is sparsely covered with trees and large exposed granite rock. It is an ideal place to set up an ambush. About forty guys get out of two Strykers and five Hummers. They all have automatic weapons of various makes. Nate walks out of the Stryker and stands there like he is General Patton. Then he walks over and up to the Hummers. He looks inside. He turns around and yells, "God damn it, there is nothing here. You five"—he points to one group that got out of one of the Hummers—"go check the house, and after you are done, burn it. If anyone is home, bring them to me."

Sam gets on the radio. "DH, watch that group over there. They are heading toward the house."

DH radios back, "Copy." He grabs his rifle. DH and Mike move through the trees to keep an eye on the group. They set up in the back where the farm family had been dumping garbage. It is perfect camouflage.

Nate and the gang start milling around. Nate is getting anxious.

Sam gets on the radio. "Mickey?"

Mickey radios back, "Copy."

Sam radios back, "I know you had friends working at the truck stop, so you get to take the first shot if you want it. See that asshole in the blue uniform with the Magnum PI sunglasses? Shoot that son of a bitch in the belly."

Mickey radios back, "My pleasure." He looks through his scope and puts Nate in the crosshairs, then squeezes the trigger.

Nate falls back and hits the ground like he just got hit with a sledgehammer. He feels a severe pain rush through his body followed by blood running down his butt and stomach. He just sits there and looks around like "What the hell was that?" Then he realizes he just got shot. The others open fire at the two Hummers. They all shot at the vehicles like they are the ones that fired the shot. Bullets ricocheted off the armored Hummers. Since men are all standing in a circle surrounding the Hummers, bullets fly everywhere. Men start dropping like hornets out of a hive being sprayed with foam insecticide. The more that are shot the more they fire. They soon start firing in to the trees and in the ground and up in the air. Sam and his group just hunker down behind rocks until the shooting stops.

When the shooting stops, only four men still stand. The others are either dead or severely wounded. There is blood, flesh, detached limbs, and shards of bone everywhere. The ground looks like a carpeted butch shop floor. Five men are missing pieces of skulls and looking around like they are trying to find the pieces. Some of the living men lie screaming with a gurgling blood-filled scream. The four men that are not injured stand there looking over the carnage in disbelief. After several minutes of silence between the four, they start arguing about who is at fault and who is going to get into trouble. Not one of them makes a motion to go help out their fallen comrades.

The five inside the farmhouse have set the house on fire while still inside. The shooting starts and they run for cover in the house. They all hide in the house as the house burns around them. The farmhouse, being old, has walls that are filled with corn husk instead of fiberglass insulation. When the flames burned through the walls, it was only a matter of minutes and the building comes crashing down to the ground. The five men are trapped in a flaming coffin. DH and Mickey watch and they never see any of them come out.

DH radios Sam, "What the hell is that?"

"We only fired one shot," Sam says in amazement. He has never seen so many people be so stupid with guns all at one time. "They shot each other. There are only four of them left standing and they are still arguing about whose fault it is. Do you still see those five men?"

DH radios back, "Sam, they went in there and started the house on fire and I never seen any of them come out. They could have jumped out the window but I think they burned in the fire. That house burned fast and hot. It was only minutes from when we saw smoke in the house till flames shot up and then it crashed to the ground." DH has a little nervous voice.

Sam radios back, "Well, just stay put till we see what these other four are going to do."

Sam then did a radio check on everyone to see if anyone is hurt. Everyone is OK.

The four guys start looking around and checking pockets on the dead and the wounded men. None of them offer assistance to the wounded. They just robbed each of the men and leaving weapons and bodies lay as they are.

"Sam, there are two tandem axial trucks headed your way," Sarah radios. "I don't know if there are any men aboard, but they are the blue and white trucks, so they must be back up or something."

"Thanks, Sarah," Sam radios back. "Did everyone copy that? Let's just keep our heads down till we see who is coming to visit."

"Copy," everyone radios back.

The two trucks pull up and four armed men jump out of both trucks. The drivers stay in the trucks, but both passengers open their doors and climb down. One of the passengers is a tall lean man dressed in navy camouflage fatigues and a beret tilted to one side of his head. Sam looked through the scope on his rifle to get a better look at the man. On the shirt above the left chest pocket is the words "Iowa YUPPI" and over the right pocket is "Brad Rutter." The other men all wore the same kind of fatigues, but they had bulletproof vests and written on those is Iowa on the front and YUPPI on the back. Sam radios, "I see that the Iowans are here. Everyone stay out of site. If I fire, you all fire!"

Everyone quietly radios back, "Copy."

The Iowa YUPPI captain's name is Brad Rutter. He is well known in the YUPPI group for running the strictest most ruthless outfit. His outfit was responsible for most of the voter intimidation that had gone on around the country. He had been in command of just about all the smaller YUPPI groups and was also in charge of ballet box security. Much of the paper and military ballets across the country just happen to get lost both during the primaries and the national elections. Many of the absentee ballots from Republican districts were never counted, nor were they ever seen. The only mess up they had was when one of the drivers got into an accident and the trunk broke open. Thousands of ballots were found by the highway patrol but it was quickly covered up by a couple of congressmen.

The eight armed men quickly ran around and search the premise. Once they are satisfied that the area is secure, they brought up the four uninjured men to Captain Rutter. The four men stand in a line in front of Captain Rutter. All four have their hands full with wallets and watches and other things that they had taken from their dead or dying comrades.

Captain Rutter asks, "What the hell went on here?"

One of the four men nervously says, "Aaahh, someone shot at us and there was a big firefight. We all laid down return fire, and when all was said and done, we were the only ones left. We were just going around and trying to help the wounded."

Captain Rutter looks around and then looks at the four men like that is the biggest bullshit story he has ever heard. He asks, "Do any of you other three have a different story, maybe one with some truth in it?"

A second of the four men gives his story. He says, "I heard a shot and then Captain Nate yelled 'Fire!' I then spotted a group of men that were hiding inside the Hummer. My little group fired on the Hummer, but with the armor, some of the bullets did ricochet and hit some of my men. The other groups spotted the men that were under the Hummer and they shot them. There was basically a whole platoon out here. After the shooting stopped, they grabbed their men and they left in a couple of heavy trucks. We just stayed down until they were gone and then we found that Captain Nate was still alive but was wounded. We didn't want to move anyone before help got here. We were still looking over the men when you all came in. We were getting the valuables from the men so those doctors won't steal it. So that is what really happened."

Captain Rutter rubs his chain and then stares at the four of them. He says with a calm authoritative voice, "We didn't see any trucks leaving this area when we came in, and it really doesn't look like anyone else was shooting back. If they had been in heavy trucks with a whole platoon, we should see some tracks leaving the area, which I see none. I reckon that you stupid assholes probably shot each other. So now I have to clean up this mess. Oh, where the hell is the money?"

The four of them all tell the captain, "There is no money. Nate was very pissed when we didn't find any money. He had paid a lot for the map." They start laughing and looking at each other like it was an inside joke.

"What is so fucking funny? I didn't hear anything funny. One of you want to tell me what is funny?" Captain Rutter asks in a very stern voice.

One of the four says while still kind of laughing, "Nate gave that shit bag that asked for a hundred grand for the map, a bag of C4, and a free stop watch. It blew the shit out of him and that fucking truck stop. Man, did it ever blow the shit out of things. Hell, they are probably still picking up the pieces."

Captain Rutter had heard that someone had blown up a truck stop. It is not out of the realm for the YUPPI group to blow things up but never something like this that would draw to much attention to the group. One of the rules is to keep things as low key as much as possible. Captain Rutter turns and looks over at the eight armed men and tells them, "Let's shut EVERYTHING up, Sergeant, you make sure these four get properly unbriefed, and I don't mean debriefed."

The sergeant nods and then takes out his .45 Colt and shoots all four men in the head before they can even react. All four men drop dead in a pile. The captain and the sergeant just turn and walk away. Then they climb into their trucks. The captain watches as the eight armed men walk around and check each man on the ground and then shoot each one of them in the head. None of Nate's men, including Nate, is left alive. The eight armed men then climb in their trucks and the drivers drive off.

Sam is aghast to see what just took place. All of Sam's group cannot believe that someone would do such a thing. Sam radios Sarah, "Hey, watch those two trucks and see where they end up at. If you are running low on fuel, go fill up now, and then get right back on them. We are going to move all these vehicles back to the farm, and then I am going to come back or someone needs to come back and call the cops in on this. We need to pretend that nothing ever happened."

Sam and group come out from the trees. They gather all the weapons and put them into the Stryker. They move Nate out of the Stryker but leave the other dead men where they lay. They take all the vehicles and drive back to the farm.

Once at the farm, Sam gathers all the people together and talks about what just happened. No one is having lasting problems with the whole thing. They all are OK. They know this kind of thing happens and are glad it didn't happen to them. What they didn't think can happen is an army of men could be so dumb and shoot each other.

They all sat down and ate. After eating, Kim goes home to see his family. Skids, Mickey, and Dan go to look at the new vehicles that they have just acquired. DH, Lisa, and Beth inventory the new weapons. Sam takes his truck to go back over to the ambush area.

When Sam gets to the ambush area, he can hardly believe what he is seeing. No bodies, no blood, no tire tracks. The ground has been worked up with a disk. Someone came and cleaned up everything. He can hardly believe that the ambush even happened. Sam gets back into his vehicle and drives back to the farm. Sam thinks as he is driving, "How the hell could anyone get this place cleaned up that fast? Did the cops clean up the mess? And if they did, then the cops are in on this whole thing. If it was the guy in the truck, then they are really organized. Shit, then we need more help or more organized help. They needed to get more organized. No more of this willy-nilly stuff, someone could get killed. What they need is a retired colonel or general. Someone that has had military strategy." He rolls it around his head for a while and then he says to himself. "Fuck it, we've been doing well up until now. Who needs someone telling me what to do? Besides, we have Gunny." Sam pulls into the farm and calls everyone over to the tent. He tells everyone about what he saw at the other farm.

As Sam is finishing up with everyone, Sarah flies on to the farm with the helicopter. Skids and DH ran over to the helicopter. DH looks the helicopter over and then motions for Mike to come over and help him with carrying all the stuff left in there by Kim and Sam. Skids immediately starts looking over the helicopter to check for stress damage and anything else he can find. Sarah walks over to the dining tent and grabs a beer and a sandwich. Sam goes over to her.

Sam asks Sarah, "Did you see the final destination of those trucks?"

"Yes, they're in Iowa. I'll fly you over there as soon as we get the helicopter refueled," Sarah says as she continues to eat.

"I don't think we need to go right away. We need to organize before we go after this group. They are more organized then any of the other groups," Sam says calmly. "What we really could use is the number of men in the group. Is there any place out there that we can put surveillance in?"

"The place is surrounded by cornfields. There are two farms about two miles away. The place is four large Quonset hut buildings and about fifteen to twenty double-wide trailer houses. Let me just fly you over there and we can look around," Sarah says with her mouth full of food.

"OK," Sam walks out of the tent and yells over to Skids. "Hey, get that helicopter fueled quickly. We need to leave again."

"We are getting on it right now," Skids says.

In about an hour, the helicopter is ready. Sarah climbs into the pilot seat. Sam and Mike climb into the back of the helicopter. Sam wants Mike to tag along when they flew over the new target site. Sarah flies over to where the Captain Rutter's convoy drove too. Sam and Mike spot a great place to set up recon for a while until they get a good troop count. They all fly back to the farm. Then Sam has Mike pick a spotter. Sam goes to find DH. DH is busy giving the two brothers hell for smoking in the barn.

"Hey, DH, I need to talk to you when you are done kicking the boys around," Sam says with a little sarcasm.

"I'm done. Those two just ain't got a lick of sense," DH says in an angry tone.

Sam tells DH, "I'm going to head home for a little while. I need to go back and do some work. I need make sure I still have a hospital.

I'm going to drive down to the train station in Omaha and catch the train home. I need someone to take me down there and drop me off. We also need to get you a truck if you are going to stay out here for a while."

"I'm going to stay here till this job is done. My wife is going to come for a visit soon as we get things organized," DH says. "So I guess we need to go get a truck tomorrow."

"Good, we will do that first thing in the morning," Sam says. "We'll figure out the next step when I get back. We need more good men to go after the next bunker area. Maybe Darwin can get some intel off the computer we confiscated."

"I'll have Kim look around for a few more good men. Maybe some of these farmers can be hired," DH says.

"That would be fine but we need some military men, some with experience in fighting. I think that this next group is a little more experienced and a hell of lot meaner. What about some of your old army buddies?" Sam asks.

DH rubs his chin and kicks some dirt as he is thinking. He says to Sam, "Don't know if any of them would be any help. I can find a couple of them, but I need help finding the rest."

"Give Darwin a list of names and he can find anyone. He can find them but you will have to talk to them," Sam says. "We need at least another twenty or thirty good man."

"I'll get a list tonight and you can take it along with you tomorrow," DH says. Then they both walk over to the tent.

Sam calls Carol and tells her, "I'm coming home for a while. I need someone to pick me up at the Staunton train station in a couple of days. I'll have to call from the train when I know what time I'm going to be there."

Carol tells Sam, "You have a lot of work to do as soon as you get back. Some of these clients only want to see you and have been waiting for several weeks. When you know when you are going to be back, call me and we will get appointments set up.

Sam says, "OK, I will do that, but I don't know why they are waiting. There are plenty of doctors there to look at their horses."

Carol says, "I know, but you know how they are. Well, I got to go so, love you."

Sam says, "Love you too."

Then they both hang up. Sam never understood why anyone would wait that long to get their lame horses fixed. Anyway, to Sam it is little flattering.

CHAPTER TWENTY

SAM ARRIVES IN VIRGINIA TWO days later. It is a cold October morning when he gets off the train. He goes right to work the minute that he gets back to the hospital. He works for a week on horses from the time the sun comes up until late at night. Sam doesn't have time to even work with Darwin for the first week. Sam has a slower second week at work. He is getting tired of working already. After twenty years of working as a veterinarian, this is the first time Sam ever said that he is tired of working. He figures that it is just hard coming back to work after having a long vacation or it doing something different. Sam knows he can get back into the swing of things, but it is going to take a little while. He figures that many shorter vacations will be better than one long vacation. Then again, he really doesn't need to work anymore, but it is something that he enjoyed.

After Sam catches up on his work, he decides it is time he works on something fun, such as his bunker busting of the governments meth labs. First thing, he has Bud and Harland bring in multiple semi loads of dehydrated food and protein drinks to stock the bunker, enough food and water for five hundred people for five years. He also calls DH and tells him to do the same after his bunker is finished. Sam has been thinking that the most valuable items in the world if everything goes wrong are family, food, and water. They already have money and weapons, but if things go bad in the country, money will be worthless. Food, water, weapons, and family will prevail as the new power. Sam's group has the money now to buy all the things they need, except loyalty, which will have to be gained and worked for. His next thing is to get caught up on the information that Darwin dug out of the computer that they had taken from the YUPPIs.

Sam goes down into the bunker and walks around for a while. A lot has changed since he had left. There are a lot of improvements and rooms added to the bunker. He guesses that when Carol had to stay down here overnight, she didn't appreciate the accommodations.

Sam says to himself, "Well, it looks very livable." Sam finally finds Darwin tucked away in his computer room. There is so much electronics in his room, it is hard to tell if Darwin is in there.

Sam works his way through the room. He has to crawl in some areas just to get under the computer cables and whatever the other stuff is that had blinking lights and fans. Sam finds Darwin sitting in a large swivel recliner chair. Darwin smelled bad, like he hadn't taken a shower for months. His clothes looked like he just mugged a homeless man and stole the clothes. Sam just wrinkles his nose and ignores the vagabond look.

"Darwin, how the heck have you been?" Sam asks.

"Hey, Sam, when did you get back? Darwin asks without looking away from the computer screens.

"A couple of weeks ago," Sam says. "Ahhh, Darwin, when is the last time you were out of this room?" The smell is starting to get to Sam. Sam had with stood many bad smells in his life growing up on the farm, but he could not stand a stinky person.

"I think I went back to my room yesterday but I can't remember. You know how it is, once you get going on something, you just lose track of time," Darwin says as he types on the keyboard, "So did you have fun back home?"

"Well, yes, I did," Sam says. "Darwin when did you leave the bunker last?" Sam looks at Darwin and he thinks, "Hogs in the pig pens that look cleaner than what Darwin looks like now."

"Once I got this place set up, I don't think, aahh, not too long ago, but I could be mistaken," Darwin says but still hasn't looked up from the computer.

"Well, Darwin, we need to go out and get some good food. But you need to go get cleaned up first. So go get cleaned up and I'll watch whatever you want me to watch on this computer," Sam says. "Ahh, what are you watching anyway?"

"I'm watching a meeting at the US embassy in China between Harriet, the ambassador and Chow Yon, China's representative. She has been trying to get China to agree to buy more American bonds in exchange for not putting any tariffs on their products. Also she agreed to make it more economically feasible for companies to move over to China than to produce goods here. They are going to increase cost of doing business here for companies by running that fucking health care bill through raising taxes and putting more regulations. Chow Yon argued that American people would never allow it to happen. She said that they could do it through the unions breaking the companies because Barrack controls the unions. She also said they are going to use the EPA. She told him not to worry about the people because most of them will be on unemployment, and with the help of the media, people will just hate corporations. So that has been going on for quite a while. I just watch and take notes on the other computer so I can bring the information together with the other information. I'll analyze it later," Darwin explains to Sam. He tells Sam that he has been analyzing all the information he has been getting by hacking into all the embassies whenever there is a meeting. He explains that the new government is trying to break the free market attitude in the US so that they can centralize control. He tells Sam that Barrack wants to make it so he can stay president forever.

"Shit, Darwin," Sam says with a little despair. "We need a new government. One that is made up of people that gives a shit about the people and America."

"Sam," Darwin says, "there is not but a handful of politicians that fit that description. Almost all of them are crooked and on the take."

Sam asks, "How the hell do you know that? I suspect that but I don't know that for sure."

Darwin says, "I listen to these politicians all the time. I just hacked in to some of the CIA and other lettered agencies that I never even heard of, spyware programs. They listen to almost everything that these politicians say. Everyplace is bugged even their bathrooms.

If I can't find it from one those agencies, I just go to the Chinese or the Russians. They got everything hacked and have been listening everyone for years."

Sam shakes his head and says, "I think we need another revolution to take our country back."

Darwin crosses his eyes and says, "I don't think we need to go that far but we do need to watch and listen."

Sam gives Darwin a piece of paper that has the list of names of people that may be useful to their little group. DH had worked with all the men on the list. Darwin takes the paper and asks, "What's this?"

Sam says, "It's a list of names of men that I need you to see if you can find them."

Darwin sits down in his chair in front of the computer and tells Sam, "I'll get on this right away."

"No! No, go get cleaned up. I'm hungry," Sam says but he wasn't really hungry. He just can't stand the smell coming from Darwin anymore. "OK, go get cleaned up and we can talk everything over while we eat. Go, go now." Sam shushes him away.

Darwin wrestles through the room and finds his way to his room. Sam calls Carol to see if she wants to come along and eat with them. She decides to stay in and go to bed early. Bud and Dakota are busy with their families, so Sam calls his Dad and Gunny to see if they want to go, but they have plans that night at the shop. Sam calls Harland. He is all in to go eat and drink. He changes his clothes and is ready in minutes. It is just Sam, Harland, and Darwin to go eat and drink.

Sam calls Bill. "Hey, Bill, why don't you grab Joy and the new van? Come and pick up me, Darwin, and Harland. We'll all go out and get something to eat."

"Well, Sam, I had a long day and I don't think we want to go out anywhere except to bed," Bill says in a very harsh and slurred voice.

"OK, then. You don't have to get mad. I'm just inviting you to supper," Sam says in a "What the hell is your problem?" voice.

"Sam, as of right now, I don't want to go eat with you or anyone else from that fucking place. Matter of fact, I'm not sure if I even will be showing up tomorrow," Bill says in a drunken, angry voice.

"Well, Bill, can you tell me why you are not coming to work tomorrow?" Sam asks like he is talking to a four-year-old.

"I've been thinking, and I know you went out west and got a lot more money and stuff out there. You've been cheating me out of what I deserve. So I ain't fucking working there anymore, and as a matter of fact, you can just fuck off," Bill tells Sam in his drunken tough-man voice.

"Now then, what do you think you deserve?" Sam asks in a calm voice.

"I want half," Bill says harshly.

"Half of what?" Sam asks. He had no idea of what half of anything that Bill deserves.

"Half of the money and half of the guns. I know you got to have at least a hundred grand and I want half," Bill yells and then burps loudly.

"OK, Bill, you come and take what you think you need too tomorrow. I'll get all of us together and we will see if it is fair to everyone," Sam says.

"I'll be over tonight and there will be no need to call in yur fuckin' brothers. I'll take what I want and you can sort out whatever," Bill demands.

"I'll be waiting to see you here," Sam says and hangs up. Then turns to Darwin and says, "Bill is drunk and is coming over here to get his SHARE."

"He's been talking to that cousin of his," Darwin explains. "His cousin is part of the YUPPI group and he's been telling Bill that he needs to bring him a bunch of money. He wants Bill to buy in to the little gang. He's been tell Bill to join the winning team because you and your brothers are about to come to an end."

"Now how the hell do you know that? You never come out of the bunker," Sam inquires.

"I listen to all the phone calls of everyone except that which your family makes. I hacked into the telephone system so I can listen to any cell phone or landline phone anywhere or anytime. All I need to do is to get a phone number or a geographic fix on a phone and I can listen. If you want, I can find where the person is that is using the phone," Darwin explains. "That Bill is no good and he is selling you out. Do you want me to take him out? I was going to do it before you got here but, aahh, I was busy."

"No, no, I'll handle it tonight," Sam says. "Will you call Bud and Kota? I think they may need to be here in case Bill brings any friends along." Sam pauses for a moment. He knows that Darwin wants to help especially after what they did in South Dakota. He goes on to say, "Um, not that you couldn't pick up the slack, but just in case he brings a bunch of men that we can't handle."

Harland leaves to go change to his work clothes. He knows they are not going to get to go out on the town.

Sam and Darwin walk through the bunker and into Sam's personal weapons room. Sam had them store all the hand-to-hand fighting weapons that he has used along the way and a bunch of new ones that Gunny has made especially for him. Darwin is talking on the phone while he walks around the room. He walks over to a trunk and pulls out a sawed-off shotgun. Sam just grabs his knife and the bladed whip chain. He clips the chain on to his belt with a carabiner. He clips the knife to the back of his belt. Sam looks over at Darwin and says, "I don't remember ever putting any guns in here."

"There's a lot of unused space in here, so I just put some things in here for safekeeping," Darwin says with a smile. "Besides, I have grown accustom to using this after the days in the Dakotas." Darwin goes through the motions of inspecting the shotgun but not really knowing what he is doing.

Sam and Darwin go up and out of the bunker to meet Bud, Harland, and Kota in the therapy building.

"So Bill is coming to get what he deserves tonight," Sam tells them. "He said he wants half of everything. I think he will be bringing help. He is drunk and stupid, but I don't think he would be showing up here and demanding stuff all alone. He knows he will get a beating. Bud, you gave him one a while back. I don't think he has forgotten. Have you guys noticed him acting strange lately?" Sam is curious if anyone noticed when Bill started acting this way.

"He's been getting lazier and not showing up when he is supposed to be here. I was going to fire him, but he knows about almost everything. I just kept him around so that I could watch him," Bud says.

"Well, he tried to hit me with his truck a couple of days ago. I jumped out of the way and he just smiled and said, "Just joking, just wanted to see if you were on your toes." I just cut the sidewalls out of his tires. Maybe he's mad about that," Kota says.

"No, Darwin said that he has been up to no good. Darwin's been monitoring him," Sam says. "I think you guys better get armed just in case."

"I got into a fight with Bill the other day," Harland tells everyone. "He was talking shit about Carol and the girls up in the hospital. I had to set him straight and we had it out. I told Carol about it and she said she would handle it. Bill hasn't talked to me since."

"Well, we'll just see what the hell he's up to here in a little bit," Sam says with excitement in his voice. "I have my suspicions that he has been cohorting with the enemy."

"I'll get the .308 and night vision scope and get up on the roof just in case we need backup," Kota says and then he goes down into the bunker to get armed along with Bud and Harland. When they come up from the bunker, Kota climbs his way up to the roof. Harland climbs up on to the hospital roof with his rifle and night scope. Bud and Darwin move chairs around in the therapy building's office where they can close the shades and still peek out the window. Sam goes outside and sits down on the bench in front of the machine shop. About five minutes later, Bill drives up in his truck with two other big moving vans following behind him. Bill, Joy, and two other men step out of Bill's truck. Bill staggers up to the shop. Sam stands up and sees that Joy is wearing sunglasses. The other two are some big guys that are more fat than brawn.

"Joy, are you OK?" Sam asks in a calm concerned voice.

"She's fine and none of your business," Bill snaps back in a snooty voice.

"She don't look like she is OK, Bill!" Sam says in a stern voice. "Joy, are you OK?" Sam asks Joy.

"No, Sam, but I'll be OK," Joy says while crying.

"What happened, Joy?" Sam asks as he looks over at Bill.

"She ain't none of your business, God damn it!" Bill yells. "Or is it you and her. You've been messin' around with my wife too, Sam. Ya want her too?"

"Bill, you are being stupid and you need to simmer down," Sam instructs Bill in a calm, loud voice.

"Shut the fuck up and go get me my stuff," Bill yells and grabs his wife by the arm. He jerks her backward. Joy falls back to the ground. One of the big guys grabs her by the hair and drags her backward until she gets up to her feet. Then he punches her in the stomach and throws her to the ground. Bill doesn't do anything except laugh. "That bitch has been back-talking the whole night. Maybe that will shut her up for a little while," Bill says in a snide tone.

Sam moves forward toward Joy but Bill and the two guys move in front of her like they were guarding the queen. Sam stops and looks over at the moving vans when he hears some doors opening.

The cab doors to the moving vans open and three men from each van get out. One of the men from each of the moving vans goes to the back doors and opens them. A total of nineteen men come out of the moving vans.

Sam is now standing there in front of twenty-one men and Bill. Sam looks them over. He checks to see what kind of weapons they may be packing and sizes them up. There are several big men that weighed in at the upper two hundreds to three hundreds. Four of the men look like they had been doing too much meth and are thin as rails. A couple of them look like they are in pretty good shape. One of them is a muscled up body builder type. He is flexing his chest and his arms spread like those guys you see in the gym that do nothing but lift weights all day. The one Sam is most worried about is the short bald guy that is warming up by doing spin hook kicks. The other ones, Sam is not too worried about. One on one he could take out any of them, but all together, he may not fare too well. Sam knows that he couldn't let any of them get ahold of him. Otherwise, he will be done. As weapons go, Sam doesn't notice any guns on them except for Bill, who is carrying a semiautomatic .45. Some of the others are carrying pipes, bats, and an assortment of machetes and knives.

Sam steps back and signals Bud and Kota from behind his back. They know that they are to be ready but just lay low as a surprise.

"So, Bill, what do you plan on doing?" Sam addresses only Bill and steps forward a little toward him. "Did you come up here to try to beat me up or just your wife?"

"I aim to take all that I want," Bill yells in a confident voice and then looks behind him like he is making sure the gang he brought is still there. "Now tell me where the money and guns are, or we will beat it out of you."

Sam noticed that the other men are moving around him. Sam steps to the right and they move a little to the left. Sam did this in order to keep them in line with Kota and he always likes to move his opponents to the left.

The men keep closing in and Sam estimates the range between him and the men and the distance between each man. Range and speed is everything when fighting in hand-to-hand combat. Sam slowly reaches down and unclips his bladed whip chain. He no more than gets the weapon unclipped when three fat men lunged forward. Sam swings the bladed chain low much like roping the heels on a steer when team roping. The blade slices through the calf muscle of one of them and he drops to the ground. Blood gushes from the cut and the man grabs his leg trying to slow the bleeding. Sam whips the bladed chain back as the other two move forward. One swings his pipe and Sam dunks as he recoils the bladed chain. Sam swings the blade and cut the belly the man that swung the bat, then sinks the blade deep though the right arm of the second one. Sam jerks the blade back, ripping the bicep muscle off the right arm. The man grabs his arm and clinched on to it to try to stop the bleeding. Sam comes back with an across the belly cut, opening a large gapping opening to the man's abdomen. Blood and intestines ooze out of both men's gapping belly wounds. The men fall back screaming and grabbing at their abdomens in an uncontrolled manner as if they are trying to slap ants off themselves. After Sam has put three of the men out commission, the others backed off. Bill had run back to his truck while the little scrimmage went on. Now he is sitting inside the truck with the two big guys guarding the doors. Sam walks over to Joy and picks her up. He carries her to the shop bench. She sits there with tears running down her face. The left side of her face is swollen and blood oozing from her mouth and the corner of her eye from the kick that one of the big guys gave her while Sam was fighting. Sam knows she is strong and will be OK.

Sam turns and notices a few of the men running back to the moving vans and are now out of his sight. Next thing Sam sees the muzzle blast of Kota's .308 Lapua. Kota fires four times and one man comes staggering out from behind the van with an AK-47. He is hopping on one leg and on the other leg, his foot is just flopping. Blood is running under his jeans. He staggers a little before he starts to fall. He has his finger on the trigger and is firing as he falls to the ground. In doing so, he shoots the shop and six of his own men. The other men that had been standing off with Sam hit the ground to trying to avoid getting shot. Sam dives for cover behind the front of Bill's truck, and when the clip empties in the AK-47, the shooting stops.

Sam peeks around the front of the truck. He takes a quick mental survey of the men left. "Six men left from the moving vans and then both big guys and then BILL."

The body builder guy and four others are crawling toward one of the moving vans. The guy that was doing spin kicks is moving in toward Sam. He has a machete in each hand and is moving wildly and quickly. Sam can tell by the way the guy is handling the machetes that he has had training in some form of Filipino martial arts. Sam readies his blade in his right hand and the chain in his left. Sam whips the chain at the guy to back him up but he keeps coming. Sam then quickly recoils the chain and whips the chain's weighted end toward the guy's forehead. The guy swings his machetes wildly at the chain but misses as a baseball player misses a fastball. The weight on the chain hits him square in the forehead. The blow knocks the man unconscious and he drops to the ground. Sam quickly recoils the chain and gets ready for more. But the rest of the five are now hiding under the truck.

Sam looks over at Joy. She is sitting up and crying. She looks over at Sam in despair. She looks into his eyes like an abused dog looks at the person who just saved them with food and water. Sam knows what abuse looks like; he had seen it many times in his life. He hates anyone that abuses man or animal. Then Sam looks over at Bill sitting in the truck drinking.

"So, Bill, are you just going to sit in your truck all night, or are you going to come out and clean up your mess?" Sam yells.

The two big guys are still standing next to the doors, acting real tough. Sam walks over the guy that had hit Joy. The guy takes a swing at Sam, but Sam is ready. He has wound the chain around his hand before walking up to him. Sam moves to the right and punches the guy in the forearm just above the thumb. The blow shatters the guy's wrist. Sam quickly comes back with a back fist to the guy's mouth, shattering his chin and breaking the front teeth. Blood and teeth erupt from the guy's mouth. Sam jumps back and sends a kick to the guy's testicles and then a punch to his frontal bone that caves in his frontal sinus. The guy drops to the ground before he even knows what hit him. The guy lies there with blood gushing from his mouth and nose. Bill in the meantime just keeps drinking. Sam walks over to the shop bench and motions for Bud and Darwin to come out to attend to Joy.

Sam yells to the men hiding under the moving vans, "Come out and collect your wounded and take them to the hospital."

The body builder guy yells, "We already called the ambulance. We ain't coming out till the cops get here."

Sam motions to Harland to lay low. He motions to Kota to get into the bunker. Kota slides off the roof and climbs down the corner of the building. He goes down through the bunker and grabs the .338 Lapua. He then goes out through the cave and to the top of the hill. He is about six hundred yards away, looking down on to the farm. He can see everything. Bud and Darwin put their weapons away along with Sam's knife, down in to the bunker. Sam keeps his chained weapon since it is pretty obvious that he had used a weapon.

Kota's .308 slugs will be much like the slug of an AK-47, so they cannot prove there was another weapon unless they do ballistics. Sam knows that the county cannot afford that type of testing.

Bud and Darwin go over to assist Joy. Sam goes over to the men that he had cut their abdomens open. Both men are unconscious but very much alive. Sam yells to Bud to get saline, skin staplers, and sterile bandages from the hospital. Bud runs in and grabs supplies and runs back out. Sam washes the few feet of small intestine that has exteriorized from the wounds and pushes them back in. Then he staples the wounds shut and bandages the abdomen. Sam knows when they get to the hospital that they take them into surgery and lavage the abdomen. He knows what he did will reduce the contamination. All the men should be OK except for the ones that were hit by the AK-47. That was not his fault, as a matter of fact; Sam knows none of it is his fault.

The state police and the county deputy sheriff Benz arrive with the ambulance and the local rescue units. The EMTs quickly go to work. The hospital helicopter flies in and takes two of the men. Most of the others are hauled in by ambulance. Joy is refusing medical attention but files charges on the man that hit her and Bill. Bill is still sitting in his truck drinking while many of the officers are taking statements from the other men that had been lying under the moving van. Bud and Darwin give their version of the story to the police. Sam calls Carol and tells her what had happened.

"I knew he was up to no good," Carol says. "He has been rude and disrespectful for the past month now. I was going to fire him but you said you wanted to keep him in sight, so I just put up with it. I really don't think it would have made a difference anyway. He would have come after you. Let me know what I can do for you."

"I will, but don't worry, I should be home soon," Sam says.

Deputy Benz walks up to Sam and says, "So, Sam, it hasn't been that long ago when I was out here before."

"Get that pool of corruption cleaned up over there yet, or did you just jump in with everyone else?" Sam asks in a sarcastic tone.

"No, we stay fairly busy cleaning up your messes," Deputy Benz says in a very sarcastic tone. "Sam, I'm going to have to take you in for questioning. Someone has to be arrested for this and you can't just claim self-defense this time. You don't have a scratch on you."

"I don't think I am going anywhere but home, Sheriff!" Sam says in stern voice. "Old Billy there brought up his friends and they wanted to clean me out, so he says. I think he just came up here to work me over, but you can ask him about that."

"Why do we have so many bodies around here?" Deputy Benz asks. "You must have been waiting for him." He knows that all the guys lying out there are troublemakers, but if he doesn't arrest someone, then he will get in trouble.

"I called him earlier to see if he and Joy wanted to go to supper with Darwin and me. He said he was coming up here to get what he deserves. He shows up with these guys. I guess he brought along the wrong help," Sam says in a kind a joking manner.

"Why do you say he brought the wrong help?" Deputy Benz asks. "Did you know what they came for?"

"Well, Sheriff, if you're going to wrestle an alligator, you should take him out of the water first," Sam says. "And the way it looked, they just came here to kill me or work me over. Bill never really asked for anything, he just sent his fat boys after me."

"Well, Sam, we are going to put you in jail. We are going to arrest you for attempted murder and probably manslaughter among many other things. We can probably find several things to put in jail for this time. The way it looks to me is that they came out here to load up something and you were waiting for them. That is premeditation. Now, Sam, I'm going to read you your rights and—" Deputy Benz tells Sam till Sam cuts him off.

"You ain't taking me anywhere. You are going to take all your buddies here and get them some medical help and then you all can leave me and the rest of my family and friends alone," Sam says in very threatening way.

"What makes you thing I won't just Tase you and cuff you?" Deputy Benz threatens Sam.

"Because somewhere out there"—Sam points all around in the dark—"there are two snipers that are very good. They will blow your fucking head off if you just even look like you are going for your weapon and there isn't one damn thing you or I can do about it. You will never find them and you will never see them," Sam says in a calm voice and then pushes Deputy Benz back with one hand. "I knew when you bastards showed up so quickly that you were all in on this. You may not be a dirty cop but you are a pawn. Now if I'm wrong, tell me."

"We're just doing are job, but you have been a pain in my ass since last year and I've about had it with you. I'll get to you later," Deputy Benz says in a threatening manner.

"You ain't going to do shit," Sam tells Deputy Benz. "Just remember, I may have someone watching you all the time. At any given time I can have you erased."

"Are threatening me?" Deputy Benz asks. He is pretty shook up by Sam's confidence and assurance. He is pretty certain that Sam will and can have him killed at any time.

"No, Sheriff, that is a promise. Now get your shit off my property and take that fucking wife-beating traitor Bill with you too," Sam says in a calm voice. "Remind him that if I see him again, no one else ever will." Sam turns and walks into the therapy building. Bud has a beer waiting for him. Sam opens it up and sits down. Sam takes a deep breath and lets it all out. "So is Kota and Harland out there or was I just blowing smoke out my ass?" Sam asks Bud.

"Kota took the .338 with him and Harland is not back here, so I reckon they are somewhere out there," Bud says. "Should I call them and find out where they are?"

"No, they will show up when they know the coast is clear," Sam says. "Darwin is the perimeter surveillance equipment up and running?"

"Sure is. I made several upgrades to it and there is no way anyone on foot or flight can get in without us knowing," Darwin says confidently. "All I have to do is turn it on again and it can call everyone and tell you how big and how fast it is moving and exactly where it is. I'll go turn it on right now and you can watch it on your phone."

"Great," Sam says and then downs his beer.

Sam watches as all the vehicles leave his place. Kota comes back through the bunker soon after everyone leaves. Harland comes through the front door of the therapy room. Darwin, Bud, Harland, Kota, and Sam sit around discussing the night's event. They have put Joy up for the night in the extra room in the shop. She is very shaken up and will not go to the hospital to get any help. None of them are quite sure what to do with her. Carol will have a talk with her in the morning. They all adjourn their little meeting and go home for the night.

Chapter Twenty-One

....

Early in the morning, Joy stands over her drunken husband that is lying a pool of blood on the floor with his head crushed in. She is holding a medieval type mace that she took from Gunny's shop. She stands there and stares at him with tears in her eyes, tears of sadness and tears of joy. She feels the weight on her taken away. She no longer has to put up with Bill beating her and his friends raping her. She knows she will go to jail, but at least the pain will stop. She knows she should have let Sam handle him. Sam would have made Bill suffer if she would have told him that Bill had been letting his knew friends gang-rape her while he watched and got high on meth. As time passed with her standing there, she realizes that she doesn't want to go to jail for this; he deserves it. He was going to kill her if she showed back up at home. She just beat him to it. She decides to call Sam.

"Sam," Joy starts crying, "Sam, I did something real bad."

"Joy?" Sam is just waking up. He looks at his phone and it is seven in the morning. "Joy, what have you done? I thought you would still be sleeping in the shop. Where are you?"

"I went on home this morning. I took one of the farm trucks, I hope you aren't mad," Joy says. "I'll bring it back."

"No, that is perfectly fine that you took the truck," Sam asks with a little more clarity. "Joy, what is the problem."

"I taught him a lesson. He will never do anything to hurt me again." Joy is still crying. "I killed him, Sam, and now I don't know what to do."

"What did you do that for?" Sam asks and sits up in bed.

Carol wakes up and asks Sam in a snippy tone, "Who are you talking to?"

"Here, Carol, talk to Joy, she just killed Bill. I'm going to get dressed," Sam tells Carol.

Joy explained everything to Carol, all about the abuse over the last month that she had to endure. Carol starts to cry because she didn't realize what was happening even though she had seen Joy several times over the last few months. She starts blaming herself for Joy's abuse much like Joy blames herself. Carol tells Joy that she will talk it over with Sam and she will call her back.

Sam walks in after taking a shower. "What is wrong? Why are you crying?" Sam asks in a compassionate and concerned voice.

"I feel so guilty for what happened to Joy. I should have seen it and I just let it go on," Carol says tearfully. She is very upset.

"Carol." Sam goes over and gives her a hug. "It is not your fault, its Bill's fault."

"Sam, I want you to go over and get rid of the problem. Go over there and burn the house down or something. Joy doesn't deserve to spend any time in jail," Carol says, almost begging him.

"I can't do that right now," Sam says. "They'll probably try to pin this murder on me since Joy used our truck and one of the weapons that Gunny made. Plus last night, my run in with Bill, hell, there is no way they won't try to pin this on me."

"Well, we got to do something," Carol says as she brainstorms. "Maybe we can send Bud or Kota over there and they can handle this problem."

"No, we need to stay away from this as far as we can get," Sam says. "We should send over Terri Logan and she can give her the legal advice that she needs. They can figure out what needs to be done."

"OK, you're right. I'll call Joy and tell her what we have planned. Then I'll call Terri and see if she can get over there right away," Carol says as she grabs the phone. She dials Joy's number.

Joy answers, "Oh, thanks for calling me back right away. Is Sam on his way yet?"

"No, Joy, I am sending over Terri Logan. She is a lawyer and she can give you some legal advice," Carol tells Joy.

"I need Sam over here to handle this, I can't go to jail. This bastard deserved it and you know it," Joy pleads with Carol.

"Probably so, but Sam is a little afraid of getting in the middle of this right now. Just last night, those two tangoed and they will try to get him for murder on this one if he gets involved," Carol explains.

"Well, OK. You go and send the lawyer over and I'll get things together on my side. I wasn't thinking that clearly before, but I'm thinking a lot more clearly right now," Joy says with confidence in her voice, but she is still a little shaky. "Well, I'll let you go now, Carol. Thank you for everything."

"I'm going to call Terri right now and I'm going to give her your number, OK?" Carol tells Joy.

"OK, thanks." Joy hangs up the phone.

Carol hangs up, then immediately calls Terri and tells her about Joy's problem. Terri tells her that she will call Joy immediately and then go over to meet her.

Joy quickly goes and takes a shower. She changes clothes. Then she packs some clothes and some of her personal belongings. She goes out to the shed that has the safe underneath it. Bill had cut a hole in the floor soon after the safe was put under the shed. He wasn't supposed to dip in to the money, but he spent it like bathwater. That is how they found him and when they did and he sang like a songbird. He told the YUPPI gang about how Sam had robbed them and how he had set up all the security around his place, but he never knew about the bunker and the cave. Joy opens the safe like she had watch Bill do so many times. Bill never locked it because he was too stupid to remember the combination. He had lost the key a long time ago, so the lid is just shut. The lid was very heavy so Bill ridge up a block and tackle to open the lid. Joy opens the lid and takes out what money remains. There is only about fifty thousand left. Bill had drunk and partied the rest away.

Joy puts all her stuff into the truck and then gets into Bill's truck, starts it up, and drives it through the wall of the house. She climbs out of the truck and drags Bill off the couch and up under the truck. She goes over to the cupboard and grabs all the vodka out. She dumps it all over the house. She then walks out of the house through the hole in the wall. She leaves a trail of vodka to the outside. She reaches in her pocket and lights a cigarette. She takes one drag, then flicks it on to the vodka trail. The vodka lights instantly. The blue flame races down the line of vodka on into the house. The house bursts into flames. Joy climbs into Sam's truck and takes off. All Joy can think of is "I'm free at last." She points the truck toward I-64 west and drives away.

Terri calls Joy like she said she would. "Joy, this is Terri. I'm coming out to your place right now. Remain calm and we will get this handled in the proper way. Now don't worry. I'll be there in about thirty minutes. Don't talk to anyone till I get there."

"Thank you, but no thank you. I already got everything under control. I will not need your services. Please thank Sam and Carol for me." Joy hangs up her phone and throws it out the window. No one ever hears from her again.

That afternoon, Deputy Sheriff Benz and Sheriff Allen along with several deputy cars drive up to the hospital. Some deputy's cars are parked on the road. Deputy Benz and Sheriff Allen along with ten other deputies get out of their vehicles. All of them have their weapons drawn and surround the hospital. Some go into the barns and other buildings. Sheriff walks in to the reception area and asks Marsha, "Where is Sam Kelley?"

"What do you want to see him for, Sheriff?" Marsha asks.

"I have a warrant for his arrest," Sheriff Allen says. Deputy Benz nods in a "hello" gesture to Marsha.

"Well, he is unavailable at this time, but if you would like to make an appointment, I can fit you in the Tuesday after next," Marsha says sarcastically.

"Don't you get sassy with me, damn it. I have a warrant. Now where the fuck is he?" Sheriff Allen starts yelling at Marsha.

Deputy Benz taps Sheriff Allen on the shoulder. He says, "Now, now. Marsha is not the problem here. She has always been cooperative."

Marsha doesn't like to get yelled at no matter who it is. She snaps back, "Well, fuck you too, Sheriff. I don't have any idea where Sam is today. He doesn't have any appointments today. Maybe he is at home. He don't fucking live here, you dumb shit."

Now Sheriff Allen is really mad. "He's not at home. Where would he be if he was not here or there?"

"I don't know. He was here about eight o'clock this morning, and then he left his office. Maybe he is outside. I don't know, I don't keep a GPS on him," Marsha yells back.

"I want you to call him and tell him to come to the office. Don't tell him that we are here," Sheriff Allen says. He wants to ambush him when he comes in to the office.

"You want him, you call him," Marsha says. "I don't work for you, so either leave or sit your ass down and wait. I don't care what you do. I have work to do."

"Ya know I can arrest you for aiding and abetting a felon," Sheriff Allen tells Marsha in a stern, threatening voice.

Deputy Benz steps in and says in a calm voice, "Marsha, it is going to be a lot better if Sam just comes up here and turns himself in. I tried to tell him last night that he needed to come in, but he was a little resistant. So if you can just assist us, we can get this all straighten out."

"I'm not aiding anyone. I'm telling you, I don't know where the hell he is. So if you have a search warrant, you can go look around the farm for him. But if you don't, then get the hell out of here." Marsha has had with the sheriff. Sheriff Allen doesn't have a search warrant to look through anything. Marsha figured that there wasn't a search warrant. Otherwise, the sheriff would have shown her as soon as she resisted.

"I'll be back. If you see Sam, tell him to come to the county jail and turn himself in. It will save him a lot of discomfort." Sheriff Allen is frustrated. He shakes his finger at Marsha and says, "Tell him."

Sam has been down in the bunker with Darwin. Darwin had picked up over the police scanner that the sheriff had found Bill's place burned and Bill is found died. Darwin has been following Sheriff Allen since he called the prosecuting attorney for the arrest warrant for Sam. Sam is safe in the bunker. No one but a few people knows about the bunker. Even if they do know where the bunker is, they will never find their way in. The entrance is a floor drain. When not in use the drain is filled with water, and when they go in and out, like last night, there is no water in it. Now that someone that may snoop around will just fill it with water, and no one will ever suspect it to be an entrance. Sam can always leave through the cave or just stay there forever. Darwin can watch the whole place on camera, which he was doing at this moment. Darwin records all the deputies snooping through all the buildings, and if needed, he can use it in court.

Marsha calls Sam and tells him what the sheriff had said. Sam tells her that he knows about it and that she needs to call Terri Logan immediately as soon as Terri is done with Joy.

Marsha calls Terri. "Terri, Sam told me to call you and fill you in on some things that are happening here." She fills her in on what Sam needs.

Terri tells her, "I'll be over in just about a half an hour. Joy didn't want me to come over and she probably left town."

Marsha tells her, "Sam doesn't think it is a good idea to come here because they are watching who comes and goes. He said he can meet you over at Tom's Pizza."

Terri says, "OK, I see him there in a half hour."

Sam takes the back way out of the place and drives about eight miles to Tom's Pizza Parlor. He goes into the place and sits in the back area of the restaurant. He sits close to the back door and keeps an eye out for any sheriff cars. Terri walks in and looks around briefly until she finds Sam. She goes to his table and sits down. They order pizza and then Sam tells her about what had happened the night before as she takes notes. Sam gives her every little detail that he can remember. Then he tells her about Deputy Benz wanting to take him into the jail so he didn't get into trouble for not arresting someone.

"I'm not going down to that jail. That sheriff I'm pretty sure is dirty. Deputy Benz may not be dirty, but I don't trust him. I saw him several times. The last time a gang of people came up to the hospital," Sam says. "Do you remember that?" Sam takes a piece of pizza and loads it with parmesan cheese.

"Do you want some pizza with that cheese?" Terri jokingly asks. Sam just smiles. Terri says, "I do remember that and they let everyone go with restraining orders. Do you remember the name of that sheriff?"

"Well, I don't know who the hell he is because he is not even this county's sheriff. I think it is the new Sheriff over where that fucking Tamms was being a sheriff," Sam says. "I think his name is Allen or something like that. Darwin would know so I can find out." Sam devoured the piece of pizza.

"Yes, that is him. He is now the sheriff around here. That jailhouse is no different than it was when Sheriff Tamms was running it. I suggest you don't go and turn yourself in until I get things worked out with the state or with the FBI," Terri says. "I'll make some calls. I have some friends that are involved in the FBI." Terri grabs a piece of pizza and nibs on it.

"Well, no one is going to find me. I may stay here or I'll go back to South Dakota." Sam says and then eats another piece of pizza. "I'm not even sure if I am dealing with the same YUPPI gang that was around before. I never saw these guys before. I do know that Bill's cousin is involved somehow with the old gang or something like that."

"I wish that we could find Joy. She may be able to clear up some of this stuff," Terri says.

"I'll have my friend look and see if he can find her somehow. He's really good at that," Sam says.

"OK, stay out of trouble. Don't—and I repeat *don't*—let them find you before I get this straightened out," Terri tells him. She stands up and grabs her purse.

Sam stands up and put the rest of the pizza into a "to go" box. Sam tells Terri, "I got the bill. You better go before someone see's you with me. See you later." Sam leaves a hundred-dollar bill on the table for a tip.

Terri leaves. Then Sam goes up and pays the bill. Sam drives back to his house but keeps on driving when he notices a truck parked about a quarter mile down the road.

"Shit! They are watching the house," Sam says to himself. Then he drives to the hospital but goes in the back entrance that is through the neighbor's pasture. He parks the truck behind Gunny's shop. Sam goes into the shop. Gunny and Darrell are sitting in there, drinking coffee and playing cards.

"Hey, Sam," they both say simultaneously.

"Now I know you two have been around each other too long," Sam says because the both spoke at the same time and look up at the same time.

"Ha, well, we are just having fun," Darrell says with a smile on his face. Sam had never seen his dad smile before.

"Are you ever going back home?" Sam asks his dad. "Not that I want you to leave."

"Your mother is getting things together and then she is going to come out here," Darrell says and then throws his cards on the table face up. Gunny cringes. Darrell informs Sam, "Gina is going to move over to the farm for a while. Your mom should be out here in a week or so."

"How are my brothers and Montana and Luke doing in their training, Gunny?" Sam asks.

"They are coming along. The two boys are doing very well. Bud and Dakota are coming along, but I am having a hard time to get them to open up to new ways of fighting. They are more interested in guns and brawling," Gunny says. "But they will come around over time. I have to say they are shooting extremely well."

"Great, well, keep up the good work," Sam says. "I am going to have to have some lessons as soon as we get time. But I may be leaving for a while." Sam sits down and puts the box of pizza on the table. Both Gunny and Darrell dig into the pizza like they haven't eaten for days. "They want to throw me in jail for killing Bill."

"Bill's dead?" The both ask in amazement.

"Yeah, this morning, Joy bashed his head in with that mace you made," Sam says.

"Huh, I wondered why I had this feeling that something is missing when I came in this morning. I just didn't put my finger on it." Gunny scratches his head.

"I noticed there was something missing, but ya know the boys borrow things," Darrell says. He is full of shit sometimes. He really didn't know anything is gone but he just has to say something.

"So they think I did it because Bill came here with a gang of people last night and we had to convince them to leave." Sam tips his hat back. "Ya know, Gunny, I really like that bladed chain you made. I think it is my favorite weapon."

"Don't just get used to using one weapon. Make sure you keep up with several. One weapon doesn't always work in all situations," Gunny says to Sam.

"I know, but I'm just saying I really like it." Sam gets up. "Well, if you see anyone snooping around, remember to hit the panic button. I'm going to stay in the bunker till I figure things out. They are watching the house."

"Do you need us to go get you anything?" Darrell asks.

"No, I got some of the special camouflage clothes that I had made. I'll just wear those clothes. They are a little warm for just sitting around in, but they will do," Sam says. "Hey, what is the weather going to do?"

Those two guys can tell you what the weather is going to be over the next year or so they thought. They discuss the weather every day.

"Going to snow about a foot of snow this weekend," Darrell tells Sam.

Gunny instantly jumps in, "That's not right, I'll bet ya it snows two to three feet with those two fronts that are closing in."

"OK, well let me know if anything changes," Sam says and then goes out the door and heads for the bunker.

This time when Sam goes into the bunker, he floods the entrance just in case the sheriff comes back. Sam tries on a new suit he had made. An old seamstress in Steeles Tavern helps to design and sews them for him. He had some other ones made but each time one is made he changes a few things. The camouflage clothes are lined with a heat reflective shield along with Gore-Tex and Thinsulate. The outer cover is waterproof but breathable. There are several pockets and areas to attach weapons and other items. It has a built in climbing harness just in case it is ever needed. The knees and elbows are padded with Kevlar-type material. The clothes open in different areas so that temperature can be controlled. There is a tubing system that attaches to a facemask that will capture the heat from your breath and distribute it throughout the clothing for cold climates. It is light and extremely comfortable. Sam loves to wear them but each pair is different. He likes to wear them for a day or two to see if anything needs to be changed. He didn't have many pairs of them. It is impossible to clean them, so once they are beyond a point of stinking, then it is time to dismantle them and get them rebuilt. Sam loves to invent new things. He always thought that he might be able to mass-produce them for sale to the military, but that will now have to wait for a later date.

CHAPTER TWENTY-TWO

SAM HEADS INTO DARWIN'S COMPUTER room. After crawling up into the computer area, he finds Darwin watching multiple screens.

"Hey," Darwin says without looking away from his computer screens. "Found telephone numbers and addresses for all those people on the list. What do you want me to do with it?"

"E-mail it to DH's phone. He's got an iPhone, so he should get it right away. He can call them," Sam says. "Have you been monitoring that fucking sheriff?"

"Yep, he's coming here right now," Darwin says.

"Why didn't you tell me, you jerk?" Sam says jokingly but semiseriously.

"I knew you were here. I've been following you all over the place and if I thought you were straying away from here, I'd called you." Darwin says with a smile on his face. "Don't you worry; I've got your back. You helped me and I will help you, just like in school."

"Thanks, Darwin." Sam rubs Darwin's head like a pet. "What ya working on now?"

"I'm hacking into a bank that I found on that hard drive that we acquired. I want to know how much money is in there from those meth labs or in OCORCS account. Then I am going to take it and spread it across the world and have it change from one bank to another until I say it can stop," Darwin says.

"You can do that?" Sam asks. He is always amazed at Darwin's cyberspace abilities. "Well, don't get caught."

"Don't worry, I am going to find all of them people and then they will be broke. As for me getting caught, I am just going in through the little piece of software that everyone stole from me. No one knows I am there." Darwin says with pride.

Sam watches Darwin for a while and then wrangles another chair into the area of the computers. Sam sits down and watches for a while until he falls asleep.

A little while later, Darwin nudges Sam. "The sheriff is coming up the driveway."

Sam shakes his head to get the sleep out.

Darwin points to two screens. "They're on camera now. Looks like one car and three vans. Over there is the road and there are several cars up and down the road. You must be pretty important to send out all those people."

"Well, it would really only take one cop, if I knew they weren't dirty cops. I'd turn myself in and this would all be over quick," Sam says. "Hey, can you hack into that sheriff's stuff or into the jail's stuff and see if they are on the take or not. Hey, see if they have a real warrant or not. I'll watch the screens."

"Sure, that will be my pleasure." Darwin goes to work as Sam watches the vehicles pull up all around the hospital.

Twelve men get out of each of the three vans and four men, including Sheriff Allen and Deputy Benz get out of the car. All the men are heavily armed with shotguns, automatic weapons, and side arms. Some have AP-90s, M-16s, and other weapons that Sam didn't know what they are. All of them are wearing bulletproof vests.

"Hey, Darwin, can you magnify this video so I can see what is written on the vest?" Sam asks.

"Sure thing," Darwin pushes a couple of keys, then slides the mouse and magnifies a still shot of the vest. "Looks like a symbol and not really writing. Doesn't look like police vest." Darwin zooms in on the back of a vest and makes it a still shot. "It says 'Fed Law' on the back."

"OK, just keep looking into that stuff and I'll try to figure this out." Sam's mind races through the possibilities of what the hell is going on. "I bet that is the YUPPI symbol. They are now the federal law?"

"Here I found this." Darwin points to his screen and says, "This is an internal memo at the jail and it says that the new men in the department are stationed there permanently and they are on classified patrol. It's signed by the sheriff, but it doesn't say where they are from. I'll keep looking."

"Shit, they are now in the office," Sam says.

In the front office, Sheriff Allen, Deputy Benz and two other men from the car go in as the others surround the hospital. They storm through the front door like it is a drug bust and scare the clients that are sitting in the reception area.

Sheriff Allen walks up to the front desk, "I want to know exactly where Sam is now. I have a warrant to bring him in. Tell where he is and we will leave now."

"I don't know where he is at," Marsha says. She is very startled.

"I know he is here. He was seen driving by his house earlier and then he took the road up to this place. I'm pretty sure that he is here, so just call him or intercom him or what the fuck ever you do," Sheriff Allen screams. He is mad. "Get him the fuck in her right now."

"Let's see the warrant, first," Marsha orders. She has regained her senses.

"I don't need a fucking warrant. I am under a new law and we don't need warrants anymore. Sam is now considered an enemy of the state," Sheriff Allen screams.

Deputy Benz and the other two men are standing behind Sheriff Allen. Deputy Benz has a look of embarrassment on his face. He nods in a greeting fashion and smiles at the clients sitting the reception room. He knows the sheriff is an unreasonable asshole. No one liked him before he was made sheriff. Now he is totally unreasonable since he has a congressman backing him. The other two men have no expression on their faces. They are just hired thugs and can't careless about anything.

"Bullshit. Get a warrant or get out. Get out now!" Marsha says sternly. She is really mad.

The sheriff turns to the other three men and says, "Take the place apart—every building, every nook and cranny. Leave no place unturned." One of the men runs outside and yells to the other men. Groups of four men are running everywhere into every building, kicking in doors, tipping shelves, braking windows, letting horses out of stalls. The doctors and techs go running outside to catch loose horses. Technicians and doctors start yelling at the men in the vests to stop.

Sam is watching it all on video.

"Here it is, Sam! They are from that YUPPI gang thing. It's all black and white. They are now part of a fusion center or something and it looks like they are now spreading across the nation. It says something about the council of governors, I don't know, I'll look into it more. They're dirty Sam, I do know that," Darwin says with excitement.

"Well, shit, I can't have them tearing shit apart. I'm going to end this little shit group once and for all. Hell, I'm supposed to be a murder so why stop at one or two. See you later, Darwin," Sam says as he goes out of the room. He grabs his emergency pack, hand weapons, parachute, and then some climbing gear. Then went and grabs the .338 Lapua and some night vision goggles. On his way out he grabs his ghillie suit. He heads down to the cave. He loads the Polaris RZR four-wheeler with all the stuff along with extra water and three homemade claymore mines. The Polaris RZR had been modified by Kota and his mechanic friend. The modifications make the vehicle go faster and hydraulics that raise and lower the deck for on road and off road use. The claymores were Gunny's specials and are extremely deadly. Sam drives the four-wheeler out of the cave vehicle entrance and then recamouflages the cave entrance. He drives to the top of the hill and sets up the .338's bipod. He spots a man that is kicking on Gunny's shop door. Sam puts the man in the crosshairs and fires a round. The man flies back about five feet and never got up. A pool of blood forms between the man and the ground. Sam had hit him in the breastplate of the bulletproof vest and the velocity of round went through the vest and plate and ripped through his chest. Shards of bone, tissue, and flesh flew out of the man's back.

Gunny opens the door and looks out then quickly closes it. He runs back and grabs an old remodified Tommy gun and hands a .45 pistol to Darrell. They both standby the door in case anyone tries to force their way in. Sam spots two men coming out of the barn; this time he takes aim at the head of the front man and waits till both lined up. Sam fires a round. The first man's head flies back and the bullet slows just enough to make it go into a tumble. The bullet goes through the first man's head and through the second man's head. Then the bullet travels through the barn wall and into the concrete floor on the inside of the barn. The second man's head explodes, completely ripping it from the torso. Both men fall to the ground dead. Two more men come out of the hospital's back door. They see the three men lying on the ground. They instantly dive to the ground. They look around in confusion. One of the men radios the others, and now they all come out from the buildings staying close to the ground and next to walls. Sam waits to see if the sheriff will come out, but he never comes around the hospital. Sam spots in another one that has a scope on his rifle and is looking around. Sam fires a round, sending it through the pelvis of the man. He drops like someone just folded him up and set him down. Sam sees another in the doorway of the hayshed. The man starts firing several rounds in all directions. When he stops to change magazines, Sam fires another round and hits him in the leg. The leg snaps like a twig and the man throws himself to the ground. Sam shots two men lying in the yard. One round goes through the shoulder of one and the other round goes through the other men's rump and exits out the leg. The leg explodes like popping a water balloon. The leg is only attached by shreds of flesh. Sam looks through the scope for anyone else looking his direction when he decides it is time to go.

Sam decided that a few dead men will get their attention off the hospital and back on to him. He also knows that they will be scared to move for a little while, so he jumps on his Polaris and heads toward the mountains.

Before the shooting started, Sheriff Allen and the two YUPPIs became very abusive to Marsha and to one of the clients in the reception area. One of the YUPPIs had grabbed Marsha and held her while the Sheriff punched her in the stomach. When she dropped to her knees, another YUPPI helped pick her up and held her. The sheriff adjusted his gloves, then punched her in the face. Marsha was knocked unconscious. A male client in the reception area jumped in when the sheriff first hit Marsha. One of the YUPPIs blindsided him with a punch to the side of the head. When the man dropped to the ground, the YUPPI began to kick and punch him until he was no longer conscious. Deputy Benz did nothing except leave the office. He gets into his car and leaves.

Darwin has it all on tape. Darwin had called Bud and Kota when it all started. They were loading hay about twenty miles away. They immediately unhooked the trailer and raced back toward the hospital. They didn't make it back in time. Harland was helping catch horses.

The YUPPIs outside radio frantically to Sheriff Allen. All of them are screaming in fear and horror. The YUPPIs are all extremely undertrained thugs. None have had any training except to point and shot. They are the type of men who were the bullies in school that picked on people whenever they were in a group. They are all tough guys as long as they are in a group but total wimps when they have to fight on their own. Now, they are all lying on the ground scattered around buildings and bushes, hiding like scared rabbits. None of them are brave enough to come out to see where the shots come from. After about ten minutes, the sheriff comes out. He gets everyone up and loads them in the vans.

One of the YUPPIs on the road had seen a muzzle flash at the top of the hill and jumped into his car. He races around the section of land on the road to tries to get the jump on the shooter. Sam sees the car coming while he is on the Polaris. Sam stays just far enough ahead just so he doesn't lose him. Sam does this on purpose so he can set a trap for them away from the hospital. Sam heads into the mountains. He has ridden horses several times up into the mountains. He knows of one perfect place for a standoff. He and Carol have ridden up and then climbed the rest of the way. They could see for miles and miles.

Sam turns on to an old logging road, he knows he will lose the guy in the car, but he has him close enough so the guy in the car will know where to look. Sam has to make some headway in order to hide the Polaris and then back track up the only pathway to the top of the mountain. Sam figures it will take those idiots most of the night before they can get things together and move up the logging trail. Sam will be ready and waiting for them when they do come. After parking the Polaris in a ravine about a half a mile away, he covers it with branches. Then he makes his way back to the base of the trail. Sam marks his trail well so it will keep them coming after him and leave his family and friends alone. He knows he will now be a fugitive for the rest of his life, but there is no way he will just give up. He knows he would just die if he had to go to jail, so he will just fight to the death. He never killed anyone before, and it really disturbed him to do it. He just lost his temper, but they are the ones that keep pushing. He knows that they will just keep pushing, and he has to end it here and now.

Sam climbs the long steep trail. The trail goes straight up the side of the mountain. All around it is cliff face much like a palisade. The dirt and gravel-like footing makes it difficult to climb. You take two steps up and slide one step back down. Under the loose footing in some areas, there is jagged rock that can shred bone if you fall. The climb is fairly dangerous, but for an experienced hiker, it would be a moderate climb. This trail is the only way to the top without rock climbing. The cliff face jets up about seven hundred feet all around the mountain. The top is rocky with a moderate amount of brush and scrub tree growth.

Sam stops and writes a message on a white handkerchief, "Please do not follow up the trail. Leave me alone or die." Sam hopes that will get the message across to some of them so they go home. Mostly he wants to come up, but he wants to do his part to warn them first. Sam moves up the trail slowly but surely. He says to himself, "I'm getting old and fat." Sam always figured the trail was a ravine and not really a trail, but it is the only way up to the top unless you had climbing gear or you can fly. Along the trail, Sam sets several traps and surprises. The first few traps are just to scare them, and the higher traps get more deadly. The top three are the claymores that Sam had grabbed when he went out. Sam says to himself, "If those guys get that far up, they will only be about a two hundred and fifty yards from me. If they do manage to make it past the claymores, I'll get them with the .338." Sam puts on his ghillie suit and moves in close to a rock ledge that has brush and sparse tree cover. Sam can see ninety percent of the trail from where he is sitting. Sam waits and watches.

The guy that was following Sam calls Sheriff Allen, "I followed that son of a bitch to the jump mountain road. He's got to be going up there to hide."

Sheriff Allen gives a little laugh. "Great! Just stay there until we get there. I'll get things wrapped up here and then get over to you."

The guy in the car says, "OK, I'll stay here." Then hangs up his phone and watches a movie on his phone.

Sheriff Allen doesn't even bat an eye nor look surprised when he sees the seven men on the ground. It is as if he knew it was going to happen. He has the seven men brought to the hospital in the van and the rest go back to the station to regroup. Once at the station, he calls in for more help. "I'm going to get him once in for all. I'll have enough men to move the mountain not just search the mountain." He calls in every one of the fusion center's men and all the YUPPI men. He also brings in Poot, ex-deputy Trevor, and ex-sheriff Cecil Tamms. All three hated Sam, and Sheriff Allen knows they will enjoy seeing Sam die.

CHAPTER TWENTY-THREE

When morning comes on the mountain there is about twelve inches of snow on the ground. Snow is unusual for this time of year in Virginia. Some of the men have a hard time making it to the station but Sheriff Allen needs all of them. Sheriff Allen waits till everyone arrives. He now has a hundred and twenty-eight men in all. He doesn't have any armored vehicles like the group out in South Dakota; they all just pile into trucks and vans. Some of them brought along four-wheelers, but all of them have an overabundance of weapons. The man that had followed Sam part of the way up the logging road stayed out all night. He gave directions to Sheriff Allen to the logging road leading to the trail to the base of the mountain. He got tired of sitting on the road, so he drove up to the trail to sleep overnight. He really isn't sure if Sam is still there but he doesn't want to tell Sheriff Allen that.

When the group stops on the logging trail, it is chaos. There are men that can't get there four-wheelers off the trucks. Some of the men are still hung over or drunk from the night before. Some of the men are already smoking meth, which then gets them so hopped up that two of them get in a knife fight. Both of those men are hauled to the hospital. Some of the vans get stuck or can't make it up the first part of the trail. Some of the men are complaining about the cold and bad weather. Most of the men don't want to go up the mountain. Most of them are too fat and out of condition for the climb up the mountain, so they argue over who is going to ride the four-wheelers. All and all it takes hours for Sheriff Allen to get the men organized.

The sheriff decides that the four-wheelers will go out and scout the area until they can find a trail or a sign that Sam is still in the area. The rest of the men will scout the area on foot as far as they can go.

Sam is completely covered with snow. The only thing that differentiated him from the surrounding environment is the end of the barrel of the rifle. Sam thinks, "This is perfect camouflage, I couldn't have asked for better luck." Through the night, Sam stays awake, thinking about his life. "I don't mind being alone. I am more productive when I have a partner to help out. If I am a group of three, then I am always the lone man out. I never did have any friends when I was young because I was working all the time on the farm. When I had time to play, it was usually with my brothers, or I'd just go off on my own. I used to like building things or trying out new inventions that never worked. But all in all, what I did when I was a kid made me a better person now. I hated killing those men, but fuck it, they deserved it. It's like killing spiders in your house. I didn't ask them to come to my place a tear shit up, so they had to pay. It's not like hunting. Those animals were just going about their own business, and I went to where they lived and killed them for fun. I can still see the fear and pain in those dying deer. I am happy not to hunt anymore, but if I have to to feed my family, I will. Now I'm a fugitive for the rest of my life. No more rules, yeah. At least those dead bastards won't bother my family or friends. I'll just head to South Dakota when I get done here. That is if I live. I'll travel around. Shit, I got a lot of money. I fucking hate politicians. I wish people would just say what they mean and do what they say. Things would be some much better if that was the case. Politicians are like con artists. They avert your attention elsewhere while they eviscerate you. It makes me so mad that they can stand up there in front of the American people and lie with no consequences. They call that shit politics. You lie to them and they throw you in prison. They do insider trading and make millions. Anyone else does that and it is jail time. Rules are for honest people kind of like locks. Those who follow the rules are incarcerated by them. Those that don't follow rules are protected by them. Those that follow rules and live an honest life still die the same as those that don't. The government tells everyone that too much debt is bad and that those who owe money should tighten their belts, yet the government spends money like a drunken college student in a whorehouse on spring break. If you are late paying taxes, it costs you a fortune with interest and penalties. It's not even the government's money—it's mine to begin with. Politicians spend millions of dollars of both their own money and of funding raising money just to get a job that pays a couple hundred thousand dollars. Then they come out multimillionaires. What the hell did they save their money? Why don't they try to go into business once? Create a product or service and the government is right there to take what they think is their share. Fuck the government and everyone involved with it. The government then says that they are entitled to forty or fifty percent. They also will make all the rules not to help you succeed but to make it harder to make money. Is it really worth it? It is now easier to have nothing than it is to try to make something of yourself. I'll always strive to be better or the best. Still after all these years, I'm not the best at anything. No matter—" Sam snaps out of it when he sees a lot of movement at the bottom of the mountain. That is when the trucks rolled in.

Sheriff Allen and his men are out scouting the area for hours and no one finds anything. They all gathered back at the base camp which is on the logging road.

All the men gather in one spot. Sheriff Allen stands in back of one of the trucks and yells, "Did anyone see anything that would lead you to believe that our fugitive is still here?"

No one person says anything.

"Has anyone been on this mountain before?" Sheriff Allen yells.

One of the men speaks up, "Hunted up here a bit."

"Well then, how would one get out of here if you had to do so? Is there any way out to the highway except the way we came in?" Sheriff Allen asks.

The hunter informs Sheriff Allen, "It would take someone a couple of days in this snow to hike out of here. Too rough out here to four-wheeler it out of here. You could take a horse though. Hell, you can probably get out of here faster if you climb over the top and go down the backside. There is only one trail and it's a hard climb.

I doubt if anyone would go that way. Once on the top, you have to either fly or climb down the cliff in the back."

"Well then, that is where we are going. Show me where this trail is. That's where that dumb bastard went. He will figure no one will know about a trail like that," Sheriff Allen says with excitement.

The four-wheelers start to haul men up to the base of the trail. Sheriff Allen and the hunter are the first ones to the trail. The sheriff notices something hanging on the tree. He takes it down and looks it over, then throws it at the hunter.

"I thought you said no one would go up this way," Sheriff Allen yells. "Why the fuck didn't anyone find this before?"

They go back to the base of the trail and Sheriff Allen gathers the scouting crew together. He tells, "That asshole is up on that peak. We are going to go get him. Who wants to go bring him down?"

Sheriff Allen repeats his question but no one says a word. They all just look around. Sheriff Allen tells all the four-wheeler people, "Take everyone to the mountain base. We will set up camp there and that will be the new base camp. Those that can drive their trucks up there follow along."

At the new base camp, everyone looks up at the trail regretting that they showed up for this manhunt. Sheriff Allen picks out some men to climb. After about an hour, all the men are in position to start climbing. The first group consists of ten men. They are energetic young men that have been doing meth all morning. They are wound tight. They quickly move up the trail. The man that is leading the group up the trail innocently steps on a stick that is lying across the trail. The men in the group hear a noise. They look up to see a large boulder slowly rolling down the trail heading directly at them. They all quickly jump to the side of the trail and let the boulder go on by them. As the boulder moves on by them, two small trees on the sides of trail come with it, sweeping all the men off the sides of the path. The trail is steep and with the snow and ice; it impossible for the men to hold on. They all fall and slide down to the where the boulder stops, which is just above the base of the trail. All the men are injured but none fatally, but none can go on. The ten men are helped to the four-wheelers and are taken back to camp. Tents have been set up for a command center and a chow tent, which is now turned into the medical tent.

Sam sees it all. He says to himself in a low whisper, "That thing worked better than I thought it would. Maybe they will think twice about messing with me and just give up and go home." He laughs a little.

Sheriff Allen is furious that his men are so dumb and careless that they started a rockslide. He doesn't realize that it was a trap set by Sam. He turns to the men and yells, "I need another group of ten men to get up that trail ahead of us and scout it out."

Twelve men yell out that they will go. Poot is one of them.

"I'll lead the men. Y'all wait here and when we get to the top, come on up," Poot says. He slings his AK-47 over his shoulder and chest. He motions the men to move up the trail.

"Don't you guys be stupid and get slapped off the trail like those last dumb asses," Sheriff Allen yells.

Poot turns and gives him the finger to tell him to fuck off and he knows what he is doing.

They move quickly up to where the others had made it too. Poot and another man named Mathew look around and notice that there had been stakes pounded into the ground. They also find the trigger cord that Sam had used in his trap. They all squat down to rest and plan things out.

"That son of bitch set that trap. Shit. We need to keep an eye out for any more traps," Mathew says. "I saw these type of traps used down in El Salvador. They are more deadly down there, usually they would be attached to spear points, saw blades, or a bucket of venomous snakes." Mathew is starting to get scared like he is reliving a nightmare.

"Well, we're not going to see any venomous snakes around here, you jackass, it's winter," Poot says in a condescending voice. "And when the hell were you in El Salvador? You've never been out of this state let alone this country."

"I have too," Mathew says. "My mom and dad were missionaries down there and that is where I was born and raised till I was ten. So go fuck yourself."

"OK, didn't know," Poot says in defense. "Let's get going." Poot motions to the men to get up and get going.

They go another hundred and some yards up the trail, then they all have to sit down and rest again. Poot pulls out his pipe and starts smoking meth, then passes it around among the men. They all took a big hit off it and become energized. Poot puts the pipe away and they all start rushing up the hill. They are moving quickly and carelessly. One of the men grabs a branch that is sticking up in the trail. When he grabs it, two small trees on the side of the trail flipped up, sending some twisted bark cord filled with small sharpened sticks whipping up the hill. Two men are knocked off their feet, sending them falling backward down the trail. Three of the men have legs and arms ripped open, sending blood, tissue and pieces of clothing flying everywhere. They fall to the ground and roll till they get wedged in the rocks alongside of the trail. When the rope whips back, it hits Poot, who is standing next to Mathew. It rips Poot's neck open like chainsaw. He falls and starts rolling down the hill. Blood is spraying everywhere as he falls head over heels down the trail. Mathew just stands there unable to make a sound. He passes out from the site of the blood. He also rolls down the hill until he gets wedged in some rocks. When Mathew hits the rocks, he comes to. He starts sliding down the trail not out of control but not in control. The rest of the men had dove over to the side of the trail and sank down low until the whip had stopped. None of the men move; they just look at each other. Then they see Poot bleeding profusely. All of them at once turn and ran down the trail. Some of them jumping and moving ten feet at a time. Some of them just slide. All of them leave the injured men lying on the trail and in the rocks along the side of the trail. When they reach the group at the bottom of the trail, they collapse. None of them can speak.

"What the fuck happened up there?" Sheriff Allen asks.

"Aahh, aahh, hill, the hill." That is all Mathew could get out of his mouth as he sits on the ground hyperventilating.

"Speak up, now what the hell happened, and where are the rest of the men?" Sheriff Allen screams.

"The hill it's trapped. It's deadly," Mathew mutters after he calms down a little. "Poot is still up there, I think he's dead. The others are probably hurt really badly. It all happened so fast. We didn't even see it happen."

"What kind of trap was it?" the sheriff started shaking Mathew.

"It was some whip thing. I don't fucking know but I'm not going up there again. I quit," Mathew yells.

Everyone is standing around the men that just have come down. Fear comes over the faces of some of the men. They have never signed on to something like this. They just wanted to shoot and have the free rein of the law on their side. Some of them yell, "Yeah, man, I ain't going up there neither."

About twenty-some men get up and say, "I quit," then they start walking out to their trucks.

Sheriff Allen shrugs and throws his arms up. He screams, "What the fuck, this is turning into the biggest cluster fuck that I have ever seen." He turns to the ex-sheriff Tamms. "Can you take some men up the trail and get those men down here so we can get on with this? Christ, is anything going to go right today?"

Sheriff Tamms motions to a group of men. "Let's head out and bring the men down." By the time the group gets up to the men on the trail, two of the men are already up and helping some of the other men. Poot is dead not from the neck wound but from hitting his head on a rock. He hit his head with such force that the rock is still imbedded into his skull when they picked him up off the ground. Tamms and the others start to bring the men down when they hear shots. They all dive up against the rocks and squat down.

The large group of men that are staying surround the small group of men that are leaving. The large group of men starts shoving the men leaving into the center of a large circle. The men in the large group pull their guns on the small group and are just waiting for the command to shoot. The men in the small group also have their weapons drawn and no one is speaking a word. All the men are nervous now. All it would take is one shot to send it into another OK Corral showdown. Sheriff Allen yells, "Just let those chicken shits go. We don't need them. It's only one man, not an army."

Sam is watching through his scope. He sees how the crowd has gathered. He has seen this before outside a street dance. A bunch of guys surround him and his friends. No one was willing to take the first swing. Then someone from outside of the rumbling groups threw a beer can into the circle, then all hell broke loose. Sam figures that this might be all these guys need. He scopes in on one of the four-wheelers and fires one round. He hits the gas tank and gas begins to leak out. He fires another round at the ground, under the four-wheeler. The round hits a rock, which causes a spark. The spark ignites the gas. The fire quickly reaches the four-wheelers gas tank and causes it to explode. As soon as the explosion happens, a gunfight brakes out. Men are shooting all directions. Bullets and blood is flying everywhere. Men are dropping like tall grass being cut down by a weed eater. The only thing the sheriff could do is to take cover. He knows the gunfight will just have to play out. He will just have to pick up the pieces when it is all done. As Sam watches, he can only think that it all looks like a scene out of an action movie. It plays out better than any trap he could have set except for his final finally.

The gunfight lasts only a few minutes. No one moves for another five minutes until the sheriff yells, "Are y'all done?" No one answers, so he yells again, "I'm going to come out and no one better fire another shot." Sheriff Allen stands and looks around. There are men littered across the ground. Blood and flesh covers the ground like sprinkles on icing. Sheriff Allen shakes his head. He is very disappointed and embarrassed that he has such incompetent men.

Men start coming out from hiding. Some of them walk over to check out who is dead and who is alive. Sheriff Allen takes a quick count of how many men are still alive. Sheriff Allen radios to the command center, "Send all the four-wheelers up here and start hauling men and bodies down. Then call for ambulance service and get them out here immediately."

"How many ambulances do you think you might need?" the man at the command center asks.

"All of them! Every single ambulance or truck or anything that can haul men to the hospital. There are about fifty to sixty men down. Some dead, some wounded," Sheriff Allen says with great anxiety. He knows that the media will get ahold of this and they will be out here nosing around. He knows there will be a lot of paperwork and investigation into what he really is doing out here. All he can say is "Shit, shit, shit." He doesn't know how he is going to justify spending thousands of dollars and all these casualties chasing someone. He doesn't even have an arrest warrant. He should have let it go, but he hates Sam. He knows that Bill's wife is the one that killed Bill. Now he is going to have to make a fake warrant or just catch him and get rid of him.

The ambulances take a long time to reach the entrance to the mountain. They could not get to the base camp because of the snow so all the men had to be taken out on sleds. It takes hours before all the men are brought out and now the sun is going down. The media trucks are all parked along the road, so it makes it easy for the sheriff to avoid any questions. He figures that he will handle everything tomorrow when they have gotten rid of Sam. Sheriff Allen tells everyone that is left to bunk down in their trucks or in the tents. That night the temperature drops into the teens, and all the men are complaining about the conditions and lack of food. Most of them, though, have enough alcohol with them that they drink themselves to sleep.

Sam is getting really stiff and sore from not moving for so long. He figured that they would be slowly coming up but not this slow. He starts to debate whether to stay or leave. It will take them all day tomorrow to get up the trail, or they will probably just get a helicopter to fly them up here. Sam figures that they may even give up. By now, most men would be long gone. Sam decides to wait it out, just to see what will happen next. He thinks it is a little sadistic but he really doesn't have much going on this time of the year. Sam is glad that he had worn his newly designed clothes. It is cold out but he is warm, warm enough that he decides that he will sleep for a few hours.

Morning comes and Sam is still sleeping. He is quickly awakened by the sound of a helicopter overhead. Sam opens his eyes. It is difficult to see through the clouds. Visibility is only about twenty feet. Sam can't understand how any idiot would fly in this weather;

maybe it is military. The military fly around this area all the time. The helicopter comes and goes, so he quits worrying. He is mad at himself for sleeping so long. Someone could have sneaked in on him and he would have never heard them. He always hated getting up in the morning, so he should have known better. Sam reaches into his pack and grabs an energy bar and a bottle of water. Sam thinks, "Aaahh, breakfast of champions. This is the best I'm going to get while running, so I had better get used to it."

Sheriff Allen and his men are up and getting ready to move to the bottom of the trail. He has called for a helicopter earlier that morning, but when they fly over, they cannot see anything. The helicopter returns to the airport until the visibility changes. Sheriff Allen decides that he will bring men in from the top and the bottom. He has sent a small team up before dark so that they can clear the way by the time he gets the rest of the men to the trail.

The small six-man team is led by the ex-sheriff Cecil Tamms. Tamms has a feeling that Sam is still on the mountain, and if Sam is there, he is going to get him. The team is very cautious as they move up the trail. No one touches anything that looks out of the ordinary. Movement is slow. It takes them two hours just to reach the point where Poot and the men had run into the trap. Ex-sheriff Tamms and the men rest there and look up. The top of the mountain is still not viable. They look around and see the braided rope that took out the other men. They all thought that no one would have seen that and even if they had, they probably wouldn't have realized that it was of any danger. After a short break, they get up and start moving up the trail. One of the men spots a branch sticking up in the middle of the trail. The last team said that the trap was sprung when one of them grabbed a stick. Everyone moves around the branch in the middle of the trail like they are avoiding a coiled rattlesnake. They step out on to the side of the trail on both sides. As soon as they get about five yards, a stick snaps they all look at each other. The guy that stepped on the stick says, "Fuck, fuck." Four small trees spring up about ten yards ahead of them, two on both sides of the trail. Sharpened sticks fly through the air, like a volley of arrows. They fly straight at the men on both sides of the trail. The arrows shower the men. All the men are hit, some in the legs, some in the chest; Tamms is hit in the chest, neck, and leg. None of the men can move. All they can do is scream.

Sam had placed the branch in the center of the trail gambling on that after the first two traps were triggered, the branch would steer the men off the trail. The trees were too far from the trail to make an effective trap on the trail, but on the sides he had many options.

Sheriff Allen can hear the men screaming from where he is standing. He just stands there and stares up the trail. He thinks that it is not worth any more men. All he has left are the drunks and meth junkies. As he stands there, he turns and looks at the men, and says to himself, "What the hell, these guys die and no one will give a shit. Payroll will be cheaper." Then he yells down to the men, "I want twenty men up that trail now. Ten of you bring down whoever needs to come down and the rest keep going up the trail. Now move it."

The men look at each other, like "I'm not going up there." Finally twenty of the men built up enough courage to go up the trail. When they reach Tamms's group, only one man is dead and that is Tamms. Tamms's wounds from the arrows had lacerated his carotid artery. He may not had died if he would have left the arrow were it was. When he pulled the arrow, the frayed edges lacerated the artery. None of the other men are in critical condition but they cannot make it down the trail, so they have to be carried down. It takes all the twenty men that went up to get the injured down.

Sheriff Allen is furious, he had told them that half were to come down and half proceed up. He looks up the mountain and decides that the visibility is good enough to get a helicopter up there. He calls the chopper pilot and tells him to stop at the base camp and pick up five men. Then he picks five of his best men, including ex–deputy sheriff Trevor to wait for pick up. He rounds up the rest of the men and has them all head up the trail. This time all the men are going and if anyone else is injured they will just have to wait till the descent. The men slowly move up the trail. Sam didn't have time to set any other traps except for his grand finally. He had thought that they would have come after him quicker.

Sam thinks it is time to leave but first he wants to make sure that they keep coming after him. He figures by now they will have sent a helicopter to the top because the sky is clear and warm. The sun is melting the snow and he is now uncovered but still camouflaged. As Sam watches the men timidly struggle up the trail, some stopping every five or ten feet, he hears a helicopter. Sam almost cheers. He can see it come into view and then descend down at their base camp. Sam decides that it was time to get his stuff together so that if he has to leave fast, he can. The other men are only about halfway up the trail when the helicopter takes off. The helicopter rises slowly and comes straight for the top of the mountain. Sam watches it circle a few times. He can see that there are five men and the pilot aboard. Sam thinks, "I wish I had my helicopter right now. It could chase this one down. I bet Sarah is a better pilot then this pilot." Sam chambers a round and takes aim. He follows the tail rotor of the helicopter. The helicopter circles and then goes into a hoover as it set to land. Sam fires and hits the tail rotor. The rotor starts wobbling and helicopter starts shaking. The pilot quickly turns the helicopter back toward base camp to try to quickly land it before crashes. Sam quickly packs the rest of his gear, puts on his parachute, then runs and dives off the cliff. Sam throws his pilot chute and the main quickly opens. Sam grabs his steering toggles and pilots his chute to the clearing he had picked out previously. He lands little hard but still safe. He is really overloaded with all his gear. He gets up from the ground and packs his chute again. Sam's adrenaline is flowing. He always loved skydiving but BASE jumping scared the hell out of him.

The pilot lands the helicopter safely. He radios Sheriff Allen, "That son of a bitch shot my rotor. I can't fly this damn thing until it gets fixed. even then, I'm not going back up there. So go get him yourself or get someone else to fly up there."

"You chicken shit! Get me another chopper out here right away and get my men up there or else," Sheriff Allen screams. He is furious.

"You don't pay me enough to go back up there and I'm not going to tell anyone else to fly up there and then get shot at. You call them, you shit head bastard," the pilot screams back.

"Screw you," Sheriff Allen screams. "We'll be to the top in another twenty minutes and then we'll get rid of this pest once and for all. So you can just stay put, you fucking pussy."

Sheriff Allen continues on up the hill. All his men are ahead of him and pushing hard up the trail.

Sam is back at his four-wheeler and stows his gear. He starts it up and takes out his cellphone. "Darwin, I'm back on the four-wheeler."

"Yeah, I know where you are," Darwin says. "Is everything all right?"

"How the hell do you know where I'm at? I turned my phone off," Sam asks.

"I put a tracking device in that new suit of yours," Darwin says as he laughs.

"Oh, well, that's a little creepy, but I need directions to the road and I need someone to pick me up. I'm going to lie low in South Dakota for a while," Sam says.

"OK, I'll call Carol and tell her that you are OK. I'll feed you direction through the phone so push the download button as soon as it beeps. Can you do that?" Darwin knows Sam doesn't know anything about computers or his phone.

"OK, OK, I got it," Sam says. Sam drives through the woods on an old logging trail toward the main highway. He hopes that Darwin will get him directions soon. Just then, the phone beeps. Sam pushes a few buttons and the GPS route comes up. Sam drives on, thinking about what will happen when the men reach the top. Sam's mind races and then the phone rings.

"Oh, Sam, I forgot to tell you. That sheriff really doesn't have a warrant for your arrest. They are already looking for Joy. They suspected that she did it. Also, all those guys that you shot, none of it was even reported. No one even knows any of this ever happened," Darwin informs him.

"What! I shot two of them in the head?" Sam is mind-boggled.

"You didn't shoot anyone in the head. No one is dead according to them," Darwin says. "I'll keep you informed. Carol is going to call you. She said that she can't pick you up because someone has been following her. Bud is following the people that are following her. Harland is going to pick you up. Talk to you later," Darwin says.

"See ya," Sam says. Now his mind is really troubled. Those guys are going to the top of the mountain to kill me and what is waiting for them is total annihilation if they are stupid and don't get off the mountain fast enough. "Shit, I left a note telling them to leave quickly because I am sure that they had tripped the trigger for the top of the mountain to explode. So if they don't leave, I'm not responsible," Sam thinks. He was worried. "Why should I worry? They are the one's trying to kill me. They started this war."

Sheriff Allen and his men reach the top of the mountain. One of the men runs over and hands the sheriff a note, "Get off this mountain right now. You have fifteen minutes before it explodes." He throws down the letter and yells to everyone to get off the mountain immediately. Men start running down the trail, and Sheriff Allen is the last one to leave. As he is heading down the trail, the three homemade claymores explode. Rocks shower down upon the men and trees are ripped to shreds. Not one of the men gets down the trail without getting injured. Some of the men are hit by rocks and splintered trees. Some of them get injured from men falling on other men. No one dies, but there is no YUPPI gang left on the mountain.

CHAPTER TWENTY-FOUR

AFTER THE INVESTIGATION IN TO the incident, the sheriff and his deputies are put on suspension FBI finds several problems with the department and a new Sheriff and deputies are hired by the fusion center.

The fusion centers are placed all across the United States. They are built and maintained by the federal government supposedly for quick response to terrorism. There is no department in the federal government that controls these centers and there for they operate without impunity. The council of governors consists of ten people. This council was established by executive order by the president, in this case, Barrack. They are to strengthen federal and state governments control over the National Guard and other military matters. In other words, synchronize government control over the people without any checks or balances going through congress. The government can do what they want with any military action or militia.

Darwin has been looking in the council of governors and the fusion centers. He finds the trail of money. Money comes from a bunch of pork barrel spending projects that never happened. Projects are tied in with social security budget, child welfare budgets, and other bills. They are not funded directly because then the congress can defund them. They are also funded through OCORC until they themselves were defunded. Now they receive money through the drug enforcement department and some from the hidden OCORC budget that Sam has been slowly taking away from them.

Harland picks Sam up along Interstate 64 a day later. He had to wait until no one was watching before picking up Sam.

Sam drives his Polaris up into the bed of the truck and they head to South Dakota.

Sam calls Carol, "How is everything going?"

"Fine, how are you?" Carol asks in a concerned voice. She knew he is all right; otherwise, he wouldn't be calling now.

"Good, we are on our way. I don't know when I will see you again but I hope it is soon," Sam says. He really hasn't seen Carol all that much over the last year. They hadn't ever taken a vacation together, not even a honeymoon. Sam knows that they are long over do for some travel time but not right now.

"Stay safe, baby. I'll be OK here with the boys watching," Carol says.

"I'll be all right. Did Bud confront your secret admirer?" Sam asks.

"He did. The guy followed me up to the house the other night. Bud and Kota grabbed both guys and took them away. I'm not sure what they did with them but no one is following me anymore," Carol says. She isn't surprised that the guys aren't back and she really didn't want to know what happened. She is sure that the boys didn't kill them, but they probably did something horrible to scare them.

"Well, good. I'll call you when we get to where we are going. Love you and be careful," Sam says and then hangs up.

Carol knows she can always find Sam; all she has to do is ask Darwin where to find him.

Sam calls DH and tells him that they should expect him in about twenty hours. DH tells him that he has a surprise for him when he gets there. Sam takes over the driving when it gets dark. Harland was driving like an old lady and kept trying to fall asleep.

Sam pulls into his parents' place the next afternoon. He is glad to see his mother and sister, but he has to leave right after he takes a shower and changes clothes. He knows if anyone is looking for him they will be watching his parents' place. It always baffled Sam why people running from the law are stupid enough to go home or to a girlfriend's home or to their parents' place. But most criminals are stupid.

Sam hugs his mom before he leaves, and Harland drives Sam over to the other farm place where the bunker is being built. DH meets them at the end of the driveway. Sam looks around and sees that the whole place has a huge wall around it. It is in the cover of trees, so from the road you cannot see it till you get to the gate. DH jumps in the back of the truck and Harland drives in. The whole place looks great. The barn looks like it did when Sam was a kid. The house has been totally remodeled. No more tents. There is only two areas where there are men still working. One is on the hill and the other is down in the pasture. The hill is about finished except for some excavating work.

Sam and Harland get out of the truck and stretch. Sam reaches out and shakes DH's hand, "Damn, DH, the place looks great."

"Well, thanks, Sam. We haven't been slacking any since you been gone. I told you I'd get this place into shape fast," DH says with a smile and a whole bunch of pride.

"You reckon you got a beer for us somewhere around here. I know it's cold, but I sure could use one," Sam says.

"Hell yeah. Come into the house and we'll get you a beer and something to eat. I hope you don't mind that we moved into the house. We got tired of sleeping in the tents, so once the house was done we moved in," DH says.

"I don't mind. My grandparents wouldn't have turned you down for shelter and a meal. So let's go in and I'll tell you all about what is happening in Virginia," Sam says and then slaps DH on the back. They all head up to the house. Bobby and Tom run up to the three of them and then shake Harland's and Sam's hand.

"Good to see y'all again," Bobby says. "Harland can I take your keys and fill your truck up with diesel? Are you leaving the four-wheeler on or you do want us to take it off and have Skids clean it up for you?"

"Take it off for now. It's been through some hell lately," Sam says. They all go into the house. Bobby takes the truck and drives off.

"DH this place looks great. It looks just like when my grandparents lived here with a few added luxuries. Wow, this just like the old table that was here. And the two buckets of water on the cart, how the hell did you know about this?" Sam asks with almost giddiness. He waltzes through the house like he is a little kid again.

"We got some pictures from your mom. Then we went from there. We added some stuff but it's close," DH says then goes to the refrigerator and grabs some beers.

Sam drinks his beer down like a man dying of thirst. DH hands him another one. Sam tells DH the whole story of how everything went down in Virginia. Harland sits and listens with a little pride like it is his son telling the story. When Sam is about done with his story, a woman comes into the kitchen. Sam has not seen her before.

"What would you guys like to eat? I can fix you just about anything you like," she asks.

They all agree on omelets. Then the woman goes to work.

"She is our chef. We had to fire the caterers because they started spreading rumors around town about what we were doing out here," DH explains. "Her name is Karissa. She was an out-of-work single mother. I hope you don't mind?"

"I'd done the same thing," Sam says and then eats his meal quickly. Harland is eating slowly so DH takes Sam and shows him around some more.

They go down to the basement. Sam was always afraid of the basement when he was a kid. Now the basement looks like the inside of a posh office building. They then go through a small door that is hidden behind a wine rack. They come out into another room that has two exits.

"This one takes you to the wall and you can go all the way around the property," DH explains as he points to the right and then to the left. "This one we will take and it goes to the garage and machine shop first and then you can go to the rest of the bunker from the shop. There are five tunnels and you can get anywhere from the shop. I know it's a downfall but the house connection was an afterthought."

DH and Sam walks in the shop. All the troop carriers and trucks are parked in there. There are four-wheelers, motorcycles, and golf carts. Sam and DH jump into the golf cart and head down one tunnel. Sam is amazed how well it looks. It doesn't look like a damp dark tunnel but more like going down a well-lit hall in a house. They stop and climb a spiral staircase.

"We are now in the barn if you can't guess," DH says with a little laugh. "The vault is inside this old grain bin that we modified a bit." They walk in and DH pushes an old wooden lever. Then part of the floor opens up to the reveal the vault door. DH climbs down and unlocks the door. Sam and DH climb down into the vault.

"Still got stacks and stacks of money," DH says. "We even paid all the contractors their bonus for getting done so soon." Sam just nods. Then they climb out, lock up, and get back into the golf cart. They turn around and head down another tunnel and stop. DH gets out and opens a door. On the other side of the door are the living quarters. DH gets back on the golf cart and they drive around. The place is very large much like the ground floor of a fancy hotel. It makes the garage look small. As they move through tunnels and hall-ways, Sam sees all of that other people have moved in while he was gone. They proceed to the large food storage area.

"I put enough no perishable food in to feed a five hundred peo-ple for at least fifteen years. We can keep track of the stock by the computer, so if anything is going out of date, it will be found and replaced," DH explains. Sam just looks around in amazement.

DH then takes the golf cart down another tunnel. "This is where the armory is," DH says. "It is far enough away from every-thing, so if it does blow up, it won't affect anything else."

"Looks great," Sam says sincerely.

Then they go on their way down another tunnel. "Everything is logged into a computer so we can keep track of stock. I have all ammunition stocked for world war three if we need it," DH explains as they drive along. "Now this is what my surprise is." DH stops and they both walk up to a door. DH opens it. The door opens to a really small closet-size room that has a door in the floor. DH grabs a headlight that is hanging in the small room. He puts it on and hands one to Sam. Sam puts the headlight on as DH opens the door in the floor. They climb on to an elevator that looks like an old dumb waiter. They go down several hundred feet. When it stops, they make their way through a tight cave area. They are now about three to four hundred feet underground. They make their way to an opening and soon they are standing on the shore of a huge underground lake. The walls just sparkled from all the quartz lining the walls. The rock ceiling looks like a cathedral with abnormal rock formations jetting down from a sparkling heaven.

Sam stands there in awe. Goose bumps formed on his arms and tears welled up in his lower eyelids just before they joined the millions of tears in the lake. The sight of this place brought back memories of childhood dreams. Sam could not speak. He is trying to choke back the tears so that he did not show any weakness.

DH looks at Sam. He slaps Sam's back and says with a whisper, "I know. That's the same reaction I had when I saw it for the first time."

Sam turns and wipes his eyes on his sleeves. He asks, "How the hell did you find this place?"

"Well, when we were digging, I wanted to put a well inside the bunker. The drill hit an opened area and it just fell in the big crack in the ground. Kim and Whiskers decided to dig a little, and then they went exploring and found it. This is such a great place," DH explains. "Everyone wanted to go swimming in it, but it is strictly off-limits. This is clean fresh water, pure water that will last a lifetime."

"This place is amazing. This is huge underground aquifer. Some days we should find out where it runs too, but for now we will keep it from contamination. I think we just need to keep the opening locked up like you have it." Sam says.

"Yes, I think so," DH says, "Let's get out of here and we can discuss some plans of what we are going to do with that Iowa YUPPI gang."

They take the elevator up and get back on the golf cart. DH takes the long way around inside the wall. They come out at the basement of the house. Then they go upstairs. Harland is up there drinking beer and telling stories to Bobby, Tom, and Karissa.

"Harland you got to take a tour. It is amazing," Sam says.

"Yes, you do! And Tom and I are going to give it to you," Bobby says with excitement.

Then the three of them go off on tour. Sam and DH stay and drink some more beer. DH gives Sam the lowdown on all the surveillance and the plan that he has come up with.

"Well, we will probably need more men," Sam says.

"I called all those guys and about twenty-six of them are going to be coming," DH says. "We'll have plenty of men to get the job done. They are all retired military. Some are ex–special forces. They know how to handle themselves and I offered them all the same deal as what we gave the others."

"Great, when will they be ready?" Sam asks as he downs another beer.

"By the end of this week they will all be here. We can go this weekend that is when these guys go party," DH says. "They'll be drunk till Monday."

"Good, we'll get it all set up when they get here but for now, we just need to relax," Sam says. "Spending those few days in the woods was pretty fun but very tiring. It was good to get out and spend some time all alone. It just lets you think long and hard about everything." Sam drinks down his beer.

DH goes over to the freezer and takes out a bottle of tequila. Then he goes to the cupboard and grabs two shot glasses. "Well, what did you think about while you were out there?" DH sets down the two shot glasses and fills them up.

"I've come to the conclusion that I am going to take a break from veterinary medicine for a while," Sam says as they both raise their glasses, and then they drink their tequila in one swallow. DH pours another round. "After all this shit that has happen with these YUPPI groups and the fucking government run amuck, I'm tired of them ruling my life. I want to destroy all their secret drug labs and take all that we can take from them."

"Well, we have a good start. Why not just finish it," DH says as he throws back another shot of tequila and then Sam follows with his tequila.

"I don't think we even began to scratch the surface with all this shit. I would bet that there is a lot more of these YUPPI groups are out there. We need Darwin to track this stuff down. Maybe if we can get a hold of more hard drives, we can find all of them," Sam says as he pours another round.

"We'll soon have enough men. If you got the time, I'm sure the men will follow if we don't screw up to much," DH says just before throwback another shot. He takes a drink of beer.

All the men and women living in the bunker come up into the kitchen of the house. The party starts for the night. Sam stays up for only a few minutes and then heads off to bed. He hadn't gotten much sleep over the last few days. Sleep will be best for now.

Two days later and Sam is completely rested. He actually felt good for once. It had been a long time since he is not tired and worn-out.

The new men show up at the bunker one at a time. The bunker is like the street in front of the red carpet at the Academy Awards. When one man drives up, Bobby or Tom take their vehicle and park it inconspicuously in the trees. Sam has the new people gather in the shop area as they arrived. By nightfall they all have arrived. Sam and DH go over the usual swear in one at a time. Then Sam gives everyone, all at one time, his lowdown on what they are about to do. Many of the men are reluctant to want to go through with his plan until Kim comes in.

Kim has way of handling military men. When Kim went into the marines, it was quickly recognized that he was a leader and a fighting man. They made him a platoon leader. During his time in the marines, he was always getting into trouble because he was not afraid of anything. He would attack when there was danger, and he would not take any slack from his men. Then while on patrol in some kind of war games, he forced a man to finish the hike that they were on. A marine officer thought that this was cruel, so they took away as a platoon leader. Kim never did mind and it really didn't slow him down much. He came home from Desert Storm with a fist full of medals and a new appreciation on how to get things done.

Kim straightens out the situation. Those that don't want to be there are told to leave. Two men get up and voice their opposition to stealing from the government.

Sam stands up. He is mad now at not only those two but at his self for not being a better judge of character. "First we are not stealing from the government because these groups don't exist. They are all drug dealers and murders. We have seen them kill people without any hesitation," Sam says in an angry voice. "Second, you two leave me no option except to make you both disappear. You know too much now."

The two men's faces turn white; they are in a very bad position. The two men are not ex-infantry, one had been a mechanical engineer, and the other had been in communications. Neither of the men had shot or fought since they had been in basic training.

"I am not disagreeing that you should not do it, but only that I cannot do it," the communications guy says trying to back pedal out of a bad situation. "I have never shot at a man, nor do I think I could shoot a man. I do communications. That's all I have ever done. I don't think I would be useful to you in a fight."

"Well, I may not have to bury you two, but maybe we can just put you both in a vault," Sam says jokingly as he looks at Kim and laughs. "Really, you two, I am not crazy and I would not kill you or anyone really. If you guys want to go, you can. If you want to stay, you both can work here in the bunker. We always need good men. You can set up a communication system along with my intelligence person. You two can talk later. We also need a mechanical engineer when we add on to the bunker. You can work with DH."

The other men are relieved that no one is going to die right away, so they start laughing. The two men then start laughing along with them.

"Well, what do you two want to do? It's now or never," Sam asks.

"I will gladly work in the bunker," the communications man says.

"And, I also," the engineer says.

"Good, then is everyone happy? If not, speak now or forever speak no disdain to our group or anyone here," Sam says.

Everyone looks around and no one says anything. Sam looks around to see that everyone looking satisfied and then says, "Well then, we will eat and drink tonight and tomorrow we will go to work."

Friday comes very quickly. The new men are still trying to settle into the bunkers accommodations. The living area is very comfortable but it is underground. There is no sound except from those that reside in the bunker. A man could fall asleep in the bunker and wake up days later without a clue if it is night or day.

Sam has Sarah fly him over the target area. There is very little activity going on in the area; only one car goes out of the target area. Sarah flies down to get a better view of the vehicle. Sam uses his binoculars to get a look at the license plate number. He knows that this is the vehicle that they are going to hit tonight. Sam texts Darwin to get an address of the person driving the vehicle and Darwin texts him back within minutes. Sam has Sarah drop him off at the tree line along cornfield and the small hill that overlooks the target area. He grabs his gear and then Sarah flies off. Sam calls into the bunker and gets the new communications guy on the radio. Sam sent the texted address of the vehicle to the guy.

"Hey, first what is your name?" Sam asks. He is tired of calling the man "Hey, you."

"Josh Carlson at your service. How may I help you? Ha!" Josh says jokingly.

"Well, Josh, get Kim, DH, and Harland on the radio," Sam says in a calm authoritative voice.

"I'll have them here in a jiffy," Josh says.

Within a few minutes, Josh radios Sam back. "They're here Sam."

"OK, here is the plan. I want Kim and two men to go and stir up some trouble with the person driving the car that came out of the target area. I texted the address and all the information you need. Make sure that they call into this IOWA captain for help so that some of those men leave. Harland and DH split the men into three groups. Pick out four of the best snipers and arm them with something that will stop an armored Hummer. The three groups need to move in from three entry points and make their way to through the buildings. I want one of you guys in each of the teams. Kim can come back right away after these guys leave from here. That way, Kim, you can lead a team. I will stay here and watch in case they decide to leave early. I want the teams sitting no farther than two miles out. Look at the map and find a place where everyone can stay until these guys move. When I call in, I want Sarah to watch them from the sky. If they head back this way, I want to know sooner than later. Now here is the kicker—don't let any of them get liquored up before this all happens. They can have fun after," Sam tells them.

"We'll get everyone going right now," Kim says. "What vehicles do you want us to use?"

"Bring what you want but don't make it look like some fucking convoy. Be a little incognito," Sam says.

"OK, we are gone," Kim says.

Kim grabs his two brothers and heads to Larchwood, Iowa, to find the person with the car. Kim knows Larchwood fairly well because he and Sam used to buck out horses there. They used to know about everyone. Kim quickly finds the car parked in an alley behind one of the bars just outside of town. The town is fairly small and only a few places that most people will hang out. Kim tells his brothers to stay in the truck and watch the car while he goes into the bar. Kim walks in to the bar. Once inside the door a middle-aged woman that looks like she has done way too many drugs in her lifetime says to Kim, "That is ten-dollar cover and there is a two-drink minimum."

Kim looks at her in disgust and a little pity. "I'm not staying and I'm not drinking."

She scoffs and says, "Listen, Mister COWBOY MAN! I just work here and it's ten dollars. Just pay and go see the ladies."

Kim looks at her as he hands over ten dollars and says, "I guess there is no arguing with stupid."

She takes his money and tells Kim, "You have to leave your hat here."

Kim just walks away and steps inside the door. He does a quick surveillance of the room. He is shocked to see that it has been turned into a strip club. He and Sam used to go to the bar on Friday nights for dances. Now it is a low-end strip club. Kim looks around, and there are only a few guys in the bar. There is a moderately overweight tattooed woman dancing completely naked on stage. Kim shakes his head and walks up to the bar.

"Do you know who owns the old orange Camaro outside in the back?" Kim asks the bartender.

"Uhm, what do ya what to know for?" the bartender asks as he leans on the bar with both hands. He tries to flex what little biceps that he has.

Kim looks the bartender over and thinks, "He thinks he is the tough guy in the bar. He probably had thrown out a few little dirtbags out the door. The guys probably were touching some of the girls and the bartender probably took it on himself to be the bouncer. He probably thinks of the girls as being all his."

"I just need to see that person," Kim says.

"I could tell ya but ya know, then I might have to kill ya," the bartender says with a sinister smile on his face.

"Well, you could try," Kim says with a straight face, "and if you don't, I'll beat it out of you."

"Well, asshole, I don't know whose car it is, so get the fuck out of here before I throw you out," the bartender says as he is backing away from the bar. He stands there with his arms crossed.

"OK! Just tell whoever's car it is that it is on fire." Kim leans over the bar. "You got that tough guy."

The bartender's eyes get big but he just stands there. Kim walks around to the back of the bar. He grabs a bottle of vodka and turns to walk away. The bartender grabs him by the shoulders and tries to pull him back. Kim quickly turns around and head-butts the bartender in the face. Blood erupts from the bartender's nose. He staggers back a little until he drops to his knees bleeding from his broken nose and only semiconscious. Kim just turns and walks out of the bar. He walks around to the alley. Bobby and Tom see Kim walk around to the back of the bar, so they get out and follow him. He opens the driver side door. He pours some vodka on and in to the cameo. He finds a jacket in the front seat of the car and rips a piece of cloth off it. Kim asks Bobby for a lighter, then he stuffs the rag into the bottle. Bobby digs a lighter out of his pocket and lights the rag. Kim let it burn for a little bit and then smashes the bottle against the window of the car.

The man who owns the Camaro is dressed in full biker apparel, including biker chaps, boots, and gloves. He has "SLAYER" tattooed on his neck along with several other face and neck tattoos. He and the bartender come running out through the back door of the bar.

"What the fuck are you doing to my car?" Slayer screams as he runs straight at Kim.

Kim doesn't say a word. He just throws a punch and Slayer's face meets Kim's fist. Slayer's face appears to explode in blood. Then he falls to the ground dazed but not unconscious. The bartender moves toward Kim, but Bobby tackles him. Bobby had been a very good wrestler in high school, and he is able to quickly hold down the bartender in a chokehold. Kim goes through the biker's pockets and finds the keys to the car. He opens the trunk, inside is a spare tire, a bunch of clothes and a couple of knives. Kim and Tom throw out all the junk out of the trunk. At the bottom under the carpet is a locked lid. Kim looks under the car and sees that there is a box attached to the bottom truck. Kim goes through the keys on the key chain and then opens the box. Inside box is a 9-mm. Sig, thirty thousand dollars in cash, and a large bag of crystal meth. Kim takes it all and then gives it to Tom. Tom puts it in to the truck. Then Kim opens up the passenger side car door. The fire has burned out and never made it to the inside of the car. Tom and Kim look through the car. Tom finds that the backseat lifts up and underneath is two AA12s, a stainless steel automatic 12-gauge shotgun. There are five thirty-round clips and about fifteen thousand dollars and more crystal meth. Kim takes everything and gives it to Tom who throws it into the truck. Then he runs back to help out.

Slayer is now sitting up. Then he wipes the blood off his face with his shirt. He looks up at Kim. "You asshole, you're going to pay for this. Do you know who I am?"

Kim smiles and gives a little laugh. "I don't know who you are, but I do know what you are and what you are going to do."

"Fuck you. I ain't doing anything for you," Slayer yells as he pulls out his phone. "You bastards are going to pay for this shit. I never forget a face."

Slayer makes a call to one of the guys in the Iowa YUPPI group, "Listen up, piss ant! Some fucking guys are here taking the entire inventory and they are fucking burning my fucking car."

The Iowa YUPPI on tells him in a panic, "AAHHH! Stop them and I'll get the captain on it right away. What is your location?"

"I'z behind the fucking stripper bar in Larchwood," Slayer screams. "Right where I'a always is."

They both hang up the phone. The Iowa YUPPI runs back and fills his captain in on what is happening.

Kim takes the keys to the car and throws them into a Dumpster in the back of the bar. Kim and Tom start walking toward the truck. Bobby lets the bartender go after giving him kick in the ribs. Then he joins Kim and Tom, who are already in the truck. Kim drives away and heads for the rendezvous point.

Sam radios DH, "Their on the move. I see about thirty men in two vans and one Hummer. They are just going out the gate and will be out of sight in about three minutes."

"Got it Sam," DH says. "Kim and the two brothers are back here. They have a little treat for you when we get back. The team is leaving in five minutes. They'll signal when they get there. ETA fifteen minutes."

"OK, out," Sam says. Sam looks to see if there is any activity in the target area. No one is stirring but he knows there are more men. He had seen a couple of them go back inside. He doesn't think that this leader is stupid enough to bring all his men on one stupid distress call. Sam just watches until his team gets there.

Fifteen minutes on the button, Sam sees men moving in the brush across the compound. Sam hears some rustling to his right. He moves slowly through the brush to see who it is. Sam moves in close enough to see only a bump in the fallen leaves but no movement. Sam waits. Then he sees one part of the bump move. Sam knows it is a man who is well camouflaged, but he cannot tell if it is one of his men. They had not radioed as of yet. Sam moves slowly at a snail's pace, trying not rustle any vegetation that he is crawling in. He gets close enough to the camouflaged man so that if it is not one of his, he can easily get the jump on him. Sam slowly draws out his tomahawk and gets ready. He then whispers on the radio, "You here?"

"Yes," DH radios back.

"Tell all our men to move their left hand," Sam whispers on the radio.

A few seconds later, the camouflaged man raises his right hand.

"Hey, Sam here," Sam says loud enough for a person sitting next to him to hear.

The camouflaged man quickly turns. Sam leaps forward to take him out if he is not recognizable. The man draws his weapon but not before Sam grabs the guy's hand and has the tomahawk inches from his throat.

"Hey, Sam. You spooked me," the guy says calmly and quietly. "It's me, Ben."

"Ben, you have great camouflage. I just had to make sure you are one of us," Sam says calmly and quietly. "Now I'm going to move down to the buildings as soon as the teams move in. I need you guys to keep in touch with everyone. You got your radio?"

Ben points to his earpiece. "OK, Sam, they'll radio up here as soon as everything is secure. I'll keep an eye on everything, and if anything changes, you'll know."

"Don't let anyone sneak up on you again," Sam said jokingly. "Oh, and your left hand is the other one."

Ben looks at Sam a little funny but then he smiles. "I won't. It has just been a long time," Ben says and then continues on scoping out the area. A great sniper is a very observant person. They can tell if a rock is out of place. They make great surveillance people. Not only can they see changes, but they can hold off a large group of men.

The three teams move into the compound quickly and with professionalism. They move into all three buildings. Each person follows the leader. Each building has an inside the door guard, which all three group leaders take out it the butt of the rifle. The other men in the building are unarmed and stunned at the sight of anyone crashing through the front doors of their heavily armed compound. The three teams take twenty-two men prisoners. Not a shot is fired and only a handful of the prisoners are injured.

DH radios Sam, "We have secured the buildings."

"I'm already on my way," Sam says as he is making his way into the compound. "Tell your men not to shoot me."

"Got it." DH radios the other men and informs them that Sam is on his way in.

Sam goes into the compound. He walks up to the first building. The first building has six armored Hummers, one Stryker personal carrier, four heavy trucks, several small trailers, and one Ferrari. The whole shop is filled with spare parts, tools, and everything that is ever needed in a shop.

Many of Sam's men are standing around staring at the Ferrari. Some of them are fighting over who is going to get the Ferrari. Sam looks over at the new men and thinks, "They are way too hungry for things. They are greedy or I don't know, but shit, this is not good. This was kind of a test and they kind of passed, but shit. This can't keep happening. What if they start really fighting? Shit won't get done. I really don't need men that want things. That is why I pay them a hell of a salary."

"OK, men, load up all the parts and tools that you can in two of the heavy trucks and a couple of trailers," Sam says sternly. "Harland, you make sure it gets done." Sam turns to walk out of the building.

"OK, Sam," Harland says.

Sam hears some of the men arguing. Sam turns and asks very loudly, "What the hell is the problem?"

"Who gets the Ferrari?" they ask with big smiles on their faces.

"We are going to leave it for them," Sam says in a calm voice. Then Sam turns to Harland. "Harland, burn the car after the vehicles are loaded and out of the building."

"OK, Sam," Harland says with authority. All the men's faces drop and a twinge of anger comes over them.

Sam goes over to the second building. Kim meets him at the door.

"Sam, you got to see this." Kim walks Sam over to a cafeteria area. Then into a large walk-in refrigerator.

"So are you saying this is set up just like the other place?" Sam asks Kim.

"Yes, it is." Kim says. "That is how I found it. The thing is that there is a hell of a lot more money than the other place. We need three trucks to haul this load."

"Why do you think they keep so much money in these places? It don't make sense. Do they actually make this much money selling crystal?" Sam asks. He didn't expect an answer. It is just puzzling why there is so much money.

"Maybe these places are just like a bunch of Fort Knox's. They just keep it here till they send it to wherever they send it," Kim speculates.

"I reckon they are," Sam says as he and Kim move on down through the refrigerator to the lower basement area. At the bottom is a money storage area. Kim has the door open already. There are four men that are duct tape to four chairs. Sam looks at Kim.

"They didn't even fire a shot," Kim says to Sam before he even asked.

Sam looks into the storage area. Sitting on the floor is five pallets of money and they are stacked higher than the last place they had confiscated money. In the back of the room is a pallet of ten small wooden boxes that are filled with small gold and silver bars.

"Well, let's load the boxes in the Hummers and as many pallets as we can on the Stryker we just found. The remainder of the money we will have to split up and put into some bags or something. Maybe we can find some garbage bags or delivery bags upstairs. We will load them on the Hummers and in the heavy trucks," Sam says while getting a little nervous about getting the money out. He didn't want the greedy men to see the money. Sam tells Kim, "I only want you, DH, and Harland to load it and no one else sees any of this. Those new guys are a little materialistic and I don't yet trust them. Now if your two brothers can keep their mouths shut, then they can help. Make sure they know the consequence of talking."

Sam leaves to go back to the first building. He finds Harland and tells him, "Move the Stryker and one heavy truck over for them to load. Now, Harland, I want you and only you to drive the vehicles over. Then help get them loaded. Then you and Kim are going to drive them over to the bunker."

"OK, Sam. I'll just keep these guys busy," Harland says.

Sam goes over to building three and DH meets him at the door. DH informs him, "This place is full of weapons, and some of them I have never seen before."

Sam walks around the building with DH pointing out all the weapons that he wants loaded first. Sam spots some crates that contained ground to air missiles according to one of the new men. Sam decides he has to have them, even though he will probably never use them.

"OK, get the men to start loading these in the Hummers, trailers, and whatever room is left in the other two heavy trucks. I want you to go help Kim load up," Sam tells DH. "Then we are going to blow up the lab that Kim found. We need to get a move on before those assholes come back."

"I'll get right on it," DH says. He runs over to the second building. He sees Kim contemplating the problem with carrying all the money up to the trucks with just the four of them.

"I don't know how the hell we are going to move all this money with just four of us and without anyone seeing?" Kim asks DH. "If we had some sacks or garbage bags, it would help."

"I know just were to find some. There are some canvas bags in the weapons depot. I don't know how many there are but any will help," DH says. "I'll go get them right now."

Just then Sam comes down to the vault area carrying an arm full of canvas bags. DH runs back and gets more. Tom and Bobby load the bags with money and Harland, Kim, and Sam carry the bags full of money and load it on to the truck and Stryker. Within a half an hour, everything is loaded and everyone is ready to move. They have even cleaned out the weapons depot by loading more into the two heavy trucks.

The men they had taken prisoners were all locked in the weapons' lockers. Sam and Kim go back into the meth lab area. Kim grabs the hard drive out of the main office area. When he is clear, Sam throws three grenades into the meth lab, then runs out of the building. The building just bellows and heaves from the blast. The lab was encased in a concrete room, which kept the blast from totally destroying the building. As Sam and his men load into the trucks, dust and smoke are still rolling out the cracks and crevices in the building. Two of the teams go back and get the vehicles they came in.

They have pulled everything off without a hitch. It takes them two hours to get back to the bunker. Sam, DH, Harland, and Kim back the Stryker and their heavy truck up to the barn and unload the money into the vault. This time the vault is full.

"Well, we aren't getting any more into that vault. I think the shop and the weapons depot will be full also. What the hell are we going to do with anything else we may find?" DH asks with a smile on his face.

"DH, you did such a great job with this place. We may just have to have you build another bunker elsewhere," Sam says.

Kim laughs like Sam is joking. Harland and the two bothers just look at each other. "So where the hell do you think we are going to build another bunker?" Kim asks.

"We will see. We will see," Sam says and then shuts the grain bin up. They all get into the vehicles and drive them into the shop. The entranceway to the shop is hidden by an old run-down building. They drive into the building and a door opens. They drive into the shop to see that all the men are busy emptying the trucks.

Two hours later the trucks are empty and the men all gather in the living quarters. The chef has a meal fit for a king already made and served up buffet style. When everyone is sitting down eating and drinking, Sam stands and addresses the men. "Well done, everyone. We all made it and no shots had to be fired. That means it was a good plan. Now I'm not saying that it is over, but it is for now. We will party tonight and rest tomorrow. Come Monday, we will be back to work. Where that will be, I do not know. We may be in Montana or Illinois, I don't know. What I do know is that everyone will get a fifty-thousand-dollar bonus tonight."

Everyone starts yelling and cheering. Sam raises his hands to quiet them down and says, "The other thing is that some of you looked a little hungry for things, specifically concerning that Ferrari." Sam looks over at the men that were arguing over the Ferrari. "Does anyone have anything to say?"

One of the men stands and announces himself, "Sam, I'm Giorgio. Now I know what you are talking about and we were just admiring a fine automobile. We didn't mean anything about it."

"Good to have you with us, Giorgio. Now you and the other few men could have cost us some lives. I am going to pay you enough money that you can buy your own fucking car or whatever you want. But from now on, we take what we can use and then destroy the rest," Sam says sternly but calmly.

"Sam, like I said we didn't mean anything about it. We know we made a mistake, it won't happen again," Giorgio says in an unconvincing, apologetic tone.

"OK, let's see that it doesn't. We got by easy today. Next time it may be a small army we may be fighting. So if anyone what's for anything, let me know, and you can either leave with your pockets full of money or we will get it for you," Sam says. "Hell, we may even have it here and you just don't know about it. So ask."

"We really would like to go town and spend some money, maybe we can do that tomorrow?" Giorgio asks.

"Now that would be pretty stupid. We just stole a whole bunch of shit from a really big gang of people. They are going to be looking for a bunch of men spending money and drinking it up. If just one of you gets drunk and little loose-lipped, then we all go down. I just don't think that would be a good idea," Sam says. Sam looks around and sees a bunch of the men nodding. "Besides, what the hell are you going to buy that you don't already have here?"

"Women!" a couple of men yell out. Everyone starts laughing.

"I know, I know. You just got to wait a week or so, and then you can head out to Rapid City or down to Omaha to party. We just don't want to raise suspicion around here," Sam says. "Do you think you can wait a week or two?" Sam asks.

A couple of men yell, "Yeah, we can wait."

"Good then we can all eat and drink now," Sam says in cheerful tone. "DH will hand out the bonuses right now." Sam looks at DH. DH has a surprise look on his face.

"Sam, I didn't bring any money with me," DH says in a whisper.

"Well then, we can go get some," Sam says in whisper out the side of his mouth. "I'll go with you. Let's get the buggy."

Kim jumps up. "Hold on Sam, we got something for you that I know you will love." Tom and Bobby come over and set the two AA12s, the full magazines, and a bag of money down on the table in front of Sam.

Sam picks the AA12 up and makes sure it is not loaded. He then bounces up and down in his hands to check the weight and the handling. "Thanks you, guys. This is great," Sam says as he opens the bag to look inside. "Oh, you shouldn't have. I appreciate it guys."

"Well, it is the least we could do for you," Kim says with a smile on his face. He knew Sam would love the new weapons. No one can even buy one of these weapons in the USA. Only the armed forces can have them. Kim knows that Sam didn't need any more money, but he thought that everyone else was getting a bonus; why not give one to Sam?

Sarah jumps up. "Hold on everyone. I have to tell you what I saw when we flew over the compound one last time. I saw those men coming back in the vans and the Hummer, so I decide to fly back and see just how many men there were in those vehicles. When I came back, they were killing those men we left behind. They were dragging them by the neck with the Hummer. Bodies were everywhere. Some of the men were being beaten with bats or big sticks. I saw one man get his belly cut open, and they were pulling on his intestines. I had to leave. I just couldn't watch anymore."

Sam and the other men didn't say a word. They are a little shocked that someone would kill his own men. After a few minutes, all the men move over to look at the new weapon. No one had ever shot one because they are so new, but they know what one of them can do. They all are a little envious.

The next day, Sam calls Darwin, "Hey, I got another hard drive for you."

"I know you crashed another place," Darwin says. "They are looking for you. They have been talking with the group out here. They know it is you but they don't know how many men you have and where you are."

"I figured they would get to finding me," Sam says with concern. "Just make sure that they are not going after my family. You let me know as soon as anything pops up about anything to do with my family."

"I have been watching. Now do you have the hard drive with you?" Darwin asks.

"Yes," Sam says.

"Plug it into the Internet and then plug your cellphone into the computer so I can find the hard drive," Darwin sarcastically instructs Sam. Sam does exactly what Darwin requests.

Darwin quickly locates the hard drive and downloads all the information off the hard drive on to his computer. Sam can hear the hard drive running and then it quits. Sam unhooks the phone.

"Well, did you get it all?" Sam asks.

"Yep, I got it. I'll look at everything and call you later," Darwin says.

Sam hangs up and calls Carol. He tells her that she needs to call him on a secure line. She goes down to the bunker and calls Sam on one of Darwin's phones. Sam tells her all about the week and about how well the new farm looks. She gives him the news about the clinic.

"I miss you, Sam," Carol says with a loving tone. "When can we be together again?"

"Pretty soon. I love you," Sam says sincerely. Then they both hang up.

CHAPTER TWENTY-FIVE

CAPTAIN BRAD RUTTER AND HIS men drive to the stripper bar to meet with Slayer. They park in the alleyway of the bar. When they arrive, they all see the scorched Camaro but it still looks functional. Several of the men and the captain enter the bar through the backdoor while some men stay with the vehicles. The bar only has a couple of men in the seats surrounding the stage and they are busy watching one of the girls dancing. The bartender and Slayer are sitting at the bar drinking. The captain and his men walk up to the bar. Some of the YUPPIs walk behind the bar and escort the bartender into the back room.

The captain sits down right next to Slayer. He takes the drink that is sitting on the bar and drinks it down. Carefully sets the glass back on the bar without making a sound. He turns to Slayer and tells him in a calm soft voice, "OK. Slayer! Tell me. TELL ME, exactly what happened?"

Slayer does not even look up from the bar. He stares at the bar like there are some answers written in it. He tells the captain in a soft but almost hysterical voice, "Well, Captain, I was in the back make'n deals when he came back said they's burnin' ma ride." Slayer rubs his eyes with his hands. "Damn, man! I fucking loved that car." He takes a deep breath and looks up then continues to say, "I ran back to the ride and an army jumped me and him."

"An army, you say? Maybe it was one man, maybe two?" The captain asks in a calm, sinister tone. He leans in closer to Slayer and looks him in the eyes. "How many men would you say, ten, twenty, thirty, or more?"

"They's about thirty or forty. They all's had guns down on me," Slayer says in a panic. His voice just got a little higher and he starts talking faster. Then he sits straight up, throws his shoulders back, and throws a cigarette in his mouth. He lights it and takes a deep draw. He is a little worried that the captain isn't buying his story but continues, "Really, Captain, I couldn't do a damn thing about it."

"OK, OK," the captain says in a calm, pretentiously compassionate voice. He pats Slayer on the head. "I will just ask the bartender how many there were since you don't remember." The captain gets up and walks to the back room. The bartender is sitting in a chair, smoking a cigarette. He walks up to the bartender and asks in a calm but stern tone, "Do you know how to count?"

The bartender just looks at him puzzled.

The captain grabs the bartender's chin and asks in a more harsh tone, "Do you speak English or Español? Are you deaf or mute?"

The bartender just starts shaking his head and says in an angry voice, "I can fucking talk. There were fucking three men. One hit Slayer and another jumped me and held me down. I couldn't get away. He was like a damn gorilla. The other one was a go-for boy."

The captain lets the bartender's chin go and says in a calm, cool voice, "Well, that is better. Now, did you see what they were driving?"

"Yes, yes. They were drive'n a Ford truck, white I think. The license plate is something, something, 2, D, something, something. That's all I know. Really!" The bartender says in a shaky voice.

"I see. You are just stupid," the captain says as walks out of the room. He goes back to the bar and sits down next to Slayer.

"Well! Slayer, Slayer, Slayer, I have a number on how big that army was," the captain says calmly and sarcastically. He slaps Slayer on the back. "BOY! With all those weapons that I have given you, I don't know how you defended yourself against all those men."

Slayer says in a shaky voice, "Well, I tried. There was just too many of them."

"I'm sure you did try," the captain says sarcastically. "You, being that tough guy and all, could probably handle how many men?" The captain looks at him straight in the eye.

Slayer puffs up his chest a little and says, "Probably eight to ten."

"Well then, it wouldn't have even been a chore to handle the three that jumped you two now, would it?" the captain says in a harsh, angry tone. He grabs the back of Slayer's head and throws him on to the floor. Then gets up and gives him a kick in the ribs. "Now I want my money and I want my drugs back. How do you propose to do that?"

"I'll go after them and I won't stop till I find them," Slayer yells in a shaky, pleading voice.

"Do you know who they are or what they were driving?" the captain asks as he looks down at Slayer.

"No, that don't matter. I'll still find them," Slayer says with certainty.

The captain takes a deep breath and walks toward the bar's exit. He looks over at his men standing at the door and tells them, "Take those two out and see how tough they are. I don't think I ever want to see them again."

Two of the YUPPIs grab Slayer by the arms and drag him out the back exit door and into the alleyway. Two other men run into the back room to get the bartender. One of the men grabs the bartender by the hair and the other grabs the back of the bartender's belt. The bartender grabs the hand that is pulling his hair to keep from getting his hair pulled out. He is being dragged too fast and couldn't keep up. His hair along with half his scalp comes off his head. The bartender falls to the floor screaming as he grabs at the top of head, thinking somehow that will stop the pain. The YUPPIs stop. The one with the scalp in his hand looks at it for a moment, and then they both start laughing. He stuffs the scalp in his pocket. Then both YUPPIs grab the bartender's legs and drag him out the door to the alleyway. The bartender just curls up into fetal position and cries. Once both men are in the alley, all the YUPPIs start beating them with liquor bottles. Slayer is finally hit so many times in the head he is in and out of consciousness. He falls to the ground next to the bartender. Slayer lies there bleeding from open wound to the head and from multiple stab wounds to the stomach and chest. The YUPPI has stabbed Slayer with broken bottles. Once Slayer hit the ground, the YUPPIs turned their attention to the bartender. One of them kicks the bartender until he rolls on to his stomach. The YUPPI jumps on the bartender's back like a trampoline. The rest of the men watch the trampoline act and cheer the man on. He jumps up and down on the bartender's back over and over. The bartender's ribs break and the chest caves in. It only takes one last jump and the bartender gives one last grunt before blood shoots out of his nose and mouth like someone pumping water. The bartender is dead. Slayer tries to crawl away, but two of the men grab him by his legs and drag him back. One of the men runs to the van and grabs a rope out of the back. He ties the rope to one of Slayer's leg, then drags Slayer closer to the burned orange Camaro. He cuts the rope and ties the rope to the front steering rod of the car. The other men see what he is doing and join in. Another man ties the rope to the other leg. They back up the van and tie the rope to the van's bumper. Slayer tries to struggle and free himself, but one of the men just kicks him in the head. Slayer is knocked unconscious. All the men watch as the van slowly pulls forward. Slayer regains consciousness just as his hips are dislocating. Slowly the van creeps forward inch by inch. The skin and muscle tissue reaches its elastic limit and Slayer's legs are ripped off. He can only scream as he feels himself getting ripped apart. The skin and muscle rips up to his abdomen, which leaves a large hole for his intestines to spill out on to the ground. He just lies on the ground with a steady scream as the men around him laugh. One of the men walks up to Slayer and sticks a liquor bottle in his mouth and holds it there as another on comes over and stomps on the bottle. Slayers jaw dislocates and then blood shoots out of his mouth. His screams turn it to gurgles. With all the loss of blood, he dies within seconds. The men pick up the bartender and Slayer and throw them in to the back of the van. They dump gasoline on the pools of blood and light them on fire. They kick dirt over all the burned blood in the alleyway. They load into the van laughing and cussing like they just won a football game.

The captain and his convoy go back to their compound. When the captain walks into the shop and sees that everything is gone. He has the men search the rest of the buildings while he goes to the refrigerator. The captain and three of the men walk down to the money storage area. He finds the men he left to guard the place are tied up. The three men start untying men.

"Hold on. Leave those bastards tied. Since they let everything get stolen, that I say is treason. They are to be hung right now," the captain yells.

"We don't have any gallows," one of the men says.

"Then take them out and put a rope around their necks and drag them behind the Hummer," the captain yells in a fiery tone. "I want it done now. Now get some men down here to get them out of here."

"Yes, sir," one of the men says and then runs out to get help.

The four men that are tied up are dragged up to the compound's yard. One YUPPI starts the Hummer and backs it up to the line of four tied up men. The four men struggle and beg, but their comrades pay no heed to their cries. A lope is placed around the first man's neck. The rope is tied to the hitch of the Hummer. The man driving the Hummer revs up the engine and then lets the clutch out. The Hummer flies forward. The YUPPI drives around the compound until the head comes off. The rest of the men cheer like they are watching their favorite team in the Super Bowl. One by one, they kill all four men. The other men that Sam left as prisoners were also found and killed. The YUPPIs get very bored with the one vehicle-hanging bit, so they come up with other ways to kill them. Some YUPPIs start beating the men with pipes and bats, whatever they can find. Some of them can't find anything, so they use their knives to stab and slash. One YUPPI decides to cut one of the prisoners belly open while several men watch. Instantly, intestines start spilling out on to the ground. Those men standing around take the opportunity to learn how to jump rope with the dying man's intestines.

The captain just stands there watching. The only time that the captain looks away is when he sees the low flying helicopter fly right over the compound.

When the last prisoner is dead, he goes in and calls his boss. He informs them what happened.

"How much of it is gone?" Congressman Bud Jacklow asks.

"All of it. Everything is gone, including the lab," the captain, says shamefully knowing full well that he should not have gone with so many men. He should have just sent a couple of guys to check out the situation. He knows he just wanted to show off and make a big strong presence.

"Get it back. Get it all back. For God's sakes, that was over a billion and a quarter you had there. You get that back or don't you come back," the congressman screams and then starts to cough. "You stupid bastard, you get that shit back. The son of bitch is probably the same one that was in South Dakota and in Virginia. I'm sending a picture of the man in Virginia that has been raising hell." Then he hangs up.

The picture comes over the fax machine. The captain grabs the fax and then rushes out of the office. He gathers up ten of his men and sends them out to find Sam, the man in the fax.

CHAPTER TWENTY-SIX

EVER SINCE JOHN BARRACK TOOK over the presidency, he has been running around the world apologizing for Americans being arrogant, selfish, and starting wars. He has been trying to turn this country into a socialist society. The government has been taking over large industries and the financial centers, spending money on entitlement programs, and no one knows where any of the money ends up. The government has been giving billions of dollars to countries with ties to terrorist organizations. The president and his congress have spent more money in the first one hundred days of his presidency than all the presidents put together. With the help of the speaker of the House of Representatives, Chelsey Palawan, and majority senate leader, Henry Remolds, they have triple the country's deficient. The government under John Barrack's administration has bankrupt this country with a joke of a national health care program and a large so-called stimulus packages to unions, banks and companies that Barrack owed for getting him elected. Barrack traveled to countries that hate the USA and buddies up to their dictators. Barrack said that all his program would keep unemployment down and bring the nation out of the recession. Nothing has worked. He has cut the budget to all of America's defense programs and allowed free reign of illegal immigrant traffic. His change for America includes breaking small businesses, increasing his and his supporters' wealth, getting rid of large privately controlled industries, and selling America off to the highest bidder.

Big cities and little towns start to see more illegal aliens move in to the low-rent housing. Crime rates have gone up in most of those areas, not just petty crimes but murders, rape, drugs, and illegal gun sales. It is not all illegals doing the crimes but there is a definite pattern. The biggest problem is that the law enforcement in those areas are understaffed and underfunded especially now since part of Barrack's plan is to cut law enforcement funding in small-town America. The local tax income that would help fund the law enforcement is lower because of many people losing their jobs and homes. This lower local tax base and the federal funds don't make up for the deficient funds. Most of the small towns only have part time police and work only in the afternoons the rest is taken up with the county sheriff departments. With only a part time police force, none of the crimes are ever followed up. Mostly these law enforcement departments do is hand out traffic tickets and make sure kids don't buy beer or cigarettes. All other crimes fall to the county and state, which doesn't have the people power or the funds to cover anything but the most publicized crimes. That also is a problem because small-town newspapers have also gone belly up. Everyone gets news from the bigger papers or from the Internet and these small-town crimes do not make either of those.

It all started out with nine hundred eleven murders across the country. All murders were by gunshots, which made congress say that there needs more gun control. Many cities tightened their gun control laws to the point where beating a man to death had a lesser penalty than possessing a gun without a license.

Only a few of these nine hundred eleven murders were solved. The convicted killers were illegal aliens from Iran, Iraq, Mexico, Venezuela, and Cuba. None of these people were sent back home, and only half of them are imprisoned. The other half are back on the street again because the liberal judges let them go on technicalities. Only a few of the crimes were publicized; those are the ones that someone was convicted.

The next month there are nine hundred eleven murders due to knife wounds and the next month was nine hundred eleven murders with blunt objects. None of these crimes made the big news because there was no legislation on knife control or blunt object control. Most of these crimes were not investigated because they were in the "ghettos" of the big cities. No one did put the numbers together or see that there is a coincidence except for Darwin and his computer analysis. Some of the murders were found or caught in action, and all were illegal aliens. Many of the illegals were people that had over-stayed their visas. But those crimes that no one was convicted were all pushed over to drug-related crimes.

Maybe if John Barrack would use the Patriot Act for finding ter-rorists instead on taking out political opposition, they would notice the coincidence between all the murders. Now the illegals from many nations run free throughout the USA. The illegals are building strength in numbers. Their gang numbers grow with home grown people, illegals overstaying visas, and those freely coming over the southern and northern borders. They integrate in to jobs throughout the country not only into labor jobs but also into top security jobs. President Barrack brags about hiring immigrants as part of his own Secret Service.

Sam is thoroughly convinced that Barrack is an implant from the Muslim Brotherhood, sent to cause the downfall of America. It is the greatest terrorist plot ever created. Get a person in to become president and have him make conditions so bad so that he can divide Americans in half, such as class warfare. Then when everyone is blam-ing everyone else, make conditions even worse for the lower class and make it even better for the upper class. Then they can yell, "See, see, they have more, you have nothing, and you deserve what they have." The lower class will keep voting for you, and since there are more people in the lower class than in the middle and upper classes, you have a "shoe in" to winning. After reelection by class warfare, buying votes, and voter fraud, the real plan can go into effect. Use executive power to change the Supreme Court and the justice system. Then through other changes, through EPA, FDA, IRS, and other agen-cies, break all the corporations and energy companies, thus causing the economic downfall to America. The people are then hungry for anyone that will save them and the Muslim Brotherhood is more than willing to move in and fill the order. Once they are in, they will tighten the grip and change America into their own image.

Sam has a lot of time on his hands. It is hard for him not to be doing any work so he stays busy practicing with his hand weapons. Gunny had given Sam several practice drills to improve speed and accuracy. Sam also practices kicks and strike drills that he had learned in karate. Sam also had several meetings with Gina. She has been making several farm loans to anyone that asks. Gina has begun to get worried because none of borrowers have paid their loans back. She is concerned about the money running out for any more loans.

"Sam, no one has paid their loans payments yet," Gina says with concern. "We have over three hundred million in loans with no interest and no collateral. How are we going to get the money back if they don't pay?"

"Those that can't really afford it will work hard and pay us when they can. Those that can afford it and didn't really need the loans probably will never pay it back," Sam says. "I guess we need to do a better job at just picking out the honest and really needy people. I don't mind giving them the money. The others, you need to make a list of those and we can send Kim and his brothers after them. Kim can see if they can afford to pay and we will let him decide. Just remember, it's not really our money."

"Yeah, OK. I guess that will work, but don't you think we should make them put some collateral on the line?" Gina asks.

"No, their collateral is their name, and Kim will take care of the rest," Sam says. "Or better yet, just find someone for that job. There has got to be someone that you loaned money too that wants to work off the loan and is a good collector."

"Well, we are about out of money," Gina says.

"We got more. I'll have Harland and a couple of the men bring you more money, and if you need more, just let me know," Sam says. "Now, here is what I really wanted to talk about. I think since the banks won't make loans to small businesses, we should do that. We will get the small businesses to put up collateral, like something that is very near and dear to them. That way we know they will pay it back, and it will show us that they really believe in what they are going to do. That should stop all those that are just willy-nilly. Also I want you to find someone to get some companies started."

"OK, I can do that. We can make small business loans but I'm charging interest," Gina insisted. "What companies do you want to start?"

"No one makes clothes here in the US, and I have several designs that I want to make. I also got several ideas on little inventions. I want to put them into production, so I need you to get me a designer, a seamstress, a chemist, a computer engineer, an electrical engineer, a textile expert, and a mechanical engineer. We also need a graphic designer, marketing people, and someone to get these things in full swing," Sam says. "I want to start right away, so find someone quick."

"I'll start on it right away," Gina says.

With the bank bailouts and the crash of the market, none of the banks would take chances on a new business. They all needed so much collateral that it was impossible to start any businesses. Sam never understood how it is going to be possible for the US to recover from the recession without industry. How can you increase the gross national product without making and selling things to other countries? China is busy taking over the world market while the United States is just swirling money through the service industry. That is why Sam starts the companies. Also people that work place more value on life, or he so hoped.

Chapter Twenty-Seven

....

Darwin is been busy with the new hard drive information. He finds names of several congressmen, senators, and governors and their bank account numbers on the hard drive. Darwin traces pay-offs from the YUPPI group to all these politicians. He has hacked into to confidential e-mails and into bank accounts. He had a lot of trouble finding the money in foreign banks but he found most of it. He is still on a revenge trip from when Congressman Jacklow killed his wife. He is bound and determined to make Jacklow and all other politicians pay by killing them where it hurts the most—their bank accounts. He drains all the bank accounts and transfers the money to many new accounts spread all over the world. Politicians' credit cards, telephones, satellite televisions, and anything that is closeable is permanently closed. He changed all their credit ratings. Their cars that they drive are all reported as stolen. Then Darwin hacks into the IRS files to put them all down for audits. Needless to say, there are several politicians that can do nothing but pray for miracles. Their families can't afford a stick of gum. Darwin is very proud about the work he has done, and for the first time in a long time, he is happy.

Darwin calls Sam. "Hey, I got great news and some not-so-great news."

"Hey, are you doing all right?" Sam asks.

"Yes, now listen up. I took care of some of those politicians and they will be busy trying to find second jobs—that is, if their wives or husbands don't kill them first. Anyway, I took them down. The bad news is that they think it was you," Darwin says as he breaks out laughing. "Oh! How stupid! They are, if only they knew that you couldn't have done this. Hell, you can barely run your cellphone. So just watch out, they are coming for you." Darwin is very excited and then throws in, "OH YEAH! They have hired every bounty-hunting service out there just to find you."

"Well, that sounds great. Do you happen to know where these bounty men are located?" Sam asks.

"Yes, and I will e-mail you all their addresses. I also took the liberty of e-mailing them that they were to cease looking for you. I don't know how many of them will listen but a lot of them may not go after you when they find out that those politicians don't have a dime," Darwin says. "I am also going to e-mail you a list of bunch more meth labs run by the group. I got addresses and how many people work there. I even got how much money they make every year."

"Well then, how much money do they make every year?" Sam asks with curiosity. He isn't really worried about the people after him. He is used to it now.

"Around thirty-two billion dollars and I mean billions with a *b*. Shit, Sam, we can buy a small country if we get all that," Darwin says.

"We are going to get all that and then some. But we ain't buying no damn country. I like this one and we are going to take it back. So keep on your toes. I'll probably be sending you some more hard drives," Sam tells Darwin. "I'll call you later."

Sam opens his e-mails and then downloads it into the server. He really didn't want anyone to see this information. Sam thinks, "I want my men fighting for the destruction of drug labs and not for money. People who fight for a cause fight harder than those who fight for money. I'm not really interested in all the money, it is just icing on the cake. I just want to bring the YUPPI group down by destroying their income."

It has been several weeks since they had raided the Iowa YUPPI compound. Sam decides that it is OK for some of the men to go to town if they want to. They all really need to get out and kick up their heels. Sam gave the OK for anyone that wants to leave to go out. He gave explicit instructions to not get into trouble and thrown in jail.

They are not to say anything about this place, the group, and especially anything about Sam or what they had done. Everyone one of them agreed to it.

Eleven of the men decide to go to town. They all leave with the fifty thousand dollar in bonus in their pockets. Sam tells them, "It is stupid to bring that much money to town, but I'm not going to stop you. You all are adults."

The men leave in the morning. They all pile into to two of the trucks. One group goes shopping for new clothes, and the others go straight to a stripper bar. When the men get to the stripper bar, they start spending money like they are buying women. By one in the afternoon, they start to grow tired of giving money to a bunch of women that are never going to do anything with them. They decide to head out and find the other group. They all meet up with the other group at a bar called Borrowed Bucks. It is a good ole country bar with lots of college students hanging out. They all start drinking fairly heavily, and by five, one group decides it is time to go home. Four of the men stay to drink and try to pick up some collage chicks. By midnight, they are really drunk and start shooting their mouths off on how much money they made and how they are paid killers. A group of three men overhear them. The three of them are part of the Iowa YUPPI group looking for Sam.

Giorgio is really drunk and starts bragging, "Yeah, I'm a paid assassin. We make more fuckin' money then the president himself."

"Really?" one of the three YUPPI men says, "My name is Richard. Let me buy you a drink."

The three YUPPI men slide their chairs over to the Giorgio's table and sit down. They wave to the waitress and she comes over and takes their order. When she leaves, the YUPPIs start cozying up to Giorgio.

"We got ourselves a sweet deal," Giorgio slurs. One Sam's men named Jamie kicks Giorgio under the table.

"Giorgio, you need to watch what you are saying," Jamie whispers harshly to Giorgio.

Giorgio reaches up and lightly slaps Jamie on the face. He tells Jamie, "Now don't you worry. Maybe these men need a job. Sam is always looking for more gunmen."

"Yeah, we are in town looking for jobs. My and I friends used to be in the military," Richard says and then looks at the other two. "How do we sign on to this job? Hell, I'll do anything for a job."

"You just need to show up and I'll get you in. Sam and I are really close," Giorgio tells Richard. The other three men grab Giorgio and start dragging him out of the bar. Giorgio yells, "Come into Hartford and go to five miles north of town on Kelley Road. Look for the big wood gate."

Sam's three men throw Giorgio on to the ground once they get out the door. Giorgio hits the ground and then rolls over. He starts to laugh and says to three men, "Ahhh! That was fun. Let's go to another bar." Then he rolls back on to his knees. He starts vomiting like a cat with a hairball.

Jamie scolds Giorgio, "Sam told you not to open your mouth about anything. He is going to be pissed that you shot your mouth off."

Giorgio wipes his mouth on his shirtsleeve and says, "Fuck, Sam. He can fucking go to hell."

The three men pick Giorgio up and throw him into the bed of the truck. Giorgio passes out until they get back to the farm.

Once at the farm, the four of them go down to the sleeping quarters and go to bed. None of them wants to wake up Sam and tell him what just happened. The next morning Jamie goes and finds Sam.

Sam, DH, Harland, and Kim are all sitting around just finishing up breakfast. Jamie comes over and sits down at the table.

"Giorgio got a little too drunk last night," Jamie tells everyone then grabs a piece of bacon and eats it.

"And?" DH asks.

Jamie finishes chewing his food and says, "Well, he started shooting his mouth off and told some guys about where Sam was and that they would be getting jobs if they just showed up. I really didn't like the looks of them, so we grabbed Giorgio and dragged him out of the bar."

Sam just sits there. Everyone can tell that Sam is mad. No one says anything for about five minutes, and then Sam tells one of the men at the table, "Go get Giorgio."

Within five minutes, Giorgio is standing in front of the table. He is very hung over and can barely stand.

"Giorgio, what did I tell you not to do when you went out on the town?" Sam asks.

"Aahh, listen Sam." Giorgio sits down before he falls and says, "I'm not feeling very well right now. Can't we just do this sometime later?"

"Fuck no. You just told, God knows who, about everything that just went on here. Now we got to go on full alert until we get this all straighten out. Then we got to figure out what the hell we are going to do with you," Sam says in angry but soft voice.

Kim jumps in with a somewhat sarcastic remark but hoping Sam will go along with it, "I think we should just fly him over to the badlands and throw him out at about five thousand feet." Kim really didn't like Giorgio anyway. He thinks Giorgio is a big mouth and very contemptuous.

"Hold on now. What the fuck you talking about?" Giorgio says in a shaky voice. "I didn't do a damn thing." He isn't sure if Kim is joking or not.

"That's not what Jamie just told us," Kim says in a very angry voice. "He said you told some guys where Sam was. Isn't that right, Jamie?"

"Yeah, that's right, Kim," Jamie says.

"I, I don't remember a thing," Giorgio says. He is a little pissed that his friend ratted him.

"I'm not sure what we are going to do with you, Giorgio," Sam speaks up. "For now, you can either go on garbage and cleaning duty until we figure out what is going to happen to you or you can leave. If you leave, you are an open target for the YUPPI group. Now what will it be?"

"I have no choice but to stay here," Giorgio says with disgust.

"Hell, we at least got to give him a beating, don't we?" Kim asks.

"No, we don't," Sam says. "Giorgio get your ass to work."

"Can't it wait till later?" Giorgio pleads.

"Kim," Sam says.

Kim gets up and grabs Giorgio by his hair. Giorgio stands and turns toward Kim. Kim lets him go. Giorgio punches Kim in the face. Kim is a little dazed. He thinks, "I can't believe this piss ant just hit me." He shakes his head. Giorgio jumps back and gets into a boxer's stance. Kim stands there for a few seconds and when Giorgio throws a jab, Kim punches him in the nose. Giorgio drops to his knees. Kim follows up with a kick to Giorgio's ribs. Giorgio falls back on to the floor screeching in pain. Vomit erupts from Giorgio's mouth, which halts the screeching. Two men come over and pick Giorgio up. They walk him to the bunker for Lisa and Beth to patch him up.

Sam calls a meeting and informs everyone to get prepared for an invasion. They all load up on weapons and ammunition. Some of them take their stations on and in the wall. Some of the men go up into gun areas in the barn, outbuildings, and the house. Four of the men including Ben and Harland take their sniper rifles and set up in the trees and the barn. When they are all set up they just wait. Sam, Kim and DH just wait in the house. Sarah and Mickey go up in the helicopter and fly around to keep surveillance. Skids had mounted a M60 machine gun on the helicopter. Skids had found it in the stuff that they had taken from the last YUPPI raid.

At two in the morning, Sarah calls in to Josh, "There are three vehicles headed down the Kelley Road. Not sure if they are going to the farm."

"Roger, I'll tell the man," Josh says. Josh calls Sam over the radio and tells him and then calls the rest of the men to warn them.

Sam tells Josh, "Call the gate and tell them to leave it open and when they go though, let no man out. And I mean, no man out. Oh, and turn on all the outside lights."

Sam grabs his bladed whip chain, a tomahawk, and a knife. Sam really didn't like to use a pistol or rifle unless he has to. Now he has enough people watching over him that are quicker on the trigger; it is stupid to carry a gun. Sam walks over to the buckets of water and drinks down a ladle of water just like his grandpa used to do before he went out to work. Sam wipes his mouth and then walks to the door. He stands their staring out the door not to look out but to concentrate. He needed to focus completely. Kim and DH walk up behind him. No one says a word. DH has seen Sam fight enough now that he isn't worried about any strategy; he knew Sam didn't have one. Sam just fought by instinct. Kim on the other hand is worried about keeping Sam safe. He hands Sam a Dragon Skin bulletproof vest. Sam quickly puts it on and then adjusts everything. Kim grabs his AA12 with a thirty-round magazine and slings it over his shoulder. Kim is ready to take out a whole platoon if he has to. Kim knows that Sam is always too focused on cutting the head off the scorpion to remember to look out for the stinger and claws. Sam often forgets about the other dangers.

Two vans and a Hummer comes speeding into the yard. The men unload quickly out of the vans and then the captain sauntered out from the Hummer. The captain walks to the front of the men and put his hands on his hips.

"Sam, we are here for our shit you stole from us," the captain yells up to the house. "Oh yeah, Sam, I'm supposed to kill you too. So get out of your hole and come here and we will get this over quick."

That is Sam's cue to go to work. Sam slowly walks out the door followed by DH and Kim. Sam slowly walks toward the captain. He did not feel apprehensive about moving toward the group of men pointing guns at him. He concentrates on just the captain. He sees the captain just standing there without his weapon pulled. He notices that none of the other men are doing anything but watching. He is a little confused but then he thinks, "Action is quicker than reaction." Sam picks up the pace with each step. He wants to get in close so that he has a chance. He thinks, "A chance at what. Hell, I just find out what I do when I get there."

The captain just stands there with a big smile on his face. Then suddenly he realizes that the man that just came out of the door is headed straight for him and it didn't look like he is going to stop. The captain reaches for his pistol but it is still holstered.

Sam by now is running as fast as his middle-aged old body will take him. When Sam sees that the captain is drawing his weapon, he leaps into the air at the same time he draws his tomahawk. On his descent, he swings down with the tomahawk completely severing the gun hand from the captain's arm. Both the captain and Sam crash to the ground. Blood shoots everywhere from the severed arm, and the captain just lays there and grabs for his severed arm. Sam rolls and jumps back on to his feet. He comes back with a circular down ward swing and buries the spear end of the tomahawk into the skull of the captain just above the right ear. The captain screams for a short second and then goes into convulsions like a fish that was just tossed out of the water. Sam jerks the tomahawk out of the captain's skull and dives to the open door of the Hummer. In doing so, the skull cracks open like a cracked boiled egg and the convulsing stops. Sam slams the door and crawls over to the driver's side and starts the vehicle.

The other men that are standing around with their weapons drawn are momentarily stunned when Sam cuts the captain's hand off. They just stand there watching for the few seconds that it all takes place. Soon as the door the Hummer shuts, it is like they all just realized that they are supposed to be doing something. They start firing at the Hummer. Sam starts driving forward. A couple of the men grab the door handles to try to get in. Next thing Sam sees is their heads exploding as Kim shoots them with the AA12. Men begin to explode around the Hummer. The flechette rounds coming from the 12-gauge rend the men to shreds. The other men in Sam's group follow Kim's lead and open fire. Within minutes, not one of the captain's men is still standing. Sam keeps on driving to the shop and never looks back. He knows it would be a gruesome sight.

Sam's men come out from everywhere. They load the dead men in the vans and then go to find Sam.

"Sam, what do you want to do with the dead?" one of the men asks. "Shit, we're going to get into trouble for sure for killing all these men."

"Don't worry about it," Sam says. He is a little nervous. He knows these men were evil and they got what they deserved. He just didn't know how all his men are going to react to just getting rid of a bunch of bodies. "Kim, come over here a minute."

"Yeah, Sam?" Kim asks. Kim pushes the other guy away from Sam.

"Does your dad still have all those pigs?" Sam whispers to Kim. He notices that the man is eavesdropping so Sam points to him. "Get the fuck out of this room until I call you back." The guy is a little shocked but then quickly leaves the room.

"Yeah, he's got about two thousand fat hogs," Kim whispers. Then a smile comes across Kim's face. "I know exactly what you are going to say and my brothers and I will take care of this right now."

"Good. Take DH or Ben with you if you need help," Sam says.

"Got it handled," Kim says with enthusiasm.

Kim, his two brothers, and Ben jump into the two vans. They drive over to Kim's dad's hog farm and back up to one of the grain bins. They unload one man at a time. Some of the men are so shot up that their limbs fell off when they are pulled out of the vehicle. They strip the men naked and pile the clothes. Bobby checks every pocket for anything worth keeping. All he finds is a few hundred dollars and some knives. Tom goes over to the machine shed and hooks up the riding lawn mower to the wood chipper. He backs it up to the feed grinder and positions the head of the blower so it will feed into the supplement tube in the grinder. They start the wood chipper and the feed grinder. They start the grain flowing into the grinder, then ran one man into the wood chipper at a time. The men grind up and mix into the batch of feed. They feed the hogs that night a little early morning snack. The fat hogs are happy to oblige. By the time the grinding is done, Bobby had all the clothes burned in the burn barrel. When they were done cleaning things up, nothing is left except for the vans.

They drive the vans back to the yard at the bunker and the men in the shop strip them all down to parts.

Kim finds Sam and tells him, "All handled. Pigs are happy and there is no mess."

"Well, just make sure that your brothers and Ben stay cool with this. I don't want any rumors buzzing around here. One thing you can do is go tell Giorgio he may end up as pig food if he doesn't learn to keep his mouth shut," Sam says.

"I will do that later. Right now I'm going to go get some sleep. I'll see you later," Kim says.

Chapter Twenty-Eight

....

Over the next few weeks, Sam and several of the other men laid out plans for the busting another meth lab compound. Sam had Darwin, Bud, and Kota flown into go over plans. The raids will take a lot of manpower and time. Darwin found twenty-seven labs to hit all across the country from the servers they took for the labs. Sam decides to do them in a random order because they didn't what to disclose any pattern.

Darwin sets his laptop computer on the table and brings up a map of the United States on the screen. He had mapped all the lab locations. He had Google Earth maps for each place along with distances, time to travel, and surrounding locations. He then attaches a device on to the computer and a holographic image of what is on the computer appears on the tabletop.

Sam looks at Darwin with surprise and mild deprecation. Sam says to Darwin, "REALLY!" Not that Sam despises Darwin's artistry of the digital cosmos but holographic projections are a little over doing it.

Darwin laughs and says, "I just want to introduce you all to the modern world. There will be no more paper in our future."

Everyone just looked at Darwin like he is nuts. Sam pointed to areas on the map and when he did, Darwin would play a little video of the area. All this computer stuff was starting to confuse Sam and he starts to lose his train of thought. He looks away from the table for a minute and then continues on with, "Let's say we start in Oxbow, Maine then move on over to Grass Valley, Oregon. If we see-saw across the country we will be harder to catch. We will then move down to California and then back up to New York. Then so on and so forth. What do you think?"

"We can't drive all that way. It will take years to do this. How are we going to get all the stuff back here?" Kim asks.

"We need a cargo plane," Sarah speaks up.

"Yes, but where the hell can we get one and who can fly the damn thing?" Sam asks.

"Do you remember that mechanic that worked here in Hartford for a long time? He was a cargo plane pilot for the military. Then he left to fly for that small plane company in Sioux Falls. Maybe we can track him down to fly for us," Bud suggests.

"I'll get you a plane," Mike jumps into the conversation. "Just send me with some money and I'll have one flying into the airport with in the next week. I'll even have a pilot and a copilot so if your other buddy doesn't work out, we have extra."

"OK, Mike, how much money do you want and when can you leave?" Sam asks.

"Maybe about four to six million. That will get us started. I'll leave right now if it is OK," Mike says. He is very excited to go out wheeling and dealing.

"DH, can you go get him some money in a couple of duffel bags. Then tell the guys in the shop to get a truck ready," Sam asks DH.

"I'm on it," DH says and leaves.

"OK, then we need to find is a place to land and take off. We can probably land in Sioux Falls, but where can we land all these other places? We need to go to all these places and recon the area. Then we need to make a plan. So far, we have been lucky and all the troops we went up against have been very stupid. Not all these guys are going to be like this, especially when we get going. We have to hit all of them fast. Otherwise, they can get a plan of their own or even build up an army. So we are going to go in two's and everyone is going to take six or seven places to recon," Sam says.

"When do we leave?" Kim asks.

"Right now. Everyone pair up and take six labs. Go down and get a couple of million dollars, drive or fly or both. Just get there and make sure you get all the locations of the police, airports, and farms. We need to know everything, including how many men, vehicles, just find out everything you can. If there is a farm around for sale, buy it. If not rent it. Whatever it takes," Sam tells everyone. "OK, so let's get going."

Everyone splits up and go down to get the money from DH. Sam takes DH and Ben with him because he wants to find a couple of places to build more bunkers. Sam has one of the new guys drive them into Sioux Falls. He goes to see Jay and buys a new truck to drive out west. Sam really doesn't like to fly, so they are driving everywhere.

Over the next week, everyone travels. It takes Sam, DH, and Ben a day to drive to Oregon. It takes them another two days to do all their reconnaissance on the area. They found the Oregon lab to be about the same size as the Iowa lab. After marking the area and determining a rendezvous, they leave for Nevada. They take all day to drive to Nevada stopping several times to enjoy the scenery. They drive around Las Vegas even after Ben pleaded with Sam and DH to stop on the strip. Both Sam and DH have been to Las Vegas and know it is just a good place to get into more trouble than it is worth. Sam has known about a small airport on the outside of Las Vegas, so they go out there to check it out. Darwin finds a great piece of property in the middle of nowhere for sale. The property is near the small airport that they are going too.

They stop at the airport. The three of them go inside. The place is full of skydivers and Sam asks to see the boss.

"Hello, my name is Sam," Sam greets the boss.

"Hi, I'm Greek," the boss says with a smile and a bit of confusion. "That is what everyone calls me anyway. Aahh, how can I help you? Did you what to go skydiving?"

"No, I love skydiving and I used to do it all the time but it has been a while. Maybe after we talk, I'll take you up on that offer." Sam says. Ben and DH are walking around looking the place over and gawking at the women divers. "Do you own this airport?" Sam asks.

"Yeah, we bought it about twenty years ago and have had this skydiving operation ever since then. We paved the runway about fifteen years ago," Greek says.

"Well then, I am talking to the right person," Sam says with no expression. "I want to buy it from you. What will you take for it?"

"I can't sell it. This is my business and a lot of people rely on this place to jump at," Greek says with a harsh tone. "Besides, I don't think you have enough money to buy me out anyway."

"How much would that be?" Sam asks.

"Fifteen million." Greek laughs. "What the hell do you what with this place anyway?"

"OK, I will give you a check or do you want cash?" Sam asks.

The Greek busts out laughing again. "I'll take cash if you got it. I'll also throw in a lifetime of jumps."

"I'll be right back," Sam says. He turns and grabs DH and Ben. They go out to the truck and grab seven large backpacks. They carry them into the office and set them on the floor in front of Greek.

"What is this?" Greek laughs as he bends over and opens one backpack up. "Holy shit."

"That's fifteen million. You can count it while we go and take a jump if you don't mind," Sam says.

Greek yells out to his workers to get everyone ready for the jump. The Greek is trembling with excitement. He had never seen this much cash in all his life.

Sam and Ben both know how to jump, but DH has never jumped before. He needs a tandem jump. They all went up to fourteen thousand feet. DH is trembling with fear and anticipation. When the plane's door opens and he looks out, he starts panicking. He grabs for Ben and almost pulled out Ben's pilot chute. Sam grabbed DH's hand and the tandem jump master pushes himself and DH out of the plane. Sam and Ben follow. Sam and Ben fly around DH and the tandem master as they fall to the ground. DH yells the whole way down. After an uneventful landing, DH walks over to Sam and Ben. He yells, "I will fucking never do that shit again. I pissed my damn pants!"

"Oh shit, that was fun. Settle down and go change your clothes." Ben says as he picks up his chute.

Sam looks at DH and says, "Y'all be OK. I saw a shower and a place to change in there. The first jump is always great or terrible. You either love it or hate it." Sam picks up his chute and they all go back to the packing floor area. The Greek greets them on the packing floor.

"Well, I'll need a little time to get things cleared out of here. Can you give me about a week or so? I'll get you the land title by tomorrow, so if you guys want to stay and jump, feel free to do so," Greek says.

DH yells, "Fuck no! I don't want to jump."

"No, you don't have to leave. I want you to stay here and keep this business going. We are now partners. I want you to get a bigger runway in here. DH will help you with this," Sam says and then introduces DH. DH and Greek shake hands. "Ben and I are going to go to California and then to New Mexico. I'll be flying back in about a month to check up on everything."

"I'll help DH out anyway I can." Greek shakes Sam's hand. "Sam, I got a small twin engine if you want to fly to California. I'll fly you. Hell, the plane is now yours anyway."

"Thank you I appreciate that but we'll drive. DH may need a ride to town to get a vehicle. If you can chauffeur him around for a while, that would be great. I may need you in the future to fly for me if you will give me a rain check," Sam says.

"That's great," Greek says.

Sam and DH go out to the truck. Sam gives DH two of the bags of money. Sam thinks, "I glad I brought a truckload of cash. I'll probably need it before the end of the run," Sam tells DH. "Go buy the piece of property that Darwin found. Let's get going on a new bunker. We will probably need it instead of hauling everything back to South Dakota. Call Darwin and see whom to contact about the property. Maybe Greek knows where the property is at." DH knows what to do and Sam is not worried about DH getting it done.

"Hey, call up headquarters and tell Ronald to come out and help you. He's some kind of engineer or something," Sam tells DH as he climbs into the truck. "See you later. Call me in a week and I will let you know where the other bunker will go. You can fly down and get that one started also."

Sam and Ben leave.

CHAPTER TWENTY-NINE

ON THE OTHER SIDE OF the country in a Holiday Inn in Manassas, Virginia, six men are gathered for a meeting. Four of them are of Middle Eastern descent and two men are of South American descent. All the men are American citizens, their birth certificates are written so, but only one is truly from the USA. His name is Sardar Arjmand; his parents were from Iran and moved to the USA forty years ago. Sardar was raised in New York City, where he became deeply involved with Islamic religion. He has a business of imports of Egyptian art and antiques. He is well known as an extremist and a person of interest by the FBI. He has been watched for years. His imports of goods are always examined by Homeland Security but no contraband has ever been found. The FBI knows full well that weapons, explosive devices, and money are being shipped in and out of the country by Sardar. They also know that he is fronting many of the Islamic extremists' movements in and out of the country. Sardar is also an expert in making explosive devices. He has degrees in chemistry and electrical engineering from MIT. He also worked in Iraq during the middle of the Iraq war. During this time, he was responsible for building many IEDs (improvised explosive devices). He was responsible for killing and wounding hundreds of American soldiers. He not only has he made and sold the IEDs but volunteered as a bomb expert for the army. He helped to disable hundreds of IEDs found by the military. To the military, he is a hero and a traitor. To the terrorist, he is a hero.

The other three men of Middle Eastern descent are not citizens at all. They had come from Iraq, Iran, and Pakistan. They flew into

Venezuela, where they met up with two men from Venezuela. They left from Puerto Capella in a boat and traveled across the Caribbean Sea to Cuba. In Cuba, they were assisted by government officials. They were given American passports, money, and weapons. They waited in Cuba for several months and waited for the right moment to travel up into the USA. When the hurricane hit the gulf coast, they traveled up into New Orleans. It was easy to get into the States because in the aftermath of the hurricane, the whole area was in chaos. They walked right off the boat and into the States. FEMA (Federal Emergency Management Agency) gave them all prepaid cards with two-thousand-dollar limits and a free ride into Texas. From there they bought a van with the money they got from FEMA and drove up to Virginia. Once in northern Virginia they met up with Sardar, who set them up with a house and high-level government connections. It was easy to assimilate them into American life with Sardar's connections. They all went to the police academy where they worked as state police in Northern Virginia area. After a year, they all applied for special agents into the Secret Service. Because of the government's plan to be more diverse in their hiring minorities and the government's plan to incorporate Muslims into high and important positions, they were easy picks to be placed into Secret Service training. The government was so set on showing the world that they were not prejudice against Muslims and Latinos. They were pushed into the Secret Service so fast that the background checks were not entirely completed. Once they completed their training, they were placed in service to guard the vice president and the president.

Tonight they are all gathered to go over the plans that are going to happen in January. Everything is going well with everything. With Sardar's connections, he is able to get anything that he wanted and how he wanted it. They all know that January 13 is a big day that will change the whole world. Nothing must go wrong, so they planned everything down to the minutest details.

The country is in a deep recession and it is very difficult to find work. Gas prices are through the roof which even makes it more difficult to make any money. The government though is spending money like it grows on trees. There are almost ninety million people on food stamps and about that many on unemployment and welfare. The presidential administration is trying to reduce government spending by cutting the military. The US military is losing its power status in the world. China is launching their own aircraft carriers and has an unknown number of nuclear submarines. North Korea is testing their three stage rockets. Iran is producing weapon grade plutonium and working to equip terrorist groups. These terrorist groups have the mind-set to rid the world of Israel and the USA. Normally these countries and groups run in fear from the US military, but now they just scoff at the United States. The president has shown that he will do nothing except bribe and talk to those who show contempt. The United Nations is a corrupt group of dictators that take money for the United States and do nothing to prevent evil around the whole. All and all, the United States politicians are killing the greatest nation on the earth without vigilance.

China takes great interest in the United States. It relies on the people of the US to buy all their copycat manufacturing goods. They make it almost impossible for US companies to produce anything more inexpensive. China has almost no development cost for most of their manufacturing. Most of their products are developed from deconstructing already made products and then reconstructing them with cheap materials and labor. Many Americans love how cheap they can purchase goods even though they are far inferior to products made in America. As more manufacturing goes over to China, so does the money. Soon America has almost nothing to sell in the global market except for services. A country cannot stay rich if it has nothing to sell. Now China has all the money, and the money left in the US is just swirled around but never adding more wealth. The US government started borrowing money from the very country they helped develop. China knows it has the wealth to buy America and it is doing so little by little. They have been sending over their women to hook up with American men that have been manipulated into thinking Oriental women are great sexual trophies. This fallacy is perpetuated by the pornography industry. These Chinese women get an American boyfriend or husband so they can buy property in the United States. Now with the housing industry in distress, the

Chinese women are buying houses at an alarming rate. China funds these women without question. After keeping the properties for a short time, Chinese banks foreclose the properties. China now owns the properties. This type of thing is happening every day on a small and large basis despite all the US laws. China is taking America slowly and silently, but it wants more, faster.

DH and Ronald found that the land in Nevada that was bought had been used by the military. The land has a missile silo on it that used to house an MX nuclear warhead. The silo has been decommissioned and the missile removed because of President Barrack's nuclear reduction agreement with Russia. Most of the living areas and elevators are still functional. Ronald just has expanded the whole bunker and added different levels inside the silo area. Since Nevada is hit hard with the recession, it wasn't hard to get several construction companies working at one time. DH has the construction crews working twenty-four hours a day seven days a week. The bunker and the runway are completed in six weeks. DH gave all the construction workers an extra year's wages for completing the project quickly.

Sam and Ben have been busy in the meantime. Sam and Ben find several out of work retired special forces men that desperately wanted a job. Sam is more than happy to give them a job. He had hired about a hundred and seventy men. All of them are paid the same. They all receive a hundred and fifty thousand. Everyone's bills are paid. Most of men are not married and don't have kids. Those that have families are sent to stay out at the bunkers for two weeks at a time and go home for a week. They also have the option of moving families to Nevada, South Dakota, or Virginia. Those with no families just move to one of the three bunkers. Now Sam has a small army. He will be able to easily move into any of the meth labs and take them over.

Also on Sam's travels, he finds a man who knows of an old military bunker in Southern New Mexico. So when they check it out, it is locked up tight and it looks as if no one has been there for years. The place has its own runway large enough for anything to land on it. Sam has Darwin find out if the property is for sale. Darwin finds that the army is selling it on the army surplus website. Sam buys it immediately. Within a few a weeks of jumping through hoops to get the title from the army, Sam finally gets the doors opened.

DH and Ronald have the Greek fly them down to New Mexico. Once they land, Sam and Ben meet the three men at the runway. Sam smiles and says, "Hey, good to see you all."

Everyone shakes hands like they haven't seen each other in years. The Greek says, "Shit, Sam, how the hell did you find this place? It's nowhere on any map." The Greek had to fly around for several hours and follow a road map just to find the place. The place is not listed anywhere as a landing area.

"Oh, we met someone that knew someone that well, you know, we just fell in to it," Sam tells everyone.

"It looks old as hell," DH says. "What does the inside look like?"

They all make their way through the bunk. Everything is old. Ronald and DH estimate that the generators, vehicles and other utilities are all from about the 1960s.

"So everything here is an antique?" Sam asks. "Is anything any good?"

"Old yes, some of the generators may be repairable. The pumps and all the wiring and plumbing is shit. The vehicles are antiques and can be sold but the rest is shit too," DH says with negativity. He is getting tired of being away from home. He hadn't been home for weeks and his wife has been giving him hell for not getting home to see the kids more often. His kids are all twenty or older.

"Well then, here is your new project. Go out and find some crews and fly them in here to fix the place up to tip-top order. I want this place like a home away from home. Make sure that any of the crews you bring in have no idea where the hell they are," Sam says. "I don't even what them to know what state they are in."

"How the hell are we going to get them in here?" DH asks in a snide tone. "We can't drive anything into here without someone knowing what state they are in."

"Well, we will just have to fly everyone in," Sam says stern but slightly sarcastic tone. "We'll fly up to Nevada and get your crews you used up there. We'll just fly everything in that you need. What do you think?"

"I'll bet them crews wouldn't mind working again. They made a hell of a lot of money the last job," DH says more calmly. "Do you know anyone with a cargo plane?"

"Well, by now we are supposed to have one, but we can probably get another one some place," Sam says calmly. "Greek, Do you know anyone we can buy a cargo plane from?"

"Matter of fact, I do," Greek says as he rubs his chin with his right hand. "Sam, did you ever jump out of the jet in Illinois?"

"Yes, but that was a long time ago," Sam says as he stares down at the ground trying to remember the good old days.

"Well, the guy that owns the jet has wanted to sell it, but none of the drop zones can afford the plane right now. It's old but it has been kept in great repair," the Greek says. "I'll call him as soon as we find a phone that works. I have a pilot that works for us that used to fly for UPS and I will get him to fly for you."

"Well, good, let's get started right now. DH, you and Ronald are in charge. Ben and I are going back to South Dakota and we are going to get started back to working on . . . ahhhh," Sam says, then remembers that the Greek is not really one of them. "Reclamation."

DH, Ronald, and the Greek fly back to Nevada to arrange all the transport of the work crews. Sam and Ben drive back to South Dakota. It takes them about fifty hours of hard driving. They had a flat tire in the New Mexico tundra because of the bad roads they had to take to get to the highway.

Sam and Ben get back to South Dakota to find that there is a lot of tension in the air among the men and women stationed there. The place is dirty and unorganized. The front gate is unattended when they came though during the middle of the day. Sam calls all the people still around the farm to a meeting.

Everyone comes to the dining hall. They come in one by one over a half an hour time. The longer everyone takes to get into the hall the angrier Sam gets. Sam wishes that Kim, Bud, Harland, or Kota were back already, but they had just called in and told Josh that it will be another week before they are back. Sam knows he could have sent one of them to get everyone rounded up and bodies would fly into the room. Since he is now alone, he will just wait and then kick some ass.

"OK, Ben and I are back. We have scouted the whole western states, and we now have new bunkers. We now have new men among us and I hope everyone has been hospitable and made them feel at home. I also have seen that this place has turned to shit since I have been gone and I would like to know why. Anyone got an explanation?" Sam asks.

About ten people all start yelling and once. Then a pushing match breaks out and is quickly broken up by others standing around them. Sam starts shouting, "Shut the fuck up until I call on you."

Giorgio starts yelling. He swaggers up to Sam. Sam just stands there. Giorgio gets closer to Sam and then throws a punch at Sam. Sam just leans way to avoid the punch and comes up with a right foot to the bottom of Giorgio's jaw. Blood instantly erupts out of Giorgio's mouth. Giorgio is stunned and on the verge of passing out. Sam follows with a right cross and a right elbow to the head. Giorgio falls to the ground. Two men come up and pick Giorgio off the ground. They drag him to the infirmary.

"Can anyone tell me what the fuck that was for?" Sam shouts. "Josh, get your ass up here now and tell me what the hell is going on."

"Giorgio has been saying a lot of shit about how you have been getting rich off what we did and that we all should get an equal split," Josh says. "He has been stirring a lot of the guys up and shooting his mouth off to the new guys about how you treat people like shit. About eighteen of us have been doing triple duty around here. The threat risks are low during the day, so we need some rest. That is why there was no one at the gate, but we were monitoring the gate."

"What the hell have the rest of the men been doing?" Sam asks.

"They have been going out every night and some of them we haven't seen for a few weeks. I know that they found the vault. Giorgio found it and has been trying to get into it since. So we posted a guard out front. Then Giorgio and a couple guys beat the guard up pretty bad. We had to take him to the hospital. We now have two guards on the vault, and then the story just goes on from there," Josh says.

"Well then, Josh, point out those who have been working," Sam says.

"I can't rat anyone out, Sam," Josh says.

"I'm not asking you to rat anyone out. I just want you to point out those who have been working so that I can reward them with a few things I picked up along the way," Sam says.

"OK." Josh calls up the eighteen people. They all look tired. Sam reached into to a large duffel bag and pulls out eighteen 1911 semiautomatic .45s that he found in the bunker in New Mexico. They were antiques and all originals still packed in wax paper. Sam hands them out to the men who had been working and thanks them for their dedication to their job.

Those that received the new weapons go and sit down together on one side of the room. They can see that Sam is mad and there is going to be hell to pay. They just didn't want to be in direct fire of Sam's wrath.

"So now," Sam says abruptly and turns to look at the twenty-seven other men sitting in the room. "What do you all have to say for yourself? Why do you all not want to work?"

One of the new men name Van says, "We new guys got here and there were no orders, so we did what we could, like clean shit up and stuff. We didn't come here to free load and shit, we came to work."

"I had no idea things were so dysfunctional around here," Sam says and then turns to Josh. "Is this true, Josh?"

"I told them to make their selves useful until we had some orders. We didn't trust the new guys to do guard duty," Josh says. "It's not the new men Sam that would not work. It's Giorgio's buddies sitting over there." Josh points to a table of twelve men.

"OK, all you new men come on up and get yourself an original .45 1911. You probably deserve it or you will deserve it. Thanks for coming." Sam hands them all out one by one.

Sam turns to the twelve men sitting in the back. "Well, do any of you men have an explanation for this mess?" Sam asks while looking at the twelve men.

"We heard you made away with a load of cash on the job we did and we all think we should get and equal split," Burt, one of the men at the table, says.

"You do, do you?" Sam says. "I paid everything upfront. You are working for me and whatever I take away from a job is my business. What the hell do you think we are doing here?"

"We didn't know you were getting rich off the jobs," Burt says. "We just thought you were going to get rid of meth labs for some personal reason or some shit. Hell, maybe we will just take over this fucking place and we could get rich doing this shit." Burt smiles and put in one of those little laughs like people do when they think they just came up with a great idea.

"Well, Burt, that will be hard for you to do when you are buried up to your fucking neck in a hog pen," Sam says. "How many of you feel this way?"

Burt is getting really brave and arrogant much like Giorgio. He stands up with a cocky stance and his arms out. "Shit, Sam, we are all in this together. You just need to talk to me and I can straighten this whole thing out." The others just sit there and shake their heads. Burt turns and looks at them, "Isn't that right, boys?"

"Fuck no, that's not right, Burt, you stupid fuck. I like it here and I was happy with everything until you and Giorgio started strong-arming everyone in to your guy's stupid plan," one of the men says.

"Yeah, Burt, shut the fuck up," the other men say.

"Looks like you are all alone on this big takeover there, Burt." Sam says in a sarcastic tone.

Burt flips everyone off at the table and turns toward Sam. Burt is thinking he will just take Sam out. Sam is older and doesn't have any military training. Burt pulls out a knife and waves it around. "OK, Sam, I can do it alone. Now when I get done with you, I'll just wait for your brothers to get back and get them too. Or you can just get me the combination to the safe and I'll take what I want and leave."

"I'd love to do that, Burt, but I know you would just blow it all and come back for more. I just couldn't stand the fact that I would have to see you again and again. So I am just going to get rid of you now and save everyone the trouble of ever having to look at you again," Sam says with a smirk on his face.

"Just how the fuck you think you are going to do that? I got the knife and you got nothing," Burt says as he is slowly circling Sam.

Sam just waits until Burt moves into the right position. Then he does a jump spin reverse crescent kick to Burt's head. Burt stumbles back and drops the knife. Sam jumps forward and kicks Burt in the face. Blood explodes from Burt's nose. Then he hits the ground and starts quivering. Sam picks up Burt's knife and cuts a notch in each of Burt's ears. Sam motions to a couple of men to drag Burt off to the infirmary.

Sam looks over at the table where Burt had been sitting and asks, "Anyone else got a problem and want to give me a try?"

Everyone shakes their heads and says, "No, we're good."

"Then get to work," Sam says sternly. "You all are on cleaning crew until this place is spotless. I will be doing a white glove walk through tomorrow. If this place is not spotless by then, you all will meet the same fate as Giorgio and Burt."

They all get up from the table and one of them says, "We'll git it done, Sam." Then they run off. When Sam leaves the dining hall, there are people cleaning everywhere.

An hour later, Sam goes to infirmary to talk to Giorgio and Burt. Sam is accompanied by Sarah and Josh.

"You both look like shit," Sam asks. "Any of you want to give it another try?"

"You asshole! If you wouldn't have sucker-punched me, I would have—" Giorgio starts off until Sarah slapped him, leaving behind a handprint on Giorgio's face.

"Well then, Giorgio, I can see I can never trust you, so I have three choices for you to choose from, but what say you, Burt? Are you with Giorgio?" Sam asks.

"I stick with him. He ain't never lied to me," Burt says as he gives a thumbs-up to Giorgio.

"OK, here are your options," Sam says. "One, I just cut your throats right here. Two, we fly you to the Mokave Desert or somewhere bad or maybe just dump you in to the ocean and let you fend for yourselves. Maybe you all live or maybe you die. But first, we remove you tongues so you can't tell anyone anything and maybe your hands so you can't write. Three, you all stay here and you're on permanent cleaning duty. You will never talk to anyone, ever. No one will talk to you, nor will they look at you. You keep your same pay, and in a year or so, if we can trust you, you can leave. If you run, we will shoot you or worse. So take your pick, you have five minutes."

Giorgio knows that Sam will kill him or have someone do it. He is a nervous. While the options were being gone through, he thinks that the last option of being caught running is being fed to the pigs alive or some other horrific thing. He tells Sam, "I choose the third option."

Burt is not nervous at all. He still considers himself a tough guy and will just wait out his time till the right moment when he can take out Sam. He tells Sam, "I guess I'll take the third option, but if I feel like leaving, I'll just leave. You bastards can't hold me here."

"Well, what would you have me do for you. I can't trust you outside of these walls and I really don't want to look over my shoulder for the rest of my life. Hmmm, I'll think on it, so for right now, Josh go get two of the men," Sam tells Josh.

Josh comes back with two of the new men. Sam points to Burt and the two men walk over to Burt. Burt jumps off his bed. He pushes one man and punches the other in the face. One man flies back and falls on the bed that Giorgio was in, and the other falls back but he catches his balance. Burt lunges toward Sam. Sam grabs Burt by the back of his head and slams him to the ground. The man that got punched in the face quickly moves over to where Burt is lying and kicks Burt in the back of the head at the base of the skull fracturing and displacing the atlas. The kick severed the spinal cord. Burt's body goes limp in Sam's arms and his eyes rolled up into his head. Sam lets Burt go and he stands up. Burt's body starts to convulse and then nothing. Josh runs over and feels for a pulse, there is none. Burt is dead.

"Did I fucking kill him?" The one man stands there in disbelief and fear. "Shit, man, I just kicked him. I didn't mean to kill him. Really I didn't."

"It's going to be OK," Sarah says as she puts an arm round the man's shoulder. "Now just keep your mouth shut and there will be no problems. OK?"

"Yeah, I know. It's not the first time I killed someone. I was in the first wave in Iraq, you know. You can trust me not to make waves," the man says.

"So what is your name?" Sam asks and looks at the man.

"Justin WindEagle," the man says.

"OK, WindEagle, how would you like to be my personal bodyguard?" Sam asks.

"I'm ready," WindEagle says.

Ben comes into the room and looks at the mess. "What the hell you want me to do with him?"

"Find out if he has any family, and if he does, dump him out along with a motorcycle somewhere in a town with no cops and make it look like he was killed in an accident. They will get him to his family, if not, dump him in the badlands. The buzzards will have an early Thanksgiving," Josh says.

Ben looks at Sam. Sam nods. Sam looks over at Josh. "Get Giorgio to his new job. If he doesn't want to work, then take both of them."

Giorgio is happy to start working, and no one hears a word out of him.

CHAPTER THIRTY

PRESIDENT BARRACK IS RUNNING AROUND all over the country bragging about killing Osama Bin Laden. The Navy SEALs went in overnight and took Bin Laden out at his house in Pakistan. It had taken Barrack months to decide to take him out. Elsewhere around the world, there are people up rising. People are taking up arms against the tyranny of their governments. Most of the uprisings are supported by President Barrack, and the rebels are given military support. President Barrack says, "We need to support these people to help them in their struggle for democracy. They are only looking to transform their states and bring their people to freedom. We cannot stand by, while the dictators of these countries are killing their own people. So through an executive order, I am ordering the navy and air force to bomb selected targets that will help the rebels of these countries. They will take out artillery and tanks that have been killing innocent civilians." Soon after the rebels killed their dictators, the new governments declared that the countries are Islamic states and that they will bring back sharia law.

In Mexico, automatic weapons are being shipped to drug cartels. These weapons are bought with drug money with the help of the ATF. The weapons are helped across the border and put into the hands of drug cartels. The ATF claims it is so that they can follow the weapons and then arrest those that have them. The guns were never tracked across the border. The real reason is to supply guns along the border in order incite fear and to control the people crossing the border. This keeps the competition of Mexican drugs out of the US, which raises the price of the available drugs. That is how so many "under the table" programs are funded. The meth labs raise billions of dollars for these special programs that are controlled by a few congressmen and senators. President Barrack also used it for his cause for gun control. He figures the American people will sympathize with the Mexican border people's fears that he can get a good following. He can easily push his agenda of a gun ban on to the American people.

Everyone is back in South Dakota, except for DH and Ronald, who are still finishing up the bunkers in New Mexico and Nevada. Sam calls a meeting with his brothers, Kim, Sarah, Harland, Mike, Dan, Whiskers, Skids, Mickey, Bozzel, Poppers, Josh, Ben, Lisa, Beth, WindEagle, and Jamie.

"OK, I'm glad that everyone made it back OK. Now is everyone ready to run and clean house?" Sam asks with some enthusiasm.

"Yeah!" everyone yells.

"OK, first things first. I need a beer, someone have Giorgio's bring some up here," Sam says. Bud runs and calls over the loud speaker. Giorgio comes running dragging a wagon full of beer. He rolls it in the center of the room and then quickly leaves. "Well, I think we found his position here." Sam laughs. "I'm going to tell about how I think we should do this whole thing and then I want you guys to jump in and tell me what you think."

"This is not going to work," Kota says. We need a table so we can throw some maps on it and we need a TV in here because we did a lot of video surveillance."

"OK, let's move over to the house and we can talk over there," Sam says.

They all move over to the kitchen in house. Kota throws down a map. "Here is the layout of Maine, two labs in New York, Illinois, Ohio, and Michigan. We bought abandoned farms all around each of the areas." Kota goes over and turns the TV and video camera on. "Here is the video surveillance we took both on the ground and in the air. There are twenty-two men in the lab in Maine, two hundred and ten men in the northern lab in New York, and three hundred fifty some in southern New York. Illinois had over four hundred. Ohio only has ninety-five men. Michigan though has the most men. For some reason, they have almost eight hundred. It is kind of hard to count because they are shipping up to Canada via boats and small airplanes. We followed one plane up to Canada, and they are not even slowing down, they just parachute the stuff it the middle of nowhere. Right now, I don't see how we are going to break in a take-over these places. They have people that are there 24/7."

"Dakota!" Sam says. "You did a great job. I am going with you to your sector to help and we will figure out something. Bud what did you come up with?"

Bud puts down his map. "We looked at Texas, Alabama, Florida, Missouri, Oklahoma, and Louisiana. We also bought farms in the general locations of all the labs. In Florida, the southern lab is right in the middle of Miami. There is at least five or six hundred men working and living in this huge warehouse. It was hard to say because people came and went like it was Walmart. Kim went in and looked around. Kim, what ya think?"

"Almost like a whole other town in there. I didn't get into the secured areas, but I did go into the garage and there are at least fifteen troop carriers, about ten to twelve armored Hummers and about twenty of those little rice burner street racers in there. They look like they transport about all the drugs in the cars and money is transported by the Hummers. The troop carries look like they never move," Kim informs everyone.

"Yeah, we followed one of the Hummer caravans, and they went to the airport and loaded everything on a twin otter. I don't know where the money ends up but the lady at the airport said the plane flies to New York all the time. Somehow, Kim got that information from her and I really don't want to know how. Anyway, Northern Florida's lab is really in the middle of nowhere. We counted about a hundred or so up there. Less traffic but it's still a very busy place. Several motorcycle gangs went in and out. They were small gangs of twenty or less. Alabama, Missouri, Oklahoma, and Louisiana each had between two to three hundred in each, and they all functioned about the same as every other lab that we already did. A bunch of drunks and druggies but not very military even though they have the weapons and vehicles. Texas though is the biggest most military place that we saw. There are probably a couple of thousand men there. Mostly motorcycle gangs, Mexicans, and some military men housed there. We will need to bomb that place to get the rats out. They have walls and constant guards. I saw at least eight to nine helicopters, an airstrip with ten airplanes, and one cargo plane. We caught a couple of the men from there at a bar. Kim got them talking about everything that goes on inside the place. Did you know that they are cooking for the drug runners in Mexico? They pretty much control all the drugs coming and going from Mexico. It's a huge business," Bud informs everyone and then goes over to plug in his video camera to show everything.

"Well, what happened to the men you caught?" Sam asks even though he knows the answer. "Are they going to go back and put the place on alert?"

"I don't think they will talk to anyone again." Kim says with a twinkle in his eye.

"OK, good job, you guys," Sam compliments. "I'll get to my little presentation later, but I was thinking we break up into two groups. Now that I know what we are up against, I am thinking we should all stay together. These places aren't going to be as big a push over as what we had before. Here is a little more information for you. We now have two more bunkers, one in New Mexico, which is huge. It's like an old government bomb shelter built for like a president to hide out in. The other is in Nevada. DH said that it is an old nuclear missile silo base. He said the place is huge and very livable. DH and Ronald should be finishing up on those places soon. We also have a hundred seventy new men and women that are all ex-military." Sam goes over and grabs a beer. "So what do you all think?"

"Sounds dangerous," Sarah says. "I'm all in and I think we should stay together."

Everyone agrees that they should stay together. And they start making plans and strategies.

"Hey, where the hell is WindEagle?" Sam asks. "Can someone get him in here."

Jamie walks over to the door and WindEagle is standing right outside of it. "WindEagle, Sam wants to see you right away," Jamie says.

WindEagle quickly turns and runs toward Sam. He stops and stands at attention two feet in front of Sam.

"Sir," WindEagle says and then salutes.

"We don't salute here but we do bow. Anyway is there any military strategist in the group you came with?" Sam asks.

"Yes, sir, Miles Drake, I fought along with him in Desert Storm and in Iraq. Shall I get him?" WindEagle asks.

"Yes, we need him right now," Sam says calmly. WindEagle bows and runs out of the room. Twenty minutes later, he comes back in with Miles.

"You rang?" Miles asks in a disgruntled voice.

"Yes, I did," Sam says with a little bitterness. "Am I troubling you by having you come over to the house?"

"No, no, these big jerks just dragged me out of bed and I am not quite with it yet." Miles rubs his eyes with his hands and then looks over at the maps and wagonload of beer. "You mind if I have a beer and look at those maps?"

"No, help yourself," Sam says with a calm tone to his voice. "We are planning twenty-seven raids on places that have us out numbered and in places that are built like military bases. We are also going to do an additional place, just to put the icing on the cake."

"What the hell are you talking about, Sam?" Jamie yells.

"There is this bank in the middle of New York City that holds all the money that these labs collect. There is billions of dollars. Darwin said that it is a secret holding area for several congressmen and senators. They use this money to pay for things like supplying weapons to the Mexican drug cartels and also weapons and money that funds rebels like those in Libya, Egypt, and also Al Qaeda, Hezbollah, Hamas, and others like those the troops have been fighting in Afghanistan. Like those people that lob rockets into Israel. They fund one side so it makes them politically important." Sam goes over and gets another beer. "This is why we are going to drive downtown New York and take it all. What do you think?" Sam asks everyone.

"Hell yeah," everyone says.

"Well, right now we are going to drink a little and tomorrow we are going to plan everything out starting with Maine. Josh, please call the Nevada bunker and tell them to get there asses over here by tomorrow afternoon. Then call the Greek and tell him to get the cargo plane over to the drop zone to pick the men up and fly over here. Then get back here and we need to drink tonight." Sam says.

The next morning, everyone is in the house bright and early. Sam has been up all night with Miles, watching surveillance videos and going over plans on how to bust the labs. Sam has also told him about a plan he has been thinking about to break into the bank. Now this morning Sam presents it to everyone else that is in the meeting the night before. Sam's plan is to keep everything simple and small as possible. First thing is to start a diversion to get as many of the YUPPIs out of the compounds and then set snipers along the roads and around the compound. Small groups of five to ten men per building move in to the compound and remove personnel and explore each building. The goal is to remove anything worth anything from the compounds. Leave buildings intact and leave as quietly as possible and never draw attention.

All the men and women from Nevada arrive at the Sioux Falls airport in the afternoon except for ten of them that stayed behind to guard the bunker. Sam hired three buses to pick them up and bring them out to the farm. Once the men and women were fed, they all were told about the plans. Ten men are going to stay behind to guard the bunker. Everyone else is going to pack up and head to Maine on two carrier airplanes. Sam figures after the first lab is busted that there would be plenty of weapons and vehicles to use to bust the others. They packed light and are going to move fast and nonstop until they are done with all the labs. This would be away of not letting the labs get ready for the attacks. Sam recalled Ho Shih rules: "Haste may be stupid, but at any rate it saves expenditure of energy and treasure. Protracted operations may be very clever, but they bring calamity in their train." Also the words of Sun Tzu, which said, "Hence a wise general makes a point of foraging on the enemy." Sam had always read a lot and now some of his reading is being utilized.

Sam gives everyone the week off to go to town or whatever they wanted to do. He wanted to leave right away, but all the people looked like they were too wound up to focus on the new adventure. This time gave Sam time to get all the plans set in stone and to get to know everyone. Sam finds out that he has ten retired marine snipers, four communications specialists, nine helicopter pilots, several special forces men and women, two marine pilots and three air force pilots, and several mechanics and engineers. He knows he has a great group of men that could do it all without him, but it is about the principle in the whole thing. He didn't start all this but he is going to finish it.

Everyone enjoyed their week off to relax and cut loose in town. Some of the men and women went over to Darrell's and Elaine's farm to ride horses. Some spent money shopping, and some went home to see their families. Everyone is refreshed and ready to go to work when they got back.

Sam had everyone ride the bus into the airport. He rode with Bud who drove a Hummer with a trailer loaded with everyone's personal weapons. They drove it and parked it on one of the cargo planes.

On the plane ride to Maine, Sam is sitting with some of the men. Many of the men are chatting about what they did with their week off. Sam is just sitting and thinking about what is to come. Terry Zenfield makes his way up to Sam from the back of the airplane, stepping and tripping over men and women that are scattered throughout the floor of the plane. Terry is a retired airborne ranger who retired because of bullet wounds to his lower leg and left side of his face. Terry now has a prosthetic lower leg and jaw. When Terry gets up to Sam, Sam stands up from his seat to let Terry sit down. Terry sits down in the seat and Sam sits on the floor of the plane. Neither one says a word for several minutes.

Terry looks at Sam, "I need to ask you a serious question."

Sam looks up. "Sure, you can ask me anything."

Terry rubs his hands together and then rubs his legs. "I just want to know, why you are doing this?"

Sam looks down and shuffles his feet around a little. Then he pulls out his can of Copenhagen and takes a dip. He offers some to Terry. Terry takes a dip and then hands it back to Sam. Sam put it back in to his front pants pocket, then pulled out his tactical knife and opens it up. He starts to clean under his fingernails. Sam always did this when he was deep in thought.

"Well, first of all, these guys started this little war. I am just a veterinarian. My brothers and I were minding our own business and they came after us. They will not let up until they are all dead. They are evil, ruthless bastards and we have seen them do things that you wouldn't expect one man would do to another. I'm sure you seen it before. It just gets under your skin and you cannot let it go. So one thing led to another and I found out it is our own government that is behind this so-called illegal drug trade. Now the government has been in my business for years and making it harder and harder to do my job. I have worked hard all my life and the more I work, the less I make. Hell, you can hardly make a living anymore. So when I found this was going on, I figured I would just take from them and give to those who really need it and deserve it, much like all of you guys. You all gave to the government and what the hell did you get back from them?" Sam asks.

Terry sits back in his seat and pulls up his pant leg. "I gave them a leg and my jaw. I would do it again because I fought for something I believe in. The great U. S. of A. and I love my country and I don't expect to get anything back. What the hell did you give?"

Sam was a little taken aback with Terry's tone. "I thank you for your service and I would commend you to anyone. I love my country and would die defending it. When I was your age, I tried to join the army and they would not take me because Old Slick Willy Clinton was in office and they were trying to get rid of people. They said that I had a hearing deficit and could not get into any of the military services. So I became a veterinarian. So what did I give to this country, I gave it loyalty, my time, my sweat, and quite of bit of my money. I give to those who need and want my help. I farmed so I gave this country food. I give and I give, much like most people in this country. You don't have to be in the military to give to your country."

Terry just stares at Sam for a moment. "I guess you are right. I haven't done anything since or before the military. I've been living off the government disability since I got back until you came along. I was so deep in debt that I could never pay it all off. I thank you for giving me a job and paying my debt off."

Sam says, "You don't have to thank me. I am just giving to someone that deserved and wanted some help and a job. Now to answer your question, I am doing this to do what is right. These politicians are getting rich off something that is killing your fellow Americans. In a way we all are protecting America by getting rid of these labs. The average meth user has approximate life span of about a year or two. We are saving lives. With the money we confiscate we can give to those in need. The government doesn't need it. They are just using it for underhanded operations. So I am doing it for you, for him, for her, for Joe and Sally America."

Terry is a little fired up after Sam's little speech. He felt energized and good just knowing he is doing well. "Sam, I glad I talked to you. I just wanted to know that you aren't doing this to get rich. I'm all behind you every step of the way. Everyone else will be too when I tell them. In truth, they all put me up to it. They said you are a real mean bastard when confronted, and I was the only one brave enough to volunteer to ask you."

Sam smiled. "No one needs to be afraid of me unless they try to hurt any of my friends or family."

Terry gets up and makes his way to the back of the airplane. Sam just sits there and then gets up. He climbs up to the cockpit to find out where the hell they are.

They land in Maine. Sam had Darwin hire three buses before they left Sioux Falls. The buses that carry all of them are rented. The farm is about ten miles from the lab compound. This location is well within walking distance. Everyone is equipped in the best body armor that is available. Weapons were chosen by individual choice. Communication is high-tech, the best that is available in the world. Everyone is good at what they are going to do.

First Sam sends his snipers and spotters, Kota included, to recon the compound and along the road. They are going to keep track of movement in and out of the compound. When the manpower is the lowest at the compound, that's when the attack will begin. Sam also sends Kim along with four five men groups to sit within five hundred yards from the compound. Several other five men teams will sit in various areas along the road to be the watch and to ambush any traffic coming and going. Several men and women, along with Bud, will stay at the farm and guard the area in case that everyone needs to move back to it for a safe hold. Sam takes ten men with him, including WindEagle.

The call comes in to Sam from one of the snipers. "Four Hummers with sixteen men are leaving the compound."

Sam calls the road crew. "Stop the Hummers, confiscate everything, and hold prisoner those that are still alive."

They all know that it has to be done quietly. They used the old "good-looking injured woman along the road" trick to stop the Hummers. One of the women on the road crew named Allie strips her shirt off so that she has on just a sports bra and her camo pants. She finds a large stick in the ditch along the road. She rips a hole in her pants' leg and rolls around in the dirt. She stands along the road using the stick as a crutch. When the Hummers drive up the road, the drivers instantly stop when they spot Allie standing on the road. Sixteen men instantly rush out and surround Allie. One of the men from the Hummers says, "My, my, pretty lady, what can we do for you, or better yet, to you?" When he reaches in to grab her arm, and as soon as he grabs for her, she jabs the end of the stick into his face. The end of the stick hits him square in the middle of the forehead. The blow knocks him back a bit. Then she swings the stick to back everyone off. As soon as they back away, they know they are done. Everyone in the road crew has surrounded them with rifles pointing in their direction. The men in the Hummers are taken without a fight. They didn't even know what hit them. Kim calls Sam, "Hummers taken, no shots, and no corpses."

Sam calls back, "Make one of them call in to their commander for some assistance. Then capture those that come out to help. Have some men take the prisoners and three of the Hummers to the farm.

Keep one Hummer and one man there on the road. Hopefully this will get them to stop."

Kim calls back, "Got it covered."

About thirty minutes later, one tow truck and two Hummers leave the compound. Kim captures those men as soon as they stop. Kim then makes one of the newly captured men call in to say that they are under attack. Within minutes, men at the compound are scurrying around arming themselves and loading on to vehicles. Three tandem trucks, two troop carriers, three armored Hummers, and two vans leave the compound. Kota calls Kim. "Kim, they are coming in heavy and are well-armed." Sam rushes to move his men into position to help Kim and his men.

The troop carriers come along first and Sam and Kim let them go by. The three heavy trucks come next. Kim and his men rain shock grenades down on the top of trucks. When the grenades go off, the trucks stop immediately and men come rolling out of the back of the trucks. Those men that were still able to fire there weapons are shot immediately by Sam's men. The three armored Hummers that are following right behind the trucks are immediately brought to a stop. Three of the men in the Hummers move into position of the .50-caliber machine guns mounted on top of them, but the men are quickly shot by sniper fire. Some of the men in the Hummers try to get out and fire at the attackers but are shot down immediately by the road crew and sniper fire.

The leader of the patrol quickly calls back to base, "We are being slaughtered out here. For the love of Allah, send more help." There is no answer from base.

Kota immediately calls Sam. "More men are moving out and headed toward you."

Sam calls back, "How many men left back at the lab?"

Kota calls back, "Not many, maybe ten or so."

Sam thinks to himself, "What a stupid mistake to send out all your men." He calls back, "Send the groups in and I'll be coming on in."

Sam calls Kim, "There are more men and trucks coming. I'm taking five men with me to move in on the lab. You got it out here?" Sam takes half of his group and moves on over to the lab.

"I got it. I have two groups going after those troop carriers," Kim calls back. "I'm just going to kill all these bastards. They are just a bunch of hired ragheads."

Sam replies, "Do as you please. Go get 'em."

By the time Sam gets to the lab, the teams have already searched all the buildings and captured twelve more prisoners. One of the prisoners is the commander that has given himself two gold stars on his collar. Sam walks in and looks over the prisoners. Then he walks up to the commander. "I presume that you are in charge here?"

The commander they call Khan replies in a Middle Eastern accent, "I am the commander and you all are the walking dead. How dare that you invade this base. It is under federal jurisdiction. You all will hang for terrorist acts against the US government."

Sam busts out laughing as he turns to Kota, Kim, and Bud, who just walked in.

Kota, Kim, and Bud all left their men to their duties and go into the compound where Sam and the prisoners are being held.

Kota smiles. "What needs to be done so we can get the hell out of here?"

Sam says, "First, get some of those trucks back here and start loading everything up. Then find out where the hell the cash is at."

The three of them leave. Sam turns back to Khan and kicks him in the nuts. Khan grabs his groin and falls to his knees. Sam leans over and asks Khan in a calm voice, "So three things. Tell me where the vault room is, who are you sending the money to, and are there any more men hidden anywhere around here?"

Khan spits at Sam. "Why the hell should I tell you anything? You are all going to jail as soon as my men get back here."

Sam laughs. "You will be waiting a long time before that happens. Looks like I won't be going to jail after all." Sam takes out his Copenhagen and takes a dip. Sam then spits back in to Khan's face. "Give some. Get some." Sam pulls his tomahawk out of the sheath.

He shows it to Khan and says, "Now you will start talking or I'm going to start carving you like a sculpture."

Khan recovers from his kick in the nuts. He looks Sam straight in the eye and says, "I will die before I tell an infidel like you anything."

Sam doesn't say anything. He grabs Khan's right ear and shaves it off with his tomahawk before Khan can even react. Khan screams as blood runs like a river from the side of his head. Khan holds his right hand up to the area to stop the pain. He stands up and starts dancing around like it will help take the pain away, all the while screaming, "Fuck, fuck, fuck . . ."

Just then Kota, Kim, and Bud come back in to room. Kim tells Sam, "The trucks are coming and we found a huge vault and something that you need to see."

Kota jumps in and says, "Yeah! But the fucking thing is locked."

Bud says, "We thought about blowing it up but I think it would be easier to have that bleeding bastard open it up."

Sam tells them, "Well, he says he is not talking. So you want to see about asking him before I start asking again." Sam holds up his tomahawk and twirls it around.

Kota walks over to Khan and looks at him. He asks him, "What's the combination to the door?"

Khan spits blood at Kota and screams, "Fuck you. I ain't opening it."

Sam says, "I'll be back so take over, Kota."

Sam walks with Bud and Kim. The walk down a long hallway, at the end is a door that opens to stairs that goes down to a lower floor. In the lower floor is an area that looks like kennel pens for dogs. In each small eight-by-eight pen is a young girl in her early teens. Each one is has a shackle on around the neck that is chained to an overhead cable. Sam walks up to one of the girls. She is wearing an old T-shirt but with nothing on underneath. She smelled like she had not bathed in months. She has arms that look like pincushions where she has been get shot up with some drugs for quite some time. She has no facial expression. Her eyes have the blank stare of a dead soul. There is nothing inside of the girl except a beating heart. Sam thought, "These bastards are kidnapping kids and using them for sex slaves. I am going to kill that fucking prick upstairs."

Sam looks around at the men and women standing around him. "Get these kids the hell out of here. Someone take one of the vehicles and take them to near fire and rescue place. They can get them to the hospital. They probably have parents that have been looking for them. As soon as we get this vault open, we can send some money with them so they can get home."

A bunch of the troopers jump in and start getting the collars off the girls. Some of the collars had been on so long that the girls had a hard time holding up their head without the neck support of the collars. They found some clothes for the girls to work. They tried to feed the girls, but all of them were too drugged up to eat.

Sam went back upstairs to where Kota has Khan. Sam is extremely mad.

Sam asks Kota, "You get anything out of the asshole rapist fuck yet?"

Kota says, "Nope, just waiting for the bastard to recover a bit so he feels the next beating more." Kota takes one step back and gives Khan a lunging kick to the nuts. This time they all hear a pop when the kick lands. Khan falls to the ground as he grabs for his crotch with his left hand while still holding on to his right face. He writhes around on the floor in pain and then he vomits. Vomit and blood covers the floor in a pool of crimson stew. Kota is getting ready to kick him again, but Sam stops him. Not that Sam cares but he needs Khan to be alive to open the safe.

Sam leans over, "I would suggest that you tell them what they want, or I'll let him back over here to finish what has started."

Khan lets out a groan. "Fuck you."

Sam steps back and let Kota give him another kick, but this time it is to the tailbone. There is a loud crack when the kick lands. Khan rolls over and flips them off. Kota tells a couple of guys to come over and take off Khan's shoes. Kota leans over. "Now you either get up and open the fucking vault or give up the combination."

Khan just shakes his head. Kota pulls out his knife and stops. He says to Khan, "Now this is going to really hurt, and I'm not going to stop till you die, which will be about two or three days from now." Kota signals two men. "You guys hold him down." Kota grabs Khan's big toe. He takes his knife and cuts the toenail off. Khan screams in pain. He struggles desperately to get away, but the two retired marines have a firm grip on him. Kota grabs another toe and is about ready to cut another nail off when Khan yells, "I'll open the fucking thing." The two men help Khan to his feet. They wrap Khan's head and foot with bandage material from their personal first aid kits. They help Khan to the vault room and up to the vault door. Khan has a sinister look on his face as he turns the dial. Khan stops turning the combination dial and steps back from the door. One of the retired marines grab the vault handle to open the door but just stands there shaking. Sam instantly notices that the marine is being electrocuted. Sam quickly takes off his belt and throws it around the man's body. He pulls him off the door's handle. The marine falls to the floor. Sam checks him for a pulse and checks for breathing. There is no pulse, so he begins CPR (cardiopulmonary resuscitation). After about two to three minutes, Sam gets the heart going again. The marine is alive but not able to stand. Two other men carry the marine to one of the trucks. After dealing with all that, Sam turns to Khan. Sam looks him in the eyes and can see the glimmer of laugher. Sam grabs Khan by the hair with his left hand and begins to punch him in the face with his right until Khan falls to the floor. Blood and teeth falls from Khan's mouth. Khan turns over and gets on one knee then spits blood.

Khan looks up at Sam and smiles with blood still packed between his the few teeth that still remain, "You bastards will never get in. I will never open it. So you can all go fuck yourselves."

Sam slaps the man. "You will open it or we will make you wish you could die."

Sam motions to a couple of men to grab Khan and tie him to a chair. Sam tells them to strip Khan naked. One takes out his knife and cuts the clothes off Khan. The men slam Khan down into the chair and tie his hands and legs to the chair.

Sam walks over to the chair and asks, "You sure you don't want to open that vault because this is going to hurt and you will never heal up from this."

Khan struggles in his bonds and there is fear in his eyes. The cunning little smile disappears from his face as he goes into desperation mode. He knows if he will open the vault, he will be killed anyway, so he really didn't know what to do. He looks at Sam and yells, "Fuck off."

Sam sends one of his men to go get a hammer and some nails. The man quickly leaves the room, and within seconds, he comes back with a hammer and some sixteen-penny nails. Sam takes the hammer and one nail. He holds the nail over one of Khan's thigh and hits it with the hammer. The nail buries deep into the Khan's femur. Khan screams in pain and tears come streaming from his eyes while the pain shots through Khan's body worse than any broken bone would ever do.

Sam asks Khan again, "Open the vault."

Khan shakes his head. Sam grabs another nail and holds it over Khan's kneecap. Sam hits the nail and drives it in through the kneecap. Khan screams in pain and yells, "STOP! STOP!"

Sam takes the hammer and pulls both nails out. They untie him. Two of the men carry Khan to the vault door. Khan twists the dial around, but this time the door comes open. Kim goes inside the room and looks around for any traps. Then Sam goes into the vault.

Inside the vault is several crates of gold bars, millions in cash, and several antiques. Sam has everything loaded on to the truck.

Two men sit Khan back into the wooden chair and keep watch over him as several men haul everything out of the vault. Once everything is loaded on to a truck, Sam comes back to deal with Khan.

Sam says, "I should just shoot you, but you did open the safe. That gives you some brownie points."

Khan screams, "As soon as I get out of here, I will kill you and all your families."

Sam says, "If I see you again, I will cut you limb from limb with no hesitation, but for now you get a chance to live."

Sam sends one of his men for a can of gas or diesel. The man runs and returns in a few minutes with a five gallon can of diesel. Sam walks over and grabs the hammer and nails up off the floor where he left them. Sam tells the two men that are watching over Khan to hold him down. Khan struggles but has no fight left in him. Sam takes two nails. He nails Khan's left hand to the arm of the chair then bends the nails over so that the arm cannot pull off the nails. Khan lets out a yell. Sam tells one of the men to grab Khan's penis and stretch it out on to the seat of the chair. Sam takes a nail and nails it to the chair. Khan screams but only for a short burst.

Sam leans over and tells Khan, "You are only going to have a short period of time to get free and then you will burn." He pulls out a knife and sticks it through the web part of the fingers into Khan's right hand. "Here is what you need to do to save your miserable life. You need to pull your right hand off the knife. Then take the knife and cut your hand and penis off and run for the door. Or you can try running for the door while you are nailed to the chair."

Sam takes the diesel and dumps it on Khan and all around the room. He throws the can toward the chair. Sam yells to Khan, "I would get going if I were you, you stupid fuck."

Everyone has already left the room. Sam is standing at the door-way with one of the retired marines.

Khan yells, "You will fucking die many horrible deaths. I will be there to remove your fucking head." He starts to try to stand up with the heavy wooden chair but cannot make it to his feet.

Sam takes a Zippo lighter from the retired marine. He lights it and throws it in to the room. They both leave before the lighter hits the ground.

Khan struggles trying to stand again for a few seconds and then realizes his only way to move is to cut himself out. He pulls his hand off the knife and starts cutting through his left hand. He gets through, but the flames are only a few feet away. He just sits there bleeding from his left arm, unwilling to cut off his penis to save his life. Flames envelop him and the chair. He screams and then cuts off his penis and runs for the door. It is too late now; he is engulfed in flames. His flesh begins to bubble from the burns. He dives out the door but cannot make it any further. He lies there unconscious until the flames burn out. A pool of blood forms as death comes for him.

They haul everything to the rented farm. Once at the farm, Sam is confronted with what to do with the prisoners. Sam gathers up all his leaders to figure out what to do with the prisoners.

"Let's just shoot them all and throw them back into the lab and then set it on fire," Kim says. He gives a laugh, but he is not joking. "Better yet, maybe we just lock them in the lab and set it afire and that will save bullets."

"No. No. We can't kill them all, even though it would be nice and easy. We can't just let them go because they will keep coming back until we kill them just like the others. Well, any other suggestions?" Sam says and then takes off his hat and rubs his head. Sam always did this when he was tired and needed to think. It was like winding up his brain.

"Let's just get about seven of those shipping containers and ship these guys to Timbuktu. Shit, by the time they get back, everything will be done and over with," Bud says with a laugh.

Everyone looks around and nods. Sam says, "That is a great idea, but they will all be dead before they get there. WindEagle, you find out where we can send the crates that will take about thirty days to get there. Maybe like Alaska or way down south in Mexico. Kim and Bud, you guys go and get the men to chain up the prisoners. Kota finds some men to get the prisoners some food and water and lots of vodka. I want them drunk and full until the crates come. We'll chain them in the crates with food and water when we ship them. Kim and Bud, after you get that done, we need to load this bounty on to the planes and get it to Virginia. We'll use as many vehicles as we need to get the men to the next lab, the rest of them ship on the plane. Everybody good? Then let's go."

Everyone goes off to do their job.

CHAPTER THIRTY-ONE

THINGS WERE NOT ONLY GOING bad in the United States but also across Europe and the Middle East. Greece, Italy, Spain, and Ireland are on the doorstep of bankruptcy. Many countries, like Germany, France, and England, have been trying to bail those countries out of their mess. A country like Greece is so deep in debt and has a huge population of government-dependent people. Greece's government is broke. The people there don't produce anything but demand huge government handouts. President Barrack has given billions to the Greece even though the US debt is so high, it is impossible to ever break even. The US is just borrowing more from China. China has begun to realize that they will never get paid back unless they take it back.

Many Americans are starting to realize that the economy is not going to bounce back with all the government regulation choking small businesses to death. The new rules of loaning money to small businesses are to never give anyone a loan unless it is short term. Basically, if they need a loan they cannot have one. If they have property and they are behind over thirty days, a letter threatening foreclosure is to be sent out. If they are sixty days, then start foreclosure procedures. If they are ninety days over with any deficiency then foreclose immediately. The rapidity of foreclosures increased every month that Barrack has been President. Many people and companies are trying to refinance but no one will refinance for the low interest rates. The economy is a mess. Banks are losing money again even after the big bailouts. The dollar is close to being worthless.

Russia has been flexing its muscles all around the world. Syria is moving chemical weapons. Iran and North Korea has got nuclear capacities. Pakistan was an ally but is now being run by Muslim extremists. Egypt and Lebanon are just getting over civil wars and being taken over by the Muslim Brotherhood. The president of the United States takes a vacation and then starts his nation tour to campaign.

President Barrack's press secretary is constantly on the news, defending the president and his policies. Darwin decided to hack into the computer system at the White House, and whatever went in or out of the president's computer, a copy comes to Darwin. He did it by finding the phone number of the president's cell phone. When the president e-mailed or tweeted, a small piece of a virus was sent to the phone and then reconstructed into the main server of the White House via the Wi-Fi system used there. Over a period of several thousand message sent from the president's phone, the virus was reconstructed. Small piece of virus are totally undetectable by any know antivirus system used today. Darwin is very proud of his ingenious virus he has named Legos. Darwin loved the toy blocks that he had when he was a kid. With the virus imbedded into the main server, Darwin is able to go in and do what he wants because the system recognizes his computer only as the president's. Darwin has taken some of the worst of the underhanded dealings and sent it to the press. Most of the time the press did not acknowledge him until Duggie Harris looked into to some the anonymous stuff and found out it to be true. Duggie is a young and very ambitious free-lance reporter. He is like a hungry rat when it comes to finding the truth to any story. He has written and done many astounding stories over the last ten years, but the problem is he has no college education and no one takes him seriously. Most of his stuff is on the web, but only some of the conspiracy theorists read it. That is until Duggie kept hounding Gerry Beckley to read his webpage. Duggie tweeted Gerry every five minutes for three days until Gerry read the web and tweeted him back. After that, they met in private and they worked together since then. Gerry has a two-hour television show and a three hour radio show that has millions of listeners. He is well known for his explanations of conspiracy theories and getting people to think. Gerry has been using the inside information to broadcast. At first, the Barrack administration wrote it off as a coincidence and told the people that none of it was true. After the public's grumbling about the Barrack administration under-handed dealings became a roar, the president went out and told everyone, "You people just don't understand what is really being done. I am trying to clean up after the previous administration and trying to restore order and openness. All the problems that we have encountered have been from stopping the corrupt policies that had been started years ago. We have been fully transparent thus far about things that are being done, and some things are going to be difficult but necessary." After congress started their investigation, the president ordered everything secret by order of executive privilege. This didn't stop Darwin though; he finally found the e-mail that he was looking for:

"We must remove anyone or anything that can or does correlate this administration with the YUPPI group. We must halt all weapons transport to Mexico and dispose those involved. I feel that the best method is to let this Sam person and his group get rid of the personnel and the labs. This will keep us from being connected with anything, since somewhere in the office there are leaks."

Darwin sent the e-mail to Sam immediately. Sam tells Darwin to keep this under wraps because it may be a trap and send out red flags. To Sam, this is great news; he pretty much now has the blessing of the president to do what he wants to do.

All things are going well with Sardar Arjmand and his small crew. Sardar has the perfect plan and has been correlating with a man named John Overagh. John is a man in his midforties and had studied at South Dakota State University and at MIT. He has two degrees, one in mechanical engineering and another in chemical engineering. John is a native born American. His father, Jake Overagh, was a marine sniper who served three tours in Vietnam. After returning home from Vietnam, he found it difficult to return to civilian life in the USA. He found a better life in Africa. He could move from country to country if he liked, and no one ever troubled him. He lived mostly in the jungles and outer plains, but after a few years, he encountered a diamond smuggler named Jacque Jean Paul that needed assistance in guarding shipments. He was happy to assist since the pay was great. While traveling through a small town in Ethiopia, the convoy that Jake was leading was halted by an angry mob. In the center of the mob was a beautiful young woman who was accused of adultery with a married man. In reality, the woman was raped by the married man, but she was still guilty and the punishment was stoning. As soon as Jake seen this woman, he instantly fell for her. Jake had his driver drive straight into the mob and surrounds the young woman. Jake grabbed her and took her away. They got married soon after. Jake moved his wife back to the United States but traveled back and forth to Africa. Jacque was delighted about Jake's move. Jacque has Jake smuggle diamonds into the USA and purchase and ship weapons out. The weapons market was hot at this time and both Jacque and Jake made a fortune. Jake had a son born a year after being in the USA and they called him John. John was raised like a spoiled rich brat, because Jake was never around to discipline him and his mother never would say no to her baby boy. While in college, John fell in with an Islamic radical group formed from Iranians that were going to school at SDSU. They made John see that he really was not a true infidel American, but his heritage was that of a Muslim. This is where Sardar and John became friends.

John and Sardar have been planning for years to do something big. Sardar had talk John into getting a mechanical engineering degree because it would be needed for their big thing. The big thing is to stop as much interstate ground transport as possible by blowing up bridges, railways, power plants, dams, and then their really big bang. They have been buying trucks for a couple of year and buying up ammonium nitrate, diesel fuel, and dynamite. The only thing left is to get enough men to do the job, and this required at least a few thousand men. Sardar has been getting men imported in secretly through Mexico and Canada but now that Barrack is in office, he just has them fly in on commercial flights. When their visas are up, no one comes and gets them. They are free to move around openly. Some of them even vote.

Sam and much of his group stop at his veterinary hospital on the way through Virginia. He and his brothers sort of miss the hustle and excitement of the hospital. Sam miss it most of all but the break away from some of his irritating clients has been refreshing.

Carol is doing a good job running the hospital and all the new doctors are doing a great job in the new and improved hospital. After the gang broke in to the hospital and tore it apart, Sam has not really worked in the hospital. He has been too busy building fortresses everywhere, staying one step ahead of the law, building an army. Maybe when all of it quiets down, he can go back into the practice of veterinary medicine, but in the meantime, he must keep up his continuing education. That night all the families have supper together with a large catered cookout. Old Gunny and Darrell wanted to do the grilling, which upset the caterers. Gunny and Darrell win the battle. Sam and his two brothers just enjoy seeing the kids run and play. Sam misses his nephews as much or more than his two brothers miss their sons. Sam always wishes he can have kids of his own. Sam and Carol leave the party early for a midnight moonlight trip to the top of the hill where you can see everything for miles. They stay and talk for hours until Carol falls asleep in Sam's arms. Sam drives them back to the garage area of the bunker, and they spend the night there. Sam misses his cats. He loves each and every one of them. He keeps pictures of them, that when times are hard, he will just look at the picture for comfort. Sam knows they miss him also, and as soon as he drives up to the house, they are at the door waiting for him.

After a week of rest and relaxation, Sam calls his entire group together for their run down south. The group is to all meet up at Coral Springs, Florida. Once everyone gathered, some took pickups, boats, and rental cars to get to Miami. They decide to spread out and come into the city separately so suspicion was not drawn to a couple of hundred heavily armed people moving in on a city, not that anyone would notice.

They all gather at a Four Seasons conference room. Sam has rented the whole motel for the day. They go over strategies and the next job. They plan their escape and a place to regroup. They decide that it is best if they go right into the next job and try to do two labs in a twenty-four-hour period. This will not give the enemy time to go on the defensive.

"We start early in the morning. I want all four angel teams in place by 4:00 a.m. I want all sniper teams to have three men instead of two. The third man is an extra lookout and firepower if needed. This man will let the sniper and spotter concentrate on their job without worry of someone coming up on them without warning. Those of you going by boat need to be in place by 5:00 a.m. The four teams of infantry will also be in place at 5:00 a.m. The three helicopter teams will leave and scout the area. I will be part of this team. I don't want any partying tonight because we will not stop until we get back to Virginia. We will be hitting both places in Florida, then to Alabama, Louisiana, Missouri, Oklahoma, Michigan, Illinois, and then Ohio. We got a lot of traveling to do and then we will lay over in Virginia until we move on to New York. It will be well worth it to everyone. So be sharp and no talking to anyone outside of this group," Sam says with authority and then looks around. "Any questions."

No one looks surprised or upset at the plans. They are all in to it and all are well versed in battle.

The next morning, everyone is in place before their designated times. Early in the morning, no one is moving in the compound except for a few guards. The compound is surrounded by a chain-link fence with razor wire on the top. There is a sign on the fence warning, "Danger! Fence is electrified. Peligro! Cerca esta electrificada!"

The infantry teams move toward the compound. Kim throws a metal rod at the fence so that is lays against the fence and touches the ground. There is no spark, making him assume the fence is not working. He sends two of his men up to cut a large opening in the fence so everyone can go through the fence. The other teams do the same. Only two guards are at the gate, six guards walking around the compound and two at each door of the building. On the building are eleven doors in all. Most of the guards are drinking beer and smoking. They all are carrying AK-47s slung over their shoulders and some have their weapons propped up against a wall. They all are wearing blue and white YUPPI uniforms and bulletproof vests. All of them look like a bunch of hippie dirtbags that were just pulled off the streets.

Sam's helicopter flies over the compound and scouts the area. Even though it is still dark, with his night vision he can see all his troopers on the ground. Sam relays and instructs the group from the air. This is the first time he has not taken the lead on the ground. He is giving them more leave way to see how ready they are to do everything on their own. The other reason, his knee is hurting so much that he cannot move as fast and as quickly as the younger men. He knows he has to get it injected again as soon as time allows for him to do so.

Sam could just use the snipers to hit the guards, but the sound may stir the hornets' nest. He usually waits outside the compounds and plays it slow, like he did with all the other compounds but this time he is in a hurry. He thinks, "I hope this don't bite me in the ass. I really don't like to rush but we know what we are doing."

Sam sends in two infantry teams to take out the guards. Half of the guards are already drunk and half are a sleep. Most of them can't fight anyway. The first two teams move up on the guards quickly and quietly. They don't have to kill them. They zip tie and gag them. Sam radios to the infantry teams and send the other two in to the compound. Team 1 takes the front door. Team 2 takes the doors in the back. Team 3 takes the roof. Team 4 is to back up and guard the compound for anyone coming in or just to keep the "way out" open. As soon as team three secures the roof, Sam, WindEagle, and two other troopers repelled to the rooftop. All the teams move in the building at once.

The rooftop looks like all the YUPPIs did is party. There is an over flowing port-a-potty near the rooftop door. Beer can, whiskey bottles, old couches, chairs and other garbage littering the rooftop. The rooftop door is not locked and there is no sign of alarm triggers. Sam and team 3 move in quickly and smoothly. The first area they come too is the sleeping quarters. Sam and half of the team go to the front door of the sleeping quarters, and the other half stays by the rooftop stairway. Sam slowly opens the door lifting slightly on the door handle so the door has a less of chance of squeaking. Sam sees everyone in the room is sleeping. He sends in four men to pick up all the bedside weapons. When the men bring back the weapons back through the door, Sam throws in several flash grenades. Sam and troopers shielded themselves from the blast. The men sleeping, jump out of bed, stunned and unorganized. Some of the YUPPIs just stand there and some look around for their weapons. As soon as they cannot find their weapons, they head for the doors, only to be stopped by Sam and his teams. All weapons are pointing in the YUPPIs' directions. A few of the men try to fight their way out the door, but Sam's troopers cut them down quickly with short swords the troopers carry. Sam makes everyone carry a bladed weapon of each trooper's choice, most chose the short sword. They quickly gather the men together and use zip ties for handcuffs. Ten of the troopers are left to guard the men. Sam and the rest of his team go on down to the next floor.

The other two teams have secured the bottom floors with no shooting. Only a few YUPPI men are killed and several are taken prisoner. Now all the teams moved in on the second floor and secure the floor quickly. The boat teams arrive and come in to secure the dock level. Once each floor is secured, Sam sends teams of five to recheck every nook and cranny of the building. After knowing that all the building and the compound is secured, two trucks with shipping containers moved in. The containers were built to Sam's specifications so that men can be shipped to other countries. He found that the last bunch he shipped away apparently did all right. With the new containers, they will all be comfortable and safe heading toward some unknown location far, far away.

Sam, Bud, Kota, Kim, and WindEagle all gather. They walk around and look over at their new bounty. There are twenty-three cars that are built for speed. Bud and Kim said they used them to carry drugs to their distribution points. The troop carriers and Hummers were used for hauling money. As they look around, something makes Sam start to worry. He always has a sixth sense about things. Many times he has chosen to ignore it and many times he has regretted it. This time, it puts a feeling of expedience.

Sam looks at the other four. "We need to get out of here quickly. Let's not mill around. Just get everything that you can and let's get moving to the farm. Did anyone find a safe or secure room yet?"

Kim notices that Sam is a little agitated and asks, "What's wrong with you, Sam?"

Sam says, "I just got this feeling that shit is going to hit the fan, and we don't really what to be here."

Kim says, "We will get everything going quickly. I'll go check on those loading the trucks and make sure the drivers are ready to roll. Are you driving or flying?"

Sam says, "I'll drive, if one of you guys wants to come with me, that would be great. WindEagle and I will go check and see if anyone found a safe. Bud can you come along and Kota if you can check and make sure the shipping containers are heading out, like now."

Everybody goes on their way. Sam, WindEagle, and Bud goes back to check every room again to make sure they didn't miss anything.

Sam turns to WindEagle. "Go find out if anyone has found the safe or computer room."

WindEagle bows "Sir!" and then takes off running.

Sam and Bud looked through the rooms quickly. They come to a door that looks like it is a door to the outside. Sam turns the doorknob, but it is locked.

"Damn it! They missed a fucking door. Remind me to give those guys a kick in the ass. This shit cannot happen," Sam says, not really to Bud but a note to himself.

Bud quickly unlocked the door with his handy automatic pick he had made. Once the door is unlocked, Bud and Sam slid up against the wall on both sides of the door. Bud turns the doorknob. Sam kicks the door wide open. He does a forward role into the room with his 1911 .45-caliber pistol in one hand and a flashlight in the other. He completes the roll standing on his feet in ready position to shoot anyone that needs to be shot. Bud walks in behind him and the quickly check out the room. It is the computer room.

Bud looks at Sam and asks, "What the hell did you do that for?"

Sam smiles and says, "I always wanted to do that and now seemed like the time. It was stupid but no harm done except I got a stiff neck now."

Bud mumbles, "Yer lucky you didn't break your fucking neck."

Sam radios WindEagle. "Get over to the south side through last hallway. I'm throwing out a glow stick. Get here now."

WindEagle instantly takes off in a dead run and grabs two more men on the way. "On my way now," he radios Sam.

Bud finds another door and is ready to open it. Sam and Bud open the door and move into the room like they did to every room, carefully and quickly.

"Shit!" Bud says. Bud and Sam holster their weapons. The room is full of women handcuffed to bedposts. Some look half-dead and starving much like they found the girls in Maine. There are twelve women in all. Some are only teenagers. Most of them are so weak or drugged that they can't even pick up their heads. Their lips are cracked and skin is dry, which made them look like they are dehydrated and starved. Their arms have evidence of multiple injections. Sam figures they had been drugged repeatedly.

"Damn it! Now what the hell are we going to do with these women? We need to bring in a medical team or transport them to the hospital. Shit, I knew we should have hired some doctors or EMTs for this group to bring along. Before we go to the next bust, I'm going to find some medical personnel," Sam says while checking the pulses and helping Bud remove the handcuffs from the women.

"Right now, we just need to send them to the hospital. There is a van in the carpool we can transport them to the hospital. I saw a hospital when we scouted this place. It is just about a mile from here," Bud says.

WindEagle and two troopers come running in with weapons ready. They stop dead in their tracks.

"We've seen this before," WindEagle said. "I'll get some men and we will get them out of here." He takes off before Sam could even send him.

WindEagle comes back with fifteen men and they take the women away.

"Have two of our female troopers take them to the hospital with the van. If they want, they can just leave the van and the women at the emergency exit and one of you guys follow with a Hummer to pick them up," Sam tells them.

Bud and the troopers had been going through a few more doors while Sam was handling the women problem. "We found the safe room and it is loaded to the hilt with money, gold, and fucking paintings," Bud says.

Sam, Bud, and the two troopers go to check the room out.

They walk in to the vault room. Sam slowly walks in and looks around like walking in to a circus tent for the first time.

"These paintings I think they are supposed to be of some value, but I don't know anything about them," Brain says and looks over to Sam for some answers.

Sam just looks back and shrugs. "Hell if I know anything about paintings. You guys know anything about painting?" Sam asks the troopers.

"That one is a Picasso. That's a Gauguin. That's a Monet. I not sure if that is a Matisse, but there was a heist a while back at a museum in the Netherlands that paintings like these were plundered. They could be them," one of the troopers informs everyone.

"Now, how the hell do you know that shit? You guys amaze me every day," Sam says with amazement.

"I was an art major in college and my father collected artwork. He had a passion for paintings as well as I do. So I just keep up with the art world," the trooper says.

Sam asks, "What is your name, sir?"

"John Hamlet, sir," the trooper says.

"Well, John, you are in charge of these paintings and get them back to the museum if that is where they belong. If they don't belong to them, give them to whoever wants them, maybe you or your father. Just make sure that no one else in are group wants them first before giving them to someone else," Sam instructs.

"I get right on it, sir," John says. Then he starts instructing men to load them on a truck.

Sam yells, "WindEagle? Where the hell is WindEagle?"

465

Bud tells Sam, "He's loading the women. Just radio him."

Sam keeps forgetting about the radio communications. He radios WindEagle, "Make sure you take a couple of hands full of cash and give each of the women a shit load of money for their troubles they endured. Now get going and get shit done. We got to go."

Men come running into the room, and within minutes, all the rooms are empty and loaded on the carriers.

Just as Sam and the teams are ready to leave, one of the angel teams radios in, "Sam, you got some trouble coming in. Six armored Hummers and one troop carrier and they look well-armed and maybe twenty-four-plus men. There is also a helicopter looking like it's going to land."

"OK. Angel teams, did you hear that? I want you guys to take-out anyone getting out of the helicopter. Team 4, if we can get those vehicles to come in here, let them in. Everyone else makes room for them and opens the doors. Stay out of site until they all are out away from their vehicles," Sam says.

"Roger," they all say.

The YUPPI convoy moves in like they had been there before. They drive right into the open doors with no hesitation. As soon as they are in, all the men get out of the Hummers. Smoke rolls out from cab as the doors open. The smell of marijuana fills the carport. All the YUPPIs are high and carrying weapons of all kinds. They are laughing and joking. One of them takes out his pistol and shoots off several rounds. He starts howling. The others start yelling and shooting in the air. A couple of men are drinking out of a Jack Daniels bottles. Sam picks out the one that looks like the leader, then radios, "I'm going to shoot the one that shot first. If the rest start shooting, everyone open up on them."

Sam shoots the first guy. The rest of them stop yelling and stand there stunned and confused. They look around and then they start shooting in all directions, and when the shooting stops, all twenty-four YUPPI men are dead.

Outside, two men got out of the helicopter and before the blades quit spinning; both are shot dead by Sam's snipers.

The angel teams radio Sam. "Pilots are out of play. Helicopter is secure."

Sam radios back, "Roger that." Sam radios to everyone, "Load up and move out. I need one pilot to fly the new helicopter to the farm."

Some of the men move the dead to the side. Everyone loads up and heads out. Kim is in the lead. Sam and Kota are driving one of the carriers loaded with gold and cash. One of the pilots flies the new helicopter up to join the formation of the other three helicopters. Team 1 lights the meth lab on fire before they leave. They all head to a farm that Bud and Kim had bought as a rally point.

After the leaving Miami, Kota looks over at Sam, who is driving the troop carrier. "You know who these guys remind me of?"

"No, but they can't fight worth a shit. They are like a bunch of punk dopers," Sam says.

"You remember that movie called *Waterworld?* Those guys that Kevin Costner was fighting and they rode around on those stupid Jet Skis, they called them Smokers? They couldn't fight and all they did was stay drunk and smoked all the time," Kota says with a laugh. He knows he pegged them correctly.

Sam laughs and says, "You are exactly right. I think we will call them Smokers from now on. Spread the word. That is a great name for them, good job."

From then on, the YUPPI troops are known as Smokers. When Kota tells the troops about it, they all laughed and said that they were thinking.

Once at the farm, Sam sends a team of troopers to Virginia with all the money, weapons, and most of the vehicles. The helicopters stay with them as well as most of the Hummers and a few troop carriers. The next day early in the morning, they hit the next meth lab the same way as they did in Miami.

Not one of the troopers had been hurt or killed. But they all knocked on wood.

They went on to each of other the meth labs in Alabama, Louisiana, Missouri, Oklahoma, and Michigan. Sam decides to go to Ohio before Illinois so that he can get all the troopers back from

Virginia before they go on to Illinois. They had been moving so fast that by the time the troopers got back from the base in Virginia the next lab was already busted. The troopers would just grab the new bounty and turn around go back to South Dakota or Virginia again.

CHAPTER THIRTY-TWO

AFTER MICHIGAN, SAM COULD SEE the fatigue growing in his runners. He knew if they didn't have at least a small break that someone is going to make a mistake. Now all the troopers are relaxing on a farm outside Hilliard, Ohio. Sam decides a good party is in order for all their hard work. Sam, Bud, and Kota make a trip back to Virginia this time so that they can see their families.

Back in Virginia

"Sam, you look like shit," Carol says, "but you still look good to me." Carol gives Sam a big hug and a kiss.

"Yeah, we've been going at it pretty hard," Sam says. "Carol, it's great to see your pretty face again."

"Have you been behaving?" Carol jokingly asks with a little laugh. She knows what Sam has been doing. Darwin has been monitoring all the radio messages and news channels along with a lot of underground chatter on secured e-mails that went through some of Darwin's favorite enemies at this nation's capital.

"How is the rehab center and hospital going?" Sam asks. He had not really thought about his business until he showed up. He looks around and the place looks beautiful. The place was mostly rebuilt after the last battle when Sam had to leave.

"It's going great," Carol says as she grabs Sam's hand and begins to lead the way for a walk. Sam and Carol always took walks around the farm every day after work. It was a way for them to have their alone time and get a little exercise. Carol says, "I hired ten new technicians and six new doctors. We had to hire three new doctors just to take your place here."

"Well, I'm glad it's doing well. I miss being here with you. I miss the cats and the dogs. I miss working on all the horses. If I could come back and go back to work, I would, but with the YUPPIs and God only knows who after me, it is too dangerous for you and everyone else for me to come back to work. If they find out I'm here, there will just be more killing," Sam says, looking over the fence at the horses running in the pasture. Elvis and Drizzle, two cats, had died, as well as Tanner, Ruby, and Seaka, three dogs, while he was gone. Sam took it very hard whenever one of his friends died. It hurt Sam just thinking about them not being around.

"I miss having you around too. Boogie, JR, Phoenix, and Harold miss you. Your clients really missed you, and it took a long time for them to except that you may not come back. They like most of the new doctors, but like always, they have their favorites. The good thing is that I only have to oversee everything, and I don't have to really manage anyone. Marsha has taken over the business manager's position. I just help her now and then," Carol says.

Sam laughs. He knows it is more than now or then. Carol never lets anything get to far away from her control. Sam says, "I'm sure it is more now than it is then."

Carol punches Sam in the arm and says, "Oh, you think so. You know me a little too well."

"I should go check on everything and make sure all is stored properly. Then we can go home and tomorrow we can spend the day together," Sam says.

"Yes, that sounds good but we are home right now," Carol says with a little smirk on her face.

Sam looks a little puzzled and then looks around. He asks, "What, did you move into the bunker?"

"I did for a while but when you left the last time I started a little building project of my own and it is about done. Can you see it?" Carol asks.

Sam looks around and did not see a thing that was out of place except the outdoor riding arena has gotten bigger and several new fences and barns were put up. "I give up." Sam shakes his head. "I think you need to show me."

Carol takes Sam's hand and leads him around along the new arena's fence. Carol is floating on her feet like a schoolgirl skipping home from school with an "all A" report card. They get to the other side of the arena where there is a retaining wall with a door in it. They walk inside and there before him is a three-story house the size of the arena.

"Damn, this is nice Carol. How the hell did you get this done so fast?" Sam eyes are wide open and he moves around like he is looking for gold.

"You would be amazed at what you can get done when you pay enough money. I gave them a two-month deadline and they got it done in about fifty days. I'm not done yet but just about. I am going to put a climate controlled building right outside the door with a jungle theme. That way the cats can go out and play and still be inside." Carol looks at Sam. "Do you like it?"

"Carol, you are amazing. This place is great. I think the climate control building would be great." Sam smiles and gives Carol a big hug.

Boogie, Sam's oldest cat and friend, heard him and comes strolling out to greet him. Close behind him comes the other three. Sam picks up Boogie and gives him a big hug. Boogie gives him a head butt and a nose nub. Sam gives him a kiss on the head. He then sits down on the floor and all his friends climb all over him. Sam falls asleep with his cats on top of him.

About two hours later, Carol kisses Sam on top of the head. Sam had already felt someone coming close but just laid there and then grabs her. Carol gives a little scream and then laughs. She says, "You were already awake."

"Kind of, I was just waiting for a kiss," Sam says. Then he sits up and extends a hand to Carol in hopes she will help him up.

"The boys told me that you need to come over to the bunker and look at something and your dad and Gunny want to talk to you today." Carol pulls on Sam's arm.

Sam and Carol go over to the bunker where Bud and Kota are waiting for him.

"We got a little problem," Kota says. "But you have to see it to believe it."

They all walk through the bunker to the opening that goes back into the hill where the vehicles are kept.

"See?" Kota points to the over flowing carport. The vehicles are crammed into the area bumper to bumper. There is not even room to walk around in the vehicles they have to walk on top of them.

"Who is managing this carport?" Sam asks.

"No one really," Bud says. "The guys said it was getting full but they never said anything about this. They just kept moving vehicles in and around until everything fit."

"Where have they been putting all the money and other stuff, like weapons and gold?" Sam asks.

"They left it in the vehicles when there was no more room in the safe room," Bud says. "We opened the safe room and it is full to the ceiling. I don't think you can even get a drop of water in the room before the seams burst open."

"Are the food storage rooms full?" Sam asks and then goes on to say. "Because if they are not, then I suggest we have Gunny and Dad go buy about ten more truckloads of dried food. Build a few more underground water storage tanks. That will make some room for more cash storage. We could build an above ground concrete garage in the trees then cover it with dirt and plant trees over it."

"That may be the quickest way of doing things," Kota says.

"Well, one of us will have to stay here and get this done." Sam looks at Kota and Bud. "Also, I want you to hire a couple of people to help get this place straightened up. I will call Wendell. Maybe he would like a new job with higher pay. You remember him? We used to go to karate tournaments together."

"I'll stay if Bud doesn't want to stay. I want to see Montana for a while." Kota looks at Bud.

"I'll go with Sam. God knows one of us has to watch him to keep him out of trouble," Bud says. "When you get this built, though, we need to switch out so I can spend time with Luke."

"Sounds good to me," Kota said.

"Carol, can you help Kota with those fast contractors you used?" Sam asks.

"We can call them right now," Carol says. "Do you want me to do that and then they can get start right away?"

"Yes, but I don't want them to know I'm here, so they need to just talk to you or Kota," Sam says.

Carol leaves and goes out to call the contractors. The brothers stand there just looking around at all the stuff they had stolen. They all start laughing.

"Shit, would you look at all this shit," Sam says. "When we started, I never meant to get this deep into it. Now I can't quit until those bastards are broke. They'll hunt me down for the rest of my life unless I get them first."

"We got a lot. I never thought we would ever be this rich. Hell, I like doing this. It beats cleaning stalls and worrying about money," Bud says. "Maybe we can all build a new house now and get a few acres of land?"

"I think that would be all right," Sam says. "Kota, maybe you and Carol can go out and buy everything around here, and I mean around here. Like a five-mile radius if possible. Just buy anything you want and run it through Gina. She can make it look like you got a loan for it and a build a dummy corporation or whatever."

"Sounds good. We can get shit started right away," Bud says. "I'm going to buy my wife a new car tomorrow."

"Great, just grab a handful of cash and go get one," Sam says. "Let's go find Darwin."

The brothers go back through the bunker and there in his computer is Darwin. He has about twenty computer screens up. He is just sitting there typing away on his computer, just cussing all the way.

"Oh fuck, you didn't just do that shit to me. I'll just do a little lateral work, then fuck you," Darwin is yelling at the computer. "There you go, you motherfucker. Die! Die! Die!"

"Darwin, who are you yelling at?" Sam asks.

Darwin looks up a little startled. "Sam! Bud! Dakota! I was expecting you earlier, but I didn't see you, so I started a new project. I'm yelling at this fucking security on this bank computer. Those bastards are trying to keep me out. So I started a virus of my own making that will fill their computer with porn, and when they can't get rid of it, they'll shut down and reboot with me in control, sort of on a subconscious level. They will never know."

"What bank?" Sam asks. Bud and Dakota just look around.

"Hey, you guys, please don't push any buttons. I got everything just right and I don't think I can do it again," Darwin says to Bud and Dakota. "It's the bank we are looking at in New York City."

"What the hell are doing in the bank?" Sam asks Darwin. "I thought you already accessed that bank."

"I am in that bank. I can tell you that as of 2:12 p.m. that is about ten minutes ago they had one hundred ten billion five hundred thirty-one million dollars, nine thousand four hundred and thirty lockboxes, two billion in gold bars, and so on. Do I need to keep going on?" Darwin said as he sat staring at his computer. "I am now trying to get the live video stream as soon as these guys get done watching all this porn and shut the computer system off, which should be fairly soon. Their security is also being monitored every fifteen minutes by another company that watches for them screwing around on the computer. They usually lose a few men a week when they get caught playing on the Internet. Oh, there they go."

"Damn, you have been watching. So when is the best time to hit the bank?" Kota asks.

"As soon as you all figure out how to drive downtown New York City and walk into the bank and carry out all that gold without getting caught. Then you have to get out of the city and lose all those police that are chasing after you," Darwin says very sarcastically to Kota. "As soon as you figure that out, let me know and I will tell you when the optimal time to go. Shit, if you figure that out, I'll eat my sock."

"If you weren't so important, I'd punch you in that smart mouth of yours." Kota grabs Darwin by the hair.

"Simmer down, you two," Sam says.

"Tomorrow, Darwin, you will be eating your sock," Kota says and then storms out of the room. He knows he shouldn't let Darwin get to him. He could kill him with a drop of a hat if he wanted to. He just doesn't like people thinking he is dumb, especially when they are being condescending.

"My, my, he is touchy," Darwin says as he looks over at Sam then leans back in his chair. "I'll just wear clean socks tomorrow just in case. Now you guys leave me alone so I can get some work done. I'm going to get you a drone, when I get my software written."

Sam grabs Bud who was tapping away on some computer. "Let's go see Dad and Gunny."

Bud and Sam go through the underground bunker and look in each room. Things are getting musty and dirty.

"We need a maid," Sam says, looking into one of the sleeping rooms.

"Yeah, this place is becoming a pig pen. Maybe Carol can hire someone to clean or we bring in a few rehabilitating Smokers and their troopers to help around here and clean this place up," Bud says as they walk through the halls. "Ya know! We never did build this place for all that we have brought into here. We were just little and now we are getting too big for our britches."

"I know, I know. One thing just led to another. Now we can't quit till we are done and you know that." Sam says as they let the water clear the water trap.

"I guess I just want to stay at home for a while and spend time with Luke. I really miss him. As soon as he gets home, I'm going to meet him at the bus." Bud says as they walked up the stairs.

"Good idea," Sam says sincerely.

Kota is already in Gunny's shop as Bud and Sam come in. Kota tells Bud and Sam, "Darwin pissed me off."

Sam walks over and gives his Dad and Gunny a hug. Then turns and sit over by Kota. Bud walks over and sits between his Dad and Gunny.

"I know, he was pissing me off too. He gets that way because he just sits down there and never socializes with people. Damn, I'm not sure he has even taken a shower for a few weeks," Sam says.

"Shit head is going to eat a sock tomorrow because I have a plan for that fucking bank. Do you want to hear it?" Kota says.

"Not at this minute, but let's get together in the morning after you and Bud go see your kids and wives," Sam says.

"OK, in the morning, and yes, I want to meet the kids at the bus. I need to take a vehicle. Do you think I can take one of the farm vehicles?" Dakota asks.

"Dakota, take whatever you want. You know it is not just mine or whoever's, it is yours also. Everything here is yours and everything is ours," Sam says. "You never have to ask me for anything unless you need my help. If you want it and we don't have it, just take some money and go buy it."

"I thought we had to watch what we spend so that it didn't raise any suspicions?" Kota asks.

Bud chuckles. "Yeah, I think Sam sort of pushed suspicions over the edge when he shot all those assholes that attacked this place. Shit, we have so much money. We need to spend it to make room for more money."

"Yeah, he's right Kota. I think you should think about building a new house over here or somewhere close. Why you are here, maybe you can get that started," Sam says.

"OK, I'm going to do just that," Kota says. "Got to go."

Gunny had been working on the forge until Kota walked in. He then dropped everything, as Kota had been giving Darrell and Gunny a short run down on what had been going on. Darrell had not been doing anything except drinking coffee and telling stories to Gunny.

"You boys have been out getting into trouble?" Gunny asks with a little laugh in his voice.

"No trouble whatsoever. You have to get caught in order to get into trouble, but we have been making trouble for those fucking YUPPIs and a few politicians are going to go broke soon," Sam says. "If all goes right, we will have a small army and enough supplies and money to handle a small war."

"You know as you grow bigger, so do your troubles of discipline," Gunny says. "Don't let discipline get lax. Someone will always be there to try you. You deal with it fast and without any hesitation."

Darrell walks over and grabs a twelve pack of Coors out of the refrigerator. He brings it over and sits down in his chair, then passes them out to everyone.

Bud pops the beer open. "I think Sam has got respect covered. We have this small army that not only will do anything for us but they are almost like family."

"You think that until you start taking casualties," Gunny says and pops his beer open. "Men will either look to you for strength when that happens or they will look to change leadership. All I'm saying is, when shit hits the fan, be strong, be decisive, be direct, and never let lack of respect be dealt with anything less than extreme punishment. If you show any sign of weakness or letting disrespect go unchecked, they will take you out. I saw it. It happened in Vietnam."

"I got it," Sam acknowledges. He downs his first beer. "I will take all your words to heart and Bud and Kota will back me up. I have been tested before and I think I handled it with extreme punishment. I know I don't have any military experience and I will keep a close grip on the men."

Sam grabs up another beer for him and Bud. Bud sits back. "We have been through a lot of shit so far. Not as much as you Gunny, but we have handled things fairly well. We have killed a lot of men, which I am not proud of, but it needed to be done. Sam has killed more in hand-to-hand combat than most of the troopers have ever killed in the wars. I think the men are a little afraid of Sam as well as respectful of Sam. They know he was never in the military, but we also treat them and reward them greatly, so I think that they are grateful also."

"Good! You guys make sure they fear you," Gunny says with a stern voice as he points his finger at both Sam and Bud. Then he gets up and walks over to the hand weapons on the wall. "If they fear you, those that don't respect you will soon appear. Those that do respect your power will stand behind you."

"Gunny, are you grabbing that little thing I made for the boys?" Darrell asks. "Gunny has been showing me a few things, so I made you all a knife."

Gunny hands each Sam and Bud a long bladed knife. The brothers both felt the weight and find its balance. Sam takes his knife and throws it. The blade sinks deep into one of the wooden post in the center of the building.

"Damn, that is a nice knife," Sam says. Then he gets up and works the knife out of the wood. "Dad, you did a great job. I just need to make a sheath for this, and I'm going to keep it with me at all times."

"I made those too," Darrell reaches under his chair and pulls out three sheaths. "I just finished them this morning. I hope you like them."

Bud sheaths his knife. "I really like it. I've got to go now and see Luke. I'll be back tomorrow." And then he leaves with a wave goodbye.

Gunny walks over to the shelf, then comes back to Sam with four new weapons. Gunny says, "I made a few things for you boys. You may have already got them or maybe not, but I made them for you all the same."

Gunny handed Sam a .44 Magnum fully automatic pistol that holds thirty bullets in a clip. It is all stainless steel. Gunny tells Sam, "I made this one for you. I made a .50 for Bud and a .410 auto rifle with AR stock that holds slugs or fragmentation shells for Dakota. The weapons are made so that the recoil is sent back and with a downward arc so that the weapon does not move in an upward motion." Next Gunny holds out a tomahawk. "I was making this when your dad was working on your knives." Gunny goes back over and opens up a box sitting on the floor. He comes back over and hands Sam a samurai sword. Sam stands up quickly and reaches under the sword and bows. Gunny says, "Your dad and I made each one of you a sword. This is a short sword. It is easier to use inside a building and easier to carry."

"Oh, thank you so much, you guys. These are such beautiful weapons. Thank you." Sam bows and sits down to look at the new weapons. Tears come to Sam's eyes. This is the first time his dad had ever made him anything or even made a real effort to do something for him.

Gunny walks to the back of the shop and comes back with a new chained weapon. He hands it to Sam. "This one is just for you. It is made from titanium. It is very light and will work just like your steel chain but lighter. It does have a stainless steel blade so that it flies faster. You need to try it out tomorrow."

"Again, thank you, thank you very much," Sam says with shame. "I am ashamed that I do not have anything made for you two."

"I just glad you guys are still doing all right. You saved my life by bring me here and making me family. Your dad is now my best friend." Gunny bows to Sam's dad more in jest than as a formal bow.

"Oh, come now. Gunny, I enjoy your company. Sam, you just coming back is a great gift," Darrell says.

They all sit down and drink beer. Sam looks his gifts over like he did with his Christmas presents when he was a kid. Gunny and Darrell just watch in excitement for Sam.

The next morning, Sam and Carol go out to eat breakfast at Carol's father's restaurant. Sam always loved to eat breakfast there. Bud and Kota stay at home and spent time with their families. They have kept the kids home from school so that they can spend time together.

Later on that morning, Bud and Kota bring their families to the farm. Sam is very excited to see the kids again. He had been teaching the kids karate before he had to leave town. Both of the nephews had to show them what they had been practicing.

"That is great!" Sam says with excitement. He is amazed that they had progressed so much. "Has Gunny been teaching you guys while I was gone?"

"Yes, sir!" they both say.

"Well, you guys keep practicing, and when I get back the next time, we can practice together." Sam tells his nephews.

"We would like that," Luke says and gives Sam a hug.

"Sam, when are you going to let my dad stay at home again?" Montana asks looking up at Sam.

Sam is sad that he has been taking up all his brothers' time. "Well, Montana, your dad is going to stay home for a while. He has to stay here and build you guys a new house. You can help him. What do you say about that?"

Montana runs over to Kota. "Really, are you going to stay here forever and ever?"

Kota gets down on his knees and grabs up all his kids. "I'm not ever going to leave for very long. I may have to go later and let Uncle Bud come home, but I will always think about you all while I'm gone. For now though, it is going to be awhile before I have to leave again."

Luke runs over to his dad. "Are you going to stay here too?"

Bud picks up Luke. "I'm going to go for just a short time and then I will be back. Your Uncle Sam needs my help for a little bit. When I get back in a week or so, we are going to spend all our time together. Maybe, we should think about building a fort when I get back. While I'm gone, we can talk on the computer." Bud tells Luke, trying not to sound disappointed. "I miss you every time I leave." Luke hugs his dad.

One of Kota's kids gets a kick ball out of the car, so they all play kickball for a couple of hours. The kids get tired and hungry so Carol calls for pizza to be delivered. Normally no one would deliver to the country, but the tips are so good, everyone fight for the business now.

Later after all the kids are in bed, the brothers, Carol, Darrell, and Gunny along with Darwin gather in the bunker. Kota lays out his plan for taking down one of the biggest money holders for the YUPPI group. All the money that leaves from the YUPPI compounds goes to the bank where it is disturbed to all the higher-ups. The money is used for buying elections, thugs, weapons, and terrorism. The thugs keep the fear going and everyone in line. The thugs that Sam's group calls Smokers are very loyal to the YUPPI group not only because of the lifestyle they get to live but out of fear. There is no leaving the group, only torture and death. Sam's group actually gives many of these men a way out of the group. Some joined Sam's group and some just leave in the containers and stay away. Darwin also found that the money is used to pay the Mexican drug cartel to cause problems along the US-Mexican border, which keeps lone drug smugglers out of the USA along with their cheaper drugs. Along with the government's war on drugs, this makes the drugs the YUPPI group are selling very profitable. Darwin still has not figured out why there is money going out of the country to very suspicious people but he is working on it.

Kota gets out some of his kid's toy cars and trucks. He sets out a piece of cardboard with streets and buildings drawn with marker out on the table. Then he explains his plan, "So here is my plan. First we send a pseudo road construction crew to repair the streets all around the city especially outside of the bank where there will be a ton of cops. Instead of repairing the street, we can plant bombs in the road so that it can be blown to bits all the way behind us. We can equip the last troop carrier to signal the explosion behind them as we move everything out. No one can chase us from the city. Once outside the city, helicopters are going to have to keep the cops out of our way. In the front of the convoy, we can have a special designed bulldozer that can remove all the obstacles in our way. We need a hide out to go too and we can do that with one of those old missile silos that are for sale all over up in northern New York. We will have to add underground parking, but I think it can be done fairly quickly. I also found two missile silos for sale up there. If you want, I will go and purchase them and get started on the parking problem. If I can't get underground parking, I can get some Amish to put up several buildings in no time. Now to get into the bank, we need to set up diversions all over the city so that the city cops, state cops and the fire department are so busy that they have no one left to send to the bank. This will give us time to load and at least be ready to move out. We also need to set up the angel teams on our route everywhere along the streets leading to the bank. They can keep the SWAT teams out of our way and stop any stray cops from coming in before it is time. When we are ready, let them all come on in. They will get the shit blown out of them. Sam, you can warn them to get the hell out if you want, but they probably won't leave. It is up to you. Now how can we load this shit? I am not sure of the bank layout but we can use skid loaders that are left behind by the road construction crews. Maybe we will need conveyor elevators also. Darwin we need to look at the layout of the building so that we have everything we need to get the job done fast. To get in, we just make a new drive through via the front door. Our Hummers and carriers can drive through a brick wall if we wanted too. The last thing is if cops show up, we need them to think that they have someone caught inside and holding everyone hostage. That will give the crew sometime to get started and on our way before the short-lived chase is on. So what do you all think?"

"I think it is a great idea," Sam says. "That is the best plan I have ever heard."

"It will work if everything goes to plan but do you have a backup plan?" Gunny asks.

"Yes, if things go to shit, everyone gets flown out with helicopters and we blow the shit out of everything anyway," Kota says.

"Yeah, but where are you going to get enough helicopters?" Gunny asks.

"Shit, we got helicopters coming out of our ears. If we flew them all together, it would look like a scene from *Apocalypse Now*. Every compound we bust has two or three and if we need more. We will just get Mike to find more," Kota says.

"Great, let's get things rolling. After this next week, we can get everyone back here and move in to the silos and work out of there," Sam says. "Anyone got anything else to say?"

Bud asks, "Has anyone heard from Harland?"

Sam tells Darwin, "Can you call Harland and see if there is any room and if everything is going OK there?"

Darwin says, "I'll do it right now. I'll also call DH and see how the bunker is coming along." Darwin heads for the door.

Kota yells in jest, "Oh, Darwin, let's see you eat your sock." Kota starts to laugh.

Darwin takes off his sock and put it in his mouth then pulls it out, "I wore new socks today."

Everyone laughs.

CHAPTER THIRTY-THREE

SAM AND BUD LEAVE THE next morning to pick up the group in Ohio. They are both revived and happy from seeing their families again. After six hours of driving, they arrive at the farm. All the troopers are gathered at the front of the barn. Sam and Bud walk in just in time to listen to one of the new member of the team who was a Smoker. The trooper in charge of him is trying to shut him up but to no avail.

The ex-Smoker rants, "This group is done for. Sam is making millions and you all wallow in squalor. You all are like trained pigs and deserve to die like pigs. Sam is living high on the hog today! Ha-ha. For tomorrow you shall all may die. He doesn't care or respect you. All he does is take and then gives you such a petty feast. You need me to lead you all to riches. I know the ins and outs of all these places you are going and I will make sure you all get your just rewards. When Sam returns, I will cast him out of our lives and I will kill him dead. Now who is—" The ex-Smoker shuts his mouth immediately when he sees Sam and Bud walk through the crowd.

Sam walks up to him and looks him straight in the eyes. He asks the ex-Smoker, "And you were—"

The man jumps back. "I am a man of my word, which is more than I can say for you. Now prepare to die." The man pulls a knife and starts to wave it around. "I'm not afraid of you. I've been trained by the best, so you are going to die like all the rest."

Sam laughs. "And you're a poet and you know it." Everyone starts laughing.

The man is enraged at Sam laughing at him. He lunges forward and Sam blocks the knife hand with his right hand and then spun to the man's back. Sam gives him a kick in the ass. The group erupts in laughter. The man is now so mad, he cannot even speak except for, "I'm going to kill you! I'm gonna kill ya! I'm gonna kill you!" The man, knowing that the lunge is not going to work, now takes short stabs and slashes at Sam. Sam has been taught in knife fighting bu,t he figures why take a chance at getting hurt. Sam quickly draws his new bladed whip chain in one motion and slashes the man across the hand. Blood explodes from the man's hand. The ex-Smoker's knife falls to the ground with two fingers still gripping the handle of the knife. The ex-Smoker looks at his hand that is two missing fingers. This seems to make him more enraged. Sam can see that the ex-Smoker is not going to quit till he is dead. The man fumbles for his pistol and then realizes he can't hold the weapon in his right hand with his fingers missing. He switches the weapon to the left hand and points the pistol at Sam. He fumbles the pistol, trying to take the safety off. He gets the safety off and starts to raise the weapon toward Sam. Before he can fire, Sam throws his new knife that his Dad made for him. The knife sinks deep into the man's forehead. Sam thinks, "That is a lucky throw." The knife entered the front of the skull and exited the back of the skull. Only a small amount of blood drips through the exit wound. The ex-Smoker stands there motionless and then his eyes go into a vertical spasm. Then he drops face first to the ground. Only the knife handle keeps the man's face from hitting the ground. The ex-Smoker's trooper in charge jumps down and rolls the man over to his back. He checks for a pulse and there is none. Sam reaches over and tries to pull his knife from the man's head but it will not come out. Sam puts his foot on the man's face and then jerks his knife out. Blood and brain oozes from the knife wound.

Sam looks at the trooper. "Can you explain this?"

"He just came out of his tent about an hour ago and went nuts. I was like he was high on something. I followed him to try to keep him from hurting anyone and I sent some men to check the tent. He had been snorting meth. I swear, everything we did could not stop him." The trooper is shaking like a boy in the principal's office.

"Take a deep breath, man," Sam says and puts a hand on the trooper's shoulder, "This is why the rule is and every one of you that are chaperones to a Smoker listen well, if they get out of line in any way. You are to kill them dead. They are only on probation and they are not to be trusted until proven otherwise. I did not wish to make my arrival so hideously. For this, I apologize. I now wish to ask each and every one of you that if you do not wish to be here with us as a group, then please leave now. You can see my brother if you want to leave and he will make sure that you get your share of the last bounty. If you wish to stay, then meet me at the vehicles because we are heading out in about an hour." Sam walks through the crowd and goes up to the farmhouse to wash the blades.

After Sam leaves, there is a lot of talking among the group. Everyone knows Sam had to kill the ex-Smoker. They know that Sam had given him a chance, but most of the ex-Smokers are not taking to the indoctrination part very well. Most of the ex-Smokers are rude and disrespectful, but the troopers try to change them only because Sam wanted them to try. No one leaves the group they all know Sam is fair and compassionate. They had a choice and choose to stay with Sam.

The trooper in charge removes the man's body with some help from other troopers. They dig a hole in the backyard to put the body in and then filled it with thermite. They stick a magnesium stick into the thermite and light it with a propane torch. The heat is powerful and burns the body to dust along with turning the sandy soil in to glass. After the fire is out, they fill the hole with dirt. Then go and pack up to leave.

Kim has been milling around with the troopers and goes in to talk with Sam.

"Hey, Sam! Did you have a good vacation?" Kim asks.

"Hey, Kim!" Sam goes over and shakes his hand. "Everything all right?" Sam can see that Kim has something to say.

"No one thinks that the chaperone thing is really working out. Those fucking Smokers are real assholes. Shit, I had to kick the shit out of two of them just the other day. Let's get rid of them and get some real troops in here," Kim says.

"You are right. May be we can just ship them before we hit Illinois," Sam says. "What do you think?"

"Sounds good to me," Kim says.

"Bud, what do you think?" Sam asks Bud.

"Get rid of them before they get us into real trouble. We can keep the good ones if the chaperones want to," Bud says.

"Well then, Kim, can you make that happen?" Sam asks.

"Hell yeah, we just got three new containers in and we only need to use one to ship. Where to this time?" Kim asks the two brothers.

"I think Venezuela," Bud says. Sam agrees.

"Venezuela it is." Then Kim goes out and rounds up all those Smokers that their chaperones didn't want anymore, which was all of them. They load them into the soundproof container and one of the troopers hauls it to the airport in Columbus, Ohio.

The rest of the group heads to Illinois.

That night the group stops at a rest stop. There is a family that pulls in behind them. Two kids get out of the car. "Wow! Look at the army men. Dad, can we talk to the army men? Please!"

"Don't bother the army men. They are busy. Let's hurry and get to the bathroom and get going," the dad says to the two kids.

"They can talk to us if it is OK with you," Sam tells the father. "Do you want to sit in the armored Hummer?"

The father's eye light up and he says, "Ah yes! You guys! Let's go see the Hummer." The father and the kids climb around in it like it is new monkey bars at the playground.

Sam remembers when he looked at the army convoys and would have loved to climb into their armored vehicles and check things out. That is why Sam took the time and let the family check the vehicle out.

The father and the kids thanked Sam and then ran into the rest stop. Sam and the convoy go on their way.

They bust into the Illinois compound just like all the rest of them. The Smokers are about the same but some are in pressed uniforms. This is the first compound that is clean and organized. There is nothing out of place. No beer cans or liquor bottles are lying around. The place doesn't smell like a portable potty in a basement.

The troopers round up the Smokers quickly. The group works like a well-organized team. Once they get through securing the compound Sam, Bud, Kim, and WindEagle check out all the rooms. Several of the rooms remind Sam of the time when Bud, and he went into their hometown bank's boardroom. That room was all red and plush. It had the biggest table that they had ever seen. The chairs had deep cushions that were better than the mattress they slept on. It was so clean and everything was in the perfect place. They go into another room and there is a large apartment that he suspects the occupant is a very rich man.

Sam whistles and says, "Shit, this room makes me want to take my shoes off." Sam looks around. "I wonder, just who the hell actually lives in this area. Let's grab one of those Smokers and get some answers. WindEagle, can you go grab a couple of our men and bring me three Smokers in here. Be nice and bring me someone that looks like he knows what is going on around here."

"Sir," WindEagle says and then bows. Sam bows back. WindEagle takes off running.

Kim comes out of one of the closets. "Hey, do you think that it is OK to take a suit or two. You've got to see all the clothes in here that I don't think anyone has ever worn," Kim asks with a gleam in his eyes. Kim really wasn't asking he knows they are going to take whatever they wanted. He just wanted to show Sam and Bud what he found.

Sam walks over and looks into the closet that was the size of most people's living rooms. "Looks like if the shoe fits, take it. Happy shopping! Matter of fact, just take everything in this room that we can load up. Make sure anyone of our troopers that want any of this stuff gets some of it also. Share and share a like." Sam turns to walk out, then stops. "Make sure you check the bathroom for gold fixtures and then get some men in here to get this shit loaded." Sam walks out and WindEagle is back with three Smokers.

Sam walks over to the first Smoker and looks him in the eyes. "I have a few questions before you all are shipped to East Africa for a vacation. My first question is, who stays in this room?"

One of the Smokers shakes himself loose from one of the troopers that is holding him. He then runs his fingers through his long hair. He looks over at Sam and spits. The spit lands on Sam's body armor. Sam walks over to the Smoker and grabs the Smoker's shirt and rips it off before the Smoker could even step back. The Smoker steps back but runs into the trooper standing behind him. He looks back and gives a scowl to the trooper then pushes him. The trooper just stays steady and doesn't budge but smirks a little.

The Smoker is embarrassed. He says "Fuck you!" to the trooper and then turns to Sam. "Fuck you, that is who."

Sam uses the Smoker's shirt to whip off the spit then drops it to the floor. Sam looks at the Smoker and then does a reverse crescent kick which knocks the Smoker to the floor. Sam follows with a punch to the throat. Everyone in the room could hear the crack of cartilage exploding in the larynx of the Smoker's throat. The punch crushes the larynx of the Smoker. The Smoker struggles to breathe. His struggles look like he is convulsing and grabbing for his throat. The other two Smokers look on in horror as blood froths out of the first Smoker's mouth and nose. Blood fills the Smoker's trachea and lungs, which is drowning him. After about two or three minutes, the convulsions stop and his eyes dilate. The Smoker dies. Sam's troopers just stand there with no change in expression. They have grown to know that it is the only way to deal with Smokers. They know that if you show power and dominance, Smokers will tell you anything. They knew that the first Smoker was going to die as soon as he disrespected Sam.

The other two Smokers look at Sam, one of them yells, "The fucking president stays here when he is in town."

The other one says, "He meets ragheads here all the time and he's coming tonight."

Sam's eyes light up a little, "Do you mean the President of the United States?"

One of the Smokers says with a slight stutter, "Yes, yes, sir. President Barrack. He comes here at least three or four times a month. He brings in a bunch of ragheads that some say they are from the Muslim Brotherhood, or they are Al Qaeda people. Sometimes congressmen and senators come here. They have many parties and take a lot of money out of here."

The other Smoker interrupts, "If you guys would have come here a week later, there won't be any money left. We were going to ship it over to Pakistan. That's why all the money is packed in those shipping containers."

Sam's eyebrows raise. "WindEagle, you make sure that we find these containers and make sure that the contents of the safe are all unloaded," Sam yells over to Kim. "Get your butt in gear. We need to get shit loaded and get the hell out of here. Shit is about to hit the fan."

Kim radios to the troopers to get help up to the room. About three minutes later, twenty armed men come in and grab everything they can. Kim goes out with them to make sure that everything is going as fast as possible. They know that everyone is doing their job and doing it well. This wasn't their first rodeo.

One of the Smokers asks, "So what are you going to do with us?"

Sam looks at them both. "Well, you have options. A—You can end up like your buddy here. B—You can get shipped to east Africa. C—You have an option to join this group if you clean up your act. You will be on a strict probation for an undetermined amount of time. You will shadow the trooper that is standing behind you and you will be their personal 'go for.' If they don't think you are going to work out and play well with us, they are going to kill you on the spot, with no debate, no remorse, and without hesitation. Then there is D—you can stay here and take the rap for all of this. The thing is that everyone has options. Your choices will define you for the rest of your life, however short or long. One thing is that we do not accept any disrespect as you see from your buddy on the floor." Sam clears his throat and looks at both of them. "The choice is yours."

One of the Smokers says, "I didn't like that asshole anyway and I need a job. I'll take C." He nods with a nervous twitch.

The other Smoker says, "Same with me." He turns and looks at the trooper behind him, "Lead the way, sir!"

The two troopers leave with their "lackeys." The troopers have the two Smokers loaded down like pack mules with stuff from the room. Sam and Bud look around in all the rooms. Most of anything that was of any value has been carried away.

Bud disappears into a room, "Hey, Sam, come here for a minute."

Sam rushes in to the room that Bud is in. "What up?"

Bud points to the floor along the wall. "See that crack along to floor and the wall. This wall moves." Bud kicks on the wall. "See, it sounds hollow. Look for a way to open it."

They both start looking around and Sam finds a remote control. Sam pushes a couple of buttons and the wall pops open. Bud takes out a can of spray paint and sprays it toward the opening in the door. A laser light lights up.

Bud says, "Thought there might be a trigger light."

Bud steps over it, as did Sam. They walk into the small room. There are monitors and several hard drives and one chair. There is a refrigerator full of snacks and beer. On the one wall is a picture of President Barrack.

Bud says with a laugh, "That bastard is awfully vain." Then he takes his tomahawk and rips the picture off the wall. Behind it is a small safe with a fingerprint lock. Bud takes his tomahawk and pops the locking mechanism off. Then takes out his multipurpose tool and cut a couple of wires. He crosses them together and the door opens. Inside is a tray with a silk cloth laid over it. Bud grabs the tray and opens the silk cloth.

Bud whistles and says, "Those are the biggest diamonds and rubies that I have ever seen."

Sam looks at the big diamond and says, "Yep! That is where all our tax money goes."

Bud grabs the silk cloth and stuffs all the contents in his armored vest pocket. "We will split it up later. Let's get the hell out of here." Bud and Sam grab the hard drives and carry them out.

"Step over the trigger," Bud reminds Sam.

They both go down to the trucks and vehicles that they had just confiscated. They put the hard drives in the vehicle that they are going to be riding in. It is a Saudi-made Al Fahd armor troop carrier. It is completely filled with gold bars and crates of weapons. There are also two crates with ground to air missiles. Sam and Bud find everyone is loaded and ready to go. Two shipping containers that are filled with Smokers are being driven to the airport to be shipped to Costa Rica. Sam decided to send the Smokers to Costa Rica because it is more of a vacation. Since the Smokers gave up the place without a fight, he thought they deserved it. Four shipping containers on trucks that are filled with money, they are going with Sam's group. The containers are the ones the two Smokers were talking about. Everything is packed. Nine pilots flew five newly acquired helicopters and four old ones. Each helicopter is loaded with the angel teams and scout teams. Then there is the twenty-two vehicles loaded to the roof that they will be moving.

Sam decides that the Virginia is just as close as the South Dakota base, so he decided they would all convoy to South Dakota. They all know what they have to do and they all move together. The helicopters will stay ahead and behind. They will act as scouts. The armored carriers with troopers are in front and behind.

Sam figures that the president will be arriving just about the time they will hit South Dakota. Sam thinks to himself, "It would be so fun to see the look on Barrack's face when he finds all the shit is gone. We are going to be in real trouble now if they find out that we did this heist. I think I will just stay and watch."

Sam radios everyone, "Stop." Then he turns to Bud and says, "I am going to stay and see what happens when the president rolls in. I need a little comedy relief."

Bud says, "Well, shit! I can't let you stay by yourself. What if they start sending out a search team or something?"

Sam says, "Shit, I'll wait a way from the compound with the video binoculars and I should be OK. Shit, when I'm done, I'll get a car and drive to South Dakota."

Bud says, "I don't like it. It's something you don't need to do."

Sam says, "It really is something I need to do. You can come if you want."

Bud says, "No, I think I will get this stuff to South Dakota. Make sure you keep in contact. Maybe Kim might want to stay. And make sure you take enough firepower."

Sam smiles and says, "Well, you can't really have a SAW while walking down the streets in Chicago. Besides, I like spending some time alone."

Sam walks in to the back of the carrier and grabs his hand weapons, daypack, and the video binoculars. Then he jumps out. When he is out, he slaps the vehicle and the convoy takes off. Sam walks around a bit until he finds the best place to view the compound without being noticed. He finds the place in a bunch of bushes and trees that lie along the backside of the compound. He takes his pack off and removes a bottle of Gatorade and a meal bar that is specially formulated by a nutritionist in Virginia. He sets up the tripod of the video binoculars and then slowly eats. As hours pass by, Sam starts to get tired. Soon he slips into sleep without him even knowing it. He is suddenly awakened by a tap on the forehead by a metal object. The metal object is an AK-47 held by some Middle Eastern man that is wearing a blue and white YUPPI uniform. Sam sits back on to the heels of his feet. He is on his knees and his toes are tucked under his feet. He is ready to spring up and forward. Sam is mad. He is thinking, "Damn it. I am so stupid to let this fucking raghead sneak up on me. That shit has an AK-47 pointed at me with his finger on the trigger. He has armor-plated vest on and he looks pissed off. I wish the raghead would speak English. What the fuck does "Lą tthrk, lą tthrk, lą tthrk" or fucking babble mean anyway? Concentrate! Concentrate!" Sam can hear two or three more men moving through the brush up behind him. He concentrated on the gunman before him to look for any sign that the gunman's concentration is removed from him. He does not move, but every muscle in his body is ready to spring forward and cover the five-foot distance between him and the gunman. When he hears the men come out of the bush, the gunman looks up and away from him. He seizes the moment. He springs forward and grabs the rifle barrel with his left hand and at the same time he pulls his new knife that his father made him. As he pushes the rifle barrel, he stabs the knife blade into the gunman's right armpit three times. As he feels the gunman release the AK-47, he dove around the gunman and stabs the knife into the base of the neck at an angle toward the left armpit. The knife blade severs the trachea and the heart. Sam leaves the knife in the gunman's neck and grabs the AK-47 with his right hand as he holds the gunman neck to him with his left. The two men that had come up behind him send a barrage of bullets in Sam's direction. The bullets hit the armor plate on the first gunman and all around him. Sam uses one hand to fire the AK-47. He finds it very difficult to shoot the weapon with one hand because the weapon keeps walking all over the places. Sam points the weapon low and letting walk up as he fires a short burst. He hits one of the men in the leg and hip and the other in the head. The last gunman's head explodes sending out shards of flesh and blood showering the brush behind him. The other is in so much pain he stops firing and grabs at his bullet wounds trying to stop the pain and blood. Sam drops the first gunman and jerks the knife from the gunman's neck. He walks over to the wounded gunman. He slowly inserts the knife just below the Adam's apple of the gunman clear through the lower neck vertebra. The gunman doesn't die immediately but slowly chokes on his own blood.

Sam notices a lot of movement down in the compound. He looks at the video screen and sees the president come storming out of the back door of the building in the compound. He is screaming at someone. Then he points to a YUPPI with a shotgun in his hand. He screams something and the YUPPI points the shotgun at the man that the president is screaming at. In an instant, the man's head explodes, and the lifeless body drops to the ground. The president stands there for a moment until some woman in a short tight dress comes out of the back door. She starts screaming and has her hands waving in the air. The president slaps her and she falls onto the dead body. The YUPPI with the shotgun sets the gun down and grabs her by the hair. He pulls out a knife and stabs her in the neck. She continues to scream and dance around while blood runs down her body. He picks up the shotgun and shoots her in the abdomen. She flies back and hits the ground. Both the YUPPI and the president go back inside.

Sam waits a little while longer, but there is no other movement. He packs up his stuff into the backpack and takes off to find a car. He ends up buying a used Yukon and heads to South Dakota.

At the O'Hara Airport, there is an accident in loading, shipping containers on to the airplane. A forklift driver who has been on an overnight drinking binge drops a container. The container rolls over on its side. Security personnel open the container and find several men inside. With further investigation, they find both containers and bring all the men in for questioning. The FBI is brought in to do the investigation because it is considered human trafficking and kidnapping.

The FBI agents Austin Wells and Carley Van Dorren interview the men in the containers. They cannot get any of the men to talk about where they came from or how they got in to the containers. The two agents are furious that no one will talk. They are about ready to the leave Illinois after the week-long investigation, but then they get some rap sheets back on the men in the container. Two of the men are on probation for armed robbery in California. The federal marshals have been looking for them for four years. Austin has both men brought back in for questioning. Most of the men are ex-cons with cases of murder, rape, theft, grand larceny, and many different drug-related crimes.

Austin had all the men housed under guard at a local motel. Austin and Carley go back to interviewing the two probation jumpers but they have somehow escaped from their room. The two agents scan the nearest bars and find them both within a half mile of the motel in a strip club. Both men are brought back to the local police station for questioning. Austin takes one room with a guy named Arthur. Arthur is a filthy twenty-five-year-old rat that has the intelligence of a rock. Carley takes a guy named Jameill. He is thirty-something and has average intelligence but is very violent.

Arthur sits in a chair at the end of a desk. Austin sits at the desk in front of his computer. "So, Arthur, it looks like you jumped bail back in California. Would you like to tell me what you have been doing?" Austin asks.

"No, no, I don't think so. Jameill says that we are never supposed to tell anyone what we were doing. We could get killed. Yep, people will come and kill us if we say. So, no can say," Arthur says in a nervous voice.

"Arthur, no one is going to kill you if you tell me what you have been doing. Now just tell me how you got into the container and maybe we can let you go," Austin says.

"I will have to ask Jameill. He gives the orders. He is a lieutenant, you know. He is in charge of a lot of people. He knows important people," Arthur brags.

"What people is he in charge of? You know Jameill just said that you can't talk about your job, but you can tell us about what a lieutenant does in your outfit." Austin tries to con Arthur.

Arthur just scratches his head and looks off into the distance. "Um, I still need to ask Jameill to be sure I get it all right."

"I'll go ask him and then I'll tell you what he says, is that OK? That way Jameill is not mad at you for asking him. I'm sure he is busy doing lieutenant 'stuff,'" Austin says.

"Yes, that's gonna work. Don't bother him if he's busy cause he'll hit ya."Arthur warns.

"Got it Arthur, I will be back in a little bit. You just stay here." Austin says and rolls his eyes. He motions a police officer to watch Arthur.

Austin goes into the room that Jameill and Carley are in. Carley has been threatening Jameill with federal prison time if he didn't talk. Austin can see that Carley is having a hard time cracking Jameill. Austin walks into the room. "You don't need to waste your time anymore with him. Arthur told me all that we need to know. We can just pack Lieutenant Jameill here and get him shipped back to California."

"Got it," Carley says. "Well, I'm through talking to you. We could have had a deal but you are definitely too late."

"He didn't talk. He would never talk. They will kill you for just thinking about talking." Jameill looks scared. "Shit, we are all probably dead. I'm surprised they haven't come for us already."

Just as Jameill is being hauled off to a jail cell, six men in all black body armor came into the police station. They are heavily armed and wearing a SEPR1 tags on the front and back.

Austin walks up to one of the SEPR1 men and asks, "Who are you and what do you want?"

Jameill is yelling, "I told you they would kill me if I told you anything, that's why I never say anything."

Austin yells, "Gentlemen, you need to stop."

One of the SEPR1 men draws his pistol without saying a work. He holds it up point blank to Austin's forehead and pulls the trigger. Blood and brains explode from the back of Austin's head and he falls back to the ground. The other men start firing, killing everyone in the jail except for Arthur and Jameill. They grab both of them and drag them out to an armored van. They take off. None of the SEPR1 men show any emotion or any hesitation. They move as a team like this has been done several times. Now Arthur and Jameill are on their way to meet a real military trained interrogator.

Once in the van, Arthur and Jameill are hauled to a large truck that looks like a mobile surgery unit. Arthur and Jameill are taken up into the truck and strapped in chairs. A man and a woman dressed in surgical scrubs come up to the chair Jameill is sitting.

"My name is Jacques. My last name does not matter to you. I only tell you this much just so we can have some proper dialogue." The man in scrubs snobbishly tells Jameill and Arthur, "I don't care what was said because everyone is dead, but I do want to know why and how our labs keep getting overrun."

The woman takes a scissor and cuts Jameill's shirt and pants off. She then hands the man a sharp probe all most like a nail to Jacques. He puts the probe over Jameill's kneecap and asks, "Who and how did the labs get overrun?"

Jameill screams, "I don't know. No one knows just some guys with an army. They came in with this army and over ran the place then threw us on a container. That's all I know."

The interrogator says with no emotion, "I was afraid you would say that, that is what everyone says. Oh well, I have to finish anyway." He takes a hammer and starts pounding nails in to the bones of Jameill. Jameill screams in pain, and when he passes out, they just wait until he comes to. Then he starts again. They never again ask any more questions. After a couple of hours, they cut Jameill's testicles off and let him bleed to death. Then they turn to Arthur. Arthur had been on the same floor when Sam killed his Smoker buddy up in the great room.

"OK, let see if you know something," Jacques says.

"I know that it is a man named Sam and a guy named Kim and I think Bud or something like that. Don't know where they are from but they probably have about fifty men and they are just stealing shit," Arthur says, scared out of his mind.

"Oh! Now that is new information." Jacques motions for one of the SEPR1 men to come over. "Unlock the chair and get this man a drink. We got a little more talking to do."

CHAPTER THIRTY-FOUR

SAM AND THE GROUP MAKE it to South Dakota without a struggle. Sam gives everyone the weekend off and then he plugs in the new server that they just found so that Darwin could download everything. Sam calls Darwin, "Hey, I just plugged in a new server and I'm going to plug in this video. You will be astonished at what you see."

Darwin asks, "Where is the video from?"

Sam tells him, "I stayed around to see who showed up at the Illinois lab. It was President Barrack."

Darwin downloads the video and watches it as Sam was talking. He says, "I'm going to send this to the news stations and see if anyone will play it. I doubt they will, and if they don't, then I'll just play it anyway."

Sam says, "Do what you want. I just thought you would enjoy seeing what the president is up to."

Darwin laughs and says, "I know what he is up to but now I got a visual. Got to go to work. Bye."

Sam says, "Bye."

Sam calls Carol. "So how is everything going with the new climate controlled room?"

"I have not had time for that. After Kota and I got the contractor going and me having to keep those jackasses you left here in line. I just have not had time for anything else," Carol says.

"Well, I'm going to get you a personal assistant or something as soon as I get back. It's about time we got you a couple of personal bodyguards anyway," Sam insists.

"I don't want anyone tagging along with me. They will just get in the way. I can do it myself, and besides, Kota is around here most of the time," Carol insists. But Sam knows she really did want some help; otherwise, she wouldn't have fussed so much.

"We can talk more about it in a few days. As soon as I get things going around here and check on everything, I'm coming home for a little while, so see you soon," Sam says. "I love you."

"Love you too," Carol says.

Sam gathers all the team leaders together. Kim, Harland, Gina, Bobby, Tom, Mike, Lisa, Beth, Dan, Whiskers, Sarah, Skids, Bozzel, Poppers, Mickey, Ben, Josh, Steve Oakland, Jamie, and the Greek, who flew in with DH and Ronald, all are in the conference room. Sam sends WindEagle to get Bud and the ten new pilots. Sam also has the leaders of the angel teams to join in. It has been sometime since everyone has been together, but Sam wants everyone on the same page before the next step.

"OK, everyone get their drinks and then have a seat," Sam says in a serious tone.

WindEagle comes in with Bud and the new pilots.

"The reason I need everyone here is to tell you all how great of a job we did. If anyone needs anything or wants anything, please just write it down and give it to my sister, Gina," Sam says. "If you all didn't know, this is my sister. Gina, please stand up." Gina stands and waves.

Everyone says, "Hi, Gina!"

"Hi, everyone! If anyone ever needs anything, just come to me. That means money or anything. Really, even if your family or a friend needs something, just ask and you can have. No questions asked," Gina says sincerely.

One of the new pilots stands up and says in a "prove it" tone, "I am Clyde Dorrin, if you don't know me. If this is true, then I have several buddies that are in the VA hospital that are just recovering. Some of them need jobs and some need legs. Some need money to help their families. What do you say to that?"

"See Gina after this and give her all the information. It will all be done," Sam says. The pilot just stands there shaking his head.

"Well, thank you, thank you very much," Clyde says as a tear falls from the corner of his right eye.

"Now anyone else, please just see Gina afterward or whenever. Now, DH, how are the two new bunkers coming?" Sam asks.

"Everything is in tip-top shape. We just need men or women to fill them. We have food for five hundred for ten years. We have a computer system that would make NASA jealous. The rooms are better than any hotel room in Vegas. We have two new Ospreys, ten new AH-6 Little Birds, and two Black Hawks. We have two Hercules cargo plans. Right now, we have them split up between the Nevada and New Mexico. We have several SUVs that have been converted with armor plating. So I think everything is ready. Everything is self-contained. We are our own country," DH says with pride.

"OWAH!" Everyone yells.

"Good, now I am going to send you back home and then up to New York. Kota will show you everything that needs to be done. Bozzel and Poppers, you want to go to Virginia and lend a hand?" Sam asks.

Bozzel and Poppers look at each other and nod, then Bozzel says, "We would love to go to Virginia for a while."

"Great. Now I need one of you pilots to fly them out there. Any volunteers?" Sam asks.

Gary James, a forty-two-year-old ex-marine pilot, stands up and says, "Well, I don't have any family or nothing. I can fly just about anything, so I'll take them. Just need a mechanical flying device."

Sam laughs. "OK, Gary, we have two Pipers out at the airstrip. One a Seminole and the other is a Lance or something. Take your pick."

"We can leave right away. I haven't been drinkin'," Gary says and looks at DH, Bozzel, and Poppers.

"Well, get packing and head out as soon as you can. It will be a long ride so pack some food and coffee," Sam says.

The men leave and Sam goes on explaining the next move. "I think that this team can go out west and down south without me at least for one or two raids. I need to be out in Virginia to set up some things. Once we get it done, we all need to go out but for right now everyone works as a team. So all of you need to do Oklahoma and Oregon. I'll meet you all in Nevada in two weeks. Kim and Bud will be the go to guys. We have great places to stay and everything is ready. So any questions?"

"From Oklahoma, are we coming back here or moving west?" one of the angel team leaders asks.

"West, you can lie low in a place in New Mexico before moving up to Oregon. The Greek can handle the transportation to Oregon. Then from Oregon, we have a safe house if need or just move on to Nevada. Anything else?" Sam explains and then points to another angel team leader.

"When we going?" the angel team leader asks.

"That's up to Bud and Kim." Sam looks over at both of them.

Bud fumbles around. "Ah, we are going in two days. Everyone have fun tonight and rest tomorrow, and then move out on the next night. It is a 640-mile trip and we need to get there early."

Sam tells Harland, Bobby, and Tom to stay behind to take care of the South Dakota bunker along with Skids and ten other men. Lisa, Beth, and Mickey are going, but one would stay behind in New Mexico and two in Nevada. Sam is taking Ronald and Sarah is going to fly them to Virginia. Sam sends Mike and Dan to go find the best armored semitrucks or find someone to build them fast.

Sam, Ronald, and Sarah leave the next day. Sarah is going to land at the airport in Weyers Cave. Sam calls Kota, "We are about an hour out from the Weyers Cave airport. Come pick us up."

Kota replies, "I'll leave right now and check things out. Don't land until I call you back."

Sam replies, "OK, will wait for your call."

When Kota gets to the airport he instantly calls Sam, "There is an overpopulation of law enforcement here at the airport. There are way too many police officers for you to chance landing here. I don't know what the hell they are doing here but don't land here."

Sarah flies the TBM 850, which is a single-engine turboprop airplane, past the airport. Sam climbs to the back on the airplane and puts on a parachute. Sam has always had a lot of anxiety about flying unless he has a parachute, so he keeps parachutes on all the airplanes just in case. Sarah flies over the farm and slows the engine. Sam pops open the side door and jumps. He loves skydiving anyway. Sarah and Ronald fly back to the airport and land.

Sam wanted to build an airstrip at the farm, but that is one thing that he has not done yet.

"Note to self. Build airstrip," Sam says to himself as he lands in the parking lot of the hospital.

Kota picks up Sarah and Ronald from the airport. He brings them back to the hospital. They all spend a few days sleeping and catching up on what has been happening.

The first thing that Sam does when he gets to Virginia is to call on one of his old Karate friends, Mr. Delker. Sam knows Carol needs a bodyguard and Sam needs someone he can trust. Mr. Delker was always an amateur philosopher and a very trustworthy person. The philosopher in Mr. Delker will keep Carol irritated just enough to keep her mind off any worries. He is perfect for the job if he will take it. Mr. Delker is a master at the art of knife fighting and a great fighter overall.

Sam doesn't like to discuss business on the phone so he has Darwin track Mr. Delker down. Darwin finds that Mr. Delker is working in a dojo in Roanoke, Virginia. Sam grabs Kota and they drive down to Roanoke.

Mr. Delker greets the two brothers with a firm handshake and asks jokingly, "It is good to see you both. Are you going to start with lessons again?" He laughs.

Sam smiles and says, "No, no, but I will do some sparring with you if you need a good butt kicking."

Mr. Delker laughs and says, "So how have you been?"

"Good, and with you?" Sam asks.

"OK. It's a little slow right now but we still have a lot of kids. I just can't get adults in here," Mr. Delker says in a concerned tone.

"Well, how would you like to have a job where you never have to worry about getting paid and you basically are going to be in charge of three to four people?" Sam asks Mr. Delker. "You will have a new car and a new house, but you do have to relocate and you will be on call every day, all day."

"I really can't leave this job. I like it and people rely on me. Master Clemons needs me to stay here," Mr. Delker says with some hesitation.

"OK, well, the job is a personal bodyguard and you will be in control of personal assistants and other bodyguards as you see fit. Your job pays one hundred fifty thousand a year and we pay for everything, including all your old bills and your family's bills or mortgage or whatever. You will get a house that will be yours," Sam tells him, knowing that he is just on the verge of coming to work for him. "So I will give you twelve hours to think about it and if I don't hear from you in that time. I will understand, but if you ever need anything, come see me first I'm in a position to help you out."

Sam walks around and looks the small dojo over and then tells Mr. Delker, "Oh, and if you know of anyone else that needs a job, let me know. This is my phone number." Sam finds a pen on the front desk and writes his number down on a piece of paper. Then he and Kota shake Mr. Delker's hand and leave.

Within an hour, Mr. Delker has thought it over and found a replacement to teach the kids karate. He does make a stipulation that Sam has to let him teach karate at his new place of business. Sam assures that he will have plenty of students. Sam will suggest to all his employees that everyone take karate.

Mr. Delker already knows Carol, so there is no real strange "get to know" period. Carol still fusses about someone tagging along, but she subconsciously feels safer.

Sam calls his other good karate friend who is now a medical doctor. Dr. Michael Washington is a fifty-something-year-old giant of a man in both structure and heart. He is a great horseman and a man that is honest as the sun. Sam needs some doctors in his bunkers and Michael is a good start if he can get him. Sam and Kota drive to Bedford to talk to Michael. Sam knocks on Michael's house door then steps back away from the door. Michael, his mother and his two brothers come out of the front door and on to the porch.

Michael looks at Sam and says in a stern voice, "What do you what old man? Git off my porch before I give your old ass a beating."

Both of Michael's younger brothers start dancing around like they are about to get in a fight. They don't know the first thing about fighting, but they know Michael does.

Sam gives a little laugh and says, "If your old dusty butt don't go back in and git your sisters too, then this will be a short fight for the likes of you."

Now Michael's mother has a worried look on her face. She had tried all her life to keep her kids out of trouble. The two brothers look around for some kind of weapon. Michael suddenly starts laughing and walks over and gives Sam a hug, then let's go. Michael's two brothers have a great look of disappointment on their faces.

Michael says with excitement, "How the heck have you been?"

Sam replies, "Just fine. Been busy and I want you to come work for me and my brothers. You remember Kota don't you?" Sam motions to Kota. Kota steps up and shakes Michael's hand along with a greeting nod.

Michael mother says to all of them. "Well, since y'all gitt'n long, we's might as well have us some tea. Come on in."

Sam and Kota both say, "Thank you, ma'am."

While sitting around the kitchen table having sweet tea, Sam fills Michael in on the job. Michael immediately jumps at the chance but has two stipulations. The one stipulation is that he and Sam spar at least once a week. The other is that he gets to see his mother at least once a week. Sam agrees to the later request but could not promise the first. Sam and Kota head back to the hospital.

Michael comes over later in the day and Sam puts him to work down in the bunker to start making room for a hospital.

"Now, Michael, you are sworn to secrecy. Is that OK with you?" Sam asks.

"Fine with me, I swear. Now what do you want me to do?" Michael asks in his friendly, sarcastic way.

"I want you to lay out plans for the greatest field hospital that money can buy. I want you to have a surgeon and a medicine person along with nurses and technicians. Keep the staff to a minimum and make sure that they are honest and can keep a secret. I don't want anyone knowing this place exists. I want MRI, CT, PET, surgery room, isolation, et cetera. I want it done fast because you have three others to put together as soon as you are done here. You just need to tell Ronald how much room you need and what you want built. He and DH will get it done immediately. If you need money, just tell Carol. When you get out west, Gina will be your contact. Any questions?" Sam says.

"Well, when do I get to kick your ass?" Michael asks.

"As soon as you get your gear on and I go get my gear on. I'll meet you in the riding area in a half an hour. OK?" Sam says.

"Half an hour? I just hope you're ready," Michael says.

Sam runs over to the new house and finds his old sparring stuff in a closet. He hasn't sparred in so long that he is a little worried that Michael might actually beat him this time. He pushes his trepidation in the back of his mind and gets dressed in his old karate pants and a T-shirt. He gives himself a pinch in the side and says to himself, "You got to lose some weight, you fat old bastard."

Sam and Michael meet in the indoor area and both are under high anxiety. The benches are full of everybody that works on the farm and in the hospital.

"Michael, did you tell them about this?" Sam asks. He looks puzzled about how everyone found about the sparring match.

"Kind of, someone asked who I was when I was getting my stuff out of the car, and I told them that I was here to kick your ass," Michael says with a little laugh. "So I guess everyone here is waiting for you to get your ass kicked. Hmm, says a lot about how they feel about you doesn't it."

"They will be sadly disappointed now, won't they?" Sam says with a laugh. "You'd better step up old man and follow your mouth."

They spar for about a half an hour. Sam can see that Michael is tired and breathing heavily. Just so that Michael doesn't feel bad he fakes a leg cramp and Michael immediately calls it quits for both of them. Sam could have gone on for longer since the pace at which they were sparring was very slow.

They both shake hands and give each other a "man hug." They both walk away together leaving the crowd disappointed because there was no grand finale. They all sit around for a moment deciding who won. All and all they decided that Sam definitely did not get his butt kicked and that Michael was going to pass out if it went on any longer.

Chapter Thirty-Five

SAM HAD HIRED TWO CHEMISTS, two textile experts, two plastic experts, two computer and mechanical engineers, and two machinists months ago. He also bought an old building in downtown Detroit, Michigan. The building was used once upon a time for building car engines but had been closed for several years. He remodeled part of the building to be apartments and a work area for his new professionals. Sam challenged them to build body armor that actually worked. Sam had always thought, "Throughout history, man had been using some form of body armor or shielding against weapons, but it never really guarded against the weapons used at that time. Even in the movie *Star Wars*, the storm troopers wore full body armor that did not protect against blasters or light sabers. Now the soldiers wear bulletproof vests that only stop some types of bullets and only cover the upper torso. The vests are heavy and uncomfortable. They don't protect against grenade blasts or even large-caliber small arms fire." Sam wants real body armor that is light and comfortable and protects at least ninety-five percent of the body. That is why he hired all these people. He gave them free reins of how they wanted to do things. Sam's only stipulation was that if they didn't work well together, they were instantly fired. No one had been fired yet.

Sam decided that it was time to go check on the progress of the armor crew. He puts on his favorite Australian made vest. Puts his blade whip chain in the inside holster area of the vest and a knife in the sheath sewn into the back of the vest that is made for his short sword. Everything is concealed but comfortable. He says goodbye to Carol. He has Sarah fly over and land on the road out front of the farm. Sam gets in and they have a clean take off. They fly to Motor City Skydiving drop zone about forty-five minutes outside of Detroit. The Greek knows the owner and introduces him to Sam. Sam kept a lightly armor modified Ford Expedition at the drop zone. After landing, Sarah and Sam drive into the city to the Armor Crews building. The area where the old factory is located, is surrounded by run-down building that is overgrown with vegetation, a place where the earth is trying to reclaim its surface. The area is surrounded by run-down old buildings that were part of a government housing project that was left to fall into ruin. The builds are still occupied by gangs, drug addicts, and some really poor people. Sam liked the area because factory is located in an area no one would look for a functioning factory. The workers all have security and drive out of the compound in armored SUVs. The factory is surrounded by dou-ble electrified concertina wire. On the roof of the factory are several M134 Miniguns that can be fired manually or via remote control inside the factory. Sam felt that with this the factory is fairly secure for the area.

Sarah calls ahead as Sam drives. She tells them to have someone open the gates and doors so that they can drive in to the factory. Sarah tells the head of security, "We will be at the front gate in twelve minutes. Be ready. Sam is driving and I don't want to wait."

The head of security says in a grumpy tone, "We'll get the gate open when you get her, so keep your panties on for Christ's sakes."

Instantly a wave of pissed off came over Sarah. She yells into the phone, "All right, shit bag, what is your fucking name?"

The head of security replies in an antagonistic tone, "I'm Digger Stevens, if you really need to know, you little mouthy bitch."

Sarah doesn't say another word on the phone. She tells Sam what just took place. Sam says, "I heard. We'll handle that as soon as we get there."

They drive up to the front gate and wait. After twenty minutes, the front gate opens and Sam drives through. He drives up to the large door to the garage in the factory but no one opens the door. Sam is irate.

Sam tells Sarah, "Drive in when I get the door open. I think I know a way in."

Sarah and Sam get out of the armored SUV. Sarah gets into the drives seat and Sam walks up to the door. He kicks on the door, but no one answers. He looks back at the front gate and the gate is still open. Sam remembers that there is a door under a grate along the wall. That door is how they got into the factory when they first bought it. He walks over to the grate and lifts it up. He then jumps down to the door. The pulls on the door handle and the door opens. He says to himself, "They are doing a damn piss-poor job of security around here."

He walks through the door and through a small dark room. The door to the room is locked but it is just a wood door. He gives it a good kick, but it does not budge. Sam takes out his cellphone and uses the light app. He looks around and decides that the walls are just sheet rock. Sam kicks the sheetrock until he hits a stud in the wall. He continues to kick a hole in the wall until there is enough room to squeeze through. He walks over and pushes the garage door open button. As soon as Sarah drives the SUV into the garage, Sam closes the door.

Sam and Sarah walk through the garage and up to the security room. Sam opens the door and looks into the room. The room is empty. Sam walks up to the video screens that are part of the video security system, but only part of the video is working. Sam walks out and they both walk through the factory toward the research room. Sam opens the door to the research room. They walk in and instantly weapons are pointed at them.

Digger walks up to Sarah and slaps her. He yells, "Around here, I'm in charge! I don't take no lip from—"

Sarah is a little stunned but before Digger finishes talking, she comes back at him with a hard kick to the nuts. Digger screams, "Ahhhh." He grabs his crotch with both hands. Sarah follows with a knee into his faces. A loud crunch is heard coming from Digger's nose as it is flattened like a pancake. Sam used the nine gunmen's attention on Digger's plight to grab his bladed whip chain. Sam grabs the barrel of the rifle of the nearest man behind him. He pushes it up into the man's face. He stabs the man in armpit, causing profuse bleeding from the axillary artery and vein. He follows with a second stab in to the man's thoracic cavity, causing a pneumothorax, making difficult for the man to breath. Sam whips the blade forward and hits a man between the eyes just above the bridge of the nose. The man drops his rifle and stands there stunned with blood flowing down his face and nose. Sam whips the chain back and the blade slices through the left eye of one of the gunman. The vitreous fluid along with the lens oozes from the eye. The man drops his rifle and grab at his eye like he is going to hold it from hurting. Sam tosses Sarah the rifle he took from the first man. She catches it and shots the first gunman in front of her. By now the other five gunmen have moved back in order to get room between Sam and his onslaught. Sam sees the gunman in front of him take aim at him. Sam does a side roll forward and comes around with his whip chain. The blade buries deep into the gunman's throat, and when Sam rips it out, blood sprays from the carotid artery. The gunman drops the rifle and grabs for his throat, but within seconds, the man bleeds to death. Sarah shoots another one of the gunman and is now aiming at another. Sam whips the blade and cuts the end of the nose off another gunman. The gunman is stunned but is still taking aim at him. He fires. The bullet grazes Sam's left forearm. The bullet stung but Sam is already rolling toward the gunman. Sam rolls up on to his feet and slashes the gunman across the neck and abdomen and from chest to pelvis. The cuts were as quick as a flag waving in the wind. Blood sprays from the neck of the gunman, and intestines erupt from his abdomen. He falls to the floor with only seconds to live. Sarah shoots another gunman. The last gunman runs for the door. Sam grabs a rifle and throws in it so that it flies like the blade of a lawn mower. The rifle hits the gunman in the legs and trips him. He falls forward and his head hits the floor knocking him unconscious. The whole fight takes less than a minute.

Blood is dripping from Sam's hand and on to the floor. He shakes his hand and whips the blood off. He puts his chain coma back into the vest holster. Sam walks over to the gunman that is on the floor and drags him next to Digger, who is still lying on the floor groaning. Sam checks the other gunmen to see who is still alive while Sarah holds Digger and his comrade at gunpoint. One gunman is missing an eye, and the other is breathing through a hole in his frontal sinus. Both gunmen are sitting on the floor clutching their wounds.

Sam gives the gunman a kick in the back and tells them, "Get the fuck over with your buddies."

As the men move slowly over to Digger, the researchers come running out from a door to one of the rooms off to the side of the research room. One woman researcher is holding a pistol and starts shooting. Sam and Sarah throw themselves to the floor. One of the bullets hits the gunman with an eye missing. The bullet hits him in the back between the shoulder blades at the base of the neck. His vertebra explodes and the spinal cord is lacerated. He falls to the floor, unable to move his arms or legs but is still alive. It is immediately difficult for him to breathe as blood starts to fill in the pleura cavity. He lies there unable to move or breathe but is fully conscious of the fact that he is dying. The woman researcher stops firing when the pistol is empty.

Sam looks over at the woman and yells, "Shelli, stop fucking shooting!"

Shelli yells, "I'm out of bullets. Umm! I think!"

Sam and Sarah look around and then stand up. Sarah immediately points her rifle at the three gunmen still alive. Sam walks over and looks at the gunman that was shot. Sam feels for a pulse and a corneal reflex but there is none. He walks back over to the three live gunmen. Sam grabs Digger by his long hair and drags him backward. He jerks him on to his back on to the floor. He puts his foot on Digger's neck and pushes his heel down on to the larynx. Digger struggles to try to remove the foot but Sam just pushes a little more and Digger stops struggling.

Sam draws out his short sword and leans over to look Digger in the eyes. He asks, "What the fuck do you think you all are doing? I brought you out here, gave you an easy, great-paying job, and you fucking try to kill me?"

Sam eases his foot off the neck so Digger can answer him. Digger screams, "Fuck you. I never did like you. You fucking think you are better than everyone else."

Sam says, "So you are now the tough guy in the place and you thought that you are going to do what when I got here?"

Digger screams, "I'm going to fucking kill you and take all your fucking money and shit."

Sam says in a calm voice, "You see what we did to the rest of your group and you still think you can get that done?"

Digger says in an angry voice, "As soon as I get up, I will show you. I ain't like that asshole Snoop."

Sam steps back and lets Digger get up off the ground. Digger looks around and says, "Fuck, it won't matter if I beat you, that bitch will shoot me. So I got to kill both of you." Digger looks over at the two gunmen sitting on the ground in front of Sarah. He gives a subtle signal to the two of them. He looks around to see where the weapons lay.

Sam and Sarah noticed the subtle signal, so they prepared to do more fighting. Sam thinks, "I should know better. I should have just killed the bastards and then we would be done. I try to be good, but the good always have to keep fighting."

Digger lifts up his pants leg and pulls out a nine-inch knife that was in a leg sheath. He swings it up and lunges forward at Sam. Sam moves out of the way at the same time slaps the knife away with the short sword and then follows with a punch to Digger's right kidney. Digger stumbles forward and does a backhand swing with the knife, which left his whole body unguarded as he misses Sam. Sam slashes Digger across the chest and then back across the abdomen. The cuts were not deep but just enough to leave blood flow from the muscle bodies. Digger responds by throwing his knife at Sam and dives toward one of the rifles on the ground. The knife misses Sam completely. Sam didn't hesitate as the knife was far from him. He jumps ahead of Digger toward the rifle. As Digger grabs the rifle, Sam sends the short sword down through the top of Digger's head and it exited out his jaw. Digger convulses and then stops moving. He falls forward on to the floor. Sam places a foot on Digger's head and jerks the blade out of his head.

While Digger and Sam fought, the other two tried to overrun Sarah. She shoots one of them and hits the other in the face with the butt end of the rifle. Sarah is pissed off and tired of the crap. She thinks to herself, "We would have let you go, but you had to keep at this shit." She continues to hit the gunman into the face until it was complete caved in. The gunman lays on the floor convulsing until he died. Sarah checks the gunman that she shot to make sure he is dead. He is dead. The bullet entered the forehead and exited out the large opening in the back of his head. This is Sarah's first hand-to-hand fight. Normally she is in a helicopter doing surveillance, but she feels nothing but contempt for these men she just killed.

Sam calls Darwin, "Is everything going all right?"

Darwin is grumpy and tells Sam, "No shit, Sam. Otherwise, I would have called you. Now enough small talk, I got a lot of shit to do."

Sam laughs, knowing the Darwin really has to accomplish almost nothing during the day. Sam says, "Tell Gary James to fly to South Dakota and pick up Tom and his brother. Bring them out here to clean up this place. Sarah and I ran into some resistance and there are bodies to get rid of. And find WindEagle! I want him around if I need him."

Darwin says, "Yeah, yeah, yeah. I'll get it done. Anything else?"

Sam says, "Yeah! Take a break and have some fun."

Darwin says, "I don't have time but I will as soon as I do."

Sam hangs up and turns to Sarah. "They are coming to clean up."

Sarah says with a little anxiety in her voice, "OK, Sam. I just need a minute or two. You should do something with that arm."

Sam says, "I'll find a Band-Aid or something around here after I talk to these guys."

Sarah walks off by herself to think about things. She is strong but the adrenaline high and then the crash left her in a mental and physical dump.

Sam walks over to the research group, who has gathered after the gunmen are killed off. Sam asks Shelli, "How long has Digger been a problem and why the hell didn't anyone tell me?"

Shelli looks over the group and steps up to tell Sam, "He was great at first, but then in the last few weeks, he and the men have been doing trips into the neighborhood. Every time they came back, they were high and they just got mean. We started locking our doors and carrying guns. When you showed up, Akin snuck up to the security office and opened the gate. We couldn't open the garage door because they caught him and sequestered us into the room over there."

Sam asks, "Why didn't you call?"

Shelli tells him, "They took our phones away a long time ago because it was a security risk. They control the landlines and no calls could go out."

Sam says, "Well, it is lucky we showed up then. Is everyone all right?"

They all mumble something, but all in all, they were OK.

Sam says, "I'll have some men clean this place up and get some new men in here. So can anyone tell me what you have been able to accomplish under these bad conditions?"

One of the textile experts named Akin Morz has a big smile on his face.

"Well, from the smile on your face, it looks like you got something," Sam says.

"Let me show you what we, and I repeat *all of us*, have come up with so far," Akin says. "Shelli can you show them some of the designs while we set up the demonstration."

Shelli shows four designs for the outer and interior parts of the armor. They had not built the prototypes yet but they are working on them. "We will have to custom fit everyone for the inner and outer shell of the suit. We have developed a computerized laser topography tailoring device. We can scan every man and woman to a perfect fit. Here stand in this booth."

Sam walks over to the booth. "Do I need to remove my vest?" Sam asks.

"Oh yes, please strip to your to your birthday suit," Shelli says.

Sam looks at everyone. He is pretty nervous about striping in front of anyone besides his wife. In his younger days, it wouldn't bother him, but now it did. Sam removes his clothing and sucks in his gut. Then he quickly steps into the booth. Shelli pushes some buttons on the computer and the doors close. Shelli yells, "Stand still or this will not work."

Sam holds his breath and the laser light spun around the booth and stops with in thirty seconds.

"OK, Sam, you are finished," Shelli says. Sam takes a deep breath. The doors open and he quickly gets dressed.

"I didn't expect to have to do any body measurements today. I think I should have lost a few pounds before getting into that thing," Sam says with a nervous and jokingly voice.

"Come and see the read out," Shelli says.

Sam goes over and looks at the screen which gives a 3-D view of his whole body. He says, "I think that reveals a little more than I wish anyone to see."

"Relax, Sam. We are all professionals here. Your body is safe with us," Shelli says. "It will be on YouTube by tonight if you wish to view it a few more times." Shelli laughs. "I am just joking."

"Just remember, I will know who to see if it does make it there." Sam smiles. "So now what are you going to do with that image?"

"We are developing something that is like a second skin. We are taking a lot of the information from NASA to build this second skin. They had been trying to develop this skin type suit for Mars mission. While wearing the suit, the people would hibernate and the suit would control hydration and body temperature. The suit is supposed to remove any water lost and bring it through a filtration system, then pump it back into the body, either orally or intravenously. They never finished it because President Barrack shut the research division down," Shelli says.

"So how did you get ahold of this stuff to do all this?" Sam asks but already could have guessed the answer.

"When everyone left, they left with their research," Shelli says. "I just simply slept with the right people." Shelli laughs. "Actually, the research scientist was my boyfriend and I just took it from him when he became a drunk. We broke up and he left everything else in the house, so it is mine and now it is yours. We perfected the material and the pump system here so it will work."

Shelli walks over to a cabinet and opens it. She takes out what looks like a cross between an ostrich skin suit and Spandex with a figure of a woman.

"It looks like you skinned a woman that was crossed with an ostrich," Sam says with a laugh.

"Kind of but this is my suit," Shelli says as she hands the suit to Sam. "I have a nice figure, don't I?" Shelli laughs.

"Ah, yes, but not that I was looking." Sam holds the suit. "Damn, this weighs about nothing."

"Two pounds, but it may weigh up to four and half pounds for a man your size," Shelli says. "If it is too heavy then I guess, someone will have to lose those few pounds." Shelli smiles.

"It is nice." Sam hands the suit back to Shelli. He is feeling a little uneasy about holding something that looks like a woman's skin. "Keep up the great work, Miss Shelli."

Sarah comes back revived from her little walk. Shelli tells her, "Ahh, Sarah. I need you to strip and get into this booth."

Sarah looks at her like she lost her mind. She says, "I'm not stripping for anyone."

Shelli tells her, "I got to get a measurement. Come on, you're beautiful. Sam did it."

Sarah looks at Sam and then looks over at Shelli. "OK, since Sam did it."

Sarah starts taking off her clothes. Sam turns and walks away. Sarah climbs into the booth, and within minutes, she is dressing. Sam had found something else to occupy himself. He is going through the gunmen's pockets and finds several different drugs. Most of them are carrying meth pipes and small bags of meth. After Sarah is clothed and ready she goes back over to find Sam.

Sarah says, "I'm finished. What's next?"

Sam says, "Good." He stands up and throws the meth pipe that he was holding, on to the chest of one of the gunmen. "Let's go see what else they have for us."

Sarah says, "Sam. Thank you for doing that."

Sam asks, "Doing what?"

Sarah says, "For not watching. It would have made it really awkward between us."

Sam says, "Yes, it would. We don't need that."

Sarah smiles.

Sam and Sarah move over to the next demonstration. It is in the back of the building far away from everything else.

"OK, now look at that one foot square on the impact dummy," Akin says. Akin hands everyone ear and eye protection. Then one of the machinists aims the .50-caliber rifle at the square from only fifty yards away. The machinist fires the rifle. The dummy flies back about five feet.

Akin points toward the computer screen. "See, the impact is low enough that a man could survive. This is from the most powerful rifle in the world and this dummy just survived it. Next we are going to fire an armor piercing round at the square. Go ahead, Andrew."

Andrew, the machinist, adjusts his eye protection and fires the .50-caliber rifle. The dummy flies back five feet but is still intact. Sam looks at the screen and it has the same reading.

"Well, I give up. What is it? Fiber? Resin? Ceramic?" Sam asks.

"We call it Jujy after the Jujyfruits candy. This is an active gel. The gel is made of custom build Nano particles and fibers that have electrical conductivity over and through the matrix of the particle. When a bullet hits the fibers, it expands and separates the particles. When the particles separate, the electrical current is stopped which causes them to instantly contract the fibers much like a muscle. With the fibers clamping down together, it becomes a solid instantly. It actually grabs the projectile instantly. The projectile doesn't bounce off the material and the impact is dispersed throughout the whole body and then disseminated to the outer shell. The protection comes from the inner material and the shape of the outer shell. The impact is reduced and there is almost no impact to anything on the inside of the Jujy shell. After a current is reapplied, it becomes a gel again so it can be used over and over. The biggest problem is it takes 0.4 seconds for it to turn to a gel again and the outer shell will have to be replaced like the shell of a race car after a wreck. The good thing, we have a great way to carry a battery pack and so far we have tested it down to forty below zero and at three hundred and fifty degrees with no change in the particle activity. The inner suit will keep you comfortable. The shell will be of a titanium composite material that is very light," Akin says proudly. Then he points to Gene, who is one of the textile experts. "Gene, can you give Sam the lowdown on your team's work?"

"Thanks, Akin." Gene holds up a one inch thick by one-foot plastic cover cloth. "This is a flexible battery. It has the capability of twelve volts. This is the first flexible battery and it is going to revolutionize the electrical clothing industry. We are also working on this helmet, which is fully bulletproof with that same material as the suit will be. The helmet will contain all the communication devices, but there will be built-in night and thermal vision that self-calibrates with the weapon you use. No aiming and no scope because the telescopic image will show up on the right eye of the helmet. We are now working on comfort items that will keep you hydrated and keep in only clean oxygenated air moving into the helmet. It should all be waterproof if all goes right, down to about fifty feet under water. I don't know if we can get that done but we will try. The outer shell of the suit is made of this," Gene hands Sam a piece that looked like a forearm.

"Damn, that is light," Sam says while he holds the arm piece. "So what do you think the whole suit may weigh when all said and done?"

"About eighteen pounds give or take a couple of pounds," Gene says. "One down side to this system may be the way a weapon will have to be held. You may not be able to shoulder a weapon, but we do not know that yet. We also have to work with the optic connections. We don't want to have to plug a cord in to a scope every time you want to shoot. We are currently working on that right at this moment, but we need a weapons maker to see if a new type of stock can be made."

"I will get you that man as soon as I get home," Sam knows this is right up Gunny's alley. "He can make any weapon you can possible imagine."

"That is the man we need," Gene says. "Thank you, Sam."

"Oh no, thank you," Sam says with sincerity.

"No, not just for sending a weapon's expert, I want to thank you for saving my life." Gene put his hand on Sam's shoulder. "Sam, I was on the edge of throwing myself in front of a train because I lost everything with the takeover of General Motors and the stock market crash. I couldn't get a job because no one needs my type of service or anything from a man my age. You gave me back my dignity and a chance at an admirable life's work. Thank you, my friend."

Sam felt uneasy with someone touching his shoulder, but Gene appears to be sincere.

"You guys have done extraordinary work. I am happy and excited to see what comes next," Sam says. "So when do you think a suit might be ready?"

"We just got this one foot sheet right now. We are making more at this time, but it will take us a year to make a suit. We need to have more equipment to speed up the Jujy production. The equipment we have is OK of very limited production, but we need about five hundred of these machines to turnout a suit within a short period of time," Akin says.

"Are there five hundred of these machines available?" Sam asks.

"There are, or there are bigger and better ones that we could probably get from China. They will be expensive, but they do have them," Akin says.

"How do you know that they have them?" Sam asks.

"Because I built them and then sold them all to the Chinese. Chinese were the only one interested in using nanotechnology and I was the only one working on it. They wanted the machines to build nano machines and I had no funding," Akin explains.

"Well, go get the machines. This is me interested in funding nanotechnology. How much money do you need?" Sam asks.

"It may cost about a billion dollars when all's said and done. I could be wrong, but that is give or take a couple hundred million.

Do we have that much money?" Akin asks with a very inquisitive look on his face.

"We have that much money. When can you go get the equipment?" Sam asks.

"I could leave now if we had a plane. We need something the size of a 747 to bring the stuff back. So whenever we can get the transportation and the funding, we can get the stuff," Akin says.

"Be ready by tonight and there will be a cargo plane, a crew and one billion in cash along with five men and a truck and two Hummers. Get the shit you need and start this going in the next week. I want this project to start rocking and rolling. Thanks and be ready. Someone will come and pick you up so start making any phone calls you need," Sam says. "Sarah, call the Nevada bunker and get a carrier over here ASAP. Have them land in South Dakota first and pick up the money and the vehicles. I want ten men on that trip. OK?"

"OK," Sarah gets on the phone immediately.

Sam calls Gina to get the money ready and the men to meet the plane at the airport. Sam knows he has more than enough money because the Illinois job was about four billion in cash.

Sarah and Sam drive back to the drop zone and then fly back to Virginia. When Sam gets back to the farm, he sends Gunny and his dad back with Sarah. Sam hands them all a handful of cash so they can get some clothes and food when they arrive in Detroit. The three fly to Detroit immediately.

Kota and DH had headed up to New York to buy a missile silo, but it had already been sold. It was supposed to be that the Realtor secured the property, but she sold it to some Australian investor that had offered her more money.

"You were supposed to get that property for me. Why the hell didn't you do it? I just talked to you a week ago and it was a done deal at that time," Kota yells at the Realtor. He is furious.

"Well, I have to do what is best for the seller and they had more money and signed a contract first. There really is nothing that can be done now. You may need to look elsewhere for some property. I have a real nice property not too far from there that is a little more money, but we can close real soon," the Realtor says.

Kota motions DH to open the suitcase full of thousand-dollar bills. Kota opens it up and shows it to the Realtor. "There is two and half million in here. It all could have been yours but you fucked us on the deal and now you get none of this. What did you make? Twenty, thirty thousand dollars on the deal? You could have made almost a million."

Kota closes the suitcase and pushes it back to DH. "Lady, go fuck yourself. We don't deal with underhanded people and we don't reward them either."

Kota and DH grabs the suitcase and leave. Kota decides that he can find someplace that is close to New York City in New York or Connecticut along the Long Island Sound.

Kota gets on the Internet and starts looking for property for sale. DH calls Darwin to start looking for property. Together they find an old prison in Orange County near Warwick, New York. Darwin immediately buys it from the state. The state has been trying to sell it for years. DH checked it out and was fully functional with only a little repairs needed on the generators. The place had a wall that secured six hundred and some acres. It was an ideal place to defend if needed. They both traveled over to Connecticut and found a farm that was in an ideal location. They drove up to the farmhouse and the farmer immediately sold when he seen cash. The farm had access to the water. DH and Dakota headed back to Virginia after a week of traveling.

Back in Kansas, just on the outside of Kansas City, Sardar Arjmand is visiting John Overagh at his junk pile looking, truck grave of a place. Every one of John's neighbors thought that he was a savage yard for truck and some just thought he was a hoarder of junk. No one knows that John is somewhat of a genius and that everything he has and does is for a reason. He has hidden hundreds of trucks out in the open and no one asks about why he has all the trucks. Sardar is there now to make sure everything is ready for the big deal that is about to happen.

"Hello, my friend," Sardar says with a little bow as he shuts the door to his Maserati.

"What up?" John throws his head up and makes an acknowledgement of Sardar.

"I need to know if we are ready for the big day," Sardar asks in a calm voice.

"We are about ninety-five percent ready, but I need at least fifty large rental trucks and maybe that many eighteen-wheelers. Everything else is ready. We have enough explosives to get rid of the moon if we want," John says with excitement.

"I will send men for those immediately and they will arrive in twenty days with which you desire," Sardar says. He is a man that when something is going to be done in twenty days, it will be twenty days, not one day more. "I also have some big surprises for you and I have chosen the place for the fireworks." Sardar motions to the armored truck that has followed him in to the lot. Four men come out of the truck and run around to the back of the truck. They quickly return with a large crate. "Here is one of the treats. It is a nuclear warhead from a Russia missile."

"Dude! Where did you score this baby?" John asks but didn't really care for an answer.

"I have four of these warheads. You need to transform them into something wonderful that will illuminate and transform Los Angeles, New York City, Saint Louis, and Seattle," Sardar says.

"Why pick these places? Hell, it don't matter," John says with excitement. "What you ask for will be done. Do you want it done all at the same fireworks show?"

"I just always thought of those places as filthy and filled with the lowest of scum. They are not worth the life that is given to them. I wish it all to be at on show," Sardar says.

"Any particular building you want us to focus on?" John asks. "Maybe like Rodeo Drive or Hollywood near Los Angeles?"

"Yes. Yes, of course. That place and that fucking arch thing in Saint Louis. Take that shit down. What else do you know to do?" Sardar is all worked up into frenzy so much that he can hardly talk.

"Maybe, if I may suggest, Times Square in New York, and just all of downtown Seattle?" John asks.

"That is wonderful. Make sure you get that thing that goes up and down in that fucking hippie town. I hate that fucking thing," Sardar says. "Those fucking hippies are so filthy, they all must be cleansed."

"I will get the Space Needle," John says. "Let us look at the plans for the big day. If it pleases you."

"No. You know what is needed." Sardar starts to calm down. "You, I can trust to do everything to perfection. I will return in one month and I will see if you require any further assistance. We will pray together at that time."

"Gotcha," John says. "Thank you for coming. It is wonderful to see you."

"Yes. Yes, I know this," Sardar says as he walks back to the car. "Goodbye."

Sardar leaves John with four men and four nuclear warheads that he had to work on. John has to fit the warheads on to a bomb that would initiate the nuclear explosion. Since they are already warheads, it is not going to be a difficult job.

Sam makes preparations for the work that needs to done in New York. Kota and DH had been busy with the construction crews building the new garage and addition to the bunker for Dr. Michael Washington's new hospital wing. Kota also has them start on a new house in the back of the property. Kota's family is all very excited about the new house because for the first time, each kid will have their own room.

Sam spends sometime practicing with the new weapons that Gunny has made for him. The new bladed whip chain is definitely a far improvement over the old one. The new .44 Mag pistol is a great improvement and easy to handle, but Sam would expect nothing less from something Gunny made. Sam also spends a lot of time with Carol and the cats. He had missed them all very much.

"Sam, maybe you should just give up on this crusade that you are on. The Brothers3 need to come home to their families before one of you guys gets killed," Carol asks one night. "Sam, what is going to happen if one of you gets killed? I don't want any of you to get hurt, especially you."

"I don't want to get any of us hurt either. It is not a crusade, it is a preemptive strike. These people will never quit coming after us until they are all dead or just gone. I need to cut all the heads of the serpent in order to kill it and that is what we are doing. I am not keeping my brothers from their families; they can stop at any time. I have told them that many times," Sam says in a calm voice.

"Sam, you should just come back and be a veterinarian again. Your clients want you back and always ask if you are coming back to work," Carol says.

"You know I can never come back here and go to work. The whole state police force would like nothing but to throw me in jail. I can't do that. I have to keep running until that lawyer of ours gets me a pardon or whatever she is going to do. Remember that they tried to rape you," Sam says and then Carol starts to cry. Sam holds her in his arms. "Carol, I love you and I wish this would have never happened. In another year, this will all be behind us, I hope."

"You are right, Sam. I just hope you guys are being careful out there." Sam and Carol sit together outside in the gazebo until early in the morning.

In the morning, Sam finds Darwin in the computer room. He had been looking through the hard drive that Sam had gotten from the Illinois compound.

Sam is carrying his cup of coffee. "Darwin do you want some coffee?"

"No, Sam, I don't drink the stuff. You know that," Darwin says without looking up from the computer screen.

"You should start. What did you find in the hard drive, anything new?" Sam asks and then finishes off the rest of his coffee.

"Let me bring it all up on the screen." Darwin types away on the keyboard and then the computer screens light up. Information starts to run across the screens and then it stops. "Well, let me show you some of their financials. I found that they were bringing money in not only from the drug sales, but they were funded by the government mostly federal funding from the so-called stimulus packages.

They got about twenty-two billion dollars about in 2009. They spent a lot of it on weapons and money that went over to the Mideast to someone named Abu Musab Al Suri. Shit, Sam. That is the Al Qaeda man that they captured in Pakistan and gave them to the Syrian government. The Syrians just let him go, and now if the Internet is correct, he is running the 'jihad in Syria.' Let me get the Internet up again. Ah, here we go—Abu Musab Al Suri is also known as the 'mufti of murder.' Nice, and they are giving those fuckers' money. Oh, now look here."

Sam just stands there staring at the screen in disbelief.

"Those bastards were also giving money to Bin Laden while he was in Pakistan. Shit, they had given him about a hundred million dollars over a two year period. Sam, do you think that they are funding the terrorist groups?" Darwin turns and looks at Sam.

"I think they are funding the groups and that way they can keep the American people in fear. That fucking Barrack knew where Bin Laden was all the time, and when he needed a political boost, he had him killed. Is it only Barrack who is doing all this or can you find others?" Sam asks.

"Ah, let me see," Darwin says as he scrolls through a bunch of files. "Well, looks like there is a Congressman Dodd, Vice President Herman Bashert, and there he is that bastard Congressman Jacklow. They have all been in the payoff, which we already knew, but they also have instructed payments to many of the overseas people. There is someone getting over a billion dollars and his name is Sardar Arjmand. They have sent weapons to Lebanon, Syria, Iraq, and a bunch of other places. They even gave a drone to Iran. I think it is the same one they said that they lost in Iran, but then said it wasn't our drone. Nothing ever came of it after that one week on the news. So what do think?"

Sam is curious about Sardar. He had heard that name before somewhere. Sam says, "See if you can find more information about that Sardar. I have heard that name somewhere, but I can't remember where or when."

Darwin says, "I'll get that done."

"I think we need to rid this country of some really bad people. We should start with the two congressmen and work our way up. But I think the congressmen are already suffering from loss of money. What do you think about hacking all their shit and making it hard for them and their families to even live a normal life? Maybe shut off their credit cards and bank accounts along with their utilities and stuff. Do you think you can do that?" Sam asks.

"Hell yeah! I already started on Jacklow. It won't take much for the rest of them. The president though is going to be hard to touch. I know I can drain his bank account, but I don't know if it will hurt him much." Darwin is really excited about his new projects. "Well, let's look at Bank of New York Melton and see what they have been up to. That is where all the money goes other than the money you all have been taking from them." Darwin types away at his keyboard until a bunch of videos popped up on several screens and some financials on another screen.

"I think we need also see when we can move on the bank. That German-owned bank has made enough off the USA and we are going to take some of it back. I think I can get the hard currency if you can get the electronic money. Maybe put it in to some Swiss and Australian banks or something like that," Sam says.

"Yeah, I'll do that as soon as you hit on the bank. That way there won't be some asshole there that is interfering in my hack. Let's see, right now the bank is worth about five hundred eighty-four billion and some. It looks like there is about sixty or so billion in hard currency, including gold and other valuables. They do have lockboxes in the bank so you might want to see what is in those if you get a chance. The best days to do the job are on any last Friday of the month. That is when the most personnel are gone. So there you have it. Now if you will leave, I can get my work done," Darwin says. "Oh, and Bud is done with the job in Oregon and they are headed to Nevada. They are not stopping at the farm and are headed straight to the bunker. I'll call Sarah in to get the plane and fly you out there. She left your dad and Gunny in Michigan."

"Good, I'll go get ready right away." Sam walks out of the room and then up to the machine shed. He gets on one of the four-wheelers and heads over to talk to Kota and DH. After talking for a while with Kota and DH, Sam goes up to the house and kiss Carol goodbye.

Sarah and Sam fly Sam to Nevada.

CHAPTER THIRTY-SIX

....

IN CHICAGO, ABOUT TWENTY UP to fifty murders happened every week. Some murders are thought to be caused by gang wars, drug crimes, domestic violence, etc. In Atlanta, about forty some murders happen every week. In Saint Louis, about twenty some murders happen every week. Murders are happening everywhere. Most of the murders were considered drug or gang related because they did not have any real motive behind them. Just about all of them were unexplained. The murder rate in 2011 was at its lowest at thirteen thousand, but it would have been even lower if they actually knew that a lot of it is terrorism at its lowest level. The drug-related homicides had almost diminished with the YUPPIs in charge of most of the drug trade. The occasional other homicides was caused by domestic violence. Many of the mass murders that occurred were actually caused by rouge new Islamic extremists that had not kept up with their quota. Nine hundred and eleven is the quota for the month. Most of the murders are done by young men that no one would ever expect would commit murder, like ten-year-old kids playing baseball in the back lot. Then on the way home, they stop down in an alleyway and beat a woman to death, or it could be the sixteen-year-old young man that goes out on his first date and then chokes her to death. These kinds of things happen all the time and are just thought to be caused from stress of the young or from playing video games. It goes unnoticed and the American people just do not care. In reality, it is the process of indoctrination to Islamic extremism.

The newspaper has that President Barrack's property in Illinois and in Hawaii was mistakenly seized for foreclosure. According to the paper, "The properties were immediately seized yesterday because of nonpayment of back taxes. President Barrack commented that it was preposterous. These banks were just acting against a black American family and that any implication that taxes were not paid is denigrating to the position of the president and to the Afro-American communities all across this great county. The seizure of the property was immediately rectified upon notification from the IRS that indeed that taxes had been paid. The IRS and the police department issued apologies to the president and his family."

The paper also read, "Vice President Bassert's yacht was seized for nonpayment of taxes. The vice president issued a statement that he had indeed paid his taxes and that the seizure of his boat was going to be investigated. The IRS was still looking into the seizure, but there were several years of nonpayment of property taxes that could amount to around six hundred thousand dollars or more with penalties and interest. The vice president had not made any further comment."

Sam starts laughing when he read the morning's paper. He knows that Darwin has been busy over the last few days. It is good news to wake up to while he is in the Nevada desert.

Sam, Bud, and Kim have their own little meeting. Sam informs them what is being done in Virginia and about their new properties in New York and in Connecticut.

"The ball is in play for our New York run. We haven't prepped the city yet but Kota and DH are working on things. Have you guys heard from Mike and Dan?" Sam asks.

"I have not heard anything. Those bastards are probably drunk and lying in some whorehouse somewhere. Do you think we should go and try to find them?" Kim asks.

"Where the hell would you even begin to look? Mike moves around like a ghost," Bud says.

"Hold on and let me call Darwin." Sam takes out his phone and dials Darwin. The phone rang for three rings and Darwin answers.

"Hey, I'm not here right now but you can call me on the party line and I may be there." The phone call disconnects.

"What the fuck is up with Darwin. He just hung up on me. He said that he wasn't there and to call the party line." Sam is a little puzzled. "Kim, do you have any more of those prepaid phones you got out of the Oregon compound?"

"Yeah, we have a couple of hundred phones. I'll go get one." Kim runs off and grabs a phone from a big box inside one of the new SUVs that they took from the Oregon compound. He runs back to Bud and Sam. "Here you are." Kim hands the phone to Sam.

Sam dials Darwin's cell phone and Darwin immediately answers, "Hey, what up dude?" Sam asks.

"Sam, your phone being tracked so break it immediately. We can talk on this phone but don't call me on at this number anymore. I will call you in ten seconds. I have your number on the computer." Darwin hangs up immediately and calls back as soon as he hangs up. Sam throws his phone to Bud and signals him to break it. Bud smashes it with his boot and goes over to the sink and runs water on it. The phone is dead.

"Hey, Sam, you have been targeted by the Secret Enforcement Service?" Darwin says.

"What the fuck is that?" Sam asks Darwin.

"It is like a personal service to the president to get rid of people that are problems. They are spooks. These people are handpicked by the president. They have been used since Old Abe Lincoln days. His problem is that he didn't kill his assassin because it was a friend of friend of his. Anyway, they will chase you till the end of the earth. You must have really pissed the president off," Darwin says.

"You pissed him off! Maybe it was the repossession or the video. Anyway, it was pretty funny. The real question is how did they find out it was me and how did they get my cell phone number?" Sam asks.

"Shit, I don't know. They just find this shit out. I will hack into the White House computer and see what is going on. Did you want something else?" Darwin asks.

"Do you have a trace on Mike or Dan?" Sam asks.

"No, but I will look for them. Hey, with all this work, do you think I can get an intern in here?" Darwin asks reluctantly.

"Sure, but you are responsible for them. If they screw up, you get to dispose of them," Sam says.

Darwin decides against any help. He really didn't want that much responsibility and he would have to go out of the bunker. To him, it just wasn't worth it.

Sam had given Carol one of the light armored Cadillac Escalades that they had acquired in Northern Florida compound. Darwin had fixed it so that the title was all clear with the department of motor vehicles just like he had done with all the vehicles that had been acquired. Mr. Delker was sent for a few weeks to a defensive driving school in the northwestern Virginia area. He now drives Carol wherever needed in one of the armored vehicles. Carol is not happy about not being able to drive herself but she understood Sam's concern.

Carol always believes that there is never too much advertising, and the vehicles are one place that she likes to advertise the hospital. She is not supposed to put anything on her vehicle because Sam is always worried that someone that hates him would decide to go after her. She thinks of her vehicle as a driving fortress and isn't worried about any of that nonsense Sam is worried about existed. She has her vehicle wrapped with the hospital logo.

Carol needs to get off the farm. She has been stuck there at for over two weeks, but when Mr. Delker comes back, his first job is to bring Carol to her father's restaurant. She not only wants to talk to her father but she wants to treat her new bodyguard and personal secretary to a good breakfast. Carol has hired a personal assistant named Tabitha Thomas. She is a young woman that is just starting out on her own. Her father has been part of a gang long ago. He had been put in prison when she was in high school. Her mother is a waitress at Carol's father's restaurant. Tabitha was always a shy girl that was never outgoing. She started working at the restaurant helping to wash dishes when she was old enough. When Carol was looking for a personal assistant, her father told her to hire Tabitha. Carol agreed to try her out. Tabitha has worked wonderfully over the last few weeks.

Mr. Delker is driving up the interstate until Carol tells him, "Get off at this exit and stop at Staples before we go to the restaurant. We need to get a new printer for my father. We can just drop it off at the restaurant while we are there."

Mr. Delker gets off at the exit. "To Staples we will go. Just give me directions. I have never been there."

Mr. Delker makes a left-hand turn. As they drive up the highway, a police car pulls up behind them. The car starts to tailgate Mr. Delker, so he slows down to let the car pass. He continues to monitor the car behind him, but it does not pass. He just keeps his cool and continues at a constant speed, and then a car pulls out in front of him from a side road. Mr. Delker hits the brakes and turns up the side road, almost rolling their vehicle as he turns the corner. The car behind him runs into the back of the SUV as it rounded the corner. Had it not been for his new training, he probably would have rolled the SUV. The man in the car flips on the police lights and Mr. Delker pulls to the side of the road and stops. Another two cars pull in behind them.

Mr. Delker turns to Carol, "Stay in here I will handle this." He grabs the registration and his license and then gets out of the car. The windows on an armored vehicle do not roll down. As soon as he gets out of the vehicle, the person in the police car gets out.

Sheriff Allen and another young man with a YUPPI uniform get out of one of the back cars. Deputy Sheriff Trevor gets out of the first car. Two uniformed YUPPI men get out of the last car.

Deputy Trevor had healed up from the severe beating that Sam had given him. He still has a disfigured face from where to metal bar hit him in the head and cracked his skull. After several surgeries to save his life, he came back to the police force back into a new position. He came back with a huge vendetta with Sam and anyone that works with him.

Sheriff Allen is still licking his wounds from Sam and the mountain explosion. He also was in the hospital for several months and went through several formal inquiries before a Congressman Dodd got him his job back a few months ago. He also has a vendetta against Sam.

The YUPPI men are just there on orders to help out the sheriff in case one of the local compounds is under attack again.

Trevor yells up to Mr. Delker, "Stop right there and get back in your vehicle."

Mr. Delker yells back, "The windows don't work in this vehicle. I'll just stand right here."

Trevor yells, "Get back in your fucking vehicle."

Mr. Delker turns and gets back in the vehicle and shuts the door. He turns to Carol, "They told me to get back in here."

Carol takes a moment to put her iPad down and turns to look who it is. She yells in a panic. "Lock the doors and don't get out. These guys I think are the same ones that are tangling with Sam and his brothers. I think that one guy helped kidnapped me before. Don't open the door and just drive away. NOW!"

Mr. Delker quickly starts the vehicle and takes off.

The other men see him take off and quickly get back in their vehicles and chase him.

Mr. Delker speeds down the side road but the side road ends. He turns into the nearest driveway, which leads to a pasture. The gate is shut, so he smashes through, breaking off the posts that are holding it up. He speeds through the pasture up to a fence. He remembers his training of not driving through the wire but to hit the post to knock the fence over. He slows down and then slowly pushes a post over with front bumper. He drives over the fence and into the next pasture and on out to the road.

Carol yells, "Go back to the farm." Mr. Delker speeds toward the farm. Carol calls Kota and tells him what is going on. Kota and DH run over to Gunny's place and grab some weapons and ammunition. They get into to one of the farm trucks and take off to head the sheriff off at the pass.

Deputy Trevor follows the path of destruction through the field, and the sheriff heads into beeline for the farm. The YUPPIs take the back roads toward the farm.

Mr. Delker is taking the back way on the side roads to the farm. He is only vaguely familiar with the back roads, so Carol is navigating, but she is only a little more familiar with the roads. The YUPPIs spot Mr. Delker on one of the back roads and call Deputy Trevor. He knows the back roads very well and quickly catches up to Mr. Delker. The YUPPIs chase close behind.

Before Mr. Delker can even react, Trevor hits the side of the SUV at about fifty miles per hour. Because of the weight of the vehicle and Mr. Delker's driving skill, the vehicle just slides over to the side of the road and down into a gully. No one gets hurt, but they are shaken up.

Deputy Trevor's car is totaled but the airbags saved him from any bodily harm. The two YUPPIs stop their car and quickly got out. They run over to Trevor's car and help him from the wreckage. All three of them move over to the SUV that is stuck in the gully and surround it. They just stand there till Sheriff Allen and the other YUPPI arrives a few minutes later.

Kota and DH had a hard time finding Carol because she had no idea what road they are on. The vehicle is equipped with a tracker, so Darwin knows where they are and they are ten minutes away.

Deputy Trevor yells to the people in the SUV, "Get the fuck out of the vehicle, now."

Mr. Delker gives him a reply back by flipping him off. This infuriates Trevor. He draws his pistol and starts shooting at the vehicle. The bullets just ricocheted off the vehicle. Carol and Tabitha lie down on the floor of the vehicle. Carol knows that Sam always has some weapons in all the vehicles, but she never listened to him when he told her where they were hidden.

Carol tells Mr. Delker and Tabitha, "Look around in here and see if you can find some guns. Sam should have put some in here. Maybe see if they are in the floor or something."

Everyone looks around then Tabitha screams, "I found it." She had opened the floor of the passenger side backseat area and there is a .45 Colt 1911.

Sheriff Allen yells, "Come on out now. Don't make this worse then what it already is."

Mr. Delker is about to give them a second hand signal when Tabitha holds up the pistol and points it at Carol and Mr. Delker, "Get out, you two."

Carol looks at Tabitha with puzzlement. Mr. Delker looks at her with rage.

Mr. Delker gets out of the vehicle first. He helps Carol out and up out of the gully. Sheriff Allen and his men keep their weapons pointed at Carol and Mr. Delker. Once Mr. Delker gets Carol out of the gully, he goes back and pretends like he is going to help Tabitha out of the vehicle. She is dumb enough to drop her weapon long enough, so it gave Mr. Delker a chance to take it away from her. He grabs the weapon in one quick movement and at the same time adds a bone-crushing punch to her chest. The punch cracks her sternum and completely knocks the breath out of her. She can still breathe but with great difficulty. She can only lie in the SUV seat and not move. Mr. Delker then swings around and takes a shot at one of the YUPPIs. The round hit him in the chest but only knocked him unconscious because he is wearing a bulletproof vest. Deputy Trevor then shoots Mr. Delker before he can fire another round. The round hits Mr. Delker in left shoulder area, ripping the clavicle and muscle from the top of his shoulder but missing any major arteries and veins. The impact of the round knocks him down and he doesn't get back up. Carol screams and then feels a sudden fear goes through her body, making her go numb. She remembers the terror she went through when they kidnapped her before. The memory that she worked so hard to bury suddenly came alive, and all she could do is cry.

Kota and DH arrive right as the men are moving in on Carol. They slide to a stop. They jump out and run behind the truck with their weapons at hand. Kota has a Mill-Tech SS-54 urban assault rifle and DH has a .45-caliber semiauto pistol. Deputy Trevor runs grabs Carol immediately as soon as Kota and DH show up. He uses Carol for a shield. Kota lies down behind the truck's back tire, and DH crouches behind the front tire. Sheriff Allen and the two YUPPIs rain bullets at the truck. When they stop to reload, Kota leans out from behind the tire and quickly shoots the two YUPPIs. This time the rounds hit both of them in the face and exiting the back of their skulls. Blood, brain tissue, and bone fragments fly from the back of their heads. The two men are dead before they hit the ground. DH is able to get off two rounds center in Sheriff Allen's chest. He is wearing a bulletproof vest under his shirt but the impact is the same as getting hit by a ten-pound sledgehammer. The sheriff is knocked to the ground with several broken ribs and a cracked sternum. He is unconscious but still alive.

Deputy Trevor keeps close to Carol pointing his pistol at Kota and DH. He yells with fear, "You both hold it right there. Put down your weapons and I'll just take this bitch. Then we can all leave. Otherwise, I'm going to kill her right now."

Kota yells, "You stupid shit. You are dead either way you look at it. We leave you alone and now you come back for another beating."

Trevor yells back in a little frustration. He knows he has no real options. "I remember someone else getting a beating. You fucking little mama's boy. Come over here and I'll give you another ass kicking that you and your fucking brothers deserve."

Kota yells, "Go and take her. Sam will skin you alive for a couple of weeks and then have the buzzards eat you alive. Hell, you should just kill yourself now and save us the trouble."

Deputy Trevor is getting really nervous. He knows if they get him alive, they would do just that. He yells, "Fuck you." He fires a few rounds at Kota and DH. Both rounds hit the truck but that is as close as it comes. As he is shooting, he didn't notice that Mr. Delker had regained consciousness. Mr. Delker moves up close to Trevor. He has his left hand tucked into his belt to hold his arm still and then pulls out his fourteen-inch blade from under his vest with his right hand. Mr. Delker being a guru of the Philippian art of knife fighting is as deadly as a shower of chainsaws. Deputy Trevor sees him coming and swings his pistol into his direction. Before he can pull the trigger, Mr. Delker leaps in and cuts his hand off. Trevor releases Carol and she runs to Kota. Mr. Delker puts six deadly cuts into Trevor as quick as the eye can blink. Deputy Trevor falls to the ground bleeding but before he hits the ground, Mr. Delker makes the last cut up from the groin to the sternum. When Deputy Trevor hits the ground, his intestines slither out of his belly. Mr. Delker falls to his knees and the pain takes over his body.

The YUPPI that Mr. Delker shot regains consciousness. He sits up and takes a couple of deep breaths and groans. He looks around and sees he has no hope of winning any battle, so he just sits there not moving. He says, "I give up. I am unarmed."

Carol runs over to help Mr. Delker up to his feet and into the truck. Kota calls some of the troopers that are working at the bunker. Ten men drive over in Hummers. They are well rehearsed in cleaning up situations very quickly. All the dead are removed. They bury dead in the compost pile at the farm. Within a couple of months, the corpses are turned into nothing but dirt. The cars are taken to the cave warehouse and stored. Later they will be used or stripped. The SUV is pulled out of the gully and driven back to the bunker for repair. The fence that was broken down is repaired and the tire tracks are covered and brushed out. All the shell casings are picked up. Nothing remains except the stench of death in the air.

Sheriff Allen, the YUPPI, and Tabitha are taken to the farm. They are blindfolded and brought to Dr. Michael Washington to care for them. They are under constant watch with two armed men.

Since the hospital is not completely finished, Dr. Michael uses Sam's surgery room in the equine hospital to repair Mr. Delker shoulder. Mr. Delker would not be able to perform his duties to the utmost perfection for couple of months. He calls in one of his trusted friends to help.

Carol sits with Tabitha at one of the morning's breakfast. Tabitha had not needed much medical assistance besides some painkillers for a couple of days. Sheriff Allen is OK, but Carol didn't care about him.

"So tell me, Tabitha," Carol leans in across the table. "What the hell?" Carol sits back and throws up her arms.

"Well," Tabitha says in a whiny voice, "they made me do it."

"Who is they and how did they make you do it?" Carol sits back and drinks some morning green tea.

"My uncle is Officer Trevor. He hates us," Tabitha says. "He is my dad's brother and has been living in our house."

"Really." Carol looks puzzled. "Why is your name and your mother's name not Trevor?"

"I don't know." Tabitha is a little clueless. "My dad always made me call him Uncle Trevor, but he makes me call him Officer Trevor. If I don't do what he says, he will give you a slapping."

"Well, you don't have to worry about that anymore. He won't ever touch another person again," Carol says with a little smile. "I don't think he is your real uncle. Maybe it is one of your dad's friends."

"You are probably right. My dad used to share mom with him. Dad always said to 'share and share alike' with friends," Tabitha says.

"Tabitha." Carol just shakes her head. "I really didn't know you were that naive. Did your dad ever share you with him?"

"No, Dad would never do that but when he went to prison everything changed. Mom tried to keep Officer Trevor away, but he would come in the house anyway. When he got in the house, he would hit my mom and said that if I made him feel good, he would stop. I used to cry when he did things to me, but I just learned not to care," Tabitha says.

"That is terrible." Carol is appalled at the idea of how long Trevor got by with all this. "You poor girl," Carol says with sincerity. "How did he get you to betray me?"

"He said he would give my mom back if I did it. I hope she is all right, I haven't seen her in a week or so. I called the cops and Sheriff Allen came right out. He said that he would look in to it. Trevor slapped me around that night and then he and one of those blue and white uniform men raped me. Then the next day, I started working with you." Tabitha is almost crying.

Carol calls Dakota and DH down to the bunker. She tells them what happened and wants them there when she confronted the sheriff.

The three of them go down to a room that is holding the sheriff and the YUPPI. Both of them are laughing seem to be enjoying life.

Kota walks in first. "Carol has some questions for you two." DH and Carol walk in the room.

"Sheriff," Carol says sarcastically, "did you find Tabitha's mother?"

"Oh, we found her! We found her over and over." The sheriff stands up and grabs his crotch.

Kota knows that Sam never tolerates this condescension and utter disrespect. Kota leaps toward the sheriff and comes down with a side kick to the knee. The knee instantly is dislocated and the sheriff drops to the floor screaming. Kota kicks him in the ribs separating some already bruised ribs. The YUPPI makes a motion to jump at Kota. Kota quickly draws the knife his dad gave him and buries it into the thigh of the YUPPI. The knife sticks into the femur and the real pain for the YUPPI is when Kota pulls it out. The YUPPI falls back onto the floor and clutches his leg.

"Now answer the fucking question. Shit is about to get real bad if you don't." Kota yells.

"Fuck you," the sheriff yells. He doesn't know whether to grab his ribs or his knee. "I fucking know where she is, and if you want to know, you need to give me something."

Kota takes his knife and imbeds into the dislocated knee joint. He makes one twist with the knife and pulls it out. He knows how painful joints can be by being around Sam at the hospital. He saw how painful the horses with foreign bodies and infections in the joint were until Sam would fix them.

The sheriff starts screaming and crying but it was all for nothing.

They turn their attention on to the YUPPI in the corner.

"OK, your turn," Carol says, "Do you know where the woman is kept?"

"Ahhh, yeah," the YUPPI says.

"Well, where is she?" Carol asks.

"She's at the farm," the YUPPI says.

"What farm is that?" A chill comes over Carol.

"You know exactly what farm, bitch," the YUPPI says.

Kota kicks the YUPPI in the face, causing him to pass out.

"What the hell did you do that for?" Carol says with a little aggravation.

"That is what Sam would do if he was here. He doesn't take disrespect lightly," Kota says.

"Well, it looks like we are going to the farm again?" DH says questioningly to Carol.

"If you want, you can take this shit and dump them over there too," Carol points to the two men on the floor.

As Kota and DH gather everything together to make a raid on the farm, Carol decides that she should call Sam first. She knows that Kota and DH could handle everything, but this could get out of hand. She goes over to Darwin to try to get Sam on the phone. She knows Sam had to get rid of his phone.

"Do you know where Sam is and how to get ahold of him?" Carol asks Darwin. She looks around the computer room for something that might have died in there, but then she noticed that it is just Darwin. He looks like he hasn't changed clothes in weeks and smells like a pile of dead skunks. Carol fans her hand in front of her face trying to clear the air of the smell.

Darwin notices Carol's crinkled up nose and turns his head to smell his armpits and gives a shrug. "I will get Sam on the phone right away."

"Darwin, when have you showered last?" Carol asks.

"Oh, it's probably been a few days or so. I've been busy trying to track down Mike and Dan. I think I found their last cell phone location, and they have been running a credit card quite frequently in Doyle, California. I don't think it's them buying shit because the signatures don't match," Darwin says. "I got Sam on the line. Here." Darwin hands the headphones to Carol.

Carol wipes the headphones on her pants. It is all greasy and sweaty. "Hey, Sam."

"Carol, how are you?" Sam asks.

"I'm fine," Carol says and then tells him all about what happened. "Sam, what should we do?"

"I think you should do exactly what you think you should do. Kota knows how to handle things and those ten troopers I left with you are very good. Just make sure you go in with armor and get in and get out. Be safe," Sam says. "As for the two you got there, I don't know what to do with them. Ship them to Cuba or something. Kota should have a shipping container but wait till after the raid, you may have more."

"OK, Sam, I love you," Carol says. "I'm going to hand Darwin over to you. He thinks he found Mike and Dan."

"Love you too," Sam says.

Carol hands the headphones to Darwin. He makes sure that Carol is looking and then wipes the headphones off on his pants just to be sarcastic. "Hey, Sam," Darwin says, "I think Mike and Dan are somewhere near Doyle, California. The cell phone is just outside of town and their credit card is being used a lot. I don't think they are using it unless they have been buying food, alcohol, and televisions for a whole town. I'll keep a trace on them, but someone is going to have to check it out. They aren't answering the phone."

"OK, thanks, Darwin. That is not too far from here so we can go look," Sam says. "Darwin, make sure that those guys get in and get out safe. Do what you can, OK."

"I'm looking after them, Sam," Darwin says. "I'll being looking after you too. I think I found the code for a drone that the State of New York has been using for surveillance. Do you want me to fly it over to you?"

"No, just leave it for now and we will use it when we get back there," Sam says.

"Got it. I'm gone," Darwin says and then kills the connection.

Sam sits down with Kim and Bud. He tells them about what is going on in Virginia. Then Sam tells them, "Darwin thinks that there is something going wrong with Mike and Dan. He thinks that someone has their credit cards and phone. We all know that they wouldn't let that happen if something isn't going wrong. I need to go and find them. Do you all think you want to go along or carry on with busting meth labs?"

Bud and Kim look at each other and then Kim says, "I think that those guys are partying it up but maybe not. We got work to do and I'm thinking we should just keep on busting labs. If you find that they are in trouble and you need more help, we can fly to the rescue."

Bud says, "I think Kim is right. We need to stick to the plan and keep going. We got momentum on our side, and if we slow down, we may not get started." Bud takes a deep breath. "Besides, I want to get home sometime and I not going till we clean this side of the states up."

"Good. I'll go find them guys. I don't think I will need any more than a few troopers. You all go on and I'll meet you all at the New Mexico bunker. Darwin can give you the GPS coordinates. If you get too bogged down then just call in the carrier. It is rough country going to that bunker."

Bud says, "We'll get it done. Don't you get into any trouble? We don't have time to rescue you too." They all laugh a little.

Sam says, "I'll leave in the morning. Anyone in particular that you think I should take or don't want along with you?"

Kim says, "Everyone is great just take whoever wants to go."

Bud says, "Take WindEagle and the six others in his group. They work great together and they need a little break. They've been getting a little trigger happy and need to settle down just a little."

Sam says, "Good, now let's eat."

Chapter Thirty-Seven

KOTA AND DH ARE READY to go. It is just about dark enough. Since they have night vision capability, they thought this will be the best time to hit the farm. They need a couple of extra drivers. Ashley and Erin, who both are Sam's old technicians, want to help. Ashley is an old sprint car driver and Erin is a marksman. Erin had been on the Olympic shooting team but was unable to go when she broke her arm in a car accident.

Carol tells Kota, "Both Erin and Ashley are big girls now, and if they want to help, then let them help. I'm sure Ashley will make a good driver and Erin maybe a sniper or something."

Kota and DH bring Ashley and Erin down into the bunker. They had no idea that it was there. They are both amazed that this was all built without them knowing about it. When they reach the cave, both could not stop saying, "OH SHIT." They walk around looking at the cars and armored vehicles.

"Where did all this come from and how did you get it in here without us knowing about it? Damn, I love this place," Ashley says with excitement.

"Well, you will find out all the little secrets as time goes on but you are sworn to secrecy and if you talk even to your significant others. You will never ever be seen again. Sam is really strict about this." Kota tells them with sincerity and authority.

"We swear we will never tell a soul." Both of them tell Kota.

Kota gives Ashley a quick driving lesson on the Stryker. She learns quickly and is ready to go with in an hour. DH takes Erin to the weapons room down in the cave. Erin picks a modified M-14 with a night vision scope. DH gave her two hundred rounds of ammunition. Both of women put on bulletproof vests, helmets, and leggings. They are ready to go.

Ashley fires up the Stryker. Kota and five troopers jump in. DH drives the other Stryker, Erin, and five men go with him. Ashley and Erin are both high on adrenaline, kind of like getting on a roller coaster and sitting at the top of the first hill. Everyone knows their job.

Kota and Erin are let out about a half a mile from the farm almost in the area of where the big fight took place a couple of years ago. Kota is carrying a Barrett Model 98B with .338 Lapua Magnum ammunition that is capable of 1,500-yard shot, and at a closer range, it can easily penetrate the best of body armor. They both make their way over the hill and through the trees using night vision. Kota has Erin set up on one corner of the farm and he sets up ninety degrees to her. They are able to see the entire farm.

The farm has changed since the original was burned to the ground a few years ago. Now there is a large two-story building that resembled an old-style motel with separate rooms that opened into the outdoors. It is built into a C-shape. In the center, there is a smaller single-floor building that looks like a dinner hall. There is another building about a hundred yards away that is a large metal building. It is a garage and underneath is the basement lab. Around the compound is a chain-link fence that has some barbed wire on the top but it is unfinished. The gate is chained and there is no sign of an alarm attachment. On the outside of the gate is a guard shack that has one person inside. The guard is sleeping with the television on. There is no activity outside in the compound. Inside the dining hall, there is loud music that fills the air. Kota can hear someone screaming over many people yelling. There are only a few lights on in the rooms.

Kota radios DH at the same time gives all the troopers the low-down on the compound.

"We are going to move in on foot and the vehicles will come in after we secure the compound. Kota, when we get into position, you take out the electrical lines. We can move in on them in the dark. We will get the guard at the shack," DH says. "Remember the objective is to get the woman and get out as easy as possible. If in the process we see something that needs to be taken, then we will load it after the objective is done. Now let's get going."

"I'm ready," Kota says. "Erin, are you ready. Erin?"

"YEAH! I'm here. I never shot anyone before," Erin says. She is very nervous and her voice has that nervous rasp to it. "I'm ready. I hope I don't let you down."

"Damn it, Erin!" Kota says sternly, "There are ten men down there that are counting on you to shot straight and in a very timely manner. If you can't do it, tell us now so we can get someone else in your position."

"I'll do it," Erin says in a pissed way. "I'm just fucking nervous."

"OK! DH, go," Kota says.

DH leaves one of the troopers in charge of his Stryker. He and nine troopers go into the compound. Three men sneak over to the dining hall. Two men take the lower level of the motel and two on the upper deck. Three men take the parking garage and lab. Half of them enter the compound by cutting a hole in the fence through the backside and half through the gate. DH walks up to the guard shack and opens the door. The guard never moves until DH throws the zip tie around the first wrist. He struggles a bit till DH knocks him out with one punch. DH ties the guard to the chair and tapes his mouth. Then he drags the guard out and tips him backward to a tree and zip ties the chair to the tree. They unlock the gate with a key from the guard shack and go into the compound. DH takes the dining hall with the other troopers. He has them put their rifles away and get out their short swords except for the two standing guard outside the door.

"Kill the lights," DH whispers into the radio.

Kota takes aim and shoots the electrical line in half right where it connected to the pole. The lights go out and the troopers go to work. The motel troopers go into each room one by one securing each room. Several of the men in the rooms have firearms, but anyone that points a weapon at a trooper is instantly killed. The troopers can see, but the men in the rooms are taking blind shots and not effective at all.

DH and one trooper go into the dining hall. Two troopers stay outside the door as back up and to take out anyone coming out. All DH can think to himself is "Does every one of these fuckers have a pistol on them?" As soon as the two of them enter the dining hall, they can see everyone has drawn their pistols. In the left-hand corner of the room, the woman they are looking for lies naked on a table with three men with their pants and underwear off standing around her. It appears to DH that they have been gang-raping her. DH and the trooper move along the wall without a sound. DH reaches for the first man without pants and runs the blade of the short sword underneath the rib cage, lacerating the lungs and vital arteries. The chest cavity fills with blood instantly, making it impossible for the man to scream. DH quietly retracts the sword from the first man and swings the sword that cut across the throat of the second man. The sword cuts through the trachea, carotid arteries, and muscles of the neck. The man's neck flips back, leaving no connection of his trachea to the larynx. The man tries to scream but all he can do is move his mouth. He drowns in his own blood. Meanwhile the trooper tries the same lung cut on the third man without pants but the blade slips off the spinal column. As the man swings around, the blade cut completely through and out his side. Intestines and blood drop out on to the floor. The man screams, and when he does, shots ring throughout the entire room. The trooper grabs the woman and pulls her to the floor. DH dive to the floor and the rest of the twenty or so men stand shooting in all directions. The two of them watch as all but two are shot down. DH quickly finishes them off with a pistol he takes from one of the men that got shot. DH and the trooper go around the dining hall to make sure everyone is dead. Neither one of them are going to give mercy to rapists. Those that are still alive get another heart shot from one of the pistols of one of the dead. The trooper grabs a couple of shirts from the dead men. He helps put them on to the woman. DH leaves the trooper with the woman and him, and the other troopers go over to the motel to help out. Men have started to come out of the rooms when they heard the shooting.

Three of the men dive out the back windows. Kota is able to shoot down two of them.

"Erin, get that one on your side of the motel," Kota tells her in a quiet yet stern voice. "Do it now before he gets around to the other side with the troopers."

"I don't think I have a shot. I don't have a shot," Erin says in a panic.

"You shoot that son of a bitch or I'm going to shoot you. Now fucking shoot!" Kota is pissed off.

"Stop yelling!" Erin is half-crying but she targets the man and kills him with the first shot with a direct hit to the neck taking out the cervical vertebrae and half the neck. The man is dead before he hits the ground.

"Good job. Now quit crying. Troopers don't cry," Kota says.

DH and the other troopers get the other men. All the men go out shooting and die with a bullet.

The garage is taken very easily. No one is in it. There are four new SUVs, one Ferrari, and two new dually trucks with forty-foot trailers attached to them. Down in the basement is a stockpile of a sorted amount of ammunition, crates of clay blocks which the troopers know to be C-4 and several different rifles and handguns. Further in the basement is something that looks like a safe or a blast door. DH goes down into the basement.

"What you guys got?" DH asks.

"A big fucking door," the one trooper says.

"Did you try to open it?" DH asks. "Check for any traps or trigger wires first."

DH takes out a can of silly string and sprays around. The silly string will stick to wires if they are there but light enough not to trigger them. They find no wires, and if it is an electrical trigger, it should be dead unless battery operated. DH takes a chance and pulls the door handle. Nothing happens expect the door comes open. They walk in to the room to find that not only are they making meth in the lab, but they are making C-4 plastic explosives. There are cases of motor oil, bottles of polyisobutylene and di-sebacate, and barrels of powdered cyclotrimethylene-trinitramine—all the ingredients for

C-4. They move out of the lab, another door is locked with a simple paddle lock. One of the troopers quickly picks the lock. Inside is the money room. Like all the other bunkers, there is a lot of money.

DH calls in the Strykers and he decides to load everything in the Strykers. They put the woman in one of the SUVs and one of the troopers takes her to the hospital. The rest of the troopers drive out in the rest of the vehicles.

Erin is still crying and still sitting in the same spot Kota put her.

"Erin let's go!" Kota radios.

"OK," Erin sniffles. "I'll be right there."

Kota waits about five minutes. "Erin, are you coming."

"I don't know my way back," Erin says. "Come and get me."

Kota had already gone to find her and is only a few seconds away from her. "Put your weapon away so you don't shoot me. I am right next to you."

Erin slings her rifle. "I put it away."

Kota walks up on her. She is still crying.

Kota grabs her hand and lead her down the hill and back to the road. "You are going to be OK. That man would have killed one of are men if you wouldn't have shot him. He is a drug dealer and probably took part in several other types of nasty shit that you couldn't even imagine. They are not good people, and they would not even think twice about killing you."

"Thanks, Dakota." Erin quit crying. "That does make a difference. How many of these guys have you killed?"

"I don't know. I never kept track. I know Sam has killed more of these guys than anyone, and he doesn't even hesitate anymore," Kota explains. "We call them Smokers, like in that *Waterworld* movie."

"Really, I never would have thought that of Sam." Erin is a little thrown aback.

Ashley is waiting for them at the insertion point. Kota and Erin climb over the mountain of stuff in the Stryker and sit up front. All the way back home, the two women just chattered with excitement of the whole night. They both got to see how stuff got in and out of the cave without them knowing.

DH just left the guard tied to the tree. He saw no reason to take him. He didn't see anyone. Before leaving the compound, one of the troopers rigged a bomb to blow up the lab using a cell phone. Using some of the C-4 ingredients, they burned the motel and dining hall. Once down the road, the trooper dials the number to the cell phone at the lab. The whole building explodes.

Carol is waiting for them when they arrive. "How did it go?"

"Good. Nobody was hurt. The woman is at the hospital and we got you a Ferrari," Kota says.

"Any people to ship?" Carol asks but she already knows the answer.

"No one. So we will ship those two out in the morning," Kota says while putting his weapons away.

"OK. I'll call Sam and let him know," Carol says. "I'll let Tabitha know about her mom."

"OK," Kota says and then goes down to look at what they took that night. Everyone celebrates a little that night.

Chapter Thirty-Eight

Sam, WindEagle, and six other troopers took off in two armored SUVs heading for Doyle, California. Bud, Kim, and the remaining trooper team head to Colorado and then to New Mexico. They will then go to Arizona and back to New Mexico. They are hoping to meet up with Sam in California in two weeks. Then they all will finish California and Texas together. Everything should be finished within a month or so. Everyone can have the Christmas holidays off and right after the first of the year it is back to work on New York.

Once Sam and his team reach Doyle he calls Darwin for the locations where the credit card transactions took place. Sam and his team are dressed in street clothes like they usually did, but this time they aren't in any military gear. Darwin tells Sam to go to Susanville because that is where most of the transactions took place.

"Ah, Sam, there is not much in Doyle, so you might go to Susanville. They have restaurants there and a few motels. There's only like eight hundred people in Doyle. There is a place called Buck Inn Bar. That is where there is credit card activity every Friday and Saturday night. I suggest you all go get some food and a nap in Susanville. Head back to the bar tomorrow night and you may catch the cardholder. I'll call you when it gets used," Darwin tells Sam.

Sam and the team go to Susanville. The whole area is beautiful with the Sierra Mountains in the background and a light dusting of snow on the tops. It reminds him of Virginia but not as much green grass.

Sam and his team go out the next morning to just drive around and get to know the area a little bit. They're target point is the Buck

Inn Bar and they go out from there. Sam, WindEagle, and two troopers drive north and Jose Santiago and three other troopers drive south.

Jose is a retired army ranger. He had fought in Grenada, Panama, the Gulf War, and sometime in the Iraq war. He retired and came home to nothing. No job, no skills, except to think and kill. In today's job market, he was unemployable except for manual labor. He had no family except a younger brother who was a stockbroker. He had sought out Sam when he had heard that someone was hiring retired military. Jose is much like the others Sam has hired. Most are trained to fight and have nothing to gain or lose except their pride. Some of others are specialty trained such as in electronic, communication, mechanics, explosives and more. Sam gives them all they need and all they could want. Sam offers them money, pride, self-worth, and a family. He treats them all like friends and family. They all have the option to leave with all they can carry at any time. They monitor themselves; when one gets out of hand, like many times families do, they all worked it out. Only a couple of times did Sam ever intervene. The small army soon became known as the Brothers3 not just because of Sam and his two brothers. They all started saying that it was when you join, "You have three brothers and me," but later they just said, "Brothers3 are we." The people all call themselves troopers and no one has rank over another. Their military rank means nothing in the Brothers3; Sam, his brothers, DH, and Kim are the boss. Anyone can give an opinion or advice at any time without fear of any recourse. Everyone bows and addresses each other with Sir and Ma'am but only during formal times. Sam thinks it is too much of a nuisance to do any of the military recognition formalities and besides, there are no set rules.

Sam and his team end up in the bar at about nine o'clock that night. Sam's team knows that it is OK to have a good time but not to get drunk. They all sit at a table. The bar is not a hopping place, only a few ranchers and a few women. The band is a local band from Susanville that plays two kinds of music, country and western.

"We don't often get new folks in here. Where are you from?" the waitress asked in one of those friendly waitress voices.

"We are just traveling through. We are from Virginia and got a little lost, then found this place so here we are." Sam looks at the waitress, who looks vaguely familiar.

"Well, I'm Bella and this is the place to be on a Friday night unless those bikers show up," she says in a nervous voice, "What are you all having?"

"Can you tell me who owns the place?" Sam asks and then orders a Coors as well did the others, except for Tails; she orders a wine cooler.

Tails is a retired Navy SEAL. She had gotten severely injured on one a mission. She honorably discharged but never received any help from the government when she got back to stateside. She had been living in homeless shelters in Chicago. She still did not have full use of her left arm, but Sam sent her to have stem cell therapy about four months ago. Now she has partial use and is getting better every day. Everyone called her Tails because she only wore her hair in a ponytail since she couldn't do much else with only one arm.

"Well, that old man up behind the bar is my father, and the other young gorgeous man is my son." She points the two bartenders. "We all own part of this place, you might say."

"Ah, good, a family-owned business," Sam says.

"What about your husband, does he work here too?" Jose asks just because he is curious and not out of disrespect.

Bella looks at Jose with a sad but a little annoyed face. "No, he doesn't work here. He was killed in Iraq."

"Ah, sorry, ma'am," Jose says. "I didn't mean any disrespect. I was also in Iraq."

"That's all right. I'm just a little jumpy with the biker problem," Bella explains. "My husband would have handled this type of stuff, but we can't do anything about it. There is no law out here." Bella turns and goes to get the drinks. "These are on the house for all military. Are you all military?"

"No, I am the only one here that is not military," Sam says. "But the rest are."

"What are you, all the A team or something?" she says with a little laugh. The A team reference is from a television show back in the seventies.

"Something like that." Tails laughs and takes a drink of her wine cooler.

Bella smiles and walks away to wait on others. The conversation in the team turns to figuring out who would be who in the show *A Team*.

Sam is about to call it a night but around eleven o'clock, male and female bikers start showing up. They are all wearing gang colors of Vega, which also stands for "the falling." These bikers are rejects from other biker gangs such as the Hells Angels and the Diablos.

As soon as they come in, the ranchers and the women leave the bar. The bikers are loud and disrespectful. They take over the whole bar very quickly. Bella tries to calm them down by waiting on them quickly. The bikers grab her and start laughing. When she screams a little, they laugh more and let her go. Some grab their crotches and say, "You're going to have this tonight." Then start laughing.

Sam looks around and notices that there is a clear leader. He is the one sitting quietly in the back of the bar with two women sitting around him. One big biker, who was about 6'5" and 260 pounds, brings the main guy drinks. Sam figures that the big biker is the second in line. Sam also notices that most of them are carrying some kind of weapon. Most of them have fixed-bladed knives, but some have a handgun stuck in the back of their pants. The biker women all are carrying small-bladed knives.

"This fucking gang is the biggest bunch of dirtbags," Jose says to the whole group.

"If those assholes come over here and start fucking with me, I will fuck kill them," Tails says and she means it.

Bella comes over to the team's table. She looks worn and ragged. She tells them, "You all might want to leave. They are pretty rowdy tonight and things may not be very good for you all."

"We'll be all right. You are the one that we are worried about," Sam says.

"You want us to throw them out?" Jose asks as a redundant question. He knows that Sam will only tolerate so much and then go ninja on the bikers. Sam hates rude people like these bikers.

The bartenders are trying to keep people from coming behind the bar as politely as they can until till one of the women bikers punch the old man. The old man's nose starts to bleed, but he just keeps on with his work. The other bikers just laugh. Then they start throwing bottles at the band, so the band grabs their stuff and leave quickly.

Sam has had about enough, and then one of the biker women comes over to the team's table.

"So why are you fuckers still here?" the biker woman asks. "This is our place and maybe you want to leave."

"Get away, you skanky whore bitch," Tails yells at the biker woman.

The biker woman walks around to Tails's side of the table. Tails jumps out of her chair and grabs the biker woman by the back of the head. She comes up with a knee in to the biker's chest and then slams her head on the table. Tails throws the biker to the floor. The biker is unconscious and bleeding on the floor. Tails broke the biker's nose and busted out all her lower front teeth.

With all the commotion, the other bikers start to take notice of the eight nonbikers sitting in the corner of the bar near the back door. Sam and his team have weapons on them. They all have two knives and two .40-caliber handguns in leg holsters except for Sam. Sam is carrying his bladed whip chain and his short sword. As the bikers move in closer, the team slowly takes out their handguns and gets them ready. They lay their handguns on their laps. Sam leaves his weapons where they are, under his vest.

Another biker woman slowly walks over to the woman on the floor like someone walking around a bucket of snakes. She tries to pick the woman up off the floor and help her back on her but she cannot stand. Soon the bar gets really quite. All the bikers start looking into the team's direction. Bella looks nervously at her father and son behind the bar. She has no idea what to do, so she goes behind the bar to get out of the way. Sam keeps an eye on the leader in the back of the bar and on the big biker. If they move, Sam is going to take them down. The team sits still until they are surrounded. One of the bikers went to grab for Tails, and she immediately shot him in the leg. That is when the place erupts. The team shoots down twenty-two men and women bikers in less than thirty seconds. Sam has incapacitated five of the men without weapons. None of the bikers are dead. Most of the gunshots are arms and legs. The rest of the bikers back up to the front door like they are going to run for it, but instead they just stand there to watch the show. The big biker walks on over to the center of the room. Sam instantly leaps for him and draws his knife. The big biker pulls his handgun out of the shoulder holster just as Sam makes his first cut through the biker's right bicep muscle. Sam follows with a punch to the chest and abdomen. He then cuts the wrists of both arms. Sam's cuts are as smooth as a painter's hand. The biker can only stand there bleeding. He doesn't move a muscle. The rest of the bikers stand staring at Sam and then look over at the biker in the corner.

"OK!" the biker leader yells and holds up his hands like he gives up. "We all had some fun tonight." The leader stands up and walks over to Sam. He stares at Sam and looks him up and down. "What the fuck are you people doing in this place?"

Sam looks the leader straight in the eyes. "We are now taking over this place."

"By all means, take it. We will just burn it tomorrow." The leader smiles a nervous smile.

"You will do nothing except maybe just bleed or die," Sam says in a calm voice.

The leader starts to laugh and makes a motion to the bikers by the door. Sam and his team notices some of them leaving, knowing they are going to go get more weapons or more men.

Sam never is one for much talk when there is going to be a fight. His thought is to fight and not stand around yelling back and forth. Sam punches the leader in the throat. The leader doesn't have a chance to even move. He just drops to the ground holding his throat and kicking. Sam kneels over the man. Soon the leader starts to breathe a little easier but is unable to talk. Sam knows that he has to leave or kill every one of the bikers.

Sam motions the team to grab the leader and load up. WindEagle and Jose keep Sam surrounded with weapons drawn. They are there to protect him from any of the chicken shits that might run up and jump Sam. Sam walks over to the bar.

"Here is what I am going to do for you all," Sam says to Bella and her dad and son. "I'm going to give you two million dollars for this bar and you can keep it or just leave. It is still yours and you can use it to do with what you want. I would give you more, but right now, I don't have any more money than that on me. Now, I would suggest we all leave together, but you do with what you want. The thing I do need is to know how they pay for their drinking."

"They use a credit card," the son says nervously.

"OK. We are leaving. You are welcome to join us," Sam says.

The three of them look at each other and then grab their personal stuff and go out the back door with Sam.

As Sam, WindEagle, and Jose start for the back door, one of the bikers by the front door draws up his handgun. Jose shoots him dead before the biker can shoot. The rest of them run out the front door.

The team along with Bella and the other two jump in their vehicles. They drive out of the parking lot.

"Where can we take you, folks?" Sam asks.

Bella gives them the direction to their house which is just outside Doyle. Sam drops the three people off at their front door and then hands them a duffel bag full of money.

"Now, if that is not enough, there is a telephone number inside where you can call my sister and she will handle the finances." Sam goes back to the SUV and then the team takes off.

Bella and the other two just stand there stunned. They just stare at the bag of money.

The team drives down the road and then stops. Sam goes back to the other SUV, where the biker leader is lying in the back, bound, gagged, and blindfolded. He opens the back door and drags the biker out feet first. WindEagle put his foot on the biker chest. Sam takes the blindfold and the gag off the biker.

"OK, you got one chance to answer the question correctly or we drag you behind this vehicle." Sam gets really close to his face. "Now where did you get the credit card that you been using?"

The biker coughs a little and spits at Sam. "Fuck you. You are all fucking dead before morning."

Sam kicks him in the ribs and then rolls him over to his stomach. He grabs the biker by the legs and slips the zip tie over the hitch of the SUV. Sam motions the driver to drive around a circle. He decides to give the biker a taste of what is in store for him. The vehicle drives down the road and turns around and comes back.

Sam rolls the biker over. The biker shirt is already completely worn through. His stomach is raw from the gravel burn. His chin is completely de-gloved of skin.

"This was just a taste of what is to come. Where did you get the card?" Sam asks very sternly.

"Aaaahh, you fucker! We took it from a guy that was at the bar." The biker starts groaning.

"Where is this guy now?" Sam asks.

"He's at the farm," the biker says.

"You will show us where the farm is or I will drag you until you are no more," Sam says sternly.

"Yeah, I don't even fucking know where we are at. You need to go right out of the parking lot of the bar. Go about nine miles and turn left at the big tree with a red sign on it. Go down that road for five miles and go over five small hills from the turn, and it is the place on the right. Got it!" the biker says as WindEagle helps him sit up. He turns to Sam to present his bond wrists. "OK, now fucking let me go."

WindEagle laughs. "I don't think we are done with you. If Mike and Dan are not all right, you will get the same as they got." WindEagle grabs the biker by his long hair and pulls him to his feet. Then WindEagle grabs the biker's hair and his belt. He throws him into the back of the SUV. The biker screams obscenities the whole time they drive toward the farm.

The team drives on past the farm and stops about a half a mile down the road. WindEagle opens the back door of the SUV and the biker quickly scoots out on to his feet. He didn't want to be dragged out again.

"Is there any traps or anything we should worry about going moving into the compound?" WindEagle asks.

The biker has a puzzled look on his face. "What the fuck are you talking about?" That question answered WindEagle's question.

The team takes out all their gear and got ready. Sam splits everyone into two-person teams. WindEagle ties the biker to a tree down in the ditch.

Each team sits just outside of the farm compound and observes the bikers. The bikers that were shot, many of them are just coming back from the hospital. The other thirty-some bikers have a bonfire going. The bikers keep throwing more branches and brush on to the fire. As the fire grows higher, the women bikers start dancing around the fire as the men sit and drink. Some of the men continued to add wood to the fire and soon the women start to strip naked. They all are yelling and screaming and look as if the whole gang is in a frenzy.

"What the fuck are they doing?" WindEagle whispers to Sam.

"Looks like some ritual war dance or something," Sam whispers. "Back in the fifteenth century, a bonfire was actually a bone fire. They probably used to use it to burn the dead not only to whip the troops into a frenzy but also so there wasn't stinking rotting corpses lying around."

WindEagle looks a little puzzled. "How the fuck do you . . . ? Oh, never mind." Everyone wondered how Sam knew tidbits of information like that but then no one ever asked him.

Some of the biker men start striping and dancing around fire naked. They danced until someone would hand them a bottle of Jack Daniels or they ran into a naked woman. They would then throw the woman to the ground. Soon there are three small piles of men and women have sex. While others just keep drinking and throwing more wood on the fire, four of the men and two women run back to the barn. They returned rolling two large wood spools. They were used as electrical wire spools at one time, but now there is a naked man tied to each of the spools. They roll the men on the spools toward the fire but then stops just short of rolling them in to the flames. Once they stop rolling the spools, both of the women and two of the men start punching and kicking the men. Sam could not see the men's faces. Then one of the bikers picks up one of the men's face, probably to see if he is still alive. Sam could see that it is Mike. Sam motions to the men to surround the compound and move in. While Sam and the teams are getting into position, one of the men bikers pulls down his pants and starts raping Dan while one of the biker women lies down on the ground and watches. Another biker starts to push Mike's spool closer to the fire, close enough that it is cooking Mike's skin. Then he rolls him back and as he starts to roll the spool back to the fire, he stops. The biker starts to try to grab at his back to try to remove the knife that Sam stuck in him.

Sam couldn't wait any longer. He just jumps into action. The first is the biker rolling Mike into the fire. The second biker to die is the one raping Dan. Sam takes the biker's head off with the bladed whip chain. The biker woman that is watching the rape from under the spool doesn't even notice that the biker is dead until the body falls on top of her and the head rolls away. She screams but no one cares. Sam just goes on through the crowd with his blade whip chain and tomahawk cutting and gouging at the necks and abdomens of the bikers. He is killing both male and female alike until the troopers catch up to him. They see Sam is in a blind rage and doesn't want to get close to him. They yell to Sam and he snaps back into reality. Sam looks around feeling a mix between shame and attainment. He is soaked in blood. Bikers are lying everywhere with intestines crawling from their open abdomens and blood spraying from open neck wounds. A few of the bikers are crawling with their intestines dragging underneath them.

Some of the bikers make it to the house and joined others that are in the house. They break out windows and start shooting at the team. WindEagle and Tails cut Mike's and Dan's bonds and drag them off the compound. Jose and partner returns fire to the house to cover them till they are safe. Sam is tired of the fucking bikers so he has two of the troopers run behind the house and light it on fire. Sam, Jose and his partner keeps the bikers heads down with cover fire while two troopers run to the back of the house. The whole house inside and out is being showered with bullets. Some of the bikers inside that are sitting behind the walls near the windows are getting shredded. Shards of bone and ribbons of flesh and bits of clothing fly from the biker's bodies.

The old farmhouse starts a blaze quickly. Sam tells the troopers to stop shooting.

Sam yells up to the house, "As you can see, your fucking house is on fire. If you come out now, unarmed, you may go. We will not shoot anymore unless one of you has a weapon."

There is no reply. Then some shots are fired in the house. One biker woman runs out of the house yelling, "Don't shoot, don't shoot!" When she is about five yards from the door, someone from inside the house shoots her in the back. She falls to the ground, gasping for breath until she goes limp.

"We ain't coming out. You come in and get us if you want us." Someone from the house yells.

Sam yells back, "You stupid bastard. You are all going to burn to death in a matter of minutes if you don't come out. I really don't give a shit if you do burn."

Shots ring out inside the house, and then from out of the front door run nine bikers. They yell, "Don't shoot, we don't have any weapons."

"Lie down on the ground with your hands out and your legs spread," Sam yells.

The bikers lie down on the ground. The two troopers that light the house on fire go check the bikers for weapons. Some of the women bikers still are naked and some of the bikers are wounded from the bar fight. None have weapons. Sam and the others keep an eye on the front door to make sure no one comes running out of the house and starts shooting. As the house falls to the ground in a fiery heap of rumble, Sam feels it is safe no one else will be coming out.

"OK. Now get the fuck out of town and don't let me see any of you all again. Next time I probably will not be in such a good mood," Sam yells.

The bikers get up and run toward a couple of old trucks. They get in and took off. They never look back.

Sam radios WindEagle and Tails to leave Mike and Dan. "Go get the vehicles and we will load up. Hurry, we need to get the hell out of this place before the law gets here. Oh, bring that fucking biker up here too."

WindEagle and Tails run the half mile through the trees and down to the road. It is a race between the two. They are both very competitive. WindEagle wins the race only by a couple of yards. He goes over and cut the ropes that have the biker leader attached to the tree. He grabs the biker by the hair and flings him into the SUV. WindEagle slams the door and jumps into the vehicle. Tails jumps into the other SUV's driver's seat. It is easier to back up the half mile then to try to turn the vehicles around so they back the vehicles to the farm's driveway. They get back to the farm within ten minutes of leaving just to see two vehicles taking off down the road.

They both got out of their vehicles and they are out of breath. Sam asks, "What is up?"

"I won," WindEagle says with a little smile.

"OK! I guess that is good. So can you go get Mike and Dan?" Sam says.

WindEagle and Jose run up to the brush line where Mike and Dan lie and rest. They are soon back partially carrying the two men.

Sam opens the back of the SUV with the biker leader. He grabs the biker by the legs and drags him out. The biker hit the ground like a lead brick. Sam grabs him by the hair and sits him up. "I told you we would do to you exactly what you did to Mike and Dan. Seeing how I'm not that sick of a person, I'm going to let them decide what to do to you." Sam motions to the two troopers. "Pick him up and cut him loose but keep a hold on him."

One of the troopers removes a wire cutter from the sheath on this harness and cut the zip ties that bound the wrist and legs. The other stands guard.

Mike and Dan are over at the other SUV putting on some clothing. Mike's back and the back of his head have been burned with second-degree burns. Tails is applying silver sulfadiazine to the burned skin. Both men are pretty beat up both physically and emotionally.

Sam goes over to the two men, "I know both of you are hurting. It is up to you what we do with this fucking biker and any of the others that might still be alive out here. That is if you are up to it."

"We got him Sam. Be right there." In an angry and tired voice Mike says speaking for him and Dan.

Sam gives them a little time while the troopers go and check the bikers on the ground to see if any of them are still alive. Sam retrieves the knife he had left in the biker that he had first killed. Sam didn't want to lose the knife; it was the one his dad made him. When Sam pulls the knife out, he finds a woman biker under the body. She had been trapped there because the biker on top of her weighed about three hundred pounds. Sam grabs her by her arm and pulls her to her feet. Sam hands her off to one of the troopers. He continues to check the rest of the bodies. No one else is alive. When Sam looks around, it reminds him of a long day on the necropsy floor in veterinary school.

"Tie that fucking biker and bitch to the spool but with his back down and her back up. That evil bitch directed all the fucking torture we got," Mike screams and points to the two bikers.

The troopers do as Mike and Dan bid. Both bikers are dragged to the spools as they go kicking and screaming. Mike and Dan are still angry to the point of enraged. Dan goes over to the pile of smoldering coals, which was once the bonfire. Dan grabs a stick that is still burning at one end and lays it on the biker leader's chest. The biker screams as the flame burned through his shirt and then through his skin. The smell of burning flesh is suspended in the still damp morning air. Mike grabs the stick but has to peel it off the biker's chest along with boiling skin. Flesh drips from the stick as he carries it toward the biker bitch. Mike grabs a knife from one of the troopers and chops at the burning end of the stick until it becomes a smoldering point. He then takes the knife and cut the pants off the biker bitch. She screams as Mike is not being delicate about removing the pants. He cuts into her skin and muscle several times before he gets her pants off. She also knows what is coming because she had done something similar to Mike the first night that they had been kidnapped. Mike kicks her legs apart, but she just keeps closing them.

He takes the knife and slashes both Achilles tendons. She screams to Mike, "Let me go. Please. Sorry, so sorry."

Mike doesn't care after what they had done to him and Dan. Mike positions her just right and sticks the smoldering point into her anus. The burning flesh sizzles and smoke rises as Mike advances the stick up her rectum. Dan comes over and walks behind Mike. Dan kicks the stick with every remaining ounce of energy he has in him. The stick plunges up through the colon and abdomen, ending impaled in to the left lung. She tries to scream, but no words come out of her mouth. Her mouth moves but not a word kind of like a fish out of water. Mike kicks the spool over on the burning coals. Sam cannot stand watching someone cook. He grabs Jose's rifle and shoots the biker bitch in the head. The shot instantly kills her and saves her from slowly cooking on the fire.

The biker leader, seeing what they just did to the biker bitch, begs and pleads for a quick death. Dan grabs the knife from Mike. He cut what remained of the charred pants from the biker. He grabs the biker by the testicles and cut them off. Blood shoots out of the biker's groin. Dan throws the testicles in the fire and proceeds to slowly cut from pelvis to sternum then crosscuts across the abdomen. Mike kicks the spool into the fire. When the biker flips over the spool, his intestines fall into the fire. Sam cannot stand the screaming any longer so he shoots the biker in the head relieving the biker from further misery.

Sam is getting antsy. He knows they need to get the hell out of there but Mike and Dan needed to get that out of their systems. Sam knows if they hadn't done this, the rage would have slowly and mercilessly killed them. Now they can both work on the healing stage.

"Let's go now," Sam yells. "Does anyone else hear those sirens? Let's go before we have to shoot are way out."

Everyone jumps in the vehicle and they take off. They turn away from the sirens and take the long way back to Nevada. Sam notices that he is still covered in crusty blood. He climbs into the back of the SUV and finds a clean T-shirt and some water. He cleans himself up and changes clothes. Sam sits in the back alone to let himself calm down. This night is the first time when he truly lost control and it made him very disappointed in himself. After a deep breath, Sam puts his negative thoughts behind him. Then grabs the first aid kit and attends to Mike's burn wounds.

Bud and Kim have been traveling quickly. They have already finished in Colorado and in Arizona. It is going a lot faster, now that they have a small army of around five hundred men and women. Any retired or discharged military person can get hired if they meet a few requirements. Not having a wife and children is the first one. Not that the three brothers have anything against a wife and children but they did not want any trooper thinking about when he is going to make it home. Also they didn't want troopers having to call back home all the time. Everything they did is on the secret side and they didn't want family members wanting to know where they were. Another requirement is that everyone had to get along with everyone. If you don't fit in, you don't get in. Slackers are not welcome. Everyone on the team has to pitch in to the best of their ability. That meant that if you are a mechanic, you work to keep everything repaired even if you are on the road. No one is assigned duties by the three brothers. People are just asked to do things, and if they can't do it, they are to say so. If they just don't want to do it, they had better have a good reason. Everyone is sworn to secrecy. They all have heard what happened to those that break the trooper code. The three brothers don't make it up, but the troopers come up with it themselves. It is much like the three brothers' unwritten code to their family and friends.

Sam and his team join up with Bud and Kim on their way to California. The Greek flies them to the Mojave Desert and drops them off. The Greek can land anywhere now that he has been flying a Bell BoeingV-22 Osprey.

Mike and Dan were taken to a hospital in Las Vegas to be treated. Both will not be able to come back to work for months. Mike and Dan's mission was to get two armored military HETs M1070 trucks. They did not get to them, but they were on their way to pick them up. When the Brothers3 hit the last meth lab in California, they will be near the area where the trucks are being held. Sam thinks it will be safer if whole team picks the trucks up. Both trucks will be needed in New York.

Chapter Thirty-Nine

Bomb threats across the United States increase drastically. High schools, colleges, military bases, and malls are the places that the threats increase the most. These places are easiest to cause maximum amount of panic from those that are there and those at home. Also there is a lot of media attention when these places are threatened. People feel very violated and weak when their family is threatened by the unknown. Terrorists love places like this for their goals. The goals are to desensitize the population to things such as bags sitting in the hallways of schools without an owner, unoccupied cars and trucks on bridges, unexplained disappearances of people, and other things. The biggest goal is just to insight fear. These things send people in to a panic after 9/11, but now with all the fake bomb threats, people just don't care. In some cases, people are afraid to say anything about suspicious activity for fear of being accused to be racists. The Barrack administration has aided in this fear for the last four years. Anyone that disagrees with any of the administration's policies are labeled as a racist. Even the mainstream media plays along with it.

The economy is in the tank. The Barrack administration is constantly out campaigning on how well everyone is doing. "The recession is over. It is just going to take a few more years before prosperity will come to everyone. Economic equality is going to come to all of those who just waited. All we need is a few more years and everyone will be the same. The poor and the middle class will live happily ever after, but the upper class and those people with businesses will have to pay." This was their motto, which persuaded millions of people that live off the government to vote President Barrack back into office for another four years.

Sam is no longer vexed by political bullshit. Through Darwin being hacked into the several if not all the congressmen's and senators' e-mails and computer files, Sam found out that all the bipartisan bickering is just a show. Politicians are all in it together to make money for themselves. All politicians do nothing if it does not benefit them.

The voting process always disturbs Sam. Your vote does not really count if you live in the rural areas of America or if you belong to the military. Only the heavily populated areas decide who is elected and who is not. Sam doesn't even bother to vote this time. He lets any trooper who wants to vote to go back home to vote but only a handful had left.

Sam's plan to shut off the administrations underhanded funding did not work very well. The administration and their underground campaigning group are hurt a little by Sam taking all the money but they have a lot of money from foreign governments. There are a lot of private corporations that stand to gain a lot if Barrack won. Also, the Barrack administration, through the secretary of state and executive order, gives a lot of money in aid to foreign governments, which is filtered right back to Barrack and his group to buy votes.

Now that the same administration is back, all the policies that they have hidden away are now going to be implemented. The policies are going to be in the way of regulations through the EPA, USDA, FDA, the Federal Reserve, and others. The EPA is going to make it almost impossible for any businesses that want to produce energy in anyway other than "green energy" to survive. Gas will soon be so expensive that people will beg for other means of energy to supply their vehicles. Price of food will skyrocket. Soon electricity will be a luxury again. People will have to depend on the government to get electricity. The USDA will make policies to control food production. The FDA will control drug production by shutting down any drug company that does not give to the administration. They control them by tightening regulations so that it shuts down all the generic drug companies. This process gives companies that pay, a way to take over the market. Takeovers have happened over the last four years such as Pfizer taking over Fort Dodge and many more buyouts. Consolidation of drug companies has caused a drug shortage all across the USA, thus making more money for the administration friendly companies. The Federal Reserve keeps printing money and making it more worthless; thus, everyone that saved money to retire now has to rely on the government. Their savings are now less than enough to live off. Over all, the government is now in a position to control the masses by their neediness. Those that don't need will be taxed and regulated into needing.

Even the military is going to be shut down to a bare minimum. The administration has made sure that no other entitlements can be cut. They finagled congress and the senate to cut a trillion dollars from the military budget. The decreased military budget cut out veteran's health care and pensions along with shutting down productions of weapons and supplies. They basically throw the military to buzzards. They will have to close bases all over the world, which will let radical Islamists take over all over the world. Egypt, Syria, Libya, and others have been running this course all ready. The giving up of our power to the United Nations via cap-and-trade taxes and the UN tax will let the United Nations decide who wins and who loses.

Overall, this will be the end of freedom.

Brothers3 have completely eliminated all the YUPPI groups and meth labs that they had known about. Some may have reopened but those labs will have to wait until New York is done. The troopers are all tired after Texas. The compound in Texas is a true firefight. The compound is heavily guarded. They have planted a land mine field all around the compound. They are armed with mortars and three Sheridan tanks, two old M1 tanks, and six helicopters equipped with weaponry. The angel teams are able to take out the helicopter pilots before they even get in the helicopters. The Smokers are more organized than any that the Brothers3 have fought. Sam feels very lucky that he has seasoned veterans on his side. The Smokers are second-rate compared to the troopers. The biggest problem is the Smokers don't give up. All but a few have to be killed. Those that live are sent packing across the border to Mexico. The good thing is that Brothers3 have captured the biggest bounty of all the compounds. The munitions alone are larger than all the National Guard's. The place is loaded with money. The money has been already loaded in to shipping containers, nine in all.

After all the bounty is safe in New Mexico, Sam gives everyone vacations for two weeks. Each trooper receives a huge one million dollars as cash bonus. Each trooper is to report to Detroit in the next two weeks to get measured for their new ostrich second skin suit. The new machinery that was bought in China is in full production. The small factory has already made a suit for Sam, Sarah, Bud, Kota, Kim, and DH. The outer shell is not smooth and round like Sam had thought it would be. The suit is very angular and rough almost resembles a wrinkled up armadillo crossed with crocodile made from small micro tubes. The design has to do with physics. The angles will absorb and transfer energy throughout the whole suit.

Sarah flies Sam to meet his brothers, DH and Kim in Detroit. They have fun for four days trying on their new body armor and getting used to moving around. The hardest part is getting used to the optics for the weapons. The second skin makes the whole body more comfortable. Even Sam's sore joints feel good while he wears the second skin.

"I think there is more of a calling for this stuff then just under battle armor clothing. We could make this for burn patients and other arthritis patients. It really makes me feel about twenty years younger," Sam says while he jumps around and did some kicks.

"We have thought of that but first things first," Shelli says.

The body armor takes about twenty minutes to put on. Most of it goes on in pieces and then quickly screws together with fast set locking screws.

"You should sell this to the military," DH says.

"The military couldn't afford a five million dollar suit for every soldier. They would just steal the process and then tuck it away in some warehouse somewhere for all eternity. They can get men cheaper than they can build a suit," Sam says with slight disgust.

DH looks around at the suit. "How the hell you going to take a piss or a shit with this thing on. Hell, it will be too late by the time I get in and out of this damn thing."

"Well, umm," Shelli says, "you can pee in the suit. It will absorb all fluids and filter them. Even sweat is absorbed and filtered. Then it is mixed with the fresh water reserve and with the tube at the side of helmet, you drink it back in. If you have to, aahh, go number 2, you have to remove the pelvic panel and then go normally."

"I'm in trouble," DH says. "I don't know if I can get out of this thing that fast."

"Oh, you will learn," Shelli says with a smile.

After testing out the suits, Sarah flies everyone to Virginia. The preparations for the New York bank heist is just about complete. The garages and the new hospital are all done. Carol has made sure that none of the contractors slacked off. Kota is about ready to move into his new house. They are just putting in new furniture in the house when they get back to Virginia.

"You know," Sam says to Kota, "You don't have to move any of your stuff. You can just hire a mover and take out what stuff you want out of your old house and give the rest of the stuff way."

"Yeah, but you know my wife. She will want to move everything," Kota says.

"Well, just get a professional mover and have them box up and carry all that stuff of yours over to the new house. You don't have time to do that," Sam says. "If you want to, just take a few of the maintenance men with you and get your 'secret personal' stuff and bring it to your house."

"OK, I'll do that right now," Kota says and takes off.

Sam and Carol decide to go out to eat. They go up to Staunton to eat at their favorite restaurant, Rowe's Family Restaurant. Carol tells Sam all about what has happened with the Sheriff Allen incident and how she got the new construction work done so fast. Sam tells her all about the California incident and how they are just about done with the whole thing. They just have one last thing to do and then they are done. Carol is excited and concerned that Sam is enjoying his new life a little too much. She knows that when he did something, he dives in, never really testing the water first. He will just play everything by the seat of his pants and he usually comes out on top but with a high chance of getting injured.

After a nice evening out, they head back home. Sam gets on the interstate and heads south. After about five minutes, Sam grows suspicious that there are a couple of vehicles following them. He speeds up and so did the vehicles behind them. With the light shining in his mirrors, he cannot make out what kind of vehicles they are but guesses that they are Cadillac Escalades. As he drives along a few more vehicles join in behind the two following him. Sam pushes a button on the mirror that used to be an OnStar button but is switched over to a secure line to Darwin.

"Darwin. Darwin," Sam says in a calm voice. Carol is growing frantic. "Darwin, are you there?"

"I'm here, I'm always here." Darwin drops his video game hand piece. "I got you on the map. You better slow down right now. There is a cop up ahead."

Sam slows to the speed limit. "Tell Bud and Kota that I have four skunks by the tail and get them on the transmission."

Darwin gets both Kota and Bud on their cell phones and tells them that there are two vehicles trailing Sam. They jump out of their chairs at home and into their armored Hummers.

"Where are they now?" Bud asks Darwin.

"Sam is getting off at the Greenville exit," Darwin says with excitement. "I'm patching you both through to Sam."

"Sam," Bud says.

"Old providence plays the miss and hit," Sam says. They use some codes just in case someone is able to tap into their secure lines. Sam is a little cautious since Darwin says that the Secret Enforcement Service is after him.

"K!" Both Brothers say.

Bud drives down a short cut road to meet Sam. Kota drives around one of the back roads so that he will end up behind all the vehicles. Darwin monitors the speed for which Sam is to drive so that the Brothers can get in place. Sam slows a little. Kota has to drive an extra mile more than Bud. Soon Kota is only a half mile behind the vehicles.

"OK, Sam, I spy four skunks coming up the road," Bud says. "I suggest you run."

Sam tromps on the gas and gets some space between him and the two trailing vehicles. Bud swings out between Sam and the first trailing vehicle. Bud slows down a little and swerves around so that the vehicles can't pass him. Kota moves in right behind them. Bud slams on the brakes and Kota smashes into the back end of the trailing vehicles. The force slams the back vehicle up into the vehicle in front of him. Because of the weight of Bud and Kota's armored Hummers, neither one of them are hurt. The four SUVs are smashed up except the windows and the doors; they were all armor-plated with bulletproof glass.

Sam stops and turns around. He has Carol get his weapons harness out from under the seat in the back. Sam drives up and quickly gets out of the vehicle and throws on his harness.

"Take off and get into the bunker. Call DH and Kim. Get them ready in case this turns bad." Sam tells Carol, "Love you."

Carol takes off. Sam runs over to the front of Bud's Hummer. Bud is still digging around looking for his weapons that had gone flying everywhere when he was hit. Kota is up on the roof of his vehicle already, lying behind a Steel plate that he had welded so that someone could hide behind or to carry luggage. No one gets out of the vehicles. Sam cannot see into the vehicle because of the tint on the windows. Even the front windows are tinted. Kota looks through his night vision scope on his rifle. Kota can see shapes but not make out anything else. With his neck communications on, he can talk to Sam and Bud.

"Hey, I can see they are rustling around in the vehicles, but I can only partially see into the vehicles from this angle," Kota says.

"I found my auto .50. Is it clear to get out," Bud asks.

"No, just stay there," Kota says looking through the scope. "I think they are planning on something. Maybe like jumping out and do something stupid and western."

"What do you got with you?" Sam asks.

"Got my AA12," Dakota says smugly. "I mounted a night vision scope on it for skunk hunting."

"Ah, Bud," Sam says. "Drive ahead and get a little sideways if you can. Turn your lights off. Maybe they can't see in the dark."

"Got it," Bud says. Sam moves a little to let Bud drive up. Now Bud is able to climb out the passenger side. Sam just hopes no one comes down the road and runs into them. It wasn't a heavily traveled road, but anytime you don't want someone to come around, they always show up.

Bud hands Sam an extra pair of night vision goggles. Now they can partially see into the vehicles. Sam can make out that the people in the vehicles are up to something. They can see that there were about four men in each vehicle.

"Darwin," Sam says. He knows that Darwin is listening.

"Present," Darwin says.

"Get Sarah in the armed helicopter and tell her to make a few passes around here to see if anyone else is coming to play," Sam says. "Tell DH and Kim to get ready for something there. Get two of those troopers that are there in the bunker to get one of the armed Strykers to come on over here. And, Darwin, tell them to hurry." Sam has a feeling that things are going to start going to shit in a big hurry and those in the vehicles are just waiting for more people to show up.

Everyone is up and going within fifteen minutes. The helicopter has been mounted with two M134D-Hs in both side hull doors and an M-61 Vulcan mounted in the front and back under the hull. Sarah and two troopers go up in the helicopter and fly around. Kim and one trooper take the Stryker out to the crash site.

"Hey, Sam," Sarah says, "I assume that code is out of vogue by now and we can talk frankly."

"Yes, I think they know we are here," Sam says. "Whoever they are."

"I see nine vehicles coming from the west and five are coming in from the east. I don't know if they are bad guys, but they are coming fast and following each other close."

"Thanks," Sam says. "You might want to stay close in case we need some help."

"Will do, but for the next few minutes. We are going to be busy. I see a couple of choppers coming this way," Sarah says. "Do you think we shoot them down or let them go by?"

"Well, shit, I don't know," Sam says. "Helicopters always fly around here. They sell the damn things somewhere around here. Try to check it out and make sure they are not private helicopters first. If they start maneuvering around, help them down."

"Will do." Sarah flies toward one of the choppers to see if they will change course. She flies straight toward the chopper and then dives underneath. The troopers in the back are happy they are harnessed in this time.

The one chopper keeps on course but the other turns around quickly. Sarah positions so the side gunner can take him out. Shots come out of the chopper. Someone is shooting with a fully automatic rifle from an open door.

Sarah yells back, "Let them have it, boys."

The trooper takes aim and fires the M-134. The weapon fires four thousand rounds per minute. The bullets shower the chopper and completely rip the copter apart with flying lead. Everyone in the copter is dead and it crashes into an old barn. The crash causes the chopper to explode and the old barn bursts into flames. Sarah flies back to the crash site to see if Sam needs any help.

"Got one, Sam, and going to get the other," Sarah says. "Looks like those vehicles will be there in about thirty seconds."

"Great." Sam can feel the adrenaline flowing through his body. The feeling is more intense then it was before any of his karate matches.

Sam tells Dakota to get back into his vehicle and drive around to the other side of Bud's Hummer, kind of like circling the wagons. Just as Kota parks, the Stryker shows up. Kim opens the back and yells, "You guys get in here."

The three brothers run up into the Stryker and shut the door.

Kim looks at them and laughs, "I brought the suits if you think we can get into them fast enough."

"What the hell? We got a little time. Let's give it a try," Sam says. In the back of his mind, he is hoping that he remembers how to put it on. Even more, he is hoping that it really worked like it did in testing.

Kim, Sam, Bud, and Kota all get naked and slip on the second skin. The trooper that is with Kim is a little taken aback. It is not every day that he sees men strip when they are getting ready for a firefight. They all have a little trouble putting things together but they did it faster than they had at the lab.

They are now ready. Optics is working and they already had calibrated the suits for their weapons. Kota and Kim use an AA12, a fully automatic 12-gauge shotgun using buckshot and fragment rounds. Sam and Bud used an M-249, better known as a SAW, which fires about 750 rounds a minute.

There are sixteen vehicles in all out on the road. The people in the vehicles get out and take position behind their vehicles. All of them have on bulletproof vests and have fully automatic AR-15s. The trooper driving the Stryker yells back, "Ah, Sam, we are surrounded."

"That is just an illusion," Sam says with a little laugh. "Open the back door."

The four of them go out and stand in a line, Kim and Bud facing one direction and Kota and Sam facing the other.

"We have you surrounded. All we what is the man named Sam. The rest of you can go," someone from the vehicles yells.

Sam pushes a button on his right wrist console. "I suggest you all go home before you get hurt. We have you out gunned and out witted."

The people that came in the vehicles all laugh. One of them says, "OK, you can think that but one of you needs to come with us."

"Who is this 'US' that you refer to?" Sam asks.

"We are special enforcement of presidential requests, troop 1. That is SEPR1 for short. We are here to take Sam Kelley in for questioning. Now you all with the funny-looking suits, put your weapons down," the man yells. "You have one minute to comply before we start shooting."

Sam pushes a button to turn off the load speaker to ask Kota, Kim, and Bud, "What do you think?"

"Fuck them," say all three of them.

Sam pushes the load speaker button and says, "We talked it over and we come to the conclusion that you are all in the wrong fucking place. Now head home or you will be buried here. You have ten seconds to comply." Sam pushes the button again.

The SEPR1 men start laughing.

Sam starts counting. Kim starts the shoot-out by shooting the man in the mouth that is yelling at them. After that bullets are flying in every direction. The suit/weapon combination is so accurate that there are almost no missed shots. The Brothers3 hit everything they aimed at. In the end, not one of them is wounded and every one of the SEPR1 men is dead.

Sam really didn't know what to do. He asks the three of them, "So what do we do with the bodies and vehicles?"

"They showed up, they can clean up," Kim says. "Fucking leave them."

"Yeah, they aren't supposed to exist so they will get cleaned up without a word," Kota says.

"OK, let's get the vehicles and get the hell out of here," Sam says. "Sarah, did you get that."

"Got it, Sam," Sarah says. "Couldn't catch the other chopper but we kept him away. We'll stay up here so that he doesn't see where you all are going and then we will make sure we don't get followed home."

"Good job," Sam says. "Meeting in the bunker. Everyone keep lights off and just drive with night vision unless we see a car coming."

"Let's get going," Kota said. "I got to pee and I don't want to have to drink it."

Everyone laughs.

Once back at the bunker. They all look at their suits. Everyone has at least fifteen or twenty rounds that went into them.

"Shit, I didn't think I even got hit. I didn't feel a thing." Kota looks at his suit.

"These things are great. Now what do we do with the suit. How do we get the holes filled and bullets removed?" Kim asks.

"I think we take the shell off and pull out the bullets and then replace the shell. I'll call the lab tomorrow and confirm that," Sam says.

They all get dressed and meet up with Carol, DH, and the other troopers. Beer is in order, not for the killing of the SEPR1 men but for the positive test of the suit.

"So that was all the king's men? I thought they would have been better fighters than that. I wonder what will happen if we have to do hand-to-hand combat. I think we need to practice in the suits a bunch more until we get really comfortable," Sam says and then drinks down a full bottle of beer.

"It took me a few minutes to get used to the suit and the optics. It is hard at first not having to shoulder the weapon," Kota says.

Sarah and two troopers come in to the bunker. Sarah says, "Well, do we know who these guys are? Are they Smokers?"

"No, they are not Smokers, they are special enforcement of presidential requests, troop 1," Kota says in a sarcastic tone. He notices that Sarah forehead wrinkled a little. He knows she is a little puzzled. "They are, in short, spooks. They said they wanted to take Sam in."

"What the hell did you do Sam, to get invited to the White House?" Sarah asks jokingly.

"Not sure where I screwed up. Maybe one of the Smokers made it back from the Chicago compound. I doubt if we left anyone behind." Sam pops open another beer.

"I just think the suit is damn good. Fuck those spooks. They didn't fight worth a shit this time and probably won't get much better. But I think we need to calibrate some more powerful weapons like an M-32 six-pack grenade launcher. Shit, we can really be a powerhouse then," Kim says and then digs through the cooler to find a Pepsi. He doesn't like to drink alcohol when he is thirsty. "That's a good idea. I'm game. We can work on it tomorrow," Bud says and then looks around at everyone to look for a sign of anyone's objection.

"Sounds great," Sam says and then drinks down another beer.

"Sam, are those men going to be back or do you think you got the problem solved?" Carol asks just because she is worried, "I think this is their way of declaring war on you. I don't think this shithole president will quit. He's a little self-consumed."

"I don't know," Sam says seriously. "I'm not really sure who the hell those people really are except that they are now missing several men. I agree that this is a declaration of war when the president of the United States attacks. Someone should go get Darwin and get him in here. He seems to know a lot more about them then any of us. Kota can you give Darwin a yell."

Kota gets up and opens the door to the hallway. When he opens the door, Darwin is standing behind it, just about to open the door. It startles Kota for a second. "Shit, Darwin! You scared the hell out of me."

"You should thank me then for making you more heavenly," Darwin says sarcastically.

"Smart ass," Kota says and let Darwin on through. "How did you know I was coming after you?"

"I hear all, I know all," Darwin says with a smile. He actually did hear just about everything that went on in the place. He had the whole place full of microphones, thermal sensors, and cameras. There is not many places you could go anywhere on any of the brother's property that he didn't have a way of watching. He even has many of the roads around the county equipped with video and radiation sensors.

"Darwin!" everyone says in sync. It is seldom that anyone ever seen him out of his room.

"Hey, can you give us any more information on SEPR1?" Sam asks but he already knows that Darwin has a lot more information.

"Well, as you already know the name of the group, which I didn't know—now you found out the name of the group, I found more information about them that is buried deep in the government archives. With the bill that was pass in the 1980s that all government—" Darwin is interrupted by Carol.

"We don't need to know all that stuff. Just tell us about the group. Will they be back?" Carol asks nicely.

Darwin clears his throat, "Yes. Well. Ahhh, they are a group that works for the president. They were organized, to keep it short, long ago. The group was to help eliminate enemies that the president may acquire throughout his term. They have not been the most loyalist group though, such as, President Lincoln knew John Wilkes Booth. The group was to kill Booth who was a Confederate extremist. Because the men in the group were all Virginians and Southerners at heart, they didn't kill Booth. They actually set up and put Lincoln in a position to be killed. Also JFK always was on the guard and kept the group really close. The group guarded the president closer than the Secret Service but with the recession looming around the corner, JFK cut their pay. He also made them work far more than most of them cared to work. Then one day, the mafia paid a bunch of money to the group. The group was then at the mafia's control. One of the higher-ups in the mafia was mad at JFK because old John was screwing his wife, who was infatuated with John. They wanted to kill him but also knew the communist underground was after JFK. Lee Harvey Oswald was a communist extremist who was flat broke. He wants to be famous and he also needed money. The mafia found him and fronted Oswald a bunch of money to do them a favor. The favor was to kill JFK. Oswald jumped at the chance and even went around shooting his mouth off about how he was going to kill JFK. John sent the SEPR1 team after him, but the mafia called them off. Oswald wanted to get caught so that he could get on television so he could be famous. The mafia was going to ship him to Cuba, which was a great desire of Oswald but he declined. LBJ had Oswald killed because he was going to be president and he wanted to show his power. LBJ used the SEPR1 to shoot Oswald and many of the mafia. Oh, there are many more of these groups. They call them troops. The president has four or five troops now because of global threats. Now the vice president has one. I don't know of any others but they may have more. They do not really answer to anyone except the president and vice president. They are free from any laws and they really don't exist. Most of the men come from all over and some are hardcore criminals. They have killed many men. So I would say they will be back to avenge their comrades."

"OK, then, we should be better prepared for the next time, if it happens. I don't think we will dwell on it. We do need to get ready for New York." Sam drinks down another beer. He is getting a little drunk but still has room for more.

"Sam, I don't think I like the fact that they probably know you are here. They could come and get us in the middle of the night." Carol is a little frightened after Darwin's profile on the group.

"We will be OK. The troopers will be back in a week or so," Sam says. "Darwin, do you know if they had satellite observations of this place?"

"No, they don't," Darwin says with great confidence and with a little laugh.

"You seem very confident. How do you know for sure?" Sam asks.

"Because I am in control of the White House's satellite right now. I pointed that damn thing straight back at them and stuck a big fat virus in it. I made it look like a Chinese virus. All they can do for the next few months is look at each other or at porn." Darwin laughs. The whole group laughs with him.

CHAPTER FORTY

THE TROOPERS ALL MEET IN Virginia. They all cannot be housed in the bunker because Sam had not built it to be there to house an army. It was only built for family and friends. The other bunkers are much bigger but the army is getting so big, Sam has to split everyone up not only because of space but to protect the other bunkers. Sam heeds the advice that his grandmother always gave: "Don't put all your eggs in one basket." Sam goes down to base X military tent manufacturers and buys all the tents that they had available. Most of them are inflatable tents, so they needed generators to run the fans. Sam sends eight men and Kim to find the biggest portable generators that can be found. He comes back with eight semitruck trailer–sized generators. There is a new town set up with in a day.

Sam decides that he needs to have refueling capabilities. In his group is a woman name Melinda Pippins. She has been in charge of the fueling depots over in Iraq. She coordinates all the refueling for thousands of vehicles. Sam puts her in charge of fueling and fuel storage for all the bunkers. She set up the fueling depot for the Virginia bunker first and then when to the other three bunkers and to the New York prison and set up tanks. She has a portable refueling station in New York. In New Mexico, fuel has to be flown in to fill tanks. Nevada is easy to truck in fuel. She is now working on solar power and wind generators, but at this time, they are not fully operational. Sam figures if he can find a nuclear energy expert to set up something like that he would set it up in New Mexico.

The three brothers assemble a road crew along with demolition and explosive experts. They bought trucks and had them painted to look like Silverite construction trucks and NYC DOT trucks. DH, Kota, Sam, and Kim go along with twenty trucks, road construction equipment, construction signs, orange barrels, and sixty men. Once in New York City, they follow the escape route in both directions. They decide to start the construction work around the Bank of New York Melton on One Wall Street in lower Manhattan. They wait till the traffic dies down after rush hour and then sets up their "road closed" street signs, barrels, and flagmen. They look like a legitimate road construction crew so much so the Manhattan police stop at the construction site.

"We didn't know there is road construction going on tonight. I'm going to have to call this in," the police office says. Kim is standing behind one of the trucks while Sam is speaking with the police. Kim quickly calls Darwin to intercept the police officers call.

"I'm already on it. I jacked all the radio transmissions in the area because I knew this would happen," Darwin says in a smartass tone.

"This is car 1501, I'm on One Wall Street. Is there supposed to be construction tonight on this street?" the police officer asks someone he thought to be dispatch.

Darwin switches to the police officer's call. Darwin clears his throat and says with a slight Irish accent, "Yes, it says here on the screen they will be doing minor work all night. It says if they need assistance, that you should do so. They need to move on before morning."

"OK, over," the police officer says. He then turns to Sam. "We'll keep the cars detoured so you can have the whole block. You need to be out by 5:00 a.m."

"Thank you for your assistance, sir," Sam says with a sigh of relief. Sam knew that being nice would go a lot further than being argumentative. So for everyone, it will be please and thank you till the whole block is completed.

By 4:00 a.m., the crew has everything in place. By 5:00 a.m. the trucks are ready to leave, which makes the police officers more than happy. Sam makes a large donation to the policemen's rehabilitation charity fund. Sam writes a check for a hundred thousand dollars, which is large enough to make the police happy but not too large to make them suspicious.

Sam wants to leave some small conveyors and skid steer loaders close to the bank. There is a parking garage next to the bank. Sam isn't sure if they would let them rent a spot. It would be very ironic if they did let him leave the stuff there and it is going to be used to rob the bank.

Sam drives over to the parking garage up to the security booth. "Sir, how are you doing this morning?" Sam asks the security guard.

The security guard looks at him inquisitively. "I am fine. What can I help you with this morning?"

"We have just come off a long shift and we need to do some more work down the block tomorrow. I would like to rent a couple of spaces and leave a couple pieces of equipment here. Do you think that is doable?" Sam asks.

"We fill up every day and I don't think there is any room to spare. You might try somewhere else," the guard says. "Why don't you just take it with you?"

"Well, if I bring everything back to the yard it will take all day. If I leave it here, I can just bring all the boys out to get breakfast and go straight home," Sam says.

"I still don't have any room," the guard says and then turns to go back to his chair in the booth.

"Well, thank you for your time. Ahh, can I ask you how many hours you put in here?" Sam asks.

"I just put in twelve hours because someone didn't show you for work today. Now I'm tired and I just want to finish it in peace," the guard says.

"Well, this is your lucky day. You will be the bearer of a ten-thou-sand-dollar bonus if you let me park my stuff up on the top level. You would be helping me out and I would help you out." Sam takes out a bundle of money from his coat pocket. He holds it out.

The guard grabs the money and puts it into his coat pocket. A big smile comes across his face. He says, "Well, I think we can spare a few spots on the upper level for a while."

"Thank you, I will be right back." Sam drives off and gets the troopers to bring in the equipment and park it in a very tidy parking configuration. Then they leave for home.

They decide not to set mines all along the entire route out of the city. It would be too dangerous for innocent bystanders. Not that anyone in New York City would care. Sam figures that as soon as an explosion goes off, everyone will run for cover anyway. Sam can use that to his advantage.

CHAPTER FORTY-ONE

OVER THE NEXT FEW WEEKS, the Brothers3 work to get everything ready for the bank heist. DH and Kota, along with several mechanics, get one of the HETs M1070s trucks fitted with front end blades that can flip cars and trucks out of the way. The blade is blunted in the center for a ram blade. The blade then Vs out on both sides with an extreme roll. It is built so that it will lift a car or truck and then tip it on to its side. The first truck carries the blade and the second truck is used for an extra push if needed. The second truck has a large V mounted on the front, but it is to connect to the back of the first truck. The inside of the cabs are rigged so that the drivers and shotgun riders can take high impact collisions without getting whiplash. Both trucks are built with armored plating. The weight alone reduces the impact to the passengers. The back of the front truck has a reverse V connection so that the back truck can connect without having to slow down. The design helps the back truck stay connected by a "cold weld" from the two connections colliding with sufficient energy.

Once the trucks are done, they take them to a savage yard for a test drive.

Kota has the troopers line up thirty cars and trucks along with two eighteen-wheelers setting side by side. Kota straps himself into the front truck and DH is in the second truck.

"OK, we are going to go about thirty miles an hour. If I start slowing down, you hit the connection and help push on through. Follow about ten feet behind," Kota tells DH.

"Got it," DH says and gives Kota the thumbs-up.

They start their trucks and they take off together with a starting run of about fifty feet. Kota hits the first two cars and both roll over on their sides. Kota keeps at a steady speed tipping cars and trucks until he gets to the two eighteen-wheelers. Kota pushes on the throttle but just don't have enough push until DH connects. With both HETs, they easily push on through. When they get to the end, DH slams on his brakes and the trucks disconnects.

Kota stops his truck and unbuckles. He climbs out. The troopers are all jumping around celebrating. "Yeah, that was great," Kota says.

"I have always wanted to do that in a traffic jam," one of the troopers says with some envy.

DH makes his way over to the celebration. DH says, "That was good. I suppose that will work." Everyone looks at him like he is the biggest downer to the celebration. "Ahh, just kidding. That was great." DH gives everyone a high-five.

They all go back to the bunker.

"They are looking at the trucks right now for any damage to the frame. The test drive went great. The combo idea worked great," Kota tells Sam.

"Good, then we will do this in two days and we will get there at night. What do you all think?" Sam asks everyone around him. Sam has gathered all the team leaders and the original team.

"Sam, did you remember that is Christmas Eve night?" Kota says. "Are you sure you want to do this on Christmas? That's just not right."

"Yeah, you are right. So when do you want to go in?" Sam asks. "I just figured no one except a few intoxicated guards would be around over Christmas. I really don't want anyone to get hurt if we don't have to get anyone hurt."

"Let's leave now and we will do it tonight, probably not a lot of people going to be working the whole week. They probably already left on Friday and taking the whole week off," Kota says.

"It's OK with me as long as everyone else is ready and willing," Sam says. "I know the perfect diversion if we do it tonight. Do we have enough trucks to haul everything?"

"Yes, Sam," Bud says. "This isn't our first rodeo you know. Everything has been ready and the last thing to get ready was the pathfinder trucks."

"Oh, is that what they are called?" Sam says with a laugh. "Very fitting name."

"We even got a few surprises for you out in the new parking garage," Kim says.

"Well, let's go if everyone is ready. First let's go look at the surprise," Sam says.

They all drive over to the new parking garage. There sitting behind a semitruck is four small all-terrain utility vehicles. They look like Polaris Rangers but with extreme modifications. One of the mechanics comes up to stand next to the ATV.

"Sam, this is Jake. He is now the chief mechanic here," Kota says. "He can do more than any of us ever could dream of. His previous job was to build those street racers and to build rally cars."

Sam walks over and shakes Jake's hand and says, "Good to have you aboard. Ahh, when did you start working here?"

"I didn't start yet. They said I am still on probation, but I have been here for two weeks, sir," Jake says and then salutes.

Sam motions to Jake to lower his hand. "We don't salute. We are not military but more like family. No one has any rank, just that some people can do more than others. You'll learn. Anyway, what do you got here?"

Jake is a little uneasy giving a presentation to the boss after he is just corrected. Sam could see that Jake is nervous.

"Don't be nervous. No need to worry," Sam says. "We are all family here."

"OK, well then, ah, this is a high-suspension, all-terrain vehicle capable of speeds up to one hundred and twenty miles an hour. It is designed to carry two people. It is loaded with crash protection such as airbags and this new rapid foam. The rapid foam can only be utilized if you know you are going to crash and you hit this switch here." Jake points to a split lock switch on the steering wheel. "The foam will flood the entire vehicle. Much like that spray foam insulation that comes in a can. Anyway, the seating is designed around the new suits you have. Dakota, DH, Kim, and Bud have already tried them out and we have already made adjustments. Also it is equipped it rear and front guns that can be used through the optics in your helmet. You also have two six-round grenade launchers with a flip of a switch."

"My, my. You have been busy." Sam looks at his brothers. "So how do they handle?"

"Like a dream. We can use them to do diversions around the city," Bud says.

"OK, good. Well, let's get ready and get going. You guys get your suits on and we need to leave in one hour," Sam says to everyone. "Jake, good job to you and those who helped. You are not on probation. They were just pulling your leg. If you didn't get your pay yet, go see Carol. She will get you paid right away. She will also go through the few rules that we do have. If you don't like them, you can leave with the full years pay," Sam says and leaves along with his brothers to get ready.

Sam goes in and finds Darwin at the computer. He tells Darwin, "I guess we are going right now."

"I know you are. I got something for you to do for me when you get into that bank," Darwin says and hands Sam a USB drive. "I need you to put this in to one of the mainframe computers. I know you don't know a damn thing about computers, so when you get in there, I'm going to tell you where to put it."

"What the hell is this for?" Sam asks.

"It will let me hack their money that is electronic and then I can send it anywhere I want without them ever tracing it," Darwin says.

"I thought you already hacked into the computer system?" Sam says.

"I am but with all the firewalls, and antivirus and other garbage they got going. It would take me a century to take all that I want out of the system. The program you are going to upload into their server just jumps around everything and within an hour, I got everything. They will be bankrupted," Darwin says and then laughs uncontrollably.

Sam looks at Darwin and thinks, "That laugh is a little creepy" then tells him, "I'll get it done. Where are you going to put the money?"

"Oh, we have several banks across the world. When we are done, you will be able to go to just about any country and take money out of a bank. If you got any charities, then I can send them a bunch of money," Darwin says.

"We can put some in the Salvation Army, the American Legion, the Veterans of Foreign Wars, the Disabled American Veteran, the Vietnam Veterans Association, Make a Wish Foundation, St. Jude Research Hospital, Lions Club, Shriners Hospital for Children, Wounded Warriors Project, Save the Rain Forest, Save the Whale Foundation, Farm Aid, foundation for any animal shelters, and any foundation for local human shelters. What do you think?" Sam asks.

"Not a problem. It will be ready by the time you get up there. Now take this and this," Darwin says and hands Sam two USB drives.

"What is the second one for?" Sam asks, taking the drives and putting them into a small wrist pouch.

"They're the same. Give one to Bud or Kota. I know you will just lose yours," Darwin says with a little laugh.

Sam walks out and hands Kota a drive and explains what needs to be done. Then Sam goes over and kisses Carol goodbye before jumping in one of the Hummers.

They have one hundred and forty-two troopers in all going up to Manhattan. Sam also has sent some men up to the harbor on boats just in case things went wrong and they need another way out. Two Ospreys and eight helicopters are already up at the old prison compound that was just purchased by DH and Kota. The rest of the men drive up in trucks, Hummers, armored SUVs, and several Strykers. They drive together up though Maryland, Pennsylvania, and then New York. Sam is just happy that he is not driving. He hates driving in traffic, and even this time of the morning, there are still a lot of cars on the street. On the way up to the New York, DH, Kota, Sam, and Kim change into their new suits.

They did not see even one state police officer the entire trip until they get on to the Newark turnpike. The state police follow the group until they all turn on Varick Street. But no one pulls any one over. They drive through town like they own the place. They unload at a nearby park. Sam calls in the helicopters for visual support. Sam and Kim take their all-terrain vehicles up the street and then circle all around the bank. Sam radios back to the trucks to make their way up and around to the back of the bank.

They go into the bank through the underground parking garage. Sam drives up to the security booth. The security guard is sleeping when a Hummer and both Sam and Kim pull up to the booth. Sam gets out of the vehicle and kicks on the door. The security guard must have been a professional. Even though he is startled, he just opens one eye. "Yeah, whatcha ya want?"

Sam thinks, "What the hell, I'm in this weird-ass looking suit and I just kicked on your fucking door and you say whatcha ya want? Is he fucking high?" Sam pushes the speaker button on his wrist console. "I need you to get up off your ass and call all your security buddies to come out here and give you a hand."

"A hand at what? Whatcha you thinkin I'm doin'?" The security guard finally sits up straight in his chair and talks through the little speaker through the window.

"You are going to need help pulling yourself together because if you don't open the door and come here, I'm going to blow this monkey cage up," Sam says and holds up the six-pack grenade launcher.

"Aaaah, just hold on now," the guard says as he tries to get his fat butt out his reclining chair. "I'm coming out." He opens the door and come out. He now shows a little nervousness after looking up the long line of vehicle setting there.

"Now I know you are a union worker and you don't really get paid all that much to save this place from us bad guys. I have a deal for you and all your friends. Everyone that comes out the door, everyone, from the janitor up to whoever, will receive one hundred thousand dollars cash. Right now. Now here is the kicker, they have exactly fifteen minutes starting when I say go. Those that stay will be shot immediately," Sam tells the guy and looks him over to see if he is even paying attention. "Do you understand?"

The guard nods and calmly says, "Yes."

"Go." Sam looks at his clock on the wrist console and points to it to show the guard.

The guard hesitates a little and then rushes to get on the radio. "Hey, man. You need to get down to the parking garage right away and tell everyone in the fucking building. You all got fifteen minutes to get down here, there is a man giving money away, but hurry."

Someone from the other end, "What the fuck are you talking about? How much money?"

"He says a hundred Gs if you get here in fifteen minutes. If you don't, they are coming in to kill everyone. I'm taking the hundred Gs," the guard says.

"Have you seen the money?" the other guy asks.

Sam hears the radio and then motions to some of the troopers to bring the bag of money. The trooper runs over and drops a large bag of money in front of Sam's feet. The trooper opens it up and shows the guard.

The guard's eyes get really big, "It's real and I'm out of here. You all have about thirteen minutes to get your asses out here so see ya."

The trooper hands the guard a bundle of cash. The guard grabs it and runs off up the ramp and out of the garage. Soon the elevator doors open and two stairwell doors opened. About sixty people come running out of the door, some are guards, some are janitors, and some are interns and technicians. The troopers hands each one a bundle of cash. Then they all leave. Sam grabs the last security guard that comes out and asks him, "Is that all of them?"

"Ah, I think so but there maybe a few people here or there that are upstairs working. We put it over the loud speaker," the security guard says.

Sam radios everyone to move in. He sends some of the men up to get the construction equipment. Sam hangs on to the security guard and asks him, "You want to make some extra money. If you do, then you will show us vault and money rooms in this place. If not, then just leave."

The guard nods and says, "Follow me."

Sam tells the troopers to watch out for anyone still left in the building. Sam tells everyone, "Do not shoot unless shot at. We want to get in and out of this place without firing a shot. We are not going to be able to recon the whole building, so just protect your zones and leave the rest alone. Now let's get in and get out."

Sam, WindEagle, and eight troopers follow the guard down a very wide hallway. The hallway goes down about three stories before ending at a very large door. The door looks like a large blast door that is in the New Mexico bunker. Sam looks the door over and then looks at the guard. He asks, "Can you open this door?"

"Yes, I can, but why should I?" the guard says.

"Is there anything worth taking behind this door?" Sam asks sternly. He hates that the guard is starting to become an asshole. "Look, open the fucking door and get paid. If you don't open the fucking door, you will only wish that we would kill you."

"I'll open the door, but I want some assurance that I'll be able to leave with my pockets full and no one is going to kill me," the guard says with a nervous and shaky voice.

"I can't give you anything for insurance, but I'm telling you, if you open the door, you leave here rich," Sam says and gives the guard the three-finger Boy Scout pledge salute. "I swear, Boy Scout's honor."

The guard looks at Sam with some doubt. "I'll take it." He goes over to the wall and punches in some numbers and then places his hand on a computer screen. Noise comes from the large door like metal sliding over metal. When the noise stops, the door starts to open slowly. WindEagle and two troopers jumped in through the doorway as soon as they can fit. They stop twenty feet inside the door. When the door is completely open Sam walks in with the guard. Inside is another door. The guard looks at Sam and says, "I can't open this door. This is as far as I have ever gone."

"Well, who the hell can open this fucking door?" Sam asks. He is mad as hell.

"The bank's big wig bean counter, he is the only one that has the combination to this door." The guard looks at Sam in fear. "Honest, I never go any farther than this."

"Where is the fucking bean counter you talk about?" Sam asks.

"He is gone until next week. Just like everyone else," the guard says.

"Shit, shit, shit," Sam says to himself. "WindEagle go get someone up there that can blast a door open and someone that knows anything about opening computer locks." WindEagle takes off and radios as he runs. Sam radios up to Kota, "Hey, we got a problem opening doors. Call Darwin and see if he can open the damn thing. Then get into whatever computer shit that Darwin wants us to put the UBS drive in and get that done. ASAP."

About five minutes later, Kota radios Sam, "Darwin is going to try to open the lock from there and I'm heading upstairs to the computer floor."

"Got it," Sam says and then starts to look at the walls. "Hey, guard, how long has this place been here?"

"The bank was built about fifty years ago over top of an old bank that had been built long before that. It gets renovated every year. I know the vault was put in about thirty years ago," the guard tells Sam.

Sam takes out his tomahawk and chips away on the concrete wall. He had noticed the concrete is old and that it looks like someone had just put layers of sealer on old concrete. He knows that some of the old concrete would crumble because it has too much lime mixed with poor sand. The combination makes the concrete cheap but also makes concrete absorb water later in time. Upon further examination of the door, the steel hinges are welded to large anchors in the concrete. Unlike the blast door, this one was an afterthought to keep out the honest people.

Sam radios up to the troopers, "Get some of those magnesium-cutting lances in here along with some skid loaders and chains. I need them right now."

Sounds of the loaders moving fills the hallway. Sam shut off his outside microphone to shut off the noise in his helmet. The troopers go to work on the door and quickly cut the anchors out of the wall. Soon the door falls to the floor.

WindEagle is back with a demolition expert and a computer guy but quickly notices that they are not needed any longer.

Kota radios Sam, "Darwin said that you are on your own. He was decoding something and then the connection went dead."

"Tell him that we just cut the damn door down. This place is old and falling apart. We can't blast in here, but we can cut. Did you get the computer uploaded yet?" Sam asks.

"I can't figure this shit out. Do we have a computer person along?" Kota asks.

"I'm sending you one now," Sam says. Sam points to the trooper who is the computer guy. "Go help Kota now. He needs some computer help. WindEagle show him the way."

The skid loaders clear the hallway and everyone moves on down. There is a small wire mesh door remaining. Everyone can see the vault room through the door. Sam turns to the guard and asks, "Is there any alarm systems, trip wires, laser triggers, or anything that you know or heard of inside this room?"

"I haven't heard of anything but I don't know for sure that there isn't anything in there," the guard tells Sam.

Sam radios Kota, "If you are talking to Darwin, push me through to him."

"I don't know how to do that. What do you need?" Kota asks.

"I need to know if there are any alarms or anything to worry about in the vault room," Sam says.

Kota radios Darwin and then radios back to Sam. "He said he doesn't see anything, but he can't be sure."

Sam has the troopers with the magnesium lances cut the last door down. Then everyone moves into the room. The room is the size of a large indoor horse arena. There is small shipping containers and covered pallets setting everywhere throughout the room. On the wall to the right are rows and rows of lockboxes. Sam radios up to the troopers, "Bring everything down to empty this place out. Leave at least twenty troopers to guard the door."

Sam goes over to one of the small containers. The container has no lock, so he just lifts the handle and slowly opens the door. As soon as the door opens, the guard just stands there mumbling to himself and drooling. "I've never seen so much money in my whole life. Do you mind if I just take some of this and we can call this good?"

"Help yourself. See if you can find a bag or a tarp so you can carry more," Sam tells the guard. "But you can't leave until we do."

"No problem," the guard says.

Meanwhile the troopers are loading trucks. Sam sends trucks on their way as soon as they are loaded. Each truck is escorted with two armored vehicles with six troopers. The helicopter team had said that nothing of concern is in the area, so Sam thinks it's safe to send them.

Kota and the trooper that is the computer guy have finally figured out how to load the USB drive into the mainframe computer system. Darwin is already busy dumping in one of his infamous viruses into the mainframe so that he could completely break the bank. Darwin is now in control of about three hundred and some billion dollars.

The troopers have almost everything loaded on to the trucks within a couple hours. They are experts by now, at getting things loaded quickly. With the help of the construction equipment that Sam had left there, it makes things go very quickly. Sam lets the guard go on his way.

The guard shakes Sam's bulletproof gloved hand. "Thank you for being honest." He laughs a little and then heaves his overly loaded duffel bag and walks slowing up the hallway. All way up he keeps laughing and repeatedly, saying, "An honest crook. An honest crook."

"Sam, we got trouble coming your way," one of the pilots calls. "There is about thirty police cars headed your way. Someone must have told on you."

"Thanks," Sam says. "Angel teams, did you copy that?"

All of them call back that they had heard, but there is no sight of any of the vehicles.

"Soon as you see them, give me a call. I think we need to deter them a bit," Sam says.

After ten minutes, "Here they come, Sam. Some of them look like they are Smoker vehicles. They are not all cop cars. I can see about fifty in all," the angel team 1 reports. "I'm going to hit the first car. Maybe that will stop them for a few minutes."

"Sounds good, I'll get the trucks out of here. Do you think they can get through or should we hold up here?" Sam asks the angel team leader.

"Just hold for now." The angel team leader looks through the scope on his .50-caliber Barrett. He sights in the first car and then fires one shot. The car instantly stops and steam shoots from the hood. The cars in the back just swerve around the broken car. The angel team leader fires another shot at another cop car. The same thing happens. Angel team 1 radios, "Angel two and three start firing." They all fire at will but the cop cars and the YUPPI's vehicle keep coming toward the bank minus about eighteen cars.

The cops and the YUPPIs surround the bank just as the sun comes up. Sam goes up to the front door of the building. He looks outside on the street to see thirty or more vehicles. The street appears to have been blocked off and more vehicles are showing up every minute. Sam radios his angel team, "What the hell is going on out there?"

"We should have brought automatic fifties. I've taken out about ten vehicles and two and three took out about eight vehicles. They are still coming and most of them are Smoker vehicles," the angel team leader says.

"Just take out what you can and let the rest come," Sam says and then radios Kim and Kota, "Hey, meet me on the second floor and we need to get a plan together really fast."

All three of them meet on the second floor where they have a clear view of the lobby and the street in the front of the building. Sam radios the recon helicopter to send video so that a full assessment can be made.

Sam gives a full assessment of the situation to Kota and Kim. DH and Bud are still loading the last of the trucks but are listening on the radio to Sam, "We are surrounded by Smokers, police, and SWAT. I don't know exactly how many of each but most of them are in the front. They must think we are just going to run out of the front of the building. Anyway, they have Brooklyn Bridge, Broadway, Trinity Plaza, and West Street blocked off. There are cars out at the back entrance and we have no way of getting out of town. Sarah in her gun ship says that there are two police helicopters and three news helicopters. So we are right where we thought we would be at this time."

"I think we should just go with plan A, and if after we get further out of the city, we will go with plan B. Have our choppers cut down all the helicopters. We definitely do not want the news helicopters following us," Kota says. "You know, these suits are very comfortable. Dexterity is mildly decreased but I am very comfortable and feel very safe."

They all laugh a little at Kota's approbation to the suit. Sam radios to Bud, "Are you loaded yet?"

"Oh shit, we have everything that you can get from this room. We checked every container before loading because some of them are empty and some of them had other shit like paintings and other artwork. We left those containers but the rest are getting strapped down. We will be able to move in about ten minutes," Bud says.

"Good. I'm sending Kota down for lead truck and I want DH in the second truck just like they practiced. I'm going to stay with one of the ATVs and cause some problems here and around town. You and Kim can take the other two ATVs and block or whatever they need to do. Load the last ATV." Sam sits there looking out the window. He looks at Kota and Kim. "OK, you guys get going and I'm going to reduce the population a little. Kota, as soon as you hear the explosion out front here, you take off."

"Got it," Kota says and then runs off with Kim. On their run to the parking garage, they radio the troopers to get ready to leave now. Everyone is waiting by the time Kim and Kota get to the garage. They start the vehicles and are ready to move on the first explosion.

Sam radios the helicopters, "Sarah, I want all the helicopters out of the sky as soon as the trucks move. Angel teams make your way to a high parking garage and call in a chopper for pickup. Sarah can you fly over and drop our note to the men sitting in the front of this building."

"Roger on all accounts," Sarah says and whips the helicopter gunship low and over the street out front of the bank. She stops and hovers. The men on the street jump for cover behind their vehicles. One of the troopers in the helicopter drops a glass jar that has a note inside. As soon as the note is dropped, Sarah takes off and goes to hunt down all the helicopters in the area.

A police officer runs out from the cover of his vehicle and grabs the note. He runs back to a SWAT panel van and hands the note to the lieutenant in charge. In the van are two FBI agents, a SWAT commander, two YUPPI commanders, a sergeant, and the lieutenant of the police. The lieutenant read the note, "Please leave now if you value your life. All the streets in the area are set to explode within five minutes of receiving this note. This is not a joke, you will die. The bank is empty and the money is all dirty money. I am just doing you all a favor. The clock is ticking. Anyone that is still alive here after the explosions will be gunned down by our gunships. Signed, Brothers3."

The lieutenant looks around at everyone in the van. "We are leaving right now. They have us at checkmate. Sergeant, tell our men to leave now." The sergeant leaves.

The two FBI agents say that they will back up until they are needed, so they leave very quickly. The FBI doesn't have any men on the street; they are just there to consult. The SWAT team commander is under the direction of the lieutenant, so they go leave but before they can step out of the door, one of the YUPPIs steps in their way. One of the YUPPI commanders grabs the note and says, "You fuckers better not be leaving. I am under direct orders that we are to hold this bank and not let anyone leave. The vice president is on his way right now and he will not want to be disappointed."

"We are leaving now," the lieutenant says. "I don't want my men dying over a bank robbery."

The two YUPPIs look at each other and grab their pistols. They point them at the SWAT commander and the lieutenant, "Call your men back in and I want you to storm the fucking building now."

The SWAT commander grabs his side arm and steps back to get ready to shoot.

The lieutenant looks at the YUPPIs and says, "Fuck no, we are leaving now." Then he turns toward the door. As he walks out the door, one of the YUPPIs shoots him in the back. The lieutenant fell dead face first into the street. The SWAT commander shoots at one of the YUPPIs but only hits the breastplate of the bulletproof vest. The YUPPIs open fire on the commander and he is shot through the face. The YUPPIs run out into the street as the sergeant is trying to get the police off the street. The YUPPIs yell to the sergeant and when he turns, the sergeant sees that the lieutenant is dead. The sergeant yells back and draws his weapon. "Stop there or I will shot." The YUPPIs point their pistols and shoot the sergeant several times in the head.

The other men in the street notice in all the chaos that there is something going wrong. Over half of the men in the street are YUPPI Smokers. The rest are SWAT and police. They all have their weapons drawn, but no one knows what to do.

One of the SWAT snipers sees everything from a building's rooftop. He takes aim on one of the YUPPIs that came out of the van and shoots him in the neck. The YUPPI's head flops forward and he dies before he hits the ground. The sniper takes aim at the second YUPPI and shoots but misses when the YUPPI dives for cover. The Smokers in the street see that one of their own just got killed. They open fire on the police and SWAT. The SWAT snipers take down several of the Smokers, but the Smokers also have their own snipers. Soon the front street of the bank is filled with bodies and blood. One of the police officers radios to his men that are on the side streets, "Don't trust the YUPPIs, they are killing us over here. Fire at will!" The men in the side streets start shooting at each other.

Sam is watching with amazement. He says to himself, "I don't even have to blow this place up. Everyone will be dead. If the Smokers win, I'm blowing it. If the cops win, I'm just leaving." Sam radios down to Kota, "You guys might as well go now. These guys are killing each other and I don't think they give a shit about us anymore. Go now."

Kota laughs and takes off with several trucks and a several armored vehicles. They start to pick up traffic as soon as they get on to the main road but then it quickly all disappears. The first roadblock is about two miles from the bank. There are ten vehicles with both Smokers and police officers. The vehicles are parked in the classic V roadblock. Kota aims for the center of the vehicles and hit them at forty miles an hour. When the blade hits, vehicles fly like someone throwing them to the side. The men standing around the vehicles run for cover and the convoy moves through without firing a shoot.

The helicopters easily ground the others in the sky without firing a shot. They just fly up alongside of the others and point the guns at them. The police and news helicopter pilots quickly turn and ran. Now the Brothers3 helicopters take turns refueling and watching guard over the convoy.

The convoy moves through the rest of city without a problem. On the streets, there is very little traffic and where there is traffic, it is moving well. On the Brooklyn Bridge, the traffic is heavy so they decided to continue up to Warwick old prison that they bought. The prison is where the others went but the second group was to head for the Connecticut farm. On the road, there is no snow so driving is great. Besides the one roadblock, no one has interrupted the convoy. No one even follows.

Meanwhile, at the New York old prison compound, the first truck arrives. The troopers quickly secure the vehicles into the compound's parking garage. They get ready for the next trucks to arrive and then take their places on the gate and on the wall. Soon the second truck arrives and they go through the same procedure. Everyone prepares for a big shoot-out.

Sam is on the second floor of the bank looking out the window, watching as the shooting dies down. Just about all the police are dead. More Smokers show up on the street out front. They have armored vehicles with .50-caliber machine guns mounted on the top. They drive up and quickly finish off all the police and SWAT officers that remain. The Smokers quickly reorganized and start to set their sights on the bank.

Sam decides it is time to leave. He runs toward his ATV that is parked in the parking garage. As he runs, he punches in a code on his wrist console. The streets around the bank explode. The streets heave and then erupt into flying blacktop, vehicles, and bodies. The body parts and debris paint the walls of the bank and buildings around it. The explosives that Sam and his crew set into the road a while back works well. There is nothing left on the streets except rubble. Sam jumps into his ATV and takes off.

Sam drives down the road dodging in and out of traffic. He comes upon a convoy of black SUVs heading toward the bank. Sam turns and drives up alongside the last vehicle's passenger side window. The passenger opens his window and sticks a rifle barrel out the window. The passenger yells, "Get the fuck out of here before I am forced to shot."

Sam could see that it is one of those SEPR1 men. Sam thinks that it may be the president's or the vice president's men. He doesn't really care and decides just follow them. Sam slows down to get behind the last vehicle. When they reach the area around the bank, the convoy stops. Several men get out of their vehicles along with someone in a long leather coat. They look at the street in the front of the bank. The man in the leather coat has a drink in his hand and when he finishes it, they bring him another.

Sam just sits on the street watching the men in black as they watch him. After about five minutes, the man in the long leather coat points to Sam. Two men walk over to Sam as he stands up next to his ATV.

"Take that fucking helmet off so that we can see who you are," one of the men in black instructs Sam.

Sam doesn't say a word. He just shakes his head. The man points his HK MP5 fully automatic weapon at Sam. Sam isn't afraid of a 9-mm. weapon while in his suit. He won't even feel the impact.

Sam touches the speaker button on the helmet. "I suggest you get that pop gun out of my chest and go on about your business or you will end up like your buddies." Sam slaps the gun away and punches the man in the nose. The cartilage and bone in the man's nose is crushed and instantly blood flows. The man falls back and he grabs for his nose. The other man in black tries to grab Sam. Sam kicks him just under his chin. The man goes stiff and starts to shake before he falls to the ground unconscious. Seeing two men go down, many of the other men in black start to take interest in Sam. Some of the men start to move toward Sam and some rush the drunk in the long leather coat into his vehicle. Sam climbs into his ATV and starts to back up when they start shooting at him. Bullets rain down on him but nothing penetrates the suit. Sam fires his grenade launcher that is mounted on the vehicle. The first grenade goes through the back window of the closest SUV. The whole vehicle explodes and the men in black dive to the ground. Sam quickly backs out. He takes off and races down the street. They see that Sam has driven off. The SEPR1 men pick up the two on the ground. They put them in one of the SUVs and start chasing after Sam. The convoy increases their speed to try to run down Sam. Some of the vehicles cut off and go down alleyways to catch up to Sam. Sam slows and speeds up and down alleyways and side streets. It is easy for him to out maneuver them. Sam races down several streets stops in the back of one of the parks in the area. The men in black surround Sam in the park. They get out and start firing on him. Sam just starts launching grenade rounds on to the SUVs. SUVs explode and bodies fly. After eleven grenade rounds, none of the SEPR1 men are alive. Sam gets out of the small all-terrain vehicle and looks at the damage to the vehicles. Inside the middle vehicle is the man in the long leather coat that Sam thinks resembles the vice president. He isn't sure but he will find out on the news tomorrow.

Sam takes off and heads toward the Warwick destination. Once out of town he stops and fills up with gas. Sam thinks himself lucky that Bud put in a small storage box in the ATV that held some money and other supplies.

By midnight everyone is safely in the old prison compound in Warwick. Sam gets out of his suit then in to some street clothes. He meets everyone to check out what they just brought in. They all talk about what had happened and then go to bed. The next morning, Bud, Kota, DH, and Kim join Sam in the mess hall for breakfast. Sam gets on the computer to read the morning news to see if there is anything about the bank. As Sam reads, the others get interested in what is on the news.

"Hey, Sam, does it say anything about the bank?" Kim asks and the others follow with. "Yeah, what does it say?"

Sam looked at them, "Gentlemen, lend me your ears so you may luxuriate in the felicific erudition of today's newspaper."

DH looks at Sam, "What the fuck did you just say?"

"Never mind, just listen." Sam reads, "The Bank of New York Melton in lower Manhattan is closed indefinitely due to a gas main explosion that destroyed the surrounding streets. Several police officers that had bravely detour traffic in the area were killed along with some of the maintenance crew. Our helicopter crew tried to get footage but was forced out of the area due to the large amount of natural gas in the air. Officials are investigating the cause of the incident but they do not suspect foul play."

"Is that it! Shit! We should rob banks every day if it is that easy," Kim says.

"We don't need any more money. We can buy a country right now," Kota says.

"We should buy an Island," Kim says.

"Then what the fuck are we going to do with that?" Kota asks, "There would be people there and we would have to feed the no working population. Fuck that."

"OK, here we are again," Sam says. "Vice President Herman Bashert died yesterday in an accident. He and his security guards were driving in Manhattan when the vehicle was hit. He was in Manhattan to do some last minute Christmas shopping to give to a homeless shelter in the Broncs. No one in either vehicles lived. The Secret Service is looking into the incident. All the country is in mourning today. He is survived by his wife and two sons. They are not taking questions. The nation's flag will fly at half-staff."

"What a load of shit the news is," Kota says. "How do you think he really died?"

"I think I killed him when I shot up that SEPR1 convoy. I think he is the drunk in the long leather coat," Sam says. "Shit, I would be in trouble if they knew it was me."

"Do you think they will find out?" Kota asks.

"I don't know how they would ever find out. I don't think there were any witnesses, but there could have been cameras," Sam says. "I had the helmet on the whole time so, no one can really prove that it was me. Oh, fuck it. I'm not going to worry about it. Those bastards started the fight, I just won."

"What are we going to do with everything?" Kim asks.

"I think we should stockpile fuel, food, seeds, ammunition, and water to all the bunkers. May be get some more helicopters and build some hospitals. We'll sell this place. It really gives me the creeps. We can give some more money to the families of the police that just died yesterday, and I always want to build a school to help kids that really want to learn something," Sam says. "But what do you all think."

"Good idea," Kim says. "But for now let's take this stuff and send it to the western bunkers. We don't have room out here."

"OK. Let's get shit rolling. We will get everything out west and then I'm going home. I don't think there is much more to do right now. We all can just sit back and take it easy for a while," Sam says.

Everyone agrees.

Chapter Forty-Two

Sam always wonders, "Why don't the American people vote for the wages of politicians and governmental workers. After all, it is the people footing the bill. Now once again, the federal government has over spent and they need more of our money. If politicians didn't get paid when they didn't do their job, would people who really cared, get in those positions instead of power mongers. Why are all the senators and congressmen multimillionaires." Sam is just thinking about those things while he is listening to all the fabricated superfluous mourning for the deceased vice president on the news. Sam's mind wonders on, "No one should have thought of that asshole drunk as a hero. He is one of the most crooked politicians in modern day government next to the Clintons. Even his sons were caught in a Ponzi scheme, but when he became vice president, that was all swept under the rug." Sam sits and listens to the news for about an hour longer on how great the vice president was and how America will miss him. Before the end of the week, the president has already replaced him with the senate majority leader Henry Reynolds. All the conspiracy theorists believe that the president had the vice president killed because the vice president was a screw up. The media always has a field day with him whenever he spoke to the public. Sam knows differently and he knows that at some day they will figure out who did it and come knocking on his door.

Sardar Arjmand meets with his men that are part of Secret Service. Sardar is stressing over his time line because two of the men has been killed along with the vice president. Now the plan that they have will not work and more men need to be recruited.

"You men need to recruit at least five more men or this will not work. I should think that you all should be ashamed that two of you have die in disgrace. I should just kill you here in this stinking room. Your families should be ashamed," Sardar screams in anger. He is not going to let all his money and time go to waste because his men are so dumb and got killed for nothing.

"Sardar, we know of a few men," one of the men speaks up with great fear. He knows that Sardar will have them and their families killed if things do not work. "They work with the First Lady. They had been with the president, but now they are guarding that fucking whore."

"Why do you think this?" Sardar asks. He knows the answer but he asks anyway.

"It is disgraceful that men should take orders from a bitch. It is very bad. No men should be killed for a woman," the man says and spits on the ground. "They will love to kill any American. This I know is true."

"OK, how long will this take?" Sardar knows in the back of his mind. "The date will have to be moved because the Barracks will be on vacation for a month. Then it will take a month or two to integrate the new men into the plan. The date for the 'big bang' will have to be moved. We will not make the state of the union address, so they need to wait for another big day when the president will gather all congress and senate in one room. Maybe if there is another 9/11."

"Not long. We will see to it, Sardar," the man says.

"See to it," Sardar says as he starts to leave. The men in the room breathe a sigh of relief.

Sardar goes to Kansas to see John Overagh to tell him about the new plans. Sardar drives into the place that looked like a junk yard last time but this time, it is different. Every truck and trailer is perfectly aligned. They all look like they are new. Some look like U-Haul trucks, some Ryders, and other rental trucks. Some have contractor signs and license numbers. Some are eighteen-wheelers that look like big company trucks like Walmart and Western. All the trucks are in perfect working order.

"Hey, Sardar, we are ready." John never thinks of Sardar as anyone better then himself. After all, Sardar is just someone with money.

"John! My friend. You have done well," Sardar says as he looks around.

"Is the plan a go? I have everything ready and we can move with a two day notice." John hands Sardar a beer. He knows that Sardar won't drink it, but oh well, more for him.

"There is a change of plans. We will not have a big bang all at once. Two of the men got themselves dead in that shameful car accident with the vice president. We are going to train some more but this will take time. The new plan is one month after the state of the union address, we will do one nuclear device in Seattle. The politicians will then gather together to make war and then we will do the big bang." Sardar puts his hand on John's shoulder. "This is good with you?"

"Good for you, good for me." John moves a little so Sardar has to remove his hand. John has a problem with people touching him. "Let me show you the trucks I put together."

Sardar and John walk through the yard. John shows how he modified each truck to make it a more effective bridge buster. "One of the changes I made is that I changed the shape of the top and the bottom of the trucks. They are very angled so that they cut like a knife. I took the model from the shaped charges they use to cut steel beams in the imploding business. This is just on a super big scale. I also am using C-4. These trucks are packed to the maximum weight so they can go over any scale, but it is much more powerful then fertilizer and diesel fuel."

"How did you afford the C-4?" Sardar asks.

"Well, you know, I bought thousands of tons of fertilizer when it was really cheap. The price of fertilizer tripled in price so I sold it all. The government doesn't care if you sell it in bulk, just if you buy too much of it. Then there was a place in Virginia making C-4 in an old meth lab. They sold it fairly cheap. In the last couple of months though, they are no longer in business. I had to make the last bit myself. We have plenty of it now," John says as he drinks down his last beer. "Yep, these things will bring down anything we set them on or over."

"Is the nuclear devices ready?" Sardar asks. He is very impressed with John's ingenuity.

"They are ready. I shielded the truck from any radiation detection. We can go anywhere we want with these trucks," John says and starts walking back to the shop to get another beer. "I am ready and all I need is for you to do is get me the men here on time."

"That is no problem. They are awaiting my call," Sardar tells John as they walk. When they reach the shop, John opens another beer. Sardar is slightly offended that John is drinking alcohol why he is here. John doesn't give a shit. He knows after the job is finished, Sardar will probably try to have him killed. John is ready though.

"Well, Sardar. I need to get some money so I can live life to the fullest before the job ends. I am thinking I won't be doing much living after the job." John drinks his can a beer in one long drink and then opens another. "Sure you don't want one."

"You, my friend, will live a long time. I intend to make you my number one," Sardar says and puts his hand on John's shoulder again. "I promise you, you will not die by my hand."

"Ah, well, um, good." John just keeps drinking.

"I must go now. We will talk soon. Remember, one month after the state of the union address and one bomb in Seattle." Sardar walks toward his car.

"I will await your call." John knows Sardar will not kill him. One of his men will try.

All the suits are ready for all the Brothers3 troopers. Sam had all the troopers go to Detroit and get trained with the suits. Sam makes a new rule that every person has to train every week on how to put on the suit. Also, every person has to wear the suit when on guard duty or if going to get into harm's way. Everyone is perfectly happy with the new rules.

The three brothers know they have more money than they can ever spend. They like to live more simple lives. They don't need to have great luxuries but they are all glad that they don't have to worry about money. They sit around now and make plans for bigger things. They put together and funded foundations for animal care and animal shelters all across the country. They funded many children hospitals and started charter schools for kids that wanted to go to school. They also make doomsday plans. Sam always felt the need to be ready for anything, all the time.

"I think we need to plan for food, water, and fuel stores. We got a large supply of water in South Dakota but not at any of the other bunkers. We need to remedy that situation. We only have some food stores but we should plan for more. Maybe stockpile seeds for growing food and mushroom farms. We need large supply of antibiotic, anesthetics, vitamins, and analgesics to last a lifetime. Also, we can produce some electricity from solar and wind power, but we still need fuel. I know there is an algae biofuel plant that went broke out in Texas. Maybe we can get that going and also get some more gas and diesel fuel storage at every bunker," Sam says. Everyone looks at Sam like he is planning for the apocalypse. "I'm just saying since we have the money now. Why not just do it and have some security. We have to spend the money before the government makes it worthless. I think we have enough weapons and ammunition since the group in Detroit and Gunny are developing that type of stuff. If we need more money, we can sell some of our patents."

"Sam, I think you are getting a little paranoid but I'm with you," Bud says.

"Yeah, so how do we get the ball rolling on all of this?" Kota asks.

"We are going to hire some business lawyers to go out and buy these companies. Then we are going to hire chemist and botanists to make and run this. I don't have any more time," Carol says.

"I know. We need to get some retired army veterinarians to run the food storages. I'll get DH and Harland on getting this done right away. I want this to go fast, like within a month or so," Sam says.

DH quickly finds retired army and air force veterinarians that want jobs. Harland and Gina buy the biofuel plant for almost nothing. The plant is already running but didn't have enough money to make up grades after the federal government pulled the funding for biofuel development. They bought an old landfill where they built a methanol distillery. It is more productive to make methanol from the waste gas coming from the ground then it is to make ethanol. Many of the plans come together quickly and are making money even though that was never their intention.

CHAPTER FORTY-THREE

CAROL'S BODYGUARD, MR. DELKER, WANTS to go on vacation. Sam thinks it is OK since Mr. Delker has found an assistant Master Clements. Master Clements was Mr. Delker's old trainer. He had been an MP in the Korean army and was a very good at his new job.

Mr. Delker goes to India and China for a three-week trip. It is fitting for him to do so because of his interest in philosophy. Carol and Master Clements go to pick him up from the airport. When they pick Mr. Delker up, he looks terrible.

"Did you eat something on your trip that is making you sick?" Carol puts her hand on Delker's head to check for a fever. "You picked up something. You are burning up."

"I got sick while in China. I may have eaten something bad but the last three days there, I only ate McDonald's food," Mr. Delker says.

"We will get you to the hospital right away. How is your arm?" Carol asks.

"It's OK. No problem," Mr. Delker says.

"Mr. Clements, please take us to AMC hospital. I don't want him to wait all the way to the farm." Carol calls Sam. "Sam, I'm taking Mr. Delker to the hospital. He is pretty sick. I'll be there for a while until we find out something."

"OK, I'll send Dr. Jackson to the hospital to help with anything that is needed. I'll be along shortly after that," Sam says. He calls Michael. "Hey, I need you to go down to AMC hospital and meet up with Carol. Mr. Delker is sick."

"I'll leave right away," Michael says.

The doctors work with Mr. Delker for hours. His condition worsens and they put him on a respirator. Dr. Michael Jackson works with the medical team but they could not identify the cause of Mr. Delker condition. Michael goes out to the waiting room where Master Pak, Sam, and Carol are waiting.

"We don't know why he is deteriorating. He cannot swallow or breathe on his own. His white count is almost zero and his temperature is 106," Michael says.

Sam and Carol look at each other and both of them says at the same time. "It's wound botulism. Look for an abscess. There has to be one that is taking all the white blood cells. Drain that thing and maybe he will get better."

"I'll tell them to look." Michael leaves and then comes back about twenty minutes later. "They are taking him to do a full body CT scan. You all just as well go home and I'll call you."

"We will go get something to eat and then come back," Carol says.

Two hours later Michael calls Carol. "We found the abscess and it is in his liver. They are going to surgery right now to try to remove it. I'll see you when you get here."

Mr. Delker makes it through surgery and the abscess is removed. They treat him with antitoxin and antibiotics. "He will be here for a month or so before he can go home. Way to go you two. How did you know?" Michael asks.

"Seen it and done it," Carol says. "You know, we are doctors too."

It was cold and snowing when John Overagh starts the yellow and brown tractor up with a JB Hunt trailer attached. It is a fake JB Hunt trailer, but it looks legitimate. Inside the trailer is a nuclear warhead. John decides to drive the truck and have a twenty-year-old Iranian man follow behind in his SUV. John is heading for Seattle and expects to be there in three days.

Sam sits at home eating breakfast with Carol. They are watching Fox News as they eat.

"Mexican troops are building up along the America's border after John Kain. The new secretary of state had a meeting with Mexico's new president, Enrique Pena Nieto. Their meeting was about the multiple and ongoing killing of innocent people along the border by the drug cartels. Mexico is to step up protection of its people with its army. The president issued, through executive order, one billion dollars to help with the response. Experts have reported that there are now close to three hundred thousand troops gathered along the border. Both their army and navy is in full force in every border town and lakes and along the Gulf of Mexico," the commentator says. "China and North Korea have begun their war games in the Pacific Ocean. Our military experts believe it is in response to our military movement of aircraft carriers movement to South Korea. Experts believe that China is just showing the world that they can move around the Pacific with their aircraft carriers like the US. North Korea and Iran have been working closely with China in the development of a new military for all three countries. The navy is watching the war games closely. We will report any new details as they happen."

Sam looks at Carol. "I swear. Our government is frickin' stupid for even letting them move that carrier out to sea. They should bomb it immediately before things get out of hand. Hell, we are probably going to get invaded and our government is footing the bill."

Carol laughs a little. "You are so paranoid. I think the government would not let that happen. We still have the strongest military in the world."

"Correction, we *did* have the strongest military until they cut all the funding. Remember the president said we don't need a military that has to fight more than one fight at a time. They pulled most of the military men home. There are probably half the military personnel as there was during the Bush administration. This military is hardly big enough to protect all sides of the continental United States and fight a war in Afghanistan and watch China run around the Pacific Ocean," Sam says to Carol. "It doesn't matter, though. We are always going to be the safest and most prepared little group in America. Right now, the troopers are practicing just like they would during war time. They like it and they are determined to always win. Knock on wood, we fought against several small armies and not even took one casualty."

"I'm not worried. I just worry that you are too consumed with this military thing. You have moved so far from being the veterinarian you once were and what you still are if you just come back to work. Can we finally relax and just get back to work on what we set out doing years ago?" Carol asks and reaches up from the breakfast counter to shut the television off. She always did this when she wanted to talk seriously to Sam.

"I guess I can try to go back to work. I just have to watch my back," Sam says. "I don't think I should go out on calls. Maybe just start out doing things in the hospital until I get back in the groove and know the coast is clear."

"OK, let's get over to the hospital and see what we can find for you to do," Carol says.

Sam goes back to work but it is slow going. He used to have a big following of clients, but since he has been gone for so long, they all start to rely on many of the new veterinarians. The new veterinarians are good. Sam just worked along with some of the doctors giving advice whether or not they wanted it. After a couple of weeks, Sam sets his sights on writing an anatomy book that clients can use. He has always wanted to do it but never had time. Now he has time and the money to do it.

John Overagh and the Iranian man drive into Seattle, Washington. The plan is to park the truck near the Sky Needle Tower and then leave the city. John parks the truck and then watches from the other vehicle. He wants to make sure that the truck will not be disturbed. After about thirty minutes, a police officer drives up to the truck and taps on the driver's side door. The Iranian man is inside of the cab just in case the truck has to be moved.

"You cannot park this truck here," the police officer tells the Iranian. "What is your business here?"

"I am lost." The Iranian says as he digs around in his truck for his papers and the logbook.

"Let me see your logbook," the police officer says and takes the logbook from the Iranian. He starts paging through the logbook and notices that there is no report for the last few days. "I see you are behind on your logbook. Can you tell me where you are going and what you are hauling?"

"I do not know. You must leave me now so I can finish my journey," the Iranian says and starts to shut the door. The police officer grabs the door. John sees that things are going badly.

"Get out of the truck now," the police officer yells to the driver but the Iranian just pulls on the door. The police officer jumps off the truck's step and down on to the street. The police officer draws his weapon just as John drives up and hits him with the SUV. The officer flies forward and John runs him over. As soon as John feels two bumps, he stops. He gets out and walks behind the vehicle where the barely conscious police officer lies in the street. The police officer is broken and barely breathing. John looks down at the police officer. Blood is coming from the officer's mouth and he reaches up to John for help. John grabs the officer's hand and holds it. John grabs a boot knife with his other hand and cuts the officer's throat. The officer dies slowly as John stands with one foot on the officer's chest and holding the officer's hand. When the officer is dead, John picks him up and throws him into the back of the truck along with the bomb.

John reaches up and opens the door to the truck. "OK, you start driving around the town. Do not go too far from this place. Just drive around on the street until I come and get you. Do you have that?" John waits for an answer.

"I know what you say. I will do that. I will drive around and stay close to this area," the Iranian says.

"OK," John says. He shuts the truck door and gets into the police officers car. He drives it to the Sky Needle's parking lot. Then goes back and gets his SUV. He drives out of town on I-90. He heads back to Kansas. He has no intention on picking up the Iranian; after all there would not be much to pick up once his work is done. After driving for three hours, John dials in a number on his cellphone. On the other end is a receiver to start the nuclear warhead. Within seconds, nothing is left of Seattle, Washington. John keeps driving and doesn't stop until he gets back to Kansas.

CHAPTER FORTY-FOUR

THE PEOPLE OF THE UNITED States instantly go into a panic after Seattle is leveled by a nuclear bomb. Airports are shut down and security everywhere is increased. The so-called Homeland Security started their exaggeratory security checks. None of the intelligence agencies can figure out who did the bombing, nor can they figure out how the bomb got into the city without any detection.

The president appears on television to try to calm the nation's panic. "Yesterday at 11:45 p.m., the nation was once again the victim of a terrorist attack. Seattle, Washington, was bombed with a nuclear device. Thousands of innocent people were killed and many more are wounded. There was no way of knowing this was going to happen, but I can guarantee that those who are responsible will be hunted down. We as a nation have survived such a thing before and we will survive this event. We have FEMA and the National Guard in the area to help out any relief efforts. Again, at this time we do not have a clear understanding of who is responsible for the tragic event. By executive order, I am immediately calling all our military back home and I mean all the military. The naval aircraft carriers are already in route to our Atlantic and Pacific borders. The rest of the military will follow in the next two weeks. We are leaving Afghanistan and all foreign bases immediately. I have also called for our troops to patrol our towns and cities along with the National Guard for a short time until we find out who has attacked our homeland." The president is speaking from a bunker somewhere in Virginia.

Across the nation, everyone points to China, North Korea, or Iran for the bombing. The experts in nuclear physics quickly determined that the plutonium came from Russia. They conclude that it is part of Russia's old nuclear arsenal from the late 1970s. Most of these nuclear warheads were supposed to be destroyed. Some of the warheads made their way out of the country and sold to the highest bidder.

Sam and the two brothers meet in Gunny's shop along with Gunny and Darrell. Darwin comes out of his reclusion to join the boys. Of course, beer and coffee flowed as everyone told stories about their adventures over the past few years.

"I have never even thought of doing so much. There were many times, I thought for sure we were going to get killed. Shit when we first tried out those suits. Bullets were hitting me and I'm just glad you can pee in those suits. Damn," Kota says and pops open a beer. "There were times I was so scared that all I could do is shake like when those bastards jumped me at the farm. I'm just glad everything has worked out."

"You boys are brave and made me proud. Our military should have had more of you during the Vietnam War. You all did well," Gunny says. "I know your dad is proud of you."

"Yes, I am, boys," Darrell says, "I think it's time you all to do some real work now. Maybe we can start a small farm on some of the property. What do you think about that?"

"We can do some farming if you want. We just need to get some equipment and get to work. Just get a plan together on what you want to do and what equipment you need," Sam says. "I'm working at the hospital again, but if Bud or Kota want to get back at it, then feel free. It would be good."

"We can go tomorrow and look over the property. Then go to the equipment dealer and see what we need," Bud says. He has always wanted to start farming again but never really had a chance. Now is his chance.

"Gunny, you been working on anything new?" Sam asks. "How are the new weapons in Detroit going?"

"I'm working on some of these collapsible kamas right now. I'll let you try them out as soon as I'm done. The weapon division in Detroit is going well. We are going to test out the new finned semi guided round. It is going to be shot from a new .60-caliber rifle. Much like the .50-caliber Barrett M107, but we are changing things to fit the bigger round and making it with the less recoil like the automatic weapons I made for you guys. It should be great," Gunny says. "Why not all of us fly out there today so we can try it out?"

"Well, I'm not sure they are letting anyone fly today since Seattle got blown up," Sam says.

Everyone looks at Sam like they just saw a ghost.

"What the hell? When did that happen? Bud asks with concern.

"Just the other day, they said they did not know who did it," Sam says. "All I know is that it was not us. I called the Nevada bunker to see if they knew anything and they had no idea that it even happened except when they saw it on the news. The president has declared martial law and he is bringing all the military back home. I think he is just using this bombing as an excuse to do what he always had intended on doing."

"What is that?" Gunny asks.

"Total tyranny," Sam says.

"Shit. I hope that radiation don't come over here or even spread," Kota says. "Darwin, you know anything about this?"

"The word in the White House is that it was probably an Old Russian warhead that got sold to some terrorist nut. The radioactive cloud is actually moving up into Canada and is quickly dissipating because of all the rain. They don't think that it will come over the mountains. Other than that, there is no chatter on cyberspace. The government is going to have a special session with the president addressing the house of representatives and the senate in a joint session. From what I gather, the president wants supreme power to control all legislation because of the terrorist threat. He basically wants to take over and run the country without congressional approval. They are going to vote on this in a couple of weeks or sooner," Darwin informs everyone in the room and then starts drinking beer.

"Darwin, I thought you didn't drink." Kota says.

"I took it up. Is there a problem with that?" Darwin asks in a sarcastic tone. He never did like Kota very much.

"Do what you want," Kota says.

"Hey, Gunny. Don't you know anyone in the National Guard?" Sam asks.

"I do know a few good men in some high places. I haven't talked to them in a long time but if you like I could try to see if they would talk to me." Gunny says.

"Yes, I would like you to do that. Since this martial law thing is supposed to go on and we need to fly, tell them we will paint B3 on all our planes and vehicles. Tell them not to shoot at them. If they do agree, we can make a substantial donation to whatever charity of their choosing. If they don't agree, then we will start our Smoker war over again but this time with the National Guard," Sam says, "Darwin can you help Gunny get in contact with whomever?"

"Let's go," Darwin says and waves his arm to motion to Gunny. They both head down to the computer room.

Everyone talks for a while and then DH shows up.

"Did you know there are National Guard men in Staunton driving armored Hummers with mounted guns?" DH asks nonchalantly. He goes over and grabs a beer from the refrigerator.

"No, we did not but it is because the president declared martial law," Kota says and motions DH to get him another beer. DH hands Kota a beer.

"Well, what are we going to do now?" DH opens his beer. "Shit, if they come up here, shit is going to hit the fucking fan."

"Gunny is trying to fix everything right now so we are just going to sit here and drink a few beers." Sam says.

Gunny comes back with Darwin, "Well, my old friend was good with everything. He said that he has informed all the branches of the National Guard. He can't guarantee that all the branches will cooperate but the army and the air force is all in."

"Gunny you must have friends in high places," Sam says with a smile.

"My friend is a lieutenant general for the Army National Guard. I carried him out of Laos when he had been shot back in Vietnam

War days. He is also good friends with the chief master sergeant of the air force. Both of them will be meeting us in Detroit," Gunny says. "Sorry, Sam, I had to tell them about the new weapon in order for them to be interested enough to help us out. They didn't want any money and I didn't think that threatening them was going to get me anywhere. I didn't tell them about the suits. You can show them if you like."

"That's OK, Gunny. We may just need to all get along when all is said and done," Sam says. "Let's get Sarah in here so that we can fly out right away. DH can you go over and get the mechanics to start painting B3 on all the rooftops of the vehicles and on the sides of any aircraft we got near here. Then contact all the other bunkers and have them do the same. I want this all done today. Let's go."

Sam goes over to the hospital to tell Carol that he is leaving for Detroit to meet with the National Guard. She is a little upset but she knows that this is what Sam really wants to do. Sam takes off with the boys.

The meeting goes well with the two men from the National Guard. The Brothers3 and the National Guard will now be working together, both see a win-win situation if they work together. The test goes well with Gunny's new guided bullets. Gunny also has been working on another project that has been started elsewhere but never perfected. Gunny also developed a bullet that shoots two projectiles at the same time. Each one shell shoots a projectile, and then within two-hundredths of a second, the other projectile follows. It is shot from an electronic trigger rifle. Sam thinks it is a great idea but if the electronics go out, the weapon will not fire. Sam also has the two men and their entourage fitted for suits. After the demonstration of the bulletproof suit, the men are very interested in keeping the place safe and sound from any intruders. They send over fifty army troops to guard the facility. Sam gives the OK for that as long as they just guard the perimeter and no one enters the facility. The men from the National Guard are OK with that request. Only the Brothers3 men are allowed in the building except this one time.

CHAPTER FORTY-FIVE

SARDAR MEETS FOR THE LAST time with his men working in the Secret Service. The indoctrination of the new men went well, so much so that they themselves convinced more of their Islamic brothers to join the cause. They know what is expected of them and feel honored to perform their duty. They think it will memorialize them and their families throughout the Islamic brotherhood.

Sardar has to have eight new vests made for the new men. Now there are thirteen men and all of them are Secret Service. Three of them work with the president, five of them for the new vice president, two for the First Lady, one is with the secretary of state, and the rest of them just work as routine security. The plan is to place several bombs throughout the US Capitol and the rest is up to the men.

"Tonight my brave warriors we pray, we drink, we bath, and we celebrate each one of you. You may go on your journey into the afterlife and know that you have done your duty for Allah and your family. Now let us celebrate for tomorrow we change the world!" Sardar tells everyone and then passes out alcohol. Normally alcohol is forbidden, but the night before they die, it is permitted.

Sardar leaves the men in the hotel suite. He has to make sure that John's men are already moving into position with the several hundreds of trucks. Most of all, the three remaining warheads need to be in the right place at the right time. It all has to be coordinated and happen all at once.

Sardar calls John, "John my friend."

"Sardar how did you like the fireworks?" John asks about the Seattle bombing. He just needs hear Sardar to give him some gratitude.

"You my friend are an amazing man. It was so wonderful. The world owes you a debt of gratitude and I owe you the world. To my dying days I will work to repay you," Sardar says as he gets very emotional.

"Why, thank you. Now I have a great treat for you and it will come tomorrow at 2:25 p.m. Make sure you watch the north sky and may I suggest you go to where you need to go," John says.

"That is perfect. Everything will be just perfect tomorrow. We will meet again soon and then we will celebrate," Sardar says.

"Remember, tomorrow at 2:25 p.m. and not a second later. Until later, man," John says. He is very happy that Sardar was so grateful. Until now, no one has showed him that much emotion and gratitude for doing anything. It makes him feel good for the first time.

"Goodbye my friend." Sardar hangs up the phone knowing that everything is in play.

The next day at 2:00 p.m. a special session of congress starts. The president, vice president, majority leader of the senate, speaker of the house, and the full senate and house of representatives all meet in one place at the Capitol. The person that is missing is the secretary of state. He is sequestered in some bunker somewhere in the United States.

The president speaks, "Since the great tragedy in Seattle, our great nation has been under martial law. We only have a limited resource of National Guard troops to secure our towns and cities against any more acts of man-made tragic events. This tragedy has led me to bring home all our military to once and for all to secure our borders against any other bad doers. They will work with our first responders and National Guard. This action will only be for a short time. Already we have seen a decline in violent crimes in our cities but more is needed to protect our children, our young people and our seniors that cannot defend themselves. Today I am calling for vote to give me and my administration to control all powers of congress. This must be done only for a short time until we know that there will not be any more attacks on our Nation's soil. I will protect—" Then nothing.

At 2:25 p.m., the twelve Secret Service men's vests explode, sending millions of titanium balls flying at two thousand feet per second throughout the chamber. Nothing is left intact. Not a single body lay in one piece. Along with the inter-chamber explosion, several hundred other explosives go off throughout the Capitol and the White House. No one in any of the buildings is left alive.

In New York City at Times Square, the nuclear warhead explodes, leveling fifteen square miles of buildings. The explosion goes into the sewer system and the subway system, causing a complete collapse of those systems for miles in all directions. The heat and wind destroys even more, several miles away. New York City is basically gone. The same thing happens in Los Angeles and Saint Louis. Millions of people are killed. Millions more will die from radiation exposure.

The majority of the trucks are loaded with C-4 that was made by the YUPPIs and sold to John Overagh. He used it to make giant shaped explosives to cut any bridge apart. Some trucks were loaded with ground-steel scraps. When the truck explodes, the steel scraps work like millions of high-speed projectiles ripping apart anything in the two square blocks. Hundreds of major bridges fell into the water with cars and trucks included. Those that lived through the fall could not be saved. Power plants, railway bridges, shipping yards, and other major buildings are decimated. All of the country is cut off from every other part.

Transportation other than by air or water is impossible. Millions of motorists that are not killed in the explosions are trapped in traffic with no way of getting off the roads. Some of the more aggressive people make their way through ditches and fields, but most are trapped. Many of them running out of gas and abandoning their vehicles, which further congested transportation. Truckloads of food and other goods are left on the interstate highways. Truckers that can make it to a truck stop soon ran out of fuel because there is no way to haul in more fuel.

Because all the politicians in the federal government are killed, many of the governors assumed leadership positions to try to control their states. Most states have been so broke because of the deficits that they had run for such a long time, they had no resources to deal with the emergencies. Most governors have no idea how to handle the devastation.

The secretary of state that is housed in a bunker proclaims he is now the president and is in charge. He gets on a secure radio system to inform the military that he is in charge, "I will now be in charge. The president, vice president, and all of congress have been killed. Therefore, I will assume the duty of the president." At that point, his man from the Secret Service reaches in and grabs his knife. He walks up behind the secretary of state and cuts his head off. Those receiving a radio signal just heard a man screaming with a gargle in his voice. The Secret Service man there detonates the explosives he had placed in the bunker. Everyone in the bunker dies.

Most grocery stores only keep enough food stored for about two days. When the bombs go off, people ran to the stores and hoard food. They buy or steal everything that they can afford or get out of the store. Stores ran out of food within hours and they could not restock in most areas.

Right after the "big bang," people are very charitable to those who could not get food. Within a week, the charity stops and those that did not have tried to take from those that did. The National Guard tries to step in and control the looting and violence but they are over whelmed. Some of the National Guard troops head home to protect their families which left less than half of the National Guard available. Soon the army and marines step in to take over. Military generals fight over who is in charge and the military falls into chaos. Some troops are moving through towns and cities like gangs. They pillage the town's food and money even robbing banks and homes. Most of the troops are not bad. Some troops even fight against those troops in small gangs.

The small groups of want-to-be terrorist that had been doing all the killing start to band together in bigger groups throughout the nation's cities. They rampage throughout the cities and suburban towns, raping and pillaging. They show no mercy when it comes to whom they kill. They kill for entertainment and to exert their power against weaker people. Without a strong police force, the small gangs are left unchallenged. The small gangs became larger from many younger people seeking refuge under a strong force. The National Guard troops regard these groups as WTBs (Want-to-Bes). They will shoot to kill anyone from these groups. They are all punks much like gnats at a picnic. The National Guard troops hate them. When WTBs come into towns, they rape the women and children and kill the men. Then they strip the towns of anything of value.

With all the food stores gone in most areas, especially in the cities and large towns, people quit going to work. Some stay home out of fear and some stay home to guard what they have. There is no electricity in most areas and soon it goes out in all areas. No one is working at the power plants to keep it going. Also no one works to repair the lines and keep the grid maintained. The same happens to the communication system. Cellphones are useless and the landlines are out without electricity. Radio is still working but only for those that have batteries or generators.

Governors soon give up any plans of reconstruction. The country falls deeply into military rule and chaos. The United States is completely devastated within a month of the "big bang."

People soon flocked to places where they may get food, drugs, or fuel. Sam and Carol's equine hospital has all three. Carol shuts down the hospital to any farm calls and only takes those that come in. Carol has all the doctors and technicians bring their families to the farm where they move into the tent town that was built just a few months ago. Sam has made sure they had plenty of food to last for years. People from the surrounding towns find out about how the hospital is still up and running. They figure that the vet clinic will be either easy prey or a place of charity. People start showing up to the hospital, some with weapons and some with handouts for charity. Carol gives those with children food, but those with weapons are turned away.

Most people start riding horses or bicycles for transportation. People start stealing horses, but most people have no idea how to ride a horse. At one time, there was an overpopulation of horses, but due to government regulations on "no using horses for food," people that raised horse greatly decreased in number. Horses are now considered a luxury item and people will give almost anything to keep them going. The equine hospital always has people waiting in line begging for Carol's doctors to work on their horses. Many people bring in food items or family heirlooms to trade. Carol has no use for most of the items, but she regifts the food and keeps the people's heirlooms in a building for safekeeping. She figures if the people want them back when things get better, it is there for them to get.

Money is worthless inside the United States, but outside the country people still accept it. Sam and Carol had an airplane that flies up to Canada every day to buy medicine and other supplies. The shipments are guarded by the National Guard fighter jets.

Some people still make moonshine and run vehicles on it. Alcohol becomes another valuable item. Even though the nation is nonfunctional and lifestyles have been thrown back a hundred years, people still like to drink. Moonshiners soon become some of the wealthiest people in the nation almost overnight.

Bud posts centuries all around the property, along with the high-tech security systems, no one is able to get on or off the property without permission. He also makes it a rule that anyone wishing to come on the property has to be cleared by Carol or him. If they are not permitted and they don't leave, appropriate force is to be used. Bud put Master Clements in charge of the front gate. Master Clements has a level head and is a veteran with security. Mr. Delker reassumes his duty as Carol's bodyguard.

The National Guard is also stationed at the hospital. Sam has an agreement with the National Guard. They are allowed to land helicopters and camp at the farm. Sam thinks it is a little extra security for his family. Many of the National Guard troops were cut off from fuel stores except what they could get from abandon gas stations. Getting fuel and food to many of these troops are difficult because the aircraft carriers are very busy. Sam has the fuel plant in Texas and it is at peak production making biofuel. The landfill methanol plant is producing about as much fuel as some oil refineries will produce gasoline or diesel. Many of the National Guard troops convert their vehicles to run on biofuel or methanol. The methanol is not as safe as gasoline or diesel but is very functional. Sam has the National Guard troops pick up fuel in small containers that can be carried with helicopters. More troops can be supplied fast this way. The refined fuel can then be used for aircraft and not wasted on vehicles.

When the "big bang" happened, Sam immediately flew to South Dakota and make sure that his mom and sister and Kim's family were moved into the bunker. They were completely safe and sound. Sam had left fifty troopers stationed there along with Harland in charge. Harland was a stickler about security. Nothing moved in or out of the old farm place. The National Guard also camped out at the farm because it is easier than trying to get out of the city. Also, the farm has more security then any of the National Guard's armories.

China, North Korea, and Iran finish their war games a few weeks prior to the "big bang." The world watches the United States military pack up and leave for home. Without the United States military presence across the world, terrorist groups quickly move into take over areas everywhere. Iran moves in to Iraq and then tries to take over Turkey. The Turks stop them at the border. Hamas and the Islamic jihad try to move in to Israel, but the Israeli army destroys them. War breaks out everywhere in the Middle East. China invades Taiwan and then picks up the North Korean army. They go to the west coast of the United States.

China and North Korea has around four million military personnel. They do not have enough transportation to carry over more than fifty thousand troops at a time, so they have to go back and forth with their ships and captured commercial airliners. The problem with the airliners is that they cannot refuel in the United States, so it is a one-way trip for commercial jets. Soon they only have ships to bring troops over.

The United States navy has been moved to the western and eastern coasts. They quickly intercept the Chinese navy. The Chinese navy is far inferior to the American navy. Only some of the ships make it to the west coast. Problems in the US Navy arise when supplies start to decrease because of decreased ammunition production. Ammunition is still being produced but has greatly diminished from lack of workers and raw materials. The military has to haul their raw materials to manufacturers because of the lack of transportation. Special metals that are used for rockets and large munitions are becoming in short supply because the power grid is down. They could use generators but only for a short period of time each day. Fuel has to be flown in to the plants because trucks are getting hijacked even with military escorts. The good thing is that the military started out with large supplies.

Some of the Chinese and Korean troops land along the coast of the US via the hijacked commercial airliners and some of the ships that slip by the navy. Our army and marines, even though they are greatly unorganized and outnumbered, greatly slowed the invasion. They intercept any airline that flies into any airport on the west coast. If any airline that does not comply with the military's instruction of landing and being inspected, it is shot down immediately.

Mexico already had their troops stationed along the border. Mexico's president Nieto sees a great chance to invade the United States when the Capitol is destroyed and there is no real government left. He is more of a revolutionist and despised the United States since his childhood days. He instructs his troops to go and reclaim Mexico's property. Mexican troops first moved up through southern California but are stopped by the army and air force at San Diego. They also move up into Arizona but again are stopped by the US military. The Mexican troops that come up through Texas are stopped by private militia groups who despise Mexicans. To them, it is more "Don't mess with Texas" and not saving the US.

When the Mexican army moves up through New Mexico, the Brothers3 go out after them. The Brothers3 is better equipped than the Mexican army. Sam and Kim fly out to the New Mexico bunker to lead the troopers. Mexico's president calls upon some of his old friends after seeing how pathetic his army performs. Troops come up from Venezuela, Colombia, and Honduras to assist the Mexican army with the invasion. Weapons and munitions come over from Russia to Mexico and then up to the front lines.

Now the United States is fighting in the Pacific Ocean and in the states of Texas, Louisiana, New Mexico, Arizona, California, Oregon, and Washington. Foreign troops have made it as far as three hundred miles north of the southern border. The United States military is so busy along the Pacific coast fighting; they leave the fighting along the southern border to the National Guard. The National Guard was never equipped or stocked with enough weapons and munitions to fight a full-scale war. Most of the resupply of munitions goes to the US military, and the National Guard basically gets scraps.

Sam is in the middle of the fighting throughout New Mexico. He moves half of his troopers down to join him and the National Guard troops from New Mexico join him. Sam has all his helicopters equipped just like Sarah's gunship. Mexico has the Panther gunships and Sam has nothing that can match them. Sam decides to do what they did best—take what they need and take what they want.

The Brothers3 are back in action. This time there will be no prisoners.

Coming next: *The Brothers3: Invasion*

ABOUT THE AUTHOR

SCOTT REINERS WAS BORN AND raised on a farm in South Dakota. After high school, he attended National College. He graduated with an associate's degree in animal health technology and completed an externship in Nairobi, Kenya. He returned home to work on the family farm while supplementing his income doing construction work so that he could rodeo. A few years later, he went back to South Dakota State University to complete a bachelor's degree in animal science. During this time, he received a black belt in tae kwon do. After graduation, he went on to complete his doctorate in veterinary medicine at Kansas State University. During his time in KSU, he stopped riding in the rodeo and started skydiving and scuba diving. After graduation, he did an internship at Ohio State University. Scott went on to complete his large animal surgery residency at Oklahoma State University. After his residency, he worked as an equine emergency clinician. He met his wife during this time, and they moved to Arizona for a short period of time. The two later built Mountain View Equine Hospital in Virginia, where they and their son now reside. Scott stays active competing in karate tournaments and his wife shows horses.

CPSIA information can be obtained
at www.ICGtesting.com
Printed in the USA
FFOW03n0217191017
41237FF

9 781640 821866